# DAEMONS, INC.

# DAEMONS, INC.

## Eye of the Daemon
## Eyes of the Empress

CAMILLE  BACON-SMITH

FANTASY

EYE OF THE DAEMON  Copyright © 1996 by Camille Bacon-Smith
　　Printing History: DAW paperback January 1996

EYES OF THE EMPRESS  Copyright © 1998 by Camille Bacon-Smith
　　Printing History: DAW paperback August 1998

First SFBC Fantasy Printing: February 1998

Published by arrangement with:
DAW Books
375 Hudson Street
New York, NY 10014

Visit our website at: *http://www.sfbc.com*
Visit DAW's website at: *http://www.dawbooks.com/daw/index.htm*

ISBN# 0-7394-0155-6

PRINTED IN THE UNITED STATES OF AMERICA

# Contents

# EYE
# OF THE
# DAEMON

# Chapter 1

*The universe comprises seven spheres, of which the outermost is the*
*abode of the Archangels. There follow the seraphim, cherubim and*
*thrones, the minor angels in which group are included those Guardian*
*Angels, and the Princes, who reside in the second sphere, closest to*
*man who holds dominion over the first sphere of creation, that of all*
*matter in the universe. As there are seven spheres, so of Princes there*
*be seven in number and their names are Azmod and Ariton, Paimon*
*and Oriens, Astarot and Magot, and Amaimon.*

BADAD, LORD OF ARITON, SLIPPED INTO HIS HUMAN PERSONA AS HE PUT ON
the charcoal pinstripe suit coat. As Kevin Bradley he entered the office
suite fronting a corner of Spruce Street. The sounds of the Porsches and
BMWs seemed out of place passing in front of the brick sidewalks, hitch-
ing post, and boot scrapes of an earlier time, but the Society Hill offices
of Bradley, Ryan, and Davis fulfilled the promise of Federal period Philadelphia just hinted at by the marble threshold. Darkly rich wainscoting
met soft blue walls. French Aubusson carpets that mirrored the sculptured
ceiling hushed Kevin Bradley's footsteps when he crossed the office furnished in the cool geometry of Hepplewhite, enough of it period authentic
to soothe and impress the clients of Bradley, Ryan, and Davis, Private
Investigators. George Washington would have felt right at home.

The woman in the reception area started nervously when he entered
the room. She was about thirty-seven, angular and sharp-featured, with hair
a nondescript brown that fell straight from a center part to her shoulders:
the type that, under better circumstances, some would call handsome. Now
tension pinched her features into a hard mask. She wore a pink suit that
seemed out of place on her, as if the limits of her straight skirt caught her
by surprise at each step. Badad led her into the tastefully austere office
reserved for meeting clients and seated her in a spindle-backed chair at a

comfortable angle to the windows. He noticed in passing the rich green of the side garden beyond the lace-paneled curtains. The azaleas would bloom soon; already the hyacinths and crocus had unfolded, the lilies of the valley that Lirion often wore in her hair just peeking out from the shadows. Lately the garden walls had begun to close in; the memory of why he stayed sometimes faded next to his restlessness to be away beyond the night and free.

A challenge might distract him, and Badad silently hoped the edgy woman in the new pink suit had more to offer than a wandering husband. He took his place at the cherrywood desk, slipped a pen from the inner breast pocket of his jacket, and opened the leather secretary in front of him.

"I'm Kevin Bradley. How can I help you?"

Badad—Kevin Bradley—smiled encouragement while the silence stretched between them. Finally, the woman reached into her handbag and pulled out a scrap of yellow paper. She twisted it nervously between her fingertips, but did not extend it immediately for Badad to see.

"My brother has been kidnapped."

"Have you called the police?" Kevin Bradley folded his hands and watched the woman across the antique desk.

The woman stared intently at the paper she threaded between thumb and forefinger. "They didn't believe me. Said it was a prank, but I know it isn't. The people who took Paul mean what they say. They'll torture him, or worse, if I don't find him in time."

"I think you'd better tell me all about it." He spoke softly, putting the woman at ease, but half ready to dismiss her as a crank. Badad stayed as far from the legal system as possible, but even he knew that the police took kidnapping seriously. With threats involved they could hardly dismiss it as a simple disappearance. She seemed to consider for a moment, then:

"Do you mean what you said in your ad?" She spread on the desk the yellow paper, a page torn from the phone book.

"Of course we do." He smiled, showing just enough of his straight white teeth to instill confidence, while he let a bit of puzzlement show in his eyes. "Which part do you mean in particular?" He understood perfectly now, but the case always went more smoothly when the client said it out loud at the beginning.

"This part." She pointed to a line in the ad. "Cases involving the occult handled with discretion."

The smile warmed his eyes now. The woman might indeed have the key to his growing discontent, but first she had to trust him.

"Complete discretion," he assured her in the tone he would use with the bank at audit time, "but I'll need all the particulars if I'm to help you. And you should know, our rates are steep. Fifteen hundred dollars per day plus expenses, the first week payable in advance as a retainer, and the same due each week for as long as we are engaged on the case. We assign as many investigators as it takes, for as long as it takes, to resolve the situation. You may of course cancel our arrangement at any time, but there are no refunds. We guarantee results only on open-ended contracts, which means that you waive the right to terminate the contract for any reason."

The woman in the pink suit glared at him. "We are talking about my brother. I want to find him whatever the cost. But even you may find it difficult to make good on your claim."

"We are not charlatans, Miss—"

"My name is Simpson. Mrs. Marnie Simpson."

"Yes, Mrs. Simpson. Should our investigators determine that there is insufficient evidence for us to continue our investigation, we would of course unilaterally terminate the contract. While I cannot guarantee that you will like what we find, you may be reassured that all of our contracts have been fulfilled to the letter. We have never had to terminate a case from our end."

Marnie Simpson frowned down at the tattered advertisement. "I'll be honest with you, Mr. Bradley. I did not choose your agency. I found your ad lying on top of the ransom note in my dining room. For some reason the kidnapper wants you, a fact that gives me no confidence in you whatsoever. But I figure it this way: if you are working with the people who took my brother, you are my best chance of getting him back. If you are not working with these people, they seem willing to use you as a go-between, and you are still my best shot. Since the police have left me few choices, I agree to your terms. That does not mean I trust you, or put any faith in your claims."

Disgruntled, Badad silently gave his sympathies to the erstwhile Mr. Simpson. He considered sending her on her way, but hesitated. Someone dealing in kidnapping and the occult wanted Bradley, Ryan, and Davis on the case. How could he turn down the challenge, even delivered through an unwilling third party?

"I see." He cleared his throat, not quite sure what to say in the face of such enthusiasm. "I'm sure we'll change your mind about our services, Mrs. Simpson. In the meantime I'll need some background information on yourself and your family, your brother in particular. And I'll have to see the ransom note, of course."

Mrs. Simpson nodded her head. "My husband is Franklin Simpson, of Simpson Enterprises. I own and operate Carter Stables under my maiden name. My brother, Paul Carter, is nineteen—here's his picture."

She handed Brad a snapshot of a young man with blond hair falling nearly to his shoulders and eyes black as the pits of hell. Paul Carter wore some loose-fitting robe, white with arcane symbols embroidered at the neck and cuffs and with an upside-down pentagram stitched over the heart. A dark stone lay at the center of the pentagram.

"Actually, Paul is my half brother. After my father died, our mother had a brief affair with a sexual adventurer who disappeared before she even knew she was pregnant. That didn't seem to matter to Mother, though. She adored Paul, we all did, in spite of the struggle he made of his life.

"You have to understand," she urged him, "Paul was searching for something. I never understood what it was, but for a while he thought he had found it with a group he met at a club in New York, a place called the Black Masque."

Brad sat up at that one. "I've dealt with the owner on an occasion or two." On a particularly memorable occasion he'd gambled with one of his own kind for the life of the half-human son he hadn't known he had. Evan, his son, had been searching, too, but he'd found only insanity at the Black Masque. Not a nice place at all. "What exactly is your brother into, Mrs. Simpson?"

"Everything. Paul had dreams; strange, frightening dreams. When we were children, he would wake up screaming from them. Therapy didn't help, drugs didn't help. Eventually he took to following every guru and fad that came along. I think he'd given up on stopping the dreams, he just wanted to understand why he had them. The Black Masque was his most recent answer, and for a while he seemed better. Then he seemed more frightened than ever. He told me he had to get away, to think, but they would never let him escape. Today I came in from the stables and found the house in shambles, Paul missing, and the message burned into the dining room table. I wrote it down for you."

Marnie Simpson pulled a slip of notepaper from her handbag and passed it to Brad. On it she had copied: "Return the Eye of Omage and death will be swift. Withhold the Eye and he will spend eternity longing for death that does not come."

"They are mad, Mr. Bradley. I don't know what this Eye of Omage is. I would give it to them if I had it, but I don't. And yet they may be torturing my brother right now because they think I am keeping it from them. I don't know what to do."

Brad stared at the message she had written, seeing not paper but his nemesis rising from flames into darkness. Omage. Not the first time the two of them would fight, nor did the focused enmity between Badad, lord of the host of Ariton, and Omage, lord of the host of Azmod, begin with the back room of a scruffy bar in the East Village. They both remembered the first time, when the lord of Azmod had battled as a god. Not his call, but saying no to the Prince of Ariton would be like this human hand saying no to his brain. A world of worshipers had died when Badad took the battle into the heart of that people's sun. Destabilized, the star sent planets scattering like the pieces from an overturned chessboard. Omage had not forgotten, would never forget Badad's interference in that little game. An old enemy. Brad wondered how Mrs. Simpson's young brother had become a pawn in a feud older than civilization on this backwater planet.

"You haven't gone to the police about this, have you, Mrs. Simpson?"

She looked at him and he held her gaze, just a flicker of what he was glinting in his eyes. She did flinch then.

"No, I couldn't. There would have been publicity, newspapers. They'd make Paul out to be some maniac looking for kicks and, ultimately, the police would shrug it off and forget it, another spoiled rich kid who got what he deserved."

"I see. And you don't believe it is some prank, or even a bizarre threat to keep your brother in line? It's been known to happen."

"Tell me that after you've seen my dining room table."

Brad nodded. "Agreed." He took the card she offered.

"I'll meet you at this address, at three tomorrow afternoon. I may have associates who will be working on the case with me. Until then, Mrs. Simpson, good day." He escorted her to the door.

# Chapter 2

*Of the second sphere, each Prince is not a being, but a mass comprised of a host of lords of daemonkind, of which each host must convoke in quorum, being 833 daemon lords, to call upon the powers of a Prince of daemons.*

AN ALMOST IMPERCEPTIBLE CHILL THAT STIRRED THE AIR IN THE WINDOWLESS study drew Evan's attention from the computer on the cluttered desk. He carefully scanned the room for the source of the disturbance. Two tapestried wingback chairs shared a standing lamp and a low table on his left, and an overstuffed leather couch faced him over a beaten brass coffee table from across the room.

All of the furniture, including the camel saddle dropped negligently in the corner behind the sofa and the dictionary stand next to the inner doorway, stood away from the walls to allow access to the bookshelves that lined the room. Evan noticed that the breeze from nowhere riffled loose papers stuffed atop a shelf of books on his right, but both the door at his left, leading to the agency's public offices and that set in the corner opposite him, leading farther into the living quarters, remained firmly shut.

A year as the junior member of the detective agency of Bradley, Ryan, and Davis had taught him that doors meant little to his unorthodox partners, but the room still seemed empty except for himself. Evan waited, watching carefully, and caught the wavering in the air that signaled an incoming daemon. Lirion was in for a rough landing—right on top of a pile of books.

He grimaced as he dived for the corner, but wicked humor glinted in his eyes. The books skittered out of the path of the incoming daemon. Evan didn't.

"Shit, Evan. Are you trying to kill me, or just break my leg? Oh, that's what you're doing!"

The daemon had taken her usual human form—hair as dark as his nightmares and skin as pale as the hour before dawn, tall enough to stare Evan straight in the eye when they were standing up, and elegantly slim. Her eyes flamed a clear, piercing blue. Evan tried to forget that in her true form Lirion *became* the fire that, for now, burned only in her eyes.

At the moment, that fire lay hidden behind closed lids while the long fingers of one hand raked through his own chestnut hair. A single, manicured fingertip traced electric currents above his heart and lower, parting shirt buttons from their buttonholes in one languid motion. He felt the laughter in her kiss and expected the mocking challenge when they broke that first lingering contact.

She lifted one eyebrow, giving him a judicious appraisal while her fingertips skimmed over his hips, tantalizing through the supple fabric of his slacks.

"Want to make the Earth move?" Her fingers wandered across his thigh, but Evan mistrusted the look in her eyes.

"Are we talking about sex, or a small earthquake?"

She nipped an earlobe, hard. "With you? Think beachfront on the Arizona coast."

To Evan's consternation a familiar voice came between them. "If you two can spare a minute, we've got work to do."

Brad. Kevin Bradley to the world, Badad in the confines of this study. Evan struggled to a sitting position wedged between corner bookcases and weighted down with a still-intent Lirion on his lap. His rueful attempts to disentangle himself met with benign amusement. Here, in the private universe they created for themselves, the daemon partners played free of the constraints of human custom, often to the acute embarrassment of the mortal in their midst.

"Your timing lacks subtlety, cousin." Lirion glared at Badad, her features blurring as blue flame crackled in her hair. "I was about to broaden Evan's education."

Sparks snapped between them when she leaned to kiss Evan fleetingly on the tip of his nose. He rubbed his abused proboscis with the palm of one hand, glad the electric shock masked the dent in his dignity.

"Later, Lily." Evan returned the kiss absently, noticing the dark things that passed across his father's face when Badad thought he wasn't looking. They always underestimated him—it was the only advantage he had in the strange menage they were forging.

"How bad is it?" The last directed at the self-contained man who rested a hand casually on the back of the leather sofa. He could have been a banker or a stockbroker in that suit, Evan thought, except for the rare

moments like now, when an unearthly wildness stormed across Brad's—
Badad's—features.

"It can wait until we've dealt with St. George." Badad navigated the
crowded study to his usual chair, a tapestried wingback. "How was
Venice?"

If Lirion sensed the brooding storm around the other daemon, she gave
no sign of it. She gathered her feet under her, reassembling most of her
usual elegance.

"Damp, as always, but unlike some I could mention, Count Alfredo
DaCosta knows how to treat a lady."

With a look that promised more retribution than he could handle, Lily
quelled the retort rising behind Evan's sudden grin, but Badad took up the
challenge. "Showed you his etchings, did he?"

She twitched an eyebrow. "Every last Master and Modern." A wholly
spurious sigh, then: "Poor Alfredo. I'm afraid the dear Count's palazzo has
a bit more empty wall space than it did yesterday."

"Does that mean you've been unfaithful again?"

Irony made a lie of Evan's indignation. Lirion tousled his hair with an
air of innocence.

"Only once. Or twice. This week. But you'll always be my pet, little
monster."

"Growl." Evan nipped at her wrist, brushed it with a fleeting kiss. He
wondered briefly if Lirion tasted the afterbite of bitterness in his playful
response. Feelings were human things; if Lily experienced them at all, she
didn't show it. Evan had seen pride and a willful capriciousness in her,
knew most humans fell beneath her notice while she saw him as a curiosity—a monster. In spite of it all, he felt himself tied to these two as to no
others on his world. They were the source of his completion.

"Mr. St. George is paying by the hour." Badad called them back to
business, the moment passing in the resettling of clothing and hair. "If the
homecoming is over, can we see the merchandise?"

"Losing a bit of canvas and paint is the most exciting thing that has
ever happened to Charles Devereaux St. George. Waiting will just add to
the suspense." Her smile had a predatory gleam and Evan pitied the art
collector. Lirion picked her teeth with righteous citizens like St. George.

"Why do you treat poor Charlie like a slug, Lily? Is it his bald head
and his paunch, or simply that he pays for what he gets instead of stealing
it?"

Evan threw himself into the high-backed office chair. With equal parts
exasperation and indignation he eyed the daemon perched on the edge of
the desk. He would never ask the real question: If you despise humans so,

why do you stay? The memory of the Black Masque, and the night that inextricably tied his life to these lords of the host of Ariton was like an angry red scar. They were all too polite to notice, but it still rankled that he owed his life to the whim of creatures he understood as little as they understood humans.

Lirion defended her displeasure with an indignant sniff. "Charlie *is* a slug, *caro mio.* He can't see two inches past his ledger books and he wouldn't know a good time if ten dancing girls set up camp on his front lawn."

"Alfredo DaCosta, on the other hand, would know just what to do with ten dancing girls." Evan drawled the words, dripping sarcasm.

"Evan can settle with St. George." Brad reentered the fray with a conciliatory smile. He went to a section of bookshelves that opened to reveal a fully stocked bar behind false book spines. He picked up a bottle with a bright red label.

"Coke, Evan?" A raised eyebrow met Evan's affirmative, but Brad filled the tumbler before gathering snifters and a bottle of the best Napoleon for himself and Lirion. Evan accepted the tumbler and set it aside, adding his own silent question to the one the daemon voiced aloud:

"You do have the painting, don't you?"

"Of course I have it." Lily pulled the canvas from the air and unrolled it atop the paperwork scattered on the desk.

"I don't know what they see in it." Lily took the snifter Badad held out to her. "Even the color is déclassé."

"It's his blue period." Evan examined the Picasso with a magnifying glass before pronouncing it genuine. Oblivious to his cousin's sneer and his father's smirk, he continued: "He couldn't afford much else, but still the talent was there. It shines out of the canvas. Ironic, isn't it? We'll get more for recovering it than he did for painting it."

Lirion shifted to the arm of Evan's chair, toying absently with the thick hair that fell stubbornly across his forehead. "You could always give your share to some poor starving artist," she suggested, more than willing to find the whole thing ironic.

"I am." Evan grinned back at her. "Should keep me in sable brushes until the year five thousand."

She rumpled Evan's hair. "You're impossible," she declared with a smile, "but I picked up this little trinket for you anyway, while I was looking for the Picasso." She drew a heavy pendant from a pocket in her slacks and draped the chain in Evan's hair, resting a smoky topaz the size of an egg on his forehead and balancing it on the bridge of his nose.

"Because it reminded me of your eyes. Am I forgiven for calling Charlie a slug?" She kissed the top of his head and laughed as he crossed the eyes in question to see the stone, then tilted his head forward to let gem and chain fall into his outstretched palm. She took the pendant from him and slipped it over his head, resting the stone over his heart. "There," she confirmed, "a perfect match."

"If Alfredo DaCosta had it, you can bet he didn't buy it," Brad reminded them. "Somebody will probably pay us for rescuing that little bauble."

Lily shrugged. "Meanwhile, they'll be looking for Alfredo, not us."

Evan wrapped his fingers around the stone where it lay. It felt warm there. Right. "I suppose Charlie St. George should thank his lucky stars you hate Picasso, Lily, or he would be out one blue period painting again."

"And he's already paid our bill," Brad reminded them. "You will get the thing back to him this afternoon, Evan?"

The human carefully rolled the canvas and slipped it into a waiting tube. "No problem. He's expecting someone from our office at four. That leaves you an hour to tell us why we are going to hate this new case."

He took a sip of his soda, while he stared consideringly at the man across the desk. Badad swirled the brandy in his glass, his eyes focused on the aromatic film that clung to the curves of the bowl. The daemon's attention seemed far away just then, and Evan guessed whatever memory played out behind those eyes brought more pain than pleasure. The idea that his father could feel pain came as a surprise; its connection with their new client started a slow curdle of dread in the pit of his stomach.

"If it's that bad, why didn't you turn it down?"

Badad really looked at him then, glanced away at Lily, but returned his attention to his son. "This time we don't have a choice. It's Omage. He's left his calling card, no question about it."

The name froze Evan where he sat. Omage. He couldn't, not again. How could Brad even suggest . . . try not to think, not to see, pretend everything is normal. . . . He had a job, worked with strangers as human as he. Daemons were a fantasy, a bad dream, they didn't exist, not anywhere—especially not in this room. It was a bad dream and he could wake up if he tried hard enough. *Wake up. Wake up.*

The room never wavered. Agitated, Lily paced between the overstuffed chairs and the low brass coffee table piled with books—Kierkegaard, Walter Scott, Robert Ludlum—and Evan turned away from her, blocking the memory of her touch. Kevin Bradley sat forward in his chair. Evan felt the force of him but dared not meet Badad's eyes. Daemon fire lurked there: power beyond his comprehension, and a hunger for places that didn't exist except in Evan's nightmares.

"Not again." The pleading in his own voice disgusted him, but Evan couldn't stop it. This time, he would go insane.

"No." Kevin Bradley's voice, so soft, almost a whisper. He held Evan with the intensity of his look. "You're staying out of this one. Spend a month painting in the south of France, surfing off the coast of Australia, photographing penguins in Antarctica—anything that takes you as far as you can go as fast as you can get there."

"We can all go. Tell them we're overcommitted." When he looked at Kevin Bradley, Evan forced himself to see a father. He'd spent a lifetime looking for the man whose only legacy had been dreams filled with horror and the certainty that he was different—not mad—different. Ultimately, it had taken madness to find him, and Evan knew beyond logic or reason that he would lose his father if they took this case.

# Chapter 3

*And the lords of a host of one Prince may create alliances between them, but no lord treats with those of another Prince unless it be in Quorum, as one Prince to Another, to create the great alliances that may do war together, side against side. The lords of a host may hold a lord or lords of another Prince his enemy, or may choose not to recognize the existence of a lord of a neutral Prince, that he not draw his Prince into battle without his Prince wills it.*

"WE CAN'T BACK DOWN FROM THIS ONE." BRAD THREW THE PHOTOGRAPH ON the desk and gave them a brief summary of his conversation with Marnie Simpson: "Paul Carter, age nineteen, brother to our client Mrs. Marnie Simpson and bastard son of the now deceased, then widowed, Ethel Carter: it looks like more than one cuckoo from the second sphere has been fouling nests on this little planet. Carter's missing from his home outside of Baltimore. Omage has him, he left our yellow pages listing on the Simpsons' dining room table—on top of the ransom note."

To the photograph he added the slip of paper with the words printed in Marnie Simpson's clear hand: "Return the Eye of Omage and death will be swift. Withhold the Eye and he will spend eternity longing for death that does not come."

Lirion winked in and out of the room as she paced her agitation between the spheres.

"Stand still, Lily!" Brad snapped. "I can't think when you do that."

Her temper, short-fused at the best of times, flared. "Why did you listen to that woman, cousin?" She said the word cousin as if it meant maniac, or masochist, or both. Blue sparks danced at her feet as she paced, her form wavered and solidified again.

"Evan's not the only one in this room with reason to stay clear of that place. Do you think Omage will cut cards with you for the life of every human who catches your sympathy? This time your battle could cost more than this planet is worth, and you can count me out. No doubt we will meet again in the second sphere once the dust settles, but don't look for me."

"We have no choice." Badad ground the words between clenched teeth. Almost as an afterthought he added for Evan: "There is more at stake here than our lives, or Paul Carter's life. Universes are at risk—yours, ours, maybe others. Lily and I are *bound* to this battle." He added the emphasis for Lirion. Words were traps for daemons, and this one—meaning the binding of a daemon to a task through its completion—carried more weight than the rest of the OED, unabridged, combined. Lirion grimaced, and he saw the memory of Ariton's binding flare in her eyes:

*Madness, at first a gentle wave, jostled the delicate balance of the second celestial sphere. The ripple effect teetered through the spheres like so many tortured dominoes, each careening into the next until it passed beyond the awareness of the Princes of Darkness. That madness was human, and more. It tasted of Ariton and unwholesome alliances across the borders of reality, its presence among the spheres boding change in the nature of all universes.*

*For the first time in millennia the seven Princes brought together their hosts and took form. Azmod and Ariton, Paimon and Oriens, Astarot and Magot, Amaimon, each drew together out of the essence of the lords who served them, each host of 833 coalescing, becoming its Prince. Old enmities were forgotten as enemies throughout infinity put aside their rivalries to make war against the invading madness. In pillars of fire the Princes burned the message across the glittering darkness: Ariton had begun it, somewhere in that abyss where the forces of the universes froze and became matter. Ariton must end it before the fabric of realities of all the seven spheres crumbled. From the host of Ariton went Badad, daemon of solitude, and Lirion, the lily of heaven, to follow the trail of human torment to its source, the back room of an East Village bar on the planet Earth.*

"This is your fault, Badad." Lirion snarled the accusation. "If we'd burnt that place to the ground and your bastard monster with it, we'd be home now and free."

Badad saw the shock on Evan's face, mortality reflected in eyes that measured a life span in the anger of Ariton's messenger. Defiant in the face of his own fear, the human threw death in the teeth of his daemon kin and dared them to take the next, irretrievable step.

"Should I blow my own brains out, or would you like the honor? Might be a kinky new thrill for you, Lily. Or maybe not that new. Is killing humans fun, Lily? Do you get off on people dying?"

Lirion raised her hand and Badad came out of his chair in a single fluid motion. He caught her wrist and drew her gaze to the fire that blazed in his own eyes.

"Omage is the enemy, Evan. No one wants you dead." It was a lie. All the hosts of the second sphere wanted this one human dead. So did Lirion, once. He let go of her wrist and she resumed her pacing.

Lily was right in her way. One lightning bolt would have solved the problem, destroyed the nightclub called Black Masque and Omage's dirty little back room. How could he explain to either of them the impulse that had stayed his hand? Even remembering it now, Brad didn't understand.

He'd passed through the barrier between the spheres, fighting the waves of disorientation to their source. The human who set all the universes trembling drew him to the imprint of his own nature in the physical universe. Lily, passing through shadows only she could know, arrived a beat of his adopted heart later.

At first, he hadn't noticed the room. His own new flesh bombarded senses he did not understand with information he could not sort and he let that form dissolve in blue flame. As flame, he recognized the burning heart of Omage of the host of Azmod within the human body this enemy of his Prince wore. Omage knelt over the figure of a creature with no consciousness at all, just a barely animal pulsing of heart and lungs. Badad resolved again in corporeal form to confront his nemesis and, gradually, as he learned again the sensations a human body fed him, the room opened up to him in the flickering gold of a hundred candles. A small group of beings who held no trace of the Princes about them clustered around the unconscious one, their attention suddenly focused on the lords of Ariton. Omage, lord of the host of Azmod, held a bowl of stone beneath the unconscious creature's arm, collecting the warm blood dripping from the open wrist.

"You've come." Omage set the bowl down and stood, dusting off his hands. He stepped over a silver chain that bound the heavy collar around the unconscious creature's neck to the clawed foot of a high gilt chair. Smiling, he spread his hands wide. "Friends, our prayers are answered in unhoped for abundance. Welcome our guests, daemon lords of the high Prince Ariton. Ours not to command, but to worship." Omage bowed low, leading his followers in their obsequies. The humans ranged themselves behind his chair; none responded to Azmod's irony. "Is it not so, old friend? Not so grand a following as the first time we met, but a beginning. This time, of course, I had your help. I suppose I should thank you, but I see you haven't let your host-cousin in on the joke."

"You play a dangerous game, old enemy," Badad countered.

"Joke?" Lirion had interposed.

He had not answered, nearly didn't register the question at all. Suddenly it was there—Ariton—burning in his mind. The creature chained at Omage's feet had awakened; more accurately, perhaps, returned, and the fire of his own Prince glinted out at him through eyes hard with madness. So this was his son.

The creature smelled. Feces and vomit. Blood, and something else. Decay. Wounds festered on its arms, on its neck where the thick silver collar chafed.

Lirion twisted in angry flames around his head. "Kill it!" Her words crackled through his mind and he looked up. More of the surrounding room fell into place. Arcane designs in blood clung everywhere in the splintered light of the candles. Some of the symbols hurt to look at, others blurred his mind with strange hungers. One burned with daemonic fire, his son's blood painted on the wall. Omage sat in the high chair and pulled at the chain, dragging the ragged figure of Badad's insane get to its knees. "If you'd phoned ahead, I'd have held the show for your arrival."

Badad had seen enough. Home was a lightning strike away, until Omage brought his attention back to the human.

"Your father." The reptilian voice hissed the words. "I promised an end to your search." Omage kissed the forehead of the human with soft, wet lips curved in a smile of lazy pleasure and sighed, a sound like the scales of a serpent slithering across sand. "I never said it would be a happy ending."

Omage had leaned back in his high chair then, pulling the human's throat taut with the chain in his hand. "I suppose they've sent you to get rid of the creature."

*Out. Out of there.* Badad wanted out of this place, this form, out of the presence of an enemy he could not fight as long as the truce among Princes held. As long as the creature Omage called Badad's son lived.

"Now!" Lirion's voice snapped, sharp next to his ear.

The room blurred and thunder rumbled off the walls. He raised his hand to strike, and daemon-fire had glinted in his son's eyes. Badad knew nothing of the meaning of fatherhood, but he read in those mad eyes the expectation of death at his father's hand and found beauty in the need that reached beyond fear or despair.

"Father." The boy's voice was a choked whisper, a voice more accustomed to screaming in the dark than speaking. But anger seemed, for the moment, to hold back the madness. With blood-streaked hands the boy lifted his chain and held it before his eyes. "If you've come to finish what you started, do it. Do it! Bastard."

Betrayal burned in that wild glare. The boy seemed barely aware of his physical injuries, his accusations touching on something that Badad could not imagine, except that Ariton shone within him, and he had grown more than twenty years in this place of frozen time with no touch of host-cousins, no knowledge of his Prince. The hand fell, and Badad watched a drop of blood seep from the wounded wrist, mix with the suppurating oozes, and slide, gracefully, across the boy's clenched fist to gild the chain.

Suddenly, the thought of this human's death left a taste of ashes in the mouth of the body he wore in Earth's reality. Badad smiled, cold and hard in the flickering light; something trembled not quite seen in the shadows. Omage's followers fell back, hiding from his view.

"You know why I am here, lord of Azmod. We've played out your whims before, at your cost, and this time even Azmod is ranged against you. But you pique my interest. Give me the boy, and you can keep your worshipers."

Omage smiled in his turn and lifted his hands, palms upturned, to express defeat. "Kill him, then. As you say, I cannot stop you. Or do you have games of your own in mind? A deal, then. One cut of the cards. I win, he dies. You win, well, whatever."

The lord of Azmod reached, and an acolyte pressed a pack of cards into his hands. He lifted a small stack from the deck, showed a ten of spades. Badad followed his lead, showed a king of hearts.

"The boy is yours. Take him. If you want him."

"You're as mad as your human get!" Lirion prepared to strike, but Badad stayed her hand.

"No." Badad considered his prize. Well, a human life, after all, was a fleeting thing. It might be worth the moment out of the long reach of his existence to explore. But not as father or son, with all the promise and pain that bled from the tortured body of the boy. If he survived, they could ride together on a different wind, as companions.

At the last, Lily had agreed, for reasons of her own that he would never fathom. Until this moment, confronting Evan across a cluttered desk in the place they now shared, she had shown no regret for the weakness that sealed their fates to the human's. Evan's death could no longer serve a purpose, but Badad recognized the danger in Lirion's undirected wrath. His son saw it, too. The human would push at their limits, it was a part of him, but no regret Lily might feel later could take back the unconsidered stroke unleashed against a mortal body.

"This is between Princes, Lirion. It was never Evan's fight."

His words brought her up short, her eyes wide with the realization that this was Evan. Once dead he would be gone forever. "Don't be stupid. It wouldn't do us a bit of good to kill him now—Omage has already found another one."

"Then in the name of the seven Princes, will you sit down? We've got work to do, and a client who expects a Picasso on his doorstep at four." Brad waved in the direction of the leather sofa, as far from Evan at the desk as the room allowed. He kept his tone casual, and hoped his son believed the danger had resided only in an overactive imagination. Maybe, if Lily would just sit down, he'd even believe it himself.

"All right." She threw herself on the sofa curled on her side, one hand carded into her hair to prop her head against the leather bolster, grumbling. "I didn't know him then. It wouldn't have been the same thing at all. Any clue as to what Omage's up to this time?"

In the fifteen billion years he'd known her, that was the closest Lirion had ever come to an apology. Brad finally let go of the breath he'd been holding. In answer to her question he shook his head.

"Just the note. He seems to have lost something and thinks we can find it for him. Like all good megalomaniacs, he's named it after himself— the Eye of Omage— totally obscuring any useful information."

"So, no facts. Any guesses?"

"Maybe." Badad took the photograph of Paul Carter from the desk and studied it, looking up at last to consider his son. Evan was still pale, and Badad suspected that he held onto the arms of his chair to still the shaking in his hands. But the half-human was alert and watchful, only his silence testifying to the aftereffects of Lily's temper. An old human expression seemed peculiarly apt: with friends like these, Evan scarcely needed enemies. By some cruel twist of fate, those enemies proved equally powerful.

Evan seemed to relax under his scrutiny, sensing that if Brad could turn his back on Lily the crisis was truly over. Brad wished the assumption were justified, but he knew the danger had just begun, and its focus rested forgotten over his son's heart. Lily was right; the gem was a perfect match for Evan's eyes.

Brad had grown accustomed to the convention of this time that men wore little jewelry, and stones only in rings. On Evan the jeweled pendant simply made everything around him look out of step. The thought scared Brad, and he didn't frighten easily.

"Couldn't you have settled for a postcard?" He dropped the photograph on the sofa beside her on his way to refill his glass and brought the bottle back with him, pouring a second for Lily. Evan's soft drink remained nearly untouched.

"It's the same stone." He watched his son over brandy almost the color of the gem, his eyes wandering to the jewel and holding there almost against his will. "I would have spared you this—" a whispered plea for understanding, the answering nod almost lost in mesmerized fascination with the stone.

"I think we've got the Eye of Omage."

"Are you sure?" Lirion moved to the desk, looking from the photograph to the jewel at Evan's breast. "It looks darker in the picture." She reached out as if to touch it, then hesitated, dropping her hand to her side.

"As sure as a guess can be," Brad confirmed. "Which leads us to two questions: How did Omage know we would have it before you stole it, Lily? And what do we do about it?"

"Shit." With feeling, then, "I need some fresh air." She disappeared in a clap of thunder and a small whirlwind.

"Evan?" Brad slumped into his armchair and watched his son. Evan stared at the photograph, his jaw clenched as if holding back the very memory of his own screams. Brad knew what his son saw, but had no comfort to give him.

There was little physical similarity between his own half-human son and the face that stared out of the picture, but Brad remembered the dead look in Evan's eyes when he'd found his son at the Black Masque. Paul Carter's eyes held that same look. More than one daemon had been seeding this little planet, but it only took one Omage to destroy them. Evan had been strong enough to survive both the dreams and Omage once. Could he ask his son to enter that pit again? Badad knew before the question shaped itself that he would never ask it, and wondered what was happening to him that it should matter.

Evan lifted the jewel from his breast and stared at it. "I don't believe in coincidences," he said. "I'm not even sure I believe in Mrs. Marnie Simpson. But I do believe in him." He dropped the necklace on the photograph and looked straight into the eyes of his father.

"I'm not afraid of dying," he explained. "It's something all humans have to do eventually. I am afraid of the emptiness that goes on forever. The dreams were bad enough, but Mac—Omage—made it real. I couldn't take that again."

Not all the wisdom of the seven Princes in all the seven spheres of heaven could tell him how Evan had survived to adulthood, had overcome Omage's ungentle ministrations. Against all reason, Badad felt fiercely proud that his son still lived, but could find no way to tell him so.

"You've been there since," Brad reminded him. "Once with Lily, a few times with the two of us. You can find your way home now, he can't trap you there against your will. But I meant what I said at the start of this. Lily and I will handle Omage. Get away somewhere until we've dealt with him, sent him back where he belongs."

"Can you? What if *he* is stronger?"

Badad waved the possibility away, but Evan wasn't buying the bravado. "What could he do to you?"

Don't ask, Badad wanted to say, don't think the unthinkable until we have to. Aloud he gave the only answer he had: "It doesn't matter. We have to try."

"And Paul Carter?"

"Omage has shown us a simple rescue will never be enough. We have to send him back where he belongs. If we can, we'll pull Carter out of there. A lot depends on how strong he is. And then again, a lot depends on how strong Omage is. None of us may get out; that's why I want you as far away from the Black Masque as possible."

Evan studied him minutely, weighing emotion betrayed in the flicker of an eyelash. Finally he nodded.

"Okay. I couldn't go back in there anyway." He gave a rueful, self-deprecating laugh. "When it's over . . ."

"We'll find you. And, Evan, don't blame yourself because you can't do twice what most humans wouldn't survive even once."

"Yeah, well, there's no reason I can't poke around a bit at Carter Stables. We can take the Mercedes—I'm not transporting. I can pack when we get back tomorrow, maybe visit Jack and Claudia Laurence in London. Is that far enough?"

"Should be." Brad reached for the pendant on the desk, but Evan was there first, sweeping the jewel into a clenched fist.

"Sorry. I don't know why I did that." Evan stared at his hand as if it had a life of its own. "Can't leave it on the desk—I'll lock it up."

"Fine."

Brad watched a section of books behind the desk slide out of the way. Evan swung open the door to the safe and laid the stone on top of the personal papers that made them all real: birth certificates, deed to the house and offices and one to the condominium in Nice, stocks and treasury certificates. When Evan turned to face him again, the embarrassment had faded, but traces of the confusion remained.

"We'll need that to get Carter back."

"I know." Evan reassured him with a wry grin. "And right now I have an appointment with a Picasso."

Brad pulled open the door to the living quarters beyond. He waited until Evan retrieved the rolled canvas and closed the door behind them with a last nervous glance at the hidden safe.

# Chapter 4

*Among the Princes of the second sphere fall great battles, for the might of Princes must ever be tested, and each strives to be greatest among the Princes. And the Princes send out their hosts to do battle, and the lightning is the sword of the daemon, and the thunder his chariot, and the bloom of a new star in the firmament signals his great victory.*

EVAN TWITCHED NERVOUSLY IN HIS SLEEP, TRYING TO ESCAPE THE DREAMS. *THIS must be what dying feels like,* he thought as some inner part of himself tried to tear loose.

He clung to the integrity of self that was more than just a soul, but included a body he was just learning to appreciate, a humanness that found expression in eating and shitting and making love and running. Inner vision was fine, but he needed his hands to work the clay and hold the brushes. He needed his smile and his scowl and the explosion in his chest when a feeling took concrete form beneath his fingertips. So he hung on, until suddenly the pressure was gone, and he was . . . someplace else.

The darkness behind his lids passed into a greater darkness. He tried to open his eyes, and knew that he had no eyes, no throat to scream, no lungs to fill. Around him stretched not black, nor any of the mind's conceptions for the absence of light, but an absence of sensory referent to translate into the human experience of not-seeing. He had no up or down, no forward or backward, nor any sense of what those words might mean in this place. He knew he wasn't alone, and didn't know how he knew. Those others weren't friendly, but his rational mind recognized that they couldn't hurt him. He wasn't really there. And "there" went on forever—no way back.

No way back. The thought echoed in his mind. He knew that somewhere a body was screaming, but he couldn't reach it. The scream went on forever, because time no longer existed. And the others were somewhere; his *nonrational* mind warned that maybe they could hurt him. Long ago Sunday School lessons hinted at hell. He thought of Jack Laurence and sins committed while a bartender named Mac watched and smiled. Not even his guilt could conjure the images of his shame to relieve the darkness in which he hung. This was hell, and he had died, and there was no way out—

Then, a voice he could not hear shivered through him.

"Evan, wake up."

He knew that hands he could not feel shook the body he'd left behind, then a presence occupied the not-space that he thought of as himself in this place.

"Get your body up here, Evan."

The not-voice thought jolted him into self-will; Evan called upon the self of taste and touch and sight. Awake now, his body responded: he felt it shudder through the skin of reality into a place it had no way to be, and he became aware of physical sensation again. Nausea. Waves of nausea hit him while his eyes denied the truth his stomach told him. He was falling, falling, and there was no end to the falling because he wasn't moving at all, in a darkness his brain still denied.

A blue flame burned with no heat beside him, and he felt a touch on his mind like a teasing kiss. Lirion's voice floated on gentle laughter inside of him.

"Do you need a little gravity?"

The flame, transformed to a pulsing cloud the color of a summer sky, surrounded him, and weight settled on Evan's shoulders. Unfortunately, the direction to which his inner ears reacted as "up" corresponded to what his eyes saw as sideways. Falling over cured that problem, and Evan almost felt human again. Or whatever he was. He slapped his sides, hard, to be certain he was really there, and discovered an awkward truth:

"I'm naked!"

Champagne laughter bubbled through him.

"That's how you left it." Lily's voice, archly innocent, licked at his imagination.

The flame that was the daemon Lirion bathed him in a blue glow that reminded him of stories from his childhood about pissing during lightning storms. He would have crossed his hands over his genitals, but refused to give her something else to laugh at.

"Let's go home."

He knew it was the wrong thing to say when the flame glinted orange around the edges, a color that signaled Lirion's displeasure in waves of energy that pricked at the hairs on his arms and pulled at the skin over his temples. The flame disappeared, the sense of Lily with it, and Evan waited until the itch at his back warned him to turn. She wrapped him in blue flame, and he let her infiltrate his mind, pass through his body, a sensation like being tickled from the inside. When she had re-formed in flame beside him, he tried to pass it off lightly:

"I meant *my* home. I'm not exactly dressed for traveling." Keep it casual, and maybe she'd pretend his screaming hadn't wakened her in the middle of the night. "Let's go back to bed."

"Fool."

The flame snapped sparks off his nose, warning him that Lily didn't buy the breezy tone one bit. She waited, and Evan felt the challenge: she was leaving it to him.

He tried to calm the racing of his heart, but he couldn't hide the fear from her. He hated this place, and would have struck out blindly for any escape. Lirion was watching from the inside of his head, though—a feat she could accomplish only in her true form in the second sphere.

Slowly he focused his common sense on this most illogical of situations. He'd been here before in his body, with Brad and with Lily herself. Evan knew how to get home now, he just had to shape in his mind the picture of the bedroom as they had left it, sheets tumbled, outlines of bed and bureau and dressing table barely discernible in the night-shadowed room. He allowed the details to slide out to the periphery, all but Lily's big four-poster swathed in Alençon lace bed curtains. He firmed the image with the tactile memory of silk covers on fat down pillows, almost inseparable from the feel of Lily's body pressed along his side.

And they were back. The filtered light of a streetlamp slipping between the curtains left lacy shadows on the breasts of the woman beside him. Evan raised himself on one elbow to look down at her face and brushed a kiss softly over her lips.

"Thank you," he said, as her arms wrapped around his neck.

"You haven't sleepwalked in the second sphere in a long time," she commented.

They both knew what had brought the old dream back and sent the daemon part of him floating in his father's reality. Omage. But Lily had brought him home.

"You did it yourself, you know," she said.

He started, wondering if she could read his mind in this universe as well as in the second sphere. He wasn't ready to argue with her now, though—the memory of where he had been was still too strong.

"I can find my way back when I'm awake for the crossover now." He accepted her praise conditionally: "The spontaneous shifts are something else. I've never had them when I was awake—I thought it was just a place I'd invented in my nightmares until Omage sent me through at the Black Masque—but I lose control when I'm sleeping."

He kissed her. Couldn't have got it up to save his soul, but he craved the physical reality of lips and teeth and clouds of black hair drifting over soft white skin.

"Why does my universe scare you so badly?"

Soft question, between nibbles, but Lily sure knew how to kill the mood. And just when—hell, it was a lost cause anyway. Evan sat up, ran the fingers of both hands through hair grown lank with sweat.

"There's nothing there," he tried to explain, failing miserably at conveying the absolute lack he felt in the second sphere. "Or, sometimes I sense something, off somewhere in a place that has no where, and it hates me."

A half laugh: "Other kids worried about monsters under the bed. My monsters dragged me into an emptiness so complete that I didn't exist there, a place where even the monsters would have been company, but they didn't exist there either, except for a touch at what consciousness they left me. I knew with that touch they would destroy everything I'd ever known to keep me there."

He saw the expressions pass across Lily's face, recognized the knowledge they both shared. Those others whose presence he almost felt in the second sphere were not the monsters. Evan was. Half of this reality, half of the other, he had no place in either. And he knew that once, all the Princes of that other place had united with one purpose: to seek his death. He touched her, running a finger lightly between her breasts, knowing that those Princes had sent her to kill him. Lucky for him that monsters turned her on.

"It isn't like that." She took his hand in hers, entwined their fingers, and nestled the basket of their palms over her right breast. Her eyes grew distant, a tiny smile compounded of memory and touch lingering in her face.

A worm twisted in the back of Evan's mind. How did she know what he was thinking? Lirion's next words reassured, her thoughts traveling a different path entirely.

"To us, the second sphere is not empty, but filled with stars and planets that *we* know as knots in the weave of energy that makes up the Universe. What your physicists are only now beginning to learn—that space is not empty, but filled with energy—we have experienced as creation itself, and all of it seethes with sensations. Not like these—" She lifted their meshed hands, kissed Evan's knuckles for an example, and snugged the hands comfortably around her breast again, "—but more like knowing, or appreciating.

"You see a painting, and feel a set of emotions you translate as appreciation. We don't pass through the process of translation, or the separation between what we are and what we experience. If you could become the painting, love your own beauty, and then pass on, become the sunset, and love your own grandeur, you'd be getting close.

"You can observe the stars through a telescope, but you can't look at your own sun directly without burning out your sense of sight. We can enter into the very heart of that star, change its nature, and pass out again unscathed."

"It sounds beautiful when you describe it," Evan admitted.

Lily paused, her head cocked thoughtfully. "Yes. It is." She smiled. "Sometimes, after fifteen billion years, one forgets." She released his hand and leaned over him, arms crossed on his chest, and kissed the frown lines between his eyes.

"But?" she coaxed.

"I'm part daemon."

"Those are some of my favorite parts," she agreed.

Evan continued in spite of the distraction of teeth gently nibbling at his chin.

"I can travel to the second sphere, sometimes I can't *stop* myself, but I've never seen anything like you describe. I've never seen anything at all."

"That's because you are trying to see." Her hand dipped beneath silk sheets, teased him with manicured nails, and gentled the touch with fingertips. "Can you see what I'm doing?"

"No."

Long stroking touches, then: "Does that mean my hand isn't real?"

Evan wrapped his arms around her, rolled her on her back, and kissed her with feeling this time, more feeling than he'd felt safe to show her before.

"You're real," he agreed, moving slowly to the rhythm she set while he planted small kisses on her breasts.

Lily's hands drifted over his body, molded her fingers to his clenched buttocks. "Maybe we've been going at this all wrong."

Evan knew she meant the second sphere, but he needed to hear her say it. "Not everything," he coaxed.

"Oh, no." She smiled, and her arms reached round his waist, rolled him over. He saw the heat in her eyes, and the laughter in the face that hovered above him. "Some things we get just right."

# Chapter 5

*Of the Princes and their daemon hosts many tales are told, but of these most are falsehoods spread by the daemon lords themselves to mock humankind. For the true nature of the Princes one must look to their names, which are the fonts of their power in their own sphere, and the means by which man can bind them in the first. And of the nature of their Prince do the host of daemon lords share, as well as the characteristics of their own names make up their natures. If a man were to bind a daemon to his bidding, therefore, he must first know the nature of the daemon he binds.*

BADAD TRIED TO SUBMERGE HIS IMPATIENCE IN THE VIEW OUTSIDE THE CAR window, but found little there to relieve the monotony.

"Why don't you pull over and let me drive? I know a shortcut."

Evan cast him a baleful look. "No, thanks. Your shortcuts don't usually include the car. Watch the scenery—people come from all over the world for this scenery."

His window offered a view of rolling hills covered in a spring-misted green, and split rail fences weathered a soft gray. Bare, spiky vines clung to the rails. In another month the vines would green, and bloom roses in June; now they looked like dead things frozen in the act of strangling their equally moribund host. The mud cast a thick brown pall over everything, including the fenders of the silver Mercedes.

"They're crazy," he decided, "and you are lost. Route 30 doesn't go to Baltimore."

"Well, Brad, it's like this. You can't breed thoroughbreds in a town-house. It upsets the neighbors when the horses get out and eat the petunias. Carter Stables is northwest of Baltimore, but who except the natives and other horse trainers ever heard of Deep Run?"

Badad let his head fall against the padded leather seat back and closed his eyes. Counting to ten didn't help. Maybe a thousand and ten. Three hours in an internal combustion vehicle, even one as lovingly crafted as the Mercedes, tested the limits of his attachment to the man at the wheel. It would be different, he supposed, if Evan Davis couldn't pass through the interface between the spheres, but his son shared in more than a human heritage. The daemon in him called to the second sphere. Lily kept a feeler out for him at night, when that part slipped past self-control and human form to drift alone in the second sphere of his father's reality.

But forced, fully awake, into the reality of Badad and his kind until he had grown quite mad, Evan's horror had once destabilized universes. Over time Badad had shown him that with someone he trusted as an anchor, he could pass through the universe of the Princes with no harm to himself or the realities he touched in his passage. Now, however, the memory of Omage and his cursed back room paralyzed his bastard son in the physical sphere, stuck in a metal box passing through miles of northern landscape, still recovering from the shock of winter in real space.

To pass the time he considered the memories that had risen up to bind Evan to the material plane. Did those memories change the essence of humanness, like the human summons changed the essence of his own kind? Twenty-five years ago a human summons had drawn Badad into the material sphere and bound him against his will to this reality out of idle mischief he now recognized as jealousy. He'd won free of the human who thought he would master a lord of Ariton, but not before he'd seduced the girl, destroyed her coming marriage, and left behind more of himself than he had bargained for.

"How is your mother? You never talk about her." He'd never thought to ask before, and Evan looked at him strangely now.

"Didn't think you'd be interested. Didn't think you'd even remembered her."

"I don't, not much at any rate." Badad shrugged in answer to the sharp glance. "Just making conversation." Trying to untangle the web that bound him here, if he were honest with himself.

Evan wasn't buying it, but he didn't push for an explanation Badad didn't have. "You didn't ruin her life, if that's what you're asking. I saw her at Christmas—you were in Madrid, and Lily was wherever she goes when the weather turns cold. She still lives on Rosemont Street and teaches Chemistry at Edgemont High. One of these days she may even marry Harvey Barnes, the principal.

"She never blamed you for what happened. I think she's glad we've gotten to know each other; I haven't told her what you are."

"Would she believe you if you did tell her?"

"She'd probably try to have me committed. Wouldn't be the first time."

Tangled webs. They both fell silent; to go farther would be to admit they had already revealed too much. Evan's bitterness demanded an apology Badad did not have to give. The sacrifice of his own freedom demanded gratitude that Evan did not owe.

He'd never asked Lirion how she had been drawn out of the second sphere by the binding spell of a human or what task that human had set her. As the human summons had changed Badad, so that long-ago summons had changed Lily forever. His kind, like the humans, could not pass the barrier between the spheres alone. Once summoned to the material sphere with a formula of sound and symbol, however, the pattern of the passage imprinted itself upon the essence of what they were. Ariton had had few choices when he sent his warriors to stop an insane human's intrusion into the seven spheres; the part of Evan that was Badad had called to him as powerfully as the summons that created him. But Lily had shaken free of her Earth-binding long ago, and her anger at Ariton's command had shaken the heavens as she passed. That she agreed to this mad charade at all had surprised him. Little given to introspection, she had dismissed it as a whim, but Badad wondered. More tangled webs.

"We're there." Past the mailbox set on a post, and before the swinging sign with the horse's head and the words "Carter Stables" in black letters, Evan made a right between the open gates that crossed a narrow lane.

From the road they could see only a cluster of oaks and evergreens beyond the low rolling fields, but as they drew closer, Badad could make out black shutters on a white frame farmhouse. Once a straightforward double-pile Georgian, the house now sprawled over two wings added by previous owners.

Evan pulled the car around to the side of the house and killed the engine. Lily Ryan waited for them in the doorway.

"What took you so long? The boy's not still afraid of flying, is he?"

Nothing of the night before showed in her expression—she quirked a smile only slightly malicious in Evan's direction and went on: "Mrs. Simpson said to tell you she'd be down before we left, but she needed a rest. In the meantime, I can give you the three dollar tour."

They rounded the back of the house, where someone had piled the broken furniture in a heap next to a cinder block fire pit. Kevin Bradley, Badad of the second sphere, gave it only a cursory glance.

"The big square building over there is the barn, and the longer lower one with the windows is the stable. Paddock and practice track are fenced off just beyond—you can see the track from here; it looks like an old dirt road going nowhere."

Badad followed the direction she pointed and found the structures, both white with black trim, about the length of a football field from the main house. At the fifty yard line an equally well tended bungalow wallowed in a sea of daffodils. "And that?"

"Used to be the foreman's house. Paul Carter has been living there off and on for a couple of years. She gave me the key. I was waiting for you to get here before I checked it out."

Brad nodded thoughtfully. He'd never seen the place where Evan Davis lived before Omage got his hands on the boy, and he wondered how alike these bastard children of two universes really were. Evan seemed to be thinking along the same line, tension tightening the corners of eyes locked on the low frame house.

"Why don't you check out the stable, see if anyone noticed anything suspicious yesterday. We'll meet at the big house when we are done."

Evan shook his head, but his eyes never left the bungalow. "I have to go in there. I have to know what it was like for him."

"He's a fool, you know." Lily addressed herself to Badad as if Evan were not there, but her follow-up remark was intended for them both: "Like father, like son. Let's get this over with."

The door opened into a roomy kitchen with little evidence of occupancy. Paul Carter had left no half-read mail on the maple chopping block table, no salt and pepper shakers on the formica countertops or cereal boxes in the cabinets. The living room showed little more of the man's presence; its rag rug and country casual furniture looked fresh from the pages of *House and Garden.*

"He doesn't live here." Evan voiced the conclusion they had all reached in their examination of the impersonal dwelling.

Lily ran a finger over an oak end table and glared at the dust she had accumulated there. "According to Marnie Simpson, Paul comes in every few months and stays a week or two. Seems to use the place as a detox center; cleans the booze and the drugs out of his system when the waking nightmares get worse than the ones he has at night, then drops out of sight again."

"Not in here he doesn't." Evan headed for the bedroom and stopped with his hand still on the knob. "Oh, my Lord."

Figuring one lord would do as well as another under the circumstances, Badad answered the summons. "What did you find?"

He stopped with a hand on Evan's shoulder and tightened his grip when the meaning of what he saw penetrated the shock. On the white bedspread Paul Carter had outlined a crude pentagram in black paint. Carter had made of the dresser a shrine to death. Pills—black ones, yellow, red, orange, and white ones—lay scattered like confetti among the weapons. The pistol was loaded, hunting knife unsheathed, razor blades scattered with the pills. On the bedside table a Jack Daniels bottle stood empty but for an amber inch evaporating at the bottom.

Badad moved past Evan into the room and stared at the shotgun tied to the high back of the room's only chair.

He barely comprehended mortality as an idea, the reality of the state of nonbeing as alien to him as were the humans whose physical form he now shared. That one of these mortal creatures would willingly contemplate his own nonbeing, would be the agent of his own nonexistence, disturbed him as nothing else he had seen in the physical sphere. Blindly he looked to his own half-human son to reason away the unthinkable, and found only memories there.

"Why?"

"Control."

Evan followed him into the room, reached to touch the pistol with his fingertips, then thought better of it and curled his hand into a fist. "Evidence." He delivered the aside with a self-deprecating smile. The reminder was for himself.

"When the dreams become more than you can bear, you always know that, ultimately, you have the power to stop them. From the time I was old enough to find someone to sell it to me, I slept with a pistol under my pillow. Sometimes knowing that I could end it was all that kept me alive."

The thought of Evan with the side of his head blown off by his own hand revolted Brad. For this he had given up his freedom, bound to a scruffy crust of dirt on the backside of the universe to preserve the life of a human who would have ended that very life with the flick of a finger. But Evan still lived, he hadn't put a bullet in his brain. Something *had* kept him alive.

"Where is it now?"

"The safe. I don't need it any more." Evan smiled.

He hadn't quite worked out the nuances of human feeling, but Badad recognized that Evan didn't find the question funny. Gratitude came to mind, and the thought embarrassed him. Probably embarrassed Evan, too. "Anything else we need to see in here?"

Evan shook his head and led the way out of the bungalow. Brad followed with Lily at his side.

"They are all mad," she grumbled.

"Maybe," he agreed, then smiled with real humor. "Or maybe we just attract the weird ones."

With one delicately raised eyebrow Lily questioned his sanity. He answered with a shrug and followed Evan into the main house.

# Chapter 6

*Each Prince of the second sphere holds within itself both the male and female aspect, but in greater or lesser proportion, so that the Prince may be seen to be characterized more as one sex than another, as can be determined by the Prince's name. Astarot, also called Astarte and worshiped as a goddess by that name, gathers her flocks with the scythe. Azmod is the tempter, patron of all impurity. His heart is stone, harder than diamond.*

THE WOMAN WAITING FOR THEM ON THE WIDE FRONT PORCH WORE WELL TAILORED but comfortably worn corduroy slacks and an Aran sweater in the same natural color over a pale blue oxford cloth shirt. Her boots looked expensive but had seen hard use. Otherwise she fit Brad's description, and her first words confirmed Evan's preliminary identification.

"I'm Marnie Simpson." She offered a callused hand in a firm handshake that belied the nervous smile.

Evan returned the smile with a reassuring one of his own and shook hands as briefly as possible. They seldom met at their best the clients who needed the special skills of Bradley, Ryan, and Davis, but to call Marnie Simpson unprepossessing would have been a charity. A bit too thin, the woman's abrupt, sharp movement reminded him of a puppet whose strings had somehow gotten tangled, as if she herself were not quite sure which limb would follow the command for any gesture. So why did he feel like she was sizing him up for lunch? The impression passed quickly, and he chalked it up to concern for her brother and his own misgivings about the case.

When Lily and Brad joined them, Marnie Simpson led the detectives through several rooms still in shambles.

"Please excuse the mess. The housekeeper was here when it happened. I found her on her knees in the pantry, a crucifix in one hand and her beads in the other. She quit on the spot with no notice, said the house was cursed and she wouldn't spend another minute in it. The stable hand hasn't quit yet, but he won't set foot in the house. Temporary help from the agency should arrive in the morning. In the meantime I'm on my own here."

Brad muttered comforting sounds that stopped when they entered the dining room in the right wing of the house. French windows overlooked a small garden, filling the room with late afternoon sunshine and, since yesterday, a chill April breeze. The glass windowpanes lay in shards amid the rhododendrons.

Lily was the first to state the obvious: "Omage's been here all right, and he didn't come in through the windows. Probably didn't break them to get out either."

"Pressure wave, no doubt about it," Brad agreed. "He was in a hurry."

Evan fingered the letters burned into the polished walnut table while memories turned to knots in his stomach. How had Paul Carter weathered the rending tear out of the here and now of sight and touch, through that other place where senses had no meaning? What was he going through this very minute? Defensively he backed away from the thought, concentrating instead on Mrs. Simpson's discovery of the ransom note.

"Paul had been staying here for a week or two. He was scared, upset, but you have to realize that he's spent most of his life that way. I had no idea he was in real danger.

"Frank and I had tickets for a charity concert and reception. It ended late, and we decided to stay in town overnight. We had a late brunch the next afternoon, then I dropped Frank off at Baltimore-Washington Airport—he had business in Dallas—and drove home.

"When I arrived, the table was as you see it, and as I said, your ad from the telephone book lay on top, like this." She centered a blank sheet of paper on the table.

"Whoever did this wanted your firm as go-between, and I'll do whatever it takes, including deal with the devil if that's what I have to do."

Brad countered her accusation smoothly, but Evan saw the anger flashing just beneath the surface. "I assume you mean that figuratively, Mrs. Simpson. We don't know much about you either, except that you have a lot of money and your brother keeps unsavory company."

Marnie Simpson reached into a pocket and pulled out a half-empty pack of Virginia Slims, tapped a cigarette out, and replaced the pack. "Point, Mr. Bradley. Insulting each other won't bring my brother home. . . ."

A shriek from the direction of the stable interrupted whatever Mrs. Simpson would have added.

"Summer Dancer!" The woman dropped the unlit cigarette and ran back through the house. "If that bastard has hurt my horse—" She slammed her way through the kitchen door, with the detectives right behind her.

"Omage?" Lily threw a calculating glance on the run, and Evan shrugged, finding himself wasting the gesture on empty air. Brad was taking the overland route past the terrified girl running toward them, so Evan matched his pace to Mrs. Simpson's.

Private school, Evan noticed absently. Plaid skirt and gray blazer with matching kneesocks and sensible shoes: someone had worked hard to make an unattractive girl even homelier.

"What was she doing in the stable?"

"She's Mary Palmer, my walker. Local tradition, the girls earn some spending money and get to work with the horses. Mary is the only walker Summer Dancer doesn't kick."

They caught up with Mary Palmer twenty yards from the kitchen door. Marnie Simpson wrapped her arms around the girl, brushing fine mouse-colored hair out of a tear-streaked face.

"What's happened, Mary? Is Summer Dancer all right?"

For a moment Mary stared at Mrs. Simpson as if she were a stranger. When the identity of the woman penetrated the shock, Mary shook her head.

"Binky. Oh, God, why would anyone do that to Binky?"

Evan saw the girl's eyes roll back and scooped her up from a grateful Marnie Simpson's slipping grasp.

"I'll get a damp cloth and a blanket," Simpson told him. They parted company at the kitchen. Evan carried the unconscious girl into the living room and arranged her as comfortably as possible on the sofa.

"Is the girl all right?" Lily materialized at his shoulder, her expression one of indifference marred only by a mild distaste.

"Seems to be. Don't see any marks on her, and her pulse has settled down. What did she see out there?"

"Something has killed something else. I'm not sure what it was, but it wasn't human. Whoever did it left no messages. Brad is looking for clues, wants you to join him if you're not needed here." The girl stirred, distracting them, then Lily dismissed him: "You're not needed here."

Marnie Simpson returned with the damp cloth, but she had forgotten the blanket. "Has Summer Dancer been hurt?"

"A man who called himself Lopi said to tell you that Summer Dancer is panicked, but otherwise uninjured," Lily told her. "He's taken the horse out to the paddock until he calms down and he'll clean out the stall when we've finished looking for clues. After that you're on your own. He's quit, says there's devil's business here and he won't come back until someone named Father Dave exercises the stable."

"Exorcise," Simpson corrected. "Cast out the demons who've possessed it."

"Why would a daemon want to live in your stable?"

Lily sounded so amazed that Evan almost laughed. Assuming they lived to have a later, he'd enjoy teasing her about bunking down in the straw. Now, however, Brad was waiting. He heard Marnie Simpson's non-answer—"You'd have to ask Lopi"—as he left the room.

The stable was cool and dim in the late afternoon. Evan followed the long whitewashed wall past several wide stalls, empty now. The horses would be brought in soon for the night, but not until the stable hand cleared away the mess in stall number four: the smell of blood would madden the other animals. Smart. He felt the rising panic himself. *Get out, get out.* Memories painted a room with human blood, his own blood. Omage's victims, his acolytes.

He slipped on something the color of old burgundy—liver? spleen?—hacked into bits too small to identify without a microscope. Warm shit-smell mingled with the ordure of stable and death. Evan gagged, rested a hand on the stall to steady himself, and felt wet paste. Threads of red and clots of dull green glistened in the bridge of congealing fluids that followed his hasty withdrawal.

His lunch never had a chance. Evan made it to the next stall, where he christened the fresh straw. Moving deeper into the shadows he fell to his knees, wiping his hand over and over on the clean straw piled there.

"Indigestion?" Kevin Bradley rested a hand on his shoulder.

It stayed there while Evan rose to his feet, gathering himself. He checked his hand, clean although nerve memory retained the feel of gut-slime. Gingerly he curled his fingers over the offending palm and stuffed the fist into his pocket, following his father into Summer Dancer's stall.

"Just a touch. I need a drink."

"There's a bottle in Paul Carter's room."

Evan met his father's gaze and held it, remembering the days he'd once spent trying to forget. He swallowed with an effort. "Coke'll do just fine, but it can wait until we're done here." With an effort he turned his mind back to the mess in stall four. "What was it?"

Whoever had killed the animal had done a thorough job—gutted the thing and left the husk for the horse to trample into an unrecognizable mass of hair and flesh and splintered bone.

Kevin Bradley squatted beside the body of what was once a small, hairy animal. "A goat, I think. A stable hand heard the girl scream. He found the horse stomping it to pieces in the stall."

"How did a goat get in the stable?" he asked. Under control now, he dropped down to examine the carcass more closely. "Was it alive or dead when it was put here?"

"The goat lived here."

Marnie Simpson answered the question. Evan hadn't heard her arrive, but he was prepared with his most professionally bland expression in place when he turned to face her. Only the tightness around her eyes hinted at her revulsion at the viscera-smeared stall.

"Binky was Summer Dancer's pet," Simpson continued her explanation, "Most of the stables provide them for their horses. They stay together in the stall—for some reason, the horses like goats, even the most nervous of them settle right down around their own pets."

"No horse could have done this," Brad pointed out, "The animal was gutted by an expert, and thrown back in the stall."

Evan agreed, examining the gut-smeared walls. "Given the redecorating, you were never intended to think otherwise, Mrs. Simpson."

"It's another warning. They could do this to my brother."

She gave Kevin Bradley a hard stare, and Evan saw something calculated flicker in her eyes.

"When I said I would deal with the devil, if that's what it took to get my brother back, I didn't realize how literally my word might be taken. Know, however, that I did and still do mean it. Do what you must to bring my brother home alive, and I will pay any price. Am I understood?"

She turned her back on them, cutting off any reply. "Mary is shaken but otherwise unharmed. Her mother is picking her up. If that is all, I have a horse to calm before he does any major damage."

She swept out of the long stable, each step punctuated with the decisive snap of boot heels on rough-hewn boards. Looking at the pulverized remains of Binky the goat, Evan wondered what she considered major damage.

"What did she mean by that?" Brad asked when she was well out of hearing range.

"I suppose a panicky horse could hurt himself and not even know it until it's too late," he ventured absently. "Let's get out of here."

Outside, Evan filled his lungs with the clean spring air. "I don't think I'll ever get that smell out of my head."

"What smell?" Lily joined them halfway to the car.

"The smell of a stable, well kept except for the dead goat beaten halfway through the floorboards," Evan elaborated.

Lily shrugged elegant shoulders, dismissing the affair as just another aberration. "Humans have some strange customs."

Evan glared at her, but Brad distracted him from an angry retort.

"I don't care about the damn horse or the goat, Evan. What was all that devil gibberish about?"

"Oh, that." Evan laughed at the bitter irony. "She must think Omage killed the goat. Your kind have had some bad press over the years, you know. You're supposed to get off on tearing living animals to pieces. Humans are supposedly top of the charts. Goats come in a close second. You are also known to take the shape of a goat and dance in the moonlight, screwing witches."

Lily wrinkled her patrician nose in distaste. "Why goats?"

"Don't know," Evan admitted, "But it's been goats and devils for thousands of years."

"By all the Princes, these people are more barbaric than even I believed. What a stupid idea!" Lily stopped, and Evan could almost see the wheels turning in her head. "Our Mrs. Simpson doesn't strike me as a stupid woman, though."

"No, she doesn't," Brad agreed. "And she wasn't talking just about Omage. She meant us as well."

"Could she know about you?" The idea made Evan nervous. He reminded himself that she'd come to them for help. Her abrasive personality had little to do with the case and nothing at all to do with the threat Omage posed to them all.

"She obviously thinks we are in this thing with Omage," Brad said, "so it's reasonable to assume she puts us in the same category. The real question is, who or what does she think has her brother?"

Lily dismissed the problem with a wave of her hand. "If she thinks Omage gets off on trashing goats, then she doesn't really know anything about him *or* us."

They had reached the parked car, and the nagging itch at the back of his mind tumbled full grown off Evan's tongue. "If it wasn't Omage, who killed the goat? Why did they kill it?"

# Chapter 7

*Oriens is the evil king of the eastern quarter; he rules the winds, and is called the devourer by flame. Paimon rules the western quarter, and is known by the sound of bells ringing out of time. He is the whisperer, carrier of evil tidings and deceit. Amaimon rules the southern quarter with violence and death. Beware the poison of his breath.*

EVAN REACHED AROUND THE COMPUTER FOR HIS COFFEE MUG AND FOUND IT empty again. A half-full coffeepot steamed on the bar set into the wall of books, but the short walk across the study seemed more effort than it was worth. Instead he picked up the Eye of Omage, absently stroking the smooth face of the topaz while he gave in to the mesmerizing flash of the cursor on the computer screen. Waiting for the computer to finish his search program, Evan let his focus drift, reaching for the connection that seemed to hover just out of his grasp.

He didn't consciously decide to put it there, but the pendant found its way around his neck. It felt comfortable, secure, and he closed his left hand around the solid warmth of it, considering his next step.

"You should leave your senses on guard when you do that. If I'd been Omage, you'd be dead." Brad entered the room by the human method—through the doorway from the living quarters. He crossed the room and picked up the empty coffee mug from the desk. "Refill?"

"Do what? Yeah, thanks."

Badad filled the mug, and another cup for himself. "Go away when you think."

"Oh, that." Evan let his hand drift away from the gem and dragged his attention back to the here and now with an effort.

"It's called concentration; humans learn to ignore the things they expect to happen, and react only to the unexpected. Omage in the study I'd have noticed. You, on the other hand, have to exert some effort to ruin my morning's work."

"Anything interesting?" Brad held out the mug and he reached for it, but his father did not let it go. "When did you develop a taste for gaudy jewelry?"

Evan craned his neck to view the pendant at rest over his heart. "Wouldn't go with a Brooks Brothers suit, but the color's not bad with the black sweatshirt."

Brad still held onto the mug, and a glare reminded Evan that his daemon kin had little sense of humor and less patience.

"I took it out of the safe for inspiration, something to focus on." He let go of the mug to slip the chain over his head. "Funny, really: I usually feel uncomfortable with anything more ostentatious than a pair of cuff links."

Evan set the gem on the desk and coiled the heavy gold chain around it. "I wore a plain silver chain for a while, but I never bothered to have it repaired when the clasp broke." Claudia had given him the chain, and he'd broken the clasp trying to escape from the Black Masque a year later. Omage's chains were not so easily broken. He hadn't worn metal near his skin since he'd gotten out of there. Until now.

"This piece is different: I like to touch it, like the weight of it around my neck. I can't stand the idea that Omage might get his hands on it."

His eyes darkened with the fury that boiled over at the thought. Primitive consciousness fed him visions of his own hands strangling the daemon with the gold chain while his more rational self whispered truth—Omage might kill him, but the daemon could not be killed.

"That's what worries me." Badad's voice intruded on the dreamlike image, drew Evan home.

"Huh? Yeah, it worries me, too."

He let Badad pick up the stone, trying to mask the shudder that passed through him. Fingertips stroked his heart, setting that muscle to beat in strange, arrhythmic patterns.

The daemon sighed. "I'm starting to think that Omage never lost this little trinket at all."

"So what's he up to?"

Badad shrugged. "Setting serpents in our garden? I really wish I knew." He put down the mug and walked away with the stone. "Drink your coffee, it's getting cold."

Subject closed. Evan copied the daemon's shrug and drank. "Where's Lily?"

"New Orleans. She wanted fresh pastries for breakfast."

Evan didn't need reminders of their strangeness today. "We have bakeries in Philadelphia," he pointed out.

"But they don't make beignet like this." Lily materialized on the sofa, and set the box of sugary pastries on the brass coffee table. "Is there any more of that coffee, or has Evan drunk it all?"

If she noticed the tension in the room, Lily didn't show it. Evan saw his father relax and relented himself. Maybe the Rolling Stones were right. As family they might not be what he wanted, but right now they needed each other. It would have to be enough.

"Help yourself." Names and dates flickered into green life as the results of the morning's search marched across the computer monitor. Evan turned gratefully to the part of the investigation over which he had some control.

"We've lost him. He's been possessed by the electronic monster."

Brad's sardonic comment slid like a dart through his concentration. He was vaguely aware of the man trading a china cup of black sludge for a beignet, knocking the sugar off before biting the doughnut.

"Oh, Evan, really. What could be more interesting than breakfast at this hour?" Lily, and impossible to ignore, especially stretched out on the wine-colored leather of the sofa. Fortunately, he had his answer.

"Two things, really. Marnie Simpson, for one. I can't find any record of her or Carter Stables before her marriage to Simpson. Not surprising, necessarily. I was lucky to find a marriage certificate—records weren't as computerized eighteen years ago—but I'd expected a bit more, a birth record for Paul Carter maybe, or a death certificate for the mother, information on the horses they've worked with, something. I've set the ferret to look for newspaper photos and cross reference against the society pages in a hundred mile radius of Baltimore, but I don't expect to find anything. With an illegitimate kid in the family they probably kept a low profile. Can't hurt, though."

"Eat." Lily handed him a beignet. "You said two things. What's the other one?"

Typical of Lily to ask him a question as soon as he had a mouthful of the pastry. He swallowed it down with a swig of coffee and hit print.

"Franklin Simpson. He must have known his wife would be upset when Omage snatched her brother, but he went on with business as usual."

"So?" Lily countered. "He married the sister. Why should he care what happens to the other one?"

Looking from his father to his cousin, Evan found no comprehension. He frowned, wondering how they could have overlooked the obvious, then stopped himself. They were different, not superior. For Lily, fast food meant interdimensional travel to her favorite restaurant, but neither she nor Brad really understood about humans and families. Sometimes he let himself forget how different they were, but he couldn't afford to make that mistake on this case.

"How do we know Omage will stop with Paul Carter?" he asked. "Marnie Simpson may be next, but the loving husband hasn't come back to safeguard his wife *or* to give her the moral support humans need when their families are in trouble. No, Franklin Simpson didn't have to care about Paul Carter—he should have come home for his wife."

"Perhaps the happy couple are not all that happy," Brad suggested. He dusted powdered sugar from his fingers and wrinkled his nose. "Damn beignet." He glared at Lily, who met the unspoken accusation with amusement.

"Tasted better than an apple, didn't it?"

"Says Eve or the serpent?"

Evan waited until Brad had washed the grease from his hands at the bar.

"If you two are finished trading Biblical references, can we get back to Franklin Simpson?" The sharp note in his voice brought his father to the printer.

"So what did you find?"

"It wasn't easy—he's got it hidden behind seven dummy corporations, but Bruce finally cracked it." Evan patted the Batman decal on the side of the monitor. "Among his many holdings, our Mr. Simpson owns an obscure little Greenwich Village nightspot. The Black Masque."

Lily did sit up at that revelation. Brad stopped at the safe and replaced the Eye of Omage—for some reason, it still made him uneasy—before going to the printer. The names of corporations marched down one side of the paper, with the dates Franklin Simpson, or one of his subsidiaries, acquired them on the other.

Evan followed the same information on the screen. A twisting trail led to the Black Masque, but it became clear with a little study that Simpson had picked up the club four years ago. Evan had been twenty then, half mad with dreams of darkness and looking for answers. Omage had been waiting for him, like a fat spider at the center of a web. But had the daemon strung that web, or had the human, Franklin Simpson, laid the trap?

Tearing off the printout, Brad handed it to Lily, who interrupted the brooding train of his thought with another disturbing question:

"Does Marnie Simpson know about her husband's connection with Omage?"

"Not from his financial statement." Evan studied the screen, typed rapidly for a moment, and frowned at the result. "He's hidden the Masque as part of his Viva Mexico chain of Mexican-motif nightclubs. I found it by cross-indexing known addresses against his records."

He pushed his chair away from the desk and pinned Brad with a measuring stare. "Omage isn't working on his own."

"No." Softly.

Evan knew his next questions would strike at the heart of his tenuous relationship with this—creature—and he felt the threat brooding in the hooded blue eyes. Out of the corner of his eye he saw Lily snap to watchful attention, but he pressed the point.

"But who is working for whom?"

"That's no concern of yours, human," Lirion snapped. She rose from the couch and paced the length of the coffee table and back. A corona of blue flame surrounded her and flared into the room. "Get on your jumbo jet and leave the fighting to your betters."

"Not yet."

Anger sparked his response, and Evan saw it, let it go. Static crawled up his legs, across his arms as Lily's temper flared, but he would not back down. Too much of his past was tied up in his next questions. They *owed* him for that, and he had no intention of forgetting the debt. First they had to understand why it mattered so much to him.

"I never told you what those years with the Black Masque were like. . . ."

"If it bothers you, see a therapist. They get paid to listen. Leave Omage to us." Lirion turned away from him, confronting Badad. "I agreed to this charade for the novelty. Don't make me regret that decision."

Brad nodded. "I know it's been hard for you, Evan, but we haven't time to indulge in soul-searching. After we've settled with Omage, if you still need to talk, we'll listen." He flashed an admonitory glare in Lily's direction. "We'll both listen."

"There may not be a later."

Without waiting for an objection, he plunged ahead and found himself lost in the past he suddenly inhabited again. "I left home when I was nineteen, looking for something. You, I guess."

He came back long enough to acknowledge Badad, who stood halfway between the desk and his cousin with one elbow propped on a bookshelf. Badad did not react to the confession. No surprise there—Evan had long ago given up looking for signs of regret on that countenance.

"At the time I just knew that the dreams were getting worse. I couldn't go on that way. I mean, sometimes it took all I had not to put the gun to my head and pull the trigger. Other times I woke up sure I was dead, and scared that I'd spend the rest of eternity trying to get back from wherever the dreams sent me. I think that was the only thing that stopped me from ending it—the idea that the dreams were what you were left with when you died.

"I must have been on my own for about six months when I met Claudia. We got really close. I loved her, or I would have if I'd been able to love anyone then. At any rate, she loved me and I needed that. We lived together for about a year in a two-room walk-up in the Village. Claudia and I had the bedroom, her brother Jack slept on a cot we used as a sofa in the corner of the kitchen. Jack found out about the Black Masque first, and before long we were regulars."

"Is that the Jack and Claudia you are seeing in London?"

Evan nodded. Caught between the past and the present, he missed the significance his father placed on the names until Brad's next remark: "I thought you were staying away from the Black Masque end of the case."

"They're not involved," Evan assured him. "They were experimenting with the underground, but Omage was exactly what I was looking for. I'd convinced myself that the dreams were my own evil side coming out when I lost control, and the Masque seemed like the perfect place to explore that part of me. That's how I knew about the goat, by the way. There was a goat's skull, with the horns intact, mounted over the bar, and I asked Claudia about it. She'd read up on it in a history course at Columbia.

"Mac was the bartender—Omage, that is—he told us to call him Mac. He said that anything we did was right as long as we wanted it badly enough. For the others it started out as drink and talk, and a little kinky sex: a dive into wickedness to wash the squeaky clean suburbs off their healthy white skin. For me it was more. I knew what I wanted, all right—an end to the dreams, or at least some validation that the experience was real—I just didn't know how to get it."

The memory mocked him. How he had looked down on the others, thrill seekers of the moment who knew little of the horror that he'd hidden behind a brittle smile. Hell itself had possessed his sleep, and he cursed the cowards who walked away, judging them too weak to face the waking reflection of his nights.

"Pretty soon Mac began to single me out. He said he could tell I wasn't like the others—something about my aura. I almost cut out when he started with the New Age babble. But he told me he knew about the dreams, described them as a place I went in my sleep. He made falling into the dreams sound more desirable than life. I *knew* better, but his eyes—he wanted it, I could feel his jealousy past the smile and the whiskey he slipped me for free."

"He would have hated you for that," Lily broke into the stream of his thoughts, and he was surprised to find that she had walked over to lean against the desk. "Imagine someone cutting up those precious Picassos you value so highly and using them for toilet paper. You won't even be close, but you get the idea."

"I know that now," Evan conceded. "At first, though, I only cared that he believed me. Then things started getting a little crazy. By then I was drinking most of the time, and Jack wasn't far behind me. Mac started telling the others about the dreams, that I was some freak with a weird power, a gateway into another universe. I thought it was all hype, fast talk to fool the locals, but even Jack started to believe him.

"One night when Claudia stayed home, Jack got carried away with it all. He stood on the bar and slashed his wrist with a butcher knife, balled his hand into a fist and held it bleeding over the goat skull until he fainted. When he fell off the bar, somebody tied a pressure bandage around his wrist and threw him in the alley.

"I tried to stop him, but Jack was too far gone to listen and my own head wasn't that clear either. I couldn't reach the bar, and when I looked over to find Omage, Mac was laughing."

Evan shuddered. "That night I started to believe the dreams actually were a place, and that Mac belonged there. Somehow he'd been trapped here, and he hated us all because of it.

"The police must have found Jack, because Claudia called the next day to tell me they were leaving town. They never came back. I would have gone home myself, but Omage had the one argument that could convince me to stay: he said my father was from the place my dreams sent me, the same place he came from. He promised he would find you."

"More like *I* would find *him*," Brad corrected. "But what has this to do with Franklin Simpson?"

Evan could see that his father knew the answer, felt the air between himself and Lily twist into nervous eddies. She walked away, putting distance between them.

"What if Simpson doesn't just own the Black Masque? What if he owns Omage as well?"

"Only a fool would remain bound this long by a human summons!" Power crackled in Lirion's response; books caught in the pressure wave of her reaction tumbled from their shelves. She raised a hand and the wind died as quickly as it had risen, barely ruffling Evan's hair when it reached the desk. "And Omage is no fool."

"He hates it here—you said so yourself. So why does he stay?" Evan persisted. "Something, or someone, keeps him here. Whether it is Simpson himself, or someone who controls them both, the man who binds Omage is a threat to you, and through you, to me."

Brad picked up one of the fallen books—Frances Yate's *The Art of Memory.*

"You have a solution?" He challenged his son through slitted eyes and Evan's fingers trembled on the computer keyboard.

"If you are already bound, he cannot trap you."

"But we are free."

Evan wondered how his father could pack such menace into four words spoken softly, as a sigh.

"Then why are you here?" He knew the risk he took challenging the daemon, but his own life, and his father's existence in the material sphere, depended on the answers that Evan needed.

Anger flared in the daemon's eyes. Almost, Evan drew back, but he managed to hold his ground while the book in his father's hand curled and blackened. Brad looked down at the volume as it burst into flame, then set it carefully on the brass coffee table. It burned with a hot blue flame and crumbled into ash.

"Host loyalty is a different matter. We exist to do battle for our Prince, here or at home." His voice betrayed no threat, only the arrogance that Evan recognized as part of him. "No human can truly understand. We are the essence of our Prince, he speaks with the voice of the host. When we guard the gateway to the second sphere, we act out of communal need, according to our nature, not out of coercion. A human binding spell twists that nature against us. No human can possibly imagine a bondage so profound."

"Can't I?" He saw doubt pass across Badad's face. They shared a memory of Evan's captivity, but he knew that no altruistic motive would convince his father. Instead, he pleaded the self-interest the daemon would believe.

"If he binds you, he will kill me."

"So he might," Badad conceded.

Not human. The not-like-us realization raised the hackles at the back of Evan's neck. The look on the daemon's face told Evan to weigh each word with care, lest it be his last.

"I could bind you, for the duration of this case. Just as a technicality, to protect us all."

Lirion interrupted then, laughing at him. "You are a fool, to risk your life for a bad joke."

The temperature in the room rose sharply. Lirion's expression told him that she found no humor in either the suggestion or the barely veiled threat.

Badad never looked at his cousin, but shifted slightly to stand between the human and his daemon kin.

"Have you been listening?" he asked, "Do you have any idea what you are asking?"

"Probably not," Evan admitted. "I'm talking about a binding that lasts days, weeks at the most. How can that matter so much against a life span so long I can't even grasp it as a concept?"

"How long did it take Omage to rape you in that back room? How long to cut your wrists and send you crashing through the second sphere?"

Evan looked away, trying to escape the fire that burned in his father's eyes, the memories that turned his gut to stone. The words he never wanted to hear pursued him. Badad went on, inexorably: "Were you driven any less insane then, because it did not last forever?"

"No." He shaped the word, but could force no sound from a throat closed tight around remembered pain. Then, more clearly, "It wouldn't be like that."

"Yes. It would. Worse, in some ways. Time doesn't exist for us, Evan. It's always 'now.' Don't expect us to put what amounts to torture in perspective; that's a human trait."

Badad's steady gaze never wavered, and the human met it with his own truth. "I don't see that we have a choice. I'm asking you to trust me."

"Does he call up old debts or host loyalty? Not our Evan." Cold menace rode on Lirion's laughter. "Only a human could ask for trust, let alone expect to get it. He's more a fool than Omage ever was."

"You're undoubtedly correct, Lily." Badad finally faced his cousin. "But you overlook one important fact. He's right. We have no choice."

"You've been here too long," she countered, but without the heat of her earlier argument. "You've grown as mad as your half-human bastard."

Evan crossed to where she leaned on the wine-dark back of the sofa, her arms planted like flying buttresses supporting her on either side. He stopped to look up at her, his right hand over her left.

"I want to protect you, Lily, not control you. Think of what he's done to Mac. I can't stand by and let that happen to you."

"Even protection is a form of control," she countered. "And you will hurt us more than Franklin Simpson ever could. At least Simpson knows what he does for the enslavement it is. Only you would blindly ask for trust even while you betray all that is Ariton within you."

Her anger crackled in the air between them. "I can't stop you from trying, but listen well, monster—" Her fingers twisted under his, nails biting into the soft skin between the tendons that ridged the back of his hand. "Be careful that you never lose control. If you do, I will surely kill you, in ways that will make your time with Omage seem like a wet dream."

Evan gave her a twisted grin. "I never expected anything else from you, cousin. I've compiled the sources I could find," he picked up a sheaf of computer paper, "and I think it's all here. Shall we begin?"

# Chapter 8

*Magot, the magician, holds sway over hidden treasure, especially precious metals, but is known for trickery and for his evil countenance. Ariton, in other times called Egyn, is the ruler of the northern quarter who lays bare the secret, hidden things. He is known for the vehement force of his temper.*

"NOT HERE."

Neither Badad's son nor his cousin had needed the reminder that the study, a room they all considered a sanctuary from the outside world, was a poor choice for the afternoon's work. If Evan were successful, they would never again recapture the sense of invulnerability stamped into every book and chair of the crowded room. If Evan were not successful, of course, little of the study, or Evan, would remain to remind them of anything.

The living room was a marked contrast to the cluttered study. A short hallway led from the street-front offices, the only part of what had originally been two townhouses that retained the Federalist ambience, past the study to the right and the kitchen on the left. Beyond the hall, the walls seemed to fall away. The cathedral-ceilinged room opened up the width of both original houses, and sliding glass doors gave way to the courtyard garden beyond. A staircase seemed to arch unsupported to the second floor gallery and bedrooms, continuing out of sight to Evan's studio on the third floor.

Brad settled himself in the corner of the living room sofa with a copy of Evan's research. Usually he liked the room, not least because it bore the unmistakable presence of Lirion in one of her brighter moods: in the furniture coverings sparsely scattered with oversized daylilies, bright orange against a cream background; in the high polish of the hardwood floors, bare but for a few bright dashes of colorful throw rugs; in the cream walls punctuated by the spare images of the abstract expressionists. Today the bright bars of afternoon light spilling across the floor mocked his yearning for the dark reaches of home, more distant with each tie to Earth. Prisoner of the light, he mused, soon to be bound to the light-dweller, his son.

Evan had opened the wall of sliding glass that led into the private garden. The breeze was too cool, too damp, but no one moved to close the doors again. Brad pretended not to notice when the boy took the nearest chair, at right angles to the sofa, and shuffled through the papers he had gathered in his hand.

Lirion stood with her back to the cream-colored wall, one hand pressed against the invisible barrier of glass. She stared into a distance where Badad had no wish to follow, her face closed and tight around the things that haunted her there. She'd never said how she had been bound the first time, nor how she had escaped. Now that it might prove to be too late, Badad wondered what memories called to the daemon who stood unmoving at the threshold to the garden.

Badad still wondered if he could let go of his own self-will and place himself into the hands of the human. He knew beyond question that Lily would fight, and wondered if Franklin Simpson would prove to be the ultimate winner in the conflict. Weakened by a struggle against Evan, they would never stand against the will that had controlled Omage for four years.

"If Franklin Simpson wanted you, why did he go to all this trouble to attract your attention? Why didn't he just bind you like he did Omage?"

Evan's question struck uncomfortably close to his own misgivings.

"We don't know yet what he wants, but we've probably been lucky so far," he conceded. "Simpson, or whoever is using his corporation to hide the Black Masque, is greedy. He needs our true names to summon us. Omage knows who we are, but he won't give Simpson the information for free. He'd trade us in a minute for his own freedom, but so far Simpson hasn't considered the expedient that would lose him one daemon and gain him two."

Shadows filled his mind. Bound to the will of the enemy, the conflicting commands of Ariton and the human would soon have him as mad as Omage. He filled his eyes with the sight of the earnest young man curled into an armchair of exploding daylilies, a memory to hold through the lifetime of creation. Brad knew that he would kill his son before he would use him as a battering ram between universes.

"Luck seldom holds forever. Omage could have given us to Simpson at any time. Even if this case hadn't come up, we should have taken the precaution."

Evan nodded once, sharply. "It may not be that easy," he admitted. "First I have to figure out how to do it, and half of this stuff contradicts the other half. I can't see the point of most of it. Couldn't you just promise to do as I say and be done with it?"

"It doesn't work that way." Badad reminded himself to be patient, but old patterns of resistance, of battle, gripped him. His human form wavered in dark flame and settled again with an effort. "A binding creates changes at the very core of what our people are."

"Think of surgery." Her voice reached them from the place where Lirion relived nightmares only she could see. "Performed without anesthesia, for the purpose of joining you to a wild dog." Her smile was bleak. "Or, maybe, to a cockroach."

"That's not what you called me last night."

"It's not quite that bad, Evan." Brad interrupted the brewing argument before his own raw nerves pushed him into action without thought, too easy in a body that felt its emotions with the skin and the muscles as well as with the mind. "But the process has never been voluntary. You have to command, to bend the forces of the second sphere to your will. In a way you are at a disadvantage. Because you are half daemon yourself, you know those forces firsthand. They have invaded your sleep since you were a child. And you care about us. Neither of us wants to hurt you now, but we'll fight you—we can't help it—using everything we've got against you, and that includes your feelings about us."

"I didn't know."

"It doesn't matter," Badad pointed out, "because you're right. Simpson would destroy us as surely as he tried using Omage to destroy you."

Lirion let out a held breath and leaned against the wall, staring out into the garden. "Better the devil you know, eh?" she admitted. "Or maybe that should be your line."

This time when she smiled, the resemblance to a piranha was gone. Brad kicked off his shoes and stretched out on the sofa, shifting a pillow under his head. "So what do you need to know?"

"Well, for starters, if this part about four months of chastity is true, we're in trouble."

"What? Let me see that?" Brad skimmed through the list of conditions and stipulations Evan had compiled and snickered in spite of the tension. Sometimes human notions were too strange to take seriously.

"I'm not sure Lily could wait four months for your body, even if we had the time. We can dispense with the child clairvoyant as well."

"That's a relief. Snatching urchins off the streets is frowned on in this century."

Brad heard the lighter tone in Evan's voice with relief. The human would need all the confidence he could muster to pull this one off. Better not to tell the boy what complete shits the most successful practitioners of this particular skill were. Sensitivity just gets in the way when you are trying for raw power, and Brad had his doubts that Evan could be ruthless enough to wield that kind of control. He continued to peruse the list for the ritual detritus that had built up over the centuries: "I suppose we could go out in the woods somewhere, but it isn't necessary."

"In the ninth century, their time, a magician in a fair-sized Ukrainian town summoned a daemon but could not hold her."

Neither man moved while Lily's voice painted word-pictures on the glass. "There's a crater where the town used to be. The townsfolk all died horribly in the fire."

Brad closed his eyes, seeing the moment, the terror and rage she would have felt, forced into corporeal form in this world more alien to their true natures than the second sphere seemed to Evan. Freedom would have been her only thought then, the cries of the dying as meaningless as the tortured screaming of the flames or the crack of the dense forests of fir trees exploding in the heat of her passing.

She turned then, and Badad regretted the knowledge without understanding that drained the color from his son's face. In Lirion's remorseless eyes Evan had found a truth, that she had destroyed the town and all the lives in it, but not all the truth her story had to tell. As well blame the tornado or the hurricane for the damage it does. The fault lay with the hubris of a magician who thought he could tame the forces of the universe to his will. Soon, the fault would lie with Evan.

"I suppose the memory may linger in the warnings you've read," she explained, and only Badad heard the terror and loathing that gripped her still.

"Is that likely to happen again?"

Lily did not answer Evan's question directly. "It was an ugly town anyway."

"And?" Evan prompted.

"And I've gotten used to this house."

She threw Badad a fleeting look that held a promise Evan didn't see. The boy would die without the death of his city on his conscience; she'd contain the damage, if she could.

"That's good." Evan let out an explosive sigh. "Short of the mountains or the Pine Barrens there's no safe place to do this without killing people. And I'm *not* using the Ariton express until Paul Carter is free and Omage is back where he belongs."

"A sensible precaution this time," Brad agreed conditionally. "But you will need a safe place to work. As an alternative to a consecrated room or a clearing in the woods, you can use the pentagram in a circle."

"Is that really necessary?" Evan asked.

"I convinced that old Russian sorcerer that it wasn't necessary." Lirion's bitter laugh rattled staccato irony. "He died, and his whole grubby little town with him, for believing me."

Brad sat up, a hand on the arm of Evan's chair. His son had to understand if he were to survive. "You are bending the forces of two universes to your will. You must believe that you can do it, and you must believe that you are safe while you do. If you lose control for even a second, and you do not have absolute faith in the barrier that you build around yourself, you will be torn to pieces by the forces you are binding."

Lily joined them. Leaning over the back of Evan's chair, she kissed him idly on the top of his head. "Once you have begun, you must not leave the circle until the binding is complete," she admonished him. "Humans die quickly."

She snapped her fingers, and Brad shuddered, knowing in the sound the feel of a neck broken with the bare hands of his human body.

"Life ends messily for the unwary who try to bind a daemon, and if you were Franklin Simpson, I would take great pleasure in your death. But you, Evan—" she carded manicured fingers through his hair, "—you are part of Ariton, of us. We will carry the memory of your terror and pain, and your ending, through all eternity. But understand me—you *will* die."

Evan turned to face her, and she stroked a familiar finger from his temple along the curve of his jaw to his chin and touched the fingertip to his lips. If he read the ambiguous message in Lily's warning—circle or not, she expected to kill him—Brad couldn't see it.

"There are other, more pleasing memories of you I'd rather carry through eternity, little monster, so be careful."

He kissed her fingertip, took her hand in his and kissed her palm. "I'll stay in the circle."

Evan let her go then, and turned to his father. "So far we've got a pentagram in a circle. What do I do from there?"

Badad looked through the various formulas until one made the blood run cold in his human body. He felt the shape waver for a moment, and firmed it up again. "This one should do the trick." He pointed.

Evan looked at the passage. "I didn't know you believed in God."

"It's not a matter of belief. We don't have any stories about a supreme ruler in the sense of your Bible or Koran, if that's what you mean."

"Then there really isn't a God?" The disappointment in Evan's tone surprised him.

"I thought you didn't believe in that sort of thing."

Brad hadn't seen that look on Evan's face since he'd caught his son watching *Peter Pan* alone in the dark. Evan shrugged. "I guess I wanted to be wrong."

"Oh." That seemed to make sense to Evan, though only a human would understand why. But then, "A human might think of the Princes as deities," Badad offered. "Since the Princes are the combined presence of the lords in their host, we would be our own gods. Of course, not even the Princes know what goes on beyond the second sphere. We know there are five more—as many spheres as there are Princes—maybe your God does exist, and we just can't reach it."

"So why this particular spell?"

Badad relaxed a bit. This, finally, was a question he could answer without picking his way through a minefield of human association and irrational emotions.

"Could be any one of a thousand or more combinations, with or without religion," he said. "Could be a grocery list if you could work up an inner resonance to it. The summons works through a sequence of sound-feelings, and the binding through the working of sound and symbol first, and meaning last of all."

"What does that mean?"

"It means," Lily cut in with a fine disregard for Evan's always tricky sensibilities, "that certain sounds, if recited forcefully and supported by a certainty in the summoner, can twist the universes, and draw through the weak spot created there a daemon called by its true name, a sound-feeling that corresponds to one creature in all the known universes. The name has to be exact, but there are almost infinite combinations of commands that can twist the universe.

"This one—" she touched the paper, "—carries the correct sound variables, but it doesn't call on images that might remind you of Omage's back room. It doesn't matter to us, but you couldn't do it if you thought you were as bad as Simpson. This God stuff is supposed to make you feel safe about performing a morally repellent act of coercion against superior beings."

"Give us a choice and I'll be the first one to grab it, and the hell with morals," Evan countered. "I don't want to know how different you are."

"Just promise me one thing," she bargained. "Let me have Simpson."

"If he is at the root of all this, he won't get away. That much I promise."

Evan accepted the kiss and turned his attention back to the maze of contradictory instructions.

"It says I need a wand of ash wood."

Badad found the directions on the paper, glad to move into less volatile territory. "Any symbol of the physical body will do," he explained. "The lords you bind must touch the symbol of materiality in your hand when they swear to obey you, but if you reach beyond the circle, you become vulnerable to attack. Besides being your symbol of sexual power, the wand has the advantage that every part of you, including your hands, stay on your side of the circle."

Evan frowned. "Lily's riding crop is about the length of the wand in most of the pictures."

The suggestion kicked the breath out of the daemon. For a moment Badad remained silent, stunned by the slow pain the words started beneath his heart.

"This afternoon will change who we are to each other for all times," he reminded his son. "Do you want the riding crop to be the symbol of what we will become?"

"NO!" Evan's horrified denial lay between them until a sly smile crept across the human's face. "My fishing pole, then."

Brad laughed, relieved to hear Lily's high clear laughter as well. She mussed Evan's hair as she might a terribly clever puppy. "You've never caught a thing with that fishing pole."

"Must have," Evan countered, "because the bait always disappears. Never had the heart to use real hooks, though. Besides, if I'd actually hooked a fish, I'd have to do something with it, and that would spoil my nap."

"You're an idiot," she pointed out, "but I like it."

"It will do," Brad conceded. With the boy thinking through his symbols, they just might have a chance. "Do you need time to rest?"

Evan shook his head. "Better to finish it now. Give me half an hour to pull something together here."

Brad considered using the half hour to drift in the second sphere, but reconsidered. No point in tempting fate or Franklin Simpson. Lily met his eyes and shook her head, the warning understood and accepted. She preceded him up the stairs and stopped in front of her bedroom door.

"Can he do it?" she asked.

"Maybe," Badad answered. "If not, he'll be dead and Simpson won't need us anymore."

"That's not what I want."

"I know."

"Now that it's a question of who instead of when, I keep getting this urge to look over my shoulder, in case Simpson is breathing down my neck." She turned away, her head hung between drawn shoulders. "I don't like any of this."

Her bedroom door closed on the last words. Brad sighed and followed her example. Nothing to do now but wait.

# Chapter 9

*The names of the seven great Princes are known to man, but the names of the daemon lords who make up their hosts are held close-guarded. But if a man can learn the name of a daemon lord, he may summon him, and bid him do his pleasure. But if his pleasure is to do evil, he will soon find his will overborne by the seduction of the daemon, who is terrible in countenance but who may take on a seemly appearance to cajole his master.*

EVAN WAITED UNTIL HE HEARD THE SECOND DOOR CLOSE, THEN HE WENT UP TO his third floor studio. He ignored the easel that faced the north window and rummaged through the bottles on a shelf over the drawing table. The white seemed right: fill his circle with brightness rather than the black and brooding pentagram that weighed down Paul Carter's bed. He grabbed the tempera paint and the wide brush he used to gesso canvases, and headed for the garden.

A high brick wall protected him from being seen. Evan cleared the lawn furniture from the center of the courtyard and opened the glass doors to the living room as far as they would go. Then he began to paint a five-pointed star on the bricks. The background hum of traffic on Spruce Street and water splashing over rough, mica-flecked stones into a shallow pool hidden behind the tulips and the daffodils wove themselves into the gritty press of brick against his knee, and he filled the star with the sound and touch and smell of spring and home. When he finished the star, he knelt at its center and stretched outward to paint a circle around it.

The final stroke closed the pattern like a gate locking, more solid than the glass behind which the daemon would appear, and Evan wondered for a fleeting moment if he had the power to leave the circle at all. He dismissed the feeling as a trick of the imagination, tightened the lid on the paint, and stepped over the white lines to clear away his supplies.

He found the fishing rod in the attic and considered making a detour to the office for the topaz hidden in the safe. He resisted the urge. His attraction to the Eye of Omage unnerved him; the sense of security it gave him felt false at its core. He turned instead to the corner of the attic where he'd stashed the few things he'd brought from his mother's house and dug through the big square box that represented the first nineteen years of his life. It was still there, and he closed his fingers around his first drawing pen, drew it from the box.

When he was ten, and the dreams were so strong he sometimes forgot where the waking world ended and the dreams began, he would draw himself real again, endlessly. Those strange, twisted images of torture and despair had frightened his mother and disturbed priests and doctors alike: they read the plea for help, but could not find him in the wild place that trapped him. Finally, it was the images themselves that saved him. If he could draw the feelings, they must be real. In the images of his pain in pen and ink he found proof that he existed.

Until he found his father at the edge of madness, his grimy rapidograph had been Evan's personal symbol of his own humanity. Now, the images meant more to him, because they represented in pictures what he had not known in words: two universes struggled for possession of his soul. Time and again in his drawings, Evan had thrown his allegiance with the material sphere. He carried the pen to remind him of his choice, made at ten and at every moment since, to be human.

He knocked first on Brad's door, then on Lirion's to alert them that he was ready to begin, and returned to the tempera-painted circle in the garden. Grabbing a cushion from a lawn chair, he sat himself cross-legged at the center of the pentagram with his fishing rod across his knees and called upon his father and his cousin to submit to his command.

"With a tranquil heart, and trusting in the Living and Only God, omnipotent and all-powerful, all-seeing and all-knowing, I conjure you, Badad, daemon of darkness, and you, Lirion, daemon of darkness, to appear before me in the human forms by which I shall know you."

Shadows thickened around his protected circle, and grew into a scream torn from hell. Wind howled its accompaniment of rage, and somewhere nearby glass exploded. Pain. Unending waves of pain danced on his nerve endings. Evan knew that only the circle protected him from the full force of that agony, but found himself drawn to the screaming faces twisting in the shadows. His determination wavered for a moment.

"I never wanted this," he whispered, but the knowledge that Franklin Simpson would have no such qualms hardened his resolve.

"Appear before me in the human shapes by which I have come to know you. Now!"

At the sharp command the shadows coalesced. Sunlight glinted off the splinters of glass that still hung in the door frame, jagged halos around his father and his lover who started toward him through the glittering shards scattered on the threshold. He recognized their forms and faces, but Evan's mind refused to accept as the same beings these creatures who paced just beyond the limits of his tempera fortress. Blood flowed from a cut on Badad's arm, left a smear on the jagged glass, and soaked its way unnoticed down his shirtsleeve, while the daemon spat threats at the human who dared summon him.

Lirion lured him with open arms, her hips thrust forward in a way that would have been enticing, except that he saw no recognition in her eyes, just the promise of death if he looked deeply enough.

"Come on, Evan. You know you want it." She unbuttoned her blouse, shed it, slipped out of her trousers, stood with her hands on hips clad in a scrap of lace as blue as her eyes, considering him.

"I can be anyone—" She smiled, and suddenly the reflection of his father stood nude before him, arms out. "Evan—" His father's voice, offering himself in counterpoint to the threats and curses of the bleeding original.

"Don't do this, Lily." Too many feelings tumbled out of locked places in his head to sort them out, but shame and sorrow lay like a wash over them all. He didn't want this knowledge, this bone-deep comprehension that they were different—not human, not bound by the feelings of a human—and that a part of him might be like them. He backed away, would have run but the circle stopped him.

"God, please don't—"

"No?" Lirion, in the form of his father, shrugged naked shoulders. "I can be anything for you."

With Badad's voice she laughed, but hatred burned out of the daemon eyes. "Risk is everything."

Lirion shifted again. Crouching before him, she became a panther— sleek and dark, with eyes that promised hell and dared him to love her. She growled, a deep animal sound that raised the hairs on the back of his neck, and he wanted to touch her, to run a hand over her back. He wanted to roll and tumble with her like they were two cubs tussling among the flowers, wrap his arms around her neck and bury his face in the thick, sleek fur that collared her. He lifted his hand and let it drop again, confused and frightened by the feelings that drove him and sickened him at the same time.

She transformed again: Lily Ryan, naked and flushed, wanting him. Evan bowed his head, buried both hands deep in his own hair, and tried to hold back his grief. What was the point of it all, if they had nothing left when he was done? Memories supplied the answer. Omage, with his father's face, driven mad until only the pain and terror of his victims made him feel whole. Lily, cold as frost, telling of a centuries-past captivity, a town dead for her freedom.

"I have to do this," he told her softly, and stood to demand the oath that would bind them to his command.

At that moment, Lily's face contorted, her lids fluttered, and she fell with a low moan into Badad's arms.

"We can finish this later," his father snapped. "Right now she needs help."

Evan took a hesitant step, and Lirion gasped, barely able to breathe, and curled in around her pain.

"Lily!" He dropped the fishing rod and went to her, dropped to one knee at her side.

Lirion looked up at him, and her smile curdled his blood. No time to retreat, they were on him. Hands reached for his throat, contorted into monstrous shapes before his eyes. In that moment he knew he was dead.

The pen in his pocket jabbed at his leg then, and he found himself suddenly unafraid. He remembered the night, dream-walking in the emptiness, and knew that the red-eyed beast that slavered over him, jagged fangs reaching for his throat, had led him home and loved away the sick dread. Whatever became of them now, she would always be the flame that had steadied him on the road home from places he once traveled in solitary madness. And Badad, whatever he might be, had once defied a universe to save Evan's life.

The shield of his certainty drove them back. Screaming foul curses in languages no human mouth could form, they hurled their own dread and pain at him, and Evan reached out, said the words to end the agony, to bring them home:

"You are summoned by the Honor and Glory of God, by my Honor that I shall cause you to do no harm or injury to others, and for the greater glory of all creation both in the physical sphere and in the second sphere. By this I demand your oath: that whenever and every time you shall be summoned, by whatever word or sign or deed, in whatever time or place, and for whatever occasion or service, you will appear immediately and without delay. You will obey the commands set for you in whatever form they shall be conveyed."

Then he realized the fishing rod still lay in the pentagram. Standing there, he felt the trap close around him. He'd left the circle. Should be dead; would be if he backed down now. But he needed the symbol of the physical body to tie them to the material realm. A wand. A pen. He drew the rapidograph from his pocket, clutched it tightly in his fist for a moment, then opened his fingers, held his palm out like an offering, and met the eyes of the creature he called father.

"Swear."

The image wavered, drew in upon itself, and strengthened again. Kevin Bradley, disheveled and shaking with rage, the blood from the wound in his arm falling, drop by drop, onto the bricks, stood before him and the daemon's words fell like stones in Evan's heart:

"I curse the seed that spawned you. I curse the world that shelters you. I curse the form and substance of your existence. You are nothing, bastard monster of two universes, wanted by neither. In other times and places your back would have been broken at birth, your twisted life sucked back into the void before your first cry. I can still correct the oversight."

"You could have, once," Evan agreed. His fear was a slinking thing gnawing at the bars of his concentration, but his hand held steady, the grimy white pen lying like a scar across his palm. "But not now. You will swear your oath to me, because we need each other."

Chaos churned in the blue eyes of the daemon, as Badad searched within himself for the lie in his son's words and found a truth he never wanted to hear. Evan read the struggle in the trembling hand that reached toward him. When Badad touched him, he closed his fingers around those of the daemon, the pen clasped tightly between their two palms.

"Swear," he repeated, calm now, and Badad nodded.

"I swear."

His father was changing subtly before his eyes, the lines of his face shifting out of old, familiar patterns into new maps of tension, but Evan had no time to ponder the transformation. A second daemon was poised to strike, growing darker and more terrible as she fought the familiar shape he had forced upon her.

"Swear," he commanded, and he projected all of his own frustration, his fear that even now Franklin Simpson might steal what was Evan's by right. Evan Davis was human, and could command if he had the strength. He was also of Ariton, and he had the right to demand loyalty of the lords of that Prince. He had the *right*.

"Swear. By Ariton."

She stood before him in the form he knew by touch in the dark and he held her gaze, waiting for the stroke that told him host loyalty held no power for half-breed monsters.

"By Ariton," Lirion answered, "I swear." Her hand bypassed the rapidograph extended on his outstretched palm, and instead rubbed familiarly between his legs. "Symbols are fine for strangers," she explained, "I prefer the real thing."

Evan sighed, his head tilted back, unsteady now that it was over and he found himself still breathing. "You can stop now," he hinted.

"Is that an order?"

She nibbled on his ear, but even her warm breath down his neck could not distract Evan from the mindless exhaustion that suddenly possessed him: "I need a nap."

She removed hand and teeth from his person with ill grace. "So that's the way it's going to be—"

Real distress crossed her face. Her grand exit ruined, Evan thought. Then he realized what that meant. He owned them. He commanded their movements now, and he hated it.

"I'm sorry. Let's get this over with right away." He stuffed the pen back into his pocket and took Lily's hand. "By my command, and until I next summon either or both of you, you will come and go as you please, and make decisions as you choose, except you may not answer the summons of any other, and you must answer my summons as you have sworn. Until and unless I formally summon and command you, you will treat me as you would do before the oath was sworn.

"In plain English," he finished, exasperation leaking out of every word, "unless we're in trouble and I have to use it, let's pretend this whole thing never happened."

He answered Brad's cocked eyebrow with a shrug and threw an arm around Lily's waist. She was working on his ear again.

"Aw, Lily, give it a break." Evan's head dropped to her shoulder.

"Is that an order?" she repeated.

Lily turned snide into a high art, but his father came to Evan's rescue. The daemon threw one arm around the shoulder of his cousin, and the other around the shoulder of his son.

"I think," he explained to his cousin, "that Evan has a headache."

This time, Lily accomplished her exit with panache. Evan's ears rang with the thunder of imploding air where she had stood. He gave his father a doleful look, and when hearing returned, informed him, "You're bleeding all over my shirt. Come into the kitchen and I'll see what I can do."

"Is that . . ."

Evan glared his father into silence. "Don't be an ass about this. I meant what I said at the start. It's just a technicality, so that Simpson can't get his hands on you."

He led the way into the kitchen and pulled the scissors and first aid kit from a drawer. "How are you going to explain this to your tailor?" Rhetorical question. Evan held up the sodden shirtsleeve, fine swiss cotton worked by Carlo Pimi from his little shop in Milan, and tossed it in the trash. "You need stitches."

Kevin Bradley shook his head. "Just bandage it, I'll take care of it later."

Evan did what he was told, almost afraid to disturb the uneasy peace with the questions he needed to ask.

"Have we lost everything?" he asked, his eyes firmly fixed on the scraps of gauze and tape that littered the counter. He didn't want to know, didn't want it put in words that would make it so.

"What do you think we had?"

"Don't know," Evan admitted.

"Maybe it is lost," Brad said, and his tone made Evan wonder what the last year had meant to his father.

"But if you mean, will Lily come back on her own, without your summons, probably. First she needs to find out for herself that it's not just a trick, that she really is free. The question is, what will you do when she does come back?"

Evan shrugged, staring into the sink as if the garbage disposal held some answer if he could only fathom it in the fall of the blades. "That wasn't Lily."

"Yes, it was."

Evan felt hands on his shoulders, turning him. He faced the man he'd found after a lifetime of searching, the father who was not a man, not human. Sorrow filled the eyes that glinted with the color by which Evan knew him in the second sphere.

"You can't keep pretending we're just folks who happen to disappear now and then. I meant everything I said to you, I still do. You make me feel things I don't understand. I believe you when you say you want to protect me because I have protected you and felt pleasure doing it. But even the pleasure of watching you struggle and succeed passes through the anger and pain of your creation. If I'd had a choice, you wouldn't exist, but I didn't, you do, it matters, and in all of creation I have no idea why that should be.

"For Lily it's different. Her rage runs deeper, and I think even she doesn't know why she agreed to stay in this sphere. But what you have to know is, to win free of you this afternoon, Lily would have offered anything she thought would pull you out of that circle. It worked the last time, because the man who summoned her wanted to use her, and more than a thousand people died for his mistake."

"But I *did* leave the circle," Evan objected.

Brad smiled. "Not to take anything from her, but to help her. In a way, your own stupid certainty saved you. Think of it as a test, and you passed. She'll come back, in her own time, if you let her."

Evan searched the calm eyes, warm now, settling back into familiar patterns.

"I hope so. In the meantime, I've got two hours before I have to leave for the airport and I'm going to spend it in bed. If the world comes to an end while I'm asleep, just leave a note."

He left Badad standing in the ruins of what had once been the living room, and ambled up the stairs without a backward look. Sleep caught him facedown on the bed, one shoe still dangling off his foot. He didn't quite waken when a soft body snuggled against his back, but his dreams grew more peaceful.

# Chapter 10

*An' a man bind a daemon he must take care that his commands be
clearly spoken and in such words as the daemon may not construe
the command to do harm to his master. For the daemon looks always
to be free, and the unconsidered word can be used against him who
binds the forces of the spheres, even to his death.*

IN THE DIM LIGHT OF EARLY EVENING, BADAD CAME TO REST IN THE FRIGIDLY
clean kitchen. None of them cared much for cooking, so the room saw
little use. The service came in once a week, collected the coffee mugs
and Coke bottles, and dusted the appliances. No memories here.

The old ceremony hadn't seemed so final with Evan in the house.
Patching up the cut that ached a little if Brad let it, or sleeping in the
studio-bedroom overhead, Evan demanded nothing. The boy acted as if he
hadn't changed all the rules between them in a single afternoon. Then Evan
was gone, and the truth hit him. Bound in blood and bone and the essence
of his being in the second sphere, Brad had wandered through the house,
absorbing the shock.

On automatic, he headed for the study. Evan's computer still blinked
on the desk. Electric tentacles reached into data banks, lifting a bit here,
a bit there that would fit together the jigsaw puzzle of Franklin Simpson's
life. Evan was a real artist, and the modem-linked PC the boy called Bruce
Wayne was his finest medium. If he hadn't had such rigid scruples, Evan
could have been a better thief than Lily. *Was* a better thief—had stolen the
freedom of two daemons who knew enough to keep from falling into any
human traps. He'd suckered them both, and realizing that the human didn't
really understand what he had done didn't help much.

Too many memories, learning to accept each other, feel safe. He'd burn
the house to the ground just to forget the ragged thing he'd brought here
a year ago to hide, to heal. Drifting between some dreadful longing and

insanity, his arms carved up like a Thanksgiving turkey, Evan had thrashed out the nightmare of his captivity in this room. Brad remembered how Lily'd sworn at him for a fool while they filled the study with foam rubber—the clutter had come later, it was just an empty room with no windows then.

For two weeks they'd taken it in turns, following the daemon essence of the hybrid human into the second sphere and bringing him home again. Later, when he trusted Badad because the daemon was his father, Evan had let them teach him something of his nature in the second sphere. He'd learned that he could survive there, could find his way back, would be safe in either universe. So much for safety.

Out of there. Avoid the living room. Shattered glass and broken furniture beat jagged memory against raw wounds of binding—bowline knotted around his spine, tethered him right through the gut to the human. Evan was flying over water; Badad felt the pull of the tide and knew the bastard didn't even notice it. There was no justice, and somehow it gave Badad no pleasure to realize he'd been right about that all along.

Coffee. Might help the head at least. That's what brought him back to the kitchen, a set piece out of someone else's house. Only the coffeemaker worked overtime here. He cleaned out the old filter and put in a new one, put too many scoops in and didn't care, watched the water drip through it in a daze, and then poured coffee—mud thick enough to pass the spoon test—a mixing spoon would stand upright in the stuff, until the bowl disintegrated. Alone in the semidarkness he sat, trying to forget.

"Any more of that in the pot?" Lily slid onto a stool at the breakfast bar and bleared at him through sleep-puffed eyes. She took the cup he passed her, drank, and grimaced. "Now I know what humans mean by suicide."

"You came back."

She quirked an eyebrow at him. "Clever of you to notice, cousin."

"Evan thought you might not forgive him."

Lily pursed her lips, considering. "I haven't decided. He hasn't asked for anything yet; that was a surprise. It's what brought me back, actually. I thought if I confronted him, he'd do something, and then I'd know."

"And?" He'd expected a shrieking virago to descend upon him with a roil of storm clouds, had looked forward to blowing off some of his own steam in the explosion. An introspective cousin just tightened the screws pressing at each temple. Her answer didn't help.

"He was asleep. It seemed like a good idea, so I took a nap. I felt him kiss me once, on the cheek. When I woke up, he was gone."

The thoughtful frown lingered for a moment, then Lirion's face smoothed into elegant neutrality that hid none of her confusion from Badad.

"I'm still trying to understand what happened. Men are pretty predictable about sex. If you can make the offer before they make the command, they're past their own defenses like their pricks are on fire. Evan was a sure thing—or so I thought. He's never turned me down before. And you were no help at all, standing there cursing him like a fishwife. When you saw I was getting nowhere with him, why didn't you try to seduce him?"

"The thought crossed my mind," Brad admitted. It really was funny, if his head didn't hurt so badly, and if the rope through his gut didn't twist when he thought about Evan. "But I knew it wouldn't work."

"You mean you don't have sex with him?"

"Never."

"You've missed a treat there." A smile tried to break through, fond memories rising through the morass of a wretched day. Then curiosity— "But if he doesn't like sex with men, you could have taken another form—"

"The form didn't matter," Brad explained as patiently as he could. It hadn't made sense to him at first either. "Would you merge with a lord of Azmod?"

Her horrified stare was enough; he knew her answer, the same as his own. Merging with one or two lords of your own host was pleasurable, but the merge created a force. When enough lords entered a merge together, a Prince rose of and out of that force. They *were* Ariton. When they merged as a Quorum, they became their Prince, the group mind shaping the will that directed wars and alliances across all of the second sphere. A lord who merged outside of his host risked entrapment in the group mind of a potential enemy. No daemon would even consider it.

Badad stated the obvious and followed with the obscure: "We don't merge with lords outside our own host, humans don't have sex inside their own kinship group. Omage in the shape of a bag lady could seduce Evan faster than I could if I created my form out of his own fantasies."

"What?" Lily's surprise took her voice into a register audible only to bats.

Brad shrugged. "I couldn't get a very clear story out of him at the time. I was trying to convince him it was an innocent suggestion, while he packed a suitcase to leave. He kept talking about idiots and two-headed babies and having me arrested."

"And which one of you was going to be mother?" Acid sarcasm, Lily's specialty, dished up with a fine supercilious curl to the lip.

Brad laughed. With Lily to goad him, thinking about Evan almost didn't hurt. "I don't think it's rational, cousin. It's just human: they're not supposed to sleep with relatives."

"So what does that make me?"

"When the discussion arose, he hadn't decided. And according to Evan-logic, if you can't figure out what the relationship is, then it must be distant enough not to count."

"Oh." Lily thought about that for a moment. "How do they do it?" she asked, then clarified the question. "For us, being human is like a game. Sex is a fun part of that, but I've never felt anything like host loyalty with anyone but Evan. The ones like Evan, though, born human with one body, one lifetime—how can they trust that to a stranger?"

"You taunted him with the answer to that one," Brad reminded her, a little proud in spite of himself. Evan was turning out to be one tough bastard, and some of that toughness was Ariton. "They risk everything."

"Like he did this afternoon." Lirion didn't mean sex.

Brad nodded, Evan's treachery, never forgotten for long, twisting the knot around his spine. "I didn't think he could do it, sure wouldn't have cooperated if I suspected he'd actually go through with it." He rubbed his head because he couldn't reach the pain in his gut. "I thought we'd taught him something about loyalty. . . ."

Lily took his hands, pulled them gently to the counter between them, and curled her fingers around his clenched fists. "You are looking at him through two sets of eyes, cousin. The body you wear believed he cared about you, and it feels this afternoon as betrayal. The lord of Ariton can only see what Evan did as unnatural—no lord can bind another to a personal will. The one set of eyes you haven't looked through is Evan's."

"And you do?"

Lily snorted, a very unladylike sound, one she usually reserved for Evan at his most obtuse. Brad wasn't sure he liked it aimed at himself.

"Let's just say I see the boy a little more clearly. He's a good lay, and affable as humans go. But he's only a human. Ariton is in there somewhere, I'll grant you that. Life burns brighter, quicker in him than in any other human I've ever seen. Sometimes I think I'll singe my fingertips just to touch him.

"But he's tried to bury that part of himself for all the short years of his life. You can't expect him to act like a lord, because he isn't one."

"Even humans don't hold slaves, and that's what he's made us. How could he do that?" His son. He'd risked so much for this human, and now the binding tore at his gut like rope tore the hands clutching for dear life and slipping, wave-dashed, into the sea. He'd trusted Evan, alone of all humans, and his payment was a harsh lesson in reality.

"It hurt him, cousin." Lily gripped his hands more tightly, urgently, as if she had to share a newly discovered truth. "He took nothing I offered but left himself defenseless when he thought I was in pain. He held us because he believed it was necessary, and he's asked for nothing."

Brad searched her face for anger like his own, and saw an uneasy peace there. Intellectually, they both understood the need that drove Evan to bind them, but:

"It hurts." Not like any physical injury this body had ever known, it was the meaning of the pain he could not bear. Hurt worse the last time, but it hadn't mattered as much. That human was just a jerk, in over his head and with a case of the nasties for a woman who'd had the good sense to reject him. Not Badad's son.

"You killed Nicodemus Minor for doing this to you. How can you defend it in your lover?"

His cousin smiled a secret smile. "What does it feel like?" she asked.

"Rope." He rubbed the place just below his heart.

"Who holds the rope?"

Brad's mood darkened, but his glare didn't seem to bother Lirion one bit. "Evan, of course."

She shook her head, slowly. "You do." Her eyes dropped to their locked hands. "I thought the same thing," she said. "Then I left. When he didn't stop me, I just let go. That's when I knew he meant what he said. He is our shield, not our master. You can let go now."

Brad needed time to think, but already the room lay in darkness. He could just make out the mass of Lily's body, deeper shadow among shadows. Only the glow of her eyes seemed real to human vision. They had a job to do, and not much time to do it in.

"It sounds like you've forgiven him."

Surprise colored her answer: "I guess I have."

Slowly he let the fingers inside his gut unclench, let the rope slide free. He was alone in the darkness with Lily, and glad she couldn't see his face. Why did he suddenly feel abandoned?

"We have a little time," she said, and uncurled his fists, laid her palms against his open hands.

Badad thought of home.

# Chapter 11

*Beware the wrath of a daemon, for his memory is long, and his rage can bring mountains to their knees, or raise up mountains where mighty oceans ruled.*

HOME. BADAD STRETCHED, FOUND JOY IN HIS OWN BOUNDLESSNESS. FOR a brief span of moments he could feel himself free again, unconstrained by a human body, a human master, or the edict of Ariton. He spread himself thin on the wind of creation, reached into the heart of stars to warm himself, felt each whorl and eddy of life that passed through him, unheeding or unknowing that he held them in the cold light of his consciousness. He longed for infinity, forever beyond the reach even of daemon lords, and reveled in that piece of the universe he filled like a lover.

A mind like his own, but brittle and sharp, full of laughter, touched him. He contracted, drew himself in on the sensation of Lirion's presence. He'd known they would merge from the moment she had taken his hands in human form and given him back his freedom. He still felt the binding, but as a tenuous link that neither let him go nor restrained him. He thought of labyrinths and balls of thread, human myths. As far as he could imagine that string would unwind. Should he find himself trapped, lost in some tangle of deception or captivity, he need only follow the thread back to its source. He'd never thought of Evan that way before—as guide, as defender.

Lily picked up the thought and teased him with it, a mind picture of Evan as a small boy, dirty-faced and ragged-kneed, stubborn and bellowing. Was that how he treated Evan? She replaced the image with one of her own—a man, mysteries begging to be discovered in smoky topaz eyes half hidden behind the chestnut hair that defied every effort short of a razor to control it. Lily would never permit that; the hair was a warning, like the muscular arms, the narrow hips, the strong, slim legs. This Evan exuded power freely, like sweat. Evan?

Laughter answered, and the two images merged. Which was true? Neither and both, but a chrysalis struggling to become what none of them could imagine. What would it mean to be of two universes, and survive the tidal pull between them? If Evan survived, he'd be the first. If they succeeded tonight, Paul Carter would be the second. Badad wondered if either sphere was ready for two of them.

The acrid thought fell between them, colored their merging with bittersweet tensions. They shared memories beyond time, relived the great beginning when the material sphere pressed relentless patterns into the flow of infinity, savored battles between Princes, quarrels and merging and separation again, a past untouched by humans.

Deliberately they avoided thoughts of the night to come, and of all the nights that had led them here. Now they would recapture what it meant to be Daemon Lords of Ariton. The essence that was Badad mingled with the essence of his cousin, and they felt the rush of purpose. They were Ariton, and the power of Princes was their being. Their minds became one mind, with room only for sensation. Dense as a point, they reached toward that unattainable infinity, and knew the sweetness of each other. The bitterness of the battle to come only brightened the pleasure of the here and now: nothing existed except the single creature they had become, and they would hold that feeling like a weapon, defying the Princes and all the universes to tear them apart.

Badad felt the thinning, lessening of what they were, held on and sensed Lirion resist the separation. He knew her sorrow for his own, alone with only the memory of her presence. Himself again, he longed for that other thing that was not self but unity, that was Ariton.

Reality tilted, shuddered with alien presence, and Badad tasted fear and madness. Paul Carter, he guessed. Omage once again storming the bastions of the universe with half-human flesh. The distortion wave rocked them, passed on.

"We have to go now." His thought flickered in the darkness, and an answering flicker told him she knew.

They entered the material sphere through a dark alley that clung to disreputability on the not-yet-rehabbed fringes of the East Village. Drizzle glistened on the discarded plastic trash bags and brought a dull sheen to the broken macadam path between two buildings of Baltimore brick that sagged in on each other overhead. Across the street, deep gutters lined with flattened beer cans, crack vials, used condoms, the death's-head still leered from the swinging board sign above the door to the Black Masque. Black door, white bones glinting on the rain-washed black sign, smoked brick walls with no windows—the bar faded into the night. The door opened and closed again, spilled sound into the street but no light. The music throbbed like a fever, died with the closing of the door.

"This place is still a pit," Lily snarled softly next to Kevin Bradley's left ear. As they usually preferred when taking human form, they both wore black, Lirion a tailored jumpsuit in soft leather, white lily stitched on her left shoulder, Brad in slacks and sweater, a loose jacket pushed up at the cuffs. A bit upscale for this part of town, the clothes gave them freedom of movement without compromising on the aesthetics. Omage would hate that.

Lily rested one hand on his shoulder for balance and pulled unidentifiable trash from a black boot heel with the other, her nostrils pinched against the smell of urine and garbage in the alley. Spent hypos crunched underfoot when she shifted in the darkness beside him.

"You do have his trinket, don't you?" she asked.

Brad wore the smoky topaz beneath the sweater, suspended from its chain around his neck. It still felt cold where it touched his skin. He reassured her with a silent nod, then: "Let's get this over with."

He checked for witnesses to their unconventional arrival, but the street was empty. They crossed and entered the bar.

It hadn't changed much since the last time. Black candles flickered in the myriad holders, shadows closing and separating in the breeze of someone passing close to the flames. Bikers in leather and drifters in whatever scrambled for a place at the long bar, their faces gaunt and twisted in the candlelight, gleaming phosphorescent in the glow of the blacklight strobe.

Brad elbowed his way to the bar and threw down a twenty. "Where's Mac?"

The bartender pocketed the twenty and went on wiping glasses beneath the skull of a goat that still hung like a trophy over the bar. Dark stains fell between the upswept horns, splashed the skull, and washed over one empty orbit. The bones looked broken in the light of the strobe, the pieces suspended in the emptiness. The back room was worse, and the memory sank its teeth in and shook Brad hard. The bartender looked him over, took in Lirion at his side, and pursed his lips in a silent whistle.

"You friends of his?"

Brad gave his coldest smile, wild blue flame lighting his eyes. *Enemy,* that look said, and, *stand clear.*

"Let's just say we come from the same old neighborhood. Wanted to look him up before we went back."

The bartender considered for a moment. His glance shifted to Lily and found the same danger curled at the corner of her smile. He shrugged.

"If you know Mac, you know where to find him."

Brad nodded and let the press of the crowd carry him away from the bar. The music, too loud, pulsed through him while around him bodies moved to its rhythm, dancing, undressing each other in the corners, in the dark, white skin of breast and buttock glowing lavender in the strobe. Lily was with him. He felt her at his side, reaching out a hand to stroke a passing crotch as they cut through the tangle of grasping fingers and heaving flesh.

At the end of the room a woman crawled up the leg of a man standing over her with his jeans dropped to his thighs. A second man, on his knees on the floor, pushed into her in time to the music. Brad stepped over the kneeling man's legs, and met the glazed eyes watching him over the woman's hips—confused, child's eyes, seventeen at the most. Trapped in the rhythm of the music, the boy seemed to sense the deadening of his own soul, accepted it. The older man reached for him over the body of the woman, and the boy moved into the touch. Brad looked away, the connection tearing like a vein.

The door to Omage's back room was in front of him. Brad turned the handle and went in.

Nothing had changed. Ranks of candles cast golden light on the symbols crusted on the walls. Blood filled his nostrils, the smell, fresh with the fear and sweat still tangy at the back of the throat, mingled with the rust and corrosion of past offerings. Sometimes taken when not offered; Omage never wasted time on the niceties. The tumbled swastika that had poured from Evan's slashed wrists caught and held him. His son hadn't offered.

Omage had seen the power in Badad's son, had twisted that glittering flame to control the drifters and thrill seekers, to turn them into followers. Within the Black Masque Evan Davis had been a god, until the god wanted out. Then Omage's promise to give him reasons, to find his father, had ended in this room, shackled to the chair on which the daemon lord now sat. Here the dreams became reality. Cast alone into the silent darkness of the second sphere, Evan Davis had gone insane.

The memory of his son's torture in this place filled him with silent rage. Badad regretted only that he had not leveled the place to the ground when he'd found Evan.

"Omage, lord of Azmod." He acknowledged his adversary with a cool nod, never relaxing his guard.

"Badad, Lirion, lords of Ariton. Welcome."

Omage sat enthroned on his raised chair. Candlelight sparked the gold threads in the robes he wore, flashed off the rings that circled each soft finger. He gestured expansively with his free hand while the other trailed fingers lazily through the lank blond hair of the man chained at his feet.

"Humble as it is, I call it home."

Brad felt Lirion tense beside him and shifted onto the balls of his feet.

"Up to your old tricks again," Brad observed.

Paul Carter slumped against one pedestaled chair leg, his eyes turned inward on his horror. His steady whimper rose to a shriek, once, and he beat his head on the leg of the chair until the blood ran into his eyes. Semiconscious, he subsided into aching whimpers again.

The sight revolted him. Badad wanted no part of this broken creature, shared Omage's rage against the humans who subjugated lords to torment each other. But he remembered another boy in this room, taut at the limits of his chains and daring his father to strike him dead. Lirion shivered next to him, and Badad knew she remembered Evan in this place as well.

Her voice broke through his memories.

"Why are you doing this, Mac?"

Omage smiled and stroked Paul Carter's hair. "Because it pleases me." His eyes mocked the lords of Ariton, settled on Badad. "They are nothing, cousin. Nothing."

"They are our children." For Evan, not for Paul Carter.

Omage pursed his lips, shook his head, a charade of concern that the lord of Ariton should bother himself over a few bastards with a glimmer of the second sphere about them. "Not *my* children, surely," the lord of Azmod pointed out with calm reason. "Nor yours, nor Pathet's. Did you enter that woman of your own free will and leave a child there? No, a human trapped you in his circle and commanded you to ruin a life here, whisper a secret there. If that one hadn't been as stupid as most of mewling humanity, you'd still be bound to his call, just like I am to my master."

Impotent fury edged Omage's voice as he finished his explanation: "I destroy them because it pleases me, and it is the only pleasure he has left me."

Omage turned to the boy chained at his feet, drawing Badad's attention to the hand stroking Paul Carter's hair.

"Speaking of pleasure, cousin, how is Evan? Well last you saw him?"

He'd been expecting it, but still the question, drifting casually out of the middle distance, tied knots in Brad's gut.

Omage looked up then and smiled. "He was special, you know—not like this vomitous wreck that Pathet produced. Evan actually tried to kill me."

He laughed. "Of course, he didn't know how it is with us, but it did give me an uncomfortable moment. Human flesh is so vulnerable to injury, you understand. Feeling it die is disconcerting. Not an experience I would like again, but something new, done once, nevertheless.

"I stranded Evan in the second sphere for a week after that little trick; it took that much to break him."

Lirion grabbed his arm before he could raise power against Omage, and Badad let the reminder guide him. A conflict of force at the level simmering just under the surface would level a square mile of crowded city real estate. As a rule, Badad left that kind of urban renewal to the humans. And they had contracted to get Paul Carter out of there alive.

"Don't you think it's time you told us what you really want?"

"Want?" Omage paused, as if considering a new concept. "I want Evan back. For now, however, I'll settle for the return of my trinket. You do have it?"

Badad spread his hands wide. "The Eye of Omage?" He mimed incredulity. "It's melodramatic enough, I'll grant you consistency on that score, but it scarcely gives us much information to go on. Why don't you let the boy go, and we can work this as a straight contract. Cut out the middleman, so to speak—he doesn't seem to want the job anyway."

"You always did act the fool, Badad. I even know the moment it passed into our dear Lily's hands. Now, would you like to return my property, or would you prefer to see Mr. Carter perform for us?"

Omage pulled on the boy's chains until Paul Carter's head rested on his knee, his neck contorted, his breath coming in labored gasps. "Fly now, boy," the lord of Azmod whispered, and flicked a knife deftly across a distended vein. Omage had used that knife to open the veins in Evan's arms, and the blood that had dripped onto his son's clenched fist seemed to mingle with Paul Carter's blood dripping slowly onto the hand that held him. Wide-eyed, Carter screamed, his entire body rigid. Badad felt the shock rip through the boundaries between the spheres and echo in the place where Evan's binding chafed at his being. Omage winked out for a moment, appeared again as life returned to the corpselike man at his feet.

"When you are free of this, you will have to answer to the Princes," Badad warned, but he took the necklace from around his neck and held it up to the flickering candlelight. He eyed the topaz with contempt, and cast the same glance wide to include its namesake. "You can have it when you let the boy go."

Carter reacted to the glint of the gem. The dull-eyed gaze drifted over Brad, past him, focused hungrily on the jewel in his hand. The boy reached out for it, but Omage shook his head, face set in mock sympathy.

"My dear, dear Badad, you still don't understand. The stone is only half the prize. Still," he brightened with artificial cheer that revealed the sneer lurking behind it, "Pathet has doubtless procured the other half by now, so we can call the bargain concluded.

"As I recall, I promised to release this young man from his misery in exchange for the Eye."

The knife flashed in midair and clattered to the floor between them. "You will take care to honor the letter of the exchange? His death should cause as little pain as possible. I'd suggest a quick thrust upward starting just below the sternum, entering the heart thus—" The knife flew into the air and hung suspended just pricking the skin of the chained man.

Too late Brad saw the light flicker in Paul Carter's eyes. The boy reached out, touched the blade with hesitant fingertips, then grasped the hilt in his right hand. He wrapped his left around the leg of the chair, fingers drifting over the intricate carvings, and steadied the hilt against the chains knotted there. With the knife caught between the chair and his body Paul Carter tightened his left arm, pushed against the knife. The blade plunged deeply. Blood spurted over the carvings on the chair, ran down the silver chains.

"Aahh." Carter smiled, released from his prison of nightmares at last. His eyes fluttered, opened with a hopeless sanity that offered Badad gratitude for long-sought peace. Finally he lay still.

"How many?" Badad asked softly, the gold chain of the Eye digging grooves in the hand clenched around it. The question was for Omage, but he never took his eyes from the body on the floor. Once, it might have been Evan's body. Could still be, if Omage had his way. "How many children who carried the fire of the Princes in their blood have you killed?"

The answer fell coldly between them. "One less than I wished. Evan still lives, until my master finishes with him."

"You are a stain upon the face of creation, Omage, and I will tolerate no more." Badad spoke softly, but the rumbling began at the sound of his voice. He gathered power and focused it deep in the bedrock on which the city rested, split stone and tore it just under the Black Masque. The floor buckled under them, tumbling candles from their sconces and heaving jagged teeth of paving stones back upon themselves.

Omage stood before them but made no move to stop the destruction. He raised his arms above his head and spun away in smoke, his laughter riding on the night while the wrath of Badad cast the Black Masque into smoldering dust.

# Chapter 12

*To the nature of a Prince of the second sphere each daemon lord brings both his nature and his talent, the first of which is his name, the second of which makes itself manifest in the employment of the secret arts. And of the daemon lords, Omage is named the Magus, magician and tempter, and in his name and the name of the Prince the summoner may demand both knowledge of the secret arts and all manner of treasure not yet known to man.*

"Need a taxi, meester?"

The voice was familiar, the accent atrocious. Evan Davis glanced around for its source, and found him easily; tall and rangy, with the long loose stride of a Midwesterner, Jack Laurence towered over the English and European travelers like a corn-fed Paul Bunyan. Evan relinquished his suitcase, grateful for a friendly face after the ordeal of Heathrow Customs.

Matching the man's pace with an effort, he cast a nervous glance at his old friend. Jack wore his blond hair short now, his features thrown into harsh relief with no gold fringe to soften them. He caught Jack looking back and laughed, embarrassed. So, they were both worried.

"Need to sleep for a week, but I'll settle for a ride into town," Evan agreed. "How's Claudia?"

He kept his tone casual, but they both knew the question carried more than polite interest behind it. Claudia, whom they once called the sensible one because she drank less and kept them fed, had loved him. She'd never liked Mac—Omage—but she'd put up with the barkeep for Evan and her brother, until the Black Masque had almost killed Jack. Evan hadn't seen her since the phone call almost two years ago, when she'd said it should have been him in that alley, and that she was taking Jack away. They were running, as far and as fast as they could, and from him, knowing Jack wouldn't have done it for Mac. Somehow, around Evan, things just got crazy.

Jack shrugged, following the train of thought with an ease he didn't hide now that Evan had brought it into the open.

"She's stopped hating you for what happened that night, but she still cries a lot when she thinks about you."

"I'm sorry."

"Yeah, well, I'm supposed to find out how sorry you really are before I bring you home."

He should have expected this. Jack had sounded pleased to hear from him on the phone, but then, Jack had never blamed him for that night. Looking at the man walking next to him, matching him stride for stride across the burgundy-and-gray mosaic carpet, he realized that Jack did accept him with no questions about the past, or his present. But he still had to convince Claudia.

"Let's drop my stuff at the hotel," he suggested. "Then we can talk over a couple of those huge English breakfasts and a cup of bad coffee."

"Not on your life," Jack grumbled. "Most of the stuff they serve here tastes like yesterday's dishwasher. I know a place on the way where the coffee may take the enamel off your teeth, but you can recognize what you are drinking. They even serve their eggs without beans if you're forceful enough. Then we'll decide where you'll be staying."

"I have reservations—"

The glare that bought him stopped Evan's objection. "Lead on, Mac-Duff," he agreed with only a twinge of foreboding at the poor choice of phrases. The last time he'd said those words, they'd just found a new little bar in the East Village. Maybe it was hindsight, but he'd felt his life turn on its axis that time, too. The feeling didn't get any better the second time around. Jack frowned, remembering, but he said nothing as he tossed Evan's case into the back of the battered yellow Volkswagen and ground the reluctant transmission into gear.

The eggs were greasy and the coffee—well, it wasn't tea, Evan had figured out that much. The place didn't even aspire to a decor, but they found a quiet table in the front window of the café, as far from the kitchen and the other patrons as possible.

"So," Jack began over his steaming mug, "you called from Philadelphia. Do you see much of the old New York crowd these days?"

"I left the Black Masque over a year ago."

Evan set his own mug down carefully, hiding the feelings the name conjured behind half-closed lids. "I would have gone sooner, but I couldn't."

He rubbed a thumb back and forth across the scars on his wrists, hidden by his shirtsleeve, knew the gesture for nervousness and suppressed it.

"I know that feeling," Jack misinterpreted, speaking of a time when they hadn't wanted to leave. "Took waking up in Bellevue with a cop and a shrink hanging over the bed to pull me out. And Claudia, of course. Don't know what I would have done if she hadn't stuck by me. She's happy here."

Evan heard the warning—don't hurt her again—and regretted his decision to come to London. Too many memories lay between them, and too little understanding. Jack had gotten out before Mac turned nasty, before chains took the place of persuasion. Any explanation of that last year would only open doors on the horror Evan had come here to escape.

"I don't want a rerun of the bad old days, or to mess up anybody's life." he answered, knowing it was only partly true. He didn't want to hurt anybody, but if their friendship were to survive, some old wounds might need a painful cleansing.

"I'm still trying to make sense of my own life, and you and Claudia are a part of that. If there's nothing left, okay, I'll let it go. But we meant something to each other, damn it, and I have to find out if there's any of that left."

"Hey, buddy, we're still the dynamic duo," Jack assured him with a thumb upturned in the flier's salute. "I've missed your weird sense of humor—haven't met anybody else stupid enough to go along with my harebrained schemes either. Catwoman speaks for herself, though, and she's been nervous as a long-tail in a room full of rocking chairs since you called. Afraid you'll lead me astray."

Evan shook his head. "Not me, Jack. I meant it when I said I'd left all that behind. I knew I had to get away from Mac the night you carved up your arm and we watched you nearly bleed to death.

"Great show. Yeah," he murmured bitterly to himself, then remembered his audience: "I wanted to stop you, to help somehow, but I couldn't move. It was like we all became part of one ugly, snarling animal—circling dinner."

The words snapped off leaving jagged edges. Evan was afraid to go on, to confess a part of that night he had never told, not even to Brad. For Jack, because he owed him the truth—sure. Would have said so once. He knew better than to lie to himself now. He needed to say it all, to be forgiven. But not here, over greasy dishes surrounded by strangers.

The café seemed smaller with the subject of the Black Masque on the table. Evan glanced nervously at the counter where the short-order cook lounged in conversation with the room's only waitress. Logic told him no one could hear, no mark announced to a disinterested world that the men reminiscing at the window table had once danced on a daemon's string. But logic had nothing to do with his sudden craving for breathing space.

"Let's get out of here."

Jack Laurence must have felt the walls leaning in to catch each whisper as well; he called for the check and paid it. Evan followed him into the gray London morning. They turned away from the car parked in a lot—car park, Jack had called it—and walked toward the river. Rush hour traffic clogged the street. Soon tourists would find their way to the water's edge, but they'd still be in bed now, or waking up over hotel breakfasts. He wondered where Brad and Lily were, and a part of his mind felt numb when he thought of them. Paul Carter was safe now, or dead. Either way he could do precious little about it—he'd run. Though it was the sensible thing to do, he still felt guilty. Maybe that's why he'd decided to come to London in the first place. He felt guilty about Jack, too, but he could do something about that.

They were alone together on the footpath along the Thames, and Jack was waiting for him to finish what he'd begun. Time to clear the slate; Evan took a deep breath.

"We—I—watched you bleed," he said. His voice faltered, then grew stronger: "Each drop fell like a caress." He could feel it still if he closed his eyes, like fingertips stroking his throat, choking him while his skin crawled with wanting. Death-drug—death. He shook his head, denied the feeling its power, felt the wind, nothing but a cold damp mist blowing off the river, and spoke of the Evan then and now:

"Part of me hated it. I felt like I, Evan Davis, had somehow gotten locked in a tiny room in my own head. I was beating on that door, frantic to get out, while my body responded to the sight of your blood like your death was my lover. Something in me reached out to you, I wanted to feel your blood on my fingers and stroke my own body, anoint myself with the sensation of your dying. Sexual, but something more—" *Like the river.* The thought wrapped itself around his tongue, another mist like the one rolling off the Thames, tiptoeing up his arms, wrapping cold fingers around his heart and squeezing—

"Death was a sacrament we all shared. Then we were touching each other—didn't matter who, or who touched us. I don't think I even saw you fall."

"Yeah. That's how it went down, all right."

Jack Laurence nodded his head, expression grown distant, and Evan realized his own self-absorption that night had blinded him to the truth.

"You felt it, too?"

"Of course I did." Jack softened the retort with a slow smile that faded almost before it began. "I'd never tell the docs this—they'd lock me up again—but, God, nothing before or since has ever turned me on like that."

Laurence paused. The Thames flowed an arm's length from where they stood, but Evan doubted the man saw it; his eyes focused somewhere beyond the river. If he gave them half a chance, the same images would be leering at Evan from behind his own eyes, but he stayed in the present, kept the Thames at his feet. The past was dead.

Without turning, Jack picked up the conversation again with an apparent non sequitur: "Remember when Claudia was taking classes at Columbia?"

Evan nodded, then realized Jack hadn't seen the silent agreement.

"She told us how the Aztecs used to sacrifice their own people, cut out their hearts, by the tens of thousands." Laurence continued without prompting, but he did flick a quick glance at Evan. A sharp nod acknowledged the memory shared, then Laurence went on:

"We thought they were crazy. How could a sane human being willingly accept his own death like that? Well, now I know.

"My blood was a gift, my life a sacrifice for the pleasure of my God. Dying, I loved him. You. I felt my energy fill the crowd and their hands were my hands, their bodies my body. I was all of them—men, women, I felt what they felt, my energy fueled their frenzy."

"I'm no god, Jack. Not even close." Evan kept his tone low, but he couldn't entirely soften the implacable edge to it. Whatever he'd come here for, it wasn't to fulfill the fantasy Omage had spun around him. Jack accepted the rebuff with a sigh.

"I know," Jack admitted, "But you're not one of us either. Behind your back we used to wonder what you were—an alien stranded here or sent to judge us, the next step in evolution, an angel."

"That was all nonsense," Evan lied. "I was somebody Mac could use, and he made up the rest."

Jack answered with a bitter laugh. "Just because I act like a fool doesn't mean I am one. Claudia was the only one you ever convinced of that line, and you had hormones working for you there.

"No, I made my mistake when I let myself believe I knew what you were, and that we were important to it. Don't ask for an encore—"

"I didn't ask the first time," Evan reminded him sharply.

"I know that, too, Evan; hear me out. I wouldn't do it again, but I've never regretted that night. If I had it to do over, I probably wouldn't change a thing."

"That's where we differ." A little of the terror that had sent him to London leached the color from his face. "If I could do it over, I'd stay on

Rosemont Street and go to Temple University like the rest of the kids in my neighborhood."

Jack shook his head. "And the nightmares?" he asked, and Evan looked away, ambushed by the shared memories.

"Does Temple give courses in night terrors and astral projection now? Health 101—how to cope with life as a displaced deity? You needed Mac more than any of us. Be that honest with yourself if not with me."

Honest. Evan felt the weight of chains again, saw the face of the creature sent to kill him—his father.

"Before you left, Mac called me a god. Afterward, when I wanted to leave, he made me his prisoner. Yes, I found what I was looking for, but the price was too high. I'm not the only one still paying it; you and Claudia were my first victims, but not my last."

He remembered his father, snarling and wishing him dead, and Lily, who had tried her hardest to kill him just hours ago. The rewards of godlike power, he realized, were not eternal worship, but the bitter anger of the captive for his jailer. If Omage hadn't called them, using Evan's own terror to destroy the barriers between the spheres, the human would still be living half a life, lost between two universes, maybe locked in a state mental hospital by now. But Lily would be free in that place she loved. Brad, his father, would never have had to stand between the child of his captivity and the destruction of his home. The price for his own peace of mind had been the freedom, almost the lives, of those he had come to love.

"Honest," he said. "Knowing what I do now, I couldn't go through it again."

"This was a mistake," Evan concluded. They stood side by side, watching the river. Like the Thames, their apparent calm concealed rapid currents pulling them farther and farther apart. "We can't change the past, but here I am trying to do just that. Could still use a ride to the hotel, then I'll be out of your life." The south of France was lovely in April. Peaceful. He could be in Nice by evening.

He turned away, putting the river behind him. "I could take a cab, but you've got my stuff in your trunk."

"Boot," Jack corrected absently. "Claudia will want to see you. It will hurt her if you leave without saying good-bye."

Evan turned his head, met the question in Jack Laurence's eyes, and smiled. "You're a bastard, Jack, and you play dirty. I'll see Claudia, but I won't stay."

"We'll cross that bridge when we come to it." Jack's confidence did nothing to reassure Evan. He suffered the hearty clap on the back with patience born of experience and followed Jack back to the car.

# Chapter 13

*Lirion is the name of the one also called Lilith, the Lily of Heaven, lover of beauty, and lover of men. If anything be stolen, command her, for she knows all things of thieving, but be cautious. Lirion returns only part of what she regains, and she has been known to steal the heart of her master, crushing it in her grasp.*

"THIS IS LAYTON," LAURENCE ANNOUNCED AS THE YELLOW BEETLE WHEEZED its way up a small hill lined with shops and turned onto a quiet residential street.

"Reminds me of Brooklyn," Evan commented.

The Volkswagen bucked to a halt in front of a narrow white house with a well-tended postage stamp of a lawn surrounded by a freshly painted white picket fence. Claudia probably had roses growing in the back garden. Evan got out of the car and stared hard at the upstairs windows, trying to see past the sheer curtains to the heart of the house beyond. The fifth floor walk-up they had once shared in the Village seemed very far away now. He remembered Lily and Brad trading Biblical badinage just days ago, and wondered if he were not himself some messenger of downfall or, less flattering still, just the apple an unsuspecting Jack Laurence carried into his sister's newfound Garden of Eden.

Jack opened the door and ushered him into the front hall next to a steep flight of stairs. "Claudia!" he called. "I've got a weary traveler here, looking for a little comfort."

"Evan!"

The squeal preceded the flying bundle of Claudia, launched from the staircase with a fine disregard for the laws of gravity or momentum. The force of her landing drove Evan backward, sandwiched between soft full breasts and a hard plaster wall covered in a faded pattern of palm fronds and bamboo lattice.

"I can't breathe," he gasped, quailing at the determined glint in her eye.

"You need mouth-to-mouth resuscitation," Claudia announced. She moved her hands to the sides of his face, traced the shape of his skull with a sculptor's attention, and pulled his head down to meet her upturned mouth.

The Red Cross might not have approved Claudia's version of first aid, but it had a certain appeal. Evan surfaced from the kiss with a grin, the dark memories of the morning burned away in the warmth of her greeting.

"Of course, I've always thought breathing was overrated," he approved with a squeeze and a nibble.

She nuzzled at his mouth, drifting lips from corner to corner, and pulled away with a smile. "I've missed you, too."

"I can tell. How are you?"

"Late for work, I'm afraid." She glared at her brother, but affection softened the exasperation. "I wanted to see you before I left, but I have to run."

Evan finally took time to look at her, and noticed the spring coat she already wore. In many ways, Claudia and Jack were opposites. Where Jack was tall and angular, Claudia only hit five feet with her shoes on, and she fought a never-ending battle with her bathroom scale. At that moment she seemed to be winning, but Evan knew from past experience she was closing in on her stalemate point. Her hair had once been as blonde as Jack's, but had turned a soft brown when Claudia was a teenager. For a while in New York she had colored it; Evan was glad to see she'd let it return to its natural color. Somehow, this Claudia belonged in a house with a picket fence and roses in the back. Sanctuary. The word rose unbidden in his mind, and labeled the feeling that grew in the light of her warmth. The past could not touch them here.

"I've made up the back room for you." Her words cut through the fog of his wandering attention. "It's barely more than a closet, but I've moved the boxes of books into the attic, and borrowed a foldaway cot from Nancy-next-door. Got to run. Jack, feed him some tea and get him settled. I took the afternoon off. Meet me at the shop at lunchtime, and we can show Evan the sights."

She gave him a quick hug. "Missed you," she repeated, and left on the run, the door slamming behind her.

"London suits her," Evan commented, pulling his eyes away from the door that still seemed to rattle on its hinges. "The question is, can London cope?"

Jack snorted. "They're used to the type," he returned, "Napoleon wasn't much bigger."

"But Napoleon didn't have Claudia's smile. I guess I'm staying."

"Too right, old chum. If you try to back out now, she'll have my head on a plate and then come looking for yours." Jack swept up his suitcase by its shoulder strap and took the stairs two at a time.

As promised, the room was the size of a moderately luxurious closet, and the foldaway cot dripped loose springs when Evan thought about lying down. But he dismissed the room waiting for him at the Savoy without a thought. Claudia's house enfolded him in her warmth; he felt her presence in the bright throws that covered the shabby sitting room furniture, in the rug loom that relegated the Victorian dining room furniture to a pile of chairs stacked on the table in a corner. Her rugs—exotic strips of velvet and lamé and glitter woven into abstract bursts of light and dark—hung on every wall. He didn't quite believe the one in the kitchen.

"Is that what I think it is?"

Jack looked up from the jar of instant coffee and rolled his eyes. "Yup. Bread wrappers. Every couple of weeks she takes it out back, sprays it with the dishwashing liquid, and hoses it down. Half the neighbors have them now. Only uses the English ones for Christmas—"

"Why Christmas?"

"The colors," Jack explained. "English supermarket bread comes in red and green packages, mostly, but Mom's bridge club in Dayton saves Wonder and Sunbeam wrappers for her and sends them over. Sort of a latter-day 'bundles for Britain.'

"The first few shipments arrived opened, then we had a visit from our local postal inspector. I don't know whether he thought we were making napalm out of hot dog bun wrappers or we were part of a colonial plot to flood the Island with Yankee refuse. Claudia sent him home with a Sunbeam yellow sunburst for his wife, and that was the last we heard of him."

Evan took the steaming mug Jack offered. "Leave it to Claudia," he laughed. "Maybe the State Department could use her in the Middle East."

"Bread wrappers for peace? Don't even think it," Jack warned. "We'll be hip-deep in plastic before the words are out of your mouth."

"She won't hear it from me." Evan raised the mug in a mock toast, bringing him face-to-face with the wide-eyed kitten painted on its side.

Jack lounged against the side of the sink. The mug in his hand had a picture of dogs playing billiards painted on its side.

"She still loves you, you know," he said too casually.

Evan stared into his coffee. He'd hoped to avoid this conversation, at least until the past day or two had faded a bit around the edges, but Jack wouldn't let it go.

"If you mean it about being done with Mac, you could pick up right where you left off. Remember how we used to plan it: you married to Claudia, us, brothers. The old trio—we'd be unstoppable."

Claudia in the bedroom, the loom in the dining room, and roses on the white picket fence. If they argued, Claudia might char the pot roast, but she wasn't likely to turn Evan into a pile of ashes on the carpet. He shook his head at the kitten on his coffee mug. Then he met Jack's eyes, defenses down and all the turmoil of the past week stamped on his features for a brief moment.

"Too much unfinished business," he explained, thinking of his father and Lily. They were tied by the command of Ariton and by his own binding for Evan's lifetime, a commitment he had made in return. Out of the corner of his eye he saw Jack Laurence rub the scar on his wrist, and he wondered again if coming here was a mistake. It seemed like he dragged shadows of the past with him wherever he went.

"I'm still trying to figure out what I am, and Claudia deserves more than that."

Laurence shrugged. "You've still got time to change your mind." Jack rinsed his mug and set it down on the drainboard. "In the meantime, we'd better get moving. When it comes to lunch, time and Claudia Laurence wait for no man."

Time. He checked his watch, still set on Philadelphia's Eastern Standard: 7:00 a.m.. If the night had gone as planned, neither Brad nor Lily would be pleased to hear from him at this hour, and Claudia was waiting for him.

"The door is this way, man." Laurence grabbed a handful of Evan's shoulder and turned him toward the back door with a solid nudge. "The tube will get us there in no time." Evan slapped his own mug on a counter and preceded his friend from the house.

They left Tottenham Court Road Station with a crowd of tourists and shoppers but after only a few short blocks Jack directed him off congested Charing Cross onto Denmark Street, a narrow, doglegged side street with more bookstores and pubs but a few less tourists. Jack led him to a shop with a swinging sign from another century that said "Thomas James, Bookseller" in Gothic script. A little bell above the door tinkled to announce them when they entered the shop, but no obsequious Uriah Heep of a clerk scurried from behind the old oak bookshelves to curl over wringing hands and beg to be of service. Instead, Claudia's cheerful but disembodied voice greeted them:

"I'll be right there. If you don't see what you want, I can check in the back for you in just a minute."

"Don't rush," Jack announced them. "It's just us chickens." He headed for the back of the shop and folded himself into the swivel chair in front of the ancient secretary desk while Evan prowled the stacks. Dickens—he'd been right about that—the shop was crammed with the novels in a variety of languages and all sorts of editions. Other shelves held the Brontës, Thackeray, and Eliot. He passed by the Browning, considered a Coleridge, and finally decided upon a copy of Walter Scott's *Ossian*. Brad would enjoy the irony of the Scots novelist and poet creating an epic with which to establish the Romantic antecedents of his dour nation. *Vanity Fair* tempted for Lily, but he decided that she wouldn't appreciate the joke.

"Excuse me, please, but you sound American."

Evan turned, found the source of the tentative comment walking toward Claudia from an aisle labeled "Travel."

"That's right," she agreed, hanging a dusty smock on a hook next to the desk.

The stranger was well dressed, tall, with sharp, dark eyes that cut to the bone and a faint hint of Europe in his Queen's English.

"Perhaps you could advise me on a matter of national etiquette," the stranger suggested. "But I haven't introduced myself. I am Count Alfredo DaCosta, and I recently made the acquaintance of a lady of American extraction."

Evan stopped, just out of DaCosta's line of sight, feeling like he was fooling no one but himself. The thief had to know he was there, somehow had linked Claudia and Jack to him through God knew what contacts the man had in the underworld. But DaCosta ignored him, playing out his game.

"I wanted to send her a gift to remind her of our visit together. I thought this might be appropriate, but—this is so embarrassing—I don't want to presume on our short acquaintanceship."

"Let me see, Mr., uh, Count—" Claudia didn't fluster easily, but DaCosta was smiling. Yep; this one would know what to do with ten dancing girls on his front lawn all right. Claudia pulled herself together with a little shake of her shoulders that reminded Evan of other days. She took the book bound in gilt and leather that DaCosta held out to her. "Ruskin's *The Stones of Venice*."

"We met in Venice, you see," DaCosta explained, "and the lady expressed a fondness for the stonework of that city."

Claudia nodded her head, reassuring the Italian count. "The Ruskin will be a nice memento, then. Shall I wrap it for you?"

"Please."

She took the volume to the cash register and rang it up. "What brings you to London?"

Polite small talk, but Evan could have kissed her. Just the question he would have asked, if he'd had a mind to add his own presence to the meeting he had given up as coincidence in its first minutes. DaCosta was as smooth as ever.

"There's an auction at Sotheby's tomorrow. They have a Matisse I'm interested in, though, Lord knows, between the Japanese and the Americans I'm not likely to get it. Sorry, I don't mean that as a slur," DaCosta hastened to add. It's just that old family fortunes don't go as far as they once did. Still, I thought I'd take a look myself. Have you lived in London long?"

"Just two years." She handed him the book. "I'm sure the lady will enjoy it." A subtle reminder, there, that flirting with one woman while buying a gift for another might not be quite appropriate, even for an American. DaCosta accepted the hint with good grace, taking his book in exchange for a traveler's check, and turned to leave the store. Evan stood his ground and DaCosta gave him a brief nod suitable for strangers passing within a foot of each other in a place both might consider their own private find, but Evan saw recognition and something else—challenge or warning—in his eyes.

Taking it as a challenge, he spoke up: "Good luck with the auction. The Ruskin should be a winner."

"I'm sure you must be right . . . as an American." DaCosta nodded again, and left the store.

Claudia looked from Evan to the closing door and back again. "What was that about?"

"Nothing." He'd leave, tonight if he could get a flight. Or maybe he'd take the ferry, rent a car in Calais, and motor up the coast, maybe stop to do some sketching along the way. He could use the warmth of Nice. Right now, he didn't think he'd ever be warm enough again.

"Right, Batman." Jack added his opinion from his chair at the back of the little store. "Tell us another one."

Evan sighed. "He may be a friend of a friend. Or he might not." May be a friend, most likely an enemy. He knew Lily had taken the Eye of Omage, but how the daemon had lost it to DaCosta in the first place remained an uncomfortable mystery. "I never met him before, if that's what you mean, and he never mentioned her name." Half-truths, but his friends seemed willing to accept them for now.

"Oho, a she. That explains it, then." Jack unfolded out of his chair and sauntered over to the cash register. "Couldn't expect you to spend the past two years as a monk, now could we?" He waggled his eyebrows suggestively.

"That's enough, Jack." Claudia took Evan's book, the Walter Scott. "Let me see that. You know Scott faked it, don't you? If you're really interested in folklore, you'd do better down the street; we can stop there after we eat."

"We can stop anywhere you want after lunch, but I know the story. Instant history—thought my father would get a kick out of it." He kept his face cheerfully neutral for her sharp scrutiny.

"You found him, then?" She hesitated for a moment, then finished wrapping the book in brown paper. Wary, her voice seemed to tiptoe around the fences Evan put between his feelings and the outside world, giving him the space he needed while she seemed to concentrate on tying off the twine. With Claudia he didn't want the fences, but he couldn't imagine just blurting out the truth either: *He's a daemon. Wasn't really happy to discover he'd left half-human get behind him, even less enthused when his boss from outer space told him he couldn't come home until I was dead. So far I've kept him intrigued enough not to off me and split. And by the way, I'm sleeping with his cousin, who is also a daemon. She gets kinky thrills having sex with human men—must think I'm okay in that department, because she hasn't offed me yet either.* No, that part of the truth was definitely out.

"Actually, he found me. He has his own detective agency: found me, got me straight, took me into the company. I work for him now, have for over a year."

"I'm so glad."

She rewarded him with a hug, enveloping him in the radiance of her goodwill. He took his package, putting aside the sudden uneasiness that he'd just been praised like a puppy who hasn't peed on the parlor carpet when he's been locked in the bathroom all day. Usually only Lily could make him feel like that—maybe it was just a guilty conscience.

Jack rescued him from drowning in introspection. The man draped one arm over Claudia's shoulder and the other over Evan's. "It's been a long time since breakfast. Can't we chew the fat over meat pasties?"

"Bad joke, brother-mine." Claudia rolled her eyes, patted Evan's hand. "You'll understand soon enough, no reason to scare you ahead of time." She called through the door to the back room, and waited until the porch-swing-in-need-of-oiling voice of her employer acknowledged her good-bye. "We're off," she announced.

Her brother dutifully picked up the straight line: "But not so crazy that we'd miss lunch." He shepherded them out of the shop.

A leisurely walk brought them to Covent Gardens—the place, Evan decided, where flea markets must go when they die. Vendors of luggage and cheap imported clothes jostled for floor space with record sellers and purveyors of china mugs with pictures of Big Ben on them. Jugglers and painted mimes and a trio of brass musicians playing marches vied for tips in the courtyard. Claudia led them past tables of questionable antiquities and the white elephant from Aunt Mary's attic to a food stall where she ordered three pasties and the same number of teas, "Because it's authentic."

"Purists," Evan accused with mock disdain as he brushed pasty crumbs from his fingertips. Not even the strong milky tea could wash away the savory and suet taste of the meat pie. "London has McDonald's now, you know." He crumpled the cardboard teacup and took aim at the cracked plastic wastebasket.

Jack Laurence blocked the shot, and the game was on then off again when Claudia took the cup from his hands and placed it meticulously in the center of the receptacle.

"Behave yourselves," she warned sternly, "or Mummy won't buy you a sweet."

"She's been here too long, Jack."

The rangy Midwesterner sighed and shook his head. "I'd have her deprogrammed," he explained, "but then I'd miss out on my sweet."

"You're both insane." Evan led the way to a flower stall and picked out a bunch of violets which he presented to Claudia with a grand flourish and a bow. "For the loveliest lady in London."

"Is that Evan Davis? Davis, it is you."

The familiar voice cut across Claudia's response, jarring Evan out of his playful mood. He turned and found the source of the voice coming around the flower stall with his hand extended. The man wasn't as bad as Lily made out—balding a bit, and the thick tortoiseshell frames of his glasses weighed heavily on his otherwise nondescript features—but what the hell was Charles Devereaux St. George doing in London?

"Mr. St. George."

Evan took the outstretched hand, surprised as always at the firmness of the grip. Lily's influence, he supposed; it wasn't Charlie's fault he had the shape and complexion of a beached flounder. He remembered a comment Lily had once made, that a man with as much money as St. George ought to own better fitting suits. This one looked like it might have fit ten pounds ago. He smothered an incipient grin and refocused on the man in front of him.

"No need for formality—strangers in a strange land together and all that. It's Charles." The newcomer addressed the correction to Claudia, bending his head in the merest hint of a bow. "And the lady is?"

"Claudia Laurence, Jack Laurence, her brother—old friends from college. And this is Charles Devereaux St. George, a client of our agency."

Evan completed the introduction, and held his breath. Since his arrival he'd been deliberately vague about the agency. The feeling that he'd abandoned his post—somehow failed that part of himself that was not human—lay too close to the surface for dispassionate discussion, and DaCosta already had ghosts walking on his grave. There were no coincidences in this business, and nothing would convince him synchronicity had brought the thief and his mark thousands of miles from their usual haunts to the same few square blocks on the same day. Knowing his client, Evan would bet that whatever was going on, Charlie would get the worst of it. But St. George beat him to the question of the day.

"So what brings you to London, Davis? An elusive Rembrandt? A disappearing Degas?"

"Just vacation, Charles. Visiting old friends, sightseeing, like any other tourist."

"I know—" St. George winked broadly and raised both hands, palms out in surrender. "You can't say."

"Not this time, Charles. Just vacation."

"They really are the best," St. George said in an aside to his avid audience of two, ignoring Evan's protestations. "But then, you must know that better than I."

He returned his attention to Evan. "And how is the charming Lily? I did so want to thank her personally for her efforts on my behalf. Having the Mont Parnass back in its place fills my soul with peace."

"Our fee was ample expression of your gratitude, Charles. But I'll pass along your appreciation when I go home."

"Thank you, my boy, but perhaps I'll call on Miss Ryan myself when I return."

"I'm sure she'd like that." Evan almost choked on the words, but he managed to keep his expression attentively neutral. Only someone who knew him very well could have seen the devil clicking his heels behind the placid smile. Jack Laurence knew him very well: The man followed the conversation as if it were match point at Wimbledon, his eyebrows arching higher at the obvious falsehood.

"In the meantime," St. George went on, apparently oblivious to the undercurrents of the conversation, "I have another matter I'd like to speak to you about. Had planned to call the agency when I returned, but you can save me a trip if you're amenable. It's not exactly your usual line of work, but I'm in a bit of a bind, time-wise, and I'd consider it a personal favor. Can we talk over dinner, perhaps? I'm at the Claridge, your friends are welcome, of course—we can discuss the confidential details later, if you decide to take the case."

He intended to beg off, planned to be gone by then, but caught the murder in Claudia's eyes. Her expression said "adventure"—a glimpse into a world of money and privilege she had only read about in books—and Evan admitted to himself there could be no harm in dinner. Charlie St. George might be as dull as Philadelphia in November, but he wasn't dangerous unless he tripped over his own feet and fell on someone. And whatever the man had on his mind could give him a graceful way to cut short his visit.

"All right, I'll listen."

St. George beamed at him, one hand on Evan's arm, the other shaking Evan's hand. "Eight thirty. I'll be looking forward to it." He shook hands with Jack Laurence, and then turned his full attention on Claudia.

"Not violets," he said, taking her hand and brushing lips just above her fingertips, "the lady should always have roses." With a final nod to Evan, he walked off briskly in the direction of the Strand.

Evan forestalled the torrent of questions poised to descend on him from his friends. "I'll tell you all about it later," he bargained, "but for now, let's pretend Charles St. George never happened. I seem to remember you promised me dessert."

# Chapter 14

*Of the great mysteries of the spheres, eternity is the greatest, for each sphere is contained within its boundaries, yet each is boundless. Each was created, and yet each existed before time, for all time.*

THE PART OF BADAD THAT BELONGED HERE, IN THE SECOND SPHERE, CAREENED in the void, propelled by the memory of pain that shrieked through him, through the universe of Princes. Sense told him he was home, that flesh had no meaning here, but the shock of meat-death held him still. The moment when mind winked out caught him in its terrifying grasp, and he reached for something solid in the void, finding only memory—

Fire. Flesh burned. Torn, flung in clods that quivered with the cell-memory of life, the body that had been Kevin Bradley hit the broken concrete of the Black Masque's foundation. So this was death, a small voice that clung to the identity of Badad the daemon whispered into the maelstrom. He sought a distance from which to observe the experience, but found his daemon self drawn into the very heart of his body-terror. Here or now twisted out of true; just the moments before the explosion in Omage's back room remained to him, watching the blood flow out of Paul Carter's body.

Then bedrock shifted, cracked. He pulled the motion into himself, collected it in the lens of his mind, and turned it on the building around him. He might have escaped then, transported out and let the damned humans shift for themselves on a world that rocked on its axis, but a face shaped itself in his mind. He owed host loyalty to that which he recognized as Ariton in his son, while the binding spell worked by his human bastard twisted his gut like an angry fist. Evan needed a place to stand, so Badad focused down, holding the damage within the burning walls of the Black Masque.

Screams reached him from beyond the door—humans dying, buried in the rubble of the falling building and burning with the bright blue flame that reminded him of Ariton, fed by the gas line snapped in the quake. He thought of human literature—the history they made for themselves—and added a touch of sulfur to the mix, even as he felt himself losing control of the backflash.

The fire reached the back room and blew. Surprised, Badad realized that he would not escape the physical shell of this body in time. He had not imagined one body, one blinding moment could hold so much pain, and he tried to break free. The sensations, more intense, more all-consuming than any he had experienced in material form, confused him. His sense of separation from the physical realm slipped away, and he became, fully and for the first time as it died, the body that he wore. Thought scattered and flew; only the demands of heart and lungs and the reptile brain at the base of his human spinal cord reached him, the imperative of the body to continue.

Then the darkness of nonbeing seeped into the body that had been Kevin Bradley, through the ghosts of missing fingertips and toes, working inward to his heart, dimming his eyes. The roaring in his ears grew louder— the sound of flame, of flowing blood, of his own heart pumping the stuff of life onto the shattered floor. Finally, when sound, too, had ceased to reach him, Badad felt the last spark of motion leave his body. Dead, trapped in flesh that began to rot as the last breath stilled.

*Top of the food chain to the bottom in the space of a heartbeat,* his last sane thought before the darkness closed mocked him for the scorn in which he had held the humans. He could never have been one of them, could never have lived at all with the knowledge that this lay at the end of it.

Badad felt the tremors of his own damaged consciousness shudder through his universe. There were others of his kind nearby, minds flung aside in his careening race through the not-space that made up the second sphere. A familiar touch flicked a tentative merge through him and fled again.

"Immortal!" His blindness raged. "Death has no hold on me!" But the words had no meaning for him as he died again and again. A mind touched his, and he remembered a human sense—smell, of lilies of the valley massed in the shadows of a garden wall. For a moment the scent cooled the fire burning his mind away, then it was gone with a shiver of separation. He was alone again, curled against the horror of dying for all eternity.

# Chapter 15

*And of the creatures of the spheres, lords and Princes and Archangels and Thrones, only those of the first sphere, the dominion of man, know the limits of time and space. Death is the one great mystery that confounds the rest.*

"EVAN!" CLAUDIA CALLED UP THE NARROW STAIRCASE, "DID YOU FALL ASLEEP UP there? We're going to be late!"

Evan shrugged his shoulders more comfortably into his dinner jacket and adjusted his shirt cuffs to show a quarter inch below the jacket sleeves, wishing he had fallen asleep. Jet lag had never left him this shaky before—not since he had done his flying for Omage, and the similarity of the feelings made him decidedly queasy. He was in no condition to negotiate for the agency with St. George, in no mood to make small talk when he just wanted to get away from there as fast as the Dover train could take him, or home, if things had gone really wrong with Paul Carter.

But he was stuck here, at least through dinner. There were limits to the amount of hurt he could inflict on Claudia, and he'd passed that limit long ago. But, dammit, if he didn't have to get away for her own protection, he'd have invited her out for a fancy dinner himself! Too late for that now. He checked the mirror one more time—hoped Claudia wouldn't notice the tension that darkened the circles under his eyes—and headed down the stairs.

"I didn't fall asleep, and we're not late. And if we were, Charlie's got enough money to hold the table all night."

He stopped at the landing and whistled under his breath.

"You are beautiful." Claudia wore black velvet iced with silver lamé; Evan remembered seeing the tag ends of the fabric in one of the rugs that hung on the walls. He kissed her on the cheek, eased the hurt she tried to

hide with a smile. "I don't want to seem too eager. After all, if St. George
has his way, my vacation is over. Have I overstayed my welcome already?"

"Not in a million years." She gave him a hug, then moved away to get
a better look at him. "Turn around, let me see you."

He complied with a full circle and took her hands when they were
face-to-face again. "Do I pass muster?"

"And then some. You didn't pick that suit up at J.C. Penney." Not quite
a question, her comment invited explanation.

"No." Nor would Carlo Pimi have appreciated the comparison. The
thought of the Milan tailor in one of his outrageous displays of temper
made Evan laugh, but Claudia was still waiting for an answer to all the
unstated "whys?" that had lain between them through the afternoon.

"My father's agency specializes in recovery—art, mostly, sometimes
jewelry. We have to be discreet, and that means blending into our clients'
surroundings. Don't worry—I turn back into a pumpkin at midnight.

"Which reminds me—mind if I call the office?" he asked, "My dime—
corporate calling card."

"Of course, call," she agreed, "but don't take too long, will you? Jack
is warming up the car." She stopped him with a hand on his arm. "Just
one question first. Are you really on vacation?"

Evan considered his options, from outright lies to the truth, and compromised, offering little information, but an answer to the question she
couldn't voice. "I'm not here on a case, if that's what you mean, and no,
I didn't plan to bump into Charlie St. George, though we did seem to be
wading knee-deep in coincidental meetings this afternoon.

"I needed to get away for a little while, and I thought of you and Jack.
We were friends once, good friends. It's taken me a while to get over that
time, but I finally decided I couldn't throw out the good with the bad, not
if there was anything left to salvage. That's really all there is to it."

"Thank you." She kissed him, gently, and let him go. "Phone's in the
sitting room, E.T. Call home."

He found the ancient telephone set on a small table in the entryway
between the sitting room with its faded palm frond paper and the hall.
Rotary dial, heavy black base and receiver—the house must have been
wired in the fifties, and no one had thought to upgrade since. Evan dialed
the overseas operator and placed his call, waited impatiently as she made
the connections. Finally, the sound of a ringing phone echoed satellite-
tinny over the line. No one answered. He checked his watch: seven o'clock.
It would be two in the afternoon back home. Brad or Lily should have
answered, or the machine should have transferred his call. Unless some-

thing had gone very wrong. An operator broke into the line and he asked her to verify the number and place the call again.

He counted the palm fronds printed on the ancient wallpaper: one frond for each ring. Still no answer. An operator intruded again, insisted that he place his call later. For a moment Evan stood there, adding up palm fronds while a dial tone shrilled at him from the receiver heavy in his hand. Slowly he returned the relic to its cradle, his mind a blank.

"Nothing?" Claudia asked softly. He hadn't noticed her come into the room, couldn't shift his expression fast enough to pretend he wasn't worried. So he shook his head, giving himself time to pull his mind away from all the ugly possibilities an unanswered phone might mean. "I'll try again later. Right now we have a date."

A maître d' in full tails and a starched white stand-up collar and bowtie led Evan Davis and his companions to a table tucked into a discreet corner of the Claridge dining room. Charles St. George smiled and half-rose to greet them as they took their seats—Claudia at St. George's right, Evan at his left, and Jack Laurence across from St. George. "Evan, Mr. Laurence, and the best for last. Claudia—may I call you Claudia?" he took her hand, held it a fraction too long.

The attention rankled in the part of Evan's brain that whispered of caves and firelight and the music of hearts beating in rhythm with each other. His rational mind said "ancient history," rights ceded. Imagination supplied a picture from an earlier conversation—Claudia picking through the wreckage of a Midwestern town in the aftermath of a tornado—wholly at odds with the muted luxury of the Claridge dining room. Covering his confusion, he returned Charlie's smile with a bland rictus of his own.

The maître d' appeared again, this time carrying two dozen roses in a crystal vase. Behind him followed a waiter with a flower stand. The roses matched the deep pink of the tablecloths and the delicate blossoms woven into the gold ivy that bordered the service. Claudia touched the petals of a bloom and smiled, first at the maître d' who set the vase in the stand next to her chair, and then at Charles St. George.

"I was right," he declared. "You should always have roses."

She smoothed his lapel where it curled over at his neck. "No one has ever given me roses before." She slid a glance sideways at Evan, and he read the accusation there. "They're beautiful. Thank you."

St. George accepted her thanks with a little bounce on the balls of his feet, and nodded toward a bottle resting label up in an ice bucket at his side. "I have champagne chilling for later—dom Perignon. And I took the liberty of ordering something special for dinner. I hope you like it."

"I'm sure I will," she reassured him with a pat on his hand. Lily would have laughed in poor Charlie's overeager face, but Evan found himself envying St. George for the gentle kindnesses Claudia showed him, and for the excitement that shone in her smile. Charlie had given her that, and Evan wondered why it mattered so much to him while the cave-brain whispered, "Mine."

"I've passed by here lots of times, but I've never been inside before," Claudia said, her eyes wide as she studied the room. She caught Evan's glance and tilted her nose ceilingward.

He got the unspoken message: This is how a lady should be treated. Back in their Village days they couldn't have paid the tip in a place like the Claridge, but he knew that look meant more than fancy restaurants. She'd always been there—a lover in bed, a mother when the nightmares came too close. Obsessed with his own search, Evan had never wooed her, had never made Claudia feel beautiful or important, or loved. With two out of three before the soup course, Charles Devereaux St. George was already ahead on points.

"All the most famous people stay here." She smiled pointedly at Charlie. "We could be sitting next to royalty this very minute and not even know it."

St. George returned her smile. "Or a rock star," he agreed. "The valet told me in confidence that Mike Jagger always stays at the Claridge when he's in town."

Jack choked into his napkin, reached for his water glass, but Claudia seemed not to notice the gaffe. Maybe she didn't listen to the Stones anymore.

"You don't say," Evan offered blandly. He took a breath to add that Lily avoided *Mick* Jagger when he showed up at the Savoy, but Claudia's glare silenced him.

When Claudia returned her attention to Charles St. George, her brother nudged Evan in the shoulder. Jack leaned over and whispered in his ear: "Watch your back, Batman. The Penguin is making off with your girl."

In the old days he would have brushed off the suggestion with a retort of his own: *Catwoman can take care of herself.* But he hadn't played in a long time, and it had always been Jack's game. *Past,* he said to himself, calling to mind Lily's cold perfection. He shivered, afraid to let go of the warmth of Claudia even as he reached for something he could touch with outstretched fingers, but could never hold. Jack brought him back to the here and now with a thud.

"This guy doesn't make his money on a press in his basement, does he?" Laurence whispered, persistent.

Evan glared at him. "He doesn't have time," he whispered back. "Too busy spending what his father left him." He turned away, hoping St. George hadn't noticed the exchange, and found the man staring at him with a little smile.

"Not quite true, Evan," St. George admonished. "Although I leave the day-to-day running of Papa's companies to others, I still take an interest in new acquisitions. But I never discuss business before dinner—"

The waiter arrived, set a slice of terrine de trois pâté in front of each of them, and Evan picked up a fruit knife and crust of French bread. Faced with a sea of cutlery, Claudia hesitated, then followed Evan's lead.

St. George took a bottle from the wine steward. "Spanish sherry, wonderful with pâté." He filled Claudia's glass and handed the bottle back to the steward to serve the remaining guests.

Jack took his gladly, but Evan shook his head. "None for me, thank you." He turned the glass upside down on the table.

"Very well, sir." The steward bowed and took a step back, but St. George stopped him with an imperious wave of his hand. "Come, come, Evan. Don't be a spoilsport. It's like drinking bottled sunshine, you'll love it."

"I don't drink anymore, Charles. I'm an alcoholic."

St. George reached for the wineglass. "The young are so dramatic," he said. "So you overindulged a bit in college. Everybody does—that doesn't make you an alcoholic, anymore than a fine wine over dinner with friends constitutes a binge."

"I'm sure you mean well, Charles, but I really don't want any wine." Evan gritted his teeth, wondering suddenly why he had ever felt sympathy for the bumbling little man.

Jack Laurence took a sip and smacked his lips appreciatively. "That leaves more for us." He lifted his glass and looked at the wine steward with a greedily hopeful expression.

No one spoke for a moment. The wine steward filled Jack's glass and drifted smoothly around the table, depositing the bottle at St. George's right. He left the tableau to the busboy removing pâté and the waiter standing ready with the asparagus bisque.

"I suppose you don't want any sherry for your soup either," Charles dismissed the unpleasantness with a grumbled attempt at humor.

Claudia smiled. She rested her hand on Charles' arm, but her eyes were on Evan, and they warmed him with the comfort and support she had always given him. "He wasn't there, Evan. He doesn't know what it was like for us in New York."

"Is that where you three met? In New York?" Charlie asked.

Evan felt the tension ease a notch between his shoulder blades, and caught Jack lifting his eyes in a silent gesture of relief.

"Yes," Evan said. "I was putting in an abortive semester at the Carnegie Institute, and Claudia was doing a little better at Columbia. Jack had his degree in accounting from Indiana University—"

"I was taking a year off to 'find myself' in the Village," Jack added. "As the oldest and wisest among us, I took it as my sacred trust to lead my companions astray."

"Evan!" St. George eyed him speculatively, rolling the stem of his wineglass between his thumb and forefinger. "You naughty boy—you never told me."

Claudia's face had grown increasingly drawn as the conversation continued, and Evan realized that she was watching him for some signal. He gave the barest hint of a shrug, but his jaw tightened. Jack wouldn't bring up the Black Masque; the man had better sense than to regale Evan's client with the sordid details of that little adventure. The thought of Omage's name bandied about the dinner table curdled the soup in Evan's stomach.

"It wasn't a very successful experiment," Claudia interrupted. "Evan and I both dropped out of school without finishing our degrees. Jack got a job in the London branch of the Bank of America, I came with him to England, and now I work in a shop."

"And I went home to work in my father's business," Evan finished. "We just weren't cut out for the unusual."

"I don't know about that." St. George refilled Jack's glass and sat back while the busboy took away the soup bowls. "Unusual may be a bit strong, but the beautiful Lily is uncommon by any standards—not that she outshines the warmth of your own glow for a moment, Claudia, my dear." He patted her hand, a beatific smile plumping his cheeks. Evan ignored the speculative curiosity that narrowed her eyes, his own attention on the soft round hand that covered hers. He almost missed Charlie's next words:

"But I can't tell you how surprised I was to see you this afternoon, my boy." St. George turned a quizzical frown on Evan. "When we last met, I had the impression things were full speed ahead at the agency. Or am I blowing your cover—that is the expression, isn't it? Is Lily lurking in the draperies? Kevin poised to apprehend some nefarious second-story man?"

"Who's Lily?" Claudia turned bland interest on Evan, but he didn't buy the politesse for a moment. She had that intent set to her eyes she used to get doing Anthro assignments, and he felt distinctly uneasily knowing how well she could read him in that mode.

"She's my cousin. And before you ask, Kevin is Kevin Bradley, my father. They work together—we work together."

St. George perked up on that. "Ah! That explains it."

Claudia again, still on the scent: "Explains what?"

"Well, how close they seem. I would have guessed a more—physical?—relationship. Family, now—that *is* refreshing. But here is the main course. I don't suppose I could tempt you with a small glass of the Bordeaux, Evan? It's a 1963, lovely year."

Evan frowned. "Charles—"

St. George raised his hands in surrender. "Just wanted to be sure, dear boy. You could have hated the sherry and didn't want to offend."

The maître d', with a waiter following a step behind, positioned a cart bearing a large flaming platter at the side of the table. Evan ignored the display, dismissed the brief exchange with St. George as Charlie's own bumbling effort at conciliation. Lily. Her name lingered like the last strains of fading laughter, and memory carried him home. Yesterday she had tried to kill him, but he could imagine no life without her, only the pit of degradation that had been the Black Masque. Claudia was all the warmth that Lily lacked, but past experience told him she could not hold against the cold, bright will of his father's kind. Unconsciously he drew on the binding spell that tied the daemon Lirion to his bidding. He owned her, didn't have to worry that she'd grow tired of life in human form, strike him dead, and go home. She was *his.*

The thought made Evan sick. "No!"

He didn't realize he had spoken aloud until the voices at the table dropped away and he found three expectant faces watching him. Charlie was the first to speak, at once flustered and apologetic:

"I'm sorry, Evan, it was presumptuous of me to order the dinner in advance. If you don't like the crown of lamb, I'll have the waiter bring a menu."

"No, Charles. I'm the one to apologize." Evan gave a self-deprecating smile, but kept his eyes expressionless—as he expected, only Claudia noticed. "The dinner is fine, lamb is a particular favorite of mine. My mind was somewhere else completely."

"I knew it," St. George fretted. "You *are* on a case. Is it the auction at Sotheby's tomorrow? I'd planned to bid on the Matisse—don't tell me I need your services already!"

"Don't worry, Charles," Evan reassured him, while Alfredo DaCosta's presence in the city clicked smoothly into place. Poor Charlie. The thief seemed to have taken a particular interest in his collection.

"As far as I know, they're expecting no trouble, but you might want to pick up a little extra security. I can recommend a good firm we've had success with here in the past, but I'm not working this trip. Lily and my father are busy on a case closer to home. I did the preliminary workup for them, and then I was free for some much-needed vacation time."

"That reminds me," Jack pushed a cut of the meat onto the back of the fork and held it poised, "did you get in touch with your office this evening?" He popped the bite into his mouth, and chewed with more attention on Evan than on his meal.

"No one was in," Evan answered abruptly.

St. George leaned forward, curiosity furrowing his brows, and Evan cut short the question he was about to utter with a noncommittal explanation. "I expected them to be out. Unfortunately, Lily must have forgotten to turn on the machine, or to alert the service—she forgets pretty regularly when I'm not there to take care of it. I should have more luck when we get back tonight."

Claudia pinned him with the stare that saw right through him. Her frown said she knew his light tone was a lie. Later, his own small nod answered. He was relieved when she let him concentrate on his plate.

Jack gave him a knowing smirk, sliding a glance in his sister's direction and raising his eyebrows mockingly. Claudia glared at them both. "I don't know what you two are cooking up between you, but I have a feeling it means trouble."

"Us?" Jack lied blandly.

Evan shook his head, exasperated. "Not *us*, Claudia. I can't help it if your brother won't behave himself in public.

"By the way, Charles, the lamb is delicious," He steered the conversation to safer ground before Jack could open his mouth and put them both in Claudia's doghouse: "Why don't you tell me why we are here while my defenses are down?"

"It's a simple project, really." St. George waved his knife dismissively. "I'm considering the purchase of a small business in Italy. The prospectus looks good, but one can never be too careful in these matters. I'd like your agency to do a little checking for me—background checks on key personnel, current investors, that sort of thing. We could fly down to Venice after the auction tomorrow, spend a couple of days looking the place over, and I could photocopy the files you will need while we are there."

Venice. Evan looked at his plate, considering. "As you know, Charles, it's not exactly our line." But he dearly wanted to know what connection Charlie's new company might have with Alfredo DaCosta. He met the man's anxious gaze, and St. George pressed his case, leaning over his elbows on the rose-colored tablecloth.

"Of course. I'm certainly not offering something as glamorous or exciting as finding the Hope Diamond, but frankly, I don't have time to find another agency I trust the way I do Bradley, Ryan, and Davis.

"Evan, I need results quickly—the board meets next week to consider my proposal, and I have to know what I am buying by then."

"I'm on vacation," Evan reminded him, but St. George persisted.

"Time is of the essence. I'm willing to pay anything within reason for the inconvenience. In fact, why don't you bring your friends along? The job shouldn't take long, and I'd love the opportunity to introduce la bella Claudia to the jewel of the Mediterranean. Can't you persuade him, my dear? You belong to Venice."

Claudia stared at St. George. "Jack and I have to work tomorrow." She stressed the word "work," a gentle reminder that a kitchen-garden life awaited her return from the glitter and light of her Cinderella evening.

"And I can't accept a case until I discuss it with Lily and my father," Evan added.

Jack just mumbled "La bella Claudia?" under his breath, but Evan could feel the irritation mounting in the man. He cut off any comment from that corner with a promise—

"When I check in later tonight, I'll present your case. If they can free up some time, I'll let you know. Then, just fax them the information you have, and they can run the search. Lily will follow up with you when we get the preliminaries." She wouldn't like it when he told her, but he thought maybe the prospect of seeing Lily again might get Charlie off his back.

"I really need this vacation, Charles."

"I can see you do, my boy. We can talk about it tomorrow—let's not spoil dessert." A look passed across St. George's face so fleetingly that, in the muted distraction of waiters clearing away the main course, Evan wasn't sure he actually saw it. Possessive beyond hunger, that look said Evan's will was nothing.

# Chapter 16

*Badad of the host of Ariton is called the solitary one, keeper of se-crets. Slow to wrath or to make alliances, his passions once aroused run deeper than the secrets he holds. Summon Badad to reveal things hidden, but beware. Badad is Ragnarok, the end of all things in fire and cold.*

"DAMN."

Evan ran the fingers of his right hand through his hair while the left clung to the phone receiver. Jet lag was setting in with a vengeance; he'd been up for thirty-five hours, at least one of them in a battle for his life. Maybe more than one—he still hadn't figured out dinner. His body craved sleep, but his mind had him by its metaphoric teeth. No answer. Still no answer.

He looked at his watch again—eleven o'clock—and figured out the time difference: it was six in the evening on the East Coast. If Brad and Lily had come home since morning, they'd have found the machine switched off when they checked for messages. Assuming all had gone well, they'd have set the machine and left him to get on with his vacation. No answer this morning could have meant anything. He rubbed at the scars on his wrists—three thin white lines—knowing what no answer this evening could mean.

Memory hit him like a wall. Omage, in that godforsaken back room, stroking his face, his chains, crooning softly over the knife. The daemon's followers—friends, until then—held him down, arms outstretched over an alabaster bowl dulled to bloody rust, while Omage opened the veins with his silver knife, the shock flinging Evan into the second sphere.

He understood now that when his body lost consciousness he lost his anchor to the physical universe. Then, he had drifted alone in the void, reaching for a handhold on reality with no fingers to grasp with and nothing to hold, his screams backed up somewhere behind a throat gone lax from blood loss.

Three times they had opened his wrists, and each time he believed was the end—he would die, this time. He'd spend eternity alone and insane in the second sphere while his body wasted slowly in its prison. Or he'd come back mad, curled gibbering against the throne of his master until Omage got bored enough with him to finish it.

A tumbled swastika crusted on a barroom wall in the Village was little enough to show for a life. He stared back from the other side of that void, and he knew he wasn't the same person now, wasn't quite where he was going either. Tempering did that to a man, like the working of a blade. Between the stages he was vulnerable, less so with each change. Not ready yet, he knew, but maybe close enough. Had to be: he was going back.

Transporting was out. Evan knew that under normal circumstances he could handle the transfer, but he had no way of knowing where Brad and Lily had run into trouble. Maybe it was safe—or maybe the fighting had spilled over into the second sphere. British Airways might be slower, but he figured he had better odds on surviving the trip. In the morning, he decided. The shape he was in he'd be useless any sooner. Worse than useless, he'd be something else for Brad to worry about.

"Did you reach anyone at home?" Claudia had moved quietly into the room. The words gentled their way past his abstraction, no sudden jolt of adrenaline shocked his return to awareness to find her in the room.

"No," he answered, the phone still resting in his lap, and then, because he owed her some explanation for what he was going to do: "They may have run into trouble on a case. We didn't expect it, but it happens sometimes. I'll try them again in the morning. If there's still no answer, I'll be leaving on the first flight out tomorrow."

"And what happens to us?"

Evan stared at her blankly for a moment, wondering what dinner had been about if Claudia still wanted to put things back together again. "I'll be back."

"When? In two weeks? Two years? Am I supposed to spend my life waiting for you to drop into it, never knowing when you are going to walk out again?"

"You left the last time," he reminded her.

He stood up, returned the phone to its stand, and grabbed his jacket, mind still refusing to let his body rest.

"Where are you going?" Claudia's voice, trying to understand, terrified to watch him go, held him at the door.

"Nowhere." He didn't want company for the dark thoughts that preyed on him tonight, needed least of all her reminder of a life he could have had, if his father had been a traveling salesman or a con artist—anything but the creature he was, with what that made Evan.

"Just for a walk." And then, because it was the one thing he could give her, "Want to come?"

"I'll get my coat."

He watched her walk away, knowing Lily would have plucked his jacket from his fingers and laughed at him when he shivered in the dark. Yesterday Lily had tried to kill him. He should be running fast and far in the other direction, not heading back into the fire. But she was Ariton, like his father. Family, and not a damned thing he could do until tomorrow. He followed Claudia out the door.

"Did you have a good time tonight?" Evan winced at his own question—asinine thing to say, like commenting on the quality of the mattress during sex. Too many ghosts followed them past the iron fences and the ones of metal links, of chains. The ease of the afternoon had gone, leaving them stranded—not strangers but pretending to be.

"One for the memory book," she answered.

So she still had the old *Webster's Unabridged,* bulkier now with a rose from the restaurant pressed between its pages—the C's, for Charles, he guessed. She always filed the memories away like that. He wondered if she still had the cocktail napkin from Black Masque filed under B, and what, if anything she had preserved in the E's.

"Right under C," she added, as if reading his mind, "for Claridge."

"You and Charlie seemed to hit it off." Right. Follow stupid with cliché. Why couldn't they just talk?

"He's *your* client, Evan," she reminded him. "Did you expect me to be rude to your business contact?"

A pause, while they both considered how far the truth of that covered the evening. "He was sweet." Her grin followed the admission. "And he *did* try so hard. Mike Jagger."

She laughed then, the sound bright and clear against the night. "Do you suppose he has any idea who the Rolling Stones are?"

"I'm not always sure Charlie knows what day it is," Evan commented, "but he pays our bill on time and he has a collection of impressionist and modern art that puts most museums to shame." He stopped. "I thought you liked Charlie."

"Fool."

Claudia reached an arm around his neck and he bent down, knowing but allowing himself not to register her purpose. She kissed him slowly, deeply, and he clung to her, remembering the feel of her in his arms and waking up in her bed in the apartment the three of them had shared in the Village. Her fingers traced the fragile line of bone at his temples, carded into his hair and held him while he returned the kiss, his arms around her waist now, holding on to Claudia and all that was normal and right between a man and a woman.

"So tell me about this Lily—" Claudia's mouth still so close to his that the words caressed, lip upon lip, and slid through his defenses like the tip of her tongue flicked across his senses when she said, "this Lily."

Evan stepped back and remembered how to breathe. "She's my father's cousin, like I said," pulling back from the question. Lily had tried to kill him yesterday—so had his father. He hadn't felt this alone since he'd tried to leave the Black Masque and discovered exactly how much Omage hated him.

Claudia stood, warm and solid, a step away and he reached out, fingertips tracing the curve of her shoulder, the line of her arm, the bend of her elbow. Wanting caught him like Mike Tyson's fist in the gut. Below the belt. He wanted to crawl up inside her and hide there in the warm, moist darkness of her body. Evan closed the space between them, knowing he had no right to do it, no right to screw up her life because he couldn't face his own life alone anymore.

"I need you," he said because it was true. If he tried hard enough, he could forget that he had to leave in the morning. He rested his forehead against the top of her head, rubbed at the silk of her hair, and wished they were home, safe behind her picket fence and her rosebushes. The longing to drop to his knees right there under the streetlight and bury his face in her belly burned up the inside of his legs, sent electric shock waves through his arms.

"Tell me why." She took his hand, started to walk again, and he followed. "It's been two years, Evan—why now?"

"Why did you leave?" He couldn't help it, the hurt at being abandoned yet again leaked into his voice. None of it had ever been his fault.

"I was afraid."

Claudia walked with her head down so that her hair fell forward and hid her face from him. Evan kept pace with her, steered her around a corner with a hand at her elbow, and slowly she explained:

"I know Jack told you about our dad dying. Heart attack on the golf course—nothing anyone could do. At the funeral, everybody kept saying how lucky he was going that way. No pain, doing what he loved, we had to be grateful for that. Grateful. God, I was furious. He never even said good-bye!

"Jack seemed to buy into the whole spiel. He went back to school after the funeral, finished his degree. When he decided to go to New York, I was angry all over again. How dare he leave us, just like Dad did!"

"I don't understand." Evan stopped her. "He was away at school, but that was okay. What made New York so different?"

"You're not from the Midwest," Claudia reminded him ruefully. "When you grow up in St. Louis, New York isn't real, it's something they make up for the movies. I had to *make* it real, so I applied to Columbia. That way I could go, too; Jack wouldn't be leaving me behind.

"That first year, I was convinced we were right in St. Louis all along— New York wasn't real. Somehow, we'd fallen into the Twilight Zone—I kept expecting to see things in black and white, figured Rod Serling's ghost was going to show up any day and tell me to click my heels three times and recite 'there's no place like home.' You weren't Rod Serling, but you made a close second. I think my anger reached out to yours: if I could make it go away in you, my own would disappear, like sympathetic magic.

"I hadn't counted on Jack. You didn't have a father. I didn't realize at the time, but Jack really envied you for that. After all, a father you don't know can't hurt you when he dies."

"You'd be surprised," Evan objected, remembering the terror when he believed he was insane. "At least you knew who you were. There were times I'd have given my life just to know what my father looked like."

"I know." Claudia raised her head, shook her hair back into place. "I recognized your anger, remember? It was a lot like mine; figures that the reasons would be a lot alike, too. Jack saw you differently, though. He couldn't be you, so he manufactured stories about you to explain why—you weren't human, you were a god. Mac fed the fantasy. Jack started believing it because he wanted it to be true.

"When the police called, I thought it was you in the hospital. I knew about your dreams—you'd woken me up with them enough—and I saw you falling for Mac's line like it was made for you. *I* wanted to be the one who helped you break free of your nightmares. Maybe it was jealousy, but I hated Mac. Bellevue just made the hatred less irrational.

"When I got to the hospital that night, I found Jack alone with the police and the doctors and the I.V. of whole blood running as fast as they could let it. You hadn't even brought him in. The doctor told me he almost died in the alley behind the Black Masque. All I could think of was 'how dare Jack do this to me.' Just like our father. I could have killed him myself, but down deep I *wanted* it to be you."

She raised her hand, forestalling Evan's objection. "I know it wasn't your fault. Mac was using you, just like he was using Jack and the others who hung out at the Black Masque. But *you* were the fantasy, not Mac. If you hadn't been a part of it, I wouldn't have come that close—" she pinched her thumb and forefinger together, almost touching, "—to losing my brother."

"I'm sorry. I should never have come here." He'd known it from the beginning, just as he'd known he couldn't let it rest with all the unspoken feelings festering in his soul.

Claudia laughed at him, at herself maybe; there was more regret than humor in the sound. "You're wrong," she said. "I got over blaming you for what happened to Jack pretty quickly, once he was on his feet again. Then I got mad because it hadn't mattered enough to you to find us again."

They had come full circle; the picket fence that girded 42 St. Mary's Road appeared out of the night mist just ahead. Claudia looked into his eyes, waiting for answers to the questions she had asked at the beginning of their walk, and it was Evan's turn to stare into the middle distance. The warmth of her hand in his anchored him to the suburban London street while he called up the memories he was never quite successful at banishing.

"At first," he explained, "I didn't have a choice. After you and Jack left, I went to Mac, told him I was leaving, too. He didn't like the idea, so he locked me up." The memory prickled at his skin, cold sweat chilling him in the evening breeze—chains at neck and wrists and feet, Omage touching him, the delicate trace of his silver knife flicking playful cuts at his throat, his groin. Sometimes the knife drew blood—pain seared his memory—sometimes Mac just teased, knifetip raising a red welt that promised more and burned anticipation into his brain. Sometimes the daemon used the human body he wore like a knife—*Don't ask for the details,* a thing whimpered in his mind—while flashback turned his stomach, set the tremors running through him again. His hands shook. He knew Claudia felt it, but she seemed to find something in his face that she didn't want to know. She turned away, but her hand squeezed his more firmly.

"But you got away," she prompted.

Evan heard the reassurance behind the questions. He had gotten away. He was safe, at least until tomorrow.

"Not on my own," he conceded. "My father found me there, tricked Mac into letting me go. Lord, I don't know why he even bothered; I was a mess. Some days I didn't even know who I was. For the first few weeks, I was sure I had died and hell was just another practical joke the universe was playing on me. With Brad's help, and with Lily's, I started to pull myself together again. Gave up the booze, even the cigarettes. I thought I was over it until this case came up. It should have been safe enough for them both, but something's gone wrong—"

"And you feel guilty because you weren't there to return the favor when they needed you," Claudia finished for him.

It sounded too pat, too trite when she put it that way. "I owe them my life," he said. "And my sanity."

"Do you love her?"

The question made him smile. "We've been lovers," he admitted. And because he owed her the truth, "We probably will be again. But actually *love* Lily?" He shook his head, at a loss for words to describe the daemon Lirion to the woman before him.

"It's not like that between us," he tried to explain, but the words wouldn't come. "She's beautiful," and he knew that was the wrong thing to say the moment the words were gone.

"I don't know what I feel for her," he finally admitted. "I suspect it's a game with Lily. Sometimes I think maybe she does feel something for me, other times just being in the same room with her is like jousting with high-tension wires." Evan stopped, backed up, and tried again.

"It's just sex for her, I know that. She has other men. She'd never think to hide it from me—I don't mean that much to her. It scares me, because she's part of what I am, what I spent my whole life looking for, and we don't even like each other a lot of the time."

He couldn't tell Claudia about the other part of their relationship, the challenge in Lily's smile, the dare that pushed him to test his body and his skill against her hunger. He wanted her to need him. In his fantasies she would come to him, beg to please him, and he would take her in his arms—a regular Rhett Butler. He settled for the fact that she let him live.

"But you wouldn't leave her."

Not a question, Evan had to answer it anyway. "Not until she loses interest. So what does that make me?"

In the Village he'd met men who sold their bodies for money; Evan figured he was going cheap, whoring for a place to call home. He knew he was being unfair as soon as he thought it. He *wanted* Lily, and hated himself for wanting her while his hand locked with Claudia's hand, while Claudia's kisses, the feel of her arms were still warm on his skin.

"Unhappy."

Evan had to back up a minute, remember the question she was answering. There didn't seem to be anything else to say. "I'm getting cold." He headed back to the house.

Claudia left him at the stairway to the second floor. "Good night," she said, and kissed him lightly on the cheek.

He watched her for a moment. She took the stairs slowly this time, not running up them like she usually did. When she disappeared around the corner, he sighed and walked back to the kitchen, looking for something to warm him, and knowing that he wouldn't find it in this lifetime. *Settle for coffee and the illusion of comfort.* Jack Laurence was waiting.

"Hey, meester, wanna sleep with my seester?" Mocking, Jack offered his own mug, steam rising from the coffee paled with too much milk.

Evan stared at him for a minute, then shook his head. "Go to hell, Jack. I'm not in the mood." He turned to leave, but Jack stopped him.

"I'm sorry, Evan. Sit down, I'll make you a cup."

Evan sat, reconsidering the coffee. "Nothing for me, I need to sleep sometime tonight. What do you want?"

"Just some company," Laurence explained. "I thought that's why you looked us up in the first place. Or did you?"

That one hit home and twisted. Evan wanted his motives kept well out of this.

"I'm leaving tomorrow," he blurted. "There's trouble at home. I already told Claudia."

"I'll bet that went over real well. Charlie have anything to do with your decision?" Cool blue eyes, with none of the fire of the lords of Ariton but a dangerous perceptiveness of their own, took his measure. "What are you running away from this time?"

"Not a thing." Evan slumped in his kitchen chair and stared at the floor between his feet planted a yard apart on the stained linoleum.

"I don't feel special, Jack, but I can't help what I am. For a long time after Brad pulled me out of the Black Masque I thought of calling, but I couldn't face you. It's my fault you almost died." He met Jack's eyes, let the man see the honesty, soul to soul. "I wanted your friendship, not your worship; finally decided it was time to look you in the face and tell you so."

"Lucky for all of us I figured that one out on my own—decided even E.T. needed a friend and elected myself to the position." Jack punched him lightly on the shoulder, then grew serious again. "But that doesn't explain why you've been jumpy as a flea on a hot skillet since you arrived."

"Mac found another one like me; it's what got me seriously thinking about that time again, and how I'd let the Black Masque destroy our friendship. His name is Paul Carter, and his sister hired us to get him back. Brad and Lily were going after him the night I came here. Brad got me out, I figured he could do it again, but something's happened. They never got home."

He sat forward on the kitchen chair, as if he could communicate his determination with his outstretched hands, but those hands kept shaking, giving away his fear: "I owe him my life, Jack. I have to go back, help if I can, or die trying."

Jack had to know he hadn't come here to hide, but to stop hiding from his friends. "I promise," Evan said. "If I make it out of there, I'll be back. Maybe we can start over then, okay?" He offered a tentative smile, realized it was wasted.

Somewhere along the line Jack Laurence had stopped tracking the conversation. He sat with his head tilted over his mug, a frown creasing his forehead.

"I didn't think you *could* die. Figured you for immortal or something. Maybe even hundreds of years old and pretending so people wouldn't get suspicious."

Evan laughed bitterly. "No such luck. My mother is as human as yours. This body is the only one I've got; I last as long as it does. My father's from somewhere else— not quite outer space. It really is a lot like Mac described it, because he's one of them." He paused, remembering.

"Anyway, I don't know if they're immortal, but I do know we can't kill them. I tried. I felt Mac stop breathing under my hands. Then his eyes opened, he grinned at me, and thanked me for an interesting experience. He threw me bodily into the second sphere—that's where they come from. By the time he brought me back, I was pretty much insane. I don't remember a hell of a lot after that."

"Is Charlie one of them?"

"St. George?" Evan started to laugh, realized he was nudging hysteria that had nothing to do with the question and everything to do with no answer at home on the phone. He grabbed Jack's mug, choked on a swallow of cold coffee before he brought the laughter under control.

"Sorry, Jack. It's not you, just, well, if you knew Lily's opinion of Charlie, you wouldn't even ask. No, he's as human as we are. I met him on a different case entirely, and he was as inept then as he was tonight."

"Not so inept, old chum." Jack took his mug back. "He was making time with your girl, after all."

Evan stood up and stretched. "She was just making sure I was paying attention," he countered with a smug grin. "Anything else can wait until I get back from Philly. Now I need some sleep."

"Sure thing, old buddy. Just don't wait two years this time."

Evan heard the sincerity, answered it. "As soon as I take care of business at home. Promise." He put out his hand, and Jack took it in a firm handshake.

"Deal," Laurence agreed. "And figure out how you really feel about

Claudia while you're at it. If you love her, fine. If you don't, get that straight, too. Like I said, I don't want her hurt."

"Deal."

Evan left the kitchen with thoughts of Claudia, the evening at the Claridge, and his fears for Brad and Lily back home warring for his attention. As much as his body craved rest, sleep seemed far away.

# Chapter 17

*Of the alliances of Princes, Oriens most often allies with Paimon, Ariton and Amaimon, and likewise Astarot most often allies with Magot and Azmod. But in battle alliances may change, except that Ariton never makes alliance with Azmod, nor Paimon with Magot.*

BADAD STARED AT HUMAN HANDS BLEACHED PALE IN THE LIGHT OF MORNING: his hands, he realized. Motionless as stone, they rested on the table in front of him.

"Drink this, you need it."

Lirion slid a cup of thick espresso between the hands and he grasped it. Holding onto the warmth and solidity of the cup, he tried to focus on the night before and how he'd gotten there, while the images slipped away like ghosts almost caught at the corner of the eye. He drank, and only when the cup was empty did he recognize it for his own service. So they had made it home.

"How did we get here?"

Lily pinned him with her own sardonic sneer. "I pulled you out of the rubble that used to be the Black Masque and transported one step ahead of the local constabulary."

The memory surfaced in splinters. Omage. Paul Carter, dead. "I could have used some help a little sooner."

Lirion shrugged. "Not my fight," she pointed out. "Your paternal aberration has already cost me my freedom. Don't expect me to take on your enemies for the miserable life of every half-human bastard our kind has ever produced on this inconsequential rock."

Marnie Simpson would have to be told, but later, when he could think. "We had a contract."

"*You* had a contract," Lily corrected him. "It was a trap, you know."

"A trap, yeah, but what was the bait? Paul Carter, or the Eye?" His hand went to his breast where the jewel had lain, cold as the whisper of death. Gone now. Where?

"I put it in the safe." Lily anticipated the question. "You weren't thinking straight at that point, but I wasn't letting Omage get his hands on it. Not if he wanted it that badly."

"You don't feel it, do you?" he asked her instead.

She shook her head. "I picked it up as a joke. I expected Evan to lecture me on taking more than the contract called for, like he usually does. The boy has no sense of humor; it usually takes him a while to realize I'm doing it just to get him going. This time he never did figure it out."

"And you've never asked yourself why you chose that in particular, which put us back in the middle of Omage's machinations again? Or why you didn't just leave it in the rubble after the explosion?"

"That bastard! But how? What is the damned thing?" Lily glinted blue flame in her rage, which was as much chagrin, he supposed. But Omage hadn't gotten what he wanted. Evan was safe, thousands of miles away from the twisted evil that Omage had become, and the stone could wait until he was thinking more clearly. He turned his attention to the more immediate problem: "How much damage did we do?"

"Not much." Lily settled into dark sarcasm. "You didn't sink Manhattan if that's what you're wondering—only half the block is in ruins. The news is calling it a gas main accident. Doesn't help the crowd in the bar, of course, but I admire your subtlety."

"I don't remember," Badad admitted.

"I'm not surprised." Lily refilled his cup and sat down with one for herself. "You lost your temper. A very impressive sight, but not smart in a human body. I think you suffered a backflash from trying to contain the damage, though I don't know why you bothered."

He answered her challenge with a look that needed no explanation. She knew the answer to that one.

"Evan. Well, you succeeded there. No one is reporting earthquakes or firestorms, and the planetary orbit remains stable, for which the locals, including your ungrateful offspring, will never show their gratitude."

Brad shrugged. "As long as I don't have to pay damages, I don't really care." As long as Evan still had a home to come back to, and he wasn't sure whether that was his choice or the effect of the binding, but it mattered.

"That's not quite all of it."

Lily stared at her cup, then caught him with a look he didn't quite recognize. Envy, fear, desire: for a moment she reminded him of the faces moving in the half-light of the Black Masque.

"Omage transformed before the walls came down, and so did I. You didn't. Your body died."

A flash of animal-memory—blind, unreasoning terror of the meat-mind dragging him into panic-paralysis—then it was gone again.

"What was it like?" Lirion, on the trail of a new sensation. Her eyes glittered with a hard blue light. "How did it feel?"

"I don't remember."

He shuddered, suddenly cold. Day-to-day, they had no trouble separating their own true natures from the instinctive drives of the bodies they wore. Pushed to extremes, the animal mind gained ascendancy—time to bail out, to transform before identity submerged in the wave of uncontrolled feeling. Death was more, a stillness past fear where identity ceased to exist at all. The memory hovered just out of reach, but the change it had wrought in him lay very near the surface. He understood now why Evan feared the dark.

"How long have we been gone?"

"Since midnight yesterday. The day before yesterday, technically. The backflash really fried you; you've spent the last thirty hours discharging all over the second sphere. The humans will be picking up a new supernova in Orion, and you involved Ariton in a host-debt to Kaitar of the host of Paimon, but I managed to keep it below the level of a battle between Princes."

Brad nodded. The last thing they needed was to push Paimon into an alliance with Azmod over this fiasco. Too tired to dwell on the politics of the second sphere, he turned to the subject closer at hand.

"Has Evan called in?" He pushed his way unsteadily to his feet and made for the study, stopped at the safe and checked that Omage's jewel was really there. A weight settled on his shoulders when he took it in his hand, and his vision grayed around the edges, cleared again when the door to the safe swung closed with the stone inside.

Lily followed, and stopped to check the answering machine. "Forgot to turn the damn thing on."

Unbidden, Omage's words returned to him: "I want Evan back . . . the stone is only half the prize."

"It isn't over yet," Brad reminded her. He grabbed the printed bits of data from Evan's search program and sank into his favorite chair.

"Your brat is more trouble than he's worth, Badad." Lirion dismissed the boy with a flutter of the fingers of one hand, returned his patient stare with sour acceptance. "All right, it couldn't hurt to warn him. He left a number here somewhere. Then sleep—you need it more than I do. Death seems to take a lot out of you."

"Yeah."

Evan dead, forever. He shivered, suddenly cold in the windowless room. "Where's that number?"

"Right here." Lily dialed, then: "Hello, Evan Davis, please. He checked in yesterday. Did he leave a forwarding number? Thank you."

She hung up. "He never checked in. Canceled the room yesterday, left no forwarding number, just a message that he was staying with friends."

Brad let his head fall back against the tapestried upholstery of his wingback chair and probed for feeling through his son's binding spell.

"I'm too tired to think," he admitted. "He's safe for the time being. Upset about something, but I don't sense any adrenaline surge. Probably jet lag."

Lily lifted one sardonically elegant eyebrow. "I thought you let go of that—what did you call it?—rope."

"So did I." Brad thought for a moment. "It's only there when I look for it. I think I'll know if he gets into trouble, but beyond that the sensation is too vague to be of much use. Don't you feel anything?"

"Not really." She shrugged. "When you talk about him, there's something. I don't give him much thought the rest of the time. And right now, all I can think about is sleep."

"You're right." Brad agreed. "We'll need to be in better shape than this when we tell Mrs. Simpson her brother is dead. I don't think she's going to take it well." He dragged himself out of his chair and dropped the printout, still unread, on the desk as he passed. "Four hours should do it. I'll meet you back here at one."

The white farmhouse had changed since their first visit. The French windows had been repaired, and the broken furniture and debris piled next to the fire pit were gone. Daffodils still bloomed in the garden, however, and the run from which the town took its name struck silver sparks in the distance as it had before. Past the foreman's house, where Paul Carter had constructed his shrine to death, horses frisked in the sunshine of a meadow. "Summer Dancer seems none the worse for the loss of his dearly beloved goat," Lily noted.

"He's a beauty." Brad ignored the sarcasm in her voice. Strong and free, the animal drew him. "Powerful. Look at him run, and he's just playing." Someday, when this case was over, when Evan set them free again—

Lily gave him a sly, sideways glance. "You'd make a fine stallion with the right handler to break you in." She laughed. "I wouldn't mind taking that ride myself."

He watched the horses play for a moment more, but they both knew the peace was deceptive. "Let's get this over with."

Marnie Simpson opened the door after only a short delay.

"I didn't hear your car pull up." She led them into the airy living room and sat at the edge of an Empire-style armchair facing the front windows over a Louis Quatorze sofa. An end table with a lamp and an ashtray stood beside her chair.

"We left the car in the lane and walked the rest of the way," Brad lied smoothly. He looked around the room: Persian carpet, chair set next to the side window, sofa, coffee table. Lots of woods polished to a warm glow, lots of brocade in muted tones, but most of it was expensive reproductions from periods that only clashed if you'd been there when. "Do you mind if we sit down?"

Marnie Simpson gestured to the Louis Quatorze sofa, and Brad settled himself awkwardly, sacrificing comfort to Twentieth Century American posture.

"I'm fine," Lily demurred. She wandered over to the side window that gave a clear view of the foreman's cottage. *Ball's in your court, cousin,* her silence told him. She would be there as backup, but it was his case, his obsession.

"Do you have news about my brother?"

Brad turned his attention to the human woman, but found no welcome in the closed set of her face. The agency seldom had bad news to report. Sitting across from Marnie Simpson, he vowed to keep it that way—he didn't like this part of the job one bit. "Yes," he said, "I'm afraid we do. Would you like to call your husband?"

Marnie Simpson dismissed the suggestion with a cutting gesture, using the side of her hand like a blade. "Paul and Frank, my husband, never liked each other. Whatever you have to say, I doubt that Frank will be particularly sympathetic."

"Very well." He leaned forward, his clasped hands resting between his knees. "We made contact with your brother's kidnappers at a place called the Black Masque."

Simpson reached into the pocket of her tailored slacks and brought out a crumpled pack of Virginia Slims. "Paul had mentioned the place, I told you that." She hooked the last cigarette with a crooked finger and brought it to her lips, returned the pack to her pocket, and withdrew a lighter. "He knew he was in danger there; that's why he came home. Did you see him?"

"I'm afraid so." Brad paused while she lit the cigarette and set the lighter down on the end table next to her chair. "You have to understand,

Omage's methods are quite vicious. Your brother was barely alive when we found him. Omage made it clear he had no intention of freeing Paul; he only agreed to see us so that he could flaunt what he perceived as our ineffectiveness against him. We goaded him, and he made the mistake we were waiting for. But Paul was too far gone. He saw that chance for the only kind of freedom he could imagine, and he took it."

"What are you trying to say, Mr. Bradley?" Mrs. Simpson's brittle voice chilled to ice.

"Your brother is dead, Mrs. Simpson. In his condition he could hardly imagine escape and, frankly, I don't think he saw rescue as freedom."

"This Omage wasn't wrong, then, was he? Ineffective just about sums it up." Simpson flicked the cigarette ash into the china ashtray with a single sharp tap of her index finger, returning the cigarette to her lips in the same motion. "What did you do—gamble my brother's life that you could get him out of there without giving up the ransom?" Agitated, Marnie Simpson stood and paced toward the window, stopped short at the cold light in Lily's eyes. "Was this Eye of Omage worth the life of my brother?"

"He means your brother took the only way out he's ever known." Lily turned deliberately to the window. "Take a walk through Paul's bedroom, Mrs. Simpson. Sit in his chair and feel the press of his rifle against the back of your head. Touch his razor blades, swallow his pills, drink his whiskey, then tell us whose fault it is Paul died."

"I tried to help him." Still as stone, Marnie Simpson whispered the words.

"You couldn't have stopped him, any more than we could." Brad leaned forward, his head caught between his hands. He was so weary. "Paul felt he had no choice. In a way, neither did Omage."

"You may be right about Paul—" she turned sharply, pinned Brad with a glare that had wheels turning wheels behind it. "I'd be a fool to live next to that house and deny it—but don't expect sympathy for his murderer. What was he looking for—what was the Eye of Omage?"

"A stone," Brad raised his head to meet her anger. "A topaz; Paul was wearing it in the picture you left us. We don't know how Omage lost it, or why he wanted it back so badly."

The intensity of Marnie Simpson's concentration on Brad's upturned face never wavered, but the anger vanished like a door closing behind her eyes. "A stone of that size must have considerable value," she suggested. "Did you find it?"

Brad met her gaze levelly. Foolish, he reminded himself, to suspect every human reaction that didn't match the ones he'd seen in Evan. Marnie Simpson had watched her brother's struggle from the outside, far from the dark and dangerous places that haunted Paul Carter's dreams. She'd been left to cope with the chaos left in the wake of his struggle. Why did that flare of anger, so quickly suppressed, make him uneasy?

"We found it," he said, "and we offered the stone for your brother's return. Omage, however, had other plans. The ransom note promised a swift end to Paul's suffering, murder instead of torture, but not his release. We had a good chance of pulling your brother out of there anyway, but Paul had given up. As it was, we barely escaped with our own lives; there was nothing more we could do."

"I'm sorry you were in danger." Brad heard no regret in her voice; the word sounded perfunctory, like good morning to a stranger on a rainy day. "But I'm not really surprised you couldn't help my brother. Paul was never strong."

The bitterness in Marnie Simpson's last words surprised Brad. Lily stood by the window; with the woman's back to her, the daemon hadn't bothered to school her expression, and Brad saw the familiar cool disinterest sharpen to attention. She met his glance with a quirk of the brow, then frowned as Marnie Simpson roused from her brief reverie to ask:

"Do you have it with you? May I at least see this stone my brother died for?"

Brad spread his hands wide. "I'm sorry, but it's locked in the safe." We don't usually walk around with evidence of capital crimes in our pockets. Brad rephrased the thought with more tact for the bereaved sister. "The police will have to be called, and of course we will hand over the jewel as evidence. Until then, it seemed most appropriate to keep it in a safe place."

"Must we call the police?" The woman twisted her hands together, distress clear on her face for the first time during the conversation. "Paul is dead, by his own hand, and you are correct. For my brother, suicide was a matter of time. But the scandal, his name in the papers—"

Brad coughed delicately, unnecessarily, but it bought him a pause in the flow of words, and Marnie Simpson's attention. "There is the matter of the body."

"My God. Of course." The woman paled. She stubbed out her cigarette and reached a trembling hand into her pocket. "Damn." The pack was empty; she crushed it, threw it into the fireplace. "I need a cigarette. I'm sorry, I'll be back in a moment."

Alone together in the formal living room, the detectives relaxed almost imperceptibly. Lily leaned against the window frame, arms wrapped in front of her, legs crossed at the ankle. "She's a cool one," she commented, her eyes pinned on the doorway through which Marnie Simpson had exited.

Brad rubbed his forehead, considering. "Until I mentioned her brother's body. It was like he hadn't really existed until then."

"Didn't like the idea of the police being involved, did she?" Lily added.

Before he could reply, Mrs. Simpson returned, a lit cigarette in one hand. "I'm sorry. I'm not accustomed to losing control, it's a weakness someone in my business can ill afford.

"Go on, please. You were talking about Paul's—" she hesitated, then finished, "—body. Where is he? I'll have to make arrangements to have him brought home. I should have the address of the place that took care of everything for us when Mother died." She fell into her chair. "The police. My God, the scandal."

Brad crossed to her side, awkward in the role of comforter. "Let me call your husband. He can deal with the police, identify the body."

"Frank is out of the country, on business." She drew on the cigarette and put it out half smoked, stared vaguely at the stub, then drew out another and lit it. "His office has the number." She clutched at Brad's arm with her free hand. "Where do they have Paul's body now?"

"That's a little difficult to explain," Brad began. Fortunately, Lily took up the story.

"There was an accident, a gas main explosion just minutes after Paul died. We escaped in the confusion, but Paul's body was buried under the rubble, along with several dozen patrons of the club Omage used as a front for his activities."

"Were there other survivors?" Simpson asked abruptly.

Lily handed off the explanation with a glance, and Brad continued. "We suspect Omage made it out in time, if that is what you are asking. As far as we could tell, the rest were dead."

"Then I can only be thankful you came to no harm. I'm sorry." Mrs. Simpson put out her third cigarette and pushed the hair away from her eyes with the back of her hand.

"This has been a shock, you understand. You are right, of course. I have to contact my husband, and then I really must rest. I'll have Frank's office contact you about your fee."

"We'll be making our report to the police, but you have the agency number, should the police start asking questions. If we can be of any help, please call on us."

"I'll keep that in mind."

Marnie Simpson led them to the door and closed it behind them. They walked until an old elm tree obscured the view of the lane, then transported home, falling unceremoniously into their accustomed places—Brad in his wingback chair, and Lily sprawled full length on the leather couch.

Lily relaxed with a gusting sigh. "I'd rather face an audit by the IRS," she declared, "than spend ten seconds in the same room with that woman."

"She's a little cool."

Brad considered the interview while he dragged himself out of his chair and collected the brandy and a pair of snifters. "I can remember thinking, 'Evan would never do that' from time to time, but I've never found humans terribly predictable. Especially Evan."

"I was watching her pretty closely when you were talking." Lily took the snifter, swirled the brandy, and sipped it. "Whatever she says, Marnie Simpson is glad her brother is dead."

Brad considered the middle distance for a moment. "You're probably right."

# Chapter 18

*Kaitar means the high place, from where the daemon sees from a distance, but his Prince is Paimon, the whisperer of deceit. Pathet is fear, and fruitfulness. His Prince is Azmod. Fear abounds where Pathet passes.*

EVAN WOKE IN A POOL OF SUNLIGHT ANGLED TOO HIGH. MUZZY WITH SLEEP, he identified the nagging urgency slowly. Late. Trouble. A phone ringing, no answer, echoed in his mind. He'd planned to be on a plane by now, on his way home. The memory burned away the last of his morning fog.

He rolled out of bed and headed for the bathroom, showered and shaved while his head made lists. Didn't have to pack much, because he hadn't bothered to unpack when he arrived. He needed a ticket on the first flight out, but first call home again, hope for a message.

Coffee at the top of the list, Evan came down the stairs two at a time and stopped in front of the telephone, conscious of the sweat clammy on his palms and prickling at his temples. He picked up the receiver, impatient with the slow return of the rotary dial, and waited for the overseas operator to come on the line:

"Hello. May I have the number you are calling?"

He gave the private number and his message code; finally, the tinny ring echoed through space. Once, twice, then the answering machine connected, passed him through to his messages.

Lily's voice grated flat and mechanical in his ear: "Evan, we're home, more or less in one piece. If you're calling before evening, your time, we're asleep. After, we'll be out again, but you can reach us through the service if you have an emergency."

Evan felt the tension leave his neck and shoulders. It may have been touch and go for a while—he could tell that from the weariness he'd never heard in her voice before—but they were safe. He still had a home, a

family. Even the rest of her message couldn't dampen his relief on that
score:

"Unfortunately, the package was damaged beyond repair," she continued. "It wasn't built for hard use. We'll be speaking to the original owner
this afternoon, but our friend in New York is already looking for a replacement, so keep your eyes open. Leave us a number where we can reach you
if anything else turns up."

Evan waited for the signal beep and read off the Laurence's telephone
number while he processed Lily's cryptic message. So Paul Carter hadn't
made it. Anger boiled behind his eyes, and outside the wind picked up,
whistled through the windows. A week ago he hadn't known another hybrid
like himself existed—he remembered his shock when he first learned about
Paul Carter, and how he'd shared Lily's revulsion in Carter's bedroom even
while he was remembering a gun under his own pillow. None of it was
Carter's fault, not his life, certainly not his death.

Evan knew that only a part of his anger was for the boy, dead in the
Black Masque's back room. As long as Paul Carter lived, Evan was only
half the freak he had been before. He knew that the survival of his kind
was possible. Omage had taken that fragile security away from him. He
clenched his fist around the telephone receiver, fighting the storm that
tightened in his chest, while outside thunderheads churned and lightning
flashed.

Omage was a son of a bitch; that was hardly news. For some reason
that only the daemon knew, Omage wanted him back. Evan figured that
staying alive and free would be his best revenge, and Charlie St. George's
offer suddenly seemed a lot more attractive, something simple, clean, and
as far from New York as he could manage on short notice. Not that distance
made a difference to Omage; it just made Evan feel safer. He might even
have time to do a little checking on Alfredo DaCosta while he was in
Venice. He added a short message about St. George's request for a corporate
background check in Venice with his recommendation that they take the
case, and rang off with a promise to call back with details later.

The storm slowly died away while Evan tapped the telephone receiver
thoughtfully with his fingertips. He'd call Charlie, take the case. But first,
coffee.


He expected to have the kitchen to himself, but Jack was waiting with
a cup of coffee and yesterday's newspaper.

"What time is it? I thought you were going to work today."

Jack stared at him, not quite frightened, Evan realized, but uneasy. "It's
ten thirty. Did I hear you on the phone just now?"

"Yes." Evan frowned. "I paid for the call on my credit card, if that's what has you worried."

"Don't treat me like an idiot, old chum."

Evan stopped on his way to the kettle, surprised, but Laurence hadn't finished:

"Did you reach your relatives from outer space?"

"Inner space, to be accurate, but yes," Evan answered. "There was a message from Lily; she and my father are fine."

The anger, so quickly suppressed a moment before, surfaced again. Omage was out of reach, but as a substitute target, Jack Laurence gone cryptic and suspicious on him did a good job of planting a bull's eye across his own chest.

"What's the matter, Jack?" he snapped. "Suddenly bored playing with the freak? Decided the game's no fun anymore?"

"Not a game, Evan," Laurence answered. "It's never been that. Let's call it trust. Since when did Batman hold out on the Boy Wonder?"

"I don't know what you're talking about." Evan filled the kettle, banged it down on the stove, and grabbed a mug—turtledoves cooing in a tree, for God's sake.

"I went to the office this morning; this was waiting on my desk." Jack nudged the tabloid with his coffee mug. "I don't read these rags myself, but someone on the staff usually leaves a copy on my desk when there's a story about the States. I thought maybe you would have an explanation for this one."

The headline read: "Sodom and Gomorrah, American Style" and below the headline was a picture of a New York neighborhood well known to Evan Davis and his host, one particular landmark lying in ruin.

Evan fell heavily onto a chair, the promise of coffee forgotten. He buried his face in his hands and ran his fingers through his hair, dragging it back off his forehead. They both knew the place, but Jack seemed to want him to say it. "The Black Masque. Has Claudia seen this?"

"Not from me, but someone may mention it to her at the shop. We'd better come up with a good story before she gets home." Laurence took the paper back and began to read aloud:

"In the United States, the New York skyline was lit by more than neon last night. A freak accident filled the darkness with a column of flame visible for miles in all directions. According to authorities, a gas main ruptured beneath a building in the city's Greenwich Village section. It was midnight—the proverbial witching hour—when blood rained down with falling brick at the location of a private drinking club notorious for its sin and corruption even in the city that never sleeps. Witnesses drawn from their beds by the shattering blast described the scene as horrible, terrifying. 'I felt the earth move,' reported one observer, 'I fell to my knees, sure that the end of the world had come.'

"Rescuers reported hearing victims, buried in the destruction, scream- ing for help, while the terrible heat and the instability of the fallen building turned back all efforts to save the dying. According to police, no survivors escaped the holocaust. At least fifty people died in the explosion. More accurate figures will be available after forensic specialists assure them- selves that they have accounted for all limbs and body parts."

Jack's voice faded, the voices of the dying heavy in the silence. Fifty people. God! Was that what Lily meant by "hard use"? The kettle shrieked; Evan didn't notice until Jack got up and filled his mug, then added coffee crystals.

Jack set the mug in front of him and waited. "What kind of trouble are you in, Evan?"

"Do you actually think I had something to do with this?" It would have sounded more convincing if he could keep his hands from shaking. Omage could have brought his own foul nest down, out of spite, but some- how he knew his father had done this, or his cousin.

Not human. The words screamed in his mind. They didn't think like humans, didn't value life like humans. They called themselves lords, and knew his world as a flicker in their endless night. Fear that had become too familiar tightened his gut, turning it over. Fifty people dead. Did he share that part of them, the part that killed without thought, the way he shared their passage into the second sphere?

"I was on a plane, two hours out of Heathrow if they got the time right." *Should have been there, should have stopped them.* The past just wasn't worth fifty lives. "If they got any of it right."

Somewhere at the bottom of his soul a knot that had been there so long he'd forgotten what it felt like not to have the pain loosened. He knew inside himself that it was true, like a prisoner in the dark knows when his shackles are undone. Omage's chamber, caked with Evan Davis' blood, had fallen. The sacrifice was over. But at what price, what price? "I swear, I had nothing to do with this."

"Drink your coffee."

Jack folded Evan's hands around the mug. Jack didn't blame him. Evan stared at the tall blond man, saw something in eyes the color of a Kansas sunrise that shook him. *I don't want to know,* his mind screamed, while his words betrayed him. "I don't understand."

"No, you never did," Laurence agreed with a rueful smile. "Your father did it, you said he was going in to rescue another, uh, what do I call you? Your kind, I mean?"

Evan shrugged. "Paul Carter didn't make it. As far as I know, that means I don't have a kind; I'm the only one."

Jack Laurence grunted. "That pretty much clinches it, then. You're mortal all right. Do you still need help? You've got it—just say the word."

"Why?" He didn't expect this, wasn't sure he wanted easy acceptance. His father had just murdered fifty people and he wasn't taking it that well himself.

"I told you." Jack shook his head, then spoke slowly, as one does to small children or shock victims after an accident: "Once I would have died for you in that place. I'm not surprised that someone would kill for you, and I can't see them going back there for a stranger. I just need to know what comes next."

"Stay out of it, Jack." How could he tell the man that it had never been for Evan, that Brad and Lily had their own reasons for doing things that mortals didn't understand—otherwise, fifty people dead were his fault, and he couldn't deal with that.

"I didn't know anything about this, certainly wasn't expecting it, but it fits with Lily's message." Evan drank, put down the mug. "Whatever took out the Black Masque isn't finished yet, because there was at least one survivor. Mac got away, and if I understood Lily's message, he wants me back. I didn't lie to you, Jack." But he realized suddenly that he had brought danger into this house, and he had promised he'd left that part of his life behind him. "I haven't done anything. I don't know why he wants me—"

"Mac doesn't care about what you've done, Evan; he never did. It's what you are."

Not human. Evan shuddered, afraid of the knowledge of his dual heritage. Did it make him a killer like his father, like Lily? What did Omage want of him?

"But why?" he said aloud. "There's nothing I can do that he can't do better, in our world or in his."

"Maybe," Jack conceded. "But how much do you know about what you can do? I mean, did you know your father could knock down buildings? Do you know you can't?"

Evan didn't like the direction that thought took him. He shrugged off the creeping sensation that pieces of his life were fitting themselves together around Jack's questions. Some things about himself he didn't want to know.

"Whatever his reason for wanting to get his hands on me, he has to find me first. I'm packed, I'll be gone as soon as a taxi can get here. Tell Claudia I'm sorry. If things had been different . . . just say I'm sorry. And you haven't seen me since New York, if anybody asks." He got up and turned toward the hall, but Laurence grabbed his arm.

"Where are you going? What are you going to do?"

"Yes, Mr. Davis, where *are* you going?"

The stranger's voice froze them in place.

"Who are you?" Evan turned to face the man who stood with his arms crossed in front of him, leaning against the refrigerator. The stranger was as tall as Jack, but thinner, pale-skinned, with light brown hair hanging almost to his shoulders.

"How did you get in here?"

"I am called Pathet, I can tell you that because you won't live long enough to use it. I'm a distant relation of your father's, and I entered in the usual way—for our kind." The man unfolded his arms, held out his empty hands, palms up. He smiled, thin lips stretched over straight white teeth, but something vicious glinted in green eyes. A predator: Omage had eyes like that.

Evan remembered another time, blue flames licking with no heat against his skin, Lily and Brad in the second sphere teaching him that he could take his body into the place his nightmares traveled and return at his own command. In their eyes he found the mark of what they were, and in these eyes he knew the stranger.

"Omage sent you. You're one of his."

"Clever boy." The stranger moved away from the refrigerator, his arms loose at his sides. "But not too clever. We are Azmod, cousins, if you will, but I do not answer to Omage. He's quite mad, you know. But then, of course you do; he's played his games with you before, hasn't he, boy?" That slow, almost sweet smile reminded Evan of chains and a silver knife, of Omage stroking his skin and flinging him into the second sphere. Did his father feel that pleasure when he killed?

Jack Laurence squeezed his arm, offering support, and turned to face the daemon in the kitchen. "Who are you? What do you want? Evan?"

The first two questions were aimed at the stranger, but the last looked to Evan for answers. The stranger, Pathet, frowned. "Control your human, half-breed, or I'll do it for you."

Evan nodded his head, once, sharply. What hope he had of keeping his friend alive depended on keeping the stranger's attention focused on himself. He answered Jack's questions, but his eyes never left Pathet's face. *This is for you,* that look said. *I know what sent you.*

"He's one of them, like Mac—his real name's Omage, by the way—and like my father. And you were right, Mac still wants me. The question is, why? What is it about us—Paul Carter, me—that Omage needs? Like I said, I keep coming up with just one answer. Nothing. But a human, now, a human might want to know what we half-breeds can do.

"Omage isn't working on his own, is he?" Evan snapped the question, and the stranger narrowed his eyes. *So.* "Whoever is running Mac has you on a string, too."

"Come with me and find out, clever boy." The smile had more than ambient malice in it now. Hatred had a name: Evan Davis.

"Evan isn't going anywhere." Jack Laurence stepped between the two creatures in human form.

"Jack." Evan grabbed his arm, spun the man around to face him. "You're out of your depth. If you understand anything I've said, you've got to know that. Let it go; I'll be all right."

Jack laughed, a short, bitter sound. "If you believed that, you wouldn't be here. Remember when I said I wouldn't do it again?"

Evan nodded, their conversation by the Thames fresh in his mind. *My blood was a gift, my life a sacrifice for the pleasure of my god. Dying I loved him. You.*

"I can't let you—"

Jack Laurence smiled. "You can't stop me." He turned to the stranger, who stood taller, green flames lighting his features. "I won't let you take him."

"No!"

The daemon Pathet smiled and raised his right hand. Green flame shot from the palm, snapped like lightning, and hit the floor where Jack Laurence had been standing. With no time for anything more elegant, Evan hit him with an awkward tackle, heard Jack's head crack on the table going down.

"Are you hurt?" Evan stood and offered his friend a hand. Jack's eyes took a moment to focus, but he took the hand and dragged himself to his feet.

"Let it go, Jack." Evan pushed the man gently back into his chair, leaning over to hold the mortal's attention on himself, not on the daemon lounging against his refrigerator. "You can't stop him. Killing you won't even slow him down. Think of Claudia."

"And what about you?"

Evan shook his head. "They want me alive for something. And you're forgetting, I have powerful allies now. It isn't like it was at the Black Masque. My father will find them; you don't want to be in the middle of this when the fighting starts."

With a reassuring squeeze to Jack's shoulder, Evan straightened and faced the daemon. "All right," he said. "Leave him alone, I'll go with you. I can transport, but I need a guide."

"No problem," Pathet agreed. "Just give me a minute—I want to leave a message for Ariton."

The daemon contemplated Jack's down-bent head. "I don't often miss," he admitted apologetically, then, "and I don't like it when I do."

He struck suddenly, with the sound of the sky tearing open, and a pile of cinders smoldered in a blackened circle of linoleum where Jack Laurence had been sitting. The kitchen chair was gone as well. "That's better," he said, dusting off his hands. "Much tidier all around."

Evan retched as the smell of burning flesh hit him. Too fast for him to intercept the strike, it was over. Evan bent on one knee, reached a hand to the charred circle and pulled back, afraid that touching the greasy ash would make it real. *Not even time to scream,* Evan realized, and the thought turned his stomach again.

"You promised to leave him alone." He should have known better, should have expected trickery and betrayal, but he'd gambled his own worth to Pathet's master against the life of his friend.

"Yes, I did," Pathet concurred seriously, then he smiled. "I lied."

"You will pay for this," Evan swore in the face of the daemon, and Pathet laughed at him.

"What can you do to me that my master hasn't already done, clever boy?"

"I can send you back to him a failure," Evan answered. Trembling, he almost doubted that he could move. But his memory fed him Lirion's voice, soothing and mocking as she led him into the second sphere. He had learned to move through that realm with his body and his senses intact, and he did so now, snapped out of reality with a clap of thunder and pushed thoughts of nausea and nothingness away. Loss swept him like the insanity he had known at Omage's hands. He screamed—endlessly, soundlessly—and the void trembled in his passing.

Something pulled him toward home and he rejected it, not ready yet to cope with his father's murders, or his own by inaction in Jack Laurence's kitchen. He shaped an image in his mind of a safe place—Covent Gardens. The stranger might be following, but Evan took an extra minute to ease into the physical universe; appearing in public in a flash of lightning would draw more attention than he could afford right now. For a moment he stood next to the stall where yesterday he had bought violets for Claudia. Then he dusted himself off and walked away.

# Chapter 19

*A daemon, bound, remains so until the master of the daemon releases him, which requires not intention but the speaking of the words that set the daemon free. So a man who would hold a daemon will refrain from converse with that daemon which will, by answer of a seeming innocent question, pronounce the words that free that spirit.*

"THERE, MATE, WATCH WHERE YOU'RE GOING." A MAN IN A SOCCER JACKET with Arsenal on the back elbowed Evan in the ribs. Dazed and confused, he stepped back, stumbling against a man behind him. A crowd surrounded him, pressing him forward, but Evan had no memory of where he was, or how he had gotten there.

Smoke caught at the back of his throat and reality kaleidoscoped, time and place recombining in dizzy patterns. The crush of people around him was real. Other people's clothing scraped roughly against his shirtsleeved arms. Evan heard the murmurs of the curious and the voices of the uniformed policemen at the center of the crowd urging them to move on. But the image of Jack Laurence, dying, swamped his senses. He saw green flame and smelled burning flesh again, gagged on the lump in his throat and wiped cold sweat from his face. Pathet's mocking smile lingered in the air like Alice's hallucinatory Cheshire cat, fading slowly.

"What happened?" Evan said, because asking the more urgent question—where am I?—would attract too much attention.

"IRA," the man in the Arsenal jacket stated with certainty. "Planted a bomb in this 'ere bookshop. Owner's dead. They took him out just a minute ago—you must have passed the ambulance leaving when you come up."

An explosion in a bookstore. Evan nodded absently, a cold weight settling in his gut. "Was anyone else hurt?" he asked, more scared to hear the answer than he had ever been of anything in his life. "I have a friend, I think she may work around here."

"Don't know yet, coppers are still looking. You're a foreigner, aren't you? You look a might peaky—'oy, over here—" The man raised his arm above his head, pointing down at Evan. "Got a Yank here says he knew someone in the shop."

"I'm not sure," Evan began, but a man in a crisp tan raincoat had him by the elbow, drew him a bit apart from the crowd.

"I'm Inspector James." The man in the raincoat flashed his identification, returned it to his inside breast pocket and drew out a small notebook. He opened it and examined the writing there for a moment before he looked up at Evan again. "I'm sure this is a bit of a shock, sir, but I need to ask a few questions."

Evan shook his head, trying without success to clear the fog that seemed to shroud all conscious thought but one. "A woman—was a woman hurt in the explosion?" he asked.

"Now should there have been, Mr.—?" Inspector James waited with bland attention.

"Davis, Evan Davis, and I don't know." Evan paused, trying to remember. "She worked in a shop like this, but I'm not sure—" He looked around him. The street seemed vaguely familiar, but he'd been to the bookstore only once. It had looked different then—no crowds, no fire brigade or policemen, no smoldering wreckage—but yes, the same place. The imperative that had driven him here asserted itself. "I have to warn her—"

"It's a bit late for a warning, sir. There was a young lady who worked in this shop; were you and she having a spot of trouble, then?"

Ponderously, like the world was passing in slow motion, Evan worked through the expressionless voice to the meaning of the words.

Too late. *Was* a young lady.

"She's dead." He twisted his way through the policemen holding back the crowd, heading for the smoking ruin of the bookstore. "Oh, God, what have I done? Claudia!"

Hands grabbed at his arms, pulled him back, away from the heat that wavered in the air around the smoldering building.

"I didn't say she was dead, Mr. Davis." The inspector took his arm, led him to a patrol car, and pushed him onto the back seat. "Now why don't you tell me exactly what you have done."

"Nothing. Everything." Evan shivered, realized he was still in his shirtsleeves.

"You seem to have lost your jacket."

Evan looked blankly at the inspector—James, he'd said, Inspector

James—saw distaste tighten the lines around the man's eyes. They both wanted the same thing, but Evan put his chances of convincing Inspector James of that at nil. And given the way they'd started, he couldn't say he blamed the man. He shrugged his shoulders, not thinking fast enough and knowing he wasn't up to a game of cat and mouse with Scotland Yard.

"I didn't realize I'd need it when I came out this morning."

Only half the truth, it explained only half the cold he felt. At the first hint of Omage's involvement in the Carter case he should have run as fast and as far as his gold card would take him in the opposite direction. Jack would still be alive. Or later, if he'd gone with Pathet, the daemon wouldn't have come after Claudia. Bad choices all down the line: starting with the gun he hadn't used on himself when he was Paul Carter's age, he'd been buying his life with other people's blood for years. Evan wondered if he would ever feel warm again.

"I see." The inspector flipped through the pages of his notebook, lips pursed. "You called out a name a moment ago—Claudia, I believe—is that the young lady's name?"

"Yes—Claudia Laurence. She's twenty-four years old, about five feet tall, shoulder-length brown hair, brown eyes—" Warm, dark eyes with soft lashes that brushed his cheek like a breath when he held her. "Light green coat, I don't know what else she was wearing today."

She was wearing that coat when he saw her yesterday, he remembered; the weight of her tingled up the inside of his arms, the press of her kiss warmed his lips for a moment and left only the cold. The memory of her touch ripped away the numbness that had held feeling at bay. Guilt brought a cold sweat to his temples. Over and over in his head the single thought taunted him: he never should have come here. The inspector's voice brought him back to the present he would have to live with.

"Yes, sir, that fits the description of the young lady who worked in this shop. Did you know her well?"

Evan stared at the inspector, fought back the pain squeezing the breath out of his chest. "She was a friend, a good friend."

"Was you say. You know for a fact, then, that she was in the shop when the explosive device went off?"

"You were telling me, Inspector." Evan glared at the man. "I arrived after the explosion." Claudia had to be alive, or none of this made sense.

"So you say, sir." Inspector James looked back in his notebook, then glanced at Evan with an air of professional indifference. "About that statement you made a moment ago, Mr. Davis—'What have I done—' What, exactly, have you done to the young lady?"

Evan tried to pull his thoughts in line, matching the policeman's anger. "Nothing, Inspector. In my business, you make enemies. I'm a private investigator with Bradley, Ryan, and Davis in the States." And past time he started acting like it, he reminded himself. He wasn't nineteen anymore, he wasn't helpless, and the police still hadn't found a second body in the mess any one of his enemies had made of the bookstore. As a corpse Claudia was useless, but as a hostage, she had trade value for one half-human who might have loved her once.

"Ah." Anger passed fleeting across the bland face of the policeman. "Have you given the details of your investigation up at the Yard, then, sir?"

"No, Inspector." A warning might have saved at least one life, maybe more, but there had been no warning. "I'm here on vacation, didn't actually have anything to report. The agency is working on a case closer to home; we specialize in recovery work, art mostly. Our clients prefer discretion to retribution, and the less scrupulous collectors we recover from usually play by the same rules. Sometimes they don't, but I can't think of anyone we've annoyed in the last year who might do something like this." But Pathet had been very annoyed. And Alfredo DaCosta had tried to tell him something yesterday. . . .

"Someone did it, Mr. Davis. A list of the most likely suspects might be helpful." The inspector jotted a line in his notebook. "In the meantime, if we should find an extra jacket in the shop, I'm sure you won't mind trying it on for us."

Here, at least, he was on safe ground. "You won't," he assured the officer. "I didn't wear a jacket this morning, and I had just arrived when that man in the crowd called you over."

"Mmhmm." The word could have meant anything. Inspector James glanced briefly at his notebook again. "But in the event we do find your jacket, where are you staying in London, sir?"

Evan rejected the truth without a backward glance. The inspector hadn't believed one word since the first, and bits of charred bone and blackened ash in the kitchen in Layton would clinch any doubts James might have. So he improvised, buying time. "Claridge's. I'm staying with a client, Charles Devereaux St. George. The room is in his name." They'd have to find Charlie to discredit the story. Then they'd have to find Evan.

Inspector James wrote down Evan's name, Charlie's, and that of the hotel, tore the sheet out of his notebook and motioned to a man in a plaid sports coat. The man was younger, and his anger was closer to the surface. He took the slip of paper, nodded at James' instructions, and gave Evan a poisonous look as he walked away. Until that moment his danger from the police had been a distant thing, an obstacle to circumvent. For a fleeting moment Evan wondered where the greater threat lay: in the open-eyed malice of his enemies, or in the blind justice of Her Majesty's judicial system.

"Just a few more questions, Mr. Davis."

"Of course, Inspector," Evan answered politely, almost grateful to have his attention drawn away from the younger policeman.

"I don't have in my notes why you were visiting the shop just now—"

"Lunch," Evan stammered, while his mind screamed at him to get moving. Two people were already dead because of him; if he didn't find her first, Claudia would make three.

"And what time were you supposed to meet Miss Laurence?"

"Noon." Evan buried his head in his hands, wishing the inspector would go away, knowing the man would stand there all day until he was satisfied that he'd wrung the last word out of his only suspect. Evan didn't fool himself. He looked as guilty as sin, and it didn't help that he felt guilty as well.

"Noon today, Mr. Davis? What time did you say you left your hotel?"

For an insane moment he considered telling the man the truth: *I left through the second celestial sphere just after a daemon of the host of Azmod burned her brother to a cinder over morning coffee in Claudia's kitchen. He would have killed me, too, but he had orders to bring me back alive. Unfortunately, my closest friends keep getting in his way.*

Instead, he gave Inspector James a curt nod, while he wondered if they had an insanity plea in England, and whether they still hung convicted murderers. "I don't know what time I left the hotel, Inspector." He held out his wrist, showed the man the watch still set for home.

"Lucky mistake for you, wasn't it?"

"I don't understand—" Evan frowned at the policeman, confused. The inspector showed him his watch.

"It's after one o'clock. You missed your lunch date by almost an hour. If you'd been on time, you might have been caught in the blast yourself."

He must have run from the house in Layton before eleven, but Evan remembered nothing from the moment he transported until the man in the soccer jacket jostled him in the crowd. Pathet already had more than an hour's lead on him.

Inspector James checked his notebook again. "We'll have to contact Miss Laurence's next of kin, let them know what's happened here. Would you happen to know who that might be, Mr. Davis?"

Evan roused himself to consider the question. Jack and Claudia had a mother still living in St. Louis; their father had died of a heart attack the year before they'd all met in New York. "In the States," he confirmed. "I don't have the address with me, but I can call home for it this afternoon."

"That would be fine." James closed his notebook with a snap and slid it into his back pocket. "You don't seem to have your passport with you—"

Evan shook his head. The passport was back in Layton, side pocket of his carry-on, but he kept that information to himself.

"Then you won't mind if I take a look at it when I drop you off at your hotel."

"That isn't necessary, Inspector. I'll take a taxi, call home for that address, and stop by your office with the passport."

"I think I'd rather see it sooner, if you don't mind. One more question. We found this lying next to the dead man—" Inspector James reached into the front seat of the car, pulled out a bundle, and handed it to Evan. The plastic bag contained a small leather-bound volume, burned and curling up at the corners from water damage. The book was open to the flyleaf, on which someone had scrawled the words Evan D—, almost illegibly, in flaky char. "Could you tell me why the dead man's last thought should be of you?"

Until he saw his own name inscribed in the ruins, a part of Evan's mind could believe that the explosion had nothing to do with him, or with the Black Masque. Pointless to try and deny the words were there for him— Omage could reach out for him anywhere, drag him back into the darkness where nothing could save him from the terrors of his own endless night. But Inspector James would never understand the message. Suddenly a hand was at his shoulder, pushing him down.

"Don't faint, Mr. Davis. And don't vomit on my shoes, if you please. Seems we have jogged something loose in your memory. Care to tell me?"

Oh, yes, just tell the good inspector. Lily would enjoy the joke, if he lived to tell it to her.

"Not a memory, Inspector. I had nothing to do with this—" He rested the fingertips of one hand on the plastic covering the blackened book, felt nothing of the daemon who murdered to taunt him. "But somebody wants you to believe I'm a cold-blooded killer. I didn't think anybody hated me that much. I was wrong, and now people are dying for that mistake. I guess that does make it my fault."

"A pretty speech, Mr. Davis." Pale blue eyes pinned Evan with a measuring look. "We haven't found the detonator or any traces of the explosive used, but it appears to be something we haven't seen before."

"And you think I have?" Evan challenged. "Being a private detective isn't usually this eventful, Inspector. I don't carry a gun, I don't chase bad guys in fast cars, and I've never fought anything more resistant than a balky computer program. I've never even seen a bomb, and as for constructing one, I flunked chemistry in high school. If it takes more mechanical expertise than screwing in a light bulb, I'm out of luck."

"But you say you have enemies who do command exactly that expertise."

"Like I said, Inspector, until today I didn't know that either. Unfortunately, whoever did this left my name, not his own."

Nobody on the material sphere had technology like that. For a slightly annoyed daemon trying to make a point, though, it had been easy. He rubbed the scars on his wrist, remembering.

"An accident with a bread knife, Mr. Davis?" Inspector James stared at the thin white lines, drawing the wrong conclusion most people did.

"Ancient history, Inspector." None of your business, Evan's tone implied.

"Perhaps." Eyes met eyes again; Evan saw uneasiness there, wondered what the policeman saw.

"We're not making any accusations yet, Mr. Davis. When we get a line on the explosives, however, you will be the first to know."

"Evan—is that you?" Charles St. George shouldered his way through the policemen, stepping gingerly over fire hoses and bits of charred wreckage.

"Charlie—"

"Can I help you, sir?" Inspector James pulled the notebook out of his pocket again. "Are you an acquaintance of Mr. Davis?"

His expression still bland, James stepped between the two men. Evan wondered if that face ever gave anything away, or if the policeman had feelings to reveal at all.

"This is Charles Devereaux St. George, Inspector. I'm staying with him at Claridge's."

Charlie passed him a sharp glance that said, *Explanations later,* but picked up the cue. "Actually, Evan works for my company on contract. He's here to arrange secure transport for a painting I plan to purchase at auction this afternoon." St. George looked from one man to the other with growing concern. "You can't possibly suspect Evan had anything to do with this!" he gestured expansively to take in the police and fire brigade as well as the blackened hole in the row of shops. "His credentials are impeccable."

"That may be, sir. We have no firm suspects as yet, but we must consider all the possibilities," Inspector James answered politely. "You say you were to purchase a painting at auction today, sir? If you needed extra security, I assume we are discussing a work of some considerable value?"

"A Matisse. It goes to auction at Sotheby's this afternoon. My agent

is authorized for the purchase, but I thought Claudia—Miss Laurence—
might find the auction exciting. I was calling to see if she might like to
take the afternoon off, sort of an impromptu adventure."

St. George stopped a moment, as if the import of the place and Evan
here in the police car finally penetrated his flustered consciousness. "My
God, Evan, was Claudia in there?"

The policeman made another note in his book. "That's not yet certain,
Mr. St. George. But tell me more about your relationship with Miss
Laurence. She seems to have been a very popular young lady."

"I came by to take Claudia to lunch," Evan explained.

"Of course, dear boy, how foolish of me not to realize. But you didn't
say anything last night. I presumed too much on dinner, I see."

"Then you haven't known Miss Laurence long, Mr. St. George."

Evan could almost feel the policeman's ears prick up. They'd call it a
lover's triangle, he guessed, and point to the innocent shop owner caught
in the spurned lover's jealous retribution when they hanged him.

"Evan introduced us yesterday, we all had a lovely dinner together at
the hotel, and I thought—"

Later, if they found her alive, Claudia could let him down gently. Evan
could see no point in shattering the man's romantic illusions now: "I already
told Inspector James that Claudia and I were just friends, Charles—"

"Yes," the inspector interrupted. "Did the young lady spend the night
at your hotel?"

Charlie bristled like an indignant hedgehog. "Of course not! After
dinner, Evan took Claudia *and* her brother home. It was all quite proper!"

"A brother. Hmmm. Wouldn't he be next of kin, Mr. Davis?" James
riffled through his notebook, apparently found the entry he was looking
for. "I thought you said Miss Laurence's family lived in the United States."

"They do," Evan persisted while the knot in his gut twisted tighter.
He had to reach Brad before the police found what was left of the
Laurences' kitchen. "Jack left town this morning."

"I see. Then you would know Miss Laurence's local address."

"Of course." Evan gave the inspector the address of the house on St.
Mary's Road. "I'm an American citizen," he reminded James. "If you plan
to arrest me, I demand to speak to the American Embassy."

"Arrested?" Charlie demanded sharply, turning to the officer. "You
said you had no firm suspects. I thought this was a simple case of the IRA
trying to scare away the tourists and you were trying to keep it a secret."

"No, sir," James objected. "We've made no final determination on the
cause of the explosion. Until we do, however, I suggest that neither of you
leave London."

"Then I assume I may take Mr. Davis back to the hotel?" St. George put a hand on Evan's shoulder, bent over, and peered into Evan's face. "You look like death, old boy. Do you need a doctor?"

Evan shook his head. "I need a phone. Have to call home."

"Of course. Wait just a moment, I'll get a cab."

"You won't get a cab down here, Mr. Devereaux; my men have cordoned off the street at the corner." Inspector James motioned a uniformed policeman over. "I'll have Sergeant Breckenridge take you back to the hotel."

Charles straightened to his full height. "Unless this is an arrest, Inspector, we'd prefer to take that taxi."

Inspector James slipped his notebook back into his pocket. "As you wish, Mr. St. George. Claridge's, you said? I'll stop by for that address and a look at your passports as soon as I've finished up here."

"And you will let us know if you hear anything about Miss Laurence?" St. George asked. "You must understand, we are most concerned."

"Of course." The policeman nodded once. "I'll see about getting a taxi down here for you."

He gave Evan a measuring look—for a noose, Evan decided—and walked away, his raincoat flaring out behind him in the late April breeze.

A suite. Charlie never did anything halfway, it seemed. The salon breathed a quiet elegance from the sculptured ceiling to the graceful chairs scattered about the room.

"Sit down before you fall down, dear boy." St. George motioned to a brocaded Queen Anne chair next to the telephone and headed for the bar.

Evan sat and looked around him. Several closed doors punctuated the ribbon-printed wallpaper, but Evan was too exhausted to wonder where they led. In one corner of the room an elaborately carved walking stick rested against the wall. Evan shivered when he looked at it, realized the shapes trailing from the rounded knob at the top were grotesque faces, mouths wide open as if frozen in mid-scream.

"Here, drink this, it will steady your nerves."

St. George pressed a glass into his hand—the smell of whiskey kicked the craving into high gear even while it brought back memories that turned Evan's stomach. The booze would take it all away for a time, but when he came down, Claudia would be dead.

"Not now, Charles." He set the glass on the desk and pushed it away, buried his face in his hands, and rubbed at his forehead with his fingertips.

"I'm sorry, Evan, I forgot." The glass disappeared, Evan heard the splash of liquid hitting the sink, the sound of running water. "Just let me call down to room service for some coffee, then I'll get out of your way. You can lie down a bit after you call home."

"Coffee would be a godsend, Charlie, but I don't need to lie down. I've got to find Claudia."

"Find?" St. George paused with his hand on the dial. "I thought, I mean from the way that policeman was speaking—"

"She's not dead, Charlie, I'm sure of it. I have to find her before the people who snatched her get tired of waiting and do something stupid."

Charlie dialed the number, waited for an answer. "Who are they—never mind, confidential, right? Did her brother really leave town, or is he missing, too? —Oh, hello? Room service? Yes, I'd like a large pot of coffee sent up, service for two, and a selection of cold sandwiches." He gave the room number and hung up.

"You seem to be taking this pretty calmly, Charles." Evan watched the man pour himself a brandy and lift it to his lips, savoring the bouquet. "Aren't you a little bit afraid that policeman might be right about me?"

"Nonsense, my boy." St. George set down his glass, and walked over to stand in front of Evan's chair. "What do these foreigners know anyway? We Americans have to stick together."

They both turned at a knock on the door, but St. George waved at the phone. "Must be the coffee. You go ahead and make your call."

Evan dialed up the switchboard and gave the operator his number. While he waited for the connection, a hand slid a china cup and saucer steaming with strong black coffee onto the desk. He looked up, a distracted "Thank you" half formed, and clenched his fist around the telephone receiver.

"You."·

Pathet smiled his predator's smug confidence and Charlie gave a nod, the good host. "You two have met. Then I don't have to make introductions."

The daemon picked up the cup of coffee and took a sip, set it down again. "Finish your call, human."

Evan ignored the command. "What have you done with Claudia?"

St. George slipped up behind him and wrapped a comradely arm around his shoulder. "All in good time, my boy. Our dear Lily took something that belongs to me. I want it back. Later, when my property has been restored, we can talk about your lady friend."

Evan glared at the man, his own temper reflected in the mirror-hard eyes that mocked him over St. George's false smile. Slowly, deliberately, he set the receiver back on its cradle.

"Tsk." Charlie shook his head in a travesty of regret. "You really should pick your friends more carefully, old boy."

Evan felt the prick of the needle, and then nothing.

# Chapter 20

*A man who would bind a daemon to his will must always remember that the daemon does his bidding in anger and always means his master ill. Accordingly, great care should be taken in the binding and ordering of the daemon, or the daemon will twist the words of the command to the greatest harm of the master, even to the master's death.*

ONCE, TWICE, THE PHONE RANG. KEVIN BRADLEY REACHED FOR THE receiver, never made it. For the second time that day the rope sensation tightened around his spine, wrenched his gut, and died on a wave of suffocating nausea. Human form wavered, steadied, then the shattered glass and broken furniture around him came back into focus.

"What's the matter with Evan?"

Lily shrugged. "I don't know that it was Evan. The operator said the call originated in England, but whoever it was hung up before I could answer. Want to take a hop over there and check?"

Badad focused his daemon sense inward. A moment ago the link with his son had surged with an adrenaline rush that screamed "danger"; now there was nothing. Alive, surely: The rope, as he had taken to calling Evan's spell, still bound him, but he caught nothing of his son through it. The emergency, whatever it was, seemed to be over. "Maybe later."

He returned his attention to the chaos that surrounded them. The glazers had repaired the glass doors, and a cleanup crew outside scrubbed at the pentagram on the bricks, removed broken glass and twisted lawn chairs from the garden before it started to rain. When the afternoon shower began, the men would move inside. Soon, only the uneasy feeling in his gut would remain as evidence that a human had bound Badad of Ariton in this place.

"I was hoping it would all go away while we were gone," he said with a rueful frown.

"Gravity," Lirion reminded him. "Broken or not, material objects have a tendency to lie where they fall until you move them." She kicked at a splinter from an end table on her way to the kitchen, and Badad watched the chip of wood skitter across the floor.

"I didn't do it, you know." She took in the destruction with a gesture. "All this, I mean." She only confirmed what he already suspected.

"Neither did I."

Lily stopped at the kitchen door. "That leaves Evan. Not the first time either. I'm not the only one throwing sparks when we argue. Do you suppose he knows?"

Brad shook his head. "I don't think so."

"Interesting." Lily gave the matter some thought and came to the conclusion, "Very interesting," before passing out of view in the doorway.

"Yeah." Badad wondered how much damage his son would do before he admitted he needed some help controlling his daemon side. Nothing he could do about it now, but they'd have to talk about it when Evan came home.

Home. The word came too easily when he thought of Evan. He picked up a shard of glass, turned it over in his hand. Blood streaked the edge—Badad remembered the cut on his arm from the other side of body-death. The new form he wore looked like the old one, reconstructed exactly, except for the damage. He'd gotten used to the face in the mirror, identified it like a map. *If I look like this, I am on the material plane. It is the late twentieth century Western Earth time, as counted from the last bloody murder that seemed to matter to these creatures.* With an abrupt gesture he set the blood-streaked shard on an end table and turned away, leaving thoughts of dying flesh amid the broken fragments of a pottery lamp.

"Coffee?" Lily returned with a cup in each hand. She gave him one and drank from the one she kept. With her free hand she shifted a thin sheaf of computer paper from under her arm and lifted it so that she could read the print. "The results of Evan's search program. Want to take a look?"

Brad took the sheaf of paper. "Not here." Memory of what had happened in this room and the garden beyond crawled like rats over his skin, from his fingertips to the base of his skull. He ignored the sensation, angry suddenly at all humans and at himself for the decisions that had put him here, and headed for the study, away from the eyes of the cleanup crew.

"Anything from Evan on the machine?" Brad settled into his chair, the printout supported on the crook of his right knee, ankle propped on his left. He sipped at the coffee and set down the cup.

"He called this morning." Lily settled behind the desk, Evan's place, ankles crossed on the desktop. "I checked the messages while you were explaining the damages to the workmen— Punk vandals on skateboards on their way to South Street?"

Brad shrugged. "It worked. For a few minutes there I didn't think the young guy on the cleanup crew would come into the garden at all."

"Smart kid," Lily agreed. "The place makes me nervous myself these days."

"Know what you mean." Evan's uneasy presence haunted the painted circle, but whether as a sense of present danger leaking through the spheres or the lingering terror of a human binding the forces of Ariton, Badad could not tell. "So what did Evan have to say?"

"He said he bumped into Charlie St. George in Covent Garden, was going to Venice tomorrow—make that today—to do a security check for one of Charlie's businesses. Seems there's trouble in paradise."

"Danger?" Brad looked up sharply, relaxed when he caught her predatory grin.

Lily waggled her eyebrows suggestively. "More like woman trouble, I suspect. Or boredom. Maybe he discovered that his old chums have settled into deserved obscurity. For all his protestations, our Evan needs the action—he is his father's son, after all." She saluted him with her coffee cup. "What did Evan's ferret program turn up this time?"

The answer lay on Brad's lap, in the printout from the computer that, for reasons too irrationally human for the lord of Ariton to understand, Evan called Bruce Wayne. Brad lifted the paper and worked his way slowly through the complex network of associations.

"This has possibilities. No record of a Marnie Carter, but there's a picture of a Madeleine Carson that's a close fit for our bereaved Mrs. Simpson, barring the hairstyle and the date. Could be the mother."

"Society pages?"

"Mug shot. Seems our Mrs. Carson was also known as Sister Madeleine, camp show psychic. Appears there was a child clairvoyant in the act. Could be our Marnie Simpson. Let's see—" He turned the page and froze. "Shit."

"Problem?" Lily dropped her feet from the desk and leaned forward to take the printout.

"Did you say Evan made contact with Charlie St. George?"

"Uh-huh. According to Evan, old Charlie's buying a business of some sort in Venice, wants us to do the security check on the current Board and some key execs. Doesn't trust Italians, I guess. Evan decided to take the job. Like I said, the vacation didn't turn out quite as expected."

"No, it wouldn't." Brad unfolded himself from his wingback chair and dropped the printout on the desk on his way to the safe. The stone was still there—he took it out, hefted the cold weight of it in his hand.

"What's Charlie's picture . . . oh. Shit." She shuffled through the pages.

"That's our perpetually-out-of-town Mr. Simpson," Brad explained unnecessarily. "Charles Devereaux St. George." Married, it appeared, to the child clairvoyant, and brother-in-law to her half-daemon brother. He didn't bother saying it, just waited, the stone a cold and mocking presence in his hand, while she followed Simpson's financial empire to its source in the printout.

"Mr. Simpson is not the self-made man he claims. In fact, he owes his start in the business world to Francis St. George, deceased." Her glance, speculative, come to rest on the smoky topaz. He reached for her hand, turned it palm upward under the stone, and closed her fingers around it, shielding his own from its unnatural chill.

"Related to our Charlie?" He moved away and sank into his own chair, grateful for something solid under him.

"His father. It appears Mr. Simpson may have been planning Omage's little coup for longer than Ariton knew. Until nineteen sixty-seven Franklin Simpson was a minor hood, no significant connections, just a couple of convictions for petty theft. It seems reasonable to assume that he upped the ante. The real Charlie St. George probably ceased to exist about the same time."

Lily ran her fingers over the smooth plane of the stone's face, her eyes closing for a moment over cool meditation. "Dead?"

"Probably," Brad agreed. "Wouldn't have been that hard to do. Francis St. George died in a boating accident. The search only turned up one body, but that doesn't mean he died alone."

"Back at the Black Masque," Lily reminded him, her eyes wide open now, "Omage said he knew we had this thing," she held up the topaz by its chain, "the moment it fell into our hands. If Charlie St. George is Franklin Simpson—"

"It's been a setup from the start," Brad finished for her.

"So, the Picasso was bait, Paul Carter, too, if Simpson is running true to form. The trinket was the target all along."

"Not just the stone," Brad corrected her. "Omage said it—he wants Evan. It's the half-breeds; Simpson probably married Marnie Carter just to get close to her brother. Do you suppose she knows?"

Lily examined the printout more closely. "She probably knows some of it. Given the dates, they must have met when they were both still nickel-

and-dime con artists. Can't imagine she knew Omage would kill her brother."

"I'll bet Mac knew, though. Probably Simpson as well. Evan would never go back to the Black Masque on his own. While Omage kept us busy stopping his latest attack on the second sphere, Simpson had a clear shot at Evan. Did he leave a number?"

"Simpson?"

Brad glared at her, and Lily sifted through the papers on the desk, came up with the London phone number Evan had left with his message. "He was staying with this Laurence woman and her brother."

A faint trace of scorn tinged her voice, and Brad crooked an eyebrow at her over the phone receiver.

"Jealous?" he suggested.

"Disappointed," she countered. "I thought he had better taste."

Brad reached for the telephone. "Maybe he does." He left the meaning ambiguous, knowing it would annoy her, and dialed the number.

"Laurence residence," a politely bureaucratic British voice answered, waited.

Jack Laurence was American. Brad said nothing.

The voice spoke again, "Who is this?"

"May I speak to Evan Davis," Brad asked, trading information in the hope of obtaining some. "This is his office calling."

"This is the police, Mr.—"

Brad wasn't giving that much away. "Is Mr. Davis there, officer? Of course we will be happy to cooperate with the police—Interpol?"

"London, Inspector James speaking."

Brad heard a murmur of voices in the background, a muffled order to trace the call.

"If you put Mr. Davis on the telephone for a moment, I'm sure he will confirm your identification and we can get on with your questions."

Rigidly polite, the policeman's annoyance still made itself heard an ocean away. "We'd like to speak to Mr. Davis ourselves—Mr. Ryan?—but the gentleman seems to have disappeared."

"Can you hold a moment, Inspector?" Brad let four minutes sweep the face of his Rolex, the telephone receiver pressed to his shoulder. He gave Inspector James plenty of time to trace the call, information the overseas operator could have given him as quickly.

"As it happens, two of our operatives are on a case in London now," Brad lied smoothly. "We've made contact, and they'll meet you at the Laurence address in about ten minutes, Inspector. I trust their on-site judgment better than any help we can supply from here."

"We'll be here, Mr.—"

Brad hung up, met Lily's curious frown. "We're too late."

"He's not dead." Lily seemed to turn inward for a moment, sensing the same internal tie that Brad felt himself. "I'd know it if he were."

She rose from Evan's chair, paced around the desk. The cold light of home glinted in the blue flames of her eyes. "Not dead—yet."

"What does that mean?"

"Cousin, cousin." Lily sat on the arm of his chair and ran long fingers, spiked with perfectly manicured nails, through his hair.

He caught her wrist, hard, and pulled her hand away. "I'm not one of your human playthings, Lirion. We may be stuck here together, but I'd still make an enemy you can't afford."

"Maybe," she agreed, her voice as hard as his own. "Or maybe you've been here too long. Maybe that half-breed monster of yours means more to you than Ariton.

"Think, cousin. If he summons us, we have no choice but to answer. If he doesn't, well, we know Franklin Simpson's not above a little murder. We'd be free, both of Evan and of Ariton's charge that holds us here."

She paced the room, from the chair to the bookcase and back again, gold chain clutched between the fingers of her clenched fist, the Eye of Omage held before her like a prize. Her voice dropped almost to a whisper, but it carried all the force of desperation as she repeated the one word: "Free."

Darkness closed over Badad's vision. Evan dead. He'd known since they'd faced each other across Omage's stone floor that he could not bear to watch the human die, could not be a part of his son's mortality. Someday, when decay had set in, when the life in the man had grown dim, he could accept death for his son. Not now, certainly not so soon after his own brief experience with life ending.

"Could you make that same choice if you had to face him with it, say, after Omage had run at him?" he asked.

"Probably not." She dropped the stone on the desk. "But I don't have to. Azmod has seen to that."

"It won't be that easy," he countered, and gave logic rather than face the accusation that came too near the mark: "Simpson didn't go to all this trouble just to kill Evan. A straight hit would have cost a lot less and he could have done it without all the globe-trotting. Paul Carter is dead. He needs Evan to break through into the second sphere."

That got through. Lily tensed. He could see host loyalty at war with self-interest in her eyes, knew she'd come to his own uncomfortable realization. She confirmed his fear: "We've made that a hell of a lot easier for him, too."

They'd spent a year training the boy to control his passage through the second sphere. His son didn't like it, but he could do it at will now. In Evan Davis, Ariton had handed the enemy a lethal weapon, trained, and pointed at the second sphere. But that weapon had a will of its own. "Evan won't do it."

Lily gave a short bark of humorless laughter. Sarcasm edged her words: "You don't know humans. He'll do it all right, he's got the same weakness they all have."

"Which is?"

"He doesn't want to die." She gave him another cold smile. "And that's your fault, too."

He had no answer to appease her. Knowing what death meant, he wouldn't blame his son for anything he did to hold mortality at bay. He did have a question: "Why? There's nothing in the second sphere for humans. Evan's made that clear enough."

Lily frowned, and Brad saw the old explanations tick over in her head, fall away. Omage, making another move in his long-standing feud with Badad, or simply gone mad, they could understand. But what stake could a human have in all of this?

"We'll have to ask Charlie, né Franklin Simpson, when we see him, won't we?" Lirion smeared a polite smile over a hunting snarl.

Brad picked up the stone, hefted it thoughtfully in his hand for a moment, and locked it in the safe. "After you."

Broken crockery lay scattered in the ashes on the floor—turtledoves on a curve of ironstone and the fragments of dogs in green eyeshades, standing on their hind legs with cue sticks stuck somehow to their forepaws. Greasy black ash streaked two words across the white enamel of the refrigerator door: Evan's name, and the word "Venice."

*How perfectly circular,* Brad thought. He remembered Lily returning from Alfredo DaCosta's palazzo in Venice with a stone the color of Evan's eyes. Just a few days ago, but it seemed like an age of human time—was this what Einstein meant by relativity? Did Einstein have a son?—Brad made an effort to corral his scattered thoughts.

The games of Azmod had never been subtle: the message, not in human blood perhaps but in the blackened bits of charcoal that once had been flesh and bone, told him where he'd find Evan. The house in London was a warning. It could have been his son's body burned to ash. It still might be.

"How did you get in here?" A young man with a face a bit too pink, in a uniform a bit too tight, confronted them across the blackened circle on the floor.

Lily pulled out her license, smiled. "I'm Lily Ryan, this is Kevin Bradley. Our office called, said an Inspector James wanted to talk to us about our associate."

The constable puffed out his cheeks while he looked at the identification. Finally he let the air out with a plosive gust. "The inspector's this way—watch you don't step on the evidence—he'll want to know how you got in here."

"Yes, he will." The man in the tan raincoat took them in with one sweep of sharp, clear eyes. He was taller than the constable, older, and more solidly built. Experienced, Brad saw, but the mass on the floor that had recently been at least one human being and breakfast for two still made him flinch. He took Lily's I.D. and scrutinized it carefully before handing it back. "How did you get in here?"

Lily put her I.D. in her coat pocket. "Through the back door. We saw the police cars out front, came through the alley to avoid the reporters."

James inspected the daemon's face as carefully as he had her I.D. "And to get a look at the scene of the crime, no doubt." Not a question. "Your office said you would answer questions about an associate, Evan Davis."

Brad matched the inspector's understatement: "Of course. What exactly seems to be the problem?"

"Murder, Mr. Bradley. We believe your Mr. Davis murdered his friend Jack Laurence here this morning, and that in an attempt to murder Mr. Laurence's sister, he set off a bomb in the bookshop where she worked, killing the proprietor early this afternoon."

"That seems out of character," Brad objected mildly.

"On the contrary." Inspector James pulled out a battered notebook, his expression grim. "According to your Federal Bureau of Investigation's computerized crime-link, Mr. Davis appears to have been associated with Mr. Laurence through a Satanist cult in the States. Police records indicate that Mr. Laurence almost lost his life at the hands of cult members two years ago. According to the police report, accusations against Evan Davis were made at the time and later dropped." The inspector paused. "For someone who has just claimed that such behavior is out of character, you don't seem surprised, Mr. Bradley."

"I'm not," Brad agreed. "Evan's past with the group you mention is no secret at the agency. He had no idea what he was getting into when he joined them, and when he tried to leave, they made him their prisoner. Believe me, he was as much their victim as Jack Laurence."

"That is Evan Davis' story, no doubt."

"That is *my* story, Inspector," Brad interrupted. "I was in the rescue party that found Evan Davis, half dead and in chains, and brought him out of there two years ago. If you had seen what I did, you would know you should be looking not for Mr. Davis, but for his captor."

"There is no captor, Mr. Bradley; if there ever was one he is dead now, in a suspiciously timed gas main explosion in New York. No, we do not suspect Mr. Davis of that crime—we know he was in transit out of Philadelphia at the time. He may have had an accomplice, but that is not Her Majesty's problem. This is." He pointed to the blackened heap of ash, then to the door of the refrigerator. "And that."

Brad followed the direction the inspector pointed in, and then turned back, barely containing his scorn. "Does the FBI report also say that he's stupid enough to sign his name to murder?"

"Not stupid, no." Inspector James put his notebook away; Brad recognized the ploy but felt the tension mount in the small silence anyway. "Insane, probably. He's been in and out of psychiatric care since childhood."

A stroke would kill the man, or a bolt of Ariton lightning—one more puddle of ash to join the first one on the floor. Brad restrained himself. Killing Inspector James would give him temporary satisfaction, but it wouldn't help Evan.

Lily stepped between the two men. Brad felt her anger like heat against his human skin, but she turned a conciliatory smile on the inspector. "Evan is missing," she pointed out. "And, for our very different reasons, we all want to find him. Until we do, I'd suggest we cooperate."

Inspector James pursed his lips and rocked back on his heels, rubbing one hand through the back of his thinning hair. "You can start," he suggested, "with the suspect's known contacts in Venice."

Brad shook his head. "None," he lied. "He's never been there, as far as I know. I suspect the second part of the message has nothing to do with Evan. Maybe it's a list. You say the murderer blew up a bookstore in London, maybe another place in the States. My guess is, Venice is his next target, someplace small but public if he keeps to his m.o."

"I'll mention that in my report," James remarked with no great conviction. "Where can we reach you if we have any more questions?"

"The Savoy," Lily offered. "We keep rooms there whenever we're in town. May we go now?"

"Of course. Constable Dodds will see you out." The inspector turned on his heels, moving past them toward the front of the house, already deep in conversation with an aggressive young man in a loud plaid sport coat.

Lily took Brad's arm until they were out of sight of the small house on St. Mary's Road. "They've taken him to Alfredo DaCosta. Pity we didn't run Evan's ferret program on him." She sighed with spurious regret. "And we had so much in common. If I didn't know better, I might have guessed he was one of ours."

"You both like champagne, sex, and other people's property," Brad objected. "That hardly qualifies him as a lord of Ariton, or of any Prince.

"It does complicate the picture," he added more seriously. "Is Simpson running Omage, or is DaCosta running them both?"

"I don't think Omage did this." Lily stared through him for a moment, and he waited for her to put his own suspicion into words: "It's not his style. Besides, your fireworks at the Black Masque rattled his teeth a bit; he could have done this job or taken out the bookstore, but not both, not so soon."

"Rival factions?" Brad asked the rhetorical question.

"Only one way to find out," Lily returned the obvious with a hunter's grin. "Inspector James is not going to like this." She vanished. Badad followed.

# Chapter 21

*In the days of Egypt, there were three prophets, and Moses was one, and Atlas the Astronomer, brother to Prometheus, but the greatest was Hermes, called Trismegistus, the thrice great, known as Thot by the Egyptians. And all that was known of philosophy was the gift of Trismegistus.*

"EVAN! WAKE UP!"

The urgent whisper filtered through a blanket of fog. Gradually awareness returned with the feel of a soft bed under his stomach and a hand on his arm—Claudia, beside him, and home, in the womb she'd made for them in the tiny apartment. He relaxed with a sigh, wondering what Jack would make of the dreams this time. They'd been weirder than usual; better lay off the Vat 69 before he started seeing pink elephants on the street. Evan reached out to draw Claudia closer, bury himself in the haze of mother-sister-lover feeling she wrapped around him. The shackle on his wrist stopped him short.

Jackhammers slammed into both temples like the granddaddy of all hangovers when he lifted his head. Not dreams, then. Jack was really dead, and Claudia lost in the explosion—no, here beside him. Pathet had kidnapped her, something to do with Omage and Paul Carter in New York. Charlie St. George was involved as well, but he couldn't figure out how. Couldn't think past the jackhammer in his head.

"Evan, are you awake yet?" Claudia's voice. She shook his shoulder, fingers digging deep into the muscle.

"I think so." The shackle cut into raw skin, distracted him. Time to transport out of there—wherever there was—find Brad and Lily. He didn't like the idea, but it beat being chained to a strange bed, God knew where.

"What did they do to you? I've been trying to wake you for hours."

Claudia. She couldn't travel the only route open to him, wouldn't much appreciate it if he left her there. So much for bugging out. "Sorry." Evan rubbed his forehead against his shirtsleeve. "Drugged, I think. Doesn't feel like he hit me. Are you all right?"

"I'm cold and scared and mad, and I'm naked as a jaybird," Claudia explained with very little patience. "They took my clothes, then you took the blanket and lost it off your side of the bed. I can't reach it, because the bastards who brought me here chained my leg to this side of the bed. They'll be back soon, and I don't want to face them stark naked, so get the damned blanket back up here."

Evan rubbed his eyes blearily and squinted. She was naked, all right, and the huge bed looked like Catherine the Great might have entertained her horse in it. Oversized pedestaled feet gave way to carved bedposts that supported the heavy Doric-style canopy overhead. The bedcover, a deep burgundy velvet cut to reveal the gold threads beneath the nap, lay in a heap near the foot of the bed.

"Give me a minute, I can't reach—" He rolled over and struggled to sit upright, his legs hanging off the side of the bed, his brain still muddy with the drug. "Here—" He stretched as far as the shackle would allow and snagged the cover with his foot, nudging it closer to the head of the bed until he could grasp it with his free hand.

"Where are we?" he asked when Claudia had settled in a steamy bundle wrapped in the heavy fabric.

She shrugged the cover off her shoulders and wrapped it around her breasts, freeing her arms to the cool breeze drifting through the windows open at either side of the bed. "It ain't Kansas," she finally answered. "More than that, I was hoping you could tell me."

Their elegant prison was a perfectly square room, walls and floor covered with delicately veined marble, pale rose on the walls, a chessboard pattern on the floor. Two brocaded armchairs sat grouped on opposite sides of a small table to the right of the door, and a low wooden chest with an elaborately carved base balanced the grouping on the left. The room held no other furniture, but a few barely noticeable marks on the floor showed that other pieces, probably chests like the one that remained, had been removed. The walls were free of decoration, but above the level of the elaborately carved lintel the ceiling rose in late Gothic splendor over carved arches limned in gilt. Between the arches, frescoes crowded the ceiling like an overheated carousel.

The paintings took his breath away. *Titian,* he thought, then back-pedaled. He wouldn't bet his reputation that the master had ever set a brush to that ceiling—probably students, but good ones, well versed in their teacher's style. The colors were so rich, the images so vibrant he almost thought that if he could reach them, he'd find flesh beneath his fingers instead of paint.

Eight scenes around a central painting, each depicting a scene important to the arcane magical cult of Hermes Trismegistes, vaulted overheard: over the door, the traditional grouping of the twelve virtues and twelve temptations appeared, with the twelve sibyls and twelve prophets facing them from over the bed. At the far left from where Evan sat on the bed, the artist had painted the seven planets with their ruling deities, and on the far right, a figure grouping that Evan guessed represented Isis, a globe showing the celestial spheres above her head, with Moses at her left hand and Hermes at her right.

Between the key representations at the cardinal points, the artist had painted a series of scenes depicting the myth of Osiris: Osiris teaching the Egyptians how to plant wheat; the Egyptian god Seth striking down Osiris on the bank of the Nile; the trial of Seth; Thot, the father of Osiris, and Isis, sister and wife of the dead god, raising Osiris from the dead. To emphasize the metaphoric relationship, in this fresco Osiris carried not the symbols of Egyptian kingship, but a Christian cross in his hand.

An elaborate pentagram filled the central apex of the vaulting ceiling. In the spaces between the five points of the star, fierce warrior angels with bows and arrows at the ready stared grimly outward, defending an angel representing one of the arts in each angle. The center of the pentagram held Evan's attention. A figure in classic Greek attire with wings at his feet—Hermes again—sat with poetry on his left and music on his right. The artist had used the same model as he had for Thot, Evan realized, but the two characterizations showed very different aspects of the man. Where Thot wore the expression of the stern judge, Hermes had the thoughtful demeanor of a teacher. Like all the frescoes, this one had an elaborate nature background suffused with light and texture. But the figure of Hermes seemed to glow of its own light, rather than reflect the rays of the sun. Analyzing the light and shadow on the trees and rocks, Evan realized that all of the light in the picture seemed to originate with the figure at its center.

The magician looked down from his lofty position with warm brown eyes, the full mouth softened in a pensive smile beneath the hawklike nose. Hair in dark waves, cut short in the classic Greek style seemed out of place on that hauntingly familiar face. *He's looking right at me,* Evan thought, *and he knows what I am, what I have been.* Was Titian's student a bastard of two universes, a monster like himself? Had he lived to see his talent wither in the torment of his soul, or had he died like Paul Carter, mad and in despair? He turned away, shaken that a long dead artist could affect him so deeply, and concentrated on the problem at hand. Where were they?

Not Rome, he decided, dismissing his first guess. Even the Borgia Popes hadn't gone this far in depicting the magical philosophy. For that matter neither had Titian, though the paintings reflected his earlier style. Together with the sounds floating through the window, however, he had enough to hazard a guess:

"Probably Venice."

"Very good." Mac. Omage. "In fact, we're visiting an old friend of Lily's."

The breath caught in Evan's throat, strangled him with memories. Not again. He turned and faced the creature of his nightmares. Charles Devereaux St. George followed the daemon, balloon glass in his hand, a hard smile on his face. At his side St. George carried the walking stick Evan had seen in his hotel, its length elaborately carved in the twisted gargoyle features of the damned. Age had smoothed the carvings and darkened the wood, but nothing could dim the sense of evil that pulsed from the thing. The awkward, hesitant movements were gone. St. George sat in one of the armchairs and rested the cane against the table beside it.

"Meet our host," St. George gestured with his glass at a third figure, in a white linen suit, who followed the others into the room. "Alfredo DaCosta."

DaCosta seemed taller, but maybe that was the company he was keeping these days. He had the chiseled features of a hawk, and Evan remembered the eyes: predator's eyes that missed nothing over a prominent nose narrowed in distaste. So the whole thing was a setup. Except the meeting in the bookstore. St. George expected the introduction to surprise Evan, and the Italian count seemed to want it that way.

Another, more recent memory ticked at him. The expression was different, but a quick look at the ceiling, found the man staring down at him from the center of the pentagram. Evan met the glance of the model for Hermes. The man said nothing, but sadness touched the hard eyes. Evan wondered how long it had been since Alfredo DaCosta had allowed the world to see the open wisdom in the painting, but he made only oblique reference.

"Did Lily find this room interesting?"

"Miss Ryan never had the pleasure," DaCosta answered softly, "Our acquaintance was very short, and the room is seldom used."

He retreated to the low chest against the wall where he sat hunched forward slightly, arms linked around his knees, his heels dug into the old wood of the chest. With a last measuring glance at Evan, he turned his brooding study to the toes of his hand-stitched shoes.

So Lily didn't know DaCosta's secret. That meant he wasn't one of theirs— Something else, then. He'd bet St. George was in the dark, wondered if Omage knew, but read only a lurking madness beneath the malevolent features of the daemon.

"What's going on, Evan?" Claudia's voice, sharpened with panic, drew his attention back to the problem at hand. She clutched the heavy bedcover tightly around her with both hands, and moved to the middle of the bed, as close to him as the shackle around her ankle would allow. With a quick, nervous glance at Omage, she entrusted modesty to the grip of one hand and reached out to him with the other.

"Tell the lady, Evan," Omage taunted from his place behind St. George's chair. "She deserves to know why her brother died."

"Dead?" Claudia looked at him, desperation in her eyes.

"He's lying. Tell me he's lying." She studied his face for a sign to hold onto, but he could give her nothing, didn't know what to say. "Oh, God, Evan, what have you done?"

He held his hands out to her, open, empty.

"I hate you!" She lunged for him across the bed and fell facedown, trapped by the shackle at her ankle, tearing at her hair and screaming into the overstuffed mattress.

"I tried to stop him." He knew it wasn't enough, had known it in the kitchen facing Pathet across a sea of ashes. He'd thought he could outrun the forces that had shaped him, and instead he'd brought disaster after him, right down on top of the only friends he'd ever had. She didn't seem to hear him, didn't notice when he covered her again with the heavy bedspread.

"God. God. God." Litany or mantra, the words fell softly into the mattress while one hand opened and closed spasmodically in her hair. She ground the knuckles of the other against her teeth, as if trying to hold back the choking sobs that punctuated the endless repetition.

"Let her go, St. George." Begging was easy with the sounds of shattered grief rising muffled from the bed. "She has nothing to do with this."

"Oh, Evan." St. George saluted him with the balloon glass. "How you have managed to survive this long with your naïveté intact is beyond me. Let her go? After all the trouble I took to bring her here?"

Evan knew better than to expect pity from Omage; the daemon was probably enjoying the whole thing. He turned instead to Alfredo DaCosta, perched solemnly on the wooden chest. An artist once had found something noble in that face, not kindness perhaps, but a strength of character for which Evan now searched in vain.

"I can't help you," the man explained. "I'm sort of a hostage here myself."

"I hadn't noticed." Evan stared pointedly at the shackle on his wrist, let his breath out in a long soft sigh, folding in on himself as he did. Senseless to argue with the thief. Whatever he was, DaCosta had made his decision to keep it well hidden. He could blow the man's cover easily enough. Even Charlie would make the connection if Evan pointed it out, but then what would he have? One more enemy, and he'd be no closer to escape than when he started. He slumped to the bed, rubbed his forehead in a vain attempt to placate the road crew blasting in his skull.

"Why?" he asked, looking for order in the chaos St. George had made of his life. "She's not like Paul Carter or me. She doesn't know anything about this."

St. George ignored the question while he sniffed at the brandy in his glass. "Delightful. Are you sure I can't offer—but we've already had this discussion.

"Of course she knows nothing, my dear boy." St. George returned to the question offhandedly over the brandy. "That is precisely her value. Against Omage, or even yourself, she's completely helpless. Fool that you are, that matters to you. So it's really quite simple. You can leave any time you want. I can't stop you, nor can my companions. Do your disappearing act, however, and she's dead before your feet hit ground again. Do what you're told and the lady lives."

"My father will find us."

St. George laughed. "I'm counting on it. He has something that belongs to me, stolen from this very house."

"The damned stone," Evan realized. "The Eye of Omage."

St. George tilted his head in confirmation. "Until he returns it, I can only control you through the girl. If Mr. Bradley cooperates, we can dispense with the young lady's services—let her go, if you will."

"Dead or alive?"

"That's entirely up to you, my boy."

From behind St. George, Omage gave a spurious sigh, followed by a deep chuckle. The daemon wandered to the window and looked out. "Give him what he wants," Omage's gaze shifted briefly in St. George's direction, returned to the scene outside the window, "and it's up to you whether she leaves through the street door or in a sack in the canal."

"Go to hell."

Mac chuckled again. "Now, son of Ariton, we both know hell's a fairy tale. You've been there, seen the beauty of it. You want it for yourself. Don't deny it, no one here will believe you." The daemon's smile told of secrets shared, of knowledge beyond the grasp of the merely human among them.

Tumblers clicked in Evan's head, pieces slotted into place. The drug-haze cleared, and suddenly, the headache didn't matter. "He doesn't know, does he?"

"Clever boy." Omage grinned. "A pretty game, and fitting, I think."

"It stopped being a game when the killing started." Evan turned to St. George. No, the name didn't fit: the softness, the timid awkwardness were gone. "Who are you?"

The man reached in his pocket for a pack of Camels, pinched off the filter, and tamped the load before putting it to his lips. He lit it with a monogrammed gold lighter. Inhaling deeply, he let the smoke curl out around a smile. "Franklin Simpson. Call me Frank, all my enemies do."

Another piece of the puzzle clicked into place. "Not real broken up about your brother-in-law, are you?"

Simpson frowned. "Oh, but I am, my boy. Think of the time and expense I've taken with Paul, and all for nothing. Still, we cut our losses and go on."

A setup from the start. Evan stared the man straight in the eyes, wouldn't give the bastard the satisfaction of even a moment's defeat. "I suppose the distraught sister will be joining us."

"Shortly," Simpson confirmed. "She hasn't the travel advantages of your sort."

"A pity." Evan winked out of real space, returned next to Simpson in the blink of an eye. Claudia lay on the bed with her face averted, exhausted in her grief, but the shackle that had bound Evan's wrist dangled empty from the bedpost. Evan gave his full attention to their captor.

"Well, Frank, I don't know what our friend has told you about the second sphere—his home—but there's nothing for humans there."

"Do make yourself comfortable." Simpson offered the pack of cigarettes, showing little surprise. Evan took one. He left the filter in place and accepted a light, staying between Franklin Simpson and the bed. He took a drag and let it out, the cigarette pinched between thumb and forefinger, cupped in the hollow of his palm.

"Nothing for me, you mean," Franklin Simpson continued. He smiled indulgently. "You want to keep it all for yourself. I can understand that, would do it myself if I could get my hands on it. But I can't, so I'm willing to cut a deal."

Claudia stirred on the bed behind him, and he turned to face her. She stared pointedly at the bracelet of raw flesh where the shackle had been. "Who did you sell out this time, Evan? God, how I hate you."

"At least let me free her leg," Evan bargained

Simpson shook his head. "Not yet. Later, perhaps, as a reward for good behavior."

Evan had no doubt whose behavior was in question. "I'm sorry," he repeated, at a loss to repair the damage he had done.

"Tell that to Jack." She pulled the bedcover more tightly around herself, drawing attention to her own nakedness while she stared accusingly at his shirt. He undid the buttons and slipped out of it, shifting the cigarette to free his arm; she took it without a thank you and glared at him while she worked her arms into the sleeves and pulled the shirt closed over her breasts.

"Did you tell any of the truth this week, Evan? You even lied about the damned cigarettes!"

"These?" Evan lifted the smoke, drew again and returned it to his side. "Some vices are harder to let go of than others." The ruddy end of the thing might be the only weapon he had in a fight. "And given the circumstances, I'm not real worried about cancer."

Simpson laughed at the exchange. "Imagine a lifetime of that, Evan," he taunted. "It's not too late. We can still sack her into the canal."

"Keep her out of this, Simpson." Evan jabbed the air with the cigarette. "If anything happens to her, you get nothing out of me. Nothing."

"Have it your way, my boy. Just trying to be helpful."

"I can do without your help. Let her go, then we'll talk."

"And have her miss the party? Patience, my boy. Soon the fun begins in earnest."

# Chapter 22

*And Hermes was called thrice great. As a king, he ruled with learning, as a philosopher he gave to the people writing and all manner of language, and as a priest he gave man the means to draw the influences of the heavens by means of words to the greater glory of his works, and described the influences of the decans and the zodiac.*

VENICE. GIVEN HIS CHOICE, BRAD PREFERRED HIS STUDY, BUT HE DID SOMETIMES wish that Evan had been born Venetian. The city breathed contradictions, felt old as no city its age should, felt wise like no city of merchants should. A city where old magic died slowly, like the old stone palaces, worn down by the fatalism of its people. A city of churches.

Badad wondered why of all places Lily had decided to transport via Basilica San Marco. She knew how he felt: churches of any kind made him nervous. They harbored mystics who stumbled upon recipes for piercing the spheres and drawing lords of the hosts of Princes into the material sphere against their will. He'd long ago decided that the only safe human was a secular humanist, the only safe public building a bank.

"Shall we go?" he asked. Lily nodded, and they made their way from a side chapel dedicated to a bejeweled Madonna, through the main basilica, and out into the square. The domes of San Marco glinted in the sunset, but Brad turned his back on the building with a frisson of foreboding.

"Ca' DaCosta, Alfredo's palazzo, is over there." Lily pointed to where the Grand Canal looped back on itself, out of sight behind the palaces and tenements that crowded the city. She linked one arm through his, cosmopolitan in black linen. Crossing the Piazza, her stiletto heels snapped gunshots on the paving stones; sharp red nails tilted the black-lacquered brim of a broad straw hat to protect her eyes from the lowering sun.

They passed an outdoor café—long impersonal rows of square tables with yellow-checked plastic tablecloths and folding metal chairs—and Lily grabbed his arm, pulling him over to sit down. "But first, we have to talk."

She gestured for a waiter, ordered a Campari and soda. Brad recognized the obdurate tilt of her chin. He ordered lemon juice in mineral water, and when the waiter had gone, he glared at her. "What are you doing?"

"Enjoying Piazza San Marco at sunset—" She smiled at the returning waiter and sipped her drink. "—Since I can't imagine why else we would be on this monster hunt."

"That should be obvious even to you, Lily." Brad moved his glass in small circles, leaving a trail of condensation on the plastic tablecloth. "Evan's missing. Azmod took him, and your friend Alfredo DaCosta is holding him, for Franklin Simpson or his own reasons, we don't know. We're here to get him back before they torture my son into punching a hole through the seven universes. That is why Ariton put us here. Remember?"

Lily set her glass down carefully and leaned forward, her elbow on the table, her chin resting on the back of her hand.

"I remember." She enunciated clearly, as if to a somewhat dimwitted child. "And if I'd known that keeping your bastard alive would bring me to this, I'd have killed him where he stood two years ago."

"You have to admit it's been interesting." The smile didn't work.

"The Chinese have a saying—"

He wasn't going to win this one. "I know."

She dismissed the argument with a flutter of blood-colored fingernails. "Think for a moment like Ariton, if you still remember how. Humans now command a lord of Azmod to force half-breeds into the second sphere where they invariably go mad, and for nothing, which, according to Evan, is what the second sphere holds for humans.

"Those humans have apparently taken prisoner your half-breed bastard, again, only now he has the training we gave him to do what he is told and stay sane while he does it. With that same training he can transport out of there any time he wants, but for reasons unknown he has not done so. And you want to rush to the rescue like the Canadian Mounties in an old movie, even though the boy can save himself if he wants, we would be free if they killed him trying, and we could kill him ourselves with the backlash if we have to fight Omage for him. And that's if Mac doesn't finish him off for spite."

"You're right," Brad agreed, "and it doesn't make sense. Evan is just a small part of the problem. I admit, I want to get him back alive."

He closed his eyes for a moment to steady himself, couldn't let Lily know how important that goal had become. When he opened them again, she was waiting. The daemon Lirion stared through him with a look that said she knew everything and cursed him for a fool.

"Maybe I have been playing human for too long," he defended himself. "I *like* the boy."

Lily returned the self-evident confidence with a wry smile. "When I think with the skin of this body, I do understand, cousin; like you, I could lose myself in this form, attach myself to places, and even your bastard monster. When I am Lily, he draws me. We share senses, human flesh and Ariton fire. But he's not Ariton, he will never understand what it means to be a lord of the second sphere and his ignorance may destroy all the known universes."

"Not just Evan," he reminded her, and sipped his mineral water with lemon, wishing irrelevantly that he'd asked for ice. Lily was right. He did attach himself too easily to the physical, to habits of flesh.

"There may be others, if not now, later. The death of my son won't stop DaCosta or Franklin Simpson, or whoever is behind this mess, from trying again. We have to find out *why* they torture the Evan Davises and Paul Carters of their world to drive them into the second sphere: what the half-humans can do that one of our own kind can't, and what their human masters stand to gain. Once we understand what they are doing and why, we'll take them down."

Lily looked at him thoughtfully for a moment, absently stirring her drink. "I suppose you've got a plan."

"The start of one. They've got Evan again, so they'll be moving their own plan ahead. We'll watch, listen, see what they do." Brad looked at the bill, drew three crisp Italian notes out of his pocket, and dropped them on the table. He held out his hand. "Shall we?"

Lily took his hand, rose smoothly like a well oiled spring. "A stakeout," she agreed while they walked along the square. "We'll have to change form. If Simpson really is St. George, he'll recognize us."

"Not human." Brad considered the problem. "We couldn't get close enough. Birds, though, might work. Who'd notice a couple of pigeons peering in their second-story window?" He poked a toe at a particularly stubborn bird pecking grit from between the paving stones of the square.

"Put a lot of thought into that one, did you?" She glared at him out of the corner of her eye, stopping to kick at a complacent pigeon that stood in her path. "Move it or die, chump.

"I won't do it. A falcon, maybe—beautiful, sleek, dangerous—" She threw back her head and grinned, showing sharp, white teeth. "—Falcons eat the damned pigeons. I could identify with that."

Brad looked at her, seeing beyond the human form to the companion of his exile, the brittle taste of her tension sharp on his tongue—innocent murderer, as he who understood death could never be. "Suits you," he agreed.

Lily sniffed, a last show of indignation. "We're a little exposed for an inconspicuous shift."

"Perhaps." Brad took her elbow, led her toward the many-porticoed building that faced the piazza. "But it's the perfect time to view the archaeological treasures of Venice."

"They don't have any," Lily objected. "And you picked a strange time to go tourist. Your bastard's in trouble, remember?"

Brad didn't answer, but as he stepped under the cover of the portico, his shape wavered and dissipated into mist. A moment later, Lily dissolved in a scattering of dust. The bright beads of her eyes, set in the sleek head of the falcon, shot lethal bolts at him. She took flight and he followed, banking north over the canal.

A Renaissance masterpiece in its own right, Ca' DaCosta turned a masked face to the canal. Arches of weathered Gothic filigree held aloft on shallow pilasters punctuated each of the three sets of two double windows on each of the three main stories. Crumbling stone balustrades underlined the window groupings to emphasize the mystic trinity. An attic turned its unadorned double windows on the canal and to each side. Most of the house lay shadowed by the growing darkness, but the attic windows were open, a soft light negotiating a compromise with the falling night.

Badad landed on the roof and settled on a windowsill that offered a view of the attic room beyond. Lirion made a pass at the lower stories before she followed, the ruff of feathers around her neck distended. Clearly, she hadn't expected to find anything in the attic but stacks of old furniture. Alfredo DaCosta was full of surprises.

The front window overlooked an elaborately carved bed. Badad saw a girl huddled at its center in a shirt he recognized as Evan's, her arms rigid bands wrapped tightly under her breasts. Evan stood with his back to the window, facing Charlie St. George—Franklin Simpson, according to Evan's ferret program. The night air carried a voice through the window, and the daemon cocked his head to listen.

"If anything happens to her, you get nothing out of me. Nothing."

Brad recognized Evan's voice, heard the strain in it, and Franklin Simpson's spurious concern:

"Have it your way, my boy. Just trying to be helpful."

"I can do without your help. Let her go, then we'll talk."

Evan again. Badad wondered for a moment who the girl was, guessed that Simpson, or DaCosta, knew they couldn't keep Evan against his will. A hostage to hold him, then; probably that girl Evan had gone to see in London. Didn't have to be—with the boy's capacity for guilt, a stranger would do just as well. Evan's captors didn't know that, though. Simpson was talking again.

"And have her miss the party? Patience, my boy. Soon the fun begins in earnest."

Brad saw the door open. Evan's back was to him, he couldn't see his son's face, but the tone of voice held no surprise, just a weary expectation. "Marnie Simpson. I can't say it's a pleasure."

A second figure followed the woman into the room. Tall, slim, with light brown hair falling straight to his shoulders, the newcomer's eyes sparked Azmod green, inhuman.

Evan identified him: "Pathet. I should have known you were the bitch-queen's lackey."

Marnie Simpson flashed a casually possessive look over her shoulder at the daemon lord behind her. "Come now, Evan. That's no way to talk about the father of my child."

A familiar voice followed with a gleeful chuckle. Omage moved out of Franklin Simpson's shadow. "Nothing like a father's love, right, Evan? Or, for that matter, a mother's."

# Chapter 23

*And Hermes, known as Mercury to the Romans, brought to man the knowledge of art and the mysteries of the planets and their movement among the stars. And Hermes told them that the sun was the center of the universe, to which the Earth turned its face in praise.*

"Paul Carter was your son?" Evan asked the question of Marnie Simpson, but his glance darted beyond her, caught the eye of the daemon, Pathet.

The daemon laughed. "Don't expect me to care, boy; I don't share in the insanity of Ariton. Alive, Paul Carter was a danger to my universe and yours. Dead, he's just slime to fertilize the ragweed."

Pathet slouched languidly into the easy chair across the table from Franklin Simpson. He lifted a glass and saluted Evan with it, an expression of amused annoyance playing across his features.

Indifference had murdered Paul, as ignorance had almost destroyed Evan. Bile crawled up his throat with the memory of a shotgun taped to the back of a chair, ready to blow Paul Carter's head off when the nightmare of his own existence grew too horrible to bear. He forced it back with a drag on the stub of cigarette in his hand.

Her walk all sharp angles, Marnie Simpson drew close enough to touch him. "Nice to see you again, Evan.

"Paul was a tool," she explained. "Like Pathet, or Mac here, or you. Yes, he was my son; unfortunately, Paul was also defective."

Evan held his muscles still against the shudder of revulsion that fought his control. Rage for the man he had never known, twisting alone in the same hell that had haunted Evan's dreams, boiled over. He wanted to destroy the woman who stood so cool and self-contained in front of him, wanted to send her careening through the second sphere and watch her body scream on the other side of that barrier, watch the silence and the darkness beyond imagining drive her mad as it had done to him, to Paul Carter.

The thin curtains tangled in the wind that twisted through the windows. It lifted his hair and pressed Marnie Simpson's blouse against the sharp angles of her body. He felt distant eyes intent on him then, darted a glance around the room. From his place behind Frank Simpson's chair, Omage licked his lips nervously. Calculated fear edged the daemon's hunger, and Evan clenched his teeth around the urge to strike at the woman in front of him, knowing the act would bring slow death at the hands of her creatures. Gradually the wind died down around them.

Evan took a deep breath, calmed the surging beat of his heart. Whatever she did to him, he owed it to Paul Carter to speak. "Why did you let it happen?" he asked, "Paul didn't have to spend his life torn to pieces by what he was. He didn't have to die. His father could have taught him control."

"Me?" The daemon shook his head slowly. "Not my style."

Marnie Simpson cast a quick glance at the father of her son, the doubt clear in her eyes. "You flatter me," she said.

She reached into her pocket and pulled out a pack of Virginia Slims, tapped out a cigarette. "A light?" The woman took the burning stub of Evan's cigarette, lit her own from the glowing ember at its tip, then dropped the butt, grinding it into the marble parquet.

"Thank you." Mocking.

She drew on the cigarette, let out the smoke again, taking a moment to collect her thoughts. "Think of Pathet as a rogue stallion, Paul a yearling with bad wind, and Mac, well you know Mac. I could only do so much with the material at hand."

Chains clinked on the bed behind him, broke the link with Marnie Simpson that held him transfixed in horror.

"Who is she? I don't understand any of this." Claudia stirred, her voice dazed as if she were trying to wake herself from a nightmare. "You're all insane."

"You're probably right," he agreed. "Mrs. Simpson," he gestured an introduction, "was a client. She said Mac had kidnapped her brother but would release him if a particular ransom were paid. According to her story, Mac left a note, instructing her to hire Brad and Lily to make the exchange, a jewel called the Eye of Omage, for Paul's life. Brad pulled me out of the Black Masque two years ago. We figured he could do it again for Paul Carter. Apparently, it was a lie from the beginning."

Claudia shifted, pulled Evan's shirt more tightly around herself, and addressed her plea to the other woman. "I'm sorry if something has happened to your son, I know how you feel. My brother is dead." She choked on the word brother. "But your fight is with Evan's father. Evan had nothing to do with it. He wasn't there, he can't possibly be responsible for what happened."

Good try, but Evan knew it wouldn't work on the woman who had given her own son to Omage as a plaything. Franklin Simpson knew it, too. From the depths of his armchair, the man chuckled.

"My dear, sweet Claudia. We did not invite Evan to join us for what he knows, child, but for what he is. As Evan's lover, you are here to persuade him to cooperate."

"I'm not—"

Simpson half-closed his eyes above a conspiratorial smile. "Don't confuse me with my dundering alter ego, sweet. Dinner last night was a wonderful performance for an audience of one. But we both know that every word, every glance for Charles St. George was an arrow pointed at Evan Davis' heart."

"Is he good?" Marnie Simpson stroked a speculative hand down Evan's arm, like checking the legs of a thoroughbred. "He should be, he's had a good teacher. Their kind understand about sex, don't they, Evan?" She tilted her head in salute to Pathet, who raised his glass in acknowledgment.

"That's none of your business," Claudia replied, more sharply than made sense if she really wanted to survive this mess. "You're wrong anyway. I don't mean anything to him. Just let me go."

"As soon as Evan gives us what we want, you'll be free," Marnie Simpson assured her.

Marnie Simpson's idea of freedom had more to do with feeding the fish than feeding the soul. Her hand ran up his arm, found the tension at the join between shoulder and neck. Evan tried to ignore the touch, but felt the adrenaline charge, fight or flight.

"I can't, you know that," he told her.

"You will." She took a drag on the cigarette, blew the smoke in his face.

"Evan!" Claudia pleaded. "Why are you doing this?"

"A lot of lives are at stake," he explained. "Yours, mine, whole worlds, maybe. I don't have a choice." He knew it wasn't enough, knew she wouldn't believe the truth, that all life, in all the spheres known and unknown, might depend on what they did in this room.

"I don't believe this is happening." She subsided into the folds of the velvet bedspread, let the shirt hang loosely while she dug the heels of both palms into her eyes. "I don't believe any of it."

He'd gotten her brother killed and Claudia kidnapped, and he wasn't sure he believed it himself. But they had one hope left—distract his captors into making a mistake, and take advantage of it when it happened—and he clung to it. In the meantime, maybe he could find out *why*. He picked the cigarette from between Marnie Simpson's fingers, took a long draw, held the smoke in his lungs while he reversed the cigarette between his thumb and forefinger. When she retrieved it, he let the smoke out in a slow, thin stream.

"I'd still like to know how you did it. We connected your husband to the Black Masque, but Paul's record was clean."

Marnie Simpson shrugged. "I'd been studying our friends for years. At first it was just part of the act. My mother contacted the spirits through the pure spirit of a child clairvoyant. I played the kid until I was sick of it, then I met Frank. I was fifteen and he was about thirty, and we set up a scam of our own. By then, I realized that some of the spells I'd been reading might really work."

"The grimoires all agreed," Frank Simpson added "that if you could control the right ones, daemons could make a man richer and more powerful than any mortal. They hinted at immortality itself. Rich was relatively simple. The spell worked, and my future wife bound a water daemon who killed St. George, along with his father, in a storm at sea. We picked the St. Georges because Charlie had been out of the country for years, and we shared similar builds; with Rachiar's unwilling assistance, I stepped into poor, ineffectual Charlie's identity. And his wealth in Philadelphia. Since Charlie had lived out of the country for years before the accident, no one considered my own long absences out of the ordinary. We used some of the St. George fortune to seed the business ventures of Frank Simpson, rising entrepreneur, elsewhere."

"So much for money." Evan looked around them: marble walls, marble floors, and Alfredo DaCosta as Hermes at the right hand of Isis on the ceiling. He focused on the man himself, bent over his knees on the wooden chest pushed up against the wall. Above DaCosta, the same face carried the heavy headdress of Thot, passing judgment on the murderous brother Seth, the Cain and Abel of the gods. Medea seemed more appropriate at the moment, but that didn't explain DaCosta. "What is his part in this little charade?"

The man looked up at him, a veneer of pained innocence covering bitter humor and something else that scared Evan to his socks. He looked again at the Judgment of Thot, saw open there the hidden message in Da-Costa's eyes. "I'm just an innocent bystander," the man explained.

Evan shook his head, rejecting the answer. "There are no innocent bystanders."

DaCosta accepted the correction. "Perhaps not so innocent. I stole the wrong Picasso, it seems, and landed in the middle of a quarrel about which I know nothing."

That was a lie, but Evan let it stand with just a glance at the painting over the man's head. He deliberately looked around him again, hoping his acting was up to the bored indifference he tried to convey to his captors.

"And this is your idea of power. Hiding in an attic—elegant," he apologized with exaggerated diplomacy in an aside to DaCosta, "—but still an attic, with two daemons who will fry your bones to cinders if you give them half a chance. Does intimidating a thief and a shop clerk really give you that much of a thrill?"

Claudia's voice cut in, wary but stronger. "Easy on the shop clerk, chum. I'm an anthropologist, temporarily out of work."

Her own warning, then, not to underestimate her. Maybe she had believed there were lives at stake, after all. Marnie Simpson ignored the interruption, but her husband snorted his contempt.

"Power over the spheres, Evan," he corrected, "over the wealth out there, where they come from and you visit, and the secret of their immortality. But you're right, we made a slight error in judgment with Rachiar."

"You made the mistake," Marnie Simpson corrected him with asperity. "The damned thing almost killed us."

"But he didn't," Frank pointed out. "We needed a better plan, something more controllable over the long haul."

"Pathet was my idea, one of my better ones, I think." She summoned the daemon with a gesture, and he came to her, held her shoulders between his hands. Twisting slightly at the waist, she patted the daemon on the cheek, turned the proprietary gesture into a caress.

Frank watched them with avid attention. "We needed a hybrid, sharing the powers of daemons but controllable as a human."

"I decided to create one," Marnie Simpson explained. "I was still fifteen—"

"And beautiful." Franklin Simpson closed his eyes, a connoisseur's smile lighting his face. "The fragility of youth in carnal communion with the powers of Darkness. Magnificent." He hunched in his chair, quivering, a flush rising to meet slowly raised eyelids. He reached out, and Evan thought the man would go to his wife, reclaim her, but he let the hand fall again. The smile turned to ice.

Pathet covered the woman's hand where it rested on his cheek, pulled it free. Her fingers bent, clawed bloody streaks into his face in parting, and hung in his grasp between them, dripping blood.

"Someday," the daemon said, "you're going to make a mistake, and I will kill you." He smiled as he said the words, turning them into a lover's promise.

"Haven't yet," she pointed out, but she let his hand fall to his side.

Evan stared at the bloody streaks for a moment, caught in the memory of blood on his father's arm. Deadly hatred had twisted Badad's face, and betrayal had shadowed his father's eyes when he bound the daemon to his will. He wondered where Brad was now, if Lily was with him, but he resisted the urge to summon them with the binding spell. He wasn't like Marnie Simpson, didn't ever again want to see his father look at him with the hatred Pathet reserved for the woman who controlled him. More important to Evan, he knew that human life was short, but the memory of daemons went with them into eternity, an immortality of its own. He wanted the memory of his life to be one of honor, if nothing else.

Marnie Simpson ignored the daemon seething at her back. "My mother was out of jail by then, and she persuaded the doctor to falsify the birth records for a slight increase in his regular fee. We were rich by then, you see. And there would have been a scandal. I was underage, and I certainly didn't want Frank to go to jail for a crime he hadn't committed." With one bloody fingertip, she slowly traced the skin stretched over Evan's breastbone.

"Nice." She leaned forward, licked the sweat from the hollow of his throat. Evan's stomach muscles fluttered with involuntary tension as her hand followed the fine line of hair to his navel.

"Mother died soon after Paul was born."

"Accidental death, no doubt," Evan volunteered. No accident at all, he was sure.

"Unfortunate, of course. Frank and I married. We spent years training the boy."

The knowledge that Paul's tormenters had inflicted that suicidal madness deliberately, for some purpose of their own, turned Evan's stomach, but he still didn't understand.

"Why? What was he supposed to do?"

Pathet answered, sardonic pleasure hiding behind the words. They shared a secret, these lords and Evan. The fleeting twist of Pathet's smile said that he knew the half-breed would enjoy the joke.

"They were training the boy to invade the second sphere, to rule there as a proxy king. Little Paul would take their orders from here and put them into action in the second sphere. For his mother, he would strip the wealth out of the purview of the Princes, bringing the lord of the hosts under the sway of his human puppet masters. There he would learn the secret of eternal life."

"That's insane." Memory of that other place, the emptiness that no half-human could long survive, settled in a ball in Evan's churning stomach.

"The forces that move humans often seem so," Pathet agreed. "You, for example, had them worried."

"Me?"

Pathet nodded, pure malice in his grin that told Evan there was nothing personal in it; he was just passing along the misery.

"From the days before you were born, when the daemon part of you first traveled alone into the second sphere, your presence was noted, the special taste of your passage recorded in the memories of Princes. I passed along the information. Paul wasn't the only monster in the universe; they had competition."

"My brother was right about you." Claudia's voice accused him, but Evan looked into her eyes and found a shaky understanding there. Not happy about it, but after years of denial, she was finally convinced. And he found something else in her wary expression: contempt for their captors. Underestimating her might be the mistake they needed; Evan answered the voice, not the eyes.

"If you mean that my father's not human, yeah, he was right. Don't expect any miracles, though. Mostly it just drives us crazy."

"Not miracles, perhaps," Marnie Simpson agreed. "But you have your uses, and your dangers. We had to find you. Mac was bait— Not the only one, but the one you found. Frank wanted you dead, but I persuaded him to keep you in reserve, in case we weren't successful with Paul. I was right, and that's why we are here."

"I'm not a bad person." Marnie Simpson held up her cigarette, stared at the burning tip before taking a slow drag. "I've kept you alive, after all, when Frank would have killed you out of hand. But you have to understand: your father murdered my son. I'm entitled to compensation. 'An eye for an eye,' you know. A son for a son."

"My father didn't kill Paul, and he won't let you kill me."

Evan hoped he sounded more sure of that than the last few days had left him. He remembered the newspaper article about the Black Masque. Fifty dead, including Paul Carter. Would his own death mean more than a ripple in the eternity his father inhabited?

Movement distracted Evan from the contemplation of his own imminent mortality. Alfredo DaCosta unfolded himself from his perch under the fresco of Thot. "If you don't mind, I'd rather not hear all of this. I'll be downstairs if you need anything."

All eyes turned to the stately thief, but Franklin Simpson spoke first. "No one leaves this room."

"Be reasonable. I'm hardly likely to go to the local police, now am I?" DaCosta countered with a gesture that took in their surroundings. "I didn't pick up my collection at Christy's; some of these works have been missing since the Nazis passed through Paris. I value them almost as much as I value my own freedom, and I have no intention of sacrificing either to a sudden attack of conscience. The less I know, however, the easier it will be to set that seldom-used organ to rest."

Simpson flicked a quick glance over the man. "Don't trust him."

"What could I tell the authorities?" DaCosta argued. "That Americans with daemon accomplices are planning to take over the universe from my attic? They are hardly likely to bring out the antiterrorist squads for that, are they? The mental institutions in this country are worse than the jails. Silence is my only option."

"Go." Marnie Simpson dismissed him, and answered her husband's objection. "You were wrong to let him hear this much."

DaCosta dipped his head in an abrupt sketch of a bow and left the room.

"Follow him." She touched Pathet on the shoulder, gestured at the door. "And kill him discreetly. We don't want any attention yet. Come back when you're done with him."

"Yes, master." The daemon bent low in a mocking travesty of DaCosta's bow.

Secrets again. Evan thought about the frescoes overhead, wondered what Pathet knew.

"I don't want to kill you, Evan." Marnie Simpson hooked an elbow around his arm, led Evan back to the bed. "I'd much rather make you a king, if only a puppet one, as Pathet so eloquently put it. But I hope you're right about your father, because he has something I need."

"The Eye of Omage," Evan supplied.

"Clever boy," Marnie Simpson approved. "The jewel works like a homing device, and your agency was more helpful than I could have hoped in tuning it. It's simple, really. I control Mac, Mac controls the jewel, and the jewel controls you. You will go where you are sent, or you will die, rather horribly, I'm afraid.

"Of course, only a fool would depend on the affection of your father's kind. You will tell us his true name, or your lady friend will die."

She pushed him down, leaned over him like a carrion bird, grinning over the bright ember of the cigarette she held in her hand.

"His name is Kevin Bradley, that's all I know," Evan objected.

Marnie Simpson laughed. "Don't treat me like a fool, boy. I haven't much patience. You'll tell me what I want to know, and you'll do what you're told." She snapped the shackle back on his wrist.

"I know you can escape this as easily as think it." She sat next to Evan on the bed and slipped the tip of her index finger between the shackle and his wrist, scratching the abrasion.

"I'll even let it go this time, because your little Houdini number told me everything I needed to know about you. But if you try it again, I'll give your girlfriend to our old friend Mac."

She turned her head, addressed the daemon seething in the corner. "You'd like that, wouldn't you?"

The daemon snarled. His eyes fixed on Claudia, a cat watching a mouse just out of reach, waiting for the wrong move that would make the girl his.

"I thought you would." Marnie Simpson turned her attention back to Evan; he shuddered as her fingertips drifted lazily over the line of his shoulder, the curve of his biceps. "Well, Evan? We know our Mac's . . . esoteric tastes, don't we, boy? I can't force you, but I think our interests run in the same direction."

"I can't tell you anything."

"You can, and you will."

Staring into the lit end of her cigarette, Marnie Simpson smiled. "Hold the girl," she ordered, "If Evan tries anything, kill her. Take your time about it, of course."

Everything she planned for him was in that smile, focused on the burning tip of the cigarette. Evan tried to separate himself from the pain he knew would follow, but instead grew hyper-aware of every sensation. Sweat bloomed in pinpricks, trickled hot trails down his temples, his armpits. With his arm chained above his head she would see the sweat beading in the hair under his arms. Illogically, the realization embarrassed him, and he tried to bring his arm down. The shackle cut into his wrist but did not let him move.

His jeans clung, too hot, too tight, around his thighs. *Don't think, don't think*—superstition crawled between his legs. She would know if he thought it. She wouldn't think of it if he kept his fear above the waist. The sheet, limp with sweat, itched at his back.

"The name, Evan."

# Chapter 24

*Trismegistus teaches that man once passed immortal through the spheres as rational mind, and seeking understanding, found in Nature great beauty, and flew to her breast, the mountains of the Earth, and mated with her and became flesh, joined in two natures, the mind and the body, mortal and immortal alone of all the spirits.*

ALFREDO DACOSTA CROUCHED OUT OF SIGHT OF THE OPEN WINDOWS. "WE HAVE to talk."

Badad cast a baleful eye on the man. Humans seldom roamed their rooftops chatting with falcons uncharacteristically roosting in their rain gutters. But Alfredo DaCosta had secrets even Lily had not discovered—the attic room was a case in point.

The man stroked a finger down Lirion's breast. She snagged the offending digit in a beak designed for tearing flesh, but did not break the skin.

"Beautiful in any form," he asserted with a smile just for her, then grew more serious. "But you stole something from me, a smoky topaz about the size of a fist, and I really must have it back."

He teased his finger away from her. "They're going to torture your son until he gives you up to them," he said to Brad. "They need the jewel to control him, and I can't let that happen—you are not the only guardians of the spheres.

"There's a café on the square. We can talk first, or I can go back inside and do what I was sent to do."

The man stood silently and picked his way around the attic projection overlooking the canal. When Badad rose into the air to follow, Alfredo DaCosta had disappeared, but the flickering candles on the tables of the café set his course. He spiraled lower, swooped under the columned portico of an unassuming church, and adjusted the cuffs of his shirt beneath his jacket. Lily followed a moment later, her hair a splash of the second sphere against the white gauze of her dress. Arms linked, they wandered among the scattered tables until they found DaCosta with his back to the rough stone wall, the fragile barricade of a cordial glass in front of him.

He stood when he saw them, held out a chair for Lily. "More beautiful than a night in Venice," he declared, "though once this city would have been a worthy rival." He smiled reminiscently at her, and Brad wondered at the affection he saw there, for the city, for Lily, and for something Brad thought he understood. Not human, then, but fond of the creatures as Brad was fond of Evan.

Lily was answering, her own smile warm with memories of Alfredo DaCosta and Venice that Brad did not share. "It still is."

"Not like it was," DaCosta insisted. "Even the stones are dying. The sea takes back its own, always."

A waiter appeared unobtrusively at DaCosta's side, with a smile and a bow for Lily.

"Three of the usual, Gianni."

Brad waited until the waiter moved away from the table, then commented, "You've been here a long time, then." He posed the statement as a question that brought another smile to DaCosta's lips.

"Since the beginning," he agreed.

"The founding of the city?" Brad asked.

Alfredo DaCosta laughed. "Of creation," he corrected. "It was a mistake." He gestured gracefully with a hand that seemed to embrace not only their small table, but land and sea and sky and more.

The waiter returned, set their drinks in front of them. When he had gone, DaCosta continued his explanation.

"Unlike the Princes, my own people suffer an inordinate curiosity about our neighbors. Like yourselves, however, we had no access to the other spheres, until in his enthusiasm, one of our searchers—humans would call them scientists—literally blew a hole between our two universes."

Alfredo DaCosta held up both hands. He spread the fingers of his right: "From what we have since learned, the searchers believe that the second sphere must consist of what, in material terms, would be considered space, but without time. You are immortal because time has no meaning in the second sphere."

He spread the fingers of his left. "We can call the third sphere the temporal sphere, since that is the aspect that concerns us most here. Time is our medium, we move in it much as fish move in the seas of Earth. Like the Princes, we are immortal according to human reckoning, though the term has no real meaning for us.

"Unfortunately, the two spheres proved incompatible. The material universe came into existence when they touched, when space and time converged." He demonstrated, intertwining his fingers. "Humans call the space-time where they met the 'big bang.'"

The moment remained vivid in Badad's memory, a marker in the eternity of home. More of the pieces fell into place. He mirrored DaCosta's earlier gesture, encompassing not only the city, but the universe that held it. "And all of this acts like a patch on a leaky boat."

"So to speak," DaCosta agreed. "The material sphere represents both barrier and access between your home and mine."

"Evan was wondering if there was a God." Lily lifted her glass in salute to DaCosta. "Now we know."

Brad added his own salute to Lily's with a sardonic tilt to the eyebrow. "I don't think he'll be pleased to find you've been sleeping with the Divinity, cousin."

"Not God, please," DaCosta corrected. "I've gone that route a time or two already."

The count lifted his glass, stared into the gold liqueur backlit by the flicker of the candle at the center of the table. Half-hidden behind the licorice-scented barricade, something implacable crossed his face, left behind only the bland insouciance of the Italian aristocrat. Brad saw judgment in that fleeting look. Not omnipotent, perhaps, but for his son, the distinction could prove moot.

Back from the place where he once walked as god, Alfredo offered a twisted smile. "Divinity is highly overrated. Too high-profile, makes it damned hard to get a date. I didn't create this universe anyway; I just watch it. A guardian angel, if you will. At most an Archangel."

"And the angel Alfredo appeared before them—do you have any parlor tricks up your sleeve?" Lily teased. A warning look told Brad she hadn't missed that fleeting glimpse behind the facade, but for now she would not see.

"A few," DaCosta admitted. "When this is all over, we can compare notes." He grew more pensive, suddenly. "I sometimes wonder, though—"

"What?" Brad asked, knowing the answer already. The same question bothered him.

"If we created the material universe, perhaps someone, something, created us as well."

"I wonder what their watchdogs think of what we're doing here today." Brad sympathized with the guardian. His own time on Earth was bounded by the life span of his human offspring. What would it be like to watch eternity tick by in the measure of the sea reclaiming the land?

"I hope they find their task more interesting than our own." DaCosta seemed firmly in control again. "Of our guardians, most travel through large expanses of this universe, maintaining a sporadic check for flaws in space-time through which the spheres might randomly touch. A very few of us keep watch over intelligent life wherever it arises.

"Until recently, the system was pretty self-regulating, dead boring when it wasn't disgusting. A handful of the persistent and unlucky would manage to bring lords of the hosts of Princes through—that's how we found out about you. Few of the human summoners lived to tell about it." Lily's eyes slitted, and DaCosta faltered, rested a hand over hers on the table. "Some crossbreeding happened from the start. Not often; your kind and theirs aren't all that compatible, and humans are obsessed with sex, not with procreation. Those rare exceptions were enough to keep me on my toes, even though they never lived long enough to cause much trouble. Most societies murdered any hybrid in childhood, as a monster, as soon as the child started behaving strangely—screaming, nightmaring, the sort of things Evan used to do. The locals didn't know what they were killing, you understand, just that it wasn't like them. Once in a while a hybrid would survive into adulthood as a social pariah, an outcast and completely mad by then. The hazards of the life usually finished the job their societies began."

"It's odd, really." DaCosta contemplated his drink. "Things have been slow for a couple hundred years. I might have been growing complacent— forgot the most important thing about this species, its talent for believing two or more mutually exclusive contradictions simultaneously, and for denying the evidence of its senses when they conflict with those beliefs. Once again, the mortals of this place began to fling daemons at their enemies."

Badad little needed the reminder. The face of a laughing woman rode the crest of a memory: Evan's mother. Flung at her indeed, a jealous suitor bringing ruin on a woman of no accomplishments and few aspirations. He'd known little of humans then; the touch of flesh, his own form, revolted him. With time and choice he'd grown accustomed to the latter. The memory of Evan, beating himself to death against the second sphere in a room with no windows still fueled his aversion to human touch. Never again. He renewed the vow he had made then: never again.

"Twice now in this age your kind have created hybrids," DaCosta continued, "who behaved as hybrids always have. Paul Carter was a failed experiment, with predictable results; he survived until he was old enough to remove himself from the horrors of his own mortal existence. In that, we've been lucky so far—they've always managed to kill themselves, or be killed, before they had the chance to procreate. Unfortunately, our friends the Simpsons are more cold-blooded about the whole thing than most. With Paul Carter gone, they've turned again to Evan Davis."

There had been nothing cold-blooded about the rage that had dragged Badad out of the second sphere, that had ruined a woman's life—except that Evan said he hadn't ruined it—that had blinded the man to the dangerous game he played when he antagonized a lord of the host of Ariton. Nothing at all like the chill purpose he heard in Marnie Simpson's voice. "But why?" he asked. "What do they hope to gain?"

"I'm afraid Pathet has been leading them a merry chase with promises of power and immortality," DaCosta said. "And Omage enjoys the joke too much to burst their bubble."

"Power over what?" Lily interrupted. "According to Evan, the second sphere holds nothing for humans."

Brad coughed a short laugh. "He means that literally. Evan says that the second sphere is empty to human senses; that's why the children go mad there."

"Interesting," DaCosta agreed. "The Simpsons seem convinced that the second sphere is like Earth, but richer and without defenses. Streets paved with gold, the whole Eldorado-New World bit straight out of the fifteenth century speculative travelogues. They came up with the notion on their own, but Pathet keeps the fiction going with casual references to wealthy merchants and a population of sheep."

"I've always found the Princes a bit more temperamental than that," Lily objected with a wry smile. "They won't like what Pathet has done at all."

DaCosta returned the smile. "I can't say; never met a Prince, just the occasional, and most unsheeplike, emissary. I can tell you this," the guardian leaned over the table, "immortality is out of the question, even for the hybrids. Time is as much a part of them as space is. When both converge, the clock starts ticking. Sooner or later, it stops. Try to separate them again, and you've got ground meat on your hands. Ground meat that rots, and not even the Simpsons can stop it."

DaCosta paused for reflection. "In spite of their efforts, just as likely because of them, Paul Carter's clock stopped sooner, the way mature hybrids always have, insane, of suicide. And that should have ended the crisis.

"You, however, have complicated things quite a bit." DaCosta stared across his drink at Brad, the guardian's grim frustration meeting the daemon's implacable will. *Don't push it.* Brad's grim countenance shouted the unspoken words. Understanding flared in DaCosta's eyes; the guardian said the words anyway:

"Evan Davis should be dead as well, or harmlessly mad in a padded cell, disturbing the business of Princes but leaving the rest of the seven universes in peace. Never in the history of the material universe has a daemon sire wasted on its progeny more than the energy it took to destroy the misbegotten creature. I don't know why you decided to intervene—"

Nor could Brad explain the pull his son had exerted on him. If the boy had begged, he would have died. The wild challenge, not for release, but for proof that his father was no saner than the creature who enslaved him, sang Ariton in the place where human cell mingled with daemon essence in the body the daemon wore. Evan lived because Evan was Ariton, not because Brad grew too human.

"—but you truly have created a monster in this man. With the training you have given him, your son is the wedge that can destroy us all."

Brad stood, turned his back on the man at the table. Ca' DaCosta pulled at him, a visceral need to be in that other place and stand between his son and the forces of three universes massed against him, but Lily answered the man with her own challenge. Brad hesitated, waiting for the answer.

"How?" she asked defensively. Brad knew she'd never understood why he'd let the boy live. But they were Ariton; host loyalty demanded a unified front. "Untrained and in Mac's hands, Evan was wreaking havoc with both our universes. With a little training, he's learned how to control his passage through the second sphere without raising a whisper."

"That's the problem." Alfredo DaCosta intertwined his fingers again, an echo of his earlier gesture. "Humans share equally in both our universes. Only the hybrids, with the balance tilted toward the second sphere, can move in that direction. We feel certain the hybrids have the potential to pass through the second sphere and breach the barrier to our own universe, with catastrophic results. Until now none has survived the second sphere with enough mind left to direct him farther. Evan is stronger than I imagined; I suspect he's more powerful than he knows."

"He is," Lily interrupted with a warning. "But he denies it. Won't transfer through the spheres unless he has to, and he's stirred up a few things, sparks, winds, that he attributes to me, or to coincidence. Nothing he can control yet, and he won't learn while he's pretending it doesn't happen, but he'll be harder to kill than you think. Push him to the wall and he'll call on the part of himself he hides from without realizing that he's done it."

"I thought as much," DaCosta confirmed. "If he chooses to fight in the material sphere, you may be the only two creatures in the universe who can stop him."

Brad dismissed the prediction with an impatient gesture. "Evan's not

the explorer type. He hates the second sphere, wouldn't go looking for
more universes if his life depended on it."

"If Marnie Simpson gets her hand on the Eye of Omage, he won't
have a choice."

"Why?" Brad sat down again, fighting the feeling that told him to
find Evan now. He needed information, and DaCosta seemed to have it.
The jewel in particular had troubled him since Lily lifted it from the man
who watched him from across the table. "It's more than just a polished
stone, but what? And what were you doing with it?"

DaCosta closed his eyes for a moment, opened them slowly on a sigh.
The cloying perfume of the anisette hung over the table. "You haven't
touched your drink," he noted, and took a sip of his own.

Brad ignored the glass in front of him, waiting.

"I can't tell you what it is—the knowledge is too dangerous. Somehow,
Omage found out about it, and with his usual hubris he called it the Eye
of Omage. I stole the jewel to keep Azmod from using it and covered my
tracks with a few emeralds and the Picasso—so far I've convinced them
I'm a harmless thief with an unfortunate attraction to gaudy jewelry. They
must have realized that Paul Carter was a lost cause, too insanely suicidal
for their plans. Evan had survived, but they needed both the boy and the
jewel to successfully put their plan into action.

"The solution was simple. As Charles St. George, Franklin Simpson
hired your agency to retrieve the stolen painting. Mac would have known
Lily couldn't resist the gem. It calls to your kind, especially if you've
been too close to Evan. I expect Evan did the rest. The Eye, as Mac
called it, would have drawn him like a magnet draws iron shavings. It
draws Omage as well. You led them to Venice, Lily. They threatened to
go to the police about my collection unless I gave them the use of my
chamber.

"The rest you must have discovered on your own, or you wouldn't be
here. With the girl as leverage, Evan will give them your names. They need
bind you only long enough to get the jewel back. For the safety of all our
universes, you will have to destroy it first."

Brad contemplated the thick, sweet-smelling liquid in his glass. "The
Simpsons won't like that. They've made a major investment in this project—Mac, Pathet, all of this—" He flicked a glance across the piazza, at
the brooding shadow of Ca' DaCosta." They aren't likely to let Evan or
his young lady go free after they have seen and heard so much."

His cousin surprised him with a possessive glare at the reference to
the Laurence woman. "If Evan is connected to this jewel as you say, its

destruction could kill him anyway," she guessed, then added, "I don't like it when my toys are broken."

"You are talking about a choice between the life of your monster or the continued existence of three universes." DaCosta drained his glass and set it down. "And the boy will die anyway in the destruction he causes."

Brad stared at the man in front of him, sick at the images he conjured. "What do you expect me to do?"

DaCosta sighed. "Give me the Eye of Omage. As for the rest, if you'd asked me two years ago, the answer would have been simple. Kill him, or let him die on his own. The spheres never mix well, and he was no exception, half mad at the best of times, pushed over the edge entirely by Mac's tender attention.

"You've got a weak spot I never thought I'd see in one of your kind. That doesn't change things, it only complicates them. Evan has to die; his life isn't worth the risk he poses even without the jewel. You can do it, make it as easy for him as you can, or you can go back to Philadelphia, read a good book, and I'll take care of it for you. I won't leave it to Marnie Simpson, I promise you that. Your job will be done, you can go back into the darkness until the next one."

Brad stared at the man, conscious of the binding that made the man's suggestion impossible, and of the thought that made it more so. Lily spoke the words ahead of him, and he smiled in spite of himself, to know what truth she finally accepted.

"Evan's too much fun to play with to give up so easily," she began, then added, "he's also Ariton. Host loyalty dictates we must protect him."

"He's also human," DaCosta countered. "A monster. If we don't destroy him now, he will bring down three universes, maybe more. And he won't stop to consider what his actions do to Ariton, because Marnie Simpson won't give him that luxury."

Brad agreed with that. "So we kill the damned Simpsons, destroy the stone, and send the lords of Azmod back where they belong."

"You think it will be that easy?" DaCosta asked.

"Easier than killing my son," Brad countered. "Much easier, since he's bound us to his will."

DaCosta stared at him blankly. "And you still defend him?"

Brad shrugged. "It isn't like the Simpsons, or any other binding. I thought it was, at first, but the feel of it is different."

"And how is that?"

Lily answered, her own bemused smile supporting her cousin. "Part of something," she realized aloud. "Like being part of Ariton."

"Not always pleasantly," Brad added. He didn't feel the pain, just Evan's shock, a gasp for breath that started at gut level and fought against a throat closed tight around a scream. He was on his feet and running before the words left his mouth: "It's begun."

# Chapter 25

*Hermes Trismegistus teaches that in Egypt at one time man grew weary of the great glory of the All, that which he encompassed in his person and his memory of the heavens, and made idols of clay and drew into them the spirits of the air, daemons commanded by the words that the Thrice Great had given them.*

HOLDING THE CIGARETTE LIKE A SCALPEL, MARNIE SIMPSON TRACED A LINE FROM the throat to the base of Evan's sternum and crossed it over his heart. The pain that followed snapped the tension, replaced it with something infinitely worse. Evan heard a scream that seemed to come from somewhere above him. *The frescoes,* he thought, *the frescoes are screaming.* Only when he stopped, his throat too raw to shape the sound, did he realize the scream was his own. Caught between the urge to tear his own burned flesh from his body and the pain that seared his nerve endings with the slightest touch, he curled away from the heat, gasping.

Slowly he recognized the sobbing next to him. Claudia, held frozen with Omage's knife resting lightly above her breast. Jack Laurence was dead and his sister soon would be. Too late for both of them now, he knew, but he had to try.

"Let her go," he begged, his voice somewhere between a gasp and a cry.

"You know I can't do that." Chill humor laced the words. They both knew better: Marnie Simpson would never let Claudia go. Until she held the Eye of Omage, only Claudia kept Evan here. If he betrayed his father, gave Marnie Simpson the jewel, Claudia would die. She'd seen too much, heard too much to walk out of this room, alive—*his fault, his fault.* His touch was a sickness as deadly as the woman's above him, no less so because he wanted it to be different.

Evan stalled for time, willing himself to believe. Brad would come for him, pull them out of there like Rambo Meets King Kong. In the meantime, he had to keep Marnie Simpson's mind off Claudia.

"I don't know anything," he pleaded.

"You're lying."

Marnie Simpson's voice, seductive, barely a whisper in his ear, warned him. He braced himself for the pain that squeezed the air from his chest. The glowing coal at the cigarette's tip found the pulse point at his throat and traced the vein with slow deliberation. Her tongue followed, licking delicately at the burn, a gesture that his clouded mind read as comfort even though it gave no relief from the pain.

"Tell me what I want to know, my sweet," she whispered. "Give me the Eye of Omage and I'll set the woman free. We can rule the universe together."

"Rule what?" he gasped, too confused by the pain to say anything but the truth, "There's nothing out there but the dark."

"Lies." The cigarette followed, burn trailing burn, as delicate as the work of a surgeon.

The muscles in Evan's back locked, arched above the bed. He screamed again, surprised that he could make the sound, and then the universe centered on the slow tracery of the ember. All sense of time, place, even his body, went away. He was in Omage's back room again and he was going to die fighting the terror and the pain and the voices in his head, this time promising relief if he would just say the name.

"DaCosta's gone." Pathet stood framed in the doorway beneath the fresco of the twelve virtues and the twelve temptations. "He's not in the house," the daemon reported.

The cigarette lifted, still close enough that Evan felt the heat, far enough not to carve another burn into his skin. He fell back on the pillow, grateful for the distraction, and dragged air into his lungs. Silver trails wept fire across his chest, his abdomen, his neck, and arms. So far she'd stayed clear of his face and his groin—*don't think, don't think; she'll hear*—he willed his imagination under control, but the pain still cut short each breath.

Claudia sobbed beside him, held fast by the shackle on her leg and the knife in Omage's hand. Evan stretched his own hand toward her, and she took it, held on tight. She was crying for him, he realized, and took comfort from her warm grasp. Help would come, Brad would find him if he just held out long enough—he tried to communicate his hope through their clasped hands.

"That's impossible." Franklin Simpson slouched open-legged in his chair, drinking in the wounds on Evan's chest. Sweat stood out at his temples and above his upper lip. He ran his tongue over his lips and took a deep breath, countering the daemon's information without taking his eyes from the figure on the bed. "The doors are sealed to humans; he must be in the house somewhere."

Marnie Simpson nodded agreement. "Forget DaCosta for now. He's here somewhere. We can take care of him when we leave."

She examined her handiwork with a thoughtful pout. "Not exactly stoical, are you, boy?" A fingernail caked with the blood of her daemon lover traced the line of a burn, asked another rhetorical question and underscored it with light pressure on a weeping scab. "Have you been telling the truth all along?"

Evan gasped, his eyes locked with hers, the vow he'd made to Lily burning in his mind. *Family.* He would not surrender Ariton to the torment that had driven Omage mad, to the woman who had caused the death of her own son.

A fingernail found pain, traced it. "It makes sense. Your father would be a fool to reveal his true identity."

"The lord who calls himself Kevin Bradley is a fool." Pathet joined Marnie Simpson at the bed, leaned over to murmur intimately in her ear. "But even he would not trust his human offspring. Others of his kind, however, know things."

The daemon slid a hand beneath her blouse and squeezed her breast, but only Evan could see his expression. Laughter and hatred mingled on his face, and triumph. "Kevin Bradley is yours, for a bargain."

"I can command you to tell me," Marnie Simpson looked into the green eyes of Azmod; Evan saw a test of wills there. "I don't make bargains."

"You can command," Pathet agreed. "But there is information, and then there is useful information. It will take longer than you've got to obtain the latter by command, but I think we can arrange a simple trade—two for the price of one, shall we say?"

"You'll give me Lily Ryan as well?"

Pathet nodded.

"In exchange for?"

"My freedom, of course."

"And mine." Forgotten in the exchange, Omage leaned over the girl on the bed, his knife drawing blood in his eagerness, "I can give them to you. Free me and keep your sex toy."

"I still need you, Mac. Your time will come."

The daemon subsided, snarling, and Marnie Simpson turned her attention to Pathet. "You've been a stunning failure so far. Your son is dead, and I'm no closer to the Eye of Omage than I have been since it was stolen."

Taking the cigarette from her hand, Pathet dropped it, crushing it out with one foot. He sat next to her on the bed, his hip grazing the burns on Evan's hyperextended underarm.

"I can change that." The daemon spread his hand wide, cupped the woman's face, and reached fingers deep into her hair. He pulled her closer and kissed her, nuzzled at her neck. Evan noticed that the marks had disappeared from Pathet's cold face. Death eyes the color of poison, of rot, fixed on him, shared with Evan the contempt of a lord of the host of Azmod for the woman in his arms while they promised death for Badad's child and the world that held them all.

So Marnie Simpson would have the lords of Ariton in spite of what he had suffered to stop her; it had all been for nothing. Trapped in the vision of echoing darkness, hope faded in black pin dots that obscured Evan's vision. The smell of blood and his own burned skin gagged him. Exhausted by fighting the madness of the creatures around him, a flash of betrayal colored his struggle. Where the hell was his father?

"Yes." The woman acquiesced with a sigh of pleasure. She pulled back far enough to read the threat in the daemon's face and smiled, aroused, Evan realized, by the danger as much as the caress. He shuddered, nauseated by the revulsion he felt for Marnie Simpson, and the waves of despair that crashed over him.

"I'll give you one more chance to redeem yourself. But I won't bargain for names. When I have them, Bradley and Ryan both bound to my will, I'll let you go. First, I need the names."

Pathet nipped at her ear. "His name is Badad, lord of the host of Ariton, and she is Lirion, also of the host of Ariton. You can command their presence, of course, but you run a greater risk of trickery that way. They are fools, but not stupid."

Marnie Simpson smiled at him, stretched her neck for him to nuzzle deeper. "What do you suggest?"

"Use the boy, he's Badad's weakness. Then, when you have them contained in the circle," his eyes flitted to the pentagram overhead, "you can bind them in safety."

The plan would fail, Evan realized. If his father cared at all, he would be here now. But caring was human. Once again the knowledge of the alienness of Ariton crawled like lice over his scalp. The binding he had done to protect them had sealed his own death. When he died, his father and his lover were free again, of him, and of Ariton's task in the material sphere. They could go home. The thought was all the more bitter with the taste of the death he had caused. The only friends he'd ever had, dead just for knowing him. His father was going to let him die.

"Your concern is touching," Marnie Simpson addressed the daemon at her side. "You will take a message for me?"

"Anything." The daemon ran a hand down Evan's leg. "Not much longer," he said. The macabre joke bubbling in his eyes turned Evan's stomach. Not much longer and he'd be dead.

Honor seemed stupid at the moment; he could command the lords of Ariton. Calling on his father for survival was not the same as the tyranny with which Marnie Simpson and her husband controlled the lords of Azmod, but that subtlety of motive would be lost on his daemon kin. The gesture seemed pointless anyway. Mind dulled with exhaustion and pain, he knew only that he could not spend a lifetime alone in his difference. Better to die now.

Marnie Simpson was looking past him, at Claudia, who listened wide-eyed while their captors decided their fate. Claudia. She had to live through this—one good thing out of the whole mess of his life had to survive. But the words that would command the lords of Ariton slipped through his mind like a breeze.

"Nice shirt," the Simpson woman said. "But not your size. How gallant of our Evan, to sacrifice fine Italian workmanship for a lady's modesty.

"Cut if off her," she ordered Omage. "I want the pocket."

Omage cut through the fabric, drawing a thin track of blood where he cut too deeply over her breast. Claudia keened between clenched teeth, her eyes locked on the knife in the daemon's hand. First, he cut out the pocket. Then, grinning, he cut each button free. Marnie Simpson took the knife and the ragged square of fabric.

"Poetic symmetry," she said, examining the knife. "Kevin Bradley will appreciate that." She stretched Evan's shackled hand palm upward, traced the threads of scar tissue on his wrist with the tip of Mac's knife, the same knife that in Omage's back room had cut the scars, an eternity ago it some-times seemed. Sometimes, like now, it seemed like yesterday.

Too much. Evan felt himself cut adrift in a part of his mind where the pain filtered dimly and time had no meaning. In that too-familiar place he drew himself into an imaginary ball and pretended that he did not exist. Almost, he didn't feel it when Marnie Simpson cut a line parallel to the silver threads. Blood welled from the cut, and the woman—*Paul Carter's mother,* the thought flitted mockingly through his mind, she knew the tricks, had seen it all before—wiped it with the ragged pocket.

"Take this to his father." She handed the dripping cloth to Pathet. "Tell Mr. Bradley that I request his presence and the return of my property, the

Eye of Omage. I'll be counting the minutes. On Evan's fine young body."
She leaned over him, kissed Evan softly on the lips.

"Go," she commanded without looking back at the daemon.

Claudia's scream, tight with hysteria, pulled him out of the safe place
in his mind. Evan squeezed her hand, felt the return grip strong and steady
that belied her horror-filled eyes. Then she pulled her hand away, covering
her mouth.

"I'm going to throw up," she moaned.

"Shut her up," Marnie Simpson ordered.

Omage leered. "Give me my knife," he pressed. "You won't hear another sound out of her."

Marnie Simpson glared at him. "Until I've got the jewel, we need her."

"It's up to you," the daemon conceded, "but I've seen it before. A lot
of them think they can take anything. Then—" He shrugged. "A little
excitement, and you've got piss and vomit all over the floor."

"I need the bathroom."

Claudia Laurence grabbed at her stomach, and Simpson dismissed the
younger woman with a disgusted curl of her lip.

"Take her to the bathroom, but leave the shirt here. She won't be going
anywhere like that. And don't let her out of your sight. We don't want her
getting into mischief, do we?"

Omage nodded, a lascivious grin lighting his features with the putres-
cent glow of something dead overlong. He stripped off her shirt and
dropped it in a heap next to the bed before he undid the shackle at Claudia's
leg. "Bathroom's this way—" He lifted her roughly to her feet by her
elbow.

Claudia bent to clutch her stomach again, and slipped out of the
daemon's grip. Two steps and she was out of the window, diving headfirst
off the roof and into the canal, her arms held stiffly above her head.

Omage followed dumbly to the window. "She's gone," he said with a
shrug. "They do that sometimes, kill themselves. I don't know why."

*Dead.* He would have raged, would have followed, but he couldn't
think past the pain to making the image real in his mind. More than grief,
he felt abandoned. Why did she leave him behind, still living, when he
would have died to save her?

Franklin Simpson came upright in his chair. "How did she get out?
You said you sealed the house."

Omage grinned, pleased with himself, and shook his head. "Not exactly. You said to seal the doors against humans. You never mentioned the
windows."

"You will be punished," Marnie Simpson informed the daemon, sharing a glance with her husband. Then she made the same promise to Evan, stroking his zipper with the tip of the silver knife. With Claudia dead, it didn't seem to matter.

From the painted ceiling above him the sad, dark eyes of Thot watched and judged. Marnie Simpson brought the knife down again, and Evan cried out, a single word like a death rattle torn from his throat:

"Father!"

# Chapter 26

*The pentagram, five-pointed star inscribed within a circle, is a symbol of protection. If a man were to call a daemon and he stands within the circle, the daemon cannot touch him. But beware not to cross outside of the circle until the daemon has been sent back to the place from whence it comes, or he will be torn limb from limb in the spirit's wrath.*

"Evan."

Badad appeared in a ripple of troubled air and reined in an anger fueled by an emotion he had never felt before. Fear, new-learned at the meat-death of his own body, screamed from human nerve endings for the shaking man on the bed. Shock, Brad realized, but not entirely from the wounds. Clear fluids oozing from shallow burns that streaked Evan's body mingled with the sheen of cold sweat. Brad felt his heart beat in the rhythm of the blood dripping slowly from an opened wrist to the pillow; had to hurt like hell, but not actually dangerous unless infection set in. Something he couldn't see was killing his son.

Haunted eyes the color of the stone lying like a dead thing on his breast opened on him. "I knew you would come," his son acknowledged. But the relief was too sharp, too sudden.

*Abandoned.* The shadows in Evan's eyes still read abandoned, and yet he had not drawn on the binding that permitted no resistance—just the one inhuman cry, too full of pain, of Brad's own fear, to carry the weight of binding in it. That call had cut through Badad like the bloody knife Marnie Simpson held over his son's heart. Brad recognized the knife. Paul Carter had died on it, Evan had painted a room with his own blood drawn by it.

"Sorry I took so long." Brad paused. "Don't you think it's time we went home?"

"Can't. Can't think, can't shape it in my head." Evan seemed to stare right through his jacket, drawn to the jewel he carried next to his skin. "The Eye—let me see it." The chain at his wrist sounded hell-chimes when Evan reached out his hand.

"Yes, Mr. Bradley, let him see it." Marnie Simpson turned to greet him, the knife held casually between them and a proprietary hand resting on Evan's abdomen.

Brad ignored the woman, his plans for a swift and vengeful rescue shot to hell in the marble room. Evan wasn't going anywhere on his own, and Marnie Simpson didn't look like the 911 type. He drew the smoky topaz from beneath his shirt. Its cold weight fell on his breast where Evan and his captors could see it.

At the window, Omage clasped his hands together, a dissipated monk in unholy prayer. "You do good work," he admitted. "The boy is more thoroughly tuned to the jewel than I could have hoped. Your dash to the rescue has discommoded our young friend quite severely.

"It's his lifeline, you see. The stone anchors the human in him to the material sphere. While the Eye of Omage," he bent his head a moment, the maestro humbly accepting the accolades of his devoted fans, "remains safely here in his human reality, young Evan can pass into the second sphere without losing himself there. The holder of the jewel controls him, draws him back, you see. When the jewel passes into the second sphere— well, let's just call it uncomfortable. If Evan should find himself in the second sphere at the same time as the jewel . . ." The daemon shrugged. "We haven't had an opportunity to test this particular eventually yet, but neither were built for the consequences. It would probably tear the boy to pieces. At the least, it would destroy his mind. Would you kill him then, Ariton? If the boy survived that far, would you finally kill your mad human bastard?"

Evan reached for the stone, let his hand fall again, but Brad ignored the gesture with an effort. "You misinterpret my presence." He held out his empty hands with a conciliatory smile. "I'm here to protect Ariton's interests. If that means saving the boy, fine. If it doesn't, I'm reasonable. For my kind." He couldn't afford to look at Evan, didn't want to know if his son believed the lie. He gave Alfredo DaCosta's hidden room a cool overview: gaudier than his own taste ran, but the aging stone walls, the chessboard floor, suited the count. Portraits on the ceiling—Thot, Egyptian god of time and lordly justice, later Hermes—told a story of the guardian moving West.

DaCosta still sat in judgment, his words echoed in Badad's being: "Evan has to die . . . make it as easy for him as you can, or . . . I'll take care of it." How could he tell the guardian, who had watched millennia of death from a distance, but who had no more real understanding of what dying meant than Lily had, that Evan would never die easily, at any hand? But DaCosta waited out there, beyond the marble walls and painted memories. Here, on the guardian's chessboard, the first moves of the battle would come. Brad assessed the forces ranged against him, found there mostly pawns.

Almost as sweaty as Evan, Franklin Simpson sprawled in an armchair at Brad's right. The human's expression mingling sour impatience with triumph: looked like he got his kicks watching. Probably interrupted at the big moment, old Frank looked like he already anticipated a bigger one. Simpson's lackey, Omage, stood next to the window with the keen joy of battle in his eyes, and Brad abandoned all hope of keeping this beneath the notice of Princes. For the first time he realized how closely Mac's human form resembled that of his master: evil little doppelganger of an evil little man. A cruel joke, and Mac never did have a sense of humor.

Marnie Simpson's smile, white queen to black knight, told him she anticipated the game. "The death of your son doesn't enter into my plans, Badad, lord of Ariton. But a bargain for his services? I think we can deal."

His true name stole the breath from Brad's human body, pulled at the very center of him where Ariton beat like a human heart. Betrayed. Quick as the thought, he knew Evan read the accusation in his face, saw hope bleeding into bleak endurance, and a challenge to believe in him or be damned. A martyr's look: why did Evan wear it now? Marnie Simpson stroked sweaty hair from the boy's brow with a gelid smile. Her eyes swept from son to father, testing, hard as old iron but pitted and brittle with it. Not far from the snapping point, Brad figured, but the thought didn't re-assure him. White Queen. Of the three, she was still the most dangerous.

That didn't count Evan, who had given away his name. The game fell apart when he looked at Evan, who lay in chains at Marnie Simpson's nonexistent mercy. Evan held the lord of Ariton in his palm, and would hand that over, too, if it kept him breathing a few minutes longer. Brad remembered death. What would he give to hold that darkness at bay, if this life were all he had? Not Ariton. Were human loyalties that different? A week ago, he would have said not. Today he looked at his son and saw no shame, just soul-killing certainty that if Marnie Simpson's insane schemes didn't kill him, his father would.

*Not yet,* Badad promised silently, *not until I understand.*

"This place will never make Michelin's; I thought I taught you better taste." He pursed his lips in mock appraisal—never let them know it mat-ters. "The accommodations aren't bad, but the service is atrocious. Minimal tip if I were you, son. And I'd have a word with housekeeping about the beds. I suppose all that blood is yours?"

"Our hostess had a bone to pick." Evan made the effort to answer in kind, but it cost him. Metal links chinged as he shifted his arm for a closer inspection. "Radius and ulna, to be exact."

He fell back, drained by a weariness that went beyond the wounds Badad could see.

"Jack and Claudia Laurence are dead." Unspoken, the words *My fault* fell heavy between them.

Brad shrugged, a veiled suggestion of hidden knowledge in his eyes. "Fire and water," he said. "How biblical. Of course, Noah had a boat."

He paused a moment, took the stone from around his neck, and held it by the chain in his outstretched hand.

"Miss Laurence said you needed this. She seemed to think it was important."

"Claudia."

Evan whispered the name, his eyes closing for a moment as he absorbed the truth of it. When he reached again to touch the stone, his arm held steady. Recovering from the effects of the stone's transfer through the second sphere, Brad guessed, and more. Claudia Laurence was alive, fished out of the Canal sputtering about kidnappers and daemons and a ransom in stolen jewelry.

"An unfortunate accident," Marnie Simpson demurred. "The girl's survival, I mean. But not critical. I have you now, Badad, and I have the stone. That should suffice to keep our young explorer in his place."

Pathet appeared at the woman's shoulder. "I found him for you—" The daemon nodded at the lord of Ariton. "As promised."

"He's here." Marnie Simpson seemed unwilling to award her own knight the point. "Where's the other one?"

Pathet shrugged. "Ask him."

"Well?" The woman rose from the bed, pulled a cigarette from the pack. "Got a light?"

Pathet snapped sparks between his thumb and middle finger, lit the cigarette.

Not Evan, then, but the fear Evan had brought into the open when they started this caper. "So Azmod cut a deal." He nodded, certain now, wanting Evan to know it, too. "But not Omage. He's tied up with the stone somehow; you may still need him. So Pathet's been whispering names in your bed."

"It could have been Evan," Marnie Simpson reminded him.

Brad shook his head. "He's my son." He smiled at the man struggling to sit upright on the bed. "I trust him."

"How warm," Franklin Simpson rumbled from his chair. "How touching. Let's get on with this before I vomit. Where is Miss Ryan? Or should I ask, where is Lirion, lord of the host of Ariton?"

"Right here." Lily usurped Marnie Simpson's place on the bed. She stayed her hand inches above the puckered lines that crossed Evan's breast, then curled her fingers into a ball to keep from touching.

"We pulled your lady friend out of the Canal for you. She's going to have one hell of a case of conjunctivitis, and you are not one of her favorite people right now, but she's safe, with a friend."

Her glance, like Brad's own, searched as much as supported. What Brad saw in his son's eyes satisfied him: not the madness or the despair he'd found at the Black Masque, but anger. Something hard, unyielding as the stone, glinted from smoky depths. Evan lay back, undefeated and waiting. Brad turned his attention to Marnie Simpson. It was time to play out the game.

"What do you want?"

The woman gave Brad a proprietary smile. "You. And Lily, of course. You did answer my summons, however indirectly issued. That makes you both mine to command for as long as I can hold you."

"You know it doesn't work that way." Lirion stood and faced the woman; Badad joined her.

Lily continued: "We have agreed to no bargain, and with so unsubtle a statement of your intentions we are hardly likely to do so."

Brad nodded his agreement. "You can't hold us. We've come for Evan, and we'll be leaving with him. Now."

A snarl from the corner out of the room reminded Brad that they were not alone. Omage's face raged out of true, and he exploded in a whirlwind of dust that Franklin Simpson settled with an upraised hand.

"Our forces seem evenly matched," Simpson pointed out.

Pathet glanced from the human to a smoldering but subdued Omage and flashed Badad a sardonic twist of a smile. No love lost there for a half-human bastard, but a grudge running deep against the human who bound him.

"When you are bound, I'm free," Pathet explained. The smile he turned on his lover was not a pleasant thing. "I'll be just as free when you are dead. Hope I don't have a choice to make in battle."

Marnie Simpson laughed. "That's why I like you—always a challenge. Badad, however, has more predictable . . . desires?"

"You said you wanted a bargain. Here are my terms." She faced Badad, all trace of humor gone. "Your allegiance, and that of Lirion, for the life of your son."

Evan would give him up to keep living, to stop the pain. *Accept it, understand it,* the part of his mind that remembered death said, and Badad realized that, yes, he could endure the twisted insanity of the Simpsons if his son still lived.

"He'll go free?"

"Give me the stone, and I'll release him right now. I'll have the occasional errand in the second sphere for him, but once he has that under control he'll be free to come and go as he pleases. We'll have no need of chains or shady little back rooms."

Brad watched his son, waiting for a word, a sign, but Evan shook his head.

Confident, Marnie Simpson watched the exchange. "Of course, your agreement is merely a formality—simpler, but not necessary.

"This room has an interesting decor, don't you agree? Particularly the ceiling art—a pentagram." She stepped out of the circle and her husband began the words of binding:

"By my will to command over the heavens and the earth, in the realms of the living and the dead and the eternally damned, I summon you Badad, lord of the host of Ariton, and you Lirion, lord of the host of Ariton. By this I conjure you: that you will appear immediately and without delay in any form I so command, whenever and every time you shall be summoned, by whatever word or sign or deed, in whatever time or place.

"You will obey the commands set for you in whatever form they shall be conveyed and for whatever purpose. If you should resist any command so issued, you will burn in the eternal fire of damnation now and until the end of time. So Swear it now by my rod, and bind it in the everlasting essence of your being."

Simpson rose from his chair and walked forward purposefully, a cane bound thick with age and the evil of the men who had carried it through time extended like a sword in his outstretched hand. The faces carved into the cane's surface screamed in Brad's ears, and he saw Lily wince, press her hands to the sides of her head.

"They can't make any bargain with you; they belong to me."

The level assertion fell like the cold darkness of home in the circle, washed away the oily taste of old torment that pulsed from the head of Franklin Simpson's cane. With the others, Brad turned to the source of the claim. Evan sat at the edge of the bed, his legs swung over the side. He rubbed absently at the chained wrist with his free hand. A memory of horror hunched his shoulders, but he faced his enemy with calm certainty.

His half-human bastard reached for him, and Badad knelt, elbows resting on his son's knees. Evan fingered the jewel in his father's hand. Smoky topaz eyes met Ariton blue. He spoke to Badad alone.

"If you hadn't taken me out of the Black Masque, I'd have been dead the way Paul Carter died, or still Mac's prisoner and insane. Fight them, yes, but don't ask me to trade your agony for my life. I can't do it."

"You disappoint me." Marnie Simpson's voice cut into the sudden silence, reminding Brad that others awaited the outcome of the conversation. "Did you believe we offered any option but complete capitulation?"

The woman took a step toward Evan, and Lirion moved between them. "You've got your own pets. Keep your hands off mine."

Sparks crackled in the air; responding to the threat, Pathet moved in, eyes slitted, a wry smile bringing a true light to his face. The lords could understand this: battle was their natural state, and Azmod had never made alliance with Ariton.

Marnie Simpson continued her explanation to Evan, the words damping the energies of Ariton building between the natural enemies.

"You belong to me. Your life for the life of my son. Tell him to give me the jewel now and you will live. If your father tries to leave here with the stone, I will send my minions to hold him in the second sphere until you are useless to either of us. When the jewel moves into the second sphere, your human reality collapses, you see. You can hold onto that reality by strength of will for a short period, but the effort costs. Your soul is being torn in two, you understand.

"But of course you understand. How long was Badad in the second sphere to come here? The flicker of a moment, and you felt—how? Like the universe had torn in two around you? Imagine that, going on for the eternity of a battle between your forces and mine. If you should try to leave here with the stone, they won't have enough left to bury when you get home.

"So. What will it be, friend Evan?"

She ignored the forces of the second sphere now, intent on the man who would bind his own father to enslavement by his enemies, or who alone could set in motion her war to conquer universes. At first only Badad seemed to notice that the energy snapping in the room flowed from that same source. A concerned glance from Lily told him she felt it, too.

"I am human, like part of yourself," Marnie Simpson circled the bed, stalking her prey. She sat where Claudia had been, reached for Evan across a tangle of burgundy velvet.

"Our lifetime is short, gone in the blink of an eye to our immortal associates. They couldn't care less for you. Is a moment of discomfort for them so great a price to pay against the next sixty years of your life?"

Badad churned through their options while he listened to the seductive reasoning. Evan had survived the jewel's presence in the second sphere once since it had attuned to him, but he was pumping out energy like a reactor gone wild. Could he live through another transfer so soon after the last if Brad made for home? Would he believe his father had abandoned him to his enemies then, or would he know to transport after, following the beacon of the jewel home?

With a quick look around the room, he gave the question up as moot. Omage would try to stop him, and Pathet—they had no choice. Here or in the second sphere, the battle would take more time than Evan could afford. Lily caught his glance; the almost imperceptible shake of her head showed that she had been considering the same options, had drawn the same conclusions. Marnie Simpson was right about that. They couldn't get Evan out with the stone, they couldn't get him out without it.

"What do you want?" Evan's voice. Brad studied his son's face, but saw no change when Marnie Simpson's tongue followed the trace of her sharp red nails along the line of Evan's jaw.

"I already told you: the jewel. And your associates' contracts. Once we have conquered the second sphere, you are, for all intents and purposes, free. From time to time I may call on you for special tasks, when I need someone I—trust—who can pass into the second sphere. Other than the aforementioned well paid jobs, you won't even know the jewel exists."

"And if I change my mind?"

Franklin Simpson raised his cane like a scepter. "I wouldn't suggest that, dear boy. Omage has wanted his freedom for a long time. I might decide to give it to him—and the jewel, as a going away gift. I don't think there's much chance he'd bring it back in your lifetime. Fun way to die, no?"

Evan searched his father's face, but Brad had no comfort to offer. "I can't transport you out, not with the stone. And we're not alone in this. Other forces want you dead."

A quick glance at the frescoed ceiling told Badad his son knew about DaCosta. "One of yours?"

"No. Not one of yours either." Not the time to tell his son he was a threat to the survival of three universes. "I don't know how strong he is, or what he can do to you. I may not be able to stop him."

His son nodded, seeing his truth, and answered his captor. "You haven't left me a lot of choices."

"I'm glad you see it my way, dear boy." Simpson grinned, showing his worn, tobacco-stained teeth. "Do we have a bargain?"

Evan look away from him then, straight into the eyes of his tormentor, and Brad shuddered at what he saw there.

"A bargain? I always thought the devil was one of their kind. Didn't know he was human." He placed both hands on Brad's shoulders. The shackle around his wrist strained at its limit, digging the raw welt deeper into his wrist, but Evan seemed to have forgotten it. Again his fierce expression demanded Badad's complete attention, shut out the rest of the room.

"You've taught me more than you know."

Badad waited.

"Give me the jewel."

Irrational anger shook him, and Brad recognized both his resistance to any forced command and his fear for the one who commanded. Couldn't his stubborn human see reason?

"I won't be able to protect you." He grabbed the chain that shackled the wrist to the bed and shook it until the pain on his son's face brought him back to sense. The damaged wrist began to bleed, but the battle to come would do much worse. Brad focused his rage on the cuff in his fist until the metal under his fingers glowed red and burst in a shower of sparks. Evan eased his arm to his side, but Brad shook the twisted metal in his face.

"If we lose, you could spend the rest of your life like this, torn to pieces by the damned stone."

Evan stopped him with a look. "Mac told us what happened at the club. I'm not Paul Carter, Father. I could have been, once, but thanks to you, and Lily, I *know* who I am. You have honored me with your contract; allow me the honor of my decision."

Lily objected with a sour laugh. "The backflash alone will kill you. A battle among our kind can destroy this little world of yours—not if we try to destroy it, but if we just don't try hard enough *not* to."

"Then take the battle to your own ground." Evan turned again to Brad. "Give me the jewel."

"You'll be trapped here, with them—"

"Choices? Looks to me like they all leave me dead or a prisoner at the end. I have the right to decide what the ending will be. Leave the stone with me and go. Fight for all of us."

Time itself seemed to hold its breath, then Badad bowed his head. He placed the gold chain around Evan's neck, touching the unruly hair lightly in passing, and placed the stone precisely over his son's heart. Evan winced—burns crossed there, a focus for Marnie Simpson's attentions— then he relaxed, as if the stone itself somehow eased the pain.

"You're a stubborn son of a bitch, Evan Davis." Brad's smile was shaky; he shared none of the confidence of the human's cocky answer:

"It runs on my father's side of the family."

Lirion shifted uneasily. "I hope you two know what you are doing."

The expressions of father and son said they were riding the wind of creation on this one, and Badad couldn't hide his conviction that it would be a stormy ride.

"That's what I thought." Taking Brad's place at Evan's side, Lily held her lover's face between her hands. "Remember what you are." While Brad stood guard over them, she kissed him deeply, searching his eyes for the knowledge he hid from himself. "You have more power than you know—Ariton is a part of you."

The moment hung between them, snapped when Omage moved toward the bed. In human form the daemons locked in battle, then together the lords of Ariton and Azmod moved into the second sphere.

# Chapter 27

*When Princes do battle, house against house, the heavens thunder.*
*New stars are born in their passing, and ancient stars die.*

FREE OF HUMAN FORM, BADAD SHIFTED INTO THE WELCOMING DARKNESS, felt the tides of creation lift and carry him, touched the sudden there-ness of what the material sphere saw as star. He spread himself thin to sense the battle, Lirion a blue flame in his mind. Pathet moved surely in a lick of green flame across his senses. Omage shivered in a nexus of acid sparks, whiplashes of feeling snapping out as he tumbled in the void—like Badad's own uncontrolled spasms after body-death in the Black Masque. But Omage, canny in his twisted madness, guided his own path.

They were not alone. Lords of the host of Ariton approached, a whisper flickering sensation growing stronger, a sense of thickening presence. Not yet the 833 that made a Quorum, but the number grew: host-cousins Sibolas and Saris; Anader the cruel, so cold he sent a shiver through the gathering host; Caromos, who filled the senses of Ariton with a swift, fierce joy. In the part of himself that had learned to shape experience by time in the material sphere, Badad remembered a past, before Evan Davis, when he merged with Caromos for the pleasure of that lord's laughing touch. In passing, Badad flicked recognition, respect. No warrior, Caromos came closer to knowing infinity than any lord, and for a point in the great continuum, Badad had almost shared that knowledge. Now they would fight together, for the honor of Ariton.

Badad sank tentacles of being into the heart of a star—not Earth's son—where Omage lay in wait. The lords of Azmod gathered in his wake, enemies of Ariton in the being and essence of the hosts. In the memory of all eternity there had never been an alliance between these two, a fact imprinted in the thoughts of Sclavak, giver of pain, and warrior Sarra, Gilarion, bloated Holba, Hifarion. Loyalty of the most obligatory bound them to their tormented host-cousin Omage, but a ceremonial hatred for Ariton met its equal in the lords of blue flame.

Sclavak moved after Lily; Badad felt the bright flare of her presence. Conjunctions of forces that were planets in another reality tore from their orbits, unraveled like string in her path. Laughing Caromos tickled fat Holba, darted from the fray to itch at Gilarion in a lick of blue flame on green. Loyal Caromos. Princes would decide the purpose of the battle, but Caromos already knew the enemy.

Badad found Omage, forced a merge with the mad daemon, heard the voices screaming in his enemy's mind, felt the tearing claws of binding wrapped throughout his being. This, he remembered, was to be bound with hatred, forced to the will of planet-crawlers in the material sphere. His own binding lay heavy in the darkness of his being, reminded him that pain and death, and better things, like brandy smooth on the tongue, were also real. Badad fought for his son's life.

Omage exploded outward. Energy driven in concentric bursts from the focus meant destruction on the material sphere, sent shock waves through the spheres beyond their own. A thousand years from now, a human standing on the Earth would look up and see the great outreaching rush of the explosion. If the Earth survived the battle. The lord of Ariton stilled in his pursuit. Conscious suddenly of fear, he waited for DaCosta's weaknesses in the fabric of the universes to bring an end to eternity.

Pathet whipped across his position, sent him tumbling with a sardonic pass. Images of Evan screaming his pain transferred in the partial merge— This is Ariton?—Pathet's scorn lingered, and Badad's memory of flesh in pain resonated in the battlefield.

Lords of Amaimon, Oriens—traditional allies of Ariton—and Paimon, sometimes friend, sometimes enemy, gathered to observe the battle. Magot, Astarot, allies to Azmod in many wars, came together, taking sides. Princes fought for honor, and the question went out: What honor is at stake? Where the advantage to settle hidden slights in the name of alliance?

Badad spread himself across the darkness to lick at the consciousness of friend and foe. Alfredo DaCosta's warning, with the images of death as he had felt it, moved like ripples through the second sphere. He became the memory even as it faded at the edges: fear, shock, pain, and felt the horror of his cousins, allies, enemies.

To Princes with no beginning, DaCosta's tale of creation and destruction meant nothing. Alien emotions, strange feelings, they were thrown back at him, some in denial, some in anger. Hifarion of the host of Azmod fed another memory into the weave of choices: ripples of insanity passing through the spheres, lords sent out to find the source and end it. Evan

Davis. Ariton had failed, the monster stilled lived to threaten the stability of the spheres. Azmod would end it for the honor of all Princes.

Badad fought back with the image of Paul Carter, monster creation of Azmod, half-human and completely mad, dying. Like Evan, Paul Carter was only an instrument. Where two had grown, others might rise up.

Harumbrub of the host of Ariton gave his presence to the battle, and drew upon the host for a Quorum. Lords shuddered in the black expanse of existence, gathered swiftly, flame in darkness. Ariton gathered in the group mind of its Prince. Out of the many voices of its lords, one thought held sway: Earth would die. First, Azmod would pay for the threat Omage had set in motion. Princes gathered, sent out scouts, warriors, and stormed through the second sphere, loosing waves of destruction.

# Chapter 28

*The God Thot, called Hermes Trismegistus by the Greeks and Mercurio Tertius by the Romans, gave to man the words by which he might travel, but only in his spirit form. For the mortal part of man is bound to the world of the flesh and does not take part in the power of the word.*

EVAN GATHERED HIS SHIRT FROM THE FLOOR AND WORKED HIS ARMS INTO THE sleeves. The cloth hurt like hell against his burns, but Evan felt safer covered. Just as well the buttons were gone, though: he couldn't have endured the rub of the cloth across his chest. Not like the Eye of Omage. The smoky topaz rested like a balm on blistered skin, as if it had always belonged there. According to Marnie Simpson, it was a part of him now.

Shaking off the physical shock of daemons shifting out of the material plane in battle status, the woman stirred on the bed. Her eyes promised retribution, and she still held the bloody knife in her hand. Evan considered a dash for home through the second sphere, dismissed the idea with a shudder. If the fighting between between Princes didn't grind him up just for being in the way, the Eye of Omage would rip him apart instead.

He'd been handed better choices in his day, but that didn't mean he was helpless. Lily's parting words still echoed in his ears: "You have more power than you know— Ariton is a part of you."

His father, a lord of Ariton, had created a small earthquake, killed fifty people with no remorse. Did he want to be a part of that, share that kind of power? No. Did he have a choice? Not, it seemed, if he wanted to live.

Alone with her husband and their stunned captive, Marnie Simpson seized her opening. "Get him—get the stone!"

Her strident voice jerked Franklin Simpson out of his frozen inertia. The man lunged for him, cane raised overhead, and Evan blocked, wrapped his hand around the heavy carved wood. The force of the blow opened the

wound on his wrist again, but the reality of his own blood scarcely penetrated the chaos that attacked his mind. The stick. Evan knew then that the
faces in torment on its surface were not simply carvings, but the desperate
souls of the men and women who had wielded the thing through time.

Loathing rose in him to batter at the chaos. His body shook with revulsion, vibrated with a fine-tuned tension. Vaguely, as if from a distance,
he sensed Marnie Simpson moving up from behind with Omage's knife,
an empty threat—he was useless to her dead. He kept his eyes locked with
the man who wielded the souls of the damned like a bludgeon. The unhu-
man strike bolted through him like lightning, into the hand that blocked
the cane. With the sound of thunder, Simpson's wand cracked. Split. Shattered. Fragments flew before the screams of freed souls fading, fading.

One scream remained: Marnie Simpson, bleeding from a dozen lac-
erations. None of the cuts seemed lethal—Evan felt the knot in his stomach
loosen—but she'd be picking splinters out of her teeth for a good long time
to come.

"My God. My God." Franklin Simpson backed away, stuttering.

"I don't think He's listening." Evan stared at his hand, where the first
layer of skin had burned away. "Shit."

"Bravo." Alfredo DaCosta stood in the doorway, an appreciative audience clapping his hands slowly while a knowing smile spread across his
features. "Lily was right. You do take after your father."

"How did you get in here?" A pale Frank Simpson stared from DaCosta
to Evan Davis.

"Seen a ghost, Frank?" Evan asked offhandedly, then turned his attention on the newcomer. "What do you want?"

"It *is* my house," DaCosta pointed out.

Evan ran his good hand through his hair. A quick scan of the room
confirmed what he already knew. "Then you'll know where the telephone
is. We have to call the police."

"And tell them what?" DaCosta asked, "What has gone on here today
that any sane carabinieri would believe?"

"Kidnapping, for a start," Evan countered, but he saw the problem.
The truth would give him the credibility of an asylum escapee.

"Unfortunately, Interpol is looking for *you*. A matter of two murders
in London. Our mad friends would most likely receive a medal for detaining
you."

"We can't just let them go!"

Evan's frustration exploded in sparks that lifted the hair on his body
and DaCosta responded with an Italian shrug, not indifference but accom-

modation. "That remains to be seen. At the moment our guests are not my concern. You are."

Frank Simpson snickered in the background, but the sound faded on the instant. Alfredo DaCosta dropped the persona of the rich dilettante, became Thot, lord of Time, passing judgment here and now. He recognized that face: a god on DaCosta's painted ceiling, a god standing before him on the marble checkerboard floor.

"Why?" Evan asked. "What are you?"

"We haven't time for explanations. Call me a guardian, if you need a category.

"As for why, you present my species with a problem." DaCosta sighed, and Evan realized that whatever the count was, he didn't like what he had to do here.

"In a better universe, there would be a place for you. As it is, your very nature threatens the continued existence not only of your world, but of all the material sphere, and several other spheres as well."

The guardian smiled ruefully. "If you were as grasping and mean-spirited as our friends, the Simpsons, this would all be much easier. Unfortunately, your good intentions don't mean a thing. You will go where you are told, do what you are told by whoever holds that little bauble presently dangling from your neck, even if it means that your worlds, and mine, will cease to have ever existed."

"Even the Simpsons wouldn't do anything that stupid," Evan objected. "They'd die, too."

"They're human," DaCosta said as if it explained everything. "Have they believed what you've told them of the second sphere?"

Evan shook his head, seeing the problem. "Do you understand yet what you've done?" he asked the woman who had retreated to the armchair by the door, then answered his own question from the look in her eyes. "No, you're halfway convinced he's lying to trick you. The other half is trying to figure a way to use it to your advantage if the count is telling the truth."

DaCosta agreed, took the logic a step further. "Our friends here may not be the only ones on this planet who have read the wrong books. The key is the stone, and you, Evan. As long as you exist, you will be a weapon that malice or stupidity can use to unmake the spheres."

Evan frowned; he didn't like the direction the guardian's argument was taking. "Let me get this straight. You're not talking about Interpol now. You plan to kill me, so that no one else can force me to destroy the universe."

"Nobody ever said you were stupid," DaCosta replied.

"And you expect me to stand here and let you do it, for some nebulous future good that will be served just as well by locking these two up for the next few decades."

"It's not that simple. Our friends here are a small problem; humans die."

Marnie Simpson whimpered a "No," but DaCosta ignored her.

"The real problem is the next time. We can't predict what it will be, so we have to clear the board now, so to speak."

He cleared his throat. "I promised your father I'd try to make it as easy as possible."

Evan stared at the man. The floor seemed to fall from under him, leaving him stranded in pain so sharp it left him gasping for breath. "My father agreed to this?"

He was alone again, in a dark more complete than the second sphere, fighting flashback while the sticky blood on his arm drew memories from his nerve endings, lost and dying in Mac's back room for reasons he had never understood.

"He couldn't," DaCosta reasoned. "You've bound him; he can't do anything, including making an agreement, that would harm you." The guardian considered him for a moment, his mouth downturned. "But that's not what you're asking, is it? Given the freedom to choose, would he have agreed?

"No, never," he admitted, and the darkness lifted, Evan's lungs rose and fell, drawing in air again.

"I expect he'll fry this little mud ball right down to its basalt roots when he realizes you're dead," the guardian finished.

Evan turned away, denying the images that filled his mind. For a moment his eyes locked on Marnie Simpson, pale and still, against the faded brocade of the chair. The woman shook her head, dazed.

"I didn't know," she whispered. "I didn't know."

"Would it have mattered if you did?" He shook his head, answering his own question and rejecting DaCosta's prediction at the same time. "You're asking me to trade not only my life but my planet for your immortality," he reminded the guardian. "I'd be a fool to agree.

"It's the jewel you're afraid of anyway," he figured. "Without it, I'm too strong for them." He smiled at that, understanding Marnie Simpson's mistake and DaCosta's real fear. "I'll bet Brad's part in that really pissed you off."

DaCosta grimaced. "Do you understand what Badad has done? Never in the history of this planet has a lord of the Princes taken more interest in the get of his human binding than to kill it. Once your father had trained you to travel between your two universes, I had to step in. You are too great a danger to us all."

"I believe you." Evan lifted the Eye of Omage from around his neck and extended it to the guardian. "So take the damned stone. Destroy it. Your home will be safe, and so will mine."

DaCosta shook his head. "I tried, when I had it in my possession, but nothing I could do would touch it. Someone has to carry it to the second sphere, and drop it into the heart of a star there."

"There aren't any stars in the second sphere."

"You can't sense them with your human equipment," DaCosta explained, "but they are there. Unfortunately, I don't have that access. Given that your relatives are tied up elsewhere, you're the only one left who can do it, but you're tuned to the damned thing now. Like Mac says, being in the second sphere with the stone will probably kill you."

"Maybe not," Evan pointed out. "Omage was working with Paul Carter when he created it. He remembers me as his prisoner," the memory made him shudder even now, "but he couldn't guess what my father has taught me. I'm stronger than he knows."

"Not that much stronger. A star in the second sphere is still a star; you'll die destroying the stone unless it destroys you first in the transfer."

Evan nodded, his eyes on the floor. He felt the sweat break out on his upper lip. *Damn, damn.* "It'll be bad, won't it?" He darted a sharp glance at DaCosta, found recognition of his own horror carved in the grim face. They were talking about a plunge into the energy nexus of a star.

"I can't say," DaCosta answered with a fleeting smile. "As I said, I've never been there. But, yes, I expect it would be pretty bad."

"But if I die in the unmaking of that thing, it was my choice, my risk. One my father will not feel honor-bound to avenge with the destruction of my world." Ideas on that scale made no sense to him, so he thought of his mother, and the house he grew up in, and Claudia's roses. Not so small a consolation, in the larger scheme of things.

"If by some freak accident you should actually survive it, I would still have to kill you." DaCosta looked genuinely sad. "As you point out, you have become too strong to control; a mistake could end the existence of your spheres and mine. I can't take that risk, and I can't ask you to endure what it will take to destroy the jewel."

The guardian withdrew a small case from his pocket. "It will be painless," he said, "I promised that much."

Evan stared at the guardian for a long minute, remembering a time when he might have said yes. He tightened his fist around the gold chain in his hand and held it close to his heart.

"I have a job to do," Evan said. "But this isn't finished."

He gestured with a nod at the Simpsons. "Keep an eye on our guests; if they contact Omage, I'm in trouble." Ironic, that. He was out of the frying pan and into the inferno already. "And I still have confidence in Europe's finest."

He slipped the chain around his neck and sent the part of him that was Ariton into the second sphere, drew his body to follow into that nonplace. The afterimage of the guardian's judgment followed, burned into his retinas.

# Chapter 29

*Trismegistus teaches that a man who leaves his body to the worms may pass through the spheres of heaven, and at each sphere the things that cling to his mortality shall fall away, like sin, until he passes beyond the reach of knowing with a pure soul. But the spheres are inimical to mortal flesh, which shall not abide there.*

EVAN FELT HIMSELF TURNED INSIDE OUT BY THE STONE AROUND HIS NECK. UP, down, sideways had no meaning. Words from childhood circled like a mantra in his mind—God help me. Please, God, make it stop. Make it go away—but no help came. He vomited, it seemed forever, alone in the void with his vomitus and the stone burning chaos into his soul. He tried to form a shape in his mind the way his father had taught him, a picture of a star cold and distant in the night sky, but the stone bound him to the chaos. Coherent images disintegrated before they could form, running away from him in scattered shards of sanity.

The sense he'd felt before, of malevolent forces set on his destruction, grew stronger, amplified in the stone. In his mind it became a wall of blue flame burning without heat in the distance. The wall of flame drew closer, and stubborn pride firmed his resolve—he would not face his father's kind like this, would not let the lords of Ariton know him for his weakness. Focused on the stone, Evan concentrated on the murky shadows at its heart, and slowly he felt the chaos fall into patterns of swirling energy pulsing, throbbing, within him. He waited, and the flame swept over him.

The host of Ariton. Evan felt the rush of personalities that were not lords but the sum of the host, not quite yet a Prince, but moving toward that group mind with thoughts that merged and flowed, no boundary where one began and another left off. Parts of the host, like the separate tongues of flame that leaped in a bonfire, crept through Evan's back brain where the reptile still lurked, tickled through the memories of running with sunshine on his face and watching the rain beat against the window, warm indoors with his pens and paper, paints and canvas. They found madness, and sex. Claudia was in his mind, and Lily—security and risk.

Out of the places he never shared with anyone, not even his father, they dragged the first time he'd night-traveled in the second sphere, a frightened child alone, the first time he'd stood next to his mother while strangers pawed at his drawings and asked him why he was so angry, so frightened. The strangers didn't like his answer, that something pulled him out of bed at night and how lost and terrified he was in the darkness where it left him. Disturbed, they called him, seriously disturbed, and shook their heads, sure they knew what ailed him better than the fatherless boy in front of them.

Ariton drew from him the memory of Omage, his despair, his pain and fear. Badad touched his mind then, one presence among the many picking through his memories, almost lost in the chorus of leaping tongues of Ariton-fire. Powerless to detach himself from the host, his father still managed to find the door he thought he had locked forever on an empty room with no windows. His own weakness sickened him, the filth and the madness and the sudden, terrifying plunge into the darkness he now traveled.

Then he had feared the second sphere as if it were death itself. Now that he knew better, he feared it more for the destruction this battle might still bring to his home. DaCosta's images—Earth a blasted, lifeless rock, a billion billion creatures murdered to revenge one death—echoed in the darkness. He met the fear with anger. Always the anger had pulled him back from the edge where Omage pushed him, and he used that anger again. He wouldn't let Omage kill him, wouldn't let DaCosta do it either. And he sure wasn't going to die over some stupid stone. But if he failed, if he didn't make it this time, his world had to survive. Call it a legacy: his death had to mean something.

His anger built, pulsed from him in waves. *My choice.* He sent the message surging back through Ariton's massed flame with the power of the binding spell. The flames licking at his mind recoiled; he felt the blistering heat of their hatred, impotent against the shield of that binding. Then he was alone with his father's oath lingering in the dark. Ariton would have him dead, but his father would protect his home against the judgment of Princes.

If his father's Prince wanted to kill him, Evan reckoned Ariton would just have to stand in line. Right now the stone around his neck had first dibs. He recognized the tug at the jewel. DaCosta said a star would draw the Eye like a magnet, but the truth was more like longing. He passed through space with the speed of thought, more and more one with the nature of the second sphere as he searched deeper into the stone for direction. The desire at the heart of the stone became his desire. The forces that gathered in his path, flames of green and indigo that twined in battle at the periphery held together against him at its center, but could not stop him. Evan felt the presence of Omage within the sickly green of Azmod's fire and burned a true blue light that flared Ariton and more. Space twisted his revulsion, and Azmod fell back, his companion fled bleeding images that it did not understand except that the end of everything approached with the swift charge of Ariton's monster.

Evan felt that fear and would have laughed, but as he penetrated the outer reach of the nearest star the pull of the stone grew stronger. Whirling eddies of energy caught and tore at him, left no room for other thought. Evan felt the energy burn him, shred him, but drawn inexorably by the stone, he could not turn away. He became the thing that drew him, stone and star and human and Ariton, all one creature reaching toward completion with a yearning that felt like home, and the horror caught him.

Earth. He was taking the stone home, to the center of his own star. Dimly he remembered Badad talking about other battles between Princes, and the deaths of stars. He was going to die, and home would die with him, torn apart in the destruction that would mark the passing of the stone. Not Ariton or DaCosta, but he himself would destroy the very thing he had come here to save.

No! His fury and rage compressed into the single syllable, he sent his denial out into the second sphere. A wall of flame like Ariton but flickering with a yellow glow drew closer with his death echoed in the minds of the lords reaching toward that density of purpose that would be a Prince. He reached for it in his wrath and felt the nature of reality shudder around him while at his touch the host tore itself into shreds that struggled to re-form as it fled.

Still the jewel drew him down, into the well of energy that danced through him. He was dying, felt nothing but the surges of power around him, heard nothing but the roar of that energy, not a sound but itself a physical pain. With his last thought he denied his death, the death of home in a well of pain that pulled all of creation after him. Dying.

Darkness moved between him and the stone. Evan found a light shimmering at its depths. Drawn to that light, he felt able to move again. He followed until he was contained within a brightness as blank as the dark that had preceded it. The roar faded; he knew that only the light separated him from the screaming whirlpool of energy that was his sun in the material sphere. Through the light he felt the swirling battle between Princes like a distant storm, but he could not react to it, could do nothing but hide in the light and question his own sanity. *Father?*

"Ungrateful fool. Badad has his own problem right now." *Lily.* Not words, but he knew her by the touch of her mind in the second sphere.

*Safe.* Could have cried, laughed, and the confusion of his feelings washing out over the universe in giddy waves that distorted the battle around them.

"Not yet," Lirion warned tartly, drifting through his head like she belonged there. "Stop attracting attention. You shouldn't be here; if it weren't for the binding, Ariton would give you up in a minute, so don't expect any help."

"I met Ariton." Evan supplied her with the memory, and he felt surprise filter through her efforts to conceal it. She probed deeper and he let her see the images of Azmod, of the other, not proud but infinitely exhausted.

"You've been a busy boy," she finally said. "I'm surprised you're still alive."

"I was angry," Evan offered, an echo of the rage he felt at his own death in the explanation. Then he added wryly, "And I was dying anyway."

He felt her doubt, saw her memory of a universe twisted out of true before it steadied itself in familiar currents of energy filled with the presence of the forming Princes. Then she laced her mind around the connection between himself and the stone, saw his intention, and shuddered.

"Why?"

He answered with images of home, and she understood then.

"Give me the misbegotten thing," she ordered him, and Evan sensed the weight lift from his soul. "Go home."

Something in her softened. He felt a cool touch, like fingertips across his heart. "You won't die today at Ariton's hand. I'm not sure the Princes can kill you now." She paused, and he felt again the feather touch of sadness in her mind, the question that still lingered. Would anything be left of him after the stone was destroyed? "I can't promise more, little monster."

With that she was gone. He thought about home, his room with the sun shining on white walls, the study where he'd learned how to be both human and daemon and survive the pull of both universes on his soul. A longing almost as strong as the pull of the stone filled him. If the destruction of the Eye of Omage killed him, he wanted to die at home. But another image took its place, a face with planes sharp as the facets of the stone, with eyes full of sorrow. The eyes of a judge. Alfredo DaCosta had once held the stone, and bereft of its presence, the part of himself that belonged to the stone followed its trace to its source.

He felt eyelids closed over sight, wind whipping at his clothes, his skin. He opened his eyes, black pawn on a white square, and saw a figure waver in front of him.

"The jewel," a distant voice insisted. "Who has the Eye of Omage?"

From a lifetime ago, before his plunge into the sun, Evan resurrected a face to go with the voice: Alfredo DaCosta, and the guardian wanted to kill him. The thought drifted like cotton candy through his mind, then vaporized in a flash of unbelievable loss. A cold hand reached through the barrier between the spheres to rip his heart out. The jewel was gone, destroyed. He collapsed in a heap at DaCosta's feet, realizing that, somewhere beyond the molten lead that pulsed through him where his blood should be, he was no longer falling.

# Chapter 30

*Hermes Trismegistus teaches that to understand the mysteries of the universe, man must become those mysteries and hold in his head the images of the sacred in the celestial spheres of the heavens. When a man attains the perfection of the art of memory that will hold the heavens in his grasp, then will he truly hold the power of the universe in his mind.*

SOMETHING SOFT BUT SOLID LAY BENEATH EVAN. A BED. HE WAS BACK, THEN. HE remembered the pain, knew Lily had destroyed the jewel, felt its absence as a dull ache, a phantom pain lingering like a Kirlian shadow around the place in his mind where the gemstone had threaded itself into his being. Slowly he opened his eyes, found Alfredo DaCosta in the flesh looking down at him. Above the man his image as Thot, god of Time, bore the same stern expression.

"You're alive." DaCosta seemed surprised. The guardian sat on the bed beside him, a small black case in his hand, and Evan tried to move away, found his arm once again shackled to the bedpost. Figured.

"You've been unconscious for about an hour," DaCosta told him. "Can you understand me?"

Evan nodded slowly, taking in his surroundings, the gentler tones of the man at his side. "Water," he said, surprised at the croak his throat produced.

"Water, if you please," he said, and Evan realized they were not alone in the attic room. Franklin Simpson handed the count a glass and moved out of sight again. DaCosta lifted Evan's head, held the glass for him, but gave way when Evan pushed himself up on one elbow and reached with his other hand for the glass. He saw the Simpsons then, Marnie Simpson sitting pale and tense in one of the room's chairs, her husband standing behind her. Both watched him like carrion birds waiting for the kill.

He turned away, realizing that for all their petty evil they didn't matter anymore. The stone was dead, had left him feeling numb, incomplete, but already he was growing physically stronger. Simpson came forward again and took the glass away, and Evan struggled to sit up under DaCosta's unwavering scrutiny. He ran tired fingers through his knotted hair and rubbed his hands over the stubble on his face. He felt like shit, figured he must smell about as bad. DaCosta was pretending not to notice. The guardian slid a chair within arm's length of Evan on the bed, and sat facing him, elbows on his knees, chin resting on hands clasped around the black case. The dark hawk's eyes stared at Evan, making him squirm like a bug on a pin.

"You surprise me," Dacosta said. "I thought you were dead for a while, your mind, if not the rest of you. Can you talk?"

Evan nodded.

"The stone. I need to know about the Eye of Omage. Who has it?"

"Why?"

"I know it's been rough for you, Evan, but try to think. Whatever else was happened here, those two still bind Omage. If they get their hands on the stone, they can try again. I can't let that happen."

"We didn't know—" Franklin Simpson protested, but his wife cut him short.

"Shut up, fool. He wants it all for himself, can't you see that?" She tried to smile at DaCosta, but Evan saw the corners of her mouth twitch. "But I'm sure we can make a deal."

"See?" DaCosta ignored the Simpsons, his attention wholly on Evan, who let his head fall back in exhaustion.

"It doesn't matter—Lily got rid of it." Evan choked on the words. "I felt it die."

For him, the jewel had become a living thing, a part of him torn out and thrown into the raging energies of a star. But he was still alive, had been cast adrift in the chaos at the heart of the stone, had passed through the outer surface of a star, stood up to Ariton and its enemies, and survived the destruction of his anchor in two universes.

*You're welcome.* Sarcasm, Evan only thought it. Pointless to expect gratitude from the creature painted on that ceiling.

DaCosta stood up, paced to the windows, and looked out. "That should be impossible. There's no way you could have survived the destruction of the stone." He continued his nervous movement to the center of the room where he turned a penetrating stare on Evan. "But, of course, you have done so, haven't you? Which makes my duty here all the more pressing.

"I'm sorry, Evan. I would have taken care of it while you were unconscious, but I had to know about the stone. I never wanted to cause you more pain."

He watched DaCosta take a hypo from the black case. The count held it up to the light and compressed the plunger a fraction, tapped the needle to break the air bubbles. So the man—or whatever he was—intended to kill him.

"You will go to sleep, and just not wake up. That easy. You know you're tired, you know the lost feeling where the Eye of Omage tied you to the Earth will never go away. Let me make it easy for you."

"Right," Evan said, and this time sarcasm cut the word. "And what would you do to keep from dying? Kill a man? Two? A hundred? Destroy a world? What right have you to make that judgment?"

"Not a right. An obligation. It's why I'm here. You are the last remaining danger to the design."

"What design?" Evan had a sick feeling he didn't want to know.

"This." DaCosta moved the hypo in a tight circle. "The material sphere. Call it science, call it art, you are the last rogue element that can destroy it all."

"We've had this conversation before." Evan let his outrage transmute into a blind, defensive fury. "I've had enough of the games," he gritted between clenched teeth. "Dying is not easy. Neither is living, but I made my choice long before I met you."

He'd spent most of his life fighting to stay alive, and he was good at it. That one talent set him apart from the Paul Carters and the Jack Laurences who succumbed to the lure of martyrdom. Outside the wind rose, blew the gauzy curtains into a twisted tangle at the windows. Lily's words, "You have more power than you know— Ariton is a part of you," echoed in his mind.

Evan called upon the power of the elements that he had seen his lover shape, that had killed fifty people in the Black Masque. He stood, snapped the chain at his wrist with a shower of smoking metal splinters, and shaped the wind into a shield with his upraised hand, forced it outward.

"Clever boy." DaCosta rocked on his feet, recovered, and deflected time. They stood again, white king on black square facing black tower on the white, while the ignorant pawns who had brought them to this point cowered in the corner.

Evan gathered the wind that battered him. "I won't let you kill me," he told the guardian. He could feel the air pressure rise in the room, and he compressed it, shaped it like a charge, while he drew energy through the soles of his feet from the house itself, from the land resting uneasily on the sea. The house rocked on the pillars of its foundation sunk deep into the mud flats of the lagoon, and Alfredo DaCosta moved them again, minutes this time: Ca' DaCosta had not shaken, air pressure was normal. The effort raised a fine mist of sweat across the guardian's brow, at his temples.

So DaCosta had limits, no more control over matter than any human, more power over time. Evan drew lightning, directed the bolt at his adversary, but the man had moved himself in time, leaving Evan in a present that ticked by slowly. A second passed, two, three, while Evan stood at the center of the attic room, his nerves strung taut, and Franklin Simpson whimpered and beat on a door that would not open. When time converged, DaCosta reappeared close behind him. The guardian threw an arm around Evan's neck and twisted with his other hand.

Evan transferred through the second sphere and emerged across the room. DaCosta moved through time again, but Evan ignored him, focused on the surge of power he gathered at his feet. The house rocked. Cracks webbed the ceiling, scarring the figures there.

DaCosta appeared at his side, one hand gripping Evan's chin, the other pressing the hypo against the vein throbbing in his neck. One part of Evan's mind seemed to detach then, wondering how long DaCosta's poison would take to do its work. He reached for the hand, tried to drag it away, and felt the strain as DaCosta forced his head around, stretching his neck beneath the needle. He felt the sharp prick of it, and let go of the energy he had compressed underfoot, using all of his strength now to push DaCosta's hand away.

For a moment the universe seemed to wink out around them, and DaCosta wavered. Then the house wobbled like a drunken dancer, cracks wide enough to stuff a fist in splitting the walls, the floor. Marble arches tumbled from where they held up the ceiling, and the pentagram began to crack. Evan felt the walls begin to disintegrate, heard the keening scream of Marnie Simpson cut off abruptly beneath the unsmiling face of Thot as he transferred out.

# Chapter 31

*The Pentagram, a star with five points within a circle, is a shape of power. If a man summon a daemon and call that daemon to appear within the circle, that daemon is held within the circle until his master bids him be away upon his task. But if the master bids not the daemon to return to the circle after the task is done, the daemon may return and slay his master, winning freedom an' the master will it not.*

THE PALAZZO CA' DACOSTA LAY IN IRREGULAR HEAPS OF BROKEN STONE, WITH here and there the glint of marble reflecting the afternoon sunlight. Evan stood in the tiny piazza, watching the police and fire brigades crawl like beetles over the wreckage. An ambulance bobbed in the canal, too late to help Marnie and Frank Simpson.

Seemed like he'd been doing a lot of that lately, watching the destruction and the mounting body count. Too many had died, and for what? A promise of riches that didn't exist? Fear of death so fierce that the Simpsons would risk the vengeance of the daemons they bound to escape it? They'd lost that one, dead under a pile of rock. His fault, and their deaths had changed him. Evan felt it all from a distance, filtered through shock and exhaustion. Tomorrow, he knew, he'd count his losses—friends, enemies, and the part of himself that could not kill another human being—and figure out how to live with it.

Across the crowded square, a somber Alfredo DaCosta leaned against a wall, watching him. Evan made his way through the crowd to face his enemy.

"A partial success," the man greeted him. "You're still alive, but you finally did eliminate our friends, the Simpsons."

Evan gave DaCosta the point. He'd done it, would carry the mark of their deaths, like the mark of their stone, on his soul forever. Was his life worth two of his enemies?

*Hell, yes,* the survivor in him answered. He didn't much like himself at that moment, but he finally accepted what he was. Not like his father, not quite human either, but enough of both to want to go on living and let his conscience deal with the cost later.

A figure in a tan raincoat picked his way through the rubble, and Evan groaned. He waited until the man reached them, and gave him a brief nod of recognition. "Inspector James."

"Mr. Davis. I came down to identify your remains. Happy to see that is unnecessary." James turned to briefly inspect the damage. "They're calling it a gas explosion," he commented. "Fire department figures a pocket of natural gas under the house ignited—maybe a spark from foundation stones settling."

"That must be it, then," Evan agreed. "Are you here to take me back, Inspector?"

"That was my original intention. Mr. Davis. Since then, I have had a long chat with your Ms. Laurence. She explained that you were both kidnapped by the couple who admitted in her presence to murdering her brother. A brave girl. Escaped the kidnappers from that very building. With a bit of help from your agency, we have determined that you are not the first rich young man to come to the Simpsons' attention. I don't suppose they were fortunate enough to escape the explosion."

"No, Inspector, I don't believe they were."

"Well, then. Just a matter of identifying the bodies, and we can close this case." Inspector James reached into his breast pocket and pulled out a passport. "I believe you lost this." He handed the document to Evan. "Your bag was impounded—very nice dinner suit, by the way—the department will return it to your legal address once the paperwork is cleaned up. You will be going home, Mr. Davis?"

"As soon as legally possible, Inspector." Evan looked beyond the man to where stretcher carriers made their way through the destruction.

"I believe you are free to go any time. And I am certain that the local caribinieri agree with my hope that you will do so with all haste. And stay there for a while, Mr. Davis. Please."

James gave a short parting nod and walked purposefully toward the stretcher bearers, leaving Evan alone again with the count.

"Are you still planning to kill me?" Evan asked, too tired to feel more than inconvenienced by the idea.

"Would it do me any good?" the guardian asked, the piercing eyes measuring Evan, summing him up, breaking him down.

Evan shook his head. "Not really. Could get messy, though. Brad never covered this kind of stuff," he nodded at the ruins, "so I don't really know what I'm doing. Maybe I'll get tired, slow down enough for you to get me. Maybe I'll just get stronger with the practice. One thing I'm sure of, though: The fight would bring this city to the ground, maybe more. I don't want to do that. I just want to go home."

"So do I." The guardian stared off into the ruins, the centuries etched in the fine lines of his face, and a moment when, perhaps, the universes they called home had almost ceased to exist. "Get that training," DaCosta advised, "I'll sleep easier nights when you know what you're doing."

Evan nodded, watched the man—the guardian—walk away. "Home." A memory drifted out of long ago childhood—*click your heels three times.* He smiled. "There's no place like home."

Someone had scrubbed the pentacle from the bricks in the garden and set the patio furniture back in place. Fortunately, they'd also replaced the sliding glass doors; beads of rain clung to his jeans when he brushed past the tall spears of tulip leaves.

He'd slept for only a couple of hours, but waking up in his own bed did more for him than a full night's sleep in a Venetian hotel. Flipping a vinyl chair cushion to the dry side, he sat under the big fringed umbrella, his elbow on the table and his hands wrapped around a thick pottery coffee mug, considering his next move.

Claudia was going home to St. Louis, didn't want to see Evan again, didn't want to be reminded of what he had done, however unintentionally, to her brother. Jack was dead, and the memory punched him in the gut, forcing the air out of his lungs. If he had stayed away, Jack would still be alive, and Claudia would have lived out her life weaving rugs and weeding the roses, selling books for the bent little man they'd carried, burned beyond recognition, out of his shop. He knew down deep that Claudia was the real victim, had been from the start all those years ago in the Village. She'd never understood the stakes the rest of them were playing for.

*Jack.* The thought lingered in spite of his efforts to expel it. Jack had been waiting to die since that night in the Black Masque when he'd made the first blood sacrifice to a monster deity Omage created out of the frightened mongrel of two universes. Evan sipped the hot coffee, wondering if he would ever understand the urge to martyrdom, and trying to forget his own aborted plunge into the sun.

One more thing to do. With a last swallow of the bitter dregs, he set the coffee mug aside and stood up, shook himself down to the fingers to loosen up the tension that was tying him in knots at the thought of what he had to do. When he was as calm as he figured he was going to get, he painstakingly retraced the pentagram on the bricks, and stood at its center. Then he began the incantation:

"With a tranquil heart, and trusting in the Living and Only God, omnipotent and all-powerful, all-seeing and all-knowing, I conjure you, Badad, daemon of darkness, and you, Lirion, daemon of darkness, to appear before me. You are summoned by the Honor and Glory of God, by my Honor that I shall cause you to do no harm or injury to others, and for the greater glory of all creation both in the physical sphere and in the second sphere."

At first nothing happened, and Evan frowned, wondering if he'd gotten it wrong. Then the itch at his skin became a low rumble and the ground beneath his feet began to shake. He'd had enough of falling buildings to last a lifetime, and he cut the pyrotechnics short with an abrupt, "Cut the shit and get back here before I lose my temper."

The flickering blue figure appeared before him in a shock wave that blew breaking glass from the sliding doors into the living room beyond, and Evan sighed. They'd lose their insurance if they put in a claim for the same glass doors twice in one week, but he'd be damned if the replacement cost was coming out of his pocket.

"Who dares interfere in the affairs of Princes?"

Evan glared at the creature, naked, sexless, and twice as tall as the brick wall surrounding the garden. It didn't look much like the pictures of the devil in his books at school, but he figured he might be damned at that.

"Who the hell are you?" he snapped. "And get down here before somebody calls the police. I have to live in this neighborhood."

The blue figure glared back. "I could kill you where you stand, human."

"I'm not human," Evan pointed out, growing weary of the conversation. "My father is a lord of the host of Ariton and my mother is a human who didn't know any better. A monster, you might call me, and don't fool yourself. I don't suffer from the limitations of humans or the loyalties of your kind.

"As for killing me, if you could have, you would have done it already, so cut the crap."

"You have no dominion over me," the Prince of daemons thundered, but he contracted himself until only the top of his three horns could be glimpsed over the garden wall.

Evan dragged the hair off his forehead, raking his fingers deep and grabbing hold, thinking.

"Ariton, I presume," he concluded. "Since I called my personal daemons by name, I also presume they are in there somewhere. I want them back. Now." He didn't expect the Prince of daemons to understand the acid commentary loaded into the statement, nor was he disappointed.

"You take risks, monster," Ariton warned. "Those you call are at war, a war of your making."

"Not my making," he contradicted, and added, "the masters of the lords of Azmod are dead, the wand that bound them is shattered, and their jewel has been destroyed. By my reckoning, the war is over."

"There are slights still to be answered," the Prince objected, expanding in the small space of the garden again, until he loomed like a dark and lightning-charged storm cloud above the treetops.

"You will have to handle them with two less lords in your host, because I have a prior claim." He remembered then how literal daemons were— worse than lawyers—and he tried the summons again: "I conjure you Badad and you Lirion of the hosts of Ariton to appear before me alone of all your kind, and in the human forms by which I have known you."

Ariton laughed then, deep and rich and dangerous, like thunder rolling before a tornado. The Prince of daemons grew and filled the sky. Winds raged, tore the branches from the trees and threw them at the housetops.

Exasperated, Evan raised a hand, gathered his fingers together and the winds with them. The storm dwindled, faded, vanished. When he looked down again, Brad and Lily were stretched out on lawn chairs, glaring at the shattered doors.

"You've got to learn to curb your destructive impulses," Lily admonished.

"That's what DaCosta said." Evan examined the broken glass with a frown. "I thought you did that, or your Prince."

Her arms around his waist warned him that she'd moved, so the words whispered in his ear did not surprise him. "It was all you, little monster."

"I think I'm starting to understand that," Evan admitted.

"What happened?" Brad asked. His father wouldn't say it, but the daemon lord didn't seem too unhappy that Evan was still alive. "By my reckoning, you should have been dead two or three times today—yesterday—whenever."

Evan shook his head, not yet ready to discuss the empty place where Omage's stone had wrapped its tentacles in his mind.

"Closer than I'd have liked," he allowed. "But I survived. Our client and her husband didn't; they were dead when the police pulled them out of the wreckage of Ca' DaCosta."

Dead, along with Paul Carter, Jack Laurence, a shopkeeper off Charing Cross Road, and for what? So that he, Evan Davis, could go on living? For the first time in almost a year he thought of the gun hidden away in the safe. Pointless, he realized. Nothing would bring back his dead.

"I haven't cost Ariton the war up there?" He rolled his eyes heavenward, though he knew that direction did not define the sphere.

Brad shook his head. "Doesn't matter anyway. We'll win the next one, or the next. It's something to do."

Evan nodded, not really comprehending the politics of immortality and distracted by Lily's ministrations. Her fingers found the track of Marnie Simpson's cigarette, traced it a breath away from the reddened pucker of the damaged skin, and Evan remembered that he hadn't changed his shirt. Claudia had worn this shirt. He closed his eyes, seeing Omage pluck the buttons while the woman gripped his hand. Claudia was still alive—he hadn't destroyed everything.

"DaCosta sent you a message," he remembered. "He said I needed training."

"I noticed," Brad muttered. "But I think Lily will keep you out of trouble for the present."

It sounded like a good idea to Evan, and then Lily was touching him, finding unmarked skin, and adding the demanding tracks of her fingertips, sweet pain next to bitter.

"Upstairs?" he suggested.

She smiled.

# EYES
# OF THE
# EMPRESS

To David and Erik,

who always keep me jumping

## Acknowledgments

Special appreciation for the Philadelphia Major Crimes Unit, especially Officer Linda Fell. I stole from you shamelessly. Breaches in procedure are my own, of course; please forgive the artistic license! My favorite sources were two books by Sterling Seagrave, *Dragon Lady* and *Lords of the Rim,* and *Wild Swans: Three Daughters in China* by Jung Chang.

# Prologue

In the ordering of the heavens there are seven spheres, each ruled by a form that the ancients had called angels, or daemons. The material sphere came to stand among them like a patch on the hole blown between incompatible states of being in what the humans called the Big Bang. And, not surprisingly for a creation formed out of error and accident, the material sphere continued to struggle toward complete annihilation of all the other spheres. In human form as Private Investigator Kevin Bradley, Badad of the host of Ariton stood in the doorway and watched one of those attempts at destruction coming toward him under the leaded glass ceiling four stories above the Furness Library.

Evan Davis wove between the long reading tables set in rows through the center of the library, a plastic champagne flute held protectively close. Crowds still made his half-human son nervous, as if he expected the dean to slit his wrists in some bloody sacrifice to the gods of academe. Of course, being half human, Evan would carry the scars of the last time that had happened forever. But the Furness Building, decked out in all its refurbished glory, bore little resemblance to the back room in New York where Omage, daemon lord of the host of Azmod, had tortured Kevin Bradley's son, disrupting all seven spheres in the process. Brad had cut a deck of cards with Omage for the life of his son then, and Evan had returned the favor, facing down the daemon Prince of Ariton in his own back yard to pull his father out of a war between Princes. He could more than take care of himself at a reception for the graduates of Penn's art history department.

"You should be proud of that young man." Harry Li handed him a plastic flute of cheap champagne and nodded in Evan's direction. "Are you putting in an appearance at the graduation tomorrow?"

Brad passed him a scathing look.

"I didn't think so," Li assured him. "Frankly, I'm surprised that Evan is bothering with all the fanfare. I expected him to leave an address for us to mail his diploma and disappear."

Evan had planned exactly that, until his mother put her foot down. It was little enough to ask, Evan had reasoned. They'd all survive one night in the same place, and tomorrow it would be over. Brad took a quick, nervous glance about the room, but he didn't see the woman or her new husband. Harvey Barnes, Evan had introduced him, the principal at Edgemont High School, where Evan's mother taught chemistry. They'd both looked nauseatingly proud, as if they'd done it all themselves, but the new Mrs. Barnes had looked decidedly unsettled at the introduction. He didn't recognize her either, of course, and would rather not have found himself in conversation with her. Hell knew what would come of that. But he didn't see her in the library or in the front hall where the refreshments were set up, and Harry Li was still talking.

". . . But then, I thought you were mad to put him back in school in the first place. He did well, though. Very well."

Brad remembered two weeks of hell, when Evan had learned that he was half daemon, not half mad, and that he could control that daemon half and survive. A year later he'd bound his teacher, the daemon Badad of the host of Ariton, to his will. Since Kevin Bradley was that daemon in his true form, he had good reason to appreciate his son's swiftness of intelligence.

"He learns quickly." Underestimating that fact had cost him dearly.

"I never had a doubt about that," Li agreed, "But he's been through a lot. I wasn't as sure he could handle the structure. He never did develop any ease with the other students."

Bradley gave Harry Li a sardonic twist of a smile. "Does not play well with his peers?" Evan had no peers. The only other of his kind had died in madness from Omage's torture and the torment of his own monstrous existence. The two parts of Evan's nature, human and daemon, did not blend comfortably. Harry didn't know that, of course, but he was sharp enough to sense something in Evan that made him different.

Harry Li tilted his head at an angle—Brad recognized the expression; Li was pulling facts together, weighing them—then he answered: "Watching Evan in a classroom was a lot like watching a shark in a room full of minnows. He terrified the rest of the students every time he opened his mouth, but he didn't seem to notice them at all."

"He can have that effect on people."

Harry Li had more interests than chess and art. Brad had often heard him mutter imprecations about the *I Ching,* even blaming his losses on the meanings recorded in books of the hexagrams. So he asked, for conversation and maybe because the question worried him:

"And what does the *I Ching* tell you about his future?"

Harry Li gave him a deeply ironic smile. "Don't jest about things you don't understand, my friend."

"Then you *have* been casting sticks!"

"Of course not. We use coins these days. Much faster and just as effective."

"And?" Brad thought he was teasing the professor, but Harry seemed to think otherwise.

"Danger, Will Robinson."

Harry could have meant a warning that the subject of the discussion was approaching. But Brad didn't think that was it.

"I don't get the reference," he admitted.

"I know you don't. And therein lies the danger."

Too late to question Harry further—Evan had closed in on them with that slightly trapped look on his face that said, "I am out of here, or here is dust."

"Professor Li. I didn't know you and my father were acquainted."

"Primarily as adversaries." Li smiled. "We play against each other at the chess club."

"I didn't realize—" Evan shook his head, then took one of his dizzying leaps of conversation: "Have you seen my mother?" he asked Brad. "She was here earlier."

"Not since you introduced us."

Brad had avoided the woman and her new husband all night. He didn't see that they had anything to discuss, and he wasn't about to find himself trapped in a private conversation with her, trying to explain why he didn't look like she remembered. He'd gotten used to this face and body and had no intention of resurrecting the one he'd used to seduce her all those years ago. It would have confused the hell out of Harry Li anyway. Fortunately, Evan didn't press the issue. Neither of them wanted to revisit the place where Badad the daemon had chosen on a slightly mad whim to let his son live in spite of the command of his own Prince. And Evan knew better than to push where his father didn't want to go.

"Lily and Alfredo left half an hour ago." Evan seemed to be cataloging his guests at the reception, checking them off some list in his head. Lily—the daemon Lirion in the second sphere—had deigned to mingle briefly at the party, but seeing Alfredo Da'Costa on her arm hadn't pleased Evan at all. Da'Costa was more than just stiff competition for Lily's attention. As a guardian of the material sphere, he had once set out to murder Evan. One life in exchange for the safety of the known universes, Da'Costa had explained, but Evan had put more value on that one life, his own, than Da'Costa was willing to pay. Venice was still sinking slowly into the mud, not toppled in a struggle between the daemon half of Kevin Bradley's son and the guardian from the third sphere. But Da'Costa had left them with a warning to train the boy or else.

Brad didn't think the University of Pennsylvania's art history department was quite what Da'Costa had in mind, but Brad himself approved. In spite of what Harry Li might have thought, Evan had needed the structure, probably more than he'd needed specific training in controlling his daemon half. He'd had both. Brad still claimed he didn't understand human emotions, but he knew this one was pride. The damned bastard had done well for himself. And maybe soon Evan would have the confidence to undo the one act that stood between them. But Evan never mentioned the binding. And Badad waited.

Evan hitched his weight from one foot to the other, his focus not on Brad but taking in their surroundings. Looking for a place to dump the glass of champagne, Brad figured. "It's getting late."

"Go." Harry Li clapped Evan on the back. "Half the faculty are in shock that you showed up at all."

Evan gave him a rueful snort. "The other half are wishing I hadn't, I'm sure."

"Not the faculty," Harry objected, "We knew about your experience with the agency from your application. You gave a few teaching assistants some bad days until we figured out what to do with you, though."

"Speaking of the agency—" Harry kept a hand on Evan's shoulder, but turned to include Brad in the conversation. "I'd like you to stop by my office tomorrow."

Here it was, then. Lately, Harry had missed more than one chess evening for board meetings at the Philadelphia Museum of Art, and Brad had figured that a recent spate of thefts must be at the root of it.

"We still don't have a line on the materials stolen from the University Museum last month," Harry continued. "In a felony burglary case like this, University policy says turn the case over to the police and let them handle it. They don't deal with outside contractors on retrieval—not with the liberals calling us post-colonial grave robbers—but I think I've finally persuaded the other board members to hire a security agency to evaluate present security arrangements for the museum."

"Are you expecting trouble?" Brad asked.

"I am," Evan interrupted. "They stole half a dozen pieces from the University Museum, but the Dowager Empress crystal ball was their big score. The Smithsonian lost their crystal six months ago, again, with a few less valuable artifacts. All of the other stolen objects were small, easy to hide and transport, which the crystals weren't—the one here at the University weighs almost fifty pounds. It looks as though the perp is trying to cover the real point of the robberies—the crystals."

"There are only three true crystal balls of that size in existence," Harry explained, "and we have no reason to think they will stop until they have the third major crystal ball." He paused, but Brad knew what was coming—"Which the Philadelphia Museum of Art has in its collection."

"Of course."

Harry hadn't expected him to be surprised, after all. "And what does Ellen have to say about it?" Inspector Ellen Li would surely have an opinion on the subject. Nothing of value moved in the city's thieves' underground that Ellen Li didn't put her finger on, eventually. And she played a better game of chess than her husband. They'd gone head-to-head across a board at the chess club most Wednesdays for the past three years, a foursome that included the incomparable Mai Sien Chong, a recently added local importer who wore silk cheongsams that showed off her legs to distraction. If Brad had trusted his secrets with any human, he'd have hired Ellen Li away from the Philadelphia Police Department long ago. But she was too sharp to miss the strange comings and goings at Bradley, Ryan, and Davis. So he thought of her as the worthy competition and tried not to look too closely at the ties he was building to the material world around him.

Harry shrugged. "The police are doing what they can, of course. They would anyway. But Ellen agrees that, unless the stolen artifacts turn up for sale, we may never find the perp. With Ellen's help, I've persuaded the board that we'd be better off stopping the thieves before they hit us than trying to find the artifacts after they are stolen. And for that we can go to outside help.

"I'd like you to take on the project. Let us know where we need to tighten security, what we can do to protect our collection and our people."

"Has anyone been hurt during the robberies to date?" Brad asked.

"Not yet. But," Li added, "we can't depend on luck forever."

"Tomorrow, then," Brad agreed. "And I assume that trapped expression on your face means you are ready to leave?" he asked Evan.

"I passed 'ready to leave' a minute and a half after we got here," Evan asserted. "Let me check the gallery—yes, there they are—"

Brad tracked the direction Evan was moving and caught sight of the couple. Harvey Barnes was taller than Evan's mother, and slim, with a trim band of closely cropped gray hair circling his bald pate. He smiled when he saw Evan coming toward him and held out a hand. When Evan took it,

Barnes pulled him closer for a quick hug before handing him off to his mother. Evan kissed her on the forehead and watched them leave together before turning his glance back to his father. He nodded in the direction of the door and headed toward it, fully expecting, Brad figured, that he'd follow without a by your leave.

"You can rein him in next week," Harry said, giving Brad a final slap on the back. "He's going to be impossible until all the fuss is over and he can get back to normal."

"Normal?" Brad asked, eyes wide with mock surprise. "Evan and normal in the same sentence is a contradiction in terms."

"Interesting, though." The sound of Harry's laughter followed Brad to the door.

# Chapter 1

TOO LATE. THE GUARD LAY FACEDOWN, EYES OPEN, ON THE FLOOR BESIDE THE broken display case in the corner of the Chinese gallery. Glass was scattered on top of the body, not under it, so the thief had taken out the guard first, then smashed the case. At least half a dozen artifacts were missing, the Moon Stone crystal ball among them. Not the best way to start a working relationship with a client. Harry Li would not be pleased; Kevin Bradley wondered if that meant chess was out this week.

Eyes like that didn't usually lie, but Brad knelt on one knee and located the pulse point at the guard's neck just to be sure. Surprise there—not dead after all. Barely a pulse though, just a feeling he wouldn't have recognized before his own body death not long enough ago. Whatever force animated human beings had gone walkabout, leaving the meat shell to cool its heels. Which took Brad back to the thief: cool customer there. Must have known that he'd blown the job, but he took the time to grab what he'd come for even knowing the police must be on their—

Footsteps. Ah. Yes.

"Stand up slowly and put your hands over your head."

Brad stood, picking glass splinters out of his hands. The man in blue who pointed the nasty looking semiautomatic at him looked too young to be out without a keeper, and he'd already developed a sheen of sweat over his upper lip. Brad considered his options. As Kevin Bradley, private investigator, he could either do as the nervous policeman said or take a nasty bullet in the gut. In his true nature as Badad, the daemon lord of the host of Ariton, however, he had a great deal more leeway. He could leave, via the second celestial sphere—a clean vanish or maybe add some bells and whistles for entertainment value. A more intimidating shape—a dragon, given their location in the Chinese exhibit—might be interesting. Would fuel the rumor machine for years, he figured.

Unfortunately, that was Evan's voice he heard through the far doorway,

"He wasn't at home, but I left him a message to join us here," followed too quickly by the source himself, trailing Harry, his wife Ellen, the curator he'd met that afternoon, and another security guard, this one with stripes on his sleeve.

"Can we get more light in here?" Ellen Li demanded.

"I intended to do just that, Lieutenant," the curator said, bringing his head up with something very like a sniff. "But some of us take a moment or two for shock when we encounter murders on our premises."

There was nothing inscrutable in the impatient glare she leveled on him. The curator winced, but he went off to locate light switches as the rest of the group detoured around the royal bed in the center of the gallery and headed toward Brad. Ellen Li's badge gleamed gold against the royal blue of her dinner dress, glinting its own reminders of rank, and a warning in the brightening light. She'd either thank Brad later for getting her out of a boring political function or damn him for ruining a night out with Harry, whose suit and tie gave him no clues at all.

Disgusted, Brad lifted his hands over his head.

Evan tracked on the motion in the corner; Brad saw recognition kick in. "Brad! How'd you get here before I did? Harry just called a few minutes ago, said the sergeant here had reported a break-in." A moment of hesitation, while Evan decided whether to play it close or ingenuous, then: "And why do you have your hands on your head?"

The police would want answers to the first question soon enough; Brad answered the last. He nodded in the direction of the policeman. "That young man suggested it. Since he was holding a gun, not too steadily, on my person, I complied with his request."

Harry waved a dismissive gesture at the policeman with the gun. "You can put that away now, son."

"I caught this man in the act, sir." The officer did not lower his gun. "He was kneeling over the body when I arrived, his hands on the guard's throat, and I believe he gave consideration to flight when I told him to stand fast. I have not yet had the opportunity to frisk him for weapons, and I believe he continues to pose a threat to this party until I do so, sir."

"Flight?" Evan raised his eyebrows, then craned his neck to scan the entrances to the gallery. "Is Lily here?"

"Lily is in Venice. With Alfredo." Personally, Brad thought that whole relationship too dangerous to contemplate, but he was sufficiently annoyed with humans at the moment to enjoy Evan's discomfort.

But he was quickly tiring of the whole circus. Fortunately for all present, Ellen Li pulled rank. "Lieutenant Li, Officer—Franks. You can put your weapon away now."

Franks peered at her badge, as if he doubted it was real, but he did finally lower the weapon. Brad figured it was safe to put his hands down; he stuffed them in his pockets just to see the young man twitch while Ellen continued to stand him down:

"You've done well, but I'll take it from here. Give the morgue a call, and—"

"Not the morgue, the hospital," Brad interrupted.

Ellen gave him a skeptical frown—she'd seen eyes like that before as well, always on corpses—but knelt and reached for the pulse point. "Nothing," she confirmed.

"Wait," Brad advised. She did, jerked her hand back in surprise. "You're right, but I don't know how . . ." she just shook her head. "Emergency it is. Tell them to have the trauma team standing by. Let them sort it out."

Brad smiled companionably at the uniformed policeman. "Aren't you going to ask Lieutenant Li to put her hands over her head now? After all, you just caught her in the same act in which you say you caught me."

Officer Franks ignored the comment. "Do you want me to cuff him?" he asked Ellen.

"No need." While she was down on the floor she gave the body of the unconscious security guard a quick check. "I don't want to move him, in case he has spinal injuries, but I don't see any wounds or blunt trauma injuries on him. Don't know what we'll find when we turn him over, though. A small caliber bullet to the chest, and the body pressure on the wound might have stopped any major external bleeds while the bullet does God knows what on the inside."

She stood up and started to brush glass off her palms, then thought better of it and began to pick the splinters off, repeating Brad's own actions. "We'll know in a few minutes."

Brad smiled at the officer Ellen Li had identified as Franks, just finishing his call on the radio.

"Appearances can be deceiving," he said.

"I am sure they are," Ellen Li agreed, and added, "but we can sort everything out at headquarters, I am sure."

"Tomorrow," Evan suggested, but Ellen Li shook her head.

"Tonight."

A commotion at the entrance interrupted them: Several more uniformed police officers arrived and began unreeling yellow crime scene tape while a brace of emergency med-techs brushed past them with a backboard and a stretcher. Forensics followed. Ellen Li left them to it and made her way to Brad's side.

"We'll want a statement from you." She picked another piece of glass from her hand. The small wound bled, and she looked around for a cloth, took the linen handkerchief that Brad held out to her. "Thanks. Officer Franks is not the only one who wants to know why you were found kneeling over an unconscious security guard next to a broken and empty display case after closing."

"We could use my office," Harry Li offered, but Ellen glared him down. She didn't tell her husband how to date Chinese Art, and he didn't tell her how to run her investigations. In the years Brad had known them both, they hadn't changed that rule and it looked as though they weren't going to start now.

"We'll use my office; the station is just a few blocks from here."

"I know it's an inconvenience, Brad." Ellen turned back to him. "We are all in for a rough night, but it's in your interest as well as ours to find as much evidence as we can while the scene is fresh. If the guard does have a bullet in him, it will help if we can prove incontrovertibly that you had no powder residue on your hands."

Brad didn't like the direction that took them.

"It just eliminates the question before someone asks it in court," Ellen explained. "More importantly, we need all the help we can get with this. You know as well as I do that we haven't had a whisper on the University job, and it doesn't take a genius to figure out that the same people paid a visit here tonight. But we didn't have a trained observer on the scene the last time. You might have heard or seen something important that you haven't connected to the burglary, and we have a better chance at shaking it loose tonight than if we wait. But I don't have to tell you that—it's your case too, after all."

"I'm not likely to forget," Brad asserted, "But I was beginning to wonder if you had. The board of trustees hired me to check out security. As we can see, it was insufficient for the purpose—you will have my recommendations and a bill on Monday, Harry. But I was hired to do a security check, not to solve a crime. And the board of trustees hasn't paid remotely enough for me to *be* the crime."

"No blood, Lieutenant," the med-tech announced. He and his partner shifted the backboard to the stretcher and snapped it in position to roll. "No sign of injury at all. May be a heart attack; we'll know soon enough."

"Thank you."

The med-tech gave her a distracted nod, focused more on the patient than the crime. "Anything else you need, they'll have it at the hospital," he said, and then the stretcher was rolling.

Ellen Li watched them disappear through the doorway, then turned back to Brad. "Looks like your mission statement just changed. Time to renegotiate." She gave him a weak imitation of her usual cocky grin, then addressed one of the police officers hovering suspiciously close to Brad.

"Don't cuff him, Coretta, just put him in my car. I'll drive him to the station myself."

She gripped his arm. Brad figured she meant it for reassurance, but he weighed the value of the Lis as chess partners against the inconvenience of a murder investigation with himself as a possible suspect and wondered if his jacket would stay in her hand or vanish with him when he transported out.

Then Evan caught his eye. Scared but determined. That combination never boded well for his father. Slowly, Evan shook his head, "No."

"Is that a command?" Brad challenged. It didn't matter that the small crowd around him stared as if he'd lost his mind. Evan was the only one that mattered, and Evan said, "Yes."

Brad glared at his son, not quite believing that he'd heard correctly. But he knew too well the hard set of Evan's jaw and the look in Evan's eyes, dying inside and braving it out, thinking he was giving nothing away. He meant it.

Always there had been war between daemons and the humans that bound them. Evan, half Ariton, and that half the stuff of the Daemon's sphere, had commanded and won an uneasy alliance with his servant, the daemon who had fathered him. The binding was real, but Evan had kept his promise to wield it only to protect, never to harm, the daemon lords he commanded. Until now.

"Don't ever lose control," Brad warned, and he saw that Evan understood. The relationship that neither could explain but that each had valued ended now in a war that Evan Davis had declared.

"Let's go." Ellen—he was beginning to think of her in adversarial terms, as Lieutenant Li—exerted slight pressure on his sleeve. "The faster we check you out and get your statement to satisfy my boss, the faster this will be over. Then we'll sit down together over one of Harry's good wines and figure out what is really going on, okay?"

She started to move him out, giving Evan a last suggestion before they left the gallery. "I don't expect there to be any trouble, but it wouldn't hurt to wake up your lawyer." She gave Evan her card. "Meet us as soon as you can, and we'll take it from there."

"You know he didn't do it . . ." Evan began. Brad wondered about the question in his voice. Did he doubt Brad's innocence or Ellen's faith?

"We'll be there within the hour," he finished without waiting for an answer. "An hour."

Was that a warning? Didn't the kid know there was nothing Brad could do about the situation right now? A command from the human who bound him left him few alternatives. From Evan's expression, Brad figured it was a promise. Not enough of one, though; nothing short of release from the binding spell would ever be enough. But then they were out the back, the folly overlooking the Schuylkill River a delicate shadow shrouded with the more solid darkness of the undergrowth that surrounded it. And Ellen had her hand on his head, guiding him into the back seat of the nondescript Ford sedan she drove for work.

He wanted out of that car, out of that body, and felt the explosion building up inside him with a yearning for the second sphere, for home and freedom from all things solid and material. And the binding seared a fire in his gut. Deep, deep, the rage boiled against the command to stay, locked in human shape and captive once again.

# Chapter 2

"THIS HAD BETTER BE IMPORTANT, MR. DAVIS. I HAVEN'T HAD A DAY OFF SINCE the first of
ay."

Khadijah Flint climbed out of the Audi parked in the timid glow of the streetlight, and Evan felt . . . better. She wore a pair of green slacks and a silk shirt in a blocky African print. A small purse hung by a narrow strap from her shoulder, and she carried a briefcase in her hand. She made a quick assessment of the neighborhood. "It never gets any better," she murmured. "Still, I suppose it will be safe enough for now."

"It's a police station, how much safer can it be?" Evan stepped around the drunk pissing against the side of the station building and opened the door for her.

"Sometimes I wonder about you, child." She shook her head, the beads in her short braids clacking softly, and entered the police station, bypassed the glass window behind which the local station operated, and headed for the stairs.

"So, how did Brad find himself in a *tête-à-tête* with the Major Crimes Unit in the middle of the night?"

"We were working on a security check for the museum." Evan let it go with a sigh, passing the responsibility to her with his explanation: "Brad decided to do a surprise inspection of the premises after closing, but the thief had already been there."

"I don't suppose he mentioned to anyone at the police, or even the agency, that he was going to be 'checking things out'?"

"You know Brad."

"Of course." Flint rolled her eyes in a patented display of disgust. "As usual, Mr. Bradley is doing as he damned well pleases and expecting the rest of us to clean up after him."

Evan shrugged. She didn't know the half of his own sense of futility.

He'd given up expecting normal human behavior of his daemon kin pretty much on making their acquaintance, but he couldn't very well discus that particular problem with Brad's lawyer. He settled for the facts of the case, as he knew them.

"Lieutenant Ellen Li took the call. Apparently she's a friend of Brad's." And when had that happened, he wondered? When had Badad, daemon of the second celestial sphere, settled into his human identity and made himself a life? "She brought him in and told me to call my lawyer."

"Well, here I am." She pushed the door open ahead of him and entered the anteroom to Major Crimes at the top of the stairs. "Let's get this over with."

He'd been here before, but not more than once or twice. Each time, the immediate impression remained the same: Someone had dumped a jumble of cast-off furniture into the abandoned shower room of a particularly run-down Y. He'd never understood why the city covered the walls and floors of its police stations with tile blocks of that particular shade of institutional green, but then, he'd worked hard at keeping his relationship with the law as distant as possible. The agency's suspects usually managed to avoid arrest, which suited Bradley, Ryan, and Davis just fine. In the more refined reaches of the art world, it was sometimes hard to tell the thieves from the victims anyway, so the agency settled for a simpler equation. Their clients paid them well to retrieve their stolen valuables with discretion. The objects returned home, the fee landed in the agency's bank account. And no one looked too closely lest they open a can of authentication and provenance worms that wouldn't go away until the art wound up in the hands of a third world dictator who would denounce the West for robbing his country and then turn around and sell the damned thing for missiles as soon as he got it back.

For a fairly large retainer and the occasional bonus, Khadijah Flint kept the legal end, until now mostly a matter of the right paperwork in the right hands, running smoothly. But they'd chosen her for the predatory intensity she could bring to the work when they needed it. He was going to need that predator tonight, Evan figured.

"Khadijah Flint." She handed her card to the officer at the window while Evan stood to the side. "I represent Kevin Bradley, and I'd like to see my client."

"He's back there—" the officer opened the door next to the pass-through window and gestured behind her—"come around." Flint entered and Evan followed. The officer closed the door after him.

"Evan Davis?" she asked him.

"That's me." He darted a quick glance after Khadijah Flint, wondering if he would need her services as well, but she was already winding her way between the desks, making her way toward the murmur of voices in the back.

"Ellen, the lieutenant, said you'd be here."

Ellen Li was Brad's friend. It would be okay.

"She said to tell you that they'd be a while, but you can wait with Harry if you'd like."

"Thanks."

Harry Li was sitting in the side chair next to an abandoned desk under a window air conditioner that rattled like a coffee grinder whenever the compressor clicked on. Evan made his way toward him across an obstacle course of abandoned desks and chairs separated by upholstered screens too low to afford any real privacy. Finally he dropped into the side chair of the next desk and stared at the professor across the narrow distance that pretended to be an aisle.

"Thanks for waiting," he said, and Harry shrugged.

"I would have, anyway. Ellen will need a ride home."

Evan wondered whether that was some sort of declaration of sides, but Harry Li seemed to recognize the thought as it played over Evan's face. "It's in the board's minutes that we hired the agency for a security review. So your father had a reason to be there even if he hadn't told anyone what he was going to do."

"Thanks. Have you seen him since they brought him in?"

Harry nodded. "Ellen sent him to the Roundhouse, to forensics first. They just brought him back a few minutes ago."

Police Headquarters, that was, shaped like a pair of handcuffs tossed like a challenge on the cityscape. Inside was a warren; it reminded Evan of other claustrophobic rooms he'd found himself trapped in. He didn't want to think about it, but the image in his mind, of Brad fighting the binding while the walls closed around him, wouldn't go away. The clammy fear sweat pricked at his temples. Hell, hell, what had he done?

Voices across the room pulled him out of the funk he'd started to slide into; Ellen Li stood on the other side of an open door in low conversation with a rumpled-looking man with thick gray hair and a slight paunch. Khadijah Flint joined them. Her hand went out, smile threatening with shiny white teeth, and she murmured something to each as she shook hands in turn.

"Who's that?" Evan asked, and Harry looked in the direction he pointed.

"Captain Marsh. Heads Major Crimes. He's Ellen's boss, and he's not real happy to be here, I gather, but politically I suppose he has to show that he's on top of the investigation." It made sense. A burglar, or a team of burglars, had walked into the museum and walked out again with a rock crystal sphere the size of his head. The newspapers would be screaming, particularly since the theft appeared to be an encore performance. Evan nodded and stood up, ready to join the group at the open door when Harry Li stopped him.

"Evan." Li hesitated, and Evan wondered why he suddenly looked so guilty.

"They asked me if I knew Brad was going to try to break into the museum tonight, to test security. I had to say no. I didn't suspect, of course. I should have, perhaps, but Ellen knew I was surprised when we got the call. I couldn't lie to her."

"Not your fault, Harry." What could he tell the man? "I've been working with my father for four years now, and I've felt as if I were one step behind the whole time. But he's good at the job, and he didn't steal your crystal ball."

"I'm sure of that too, Evan." Harry Li hesitated, as if he were sifting carefully through his thoughts to winnow out what he could say.

"Will you come to my office tomorrow?" he finally asked. "Ellen would say that I am being foolish, but I believe there is more at work here than meets the eye."

"I'll listen to anything that can help us solve the case, Harry, no matter how strange it may sound." And, he figured, if Harry Li had even a hint of a suspicion about Kevin Bradley's true identity, he'd best deal with it quickly. He wondered how much, if anything, Brad had told his good friends, the Lis. Shit. For someone who wasn't even human, Brad sure knew how to complicate a life. "But right now, I want to see Brad."

The cluster in front of the doorway moved out of his way for a moment, and Evan caught a glimpse of his father. Brad sat motionless on a steel bench against the wall of a tiny room crammed uncomfortably tight with a single chair and a table half the size of the desk where he sat with Harry. He wanted to tell his father he was sorry, but he couldn't figure out how to start and was frankly afraid that if he released the daemon from his command, all hell would break loose.

"It will be all right."

Evan wondered what Harry Li saw in his face and damned himself for showing more than he intended. But Harry wasn't finished.

"He's just a witness. And, since he had no weapon, had nothing to cut the glass case with, and he had none of the artifacts on his person, there is no reason to think that will change. His presence perhaps demonstrates poor judgment, but Ellen will sort it out."

Evan couldn't think of anything to say, except, "I have to find Lily. She's going to be furious with me."

Li frowned. "Furious with Brad, maybe. He's the one who put himself in this position, not you."

"I don't think Lily will see it that way."

Evan stood up, wandered past the small group talking in low voices outside the room where Brad waited with blood simmering in his eyes, to an ell extension off the cramped bullpen. He poured coffee from a pot warming on a table into a styrofoam cup and stared at the glass display of a vending machine, seeing nothing.

He'd be lucky to get away with his life after this stunt, he figured. Lily would kill him if Brad didn't. Couldn't really blame them, either. He'd broken the one solemn promise he'd ever made to them. One slender thread of words had held them in a balance of power and obligation for three years, since Evan Davis had bound his daemonic relatives to protect them from the predatory clutches of Franklin Simpson and his wife. Evan remembered the day, the words—

*"With a tranquil heart, and trusting in the Living and Only God, omnipotent and all-powerful, all-seeing and all-knowing, I conjure you, Badad, daemon of darkness, and you, Lirion, daemon of darkness, to appear before me . . . by this I command your oath: that whenever and every time you shall be summoned, by whatever word or sign or deed, in whatever time or place, and for whatever occasion or service, you will appear immediately and without delay. You will obey all commands set for you in whatever form they shall be conveyed . . . swear."*

He'd sworn in his turn never to use the binding spell for his own benefit, but only to protect them from the threat of others. They had believed him because he, like them, was of Ariton, the Daemon Prince of which his father and Lily were eternal lords. His own relationship to the Prince, and his daemon kin in general, would last only the length of his human lifetime but he'd meant his oath to them for as long as the binding held them. And he'd broken his word, for what? If he hadn't given the command to stay, where would they be now? Anywhere but here, which had serious appeal.

"Evan? Evan Davis?"

Evan's hand jumped, spilling hot coffee on his thumb. Where had Joe Dougherty come from, and how had he gotten so close without Evan hearing a thing? He hadn't heard that voice since high school, and he could have lived his life quite happily never hearing it again.

"What are you doing here," he asked, mopping at his hand with paper napkins. "I thought you worked out of the Northeast."

"I do, as a rule." Dougherty poured coffee into a styrofoam cup and sipped it, grimacing. "I had a call from your mother a few days ago. She seemed to think you might need a friend. Looks like she was right."

Joe and he had never been friends, certainly not in high school, when Evan had been out of control and hell-bent for suicide. Joe had been a jock in those days. No need to ask where he knew Evan's mom from, though—Dougherty had been twice through basic chemistry. He'd probably still be trying to pass it if Evan's mother hadn't tutored him three afternoons a week that second time through. Which didn't make him Evan Davis' confidant.

"My father has a lawyer, one of the best. Since he's innocent, that's all the help he should need."

Evan pretended sudden interest in the chips and candy bars displayed in the glass window of the vending machine, but Dougherty wasn't convinced. He grabbed Evan's arm and physically turned him away from the vending machine.

"Either buy something or sit down. You're making me nervous."

"I don't want anything." He wanted a drink, wanted it so badly that the longing for the burn of it down his throat and the heat of it in his gut sang in his nerve endings. But Evan wasn't going to share that with Joe Dougherty.

Dougherty led him to a desk between the one where Harry Li sat and the room where Ellen Li was taking Brad's statement; he pushed him down into the side chair and took the chair behind the desk for himself.

"Your mother is worried about *you,* Evan, not Kevin Bradley."

He picked up a pencil and bounced the eraser end against the telephone on the desk. When he next spoke, Dougherty didn't look up at him, and Evan realized the man was giving them both the privacy of their eyes, if nothing else.

"She doesn't know what you've gotten yourself into with these people, but she's sure of one thing: Kevin Bradley isn't your father."

"You're crazy—"

Dougherty waved a warning finger in Evan's face then, and held him glance for glance, metaphoric gloves off.

"Listen to somebody for a change, Evan! That always was your problem, even in high school—you wouldn't listen to a damned thing anybody said. Now you will listen, not because I like you, but because I'd be flipping burgers if it weren't for your mother. And you owe her more than I do, for those years of hell you put her through. Listening to what I have to say won't begin to even that score, but it's a start."

"You can't begin to understand my life—" Fury built behind Evan's eyes, reducing him to inarticulate sputtering. He wasn't responsible for what his birth had made him. He owed Brad his life, literally and for the shape it had taken since they'd met across Omage's knife four years ago, but he was sick and tired of taking the blame for not being what everyone on Rosemont Street expected of the chemistry teacher's son.

But Dougherty wasn't giving him time to explode, and he did the one thing that would cut through the haze of Evan's anger. He stopped yelling.

"She saw him at the reception two nights ago. And he wasn't the man, Evan. He's not the one. I know what he's done for you, but see her point of view. He pulls you out of a situation in New York that I'm sure she doesn't know the half of, cleans you up, uses his contacts to get you into a college you couldn't have passed the entrance qualifiers for, pays for an education you couldn't even afford to dream about on your own. And what did he get in return?

"When she believed that you'd found your father, it made some sense. We don't see it nearly often enough, but sometimes a man does take responsibility for a child he didn't know he had, especially if he's rich and he has no other family. Now she knows he's not the man she slept with way back when, and she's got to wonder. So she calls, asks for my help, because she's scared for you, Evan, really scared.

"Now, I figure, no surprise here. Rich older man falls for a younger one, sets him up with some social polish so that they can go out in public together. Explains the whole setup. Not my scene, but, hey, whatever floats your boat. If you want to spend your days wandering naked around some rich pervert's house with a leash around your cock, that's your business. He may even care about you in his own way, I'm willing to grant you that. But you ought to tell your mother something that she can believe, because expecting a woman to forget what the first man she slept with looks like isn't working."

"It isn't like that," Evan insisted, but Dougherty waved his protest away.

"Like I said, what you tell her about your sex life is your business. But she asked me to investigate, I did, and now Bradley, Ryan, and Davis is *my* business. This guy isn't just some rich and misunderstood perv, Evan. He's dangerous. He appeared here in Philadelphia about four years ago with a paper trail that doesn't bear up under close scrutiny. And three years ago, while you were on vacation in England, he took on a case for a Mrs. Marnie Simpson, who wound up dead, along with her husband and her son and a bar full of people in New York who had no other connection with the case than to be in the wrong place at the wrong time.

"Now I'll admit that the Simpsons were not exactly Ozzie and Harriet.

In fact, they'd be in prison now if they hadn't died, but the fact is that they did die."

Evan froze. He could see in Dougherty's calculating glance that the policeman in him knew he'd touched a nerve and was waiting to see what he'd shaken loose. Beyond caution, Evan answered the accusation out of the raw place where old battle wounds might never heal and figured Dougherty could make of it what he wanted.

"The Simpsons died when a building fell on them. I was their prisoner in the building and barely escaped with my own life, as Interpol will be happy to corroborate. If you can explain to me how my father—and he is my father, not my lover or my master, no matter what my mother does or does not remember—could have been responsible for the Simpsons' deaths when the London police placed him a thousand miles from Venice at the time, I may listen."

*But you won't, Joe,* he thought, *because that one was mine.* Collateral deaths, not even part of the endgame, though they'd set the whole wretched business into motion twenty years before. *And you couldn't handle that any more than you could handle the rest of my truth, so don't push where you can't follow.*

"Then you can explain how he blew up a gas line buried in the original concrete floor of a sixty-year-old building. But until you have evidence— evidence, Joe, not suspicion—that my father has done something illegal, stay out of my life."

*—You aren't up to my caliber of enemy—*

"I can't."

And Evan knew that Dougherty had seen more than he'd wanted the man to see but that he'd never understand enough.

"It isn't a matter of your mother and a favor anymore. When Officer Franks found Kevin Bradley standing over the body of an unconscious security guard, surrounded by the evidence of a botched burglary, investigating him stopped being a favor for your mother. Even if he is your father, that doesn't change a thing.

"Frankly, I don't care what your relationship with him is. I think he's dangerous, I think he's guilty, and I am going to nail him before he gets you killed. And the last is the only part that has anything to do with your mother.

"Now, if you will excuse me, I am about to put my career on the chopping block over Lieutenant Li's obvious conflict of interest in this case. When you see your mother, tell her she got payback in spades.

"And Evan, whatever your lifestyle these days, tell her, or as much of it as you can. She sees how well you've done. She'll understand. And you are going to need someone in your corner when this case goes south for Kevin Bradley."

Dougherty dropped the pencil on the desk and headed not toward the tiny interview room but toward the corner office where Captain Marsh sat, taking the fight out of Evan with him. He still believed that the truth— however much of it they could tell—would see them clear. But he figured that Dougherty was going to make it a hell of a lot harder to prove Brad's innocence. And if Dougherty kept digging, in the long run it might prove impossible.

# Chapter 3

FORENSICS COULD HAVE BEEN WORSE, BRAD FIGURED. IT HAD, AT LEAST, KEPT him moving. The police already had his fingerprints on record with his application for a license for the agency, so the officer, Coretta something or other, had taken just a quick look at his hands. She'd explained that, since there was no evidence that a weapon had been used on the unconscious guard and they'd found no weapons on him or in the vicinity where Officer Franks had found him, there was no point in looking for evidence of them on his hands. She'd borrowed his jacket for a quick shake over a white table, asked him if he'd touched anything, and marked down his answer when he told her he'd gotten a few bits of glass on his hands when he checked the guard for a pulse.

"Nothing else?" she pushed, then asked outright, "Did you touch anything inside the display case, maybe to check it for damage?"

Brad had given his assurance that no fingerprints of his could possibly appear on any of the artifacts, those stolen or those remaining. She'd thanked him with absentminded courtesy and sent him back to 39th Street in the back of a police cruiser. Now he was sitting in a green block-tiled box half the size of his closet. He shared the space with a bench, a chair, and a small table, which left barely room for him to stand and none at all for pacing. The requisite two-way mirror, not much bigger than the one he used when he combed his hair in the morning, covered the hole in the wall that opened to the spy cubby next door. Ellen had called it an interview room, giving it more dignity than it deserved.

He figured the space on the other side of the mirror was empty now—everyone involved in the case already stood in the bullpen, darting an occasional look in his direction but mostly paying no attention to him at all. Even Ellen was ignoring him for the moment, while she finished bringing her boss up to date, and the two of them—Ellen and the captain with the slight paunch and the irritated expression—gave Harry instructions for what they would need from the museum. Photographs of the missing objects, mostly, and descriptions of same. And a list of known collectors of historic Chinese art, the reputable ones they could ask to let them know if the missing items came on the market and those less scrupulous who might bear watching. Brad had already collected that information, but Harry made his promises anyway and accepted with good grace Ellen's request that he wait by her desk. It seemed pretty clear that Ellen wouldn't proceed with the interview until Khadijah Flint arrived. They were friends, he reminded himself; Ellen Li was trying to protect his interests by waiting.

Brad leaned gingerly against the green block-tiled wall and tried to think of the Lis in terms of the host-kin of daemonkind, but it didn't work. They were human, and they tried to control him with their cell and their lawyers just as Evan had done with his command and the spell he tricked them into years ago. His son, who knew what it meant to bind a daemon and command it against its will, who had himself nearly died as Omage's prisoner, had left him in this place where his true nature beat against the constraints of the walls closing tight around him and the bonds that held him fast through human gut and daemon essence. Power built throughout his being, and he felt the floor tremble with the effort to break free while the binding spell locked the pressure deep inside. They would die, all of them, the city would crumble beneath his rage, and he would fly home—free, free—but the wall behind his back mocked him, and he felt the binding like chains crushing him beneath their weight.

A scream nearly escaped him, until his throat felt raw with the effort to suppress it. Claustrophobia, on a scale no human could understand because no human had ever experienced the endless freedom of the second sphere as a daemon of that reality knew it, obliterated his power to think, and Brad felt the panic ooze cold sweat from his pores.

He needed a distraction, and he found it in imagining the varied lethal forms of retribution he would take when Evan slipped up and released the command that bound him to this windowless hole the size and ambiance of a bus station lavatory stall. But he had scarcely time to rehearse the disemboweling of his son and the burning of his entrails for this little trick when he heard the voice of said offspring and, more importantly, the voice of Khadijah Flint. In a moment, Flint's dark face smiled at him over the shoulder of Ellen Li's captain.

"Nice to see you again," she said while shaking the captain's hand. "I'm not really sure why you need me here, but I'm happy to help in any way I can."

Ellen picked up the answer, shaking hands in her turn: "Just a bit of confusion, I'm sure, Khadijah, but we've got a security guard in a coma, and one of our uniformed officers found Mr. Bradley kneeling over the unconscious body."

"Mr. Bradley is a private investigator. As I understand it, the museum hired his agency to review security procedures and Mr. Bradley was acting on that mandate when he stumbled upon the scene of the crime. The actions your officer describe seem to be the reasonable efforts of a man trying to determine whether the body on the floor was dead, or injured and in need of assistance. Isn't that so, Mr. Bradley?"

Khadijah Flint angled her body around that of Ellen Li and addressed Brad directly, her eyes wide, her tone open and ingenuous. Good. Evan had briefed her, and Khadijah was already on the offensive. Brad smiled his most accommodating smile.

"Exactly." He nodded his agreement. "In fact," he added, matching the innocence of her tone, "the lieutenant did the very same thing when she came into the gallery and saw the body lying on the floor. Anyone would have done the same. Even Officer Franks, eventually."

"I knew we had no problem here." Flint gave a sharp assenting nod. "Reasonably, you would like a statement from my client as to what he saw during the carrying out of his duties to make a security check. Mr. Bradley is here graciously, of his own free will, to assist in your investigation. And I'll just sit right here"—she made an elaborate show of looking for a chair and rolled one to the door of the interview room—"and make sure that everything is as it should be—all friends, right?"

"Of course," Ellen agreed. She turned her head, distracted for a moment, and Brad followed her gaze, saw Evan thread his way between the desks and disappear into an alcove next to the spy cubby. He looked as though he'd been bludgeoned with something. Good. Let him worry.

Brad smiled. "Shall we begin?"

Ellen sat in the chair next to the table. Brad realized that someone in the spy cubby could see him, sitting on the bench, but could not see Ellen on the chair. It seemed, however, that they found it easier to lounge around the open door, arms hanging over the upholstered privacy screens, and eavesdrop openly.

Khadijah Flint pulled a notebook from her briefcase. "I want to restate that my client is cooperating with your investigation as a witness in the burglary of the Philadelphia Museum of Art," she said. "He is not considered a suspect. As his lawyer, I am here at Mr. Bradley's request to advise and protect his interests as a witness."

"Fine," Ellen Li agreed. "Can we begin?"

"Any time." Flint settled herself with an alert expression, Brad's cue.

"What can I do to help?" he asked.

Ellen looked down briefly at the interview form in front of her. "We'd like to start with a few simple questions, then we'll move on to the burglary proper. Can you give us your name, please?"

"Kevin Bradley."

"And your address?"

"Seventh and Spruce. If you want the zip code, you will have to call the office in the morning, because I can never remember it."

"We can do that," Li agreed. "Your mother's name and address?"

"Mary Bradley. Deceased."

"And your father?"

"John Bradley, deceased."

"Any living relatives?"

"Evan Davis. My son. But of course you know that. He lives at the same address. And Lily, of course. My cousin, Lily Ryan. She lives with us as well. Bradley, Ryan, and Davis is a small family company. We live together, more or less in back of the shop. Out front, we work at the highest levels of independent art retrieval."

"You must have this on record, Ellen," Khadijah Flint interrupted.

"Harry does." Brad added, "That's why the museum hired us to review their security measures in the first place."

"I know, Brad." Li pointed to the form in front of her. "And you know I have to ask these questions."

"I know you want next of kin in case the witness gets cold feet and decides to do a bunk," he argued. She was right, of course, and following the standard interview routine to the letter. But the questions, with answers that wouldn't bear up under close scrutiny, made him edgy. "Given that our business is here, our case is here, and we are working toward the same goal—returning the Moon Stone crystal ball to its rightful owner—that seems unlikely."

Khadijah Flint took a breath to respond, but Ellen got in there first: "A small, family-owned company has a major advantage over us poor cops, Brad. They don't have to follow procedures set down by bureaucrats for situations that may not happen *this time*. So give me a break here, huh? We'll finish a hell of a lot faster that way, and we can all go home to bed."

"Sorry." Brad dragged his fingers through his hair in a gesture he recognized as Evan's as soon as he had done it. "Former address, Nice. Apartment 4, Place de la Mer. That was your next question, wasn't it?"

Ellen raised an eyebrow at him, but nodded. "Yes. American citizen?"

"Yes."

"Naturalized when?"

"Naturalized?"

"You said your former place of residence was Nice. That's in France. So, when did you become a citizen of the United States? According to your agency's license application, you've only been in Philadelphia four years. I wouldn't have thought you were French, though."

"I'm not. I lived in Nice for a few years before coming to Philadelphia."

"So, where were you born? In the United States? If not—"

"In the States, yes, but I don't remember exactly where. I was orphaned at an early age, you know." He had a birth certificate in the safe, had a whole identity worked out on paper. But he'd never bothered to learn it by heart, had never needed to know those things about a human life that most of them seemed to take for granted. "If you need to know that badly, I can bring the documents around tomorrow."

"I don't suppose it matters," she said. "If it's painful for you, we can wait."

Brad glared at her. "Is there anything else of a personal nature you'd like to know before we get to the case at hand? What I had for breakfast, perhaps—or who I had breakfast with, after a wild night in bed?"

He hadn't, actually, had a wild night in bed since he'd planted Evan in a young, infatuated girl twenty-eight years ago. He didn't like humans, certainly didn't want to get that close to one again, but he couldn't imagine explaining that to Ellen Li. "Mr. Bradley!" Flint rebuked him with a frown. "Sarcasm won't bring the museum's property back, and it won't help any of us get back to our beds where we belong at this hour."

Brad shook his head and tried to look sheepish. "I apologize. From now on, I shall try to contain my sarcasm to Harry and the chessboard."

"We're all a little tense." Ellen seemed willing to give him an out, but she seemed to sense the explosive tension in him. "Can you tell me how you got into the museum after hours?"

"I didn't. I waited inside until the museum closed."

"How did you avoid the heat and pressure sensors?"

The museum had sensors in some of its floors but not in all of the galleries, and he'd been careful not to let any gravity-mass impact the floor until he'd seen the guard down and realized it didn't much matter anyway. He couldn't very well tell her that, either, so he settled for half the truth.

"I didn't. The museum doesn't have sensors in all of the floors, just those with objects that are portable, easily accessed, and potentially valuable to a collector. Rooms that contain art that isn't generally considered portable, like temple pillars and the naves of churches, don't have extensive protections.

"As part of the security review I wanted to see how much freedom of movement a thief would normally have at night. I also wanted to make sure that the guards did in fact activate the alarm systems in galleries where the museum had installed them. When I saw the injured guard, I stopped worrying about not setting off alarms and went immediately to see if I could help."

He'd actually transported directly into the room with the treasures from the imperial palace and had stumbled on the guard by accident. But the police didn't need to know that. Thinking back to the moment he saw the downed guard, he remembered something else; his focus drifted, wide-angled, while he reviewed everything he had seen. There should have been laser detectors active in the gallery as well. The lasers were a cinch to circumvent—all a human being really needed was a handful of talc and a flexible body with good balance. He usually tuned his vision up to pull in their wavelength when working around lasers, but this time, he hadn't needed to—

Ellen Li had waited out his distraction, but she sat forward, eager, when he spoke.

"I don't know if the guards had set the floor sensors in the imperial palace room because I didn't have a chance to check them before I saw the guard, but someone had deactivated the lasers."

He thought about it a moment more. "Something must have been set, though, or your Officer Franks would not have wandered in and caught me in the act of checking the security guard for a pulse."

She riffled back a few pages in her notebook and stopped, read a bit. "Ah. Here it is. The alarm on a side emergency door sounded. That door was locked from the outside, but by law it always opens from the inside. The museum's own guard station had a key, and their guard on duty let Officer Franks inside to investigate while he called the director, who called Harry. Who called you. You weren't in, of course, but Evan took the message and caught up with us at the door. You know the rest. Now how about answering my questions for a change."

Brad stared at her for a moment, thinking. "Just one more, and I'll answer anything you want." He didn't promise true answers, of course, but then, she wouldn't believe the truth anyway. It made lying a hell of a lot easier.

"And that is?"

"The guard. What was he doing in the imperial palace room?" Unlike the rooms on either side, Brad knew, that particular gallery did have sensors in the floor. So a guard shouldn't have been in there at all.

"Officer Franks seems to think that the guard heard you break the case, came in to investigate, and you hit him."

"There were no marks," he pointed out.

"No," Ellen agreed, "there weren't. Now it's my turn. What were you doing there in the first place?"

"My job," he answered, and hated the fact that it was the truth. "Checking security. It didn't measure up."

"You're asking me to believe that you *coincidentally* broke into the museum to check the security the same night our perp decides to commit a burglary there? And you *coincidentally* miss said perp by minutes?"

"No coincidence," he objected. "But the wrong question. The first night we had the contract I tested the system—no reason to do it before, no reason to wait after. So who knew the museum was bringing in a security firm? Somebody knew they'd have to move fast, before we changed the systems. Unfortunately, they succeeded. But the question is, how did they know?"

He had her thinking, but before she could frame a response they were interrupted by the captain, accompanied by a man about Evan's age wearing a trenchcoat and a surly expression.

"Ellen," the captain leaned around the doorjamb and crooked a finger at the lieutenant. "Can I see you for a minute?"

"Not without me." Khadijah Flint made much of hauling herself out of her chair, beads clacking in her braids. "I'll be right back," she told Brad. For the first time since she'd blown into the station with a brisk manner and a sure confidence, Brad was worried.

He realized, at some level, that the time he waited for Ellen Li and Khadijah Flint to return was shorter than it seemed. Had to be, since it felt like eternity. He closed his eyes and let himself go limp against the wall behind him. He couldn't do it, couldn't live another second trapped in a body that was beginning to offend his own nose like something left in the sun too long, while the walls closed in and squeezed the air out of his chest. He had to get out, free, and if he took Evan Davis and the entire solar system with him when he went, well at least he wouldn't have to come back, ever again.

"Lirion," he called. A whisper in human sound, it reverberated with the power of a million despairing souls crying agony through the second sphere. She appeared at his call, stood in front of him in the cell when he opened his eyes. She wore the form she liked best in this place and time— tall, sleek, with dark hair falling to the shoulders of a leather jumpsuit, black except for the white lily that curved across her left breast and the hollow of her shoulder.

"What in the name of Ariton are you doing in this dump?" she asked with no preliminaries.

"Ask Evan," he answered bitterly, then shook his head. "Harry Li's security review turned into a burglary investigation while I was on the premises. Up until about five minutes ago, I was miserably failing an eye-witness interview. If the nervous expression on Khadijah Flint's face is anything to go by, I just took first place as suspect."

"Did you do it?"

He gave her a filthy glare, and she shrugged. "So, what makes them think you did?"

"The man in the trenchcoat. He looked as though he was holding a grudge. And he was talking to Evan."

"What's Evan got to do . . . he didn't."

He waited out her brief foray into disbelief and shook his head as she put it together.

"He told you to stay."

"An invitation he made sure I couldn't refuse," Brad agreed, while Lirion examined her fingernails.

"Do you want me to kill him?" she asked.

"You can't, unless he's released you in the past three days." Evan had them both by the honor of Ariton and the command of an old cabalist dead centuries ago. Brad sincerely wished Evan with the old goat-worshiper, but there was nothing he could do about it now.

"You said you were just a witness until the trenchcoat showed up." Lirion tried to pace and bumped into the table. "Damn." She rubbed her hip. "So, I kill trenchcoat."

"And Ellen Li? And her captain? And Khadijah Flint?"

"No." He closed his eyes again, but the narrow confines of the inter-view room pressed in on him until he couldn't breathe. "It has to be Evan. Somehow."

She sighed, brushed nonexistent dirt from the lily on her breast. "I'd gotten out of the habit of expecting something like this," she said, and Brad knew what she meant. He'd learned to trust Evan over the years, learned to think of him as Ariton, kin to the daemon host and loyal to his kind. And Evan, he'd thought, had begun to understand something of what it meant to be Ariton and to be trapped in human form. So he'd been wrong.

They heard voices growing louder, and Lirion reached out to him, touched his face. Brad flinched, and she curled her fingers away from his skin, into a tight fist. She disappeared from human sight then, but he felt her presence wrapped around him like a cloud, and he managed a thin smile when Khadijah Flint walked in and sat in the chair at the table where Ellen had been conducting her interview.

"There's been a complication," she said. "They are going to hold you overnight. They'll probably charge you with the burglary at the least. Sergeant Dougherty claims you are responsible for a number of murders here and in Europe, but he has no evidence, and at least two of them appear to have happened when you were a continent away, so I don't expect any of that to hold up.

"They don't have anything solid linking you to the burglary tonight either, but Dougherty's stirred up enough suspicion to make Captain Marsh nervous. I worked every angle I could to have you released tonight, but Sergeant Dougherty did his homework and, on the face of it, it doesn't look good."

She waited a moment, giving him a chance to speak, but Brad said nothing. Lirion would find a way to trick Evan into releasing at least one of them, and then they'd be home and free, Earth a little cinder floating in the dark. But it wouldn't do to tell his lawyer that.

"Okay," she finally said. "Evan is waiting outside. I'll let him know what happened, and then I'll be back. Ellen will want to finish the interview that Dougherty interrupted, but I will be back before she begins . . ."

As she rose to leave the tiny room, the young man in the trenchcoat pushed his way past.

"You are under arrest," he said, and cuffed Brad to the bench. Fire ran up Brad's nerve endings and Lirion fed the sensation of her own outrage back to him until the unearthly blue flame of Ariton surrounded him at the edges of human perception. His hair rose on end and crackled in the electric snap of the aura; the energy surged through the cuff at his wrist, blowing Dougherty off his feet.

"What the hell are you?" Dougherty fell back, shook his head and crawled to the table while Khadijah Flint muttered, "Lord, have mercy," under her breath.

Dougherty started to pull a gun from the holster at his back, but Khadijah Flint stopped him with a hand on top of his. He'd be better off if they shot him, Brad figured, but there was no guarantee that Dougherty would hit the right target or that Evan wouldn't find some other way to make an agony of his daemon kin's existence. He just wasn't sure he could survive this one with his sanity intact. But Flint had regained some of her composure, and Brad helped her along by damping the fire that had crackled with the sharp snap of electricity but no heat in the room.

"You have no jurisdiction here, Sergeant Dougherty." Flint was on the attack now, her long dark finger spearing Dougherty right over the heart as she punctuated each statement with another emphatic jab pushing him farther and farther out the door. "It is not your place to charge the prisoner, or to restrain the prisoner, or to try to intimidate the prisoner. And it is surely not your place to shoot the prisoner. So I suggest that you go tell Captain Marsh that we've had some sort of short circuit and he'd better get an electrician in here before he tries confining another prisoner."

"Say what you want," Dougherty retorted, "that was not natural. I don't know what he is, but it is evil, by God, and I'm going to prove it."

"God is merciful, Sergeant Dougherty, unlike some humans." Flint glared him down. "I don't know what you think you saw, but your moral posturing is not the law. Now get Ellen Li in here so we can get these cuffs off and move my client to a safe environment to complete this interview."

"We'll see who has the law on their side, Ms. Flint." Dougherty turned and walked away.

Brad noticed the argument with only the smallest part of his mind. Most of his attention focused on the metal chaining him to the bench. He could not, could not—

"Mr. Bradley." Khadijah Flint was sitting next to him on the bench, talking softly. She touched his shoulder, his hair, like she might a child, and he wondered what she saw that put that worried look on her face.

"Don't touch the prisoner." Ellen Li stood in the doorway, looking as worried as Khadijah Flint. It might have been a coincidence, but she didn't warn Flint away until Brad opened his eyes and looked at her.

Flint didn't move. "That maniac almost shot him!"

"No, he didn't." It seemed to Brad that Ellen should have sounded angrier at Khadijah Flint, or at him, or even at Dougherty, who'd acted like a moron and nearly gotten himself killed, which would have annoyed Evan no end. Instead she spoke softly, as Flint did, and he knew they must see too much in his face, to tiptoe around him quite so carefully. It didn't matter, he decided. Evan could force his physical body to stay in this place, and he could keep Badad of the host of Ariton from escaping into the second sphere. But Brad had learned a thing or two about being human in the past few years. So he pulled a trick out of his bag he'd never thought to use and simply went away inside his head.

"Damn," he heard Flint say dimly, as if at a distance, "this is going to take a while. I'd better talk to Evan." She stood up—he could tell without opening his eyes because her warmth along his side suddenly went away.

"Can you get those cuffs off him while I'm gone?" she asked, and then he heard her footsteps leaving, heard her voice somewhere outside of the room that had come to be his universe, and heard Evan answer, anger and desperation in his voice. Closer, Ellen Li's soft voice recited his right to an attorney. She was wrong, of course. He ought to explain to her that he had no rights, just an absolute bondage to the command of his son. But it took too much effort to think with his body chained to the bench and the universe growing smaller, smaller, until it was too small to hold him.

The room inside his head had a door, and so he closed it.

# Chapter 4

EVAN PICKED UP THE PENCIL LEFT BEHIND IN JOE DOUGHERTY'S WAKE AND rolled it absently between his thumb and second finger. He should go back and sit with Harry Li, waiting calmly at his wife's desk, but he didn't want teaching tonight—especially if the lesson was patience. He wanted to run as fast and as far as he could get, then find himself a hole to hide in and a bottle of Jack Daniels to hide there with him. The door to the office in the back was closed, but muffled voices rose and fell behind the drawn blinds. What the hell were they doing in there?

Khadijah Flint left the captain's office first. Looking grim, she headed for the room where Brad sat alone. Dougherty followed soon after, then the two of them were yelling at each other, and suddenly Evan felt the tingle of daemon power rolling toward him. He stood up, not sure what he could do to stop his father but knowing that he had to get Dougherty out of there, now. He tried to remember what kind of loopholes he could have left in his tersely worded command to the daemon Badad, and if those loopholes were about to kill them all.

"Let Ellen handle it." Harry Li grabbed Evan by the arm, dragged him back to his chair and shook him to make him listen.

—"You can only make the situation worse."

"What situation?" Evan tried to rein in the anger, knew that he wasn't succeeding very well and that Harry seemed oblivious to the electric surge of power that hit Evan like a pressure wave.

"I don't know," Li admitted, "but it looks like you do. Whatever it is, you have to trust Ellen to handle it."

"Brad didn't do anything wrong. Why can't he go home and fill out a statement tomorrow? And what is Joe Dougherty doing in there?"

He couldn't ask Harry Li the only one of his questions that counted: *What did Joe Dougherty do to my father that nearly drew out his daemon aspect in spite of a command that bound him in his very essence?* Harry would think he was insane. Evan had been there before and knew he couldn't afford doubts now.

"I have to go to my father—"

Harry shook his head. "Wait."

Suddenly, Dougherty stormed out of the interview room looking angry and afraid and stubborn as hell. With the exception of afraid, none of that was new on Joe. Khadijah Flint stood in the doorway of the interview room glaring after him for a moment, then disappeared inside again, followed by Ellen Li.

After a moment or two Khadijah Flint came out again, alone, and looked around as if she were trying to regain her balance. She caught sight of Evan then, made her way toward him. She didn't look happy.

"I'm sorry, Evan. They are going to charge him. There wasn't anything I could do." She started to reach out to him and stopped before her hand touched his.

*No,* Evan thought, *I don't need your comfort. I need to punch something, or somebody.* In the back of his mind raged the voice that doubted. Why hadn't Brad told him what he planned for tonight? But Ellen Li had come up beside them while Khadijah had been talking. She sat down behind the desk and they waited while she collected her thoughts. Something that she'd seen inside that room had shaken her, and it seemed to have built a low-grade fury in Khadijah Flint as well. The two women avoided looking at each other, as if by not seeing the knowledge in the face of the other each could pretend she hadn't seen and did not know. They were scaring the life out of Evan, but he kept himself still, reminding himself that blowing up in the police station wouldn't help Brad or the case.

Finally, her eyes fixed on the desk blotter, Ellen Li began to talk.

"Your friend Dougherty has no real evidence to back any of his claims, but he cast considerable doubt on the answers Brad gave us about his background." She looked up at him for a moment.

"Normally, if Brad were a suspect with this little concrete evidence against him, we'd rattle his cage and let him go, to see what we shook loose, but Dougherty was convincing enough to persuade the captain that we couldn't afford to wait. He seemed certain there was a risk of flight, and since records on your father are pretty thin before he started the business here four years ago, the captain agreed."

She shifted her gaze sideways before dropping her eyes back to the desk blotter. So Dougherty was the key, but not just to the fight in the captain's office, Evan figured. "I am sorry, Evan. I tried. Ultimately, Dougherty made the better case."

A good enough case that even Brad's friends were doubting him, Evan realized. The desire to punch something narrowed to a focused target, Joe Dougherty, and the feeling had a familiar weight to it. He'd wanted to hit Joe Dougherty all through high school, for his easy self-assurance and the casual cruelty of his thoughtlessness. Still batting a thousand, Dougherty shredded his carefully constructed life and called it a favor.

Khadijah Flint was giving him a warning frown, and he answered with a tiny nod. Tracking again, he closed the anger away from view. He knew he'd succeeded as well as he was going to when Harry raised an eyebrow, reading the change of expression with interest but no surprise. Evan didn't want to think about how well his old teacher had learned to read him, or how badly he needed the life he'd built in the last four years. Ellen Li watched the exchange with more sharpness than Evan liked as well.

She rubbed at tension lines above her eyes. "I didn't mean that as cold as it sounded, Evan. I'm tired, losing my bedside manner, I'm afraid."

*And something has upset you more than you are willing to admit,* Evan thought, but he kept the notion to himself and let Ellen Li finish her spiel.

"I'm heading the investigation and reporting to Captain Marsh. Detective Mike Jaworski will be handling most of the legwork. He has a low opinion of private agencies in general, but he's a stickler for details. Dougherty wanted in, but he's out of his jurisdiction here, and we'd have to ask for him on special assignment. I declined the suggestion."

At the mention of Dougherty she frowned. "He seems to have some kind of grudge against Brad, so he could be trouble if there is anything you are trying to hide."

She paused, and Evan wondered if she expected him to confess some deep family secret that only Joe Dougherty knew. When Evan gave her nothing, she continued. "Right now, the best that we can do for your father is to take everything by the book. Shortcuts will just come back to haunt us later."

"Shortcuts? That means—?"

"It means, Evan"—Khadijah Flint rested her hand lightly over his, whether as warning or reassurance he couldn't exactly tell—"that the police are going to hold your father for twenty-four hours."

"Oh, God. You didn't tell him that, did you?" Evan looked from one woman to the other and saw the answer in their eyes.

"Listen, Evan." Flint gripped his hand more tightly, holding him in place and focusing him on her broad black face. "Dougherty has stirred up some suspicion about that Simpson case some years back, so I'm guessing they want to run Brad's fingerprints through the FBI and Interpol databases. And they'll want the day shift in the labs to do some preliminary work on the forensic evidence before they take it to the judge for a bail hearing. Fortunately, the security guard from the museum seems in no immediate danger of dying, so the process should be simple and the bail reasonable."

The words just flowed over him without meaning. Inside, he knew that he must have expected it, or he wouldn't have felt the need to bind his father to the will of the police. But he'd been able to pretend to himself that he'd only meant his father to stay for the usual statement that Brad would have given on any case that involved the police. The daemon fury that had rolled through the station made sense now. God, God, he was lucky Brad hadn't killed them all.

"I'm sorry, Evan," Ellen said. She stood up and held out her hand, withdrew it when he didn't move to take it. "I wish we had met under happier circumstances, but I'm sure we can work all this out tomorrow. In the meantime, you should go home and get some sleep. Knowing Brad, he will leave here with a list of things he wants you to do first thing tomorrow, and he'll want you alert and ready to work."

*If you really knew Brad,* Evan figured, *you wouldn't be locking up a daemon of the host of Ariton. Not if you valued West Philly.*

"I have to see him before I leave." Evan knew he sounded desperate and didn't want to think about what they'd make of it.

Ellen Li's brow furrowed for a moment; Evan wondered if she was judging his reactions against Dougherty's claims and had to swallow panic hard. The last thing they needed was the suspicion of secrets. With Ellen's next words he released a breath he didn't realize he was holding.

"We still have a lot of work to do here tonight. You can see him for a moment, I suppose, but don't try to touch him or pass him anything. After you've seen him, go home and get some rest."

*Sure,* Evan thought. *After I find Lily and explain to her what I've done. And if I'm still alive, maybe I'll lie down and pretend I can sleep while I wait for the planet to explode.*

"There he is." Khadijah Flint gave Evan a gentle push toward the interview room. "Go make sure he's all right—I'll be here if you need me."

Kevin Bradley was clearly not all right. He slumped in the corner of a bench along the back wall of a dingy little room, his eyes closed. His right arm hung at an awkward angle, wrist blistered where the cuff had burned him. Evan fell to one knee beside him but didn't dare touch the burns. Suddenly short of breath, he knew that if they locked him in there he would scream until his throat bled and beat himself to death against the door.

Overdramatic, Evan warned himself. This was the police department, not Omage's back room. They would pull him out before he went insane again. Looking at his father, though, he wasn't sure they hadn't gone too far already, or that they'd know if they had. Joe was self-satisfied and overbearing, but he wasn't deliberately cruel. The cuffs wouldn't be too tight for a human being. But Kevin Bradley wasn't human. He was Badad, lord of the host of Ariton, a daemon for whom time did not exist, so the hope that tomorrow he would be free did not exist either. Captivity was torture, and only Evan held the key to that captivity. In a way, Evan had put those blisters on his father's wrist.

He couldn't close the door. Just . . . couldn't . . . and he figured it wouldn't matter anyway—the mirror had to be two-way. Not enough privacy to say the important things, to explain that Evan needed his father, here, not somewhere in the universe with another face and another identity that didn't include a mutant monster of a son. For four years Evan had played the dutiful son, been grateful that his father had chosen to let him live and hadn't killed him where he lay, naked in his own filth, insane and already half dead in Omage's back room. The daemon lord owed him more than this absent husk sulking in the corner. And so he addressed Badad of the host of Ariton, and ignored the shell the daemon wore as Kevin Bradley in the human world.

"Payback is a bitch," Evan said.

Kevin Bradley opened eyes of daemon fire, and Evan felt the waves of anger snapping at the ends of his hair, felt his own anger rise up to meet it. The station rumbled on its foundation.

"If you knock down this building while you're in it," Badad noted in the harsh whisper of a wind howling in flames, "you will die, and I will be free. So go ahead, do it."

Somewhere beyond the narrow cell of the interview room someone screamed, and Ellen Li appeared in the doorway, her face stark, but more knowing than it had any right to be. Later. He'd think about it later. Right now, he had to remember what losing control meant. People died. So he took a deep breath and tried to think past the moment, to tomorrow.

"It's just one night," he said, and "I survived a year of Omage's chains to find you. One night in a cell shouldn't be too much to pay for keeping our life here."

Badad, in his human form, reached out and touched Evan's face. "But it is, Evan," he said, and the trace of his fingers left bruises in their wake. "It is."

Evan closed his eyes and breathed deeply, embracing the touch as his due. A reminder, for when he looked in the mirror, that a reckoning was coming.

"And still"—he opened his eyes to confront the anger of his father—"I will it."

He turned and left the cell to hide the exhaustion that drained him and met the shock in Ellen Li's eyes.

"Don't ask," he said.

She searched his face for so long he was afraid he would fall. If it weren't so damned dangerous, Evan figured collapsing at Brad's feet would be the fitting end to a perfectly wretched day. But showing weakness now could be lethal. So he said again, "Don't ask," and brushed past her. He didn't turn around until he had again reached Khadijah Flint's side. By then, Ellen had gone back into the cell, and there was no more time to tell Brad any of the things that would have made it somehow okay.

"What was that about?"

Evan shook his head. "Long story." Alone with Khadijah for the first time since they'd met outside the station, hours ago now, Evan could think of no words to express what he wanted to tell her.

"He's my father," he said, and meant, "The things Joe Dougherty said weren't true," and, "Save us," as well.

"I know, Evan," she said, and he wondered which of his meanings, stated and unstated, she answered.

"There is nothing you can do for him tonight." And he wondered if she'd understood his plea for help, and if she was telling him, "I can't save you, Evan. It is too late."

"I'll stop by to pick you up first thing in the morning. Be ready to post bond, and we'll get him out of there as soon as the judge sets an amount. For now, go home. Get some rest—you'll need to be sharp tomorrow. And I need to be in that room, for your father."

Evan needed to be sharp *tonight*—he still had Lily to deal with. He wondered if he would find her at home, or if he would have to go to Venice to find her; he didn't relish giving her the news while she was in bed with Alfredo Da'Costa. Shit.

Flint took him by the arm and walked him to the door. "Can you drive, or do you want me to call you a cab?"

"I can drive," he answered, and didn't tell her the car wouldn't take him where he had to go tonight. But summoning Lily would be pressing his luck.

# Chapter 5

"JOE DOUGHERTY MEANS WELL, KHADIJAH" ELLEN LI'S VOICE CAME TO HIM from outside the interview room. Brad couldn't see her, didn't know if she meant for him to hear the conversation or if the room, the place, had somehow transformed him into a nonbeing. He didn't like that idea much, but he'd split hairs later—right now, he listened.

"Dougherty says he grew up with Evan Davis," Ellen said. "The family asked for his help, and you can't really blame them. We know Brad, but what did Evan's family know, except that Evan seemed convinced that Bradley was his father and had pretty much turned his life over to a stranger? Evan wasn't always the healthiest young man, emotionally. Brad could have been anything, a cultist, a con artist, even a thief. So Joe checked him out. It isn't Joe's fault that Bradley's story only holds together for the four years since he arrived in Philadelphia with Evan Davis in tow."

"I'm not convinced we don't have an infringement of my client's Fourth Amendment rights, Ellen."

"I don't think so," Ellen countered the argument. "She only knew him for that one week, but Gwen Davis, or Gwen Davis Barnes, now, seems pretty sure she'd recognize Evan's father if she saw him again. And she's sure that Kevin Bradley isn't the man. Joe Dougherty says she described him as having a shorter, slighter build, with lighter hair and freckles."

Yes, that had been the body Badad of the host of Ariton had used to seduce the young woman. Hadn't been his idea, but then nothing on this dirt ball ever was. He'd tricked his way free that time and killed the man who had trapped the daemon to ruin the girl who had spurned him. It sounded like a plan he could use again.

"People change—" Khadijah Flint entered the room; awareness of her presence was almost enough to persuade him to open his eyes.

"Mr. Bradley, can you hear me?" She sat beside him on the bench, and he felt her fingertips on the inside of his wrist, delicately tracing the

ring of blisters. Tension that seemed to charge her whole body drew her
upright on the bench. "Jesus in heaven! Ellen, he's hurt. You've got to get
these cuffs off him now!"

A sigh followed, then Ellen Li spoke again, drawing him closer to full
awareness, like a drowner being dragged to the water's surface against his
will.

"You know procedure—"

He'd heard that drowning was a good way to die. Perhaps he would
drown Evan. But the two women continued to argue.

"Your Sergeant Dougherty has injured my client," Khadijah Flint interrupted in the tone of quiet threat for which Brad had hired her in the
first place, "Procedure can go to hell—Mr.Bradley needs a hospital."

"That isn't possible." Ellen Li leaned over Khadijah Flint and took
Brad's hand. "Ouch. Okay, I'll grant you possible. It still doesn't make
sense. Those are second-degree burns. If the cuffs had been hot enough to
do that much damage, Joe Dougherty couldn't have handled them long
enough to put them on."

"That blue flash came afterward, though." Khadijah Flint answered.
She waited just long enough not to seem too eager to remove herself from
the locus of danger, Brad figured, and then she rose from the bench where
he remained sitting.

"There's an electrical short someplace in that wall, and it sent a nasty
shock through those cuffs. This room isn't safe—we have to get him out
of here."

"There's no electricity in that wall to short out," Ellen objected, but
she knelt at his side, and he heard the key click in the lock. The cuff fell
open. "Come on, Brad. I know you are in there."

He opened his eyes to her, a gift for releasing the cuff, and found
himself staring into a wryly knowing smile.

"I'll agree that there is something dangerous in this room," she said,
"but I don't think an electrician will help. Let's get this over with, Brad.
We can do this at my desk. Answer the questions, and maybe we can resolve
this mess without any more pyrotechnics."

"I don't know what you mean, Lieutenant."

"Play nice, Mr. Bradley," Khadijah warned him, "and we may be able
to persuade the good lieutenant to let you go home when you are done."

"I didn't realize we were playing a game." Still, it was enough to
pull Brad to his feet. He followed Khadijah Flint out of the interview
room that had become his prison, figuring he could play nice for as long
as it took her to get him out of here. After that he wasn't making any
promises.

He followed Ellen to her desk and sat politely in a chair with his back against a padded gray privacy screen with Khadijah Flint at his side. The wrist hurt, and memory skittered away from the little room where he'd been bound physically as well as through his oath to Evan.

"What do you want to know?"

# Chapter 6

At two o'clock in the morning, 39th and Lancaster reeked of stale exhaust fumes and dust and of the yeasty smell of urine doing a bad job of cleaning alcohol out of the system of the grubby derelict in the alley behind the police station. Evan wondered, briefly, if the drunk had chosen this particular alley as a political statement. He weighed the chances of finding his car in the spot he'd parked it if he took the shortcut home through the second celestial sphere. Given the way his luck was running, the locals would strip the car and the police would ticket him for leaving a wrecked automobile on the street. So he slid behind the wheel and turned on the ignition.

"Home," he muttered to himself, and let his back brain do the driving, too numb to think and just glad there wasn't much to run into at this time of night. He'd have to tell Lily; he didn't know if he could do it without a drink, but he knew if he started, he'd wind up in an alley just like the drunk he'd left behind the police station. Or he'd be dead, quickly. Along with the art history and the aesthetics, he'd learned over the past few years how to use the power of the daemon nature that had once driven him mad. But he'd picked up a few daemons of the human variety in the dark time in his life, and he didn't dare let them out of their bottle. Apt image. It had taken all of his self control not to ask the drunk in the alley for a slug of whatever he had in his brown paper bag.

He pulled the car into the garage and turned off the ignition, giving one last self-indulgent moment to the consideration of a sulking, half daemon monster out of control on booze. All things considered, he wasn't doing all that well sober. The other didn't bear thinking about.

The kitchen was empty, lit only by the dim rose glow of the streetlight on the corner. Evan left the lights off, soaking up the quiet of the empty house. Jumbled feelings started creeping out of the corners where he'd locked them, and he made his way through the darkness to the windowless study where a single lamp cast a green-shaded light on the desk. He passed the wine-colored leather sofa, avoided looking at the tapestry wing chairs— they'd stay empty as a reminder to him of what he had done until Brad came home—and went to the section of book-lined wall behind Brad's chair. Pressing the leather spine of a non-existent book, he opened the bar hidden behind them and reached for a glass.

"Need a drink, Evan? Or maybe a bottle?"

Lily, acid dripping from her tone. She slipped up behind him, wrapped her arms around his neck, and took a long, slow tug at the lobe of his ear caught between her sharp incisors. "After all, what's a promise, to a human?"

"Damn!" He wished she wouldn't do that!

He also wished that the soft breath of her whisper, the tug on his ear, didn't have such a direct effect on his crotch. Or, that the combined effect of her anatomy on his didn't leave his brain out of the loop. She was dangerous at the best of times, and he could tell this didn't fit the category by a long shot.

"Where's Alfredo?"

Right, goad her. He remembered another time, when she'd taken the shape of a panther, pacing, impatiently waiting for him to make a mistake while he rocked in fear and longing at the center of a pentagram. He wished he'd never had to know the true nature of his daemon kin as they had revealed it to him that day. And here he was, still alive, still testing his hold on them.

Lily lifted her head from his ear for a moment, as if giving the question serious consideration. Then she smiled.

"Waiting," she said. She licked at the little wound left by her teeth on his lobe, and slipped a hand inside his shirt stroking absent fingertips across his nipple. "He does it very well."

She wouldn't kill him where he stood because she was bound to his will, just as Brad couldn't leave police custody until Evan lifted the command he'd barely uttered over the body of the unconscious security guard. But she would taunt him with her lover while she drove him quietly mad with her body, and she let him know, with the challenge of her smile, that she would kill him if he gave her half a chance.

"You've heard about Brad." He read the answer in her fingertips on his chest, stilled in their wandering for a moment before they began their lazy play again.

Of course. "In that case, I'll need the whole bottle." He pulled a Coke from the undercounter refrigerator and knew he'd surprised her as he twisted off the cap.

"I may have been suicidal once," he explained, raising his cola bottle in salute to her before he took a drink, "but I'm not stupid enough to get into an argument with you when I am drunk, no matter how much the idea of oblivion may appeal on a temporary basis.

"So let's talk, before this little game of tease the monster goes past the place where we can find our way home again."

"Your home, little monster, not mine," she said. "Never mine."

"Point taken," he agreed. "I'll settle for getting us back to where we were last week." With an effort of will he removed her hands and put the desk between them. "You first."

Lily splashed a bit of brandy in the bowl of a snifter and draped herself in a bone-defying languid pose on the leather sofa.

"You're not going to survive this one, Evan. Until now, he hasn't really tried to break free of the oath you imposed upon us. He trusted you. That's over now. More to the point, I suspect that by morning he will be as mad as Omage was. Captivity has that effect on our kind. He will outwit you and kill you, and the only thought he will give the process is how to stop his own pain."

Evan leaned the executive desk chair as far back as it would go. He didn't want to look at her when he explained. Didn't want to see the disdain or the loathing he knew was coming.

"He was going to leave," he began, keeping his voice level because she would sneer at the indignation, the sense of betrayal he'd felt standing in that gallery and knowing that he'd never see his father again. "He could see he was in a bad situation. The guard was the only real witness, and he was unconscious, in some kind of coma, though they couldn't find a mark or a sign of a struggle. And he was just going to leave—to vanish at the first chance he had at some privacy. Hell, if the opportunity hadn't come soon enough, he might have disappeared in front of the police and Harry Li. He'd have a new body, new location, new life, and you'd be with him or with Alfredo Da'Costa. I'd be left picking up the pieces, trying to find an explanation for where he'd gone, and how, and what we had done with you. And it wouldn't have ended there. Even if I'd solved the damned case and brought back the artifacts, they'd have kept on looking for him. He'd never get out from under the suspicion that he had something to do with the job, and so they'd never stop watching me."

"And that is supposed to make it acceptable to break your oath to a lord of Ariton?" Lily swirled her snifter and took a deep breath, watching him over the rim of the bowl.

"No." Evan let his chair right itself and dropped his forehead against the palms of his hands. "Not an excuse, an explanation. It was wrong, but I didn't have time to think, I just reacted to the threat at hand."

"Which was?"

Evan looked up at her, startled by the question. But then, what could she know about being alone in all the universe and losing the only anchor to the half-world he inhabited. The fact that she wouldn't understand just underscored how absolute his solitude was.

"He is my father, and I was about to lose him," he said. "I thought Professor Li's wife would ask Brad a few questions and we'd all go home until morning. Then, I figured, I could explain it to him and release him. I even imagined we could all sit down together over breakfast and try to figure out what had happened at the museum.

"I had no idea it would be that bad at the police station. Hell, it *wasn't* that bad until Joe Dougherty showed up. Just as I thought, Ellen Li wanted to find out what he'd seen and what he knew that could help the police investigation. Then Joe Dougherty stormed in like the seventh cavalry, and suddenly Brad wasn't a friendly witness anymore. They were arresting him and Dougherty was cuffing him to the bench and it was too late to undo any of it!"

"I was there." Lily stood up and paced to the bar, considered the bottle of brandy and put it down in favor of a mineral water. Evan figured she didn't feel much like celebrating. "I saw him." She shuddered.

"So did I." That was a nightmare they shared, then. Brad, withdrawing into the dark corners of the meat brain. "I don't know how to stop it."

"You can start by realizing that when you bind a daemon, you are no more innocent than Franklin Simpson was when he bound Omage to hold you captive. And in that cell where you left him, your father will become what Omage was."

Evan rubbed his face, fighting the exhaustion. He wasn't sharp enough at this hour to argue with Lily; he knew he was in trouble but figured he'd brought it on himself this time. Besides, fighting with Lily protected him from the image of his father in the holding cell that rose up to haunt him whenever he tried to think through his answers.

"So, we'll get him out." His mistake, time to fix it.

"You mean you are going to free him?"

"If that's what it takes." Evan did know what he was saying. Lily wouldn't credit it, though. She probably figured he was stumbling into trouble, not walking in with his eyes wide—well, halfway—open.

"When?"

He reached for her hand and she gave it. "Now," he said, holding tight, and "Lily—"

"Say it!"

She loomed over him, sharp teeth grimacing, and he smiled.

"Be free."

He felt a lightness of spirit, as though a weight of guilt had been lifted from his soul and raised him up, floating, and free. But no, he realized that he didn't feel the floor, that he couldn't breathe, and that books and papers flew about the room. A lamp hit him on the head right above his left temple and he was falling, falling. He hit something hard, felt the last of the air kicked out of his lungs with the impact. Blood slicked the back of his head; he could feel it pulsing in a familiar rhythm that faded into darkness. Near the edge of the abyss, a stray thought flitted through the red haze. *Daddy's home.*

# Chapter 7

"WE HAVE PHOTOGRAPHS OF THE STOLEN OBJECTS AT THE OFFICE. EVAN IS supposed to be searching net-based information on transactions between dealers and collectors in Chinese art, but he's been rather busy tonight."

Brad rubbed absently at the bandage on his wrist and flinched. The sharp pain of the touch surprised him in spite of the hours of gnawing discomfort. Earlier, when Ellen Li had first released him from the cell, he had tried to shift out of human form long enough to recreate the flesh of his body to heal the damage. He'd failed, because the essence that was Badad of the host of Ariton responded literally to Evan's binding spell, and Evan's command had told him to stay. The ache of the spell centered itself on the blistered skin of his wrist and didn't stop. Wouldn't, he figured, until he was free and Evan was dead.

Bitter and exhausted, he'd refused the hospital but let Khadijah Flint clean and bandage the burns with an offhanded, "Put it on the bill." To shut himself away in his head again would mean returning to the cell, so he would answer their questions and hoard the pain like a promise.

While Flint worked on Brad's hand, one and then another officer wandered into the cluttered bullpen to start digging in old files. Mostly they looked as though they'd just been dragged out of bed, which he figured they probably had been. By the time she had him cleaned up, Jaworski had grabbed a mug of thick coffee, reported in, and Ellen Li had given him an ambiguous explanation for Brad's presence. The man didn't look pleased to see a private investigator sitting at the lieutenant's desk, but he didn't have that guard-dog-fixed-on-dinner expression either. Yet. He pulled up a chair and made an effort to look alert. Brad tried to do the same, with little more success. A body in pain, he realized, didn't think very clearly.

"You won't mind letting us take a look at your records?" Ellen Li asked.

"Within limits," Brad agreed. "We guarantee our clients complete confidentiality, and we take that guarantee very seriously. It's how we stay in business."

"Bring a search warrant," Khadijah Flint suggested. "Mr. Bradley will be happy to show you any of his records that deal directly with this case, or any that your office deems related—"

She turned to Brad and he shook his head. "Can't think of any. We didn't work on the burglaries at the University or the Smithsonian gem collection. They are the cases we are looking at as related jobs, but we are getting the same information you are, only we're getting it secondhand."

Not really, but Ellen Li didn't have to know about Evan's gift for picking the virtual pockets of law enforcement computer nets.

Khadijah Flint nodded. "Okay. We are happy to show you anything specified on the warrant. Any records not on the warrant will be considered beyond the scope of this investigation, and we will not breach confidentiality on those."

Brad felt dizzy suddenly. It had something to do with Evan, but when he reached for it, the feeling slipped away. Ellen was looking at him strangely, as if she had seen the change come over him, but Jaworski didn't seem to notice.

"Where were you on September 17th?" Jaworski asked, as if the date should have some significance to him. Ellen had the answer—

"Brad couldn't have committed the University job, Mike. He was with Harry and me. I remember because the seventeenth was a Wednesday. They beeped me at the chess club, where I was trouncing Mr. Bradley rather soundly, and I had to concede the game and leave."

She didn't add the part of the occasion that almost brought a smile to Brad's face in spite of his current surroundings. Mai Sien Chong had trounced Harry into the proverbial dust that night, and Ellen had teased later that in her absence Harry had allowed himself to be distracted by more than Chong's game. Mai Sien Chong didn't mind taking advantage of her sex appeal with casual partners, but the only game she played with Harry was chess. Ellen remembered, of course. And she wasn't one bit happy about arresting a friend.

Jaworski gave Brad a long, thoughtful look. "If he couldn't have done the last one," he asked Li, without breaking contact when Brad returned studied consideration, "why does Marsh think he committed this one?"

"His background check turned up some problems." Now Ellen Li gave Brad a measuring stare. Finally she let go a tiny sigh.

"Confucius says, you are out of your mind," she muttered. Then she turned to Jaworski. "Stay here. I'm going to talk to Marsh."

Jaworski nodded and took her place behind the desk. He was saying something, but Brad didn't hear it. He felt lighter, suddenly.

Agh! There it was, stronger this time, like an explosion in his heart. It hurt, by Ariton it hurt, the letting go of bindings tied to the very center of what Evan would call his soul. Evan had broken the spell. Badad, daemon lord of the host of Ariton was free, and as Kevin Bradley he stood, lifted, turned, and laughed. Then he vanished in a blinding snap of blue light with an implosion of displaced air like thunder behind him.

The second sphere was before him and he soared, free of a body and the small pain in his wrist and the monstrous pain of the chains that had bound him to the Earth and his human form and the son he should have murdered when he'd first laid eyes on him. But that didn't matter now, because he was free, he was free, and he headed for the endless dark of home and grew until he filled the universe with waves of feeling that tumbled one after the other into the sphere of princes: anger. Anger so huge that it rolled through the darkness a tsunami of feeling and stopped the Princes in mid-battle and brought the hosts to find the source of this new disturbance. And joy, boundless and exultant, and the Princes and all their hosts rejoiced that another of their kind had won free of humans.

Evan. Badad found the center of his anger and followed it home to the material sphere. Lily was gone, the study lay in shambles, and Evan lay in a heap on the floor, bleeding steadily from a wound at the back of his head. Rage shimmered in blue flame, and Badad raised a monstrous blue-scaled fist, summoned fire to put the universe out of this creature's misery. Memory—the fall of blood, the metallic smell of it at the back of his throat—stopped him like a blow. He stood in Omage's back room again, sent by the seven Princes to end the chaos rippling through the universes. At first he hadn't noticed the room, drawn only to the burning heart of his nemesis, Omage of the host of Azmod, who knelt over the figure of a young man with no consciousness at all, just the animal pulsing of heart and lungs. Omage held a bowl of stone beneath the arm of the creature, collecting the warm blood that fell from its open wrist.

"You've come." Omage set the bowl down and rose to his feet. "I knew you would." He stepped over a silver chain that bound the unconscious man to the foot of a golden throne set on a pedestal at the center of the room. The creature smelled, of feces and vomit and sweat and blood and more, of decayed flesh. Wounds festered on its arms, on its neck where the thick silver collar chafed.

Smiling, Omage spread his hands wide, taking in the unconscious youth and the room itself. Badad realized Omage had set himself up with an audience—humans, and greedy for something he did not understand.

He dismissed them as irrelevant. And then, in the flickering light of a hundred candles, he saw the symbols on the walls. The shapes seemed to move and flow from wall to wall in the candlelight. Some of them hurt to look at, and others blurred his mind with strange hungers. One, a tumbled swastika, glowed with the fire of Ariton.

Omage sat on his throne and pulled at the chains, dragging at the collar around the neck of Badad's son. The creature at Omage's feet had awakened then, and Badad felt the stir of daemon fire at its center.

"Your father." Omage bent to the human's ear, his voice a reptilian hiss. He kissed Evan's forehead then, soft, wet lips curved in a smile of lazy pleasure. "As I promised, an end to your search. I never said it would be a happy ending."

*Kill it!* Badad's first instinct was to kill it. But Omage, on his grotesque throne, pulled the chain taut, dragging Evan's head up and nearly strangling the boy. And Evan had opened his eyes.

"Father." The boy knew he was going to die, dared his father to strike him dead—"Do it, bastard. Do it." But beneath the madness Badad saw a need that reached beyond fear or despair. That need, and the boy's denial of it in that transcendent challenge to kill him and be damned, had drawn Badad to his son as no pleading could. And he had, in that moment of personal insanity, stayed his hand. So he'd cut a deck of cards with Omage for Evan's life and won. Lily would say that he'd lost. She claimed not to understand why he'd tied himself to this planet, this perversion of two universes. But she'd left Evan alive when she'd gone.

Damn. He uncurled the fingers of his blue-scaled hand. Once, he knew, something called pain had bitten at his wrist, and once a binding spell, cast by this half-human creation of bad luck and two universes, had chafed at his being like thick rope tied right through his gut, anchoring his very essence to this world. But he was free now.

Right. He found the phone and plugged it in, called 911 and left an anonymous call for help. And then he became the wind and let himself forget his ties to Earth. Turning in cyclonic ecstasy, he vanished, heading home.

# Chapter 8

E<small>VAN OPENED HIS EYES, BUT THE LIGHT HURT, SO HE CLOSED THEM AGAIN.</small> T<small>HAT</small> one glimpse confirmed what the lumpy mattress pressing into his back already told him: not home, but the hospital. How?

He vaguely recalled going home alone in the early hours of the morning, a fight with Lily, and then his brain skidded to a stop on the edge of the precipice. He'd done it. He'd released his father and his cousin from the binding spell that had tied them to his will the past three years. Only an idiot would believe he could force his daemon kin to love him. It seemed dumb luck had held again, though, because he wasn't, for the moment, a dead idiot. Which, he figured, must pretty much put him in the clear. He couldn't think of a single thing he could do that was worse than what he'd done to them already; if they hadn't killed him this time, they weren't likely to.

He figured it might just be time to stop reaching for something it wasn't in their makeup to understand, let alone give to the accidental monster Brad had created with his mother. Better to settle for the fact that they valued him alive more than they wanted him dead, something he hadn't been sure of until now. When it came to the loyalties of daemons, that was a lot more than he had a right to expect of them in the first place. He'd take a minute to feel smug about it later, when his head didn't hurt like hell.

"Evan? Are you awake? Harvey, get the nurse. I think he opened his eyes."

His mother, her voice edged with that long-suffering desperation he hadn't heard since Brad and Lily had dragged him back to sanity four years ago. Footsteps sounded on the tile floor—Harvey wore soft-soled shoes—the door opened and closed.

Running his errand of mercy, Harvey Barnes probably wondered what he'd gotten himself into when he'd married the chemistry teacher at Edge-ment High. Cross your fingers, Harvey, that you never find out. His mother had his hand; her wedding ring pressed painfully against his fingers. Time to come out and face the music. Evan opened his eyes and turned his head toward the sound of her voice. When the fireworks behind his eyes cleared, he was looking into her eyes, dark with worry and anger.

"He did this to you, didn't he? I was afraid something like this would happen."

"What *did* happen?" Past history gave him a general idea of what must have gone down after he'd released the binding spell, but when he looked for the memory, all he found were locked doors with "You don't want to go there" warnings pasted on the front.

"We think it must have been a concussion bomb of some sort." That was Ellen Li, following a doctor and a nurse.

"That can wait, Lieutenant, until we've examined Mr. Davis," the doctor stopped her with a glare. "Since he's just returned to consciousness, why don't we find out if he brought all his faculties back with him before you try to question him."

Evan winced at the volume at which the doctor spoke, but no one else seemed to notice. Must be his head. His mother stood up and moved out of the way to let the doctor stand by the bed.

"Can you sit up for me?"

Evan gave it a try, but the world grayed around the edges.

"Whoa, there." The doctor grabbed him by the shoulders, and Evan clutched at him like a life preserver in a very rocky sea. Then he was lying on his back again with the doctor driving spikes of light into Evan's eyes with a small focused flashlight.

"Equal and reactive," the doctor marked his chart. "Just a few questions and I'll leave you alone. How many fingers am I holding up?"

"Three."

"Right. What is your full name?"

"Evan Davis."

"The date?"

"May 30th."

"June first, but I believe you came in on the thirtieth. Capital of Pennsylvania?"

"Harrisburg."

"Not only recovered but reasonably well educated as well."

The doctor, who never introduced himself or gave his name, pronounced Evan vastly improved. Promising an early discharge in the morning, doubtless when the insurance for a cracked head ran out, he swept back out again. Ellen Li took the chair recently vacated by Evan's mother.

"Are you up to this?" she asked.

He started to nod, but thought better of it. "I want to know," he said.

"All right, then. Police received a 911 call about an explosion at your address. They found your side door open; after trying to raise the alarm, they entered and found you on the floor of an inside office. The office was in shambles, and you were bleeding from a head wound. There was blood on the corner of a computer monitor the police found on the floor. Bomb control seems to think that a nonflammable concussion bomb had gone off in there. A second bomb, we think it must have been the same type, went off right about the same time in the Major Crimes Unit."

God. "Was anybody hurt?"

Ellen Li gave him an ironic smile. "You were," she said. "Mike Jaworski will have a bruise on his bottom and a funny walk for a few days, and his account of what happened is a bit scrambled. His most severe injury seems to have been to his pride. You are the only victim still in the hospital. The rest is minor property damage—sound and fury, signifying overtime for the cleaning staff and nothing else, except—"

He waited, knowing what she would say, and trying to keep the foreknowledge out of his face.

"Even, we can't find your father."

Hearing it said out loud was a shock, even if he had known. And he didn't have to pretend his concern. But he'd forgotten his mother, standing out of his line of sight at the head of the bed.

"He's not your father, Evan."

He heard the anguish in her voice but couldn't find it in himself to sympathize. He couldn't blame her for where he was right now, either. Once, her jealous ex-boyfriend had bound the daemon Badad to ruin her life, and later her son had bound the same daemon to save his own life. But Gwen Davis had been an innocent bystander in all but her weakness for the man Badad had pretended to be. And she didn't want him making a similar mistake.

"I don't know what your relationship with Mr. Bradley is, or what he wants of you, but he isn't your father. If he's taken advantage of your feelings for him in any way . . ."

"It isn't like that." He didn't think she'd appreciate the only explanation he could give her, and he wasn't sure beyond the facts of metaphysics what he could say about the relationship when he didn't understand it himself. Brad was his father all right. They were kin beyond flesh in the realm of the second sphere that the daemon host of Ariton called home, a place where Evan was vulnerable to attack but could follow if he chose. And he would follow. Just as soon as his head stopped hurting and he could concentrate.

Thank God Ellen Li saw the stubborn set of his jaw. "I can't refute your memories," she told Gwen Barnes, "but I have known Kevin Bradley for over three years, and my husband and he have been friends somewhat longer, certainly since they conspired together to put Evan back in school. I can tell you from personal knowledge that he believes Evan is his son, and he has always based his actions toward Evan on that belief. He may be mistaken, but if so it is his information that is wrong, not his motives."

She patted Evan's hand. "It's all right to love him as your father, Evan. I know he loves you as his son."

Not exactly, but he didn't see that pointing out the nature of daemonic relationships would make the situation any clearer for anyone concerned, so he just said, "Thanks."

"He didn't seem to be hurt in the explosion," Ellen Li was quick to assure him. "He may have been stunned. In the shock, I suspect he just walked out and no one noticed during the commotion. We don't have a fugitive warrant out on him. Marsh agreed we didn't have enough to hold him before the explosion occurred. But he was close to the blast; he may have been disoriented, or there may have been injuries we didn't see."

She couldn't hide the real worry, though. A blast, yes, but they wouldn't have found any residue of explosives or any other evidence of a bomb, either in the police station or at the agency, which didn't surprise Evan at all. When a human summoned a daemon and bound him to the humans' bidding, that summons created changes in the very essence of that daemon. Few spells of binding lasted very long, even by human standards. The summoner would make a mistake, and die for it. When that happened, the daemon would be free, but the paths between the spheres, burned into the memory of captivity, remained. A daemon so transformed could pass between the spheres without raising a whisper. Or the daemon's rage could destroy planets in his passing.

Brad had been angrier than Lily; Evan stifled his surprise that his father hadn't turned the station at 39th and Lancaster into a puddle of glass at the bottom of a crater. Ellen Li would think he was insane if he told her that, and she was probably better off not knowing anyway. So he closed his eyes against the shards of light stabbing at his retinas and listened with half his mind, while the other half wondered just exactly why he was still alive.

"We think that whoever broke into the museum set the bombs, probably to destroy evidence, not lives. They came close to miscalculating on the one they planted at your home. They couldn't have guessed that you would be working at that hour. I'd say Brad did the math the same way I did. He had to be concerned about your safety, and Lily's. And he'll want to catch whoever did this before they have a chance to up the stakes."

"I don't know what he'll do." He figured that the daemon Badad, whom Ellen knew as Kevin Bradley, had already found Lily and they were both likely to be farther away than human minds could calculate by now. No, Evan didn't expect to see his father again unless he went looking, and he needed time alone to think, and rest, and decide on a plan of action. Objectively, he could survive on his own in both the spheres that were his birthright—could pass through the second sphere without the nightmares and return home at his own will. He'd learned control, but the accomplishment seemed empty without his father to share it and Lily to bat him in the head and call him a fool while she did delicious things to his body and promised more if he would let go of the material universe and join her in the endless dark of the second celestial sphere.

"I need to rest," he said, because he didn't have the strength to hide his feelings and didn't have the heart to defend them when he knew he was a fool for wanting so badly in the first place.

"We'll leave you alone then." Ellen Li stood up to leave. "Harry wanted to visit, but we both decided you had enough to deal with right now. He'll stop by to see you at home tomorrow afternoon, if that is all right?"

"Do you know what he wants?" It sounded more cynical than he intended, but that's how he felt: as if he could measure all of his relationships in what the other person wanted from him.

"I'm sorry," he said anyway. "I didn't mean it like that."

"Yes you did," Li corrected him, "but under the circumstances you have the right to doubt. He wants to see for himself that you really are going to recover." She paused, but he wasn't letting her off the hook.

"He asked me not to discuss it," she finally conceded. "He wants to do it himself."

She didn't wait for him to say anything else but left with a suggestion of a bow of acknowledgment to his mother, who had moved to the window to stand with Harvey Barnes.

"I really need to sleep now," he said.

"I know." His mother reached out to him, but Harvey Barnes took her hand, drew it back to hold between them. Good for Harvey.

"We're leaving," he said. "That head must hurt like hell. If it's okay with you, we can pick you up tomorrow morning and take you home with us to recuperate."

Evan closed his eyes, but he knew he couldn't hide by pretending to be asleep.

"I'd like a ride," he compromised, "but I want to go back to Spruce Street."

"What if these mad bombers come back?" His mother had the same tone in her voice she'd once used to tell the Fundie preacher, who called uninvited to denounce her son as the spawn of Satan, to go to hell. In that mode, she reminded him of mamma grizzlies and female lions defending their cubs. He almost smiled, maybe would have if that Fundie preacher hadn't been so close to the mark.

"They won't," he said. He kept his eyes firmly shut and said nothing more. After a moment or two, he heard them leave, his mother's step lighter than Harvey Barnes', two for each of his one. Tomorrow. He didn't want to think about tomorrow, and before he had realized it, the pretense of sleep drifted into reality.

Somewhere at the edges of consciousness he felt a presence, knew it for Ariton, but realized he was just too weary to drum up the appropriate level of fear or expectation. So he went to sleep.

# Chapter 9

EVAN WAS SLEEPING, HIS MOUTH PRESSED THIN AS HE FOUGHT THE DISCOMFORT. Long lashes twitched where they lay against the bruises on his face. Lirion had given him the big purple and indigo one that swelled the side of his head around the bandaged sutures. Badad had put the thin streaks of red and purple across his cheekbone. Restless, Evan fought the metal hospital bed and the sterile watchfulness of the dim light beside it, braced himself against the impersonal intrusion of nurses in shoes that squeaked on the faded floor tiles, their watches glowing in the dark when they lifted his arm by the wrist to take his pulse. He was hurting. Not dead, though. Badad of the host of Ariton gave that some serious thought.

Human flesh was fragile, as Badad had learned to his cost. It died more easily than it lived, and forced humans into narrow lives stuck to one insignificant ball of rock. Constrained by a universe that had no use for butterflies or the fleeting defiance of muscle and bone, the needs of that flesh defined their actions, birth to death.

Humans who defied those constraints to bind a daemon didn't survive the experience for long. Half-daemon monsters like Evan didn't live long enough to bind a daemon if they wanted to. If they didn't die early, murdered by the justifiably terrified humans around them, they went insane and died violently at their own hands. But Evan had survived all of it, the madness of two universes at war in his body and then captivity and torture as the enemies of Ariton used his mind and body as a weapon against the second celestial sphere. He'd survived the edict of all the Princes ranged against him and the verdict of the guardian, Alfredo Da'Costa in this lifetime, that to save all the seven spheres Evan had to die.

It wouldn't take much to end that streak of luck. All Badad had to do was reach invisible fingers into Evan's chest and wrap them around Evan's heart. Simple as making a fist. As he stood watching, he thought of a thousand ways to kill this creature who had stolen his freedom and given it back again. His son. None of those very personal murders would give him the one thing he wanted from Evan.

He felt Lirion's presence in his mind, her mocking laughter a reminder of home and the darkness that awaited him. But still he watched for some sign that would make sense of it all. "Why?" he asked in his mind, and she showed him a memory: Evan, at his desk, explaining why he wanted to bind the daemons to his will.

"You once accused me of seeing him as stronger and more powerful than he really is," she reminded him, "but now you are doing the same. You think that, because he acted out of logic when we went after the Simpsons, he did the same when he commanded you to stay."

"And?"

She laughed at him, a sparkle of blue flame in his mind. "Evan isn't logical. He wasn't, really, when he first tried to convince you that the binding would protect us. He certainly wasn't thinking with his frontal lobes when your human friend took you into custody."

"If not logic, then what?"

If she'd been wearing flesh, it would have been a sigh, or a shrug. Badad felt it as a wistful thoughtfulness. "Humans are possessive, and Evan is human. He told the truth when he said the binding was to make it impossible for someone else to command you. He wanted you—both of us, really—for himself. Not to command, necessarily, but to *have* for his own. As long as he had us in his reach, he didn't need more. You scared him at the museum."

"How?"

She didn't answer in words, but the image she reflected back made him bristle. He wasn't as dense as that!

"You weren't going to bug out and set up shop somewhere else? Brazil or Hong Kong, maybe, or New South Wales?"

Lirion had seen it in his mind and fed it back to him like a mirror, so there was no point in denying it.

"He was afraid he would lose you. And Ellen Li was a shock. He's always known he couldn't control what I do or who I do it with—Alfredo is my business, put that thought where it belongs—but you never seemed to enjoy living in human flesh. Evan thought you only had him."

"You mean he was jealous."

She laughed at him again.

Brad didn't care if she did find it funny. He was confused. How could Evan be afraid of losing what Brad had never offered in the first place? The boy was a guinea pig, an experiment. Brad didn't love him, didn't care at all, except to see what he'd do next. Monsters were, by definition, curiosities. So he was curious. "He was just . . . interesting, nothing more. I never told him I liked him."

"I said he wasn't logical, but I never said he was stupid. You didn't have to tell him. He's met others of our kind. The fact that you never seriously tried to kill him was enough."

"He's a fool."

"But he's your fool. Are you going to kill him now?"

Brad thought he was giving the idea serious consideration, but Lirion was laughing at him again, bright bubbles of light tickling his mind. Evan was still a puzzle he hadn't solved, and she knew it. Maybe when Badad figured out his son he would tire of the game.

"He's right about you, you know." She gave Evan a moment of her attention. "But I have more interesting things to do than stare at your sleeping monster." She shivered a finger of sensual pleasure through his being. "And Alfredo Da'Costa does those things so very well."

She left him alone with Evan and a last lingering thought: "He is right about you."

Evan turned his head, as if he felt her passing even in his sleep. He probably had, the part of him that was Ariton drawn to her life, flame to flame. But Evan wasn't going anywhere soon, Badad figured. He followed Lirion into the second sphere, heading out into the endless night of home.

Without realizing quite why, he found himself coming to Earth again in the turn of the stairwell to the chess club. He couldn't think of a more dismal place to be. The elevator stopped at the floor below, and the intrepid chess competitor had to brave the fire tower to reach the Franklin Mercantile Club, which pretty much lived up to the promise of the stairwell. He wouldn't have admitted it to Lily, but he liked the old place, in spite of too many layers of cheap paint covering the walls and the scattering of cheap tables and decrepit chairs for furnishings. That didn't explain, even to himself, what he was doing here, except that it was Wednesday, his regular chess night, and he couldn't face the thought of going home.

The club was busy—five tables were in active play. The Lis were absent, which left the ratio ten men to one woman, Mai Sien Chong, who was running Tony Donelli through his paces at the corner table of the club's largest room. Mai Sien sat beneath the plaque of a club win in 1977, taking full advantage of her partner's distraction to rack up ratings points. She wore a green brocaded satin cheongsam slit well above her knee, and, as usual, she'd caught her thick dark hair into a little twist of a knot from the top of which the long hair emerged again to hang tantalizingly over her left breast. Her eyes glittered with mocking laughter, but Tony probably couldn't see that. Mai Sien took full advantage of her heavy eyelids, dropping them farther to accentuate their tilt. She had once explained to him that most men found that particular look irresistible, since it appeared both saucily demure, evoking images of compliant Asian Woman, and sleepy, which reminded them of bed.

Poor Tony didn't have a chance. When Mai Sien leaned forward over the board to examine the pieces, her breasts pressed against the tight satin where her hair marked a drifting circle around her left nipple. And when that happened, Tony's eyes glazed over, and heavy beads of sweat broke out on his upper lip. Brad watched, smiling, as she crossed her legs, right over left, and Tony knocked his queen off the table. Brad figured the chess piece did it on purpose—Tony's performance would disgust even a woman made out of wood. Mai Sien seemed to enjoy it, though. When Tony leaned down to pick up the chess piece, she swung her right leg, exposing it from ankle nearly to hip. Brad figured he'd better rescue the poor guy or Tony was going to need clean underwear.

Mai Sien must have come to the same conclusion. She caught his eye and smiled an invitation, and Brad walked forward to greet her. Tony managed to drag himself out from under the table, but he viewed Brad's approach with obvious dismay. With a challenge in his eye that he couldn't quite back up, Tony set his queen firmly in place. This was *his* game, and just because Brad was taller, smarter, and better looking didn't mean he got the girl. At least not until she'd taken Tony's king. Brad sat politely by while the game progressed, but the occasional glance from Mai Sien told him she was thinking the same thing he was. Not to get too Freudian about it, Tony was about to have his wood shortened. By an expert.

When Tony finally knocked over his king to acknowledge defeat, Brad wondered if the gesture was symbolic of the action taking place on his anatomy. It must have been, because Tony managed to leave the table with the outer trappings of his dignity intact. But Brad pulled his own chair up to the chessboard.

"It's almost closing time." Mai Sien kept her eyes on the chess pieces as she reset the board. "I had begun to think you wouldn't show up tonight."

For a moment Brad had the impression of long fingernails encased in gold, but the image vanished as fast as it registered.

"I was detained." He focused on the chess pieces, hiding the feelings that passed behind his eyes. "Business. Nothing serious."

"Why do I think you are lying?" She did look up then, and Brad could almost feel the heat of her eyes on him, taking him in, measuring, weighing. "Harry and Ellen didn't show up either. And when you walked in the door, you had a look on your face that would have turned our chess pro to stone. It gave me quite a chill myself."

"I noticed your concern," Brad countered wryly. He took his first move . . .

Ah, there it was, and perfectly timed. She cocked her head, slitted her eyes, and gave him the laughing glance that had returned poor Tony to a state of pimpled adolescence.

"But I was concerned," she pouted. "I rattled poor Tony just to cheer you up. It worked, too."

"Yes, it did," he admitted. "But you can put it away now. I just came for chess."

"That's all you ever want." She sighed in a forlorn burlesque of her usual seduction game. "I don't know what I see in you."

"The challenge?" he suggested. Then he hit the timer and her expression narrowed in concentration. Minutes passed in wordless, focused attention, the silence broken only by the snap of chess pieces on the wooden board and the click of the timer turning over the move. Finally, as the last second ticked off, Mai Sien admitted defeat.

"A gentleman would spot a lady a pawn or two," she complained.

"Yes, he would," Brad agreed affably as he set up the black pieces. "If he were a gentleman."

He waited until she was in mid move to finish—"And if she were a lady."

She set the pawn down with an arch acknowledgment of the hit. The game didn't take five minutes this time, nor did Brad win it.

"Next time," she suggested, "perhaps we could play for higher stakes."

"Playing for the honor of the win isn't enough for you?" he asked, and wondered at the fizz that bubbled through his veins when she licked her upper lip thoughtfully.

"Playing for honor. Hmmm. I suppose the loser must then relinquish his honor?"

"Or hers," he corrected, and saw the trap as she closed it.

Sharp white teeth showed in a predator's smile. "I think we have a bet," she agreed. "Perhaps we should find a more private venue?"

"Not tonight—"

He stood up to the sound of her laughter. "You have a headache?"

"Not for long," he answered, although he knew she wouldn't understand his reference. For the present, he needed somewhere comfortable and quiet to spend the night and maybe do a little thinking. And adding Mai Sien Chong to the list of things to think about just complicated his mortal life more than he was ready to accept.

"How about Friday?" he asked, and she answered, "Your place or mine."

"This place?"

"Spoilsport." But she rose from her chair and took his arm, tugging his head down for a confidential chat as they walked each other to the fire tower. "But we *will* continue this conversation. Ellen Li can't protect you forever."

He hadn't realized Ellen had done that, but perhaps she and Harry had run a little interference. He must have been glad for it at the time. At the moment, the idea rankled.

# Chapter 10

HARVEY BARNES LOOKED AS THOUGH HE'D HAD A LONG NIGHT. IN SPITE OF THE signs of exhaustion, or perhaps because of them, whatever his stepfather had said or done seemed to have worked. Evan's mother rode in near silence in the front seat, turning once in a while to check surreptitiously on Evan and to make the kind of casual chitchat meant to reassure him that she wouldn't bring up the topic of his father on the trip. As they drew closer to the house at Seventh and Spruce, her chatter grew more nervous. She'd never been inside, he remembered, and wondered what she expected. She didn't, to his knowledge, have quite the imagination that Joe Dougherty had shown, but there had been times when she'd pretty thoroughly avoided his room when he still lived in the house on Rosemont Street—funny how he'd never thought of it as home. It was all too human, too normal. That life had given him no space for the daemon part of him that needed to test its measure and fly.

Mr. Barnes—it was still hard to call him Harvey, even after all these years—pulled the car up to the curb just out of parking-ticket reach of the hydrant on the corner. So, now she'd know. He led them through the iron gate set into the high brick wall, and they stopped to admire the garden— phlox and sweet william, daisies and marigolds. At the back of the garden, a man-made waterfall trickled over low rocks between the irises and the day lilies.

"It's nice here." Evan's mother idly picked the last dead blossoms from the azaleas, but she seemed more relaxed than she had on the street.

"It's mostly Brad's project," he said. Brad had developed a fascination with the myriad colors and shapes that flowers came in. He didn't actually enjoy working in dirt, but he had hired the gardener. "The lilies are for Lily Ryan, Brad's cousin." He smiled, thinking about her one contribution to the planting scheme: "We have a namesake flower for each season."

He unlocked the sliding glass doors and stood aside for his mother to step into the living room he shared with Lily and his father.

"The office is at the front of the house, so we use the back door when we are coming home from street level," Evan explained. "And there's a door into the kitchen from the garage."

"Very nice." Gwen Davis peered around, trying not to look as if she was prying. The room was still furnished in a spare, clean style, though Lily had replaced the chairs with a pair in putty-colored canvas. The new sofa looked as though they'd used Jackson Pollack's drop cloth for upholstery fabric, but it was incredibly comfortable for napping, which was fortunate under the circumstances.

Evan headed toward the kitchen, but his mother stopped under the cathedral ceiling in the living room, looking up along the path of the freestanding staircase that led to the upper levels at the front of the house.

"Is your room up there?" she asked, doubt coloring the question.

"I'll be sleeping on the sofa tonight," he admitted.

"Smart."

Why did she sound so surprised?

"If you tell me where to find them, I'll bring down some sheets and clean clothes," she offered, still looking up at the narrow balconies overhanging the living room across the second and third floors of the house.

Evan considered the suggestion. He figured she needed to reassure herself that he wasn't mad as a hatter anymore, and he did need the clothes. His mother had washed the ones he'd been wearing when they took him to the hospital, and she'd bought him a new shirt so he didn't have to wear the one with the bloodstains to come home, but he wanted something a little more businesslike to wear when he talked to Harry Li.

"Third floor," he finally conceded. "Linens are in the hall closet, clothes in the closet inside the room. I'll need a jacket and a shirt and tie."

"You are supposed to be resting," she objected.

"After I clear up some details of the case."

The detail he had in mind was clearing his father of the burglary and attack on the guard, but she didn't have to know that. Not unless he wanted her camped out on his chest until she decided he was well enough to take care of himself. She seemed to recognize that pushing wouldn't win her any more concessions than she'd already wrung out of him, so she headed up the stairs.

"I'll make some coffee," he offered.

Harvey Barnes followed him into the kitchen and grabbed a chair at the table, watching as Evan worked.

"She worries about you," Barnes explained. Evan wondered if the man was apologizing for his mother's fussing or accusing him of being insensitive.

Barnes' tone wasn't giving him the clues he needed, so he answered just as noncommitally, "I know."

"I put your things on the couch." Evan's mother smiled weakly at him from the doorway. "Let me do that for you."

"Already done." Evan poured coffee and set out milk and sugar on the table. He didn't sit down, but leaned against the counter drinking from the thick pottery mug and trying to read his mother's mind from over the rim.

"You have a very nice house," she said between sips.

"We do well enough."

That made her wince. She clearly didn't want to be reminded that he didn't live here alone. But she didn't back down either.

"I noticed the easel in your room. You're painting again," she said between sips.

"A little bit, to relax." He wondered what she'd thought of the painting, a nude of Lily in one of her more playful moods.

"You've changed." She put her cup down, a sign that she wasn't making small talk. "It used to hurt to look at your paintings. They were terrifying." She looked into his eyes, searching deep for something. "Now you're happy. Oh, I don't mean to say that someone planting a bomb in your office hasn't upset you, but, in general, your life is happy now. And the lady in the painting looks like she enjoys leading you on a merry chase."

Harvey chuckled, not the least surprised. Evan wondered if he'd missed something about his mother when he was growing up, something he might have seen more if his daemon side hadn't driven both of them to the brink of despair.

Harvey—and Evan didn't know when during the homey chore of fixing coffee he'd started thinking of his mother's husband as Harvey—took the mugs to the sink and rinsed them. "I think we'd better be on our way, Gwen, and let Evan rest. You know damned well he's too stubborn to lie down while you're here to see it."

"I'll take you out through the office." A consolation prize, he figured, but she smiled when she stood up, and she gave him a peck on the cheek.

At the front door she held onto his hand for a minute, and he thought she might cry. She didn't though. She turned, seeming to be studying the passing traffic, but her hold on his hand tightened. "I don't know who Kevin Bradley is," she finally told him, "but I can see he's been good for you. I hope some day you can trust me enough to tell me what he is to you. I had thought, maybe, that you were lovers. Oh, I know, I'm your mother and I'm not supposed to wonder about things like that. But I can tell from the painting in your room that there is something between you and that woman." She put up her free hand, palm out, to stop him from trying to explain. "Not now," she said. "I can tell from the look in your eyes that anything you say will be a lie. But later, when you think about it, remember that you can trust me with the truth. I do love you, you know."

"I know," he said, and brought their clasped hands to his lips, eased the tension in her white knuckles with a brief kiss. So, her imagination didn't fall far from Dougherty's after all. He'd have to tell her something soon, and she wouldn't settle for a lie. He hoped he'd have time to figure out what to say.

"Evan!" Harry Li walked briskly toward them along the brick Society Hill sidewalk. "You're looking dreadful. But excuse me—I can come back if you are busy."

"My mother and her husband were just leaving," Evan assured him. He disentangled his hand from his mother's clasp and shook hands with Harvey Barnes. "Thanks for the ride." His tone said good-bye quite emphatically, and Harvey grinned back at him.

"I can take a hint. We'll stop by tomorrow to see that you are all right." He took his wife by the elbow. "But I'll make sure Gwen gives you a call first."

She punched Harvey Barnes playfully in the arm, and Evan wondered, once again, if he really knew his mother at all. But the couple had reached the corner, and Evan turned his attention back to his new guest.

He'd hoped for a shower and change of clothes before Harry Li arrived, but the fates were not with him this week. So he led his former teacher into the office where they saw clients, motioned him to a spindle-backed chair with its back to the window on the side garden, and sat behind the desk. Brad's desk. He tried to put aside the sharp pang the thought caused. He'd been lonely most of his life; he could get used to it again if he had to. But right now he had work to do.

"What was it you wanted to tell me, Harry?"

"Has Brad turned up yet?"

"I haven't seen him, no." And not the question Evan wanted to hear right now, either. "You said you had something you wanted to discuss."

"I'm sorry, my boy. When he does show up, will you have him call Ellen? We are both rather worried about him."

"I will. I'm worried too, Harry. We've checked the hospitals and the morgue; there's nothing else we can do until he comes home." Nothing but the first and the last were true, but knowing that somewhere Badad the daemon was enjoying his freedom without a thought for his mortal son didn't help Evan to worry any less. "But you *did* say you wanted to talk to me about something—"

"Nothing concrete. I wanted you to see this." Harry pulled a battered leather-bound book from his inside breast pocket. "As you know, I have studied the *I Ching* for many years. My interest in art actually began with my interest in Chinese calligraphy, which itself was piqued by the ancient calligraphed texts of the *I Ching*.

"You've mentioned that in class," Evan smiled, reminiscing. "I even participated in one of your demonstrations at a colloquium for the religious studies department. You cast my coins and said that I would have success in the material world. Which, given the Beemer in the parking garage, wasn't much of a stretch."

"The fact that the future is not difficult to see does not change the fact that the *I Ching* saw it."

"A tautology doesn't leave much room for argument," Evan protested. "I don't see how that will bring back the Moon Stone, or the Dowager Empress Crystal, for that matter." Or my father. But he kept the last to himself. He didn't want Harry Li to know that Brad had disappeared, not with Harry's wife in charge of the investigation and Brad somewhere at the top of the list of suspects.

"Not all futures are as clear as yours was on that day. And even that future doesn't mean forever. The answers change with the question, and the future changes with each choice we make on our path."

Evan rubbed his hands across his face and regretted it. The bruises hurt more than they had when he'd first won them in a one-on-one with the desk lamp. Well, not exactly. The force of Ariton had given the lamp an unfair advantage. The back of his head didn't bear thinking about. And they'd probably have to replace the damned monitor.

"I'm tired, Harry." And let Harry take that as the statement of fact it was or as the beginning of the end of this discussion, which it also was. Evan was too tired to care, and he suspected that his mother had been right. He wasn't ready to go back to work yet. "Unless the *I Ching* has told you who took the crystals and where they put them, this will have to wait."

"Not yet," Harry conceded, "but it has given a clue, at least. Only, I need your help to decipher it."

"I don't know anything about the *I Ching*, Harry."

"No, but you do know something about your father. Certainly something your mother is not ready to hear."

"He didn't do it. And he is my father, real as it gets. My mother is mistaken."

"You may be correct on all three points. In fact, I'm inclined to believe you are. That does not mean we have the truth. To your first point, your father didn't commit the burglary, but the *I Ching* says that it is tied up with him, or will be. To your second and third points, I have listened to Brad chat over a game of chess often enough to know that in spite of what your mother remembers, he is equally certain that he is your father. But that is the only truth about Kevin Bradley in a forest of untruths, spurious tales, and gross exaggerations.

"I'm afraid for you, Evan. He may run away rather than face his truths, and you're not ready to lose him. And because of his connection, in some way, to the burglary, if he does run, we will never find the Empress."

Evan started to rub his forehead and stopped just in time. His face hurt worse than the headache. "I don't know what you're talking about, Harry."

"The book, Evan. The *I Ching*." Harry shook the leather-bound volume for emphasis. "When your father first came to me to ask my help with your application, I ran your fortune, and his."

That threw Evan completely off the track he was trying, with little success, to follow in the first place. "My father did what?"

"Your father knew better than anyone how much you had matured since you had joined the agency, and he felt he owed you greatly for the work you did for him."

"He pays me very well." Evan hadn't done it for the money or for any material payback. He'd thought of it as stocking up karma points, if anything, to weigh against his father's in the scales of who owed whom. But even there he'd been outmaneuvered, which was a pretty stupid way of thinking about the kind of help that fathers give their sons. But Evan didn't have that kind of relationship with Brad. He didn't have any relationship at all with Brad now, it seemed.

Harry shrugged. "If you wanted Penn, he felt you had earned that chance. And he never had a doubt you would succeed if you really wanted it. He was right, of course, but I wasn't as sure. I needed evidence, so I ran your fortunes."

"And?"

Evan squirmed under his teacher's puzzled gaze.

"Westerners usually have one of two reactions to the *I Ching*," Harry finally said. "They scorn the idea, along with all forms of fortune-telling, as unscientific, or they naively assume that the mystical East must have some otherworldly telephone line to the future which they write down in a little black book. You, however, look as if you are waiting for the other shoe to drop. Which makes me wonder about the first shoe."

"I've had three years of practice at showing no surprise at anything you say, Professor. But so far, you haven't said anything."

Harry wasn't buying it, of course, but Evan had put him back on track. He opened the book and pulled out a piece of scrap paper, a jagged corner off a larger sheet, and turned it until Evan could see the characters scrawled on it.

"I'd forgotten, but look."

"I don't read Chinese, Harry," Evan reminded him.

"Of course not, my boy. Look and learn." He pointed to the first character. "It's *Chin,* the symbol for progress. Your father was in a very favorable position when I tossed the coins: strong, powerful, like the sunrise. But the future, look, *Wei Chi,* is the last of the hexagrams and marks trouble before completion. Nothing goes as planned, and children are particularly troublesome. Frankly, I would have suggested that your father not pursue your schooling based on his own reading. Things were going well for him, but the future looked troubled, and you, it seemed, were the cause."

"You did help him, though."

"Ayeea, yes." Harry ran his fingers through his hair. Then he jabbed his finger at a third character. "*Kun,* exhaustion, borne down by too many burdens. Nothing goes well. I could not turn away your father when he so wanted to help you and you needed that help so badly. And it seemed that we were right. You prospered in your learning, and I forgot."

"Forgot what, Harry? I'd rather we didn't turn this into a Chinese opera."

"Obstruction. *Chien.* Ties with family broken. The character even predicts involvement in a burglary."

"Well, hell." Since he'd grown to understand his own dual nature and the nature of the spheres, Evan had come to respect those figures lost in history who had risked their lives and their homes to chart an understanding of the realms of reality beyond their own. But this was both too much and not enough. "Our business is finding stolen property, Harry. There is a name for the times when I am not involved in a burglary. It's called a vacation."

"I know, Evan. But don't you see? Your father is suddenly blocked, your relationship with him . . . troubled . . . I won't pry by asking about your relationship with Lily Ryan, but I would have expected to see her, and your father, at the hospital. Or here, tending to business while you rest. I haven't. Somehow, this particular burglary involves your father and yourself more than we can see on the surface. No, he didn't do it. I think I know him well enough to say that without the Book, and Ellen agrees. But it is an obstacle in your relationship with him, and until—unless—it is resolved, your life, and his, stops at this point. Not dead, but beating your head against the wall of your mutual anger."

"Harry." Evan raised his hands, as if to make a gesture that failed him. "Your coins or sticks or however you read the characters in that book of yours aren't telling me anything I don't already know. None of it helps solve the case."

Harry Li smiled. "The museum is now paying your agency to do that. Which doesn't mean the *I Ching* can't help. But right now it predicts trouble—personal trouble for you and your father. I want the museum's property back, but I also want to help a friend."

Evan sat up expectantly, which caused the world to blur dangerously around the edges. His head did not like this newfound enthusiasm.

"Later?" he asked, and set his elbows on the desk to help support his head.

"You should have told me that you were too tired for this today, Evan. You don't have anything to prove, you know. Or if you did, it's three years too late to start worrying about it. We'll do this tomorrow, when you are rested." Harry frowned his disapproval as he picked up his book and coins, but Evan saw the concern under the fussing. "Let me help you into the house."

"I'll manage." Evan stood up and tried to look alert, but the bruises on the left side of his face nearly closed that eye, and the other wasn't seeing all that clearly either. Harry shook his hand and headed for the door. After a moment to summon his strength, Evan left the office through the side door into the study. His father was sitting in his tapestried wing chair, waiting.

# Chapter 11

"YOU'RE BACK."

He supposed Evan expected some kind of response, but the answer was obvious. Brad sat in his chair, a brandy on the table at his elbow and a book that he'd been ignoring propped on his knee, and watched Evan cross to the desk and sit behind it. The room still showed most of the signs of Lily's hasty exit. Books and papers were scattered about the room, and the dictionary stand had toppled, dumping the unabridged dictionary in a heap. Someone had righted the lamp and put the computer back on the desk, but no one had cleaned the smear of dried blood from the corner of the monitor that had collided with Evan's head. Fortunately for Evan, the boy had a very hard head. Not much patience, though.

"I didn't expect to see you again." He paused as if waiting for an answer. Brad didn't have one handy at the moment, but Evan pushed on: "I'm sorry. I didn't think." As if that made a difference.

Brad remembered the handcuffs chaining him to the bench in that small room, the metal burning not-quite-human flesh, and knew he could not forgive. That would have required acceptance, a thing for saints, or humans, not for a daemon betrayed by a monster who should have carried the host loyalty to his Prince within him.

"Once I'd done it, I knew it was a mistake," Evan explained into the thick silence, "but I was afraid to let you go. I thought you would kill me, or that Lily would."

Brad had thought the same, was a little surprised that Evan had escaped that part of it with nothing but a technicolor face and a few stitches. But he still needed his own answer, and this time Evan was awake. He put the book on the little table next to his chair. He couldn't even remember the title, but as a prop it had begun to annoy him. The action gave him time to think, but his mind had locked on a single question and wouldn't budge till he had an answer.

"You did release the binding spell," he began, which Evan seemed to take as partial absolution, and then he asked: "Why?"

Evan's hand started the characteristic drag through his hair. Then stopped. He winced and extricated his fingers from the clotted tangles. "I needed time, and I knew you wouldn't wait. And I didn't realize what it would be like for you in the holding cell until Lily explained it to me."

Brad shook his head. "Not why did you make the command. You knew I would kill you, but you released the spell anyway. Why?" And Brad knew that his rage still burned, that Evan still could die for this.

"The reasons are the same." Evan twirled a pen between his fingers, his eyes caught on the bloody corner of the monitor. When he spoke, he did not look up. "I thought it would be better for all of us if you stayed, and I knew you wouldn't, on your own. And it seemed safe enough. I don't know Ellen Li, but apparently you did. And I know Harry. I figured she had to be smart and fair for either of you to like her. And she didn't seem the type to pull out the truncheons and work you over—I figured the worst part of the whole experience would be drinking the stale coffee."

Evan seemed to find something funny in that idea. Brad didn't appreciate the humor.

"Then Dougherty showed up, and they were planning to keep you there. I still figured Ellen would make sure you were okay, but Lily explained to me what captivity meant to your kind. She said it was worse than when Omage held me prisoner at the Black Masque. Was she right?"

Evan did meet his gaze then, and he knew that his son was remembering horrors of which Brad had only seen the surface. Madness and rape and his living blood painted on the wall of Omage's back room dwelt deep in his son's eyes, with the greater horror that he had done worse to his father. The hell of it was, the boy had. Brad didn't speak, but Evan knew. Lily never lied to him.

"At the end, I knew I wasn't sane anymore, you know?"

Brad nodded, letting Evan take his own path to his answer.

"But waiting for you kept me alive. Then you actually showed up. I wanted you to kill me, but you didn't."

Brad remembered the defiance in his son, and the madness. But Evan still hadn't answered the question: "Why?"

"I tried to imagine what it would be like, going through that kind of terror and pain with no hope that it would end, and I knew I couldn't have lived."

Evan shrugged. "Once I knew, I didn't have a choice. You had to be free even if I died in the process."

It made sense, in an Evan sort of way. Brad nodded.

"And if I kill you now."

"You won't." Evan smiled at him. Not one of the happy ones, this came from the place where Evan balanced risk against pride.

"You could have. I don't fool myself; if I'd been close by when I said the words that set you free, you would have killed me where I stood. I remember, just as I passed out, thinking that Lily *had* killed me, or that you'd come back long enough to relieve me of my mortal existence. I didn't expect to wake up, figured I'd never have the chance to tell you it was a mistake, and I am sorry.

"If you are here, sitting in your favorite chair with a glass of slightly charred brandy in your hand, you've already gotten past turning me into a puddle of ashes on the floor. But you are leaving—"

"I have to." Brad stared into a distance reflected in the brandy in his glass. "Before I forget that I wanted you alive more than I wanted to go home."

Funny how things worked on the material sphere. He'd thought that he would learn to understand time using the rational part of his human mind, but it turned out that the past was all about emotions and how one action, one moment in time, could change everything that came before it as well as what came after. He set the brandy snifter next to the book on the table and stood up.

"I expect Lily will return soon. Tell Harry I may see him around but that you are the key investigator for the museum case." He chose not to vanish into the second sphere but to walk from the study and head for his room for a change of clothes. Mai Sien Chong crossed his mind with the smell of incense, and he considered the challenge she had offered. If he was stuck here, he might as well take a lesson from Lirion and learn to enjoy it.

# Chapter 12

EVAN WOKE FROM A TROUBLED SLEEP TO THE FEEL OF SOFT BREASTS AGAINST HIS naked back. He didn't remember climbing the stairs or falling into bed, but he had. And he'd even managed to take off his clothes. All of them, he realized, as warm hips tucked up against his equally bare buttocks. Lily was home, her dark hair spread across his shoulder the way her body sprawled across his back. When he wriggled around to look at her, a slow smile started on her lips.

"You have a wonderful body." She snuggled more tightly against him, her arms reaching around his back to hold him close. "But your face belongs in a circus. Did I do that?"

"The furniture you threw at my head did it," he amended with precision.

"Oh, my." She kissed the bruise, lightly, then moved away just enough to give him a more careful inspection. "The important parts of your anatomy seem to be in working order, anyway," she confirmed, moving back into his arms.

The feel of her body against his raised the old familiar ache of longing and sorrow. She meant too much to him, and the sex was just a part of it. He could never tell her, though. Knowledge was power in the universe of daemonkind, and in the unequal balance of their relationship, he couldn't afford to give her any more advantage than she already had. Her laughter cut deeper than Omage's knife, and he had his pride. Which was beginning to matter a lot less to him while the sex part of the equation grew more urgent by the second. But the graduation reception still rankled.

"I thought you preferred the Alfredo Da'Costa model this month." He hoped that didn't sound as petulant to her as it did to him.

"That's different."

He moved out of her reach, a hand on her shoulder. His fingers itched to wander over her soft skin, but he resisted the urge. Lily shrugged, and his hand slipped to her back, but still he waited. No question that he wanted her; all she had to do was look. But he held his body completely still while the spark of challenge heated up the desire that crackled in her eyes.

"Alfredo can be anything, anybody. Sometimes, when we are in bed together, I pretend he is you." She grinned a promise of dangerous pleasure. "Sometimes, Alfredo takes on your shape, and we both pretend I am making love to you." She reached out to touch him.

Evan didn't let her come nearer, though her words had set the nerve endings in his skin pounding in time with his pulse beat. Did that body Alfredo Da'Costa wore feel like his? Did it smell like his? Did it move as he did? No. Whatever the physical shell, it was still Alfredo Da'Costa making love. Evan's body would thrust to Alfredo Da'Costa's rhythms, not his own. He wanted to ask her, did she prefer the original or the copy? Who was better at giving her body pleasure? But he was afraid to hear the answer. She was laughing, daring him with that body to ask, and he refused. He would not lose his pride to her game, not even when she stretched, her arms over her head, and her breasts seemed to reach for him, pressed forward by the taut bowing of her back.

"Take me home?" she asked, a knowing quirk to her brow, and her arms fell around his neck. "I love it when you take me home."

In some respects, Evan conceded, he was only human. But in some respects he was not; he stifled the whimper begging for release when he pulled her close.

He knew every inch of her, had learned her body with careful study over the past four years. Knew that when he nipped at her lip just so she would grab his head between her hands in frustration—"Ouch! Watch the stitches!"—but she gentled the touch with a kiss on the purple and yellow skin at the corner of his eye before she moved on to explore every chipped tooth and ridge on the roof of his mouth with determined energy. He knew that when his hands slid down her back to caress the round luxury of her buttocks, his fingertips teasing at the crack between them, she would roll him over and mount him with the little growl deep in her throat that promised a hard and sweaty ride, while his hands moved to her breasts and kneaded them, pulling her down to meet him, mouth to nipple, to mouth, to throat, while she picked up his rhythm and then, at the moment when his body made its final thrusts into hers, they would shift, exploding into the second celestial sphere with just the essence of their being, and Evan shared with her for a brief moment the joining of daemonkind, filling the universe as he filled her human body.

Let Alfredo Da'Costa try that, he thought, and remembered too late that in the sphere where no material objects existed, where he himself could only exist for any space of time in noncorporeal form, Lily could read his mind. From inside it.

"That wouldn't be healthy," she pointed out, "for any of us."

The last time the guardians had penetrated the second celestial sphere, they'd started the big bang that created the material universe—a dandy metaphor for how he was feeling, but not healthy as a reality.

He saw something else while their minds mingled like their tangled limbs. Alfredo was interesting and fun, more so than the human men, and the occasional women, Lily took to her bed. But only Evan had the fire of Ariton in his human veins. Her warmth enveloped him like a slow fire on a cold day, and he saw what the binding spell had obscured for most of the years he had known her. The connection between them went deep, deeper than any loyalty he could have imagined from her kind. The deeper it went, the more entangled it became with host loyalty and what it meant to join with others of the host of Ariton, reaching a quorum of individual minds that fused, became one entity more powerful than any on Earth—a Prince of the second celestial sphere.

Lily Ryan was just a name she'd made up, an identity behind which she could hide her power and pass for human in the material sphere. As her true self, Lirion of the host of Ariton, she did not simply owe loyalty to her Prince. In a true and complete sense she was her Prince, as Badad was, and eight hundred other beings who resonated with the flame in Evan's soul. Lirion belonged here in this eternal dark. She would live forever among the energy vortices and endless stillness broken only by the battles of Princes and the curious energy that bound one daemon to another. And somewhere in the tangle of relationships beyond loyalty, in the realm of shared identity, Badad's monstrous get had moved from the outside to the inside. Da'Costa was no threat because Da'Costa was not, could not ever be, Ariton.

Evan would have smiled if he'd had a mouth with him, but he'd left it with his body back in his bed on the material sphere. Lily read the feeling, though, and flicked a snap of electricity through him. "Silly puppy," she whispered in his mind, and he caught at the edge of the thought her curious teasing at the nature of his existence. Her kind were immortal. She had seen death in the process of their work, but she still didn't quite understand this ceasing to exist. Most of all, she couldn't quite equate it with Evan.

"Me neither," he admitted as the body in question drew him back. Lily followed him and gave him a dirty look: While they'd been gone, their bodies had grown sticky and chill. His first coherent word didn't improve her mood.

"Brad?" he asked, and she stopped halfway out of the bed. She wouldn't need to ask "What?" of course. The thought still lingered in both of their minds.

"I don't know anymore," she said. "He recognized Ariton in you before I did. Even so, I expected to find you dead when I came back."

He had to snort at that. The back of his head where she'd smacked him with the computer monitor still hurt like hell, and his bruised and swollen face could frighten small children. But she hadn't answered his question.

"Will he come back?"

She thought about it, and Evan wondered if she was checking some interdimensional telegraph system, but she finally shook her head. "I don't know," she said. "If you had forced me to sit in that cell with chains eating at my soul, I would have killed you."

"Hardly chains," he protested, "one handcuff, for a matter of hours." Nothing like the year he'd spent with Omage's chains at wrists and neck and ankles, tortured in the material sphere and sent careening madly through the darkness he didn't understand, filled with monsters he couldn't see.

"Enough, though." She'd already explained that, to Badad of Ariton, with no hope and no tomorrow, it had been every bit as bad. Worse, because his son had done it. Evan had given his word, and Evan was Ariton, so Brad had trusted him and had suffered for that trust.

"He can't go home until you are dead, of course. You no longer bind us here, but we still have the command of the Princes to fulfill; kill you, or make sure you don't endanger the spheres. Which we pretty much have to do from this planet in the material sphere. Since he didn't kill you, he will be around somewhere."

She didn't touch him to soften her next words. "You may bump into him on the street, or he may come back some day. But if you try to force him, you will lose him, and you will probably lose your life as well."

Evan knew better. He didn't pretend to understand the bond between them, but sitting across from his father in the study, he'd let go of the fear that had nipped at his heels since he'd come to his senses in this house, no more than halfway sane, to discover he had a father who wasn't human and didn't have a lot of patience with a pretty repulsive object lesson in cross-universe interbreeding. After everything he'd done, he was still alive and likely to stay that way if his father had anything to do with it. That didn't mean Brad was going to make this easy, but Evan was as stubborn as his father and just as motivated.

But then Lily was walking away from the bed, leaning over to pick up a robe from a chair, and Brad didn't seem important all of a sudden. Evan followed her, drawn like a magnet by the color of her flesh and the angle of her body, legs slightly apart, offering her secrets in tantalizing glimpses.

"You don't need that yet." He snugged his hips up tight to hers, his erection teasing at her crack, and took the robe from her fingers and dropped it onto the floor.

She opened her legs a bit more to give him access, and reached an arm around his neck to drag his head to her shoulder. Turning so that she could whisper in his ear, she first licked contemplatively along the length of the bruise on his face. Then she whispered a breathy invitation in his ear. "Come into my parlor, said the spider to the fly."

And he did.

# Chapter 13

MORNING FOUND EVAN ALONE IN BED, SOMEWHAT MORE RESTED AND, AS HE discovered upon checking his face in the bathroom mirror, sporting an even more interesting variety of colors on his face. The purple bruises had turned black with tones of yellow and green around the edges. The blood around his stitches had also turned black, which contrasted darkly with the bright red of the antiseptic the emergency room physician had swabbed on the cut. If he'd been a canvas, they'd have locked up the painter. He shaved around the worst of it. It didn't cut down much on the brawling streetcorner look he'd had on waking, but at least he'd made an effort.

In the kitchen he poured himself a mug of strong coffee, thick the way only Lily could make it, and pulled the sticky-note off the coffeepot.

"Let you sleep," the note said. "You need your strength! Went to check in with Lieutenant Li and have chat with Liz at major crimes—left the museum for you."

He smiled in spite of the fact that she'd left him the dirtier job. The police already had Brad's and Evan's statements. Lily had been out of town—way out of town—when the burglary occurred, so she had little to add. She'd be doing the PR work, showing the agency's interest in recovering the stolen objects, voicing their concern that the materials were stolen before they could initiate security reforms, and squeezing as much information out of the officers working on the investigation as she could.

The museum trustees, on the other hand, would want to know why they'd lost their valuable exhibits the day they hired the agency to do a security review, and they might be as suspicious as Joe Dougherty that the company was somehow involved. They would want to know why the agency hadn't already found the stolen objects. And they would doubtless wonder why the agency expected a fee for the recovery of the objects when they had been stolen from under the nose of their chief investigator. As the initial contact on the job and its chief investigator, Brad should have handled the trustees. But that presented two problems. The chief investigator was also the chief suspect, which fact would seriously impair his credibility with the client. And as far as Evan knew, Brad had disappeared.

Lily might have figured Harry Li would take it easy on him, considering the student-teacher relationship they had recently shared. But more likely she had decided that he deserved the uncomfortable parts of the job since it was his fault they needed the cover of real work in the first place. Which was pretty difficult to argue, so he didn't bother anymore.

He thought about calling from the office to make the appointment with Harry, but he remembered the chaos left in the wake of an escaping daemon with a shiver. Lily'd come home, but the books didn't leap onto their shelves on that account. He took a sip of coffee and levered himself carefully onto a kitchen stool. By no coincidence a phone hung on the wall next to the coffeepot. First, he contacted the housekeeping service to warn them that the back office would need extra time. The service had more or less gotten used to requests like that from Bradley, Ryan, and Davis; the cleaning staff had taken to wearing large crosses on the outside of their clothing, but they did a good job whatever they thought of the client. Then he dialed Harry Li's cell phone number.

"Li," the voice at the other end of the line said in that distant tone that told him Harry was reading and not really paying attention to the caller.

"It's Evan, Harry." He waited for his teacher's mind to dig its way back to the surface and was rewarded a moment later.

"Evan. It's good that you called. I've been looking to the *I Ching* to see where we stand on the Moon Stone, but I'm going to need your help to interpret the reading."

"Harry. The other trustees—remember them? They'll want a report."

Li dismissed the objection; Evan could almost see the wave of his hand when he said, "You have an appointment at two this afternoon. In the meantime, I want you to come to my office on campus. I know the answer is here, but I'm not sure what it means."

"Here," of course, meant the ideograms Harry constructed out of the toss of three coins. Which summed up Evan's understanding of the *I Ching*. He didn't know how Li expected him to help, but he agreed to the meeting.

"Give me an hour to get the ferrets running," he said.

"The what?"

Evan realized after he said it that his statement made as much sense to Harry Li as Harry's ideograms meant to him. "I want to start some computer searches," he amended, "and I have to inventory the damages here."

"Of course, Evan. I'd forgotten that the agency had a break-in as well. Curious indeed."

Still muttering, Harry let him go, and Evan headed for the study. As he'd expected, the monitor was dead, but the cpu still functioned. After calling to have a new monitor delivered, he dug the laptop out of the bottom desk drawer and slaved it to the cpu. Pulling up the programs he wanted, he set them to search the national insurance claims and police investigation databases. No point in bothering with Interpol; the databases would be pouring the relevant search information into the local system where he'd pick it up anyway. Then he added a few keywords to the ongoing watch he maintained on several less savory but considerably more useful sources of information on the movement of stolen art. Like everybody else, the fences were online these days.

Evan figured the police were probably watching the same sites, but he didn't like to depend on their analysis of the data. Codes tended toward the more esoterically intuitive in those online chat rooms where the virtual appreciation of art covered clandestine transactions for the real thing. There was a woman in Major Crimes and a guy over at the FBI he'd trust to see the links as fast as he did, but he couldn't hang the agency's investigation on the hope they'd be assigned to this case. So he set his keywords with a thesaurus link of his own, set the whole thing running and unlinked the laptop. It had taken him more than the hour he'd promised Harry, but not much more. He hesitated a moment with the laptop in his hand, then tucked it under his arm. With Harry, you just never knew what you'd need.

The cleaning staff had arrived while he worked, and the supervisor, a black woman in her forties, didn't bother to conceal her disapproval when she saw the study.

"Break-in, not a party," he explained. She examined the battered side of his face with narrow-eyed concentration, then nodded.

"You can replace books. You only get one head."

As sympathy went, it didn't go far, but it worked an almost magical effect on the team of one man and two women with her. He didn't know how he sensed it, hadn't noticed it except in the supervisor, but a weight of weary resentment seemed to lift from their shoulders.

"Thanks for coming over so quickly. I didn't know where to begin." He realized he was babbling and didn't know why, except that the exchange seemed to require some continuation of the contact. The supervisor looked around her, and Evan caught the moment when she saw the blood on the monitor and connected it to the bandage on his face.

"Mary," she said, as if she knew what he was looking for. "When we are done, you won't know anyone was here."

She didn't mean her staff, but that they would remove all traces of the damage the invaders of his home had left behind. Except it hadn't been invaders, but Lily. He wondered if Mary knew how vulnerable he felt standing in the chaos he hadn't been able to control, or how angry he felt that he should be so vulnerable in his own home. She seemed to understand that much, and he wasn't ready to take self-discovery any deeper.

"Thank you," he said. And she gave him a slow nod, accepting all the things he meant by that and all the things it didn't mean. Heading for the garage, he tucked away somewhere safe, where he wouldn't have to look at it, the knowledge of who had done this, and thought about Lily in his bed instead.

The BMW was in its usual place. Sliding behind the wheel, he could pretend that he lived in a perfectly normal if slightly upscale universe. Harry would knock that fantasy out of him, but for the moment he let himself attack the downtown traffic as if nothing else mattered. His pretense of competence lasted until he faced the staircase at the Furness Building— four flights, rising in a delicate tracery of decorative ironwork balustrades with Harry's office at the very top, overlooking the library below. For most of the past three years Evan had enjoyed climbing those stairs, passing the leaded-glass windows that opened into a center atrium that held the fine arts library. He'd landed at the wrong end of a fist often enough to know that he wouldn't make it to the top in his present condition, though, and headed for the elevator.

Harry was waiting behind his wide mahogany desk, almost invisible behind the piled books, newspaper clippings of the Smithsonian break-in, and the insurance photographs of the two crystal balls stolen in Philadelphia. Both stones were amazing examples of an art that was pretty much dead, but of the two the university's Dowager Empress stone outweighed the PMA's Moon Stone by quite a bit. Evan remembered when he'd first seen the Empress crystal, on a field trip during junior high. About the size of a basketball, it had reminded him of a perfectly round drop of water, and he'd felt it pulling him in, as if he were falling down, down, into a well with the most amazing things at the bottom, where the walls and ceiling appeared all turned around.

His junior high teacher might have left him there, lost in the depths just beyond the crystal's lambent surface, but his classmates had jostled him away. After that he'd come back to look at it alone, but he had never reached quite the level of absorption in it that he had achieved that first time. He almost felt that the crystal had taken his measure in that meeting and had no further need of him. But he remembered feeling a personal sense of outrage when it had disappeared, as if the thieves had stolen part of his soul.

He'd never had quite as strong a connection to the PMA's Moon Stone, but this time he could help to bring it back. If only he could finish with Harry and the board and get back to his computer.

"Evan!" Harry stood up but didn't come around the desk to greet his visitor, nor did Evan expect him to. Instead, he sat back down, his hands folded on the desk in front of him, and waited. Usually the approach made sense; students opened up more if they weren't pressed. Evan knew Harry's style cold by now; he'd come here often to argue some point that had passed over the heads of his classmates or just to make contact with a human being. But this time, it was Harry's call.

"What has you stumped, Professor, and how do you figure I can help?" Evan gave up and threw himself into the battered leather chair set at an angle to the desk. He fidgeted a moment with the books on the overcrowded wall behind him—old habits, and hard to break. Finally giving the desk his closer attention, he saw the *Book of Changes* open on top of the photographs and the three coins scattered there as well. A yellow lined tablet rested to the right of the book with a stylus nearby.

"I didn't think that even the *I Ching* could surprise you."

"This time it has." Harry gave him that deep, measuring look, the one that said he hoped for the truth but was prepared to spot a lie.

"I know what your agency's ad in the Yellow Pages says. That you handle the occult, discreetly."

"And?" Evan didn't like the direction this was going, though the book and the coins should have warned him.

"I would surmise, therefore, that you have encountered certain of these occult investigations."

"Yes." This conversation felt like a train running out of track at high speed. If he could figure out what to say he might be able to stop it before it crashed, but he still hadn't figured out where Harry Li was going.

"Were they always hoaxes?"

"If this is about the *I Ching,* I've already told you what I think. It seems to work for you. I don't have to understand why."

Harry waved that dismissive hand. "Not the book. That is knowledge. I mean, have you ever encountered otherworldly entities in your work?"

Well, he was hung out to dry now. If he said "yes," he'd look gullible as sin. But if he said "no," Harry would know it for a lie. And he absolutely did not want to get into how he knew, incontrovertibly, that otherworldly creatures did exist. He could just imagine Harry's reaction if he told him that truth: Sure I've met otherworldly creatures. In fact, I am one. That's how I know Kevin Bradley is my father—we share a family resemblance in the second celestial sphere. No, that conversation wasn't going to happen.

"If you are asking me, do I believe in the occult, Professor, the answer is a qualified yes. Most often we find that imagination, trickery, or both working in concert, produce the effect that the client believes to be supernatural."

He hesitated a moment to consider how he could phrase the other side of the argument, and tiptoed through an answer as vague as he could make it. "But the universe is more complex than we give it credit for. In rare cases, human beings do experience something that we can't explain logically. Does that answer your question?"

Harry was weighing that answer. "And you have experienced this illogical side of the universe?"

*I had some amazing otherworldly sex with it last night, and I gather you've played chess on a regular basis with an aspect of that great beyond as well.* But he didn't say it out loud, instead offering, "I'm as much a mortal being as you are, Professor, but yes, I have had experiences that convinced me I was working with the supernatural or paranormal."

"Maybe someday you will tell me about it." Harry Li was letting him off the hook for the present, but Evan knew that he hadn't heard the last of the professor's questions. He still didn't understand why Harry was so keen on hearing about the subject, but Harry picked up the photo of the Moon Stone and glared at it. Putting it down again, he took up the stylus and said, "Then perhaps you can help me interpret this."

He pointed with the stylus to one of three hexagrams sketched on the pad of yellow paper. "Since we had a few clues about the thief, I asked the *I Ching* for advice to identify who stole the Moon Stone. I received this answer, which makes little sense unless we consider a supernatural component to the case."

"Would that surprise you?" Evan asked. "The most valuable items stolen were crystal balls, after all. Maybe the thieves are using the crystals to predict what the police will do next, and your reading reflects a battle between fortune-tellers."

"You are being facetious now, boy." Harry tapped the paper with the stylus. "Crystals such as the Empress Dowager stone, or the Moon Stone, have no power to foretell the future. They are beautiful, and for that they have value enough. But their spirit-value is in the present. Or, perhaps more properly, their mystery resides in their capacity to stop time. Looking into the stone is like looking into a moment frozen just before it dashes itself to pieces on the future. Captured within the stone you find your surroundings, even yourself, but distorted, displaced, and again, frozen in time. In a sense, the crystals are the antithesis of prognostication, holding the present captive in water turned to stone."

As the professor talked, Evan felt himself displaced in time. He was a child again and staring into the crystal ball on its stand, waves of the sea captured in silver. He felt himself falling, trapped, as if it would gobble him up. Harry's voice droned from a distance.

"I think," Harry said, "that we may be working with a reincarnated spirit carrying out the dictates of its former life."

That woke Evan up. "What could give you an idea like that?" he asked.

"Look for yourself." Harry traced the hexagram with his stylus. "*Ta Kuo*. It stands for force of effort beyond the will that drives it. The *Ta Kuo* person is joyous, creative, but out of control. His intentions may be mild, but his actions show no restraint, so the reaction far exceeds his original intent."

"Sounds like half the people taking life-drawing class, but that doesn't make them supernatural."

"The clues are in the image and in the individual lines," Harry objected. "See here, the hexagram shows a forest overwhelmed by water. This can be one life overwhelmed by another, because look here, lines two and five, the withered tree shows new life, and the withered tree flowers, the lines reinforce the message because they give the interpretation for both yin and yang. And the top place, a man crossing the stream is submerged by rising water. Here again, one life overwhelming another."

"Isn't it more likely to mean that there are two burglars, and one is the leader and the other does what he is told?"

"No," Harry asserted, and he turned to another hexagram on the paper. "If there was another person involved, I would expect a hexagram with changing lines, and the dominant partner would be the first hexagram, and his follower would be the hexagram formed by the changing lines. In this case, there are no changing lines, so there can be only one person, but perhaps driven by the imperative of another life. There is something else you should know about *Ta Kuo*. It is a sign of an unstable situation. And items lost under this hexagram are not easy to find again. In this situation, however, it is difficult to tell if the thief is looking for lost items and cannot find them, or if the items the thief steals will be difficult for the police and your agency to find."

"And this other hexagram you are pointing to," Evan asked, though he knew he'd be sorry for doing it, "what does this one mean?"

"Nothing we didn't know before." Harry laughed softly and shook his head. "I wanted to know what your father's involvement in this crime was."

"He didn't—" It was becoming a knee-jerk reaction by now.

"I know he didn't steal the crystals, Evan. I have already told you that; asking the question again won't change the answer." Patient teacher, with just a trace of having said it too many times already, surfaced in Harry Li's response. "I also feel sure he does not consciously know who has stolen them. But I feel certain there is some connection, some relationship that we don't yet understand."

"Did you find one?"

"Yes. Again, not to our advantage. See this, *Chieh,* restraint or limits. This is a person who loves danger, but if he does not respect order, if he breaks regulations, he will suffer setbacks and hardship. Patient work can be successful, especially in finding lost objects, but this person doesn't know the meaning of patience!"

"And what is this one?" Evan pointed to the third hexagram on the paper, wondering who the third person would be, and what Harry had asked the book about them.

Li shook his head. "The question I asked about your father produced a changing hexagram, and this is its changed form. It indicates that the lost item, if found, will be lost again, and the person who stole it may escape beyond the reach of the law. Not dead, simply distant."

Evan stared at the hexagram, wondering what it said about a wandering investigator. Was it only the thief who would run away, or would Brad move beyond their reach as well?

"If that was meant as a pep talk before we meet with the board of trustees, Harry, you did a lousy job."

"I am sorry, Evan. I didn't mean it that way." Harry checked his watch and dragged his suit jacket from the back of his chair. "I have always felt that your experiences have perhaps given you more insight into the un-knowable than most. You have a way of looking out into the world some-times, that makes one wonder what you see that the rest of us are missing. I have always valued that in you, Evan, and never more than now, when we will need that special vision of yours to bring the Moon Stone home."

Harry had turned to put on his jacket; he spoke so matter-of-factly that for a moment Evan didn't process the meaning of what he said. When he did, he could think of nothing to say. Harry seemed to expect that, though.

"Just think about it, my boy," he came around the desk and waited for Evan to stand and exit ahead of him. "In the meantime, I hope you have something more substantial to give the board!"

While Li closed and locked his office door, Evan pulled his cell phone from his breast pocket. "I haven't been conscious long enough to have any results on the computer searches yet, but Lily visited with Liz down at Major Crimes this morning. If you drive, I'll get her report."

"That should keep them from pushing their noses in where they don't belong," Harry agreed. Which set Evan back a step.

"Harry, you are one of them."

Li brought himself up to his full, if slight, height, indignation exaggerated in his stern frown. "I won't tell if you won't," he retorted, then added, "Do I get to drive the excess-mobile?"

"Yes, Harry." Evan dangled the keys to the BMW in one hand and laughed when the professor snatched them up and gave them a little toss in the air. Then he followed Harry Li down the steps. Halfway down, he remembered why he'd taken the elevator up. But by then Harry was far ahead of him, and it didn't seem worth the wait. At least he wouldn't have to drive. All he had to do was talk to Lily.

# Chapter 14

Rooms at the four seasons were as good as a traveler could do away from home, so Brad found himself puzzled that his second night at the hotel had put him in such a foul mood. Home sang to him of darkness and the power to fill the universe with no limits or boundaries. Home meant battles waged between Princes that spanned infinity in the realm that perceived the material sphere as a sea of energy, its whorls and eddies the stars and galaxies of Evan's universe. Home gave unified purpose to the host of daemons. They were Ariton: Badad and Lirion and the hundreds more of their host brothers, Apolhun the destroyer and Erdulon, despoiler. Sachiad, and Sched who filled the universe with a terrible female power. Anader the cruel, and Caramos, who loved with joy, even to the 833. When merged in quorum, the host did not just serve its Prince: It *became* its Prince. Badad truly was Ariton, as were all his host brothers. When he obeyed his Prince, he obeyed the dictates of his own essence.

Home was eternity, bound in alliances—Amaimon, Oriens, Paimon locked in battle with ancient enemies—Azmod, Magot, Astarot. Scouts and warriors contended in a game of balance that killed planets and their suns on the material sphere, dead without a thought for the glory of the Princes.

Home most definitely was *not* a bed in a room looking out onto a tree-lined street, or a tapestried wing chair with a standing lamp next to a small table for his brandy and a book. Home had nothing to do with a completely undistinguished ball of dirt traveling around a fourth-rate star with a tendency to wobble. Lirion was home, but Evan was not. So he could not understand why the bed in the hotel, reputed for its quality, annoyed him so, or why he found himself standing in front of the window looking out over the fountains at Logan Circle and wishing for his comfortable chair and the sound of Evan bickering over the coffee with Lily in the kitchen. Or, more to the point, perhaps, why he planned to smooth things over with Khadijah Flint at lunch in the Fountain Room downstairs.

For whatever reason, he found himself approaching the maître d' at precisely twelve-thirty, his suit neatly pressed and his tie knotted in a full Windsor. Flint had arrived ahead of him; the maître d' led him past dark wood tables covered by crisp white cloths glinting with crystal and heavy silver flatware to a booth tucked into the corner and shrouded by a cluster of potted palms along the length of the banquette where she already sat looking at the menu. The tiny beads in her short braids clacked softly as she turned to greet him. As usual, she was wearing her corporate version of African chic—a purple linen suit, the jacket open, and a blouse in a mud-cloth print beneath it. Brad had seen her work in the courtroom and had to admit that Flint's style worked. The look told the opposition, "I'm black. Get used to it, because I'm taking all your money today."

A very good person to have on his side. Hoping that she would still be on his side after lunch, Brad joined her on the banquette at right angles to hers. From where he sat he could scan the entire room, which gave him a sense of security he hadn't realized he needed.

"How bad is it?" he asked her, and picked up the wine list as if he had asked her what vintage she preferred.

"I assume you mean your situation and not the prices of the wine," she answered over her menu. "Bad enough that I would suggest we keep a clear head for the main course. Then, if you are still feeling generous by dessert, we'll see."

Brad refrained from taking up that challenge until the waiter had returned and he had placed their order for lunch and a single malt scotch for himself.

Khadijah Flint relinquished her menu. "Shall we take your current difficulties in order?" she asked him.

Without a glass in his hand, Brad wasn't sure he wanted to hear what Khadijah Flint had to say. Fortunately, the waiter returned promptly with the scotch and departed with all due circumspection. Glass firmly in hand, he felt a bit less exposed. It was false comfort; Flint could see right through the amber liquor, and he occasionally wondered how deeply she saw into him. He didn't really want to know, but it looked as though he was about to find out anyway.

"The clock is ticking," he said in the age-old reference to a lawyer's hourly fee.

With the retainer Bradley, Ryan, and Davis paid it wasn't an accurate assessment of lunch, and she dismissed the obvious effort to keep this completely professional with an eloquent quirk of her eyebrow. He wondered if she'd learned it from Lily, or if all female bodies came equipped with that particular "loathsome object" expression.

He'd managed to bicker them into the first course, a canteloupe soup with bits of sundried tomato floating in it. Flint thanked the waiter with a smile that disappeared as fast as his back was turned. "To start," she said, "you are not an escaped criminal, though the tap dance I had to do to keep you out of Joe Dougherty's clutches will appear prominently on your bill. Ellen had decided that the police didn't have enough to hold you before the explosion. Your disappearance in the confusion wasn't very chivalrous, but it didn't, at that point, make you a fugitive from justice.

"Ellen pointed out that, since you were never out of the sight of an officer from the moment you were picked up at the museum until you disappeared, you could not have planted any explosives. Any explosives on your person, of course, would have explained your disappearance but would make searching for you a moot point. Since I was with Ellen at the time, I had no explanation to give her, but I promised to advise you to return to the division headquarters and give a suitable explanation. If you apologize, she may even speak to you again."

Brad stared at his plate for a long moment, picking through his reactions and the feelings that tumbled in his chest. Relief, which made no particular sense, and a sense of loss, of what he didn't know. The freedom Evan had returned to him that night was the only one that should have mattered, but he liked Ellen Li, didn't want to cause her trouble if he could help it.

"I'll talk to her."

"I knew you would." Khadijah rewarded him with a smile over her soup spoon. "You are too smart an operator to alienate the only person on the case who actually believed you when you claimed you didn't do it."

"Your soup is getting cold." And the conversation was getting too close to personal. He covered his discomfort with a spoonful of soup before the waiter could ask if he would prefer something else. The tang laced through the sweet of the soup was the first pleasant surprise in a long week, and eating gave him an excuse not to talk while he sorted through the sudden realizations that had come tumbling out of nowhere. If he were honest with himself, which he tried *not* to be as often as possible, he didn't want to lose Ellen's friendship. Or Harry's. Khadijah's either, for that matter, though he supposed he hadn't put her in that category until she'd shown up at two o'clock in the morning so that he didn't have to face Joe Dougherty's little cell alone. And that thought shocked him as well. He hadn't quite thought of it as a cell until Evan's friend showed up and chained him to the bench.

The busboy took the soup plates away, and with them Brad's excuse for silence. He'd have appreciated more the pan-seared gravlax the waiter set in front of him if the memory of metal blistering his wrist hadn't knotted his stomach. Khadijah Flint took the opportunity to give him a warning that did nothing to loosen those knots:

"We can work on your statement for the police right now if you want. I'd like to know where you got to myself. Frankly, we were worried about you. Harry thought you'd been injured in the blast and wandered off in shock. He half expected they'd find you dead in a gutter somewhere in West Philadelphia."

"Later," he said, and she put her fork down.

"Take the advice you are paying for, Mr. Bradley. 'Not enough to hold you' doesn't take you off the hook entirely. You still owe Ellen a statement, and I would not count on Mike Jaworski lining up on your side of the field. I know she'd feel better about her decision to release you if I could promise you will stay in town until the police have cleared you." Khadijah picked up her fork again and gestured at him with the chilled scallop skewered on the end of it, then popped the fork in her mouth. "Oh, lovely," she said, a beatific smile stealing across her face.

"It usually is," he agreed, handling the question that didn't have him clearing flight paths to the second sphere in his head, though he scarcely tasted the food himself. So Ellen had taken a risk by setting him free, and he had heard concern for a friend in Khadijah's conversational gambit. He, too, was Ellen's friend, and Khadijah Flint expected him to answer that way.

"If I go anywhere," he said, and he damned himself for a fool because he was giving the oath of Ariton, for all that she had no idea of the honor he granted her, "I will be following the same trail Ellen is. If she wants, she can do the driving."

"Ellen will be glad to hear." Flint gave him an approving nod. "And if that day comes, Mr. Bradley, just you make sure I'm in the back seat."

"Deal," he agreed.

"We can draft your statement in my office, but I assume you'll want to reassure her yourself?"

"Over a chessboard tonight, unless it constitutes a conflict of interest."

"An apology is never a conflict of interest, Mr. Bradley, but chess may be," Flint warned him. "Don't be offended if she makes her excuses tonight. She is still your friend, but the less you demand of her now, the less you will have to apologize for when it is all over."

"Her office it will be, then. Tomorrow is soon enough?" He wasn't ready to face that crowded room yet, but knew he couldn't put it off much longer than a day.

Friendship. Odd, how the feeling had grown before the idea had ever surfaced in his mind. Sometimes it almost felt like host loyalty. Not quite, of course. The awareness that confidence could be betrayed set each rela-

tionship with a human at a careful distance. No friend on the material
sphere could ever share the mind and spirit of a joining in the host of the
Prince; he could never really know a friend as intimately as the self in the
way that he knew Lily or Caramos or Sched.

Or Evan, though he often discovered he didn't know Evan at all, even
after a wander through his son's mind. He changed as the daemons, Badad's
host-cousins, did not. And there were hidden places in his mind that even
Evan didn't know about. Evan was more human than daemon, not self but
other, just as Harry and Ellen and Khadijah Flint were. But Evan shared
just enough of Ariton to make that distinction difficult to maintain.

"How is Evan doing? I understand he came home from the hospital
yesterday."

And when had Khadijah Flint taken to reading minds?

"I don't know," he answered gruffly, and motioned for the waiter to
bring him his brandy. The hotel already had his preference on file, and the
sommelier brought the bottle and two glasses with a minimum of intrusion.

"But surely you—"

"Stayed at the hotel last night," he finished her sentence, "which is
why we are having lunch here instead of downtown, where we both have
offices."

"I see."

Brad hated the knowing sympathy that crossed her face. She fidgeted
with her coffee spoon for a moment, as if he needed the little privacy she
could give him in this public place to hide whatever feelings his admission
might have evoked.

"You are a fine detective, in an agency with a deserved reputation for
recovery work." She seemed to make up her mind about something, and
set the spoon down. When she looked up at him again, Brad saw that she
had focused the full force of her legal mind on him.

"I can't imagine you didn't investigate Evan's background when you
first suspected he might be your son."

"There was little need."

"So you may have thought at the time. Now he owns a third of your
agency, and he's listed as co-owner on the rest of the property as well. You
won't get his share of the agency back. Evan has been an equal working
partner almost from the beginning, and no judge will take away his livelihood
without due cause. If he'd come to you claiming kinship, maybe. But you
were the older party, you approached him, and you had recourse to the full
arsenal of laboratory verification testing. A judge would have to assume you
knew what you were doing; you'd be furious if he did otherwise."

"I did know what I was doing." On the other hand, Brad didn't know where Khadijah Flint was heading with this. His anger had nothing to do with money, and he told her so. It did, however, have everything to do with betrayal. Utter destruction down to the atomic bonds that held his energy bound into the matter of flesh would not be enough to punish Evan for what he had done. Sensibly, Brad kept that opinion to himself.

"Even if you are willing to part with the money, it would have been wiser to make sure you had the right boy before you told him you were his father," she chided him. "A couple of tests early on and an immediate apology for raising his hopes would certainly have been easier on that boy than having the police break the news while they arrest you. And then what? You walked out on him while he was in the hospital? 'Sorry for all the fuss, kid, but it turns out you're not mine after all, so good luck to you?' "

She stared at him a moment as if she had never truly seen him before. "I would have sworn you loved that young man because he deserved it and not because you spilled some seed in his mother's womb so long ago you don't even remember who she was."

Love. She knew nothing of the ways of daemons. He tolerated Evan for the spark of Ariton that burned within him, no more. But he couldn't figure out why—oh. He'd forgotten. Khadijah Flint had followed right behind Sergeant Joe Dougherty when he'd confronted Brad at the police station and she'd heard his accusations. He figured it was past time to correct that impression.

"Dougherty was wrong. Evan is my son."

"But his mother—"

"Is also wrong. I didn't bother with lab tests because I didn't need them. There are certain family traits he shares that make his parentage impossible to mistake."

"Then you haven't thrown him out?"

"I'm the one staying in a hotel," he reminded her, then admitted, "I expect to be sleeping in my own bed tonight. I don't know where Evan will be sleeping. He was too old for a curfew when I met him."

She positively basked in a glow of approval. It nearly unsettled his lunch. "I'm so glad to hear it. But you should get some tests done. A heart shaped mole on the left shoulder may suffice for now, but it won't hold up in court if the next falling out is more serious."

"Evan doesn't have a mole on his shoulder." He didn't bother pointing out that Evan had already gone off the scale when it came to offenses.

"It's a figure of speech, Papa Bradley." She sighed. "I've worked on cases of parental identification before. Let me give you some advice for free, and maybe I won't have to watch you and Evan go through that in court some day.

"When the Moon Stone is back in the museum and you've put this case and all its upsetness behind you, get some DNA tests done. When the results come back, talk to the doctor alone. Give yourself time to get used to the results. If they prove you are Evan's father, then fine. You share a bottle of champagne and go on as usual. If the test proves that you've allowed your desire to find your son to outrun your good sense, talk to someone. After all, a negative result means your biological son could still be out there waiting to be found, and you once wanted to find him very badly.

"Decide what you want to do about it. Then sit down with Evan and calmly, compassionately, explain to him where you stand. Not telling him may seem like a kindness, but remember, you have said he was looking for his father when you found him, just as you were looking for your son. If you are not his father and you don't tell him, you will be denying him the right to search for half of what he is. But whatever you do, don't wait until you are having an argument to find out. Denying parentage is a devastating weapon. You may find that you've won the battle but lost everything that you valued in the process."

"Thank you for the advice. In this case—believe me—it is unnecessary." Brad wrote his room number on the check and rose to hand Khadijah Flint from the banquette. Falling in beside her, they walked through the lobby to the front entrance on Seventeenth Street.

While they waited for the valet to bring her car around, he continued the conversation. "When it comes to the matter of who fathered Evan Davis, my only concern is how to stop Mr. Dougherty from spreading his malicious lies."

"Take a DNA test—that's my car"—she climbed into the Audi and gave him a wry grin—"and we can take him to court."

"Thank you, Ms. Flint, I will take it under advisement."

He wouldn't, and she knew that. She was still laughing softly under her breath as she drove away. He thought about home, but this time the image of the office on Spruce Street came to mind. Time to check on what Evan had been doing on his own. It had nothing to do with the habits of human flesh and human emotion, of course. Badad had a responsibility to his Prince. And Kevin Bradley had a date for chess at eight-thirty, because now that he'd discovered time, he needed to do something to fill it. And the smell of Mai Sien Chong's perfume had nothing to do with the appointment at all.

# Chapter 15

IN THE SEVENTIES, THE MOVIE *ROCKY* HAD MADE THE PANORAMIC VIEW OF Philadelphia from the front steps of the Museum of Art famous throughout the world. Evan preferred the view from the rear exit, where the museum itself seemed to keep on going, exploring the aesthetic beauty of the river and gardens that it could not contain within stone walls. The waterworks needed a fresh paint job, but the folly overlooking the river still seemed like a found object from another age, come upon by accident amid the unkempt growth of trees and shrubs.

Upper Class Victorian America had loved the idea of ruins. Too young as a country to have its own, America constructed its relics of the past out of whole cloth and a fondness for classical Greek architecture. A hundred years later, every bride in the city seemed to stop at the folly for pictures, in spite of the fact that many of their families had left countries with real ancient ruins, and a good number of more recent ones, to come to the New World long after the Victorians had gone. Or their ancestors had arrived on slave ships long before the Victorian yearning for a purer history had dotted the landscape with Doric columns.

In spite of the distance that an inborn cynicism and three years of art history had given him, Evan had to admit that this place struck a chord in the heart of the city. And he, or the part of him that shaped his mortal life, was part of that. It pulled him off the steps of the museum and past the folly, down the path that wandered along the river, past the boathouses with their gingerbread exteriors that gave him brief glimpses of the slightly grubby interiors, rowing shells racked against the walls, and past the whispering wall where Evan had seen classmates telling each other secrets from its opposite ends. Sometimes the memories of that part of his life swept him with the force of the present, and he would have to leave or the pain and the anger would overwhelm him.

He remembered a day, watching his eighth-grade class sort itself into status groups and friendship cliques, jostling each other and laughing until the group had formed a map of relationships with just a scattering of loose satellites who refused to make eye contact lest the others see the isolation in his eyes and know he was the same. He remembered watching the old men fishing from the grassy bank and the shells arrowing down the river with the call of the coxswain and the rhythmic rise and fall of the oars.

And he'd thought about letting go. Just falling in and letting the river take him. He hadn't, of course, and his teacher had come along to hurry him after the rest of the class. He'd gone home after the class trip afraid of what he'd felt that day and hadn't come back till he was fully grown and accustomed to fighting his night terrors with challenges of his own. The river, Evan had known even then, was stronger than his will to live because, of all the deaths he had imagined in a tormented childhood, only the river held the promise of peace.

Today was different. He'd grown up, faced his demons, quite literally, and put the pieces of his life together in a way that made sense to him, if to no one else. He still had his father to deal with, but he'd managed to convince the board of trustees of the museum that the agency was actually making progress on their investigation. More to the point, the sun was striking sparks off the wavelets raised by the swift currents in the river and glinting off the sweat on the backs of the rowers pulling against those same currents. The grass was green, the breeze was soft against his face, and he had the most beautiful woman he'd ever seen at his side, so close that his body tingled with memories of its own. So he tugged at her hand, drawing her after him to walk in the green and gold afternoon.

"I think we pulled that off pretty well," he said. "We've got the job, Harry managed to deflect the discussion away from Brad's absence—"

"Harry told them Brad was pursuing a lead!" Lily tried to manage outrage, but the laughter bubbled through.

Evan gave her an elaborate, self-mocking shrug. "He could be working on the case. After all, we don't know what he is doing, right?"

"Mmmm."

Something about that noncommittal sound reminded Evan of what he had lost in this case, and he couldn't escape the knowledge that he brought it on himself. Perhaps he hadn't faced all his demons. "All my life I wondered what it would be like to have a father, you know."

Maybe it was the river; he always seemed to find himself spilling his emotional baggage all over riverbanks.

"Not really."

Lily's voice had that astringent drawl to it, the way it usually did when she was pointing out the obvious to him. But that never told the whole story with Lily, who often saw him with a microscopic clarity she'd gained in joinings they shared in the second celestial sphere. He often found it unnerving to be known that well, in all his flaws and weaknesses, from the inside out. He turned to face her anyway, hoping to gauge her understanding in the play of never-quite-human emotions in her eyes.

He was looking at her forehead instead. With a quick scan down her body, pausing briefly at the best bits, he figured out where the extra inches had gone. Somewhere along the way she had changed her high heels into sneakers. Evan hoped no one had seen it happen, and the brief nervous twitch it gave him bumped his mood out of the bleakly introspective. His father *knew* what was in Evan's head. They'd fought battles together, saved the universe together, more or less. He'd gotten used to not having secrets around his daemon kin, but he sometimes forgot exactly what that meant.

"He knows how I feel about him."

"He couldn't help but," Lily affirmed. "You maintain a pretense at balance on the material sphere, but you wander around the second celestial sphere like a puppy after a bone."

Evan gave that some thought. He had learned that he could exist in the second sphere, could travel through it without panicking, and he had to admit that learning to move from the material to the daemon spheres during sex with Lily had pretty much spoiled him for any other kind. But he'd never figured out how to hide a thing. So Brad knew. Had probably seen Evan's panic when he'd made that desperate command.

"He feels something for me too." He couldn't quite keep the question out of his voice. Some of the time he forgot what they were, and expected human feelings from them. Then, when he least expected it, they'd react like the monsters that had bedeviled his sleep for most of the years of his life, and the carefully constructed reality he had built around himself would shatter. By now it had shattered and he had rebuilt it so many times that he could almost see the seams of scar tissue pulling at the flex-points of his worldview. This was one of those times. It didn't quite hurt, yet, but the reminder of pain waiting in the dark was there.

"You'd have to ask him."

Lily was staring out over the water, or at something inside her head that she'd projected out there. It gave him the privacy to ask, "How?"

She shrugged. "Think about him."

"I've done nothing but think about him since we found him standing over the guard in the Chinese Gallery."

"No."

She did look at him then, and the expression in her eyes made him flinch.

"You've been thinking about Evan: Will Badad the daemon lord remember that he has a choice about staying in the material sphere and flash-incinerate his monster-spawn—Evan? Will Kevin Bradley the father remember that human fathers have no legal obligation to their adult children and turn away his son—Evan? Or perhaps, will Badad the daemon lord compromise, leave his monster spawn alive but create a new identity, new life, somewhere like Maçao or Calcutta or Johannesburg, while his son is left behind with a business he can't run alone and the police watching him in case Kevin Bradley should try to contact him, which of course he never will.

"It's all Evan, so when you look for him in your heart, all you find is yourself."

"I sound like a real shit when you put it that way." And he felt damned stupid as well.

"Actually," she admitted, "it is the one place where daemon and human sensibilities meet. We need each other. We don't have to like each other, we just have to fulfill that need for our Prince."

Oh. He knew that, had from the start, he figured, not consciously but as an underlying certainty that had colored every challenge he threw at his daemon kin. Lily gave him a knowing smile—she'd been in his head, knew the connections he was making. But she disappeared before he could answer.

He really wished she wouldn't do that! The couple necking on the bench hadn't noticed, but at least one old man with a fishing pole was blinking as though he had something in his eye. Evan gave the man a patently false smile, and the man shook his head and turned away.

So. He hadn't been thinking about his father at all. He could fix that. He looked out at the water, clearing his mind of everything but the glint of gold on the fragile tips of the wavelets, then gradually called upon his memory of his father. Not Kevin Bradley, but Badad of the host of Ariton, blue flame in darkness. Evan felt the strength of the daemon lord's presence, edged with danger and a terrifying knowledge. It tickled at his backbrain, stronger than memory, and he reached for it through the second celestial sphere. His body followed, and Evan fought the moment of disorientation in the place where up or down did not exist. Then he was home. Not just in the material sphere, but home, in the study of the house on Spruce Street, where Kevin Bradley, the daemon lord Badad, sat in the familiar wing chair with a folded printout on his lap. Lily, at the bar, turned around and laughed.

"Clever boy," she said, but Kevin Bradley did not smile.

Evan took the glass she handed him without noticing that he had done it, or even that he had taken a drink until he choked on the bubbles. Coke, of course. At some level he'd trusted in that implicitly. He set the glass on the desk and threw himself into his chair behind it.

Half a dozen things to say passed through Evan's mind as he stared blankly into the space the soda occupied. Shifting his gaze to his father, he knew that his next words would be judged, and his relationship would stand or fall on how he played this moment. Daemon lords fed on the weak.

"Did the new monitor arrive?" he asked, gesturing at the printout on Brad's lap.

"While we were out. The work order was on the desk, so the cleaning service let them in. Someone named Mary left you a note about it."

Evan nodded. So far, so good. "Find anything?"

"Not much." His father stood up and walked over to the computer—his take-charge mode—and Evan let go a breath he'd been holding since he'd arrived to see his father in his chair.

Brad dropped the printout on the blotter and leaned back on the corner of the desk, planting himself between Evan and Lily, who sat curled on the leather sofa. "We might as well take this in turn. Lily?"

She pulled herself into a greater semblance of attention, but Evan half wondered if Lily shifted positions just to make that expressive shrug possible.

"Ellen is not happy with you, but I told her you were at home with very little memory about what happened the night they brought you in. She blamed that on the explosion, and I didn't correct her. She would appreciate it if you would stop at the division and finish your statement. If she is not there, she said to ask for a Detective Mike Jaworski. Joe Dougherty is not supposed to be working on the case, but since he claims to have received a complaint about you, Major Crimes is required to keep him advised."

His mother. Damn. Evan had to tell her something, and soon. If only he could figure out what. His father had more practical concerns.

"Has she filed a formal charge?"

"For what?" Lily asked.

"Impersonating a father?" Evan suggested. The irony almost made it.

"Baby snatching?" Lily arched an eyebrow, demanding that he concede that the barb had hit home.

"Rescuing the wrong person from a fate worse than death?" As thank you and I'm sorry, it was better than anything else Evan had said to his father lately. Funny how exaggerated it sounded and how utterly true it was. A new place, learning to call his father by a new name and to recognize him by a different face, seemed small adjustments compared to the life he had before his father came along.

He shrugged. "Why waste a mistake on a small one, when you have an opportunity to screw up big time?" he asked. Brad turned to look at him, and Ariton burned in his eyes, but he said nothing. Not ready to accept the apology. Evan tacked a "yet" onto that while Lily broke the tension with her report:

"No formal charges, but Dougherty has raised some suspicions, and we can't dismiss him out of hand." She paused a moment, theatrically. "We could kill him. He would have to stop sniffing around then."

"I don't think it would do much to allay suspicion," Evan pointed out. "He's my problem; I'll take care of it."

Lily gave him a skeptical look. "How? Will you tell Sergeant Dougherty that your mum has a bad memory for the men she sleeps with? Or that the man in question isn't one, and is likely to fry him to cinders if he doesn't back off?"

His father was looking at him too, his arms crossed over his chest, waiting for him to answer Lily's questions.

"Joe Dougherty isn't the problem," he said. "My mother put him up to it, and she is the only person who can stop him."

Lily grinned, her face lighting up with a fierce glow of unearthly fire. "Good idea! We'll kill mum instead!"

Not funny. Moments like these shook Evan mostly because he didn't like to face the violence in his own soul. But it was there, a blue-hot flame that rocked the house on its foundation.

Expressionless except for the frozen tightness of the skin around his eyes, he faced his lover across the roiling churn of emotion, his and hers. "Just remember," he said, his voice as frozen as his face, "I know your name."

"You press your luck, boy."

"So do you."

Lily was on her feet, her form wavering in the crackle of blue light.

A thought whispered through his mind, not Lily's or his own but his father's, carried on the wave of Ariton flame that licked at the tips of Evan's hair. Evan saw what his kin saw: the power of daemonkind, and their swiftness to action, coupled with a savage urge to destroy anything that threatened him that arose from his human, mortal side. No wonder Alfredo Da'Costa had wanted him dead. He had the power to destroy worlds with a thought. He could do a job on his relationships without thinking. Which, he figured, was part of the problem—not thinking.

"Your name is Lily Ryan." Still batting a thousand on apologies, he'd be lucky she didn't turn him into a cockroach. "I will talk to my mother. She has to find out some time." Given the hell of his growing up, Evan wondered if the truth would surprise his mother at all. "And if she tells Joe Dougherty, so what? No one will believe it. He'll assume the stress of seeing her old mistakes come back to haunt her sent her over the edge."

Lily still glared at him from behind the sofa where she'd put as much distance between them as possible. She didn't care about his mother or Joe Dougherty, but he'd be lucky to make it through the afternoon with his limbs intact if he goaded her any more. The devil in him whispered, "Try."

Brad shook his head. "What makes you think she'll believe you?"

His mother. Back on track, Evan took a pencil from the cup on his desk. Holding it up between them, fingertips clamped tightly on the eraser end, he focused on it, calling on the fire of Ariton rising within him, and narrowed the focus still more, until, with surprisingly little effort, the pencil exploded in his hand.

"She won't like the explanation," he said, "but she'll have to accept it."

Brad pulled the pencil's sharpened end out of the flesh between the finger and thumb of his left hand. "I suppose a dramatic presentation will get the point across," he agreed. "We will consider the matter of Joe Dougherty closed for the time being. Anything else, Lily?"

"Liz is running her searches, but we didn't discuss them much. She knows we are looking over her shoulder, but as long as no one says anything, we can all pretend Evan hasn't cracked the access codes. They are working under the assumption that the same thief, or ring of thieves, did this job and the university job. Probably the Smithsonian job as well. She's checking with the Smithsonian to compare security systems on the off chance we've got a match.

"The museum guard is still unconscious, but the doctors can't find anything physically wrong with him. One theory is that he's in a kind of psychological shock and won't wake up until he's ready. Liz isn't sure. In her words, 'It's spooky.' "

"Funny," Evan added. "Harry said the same thing."

Brad gave him a skeptical look and Evan conceded, "Not in those words. He decided to help by applying the *I Ching* to the investigation, and he thinks the perp is being driven by a past life. He also thinks we are connected to the robberies, or to the thief, in some way. Not as co-conspirators. He doesn't just believe you are innocent, Brad; he seems to know it in his bones. And he doesn't know what the connection is, but he is afraid that we'll lose the perp if you aren't patient."

That last took almost more nerve to deliver than he had left. Fortunately, Brad accepted it as the report it was rather than as editorial comment.

"Past life. Has Alfredo developed an interest in Asian art recently, Lily?"

"Not that I've seen," she answered.

Keep it in report mode, Evan reminded himself. Right now it didn't matter how she knew, and later, in bed, she'd laugh at him for caring that she'd been with Da'Costa the week before. He took a swallow of his Coke and tried to obliterate the sudden desire to take her right there and prove that he could satisfy her, that she didn't need Alfredo Da'Costa or any other men to feed her hunger. She saw it in his eyes, of course, and in the sudden tension of his body, and she licked her lips, laughing at him while the muscles in his lower abdomen fluttered and he wondered if he were going to be sick or faint dead away from the effort it took to keep his hand wrapped around the Coke glass.

"Was there anything of value in the printouts?" Lily asked.

Evan heard her only dimly. In his mind he held the icy glass against her belly and watched her muscles twitch from the cold, knowing he could warm them up again with his tongue, his body.

"Nothing," Brad answered her. "San Francisco had a robbery of Chinese artifacts, mostly small jade items, with a carved ivory screen and a few wall hangings. Point of origin of the artifacts seems to be the only connection, other than the reasonably clean getaway and the fact that none of those items has shown up in the usual marketplaces either."

"Then why don't you find something else to do for a while?" Lily asked him.

"There was something else—"

"Later."

Lily flashed Brad a feral smile that almost brought Evan over the desk. Brad turned to look at him, a realization that Evan brushed off as an unnecessary distraction. He wanted to eat Lily's smile, rip her to shreds and put her back together again.

"Oh."

She was off the sofa, up on her knees on top of the desk, unbuttoning her blouse and without willing it, Evan's hands reached for her belt. He worked clumsily at the buckle, defeated it. He found the clasp on her pants and opened it, wondering at how the touch of her skin on his fingertips almost paralyzed him with shock.

"Enjoy yourselves."

Evan was aware only dimly that Brad had gone. In a fleeting lucid moment he couldn't quite believe what he'd done in front of his father, or what he would have done in front of him if Brad hadn't left. Nor did enjoyment seem to have anything to do with it, though the feelings he did have were too complex to face, let alone understand.

He wanted more, more, and dragged her slacks low enough to bury his face in her belly, wrapping his mouth around soft flesh. He sank his teeth into the graceful curve of muscle and skin and breathed her scent in deeply, deeply, his hands wrapped around her hips pressing her close until she dragged his face up to hers. He didn't care about the pain of her fingers clenched in the bruises along the side of his face because her teeth were scraping at his tongue, balancing promises with threats, and she fought him teeth against teeth for her pleasure.

She released his mouth long enough to order him, "Touch me," and took one of his hands and guided it between her legs. "Touch me." And she took his mouth again and moved against his hand until he couldn't bear it anymore and he stood over her, dragging at his own buckle until she batted his hand away and opened his pants. "Sit," she said, and he did. She sat on his desk and slipped her slacks and panties off, then grabbed his shoulders and Evan lifted her onto the chair, and she rocked him, played him, while she tore at his shirt buttons and bit him, tiny nips that threatened to devour him.

It wasn't enough. He needed to be inside her, and so he lifted her and set her down, slowly, over his erection, and she growled and clenched her muscles around him, wrapped his body with her own, legs tight around his back, arms holding them breast to breast while he took control of her mouth in a clash of teeth. Her lips drew back in an animal snarl that rolled in her throat. Again, again, he moved, and she bit him hard at the join of his shoulder and throat, then he was coming inside of her and her muscles rippled in greedy harmony until she fell against him, her arms draped across his shoulders.

Evan shuddered breath after breath, confused by his anger and the sadness that threatened his composure.

"Don't ever leave me."

It was a stupid thing to say, but the compulsion to say something was as powerful as the urge to sex had been.

She dug her hands deep into his unruly hair and pressed his head into the high back of the chair. Then she arched away from him, so that their lower bodies remained joined while their upper bodies had pulled apart, looking across the distance again.

"Don't ask," she said.

He closed his eyes so that she could not see inside him, where something raged at the thought that Alfredo Da'Costa had seen her like this, had entered her body, and she had held Alfredo Da'Costa in her arms, between her legs. She had battled Da'Costa for pleasure and would do it again. And for Evan the sex would never be enough, because he was human and had to own her heart, her passion.

He would have wept, but his body was not ready to give up its possession of her, and he stood up, holding her tight against him so that they remained joined, and leaned over the desk, laying her down on it, and pushed as deep inside her as he could get. She sensed the bitter edge to his mood, perhaps. Her teeth grabbed hold of the skin over his collar bone, just below the vulnerable expanse of his throat, and she bit deep and sucked at the spot, marking him on the outside as he tried to mark her on the inside. Mine. Mine. They claimed each other in the language of sex because they could not bear to speak out loud. And, Yours. Yours, they gave to each other with no promises. And they clung to each other through the swirling confusion of two universes, making promises with their bodies they would never speak.

# Chapter 16

STANDING NEXT TO A BUCKET AND MOP IN THE STAIRWELL LEADING TO THE Franklin Mercantile, Brad made his one concession to the casual style of the chess players roosting on the other side of the door. He took off his suitcoat and folded it over his arm. Then he undid his shirt cuffs and turned them back one neat roll. Satisfied, he entered the club.

They had quite a crowd tonight—unusual, but then he didn't show up on Fridays himself, as a rule. He nodded companionably at the Russian pro who was giving one of the younger players a lesson in humility. Brad rather liked Sasha, but he never played chess against him. At his present skill level, he'd have to learn to lose gracefully or seriously improve his game. Losing wasn't an option, and he preferred to keep a low profile, so he wandered back to the main competition room looking for a cool, sharp game or three to blunt his agitation.

For some reason, Evan's fevered response to Lily's performance on his desk had unsettled Brad in a way that their antics had never done before. Using the meat body he wore for sex repelled him, and had done since Gwen Davis' jealous ex lover had summoned him from the second celestial sphere and bound him to the task of seducing and then abandoning her. It hadn't worked out quite the way the jealous man intended. He'd made a mistake, as they all did, and Badad had killed him. Evan said he hadn't succeeded in ruining his mother, though she called off her wedding and spent the next twenty-three years of her life coping with a son whose daemon nature drove him insane on a fairly regular basis.

When the Princes had sent him, with Lirion his host-cousin, to eliminate that madness, he hadn't realized what it would mean to spare his son's life. Hadn't realized he would grow accustomed to living in a meat body and would even find pleasure in its senses. Good food, good books, good art: He'd learned to appreciate them all. Then he discovered chess and learned that he could enjoy the company of humans who might try to master him in equal competition but who did not try to bind him with the old knowledge. But that was an engagement of the intellect, not of the flesh. Watching Evan and Lily for even that brief few moments hadn't changed his mind. Whatever emotions fueled their bodies today, joy wasn't one of them. Play wasn't either; he'd seen Lily and Evan indulge in occasional sex play before, and he knew the difference. That love thing that Evan went on about seemed as remote to the furious coupling as opposites could be. But whatever had charged the encounter with raw aggression had also touched something in him, though he couldn't quite tell if that something rose within Badad daemon lord of Ariton or had sneaked out of the backbrain of the body he wore.

He almost considered returning to the house and dragging Lily into the second sphere to rediscover what the dawn of creation had been like, but when he thought about it, Brad didn't feel the daemon essence of his host-cousin but the touch of his fingers on skin the color of sunlight on a summer day. He'd been human too long; soon he'd be as mad as Omage had been. Except that he didn't want to cut the flesh of the humans and watch them bleed and die. He wanted something else. It made him decidedly nervous, and a nice uncomplicated game of chess was . . . not what he was going to get tonight.

Mai Sien Chong sat in their usual Wednesday corner playing against Jim, who handled the experience with a great deal more panache than Poor Tony had. He would, of course. Jim had a green-eyed blonde wife who wore his money well and showed up with the two kids to cheer him on at regionals. Brad would have smiled a greeting, but Ellen and Harry Li shared the next table over. And they'd seen him—too late to back out now. No fool, Jim scanned the room to find the cause of the sudden chill in his corner of the room. Catching sight of Brad, he tipped over his king with a sardonic twist of a smile.

"A pleasure, as always," he said to his opponent. On his way out of the room he stopped next to Brad to mutter, "The handcuffs are a psych-out. Don't let Ellen intimidate you."

He was gone before Brad recovered from the comment. Of course, Jim hadn't known about Wednesday night, or Thursday morning. It was an old joke, because Ellen was a cop and she wasn't above reaching into her purse and dropping the cuffs on the table at the beginning of a game. As a ploy to make an opponent nervous it beat the hell out of rattling chewing gum wrappers. But he hadn't needed the reminder of his rage and humiliation and—it was there, rattling around in his backbrain like an intimation of what humans called hell—his terror when Joe Dougherty had cuffed him to a bench in a cell too small to breath in.

Ellen Li had allowed that to happen, and he wanted to scream at her, to transform himself into a monster out of legends and roar his anger until she cowered with the kind of dread and despair that he had felt trapped in that cell. But if he wanted to hold onto this life he had made around a son and a physical place to call home, he had to apologize. Khadijah Flint had made that absolutely clear. As he stood there, trying to think of what to say, Brad realized he didn't know how to apologize. He knew the beginning words, "I'm sorry," but not what would follow, or how to make the words sound sincere.

Ellen made it easier. "Brad!" she said, and jumped from her chair to give him a closer look. "What happened to you the other night? You had us scared to death; we thought you'd been hurt in the blast. We even faxed your picture to the local hospitals in case you showed up in an emergency room and couldn't answer questions when you got there."

"Sergeant Dougherty thought you'd taken advantage of the confusion to escape," Harry added, "but Ellen set him straight about whose investigation it was, and who had better keep his nose where it belonged or she'd cut it off." He gave his wife an impish grin over the chessboard where he had just shifted her queen onto a square that put her in line with his bishop. "My wife can be very forceful when she is excited."

"Which she is about to become if you don't put that queen back where you found it, Harry Li," Ellen retorted without looking at the chessboard. "Lily came by this afternoon, but she worried me more instead of less. Have you seen a doctor?"

"I'm fine," he assured her. "It was just the shock." Which was the truth, even if she didn't comprehend the effect that release from a binding spell could have on a daemon. "I'm sorry if I worried you." Being true, it turned out to be easier to say than he expected. "I saw Khadijah Flint this afternoon, and she mentioned you hadn't finished asking questions when all hell broke loose on Wednesday—"

More literally true than she needed to know, but he rather enjoyed playing cat and mouse with answers that ran deeper than her human understanding. He didn't much like the stillness that came over Harry, though, as if pieces to an arcane puzzle were falling into place in his head. Brad definitely had to check out what the ancient Chinese wizards had to say about his kind, because he had an uncomfortable feeling that Harry already knew the answer to that one.

"—I can come in tomorrow afternoon if you'd like and answer any questions we missed."

"About one, then. I'll have Mike Jaworski come in and witness. You met him last night, but the circumstances weren't the best; he's doing most

of the legwork, so you will probably want to turn the tables on him when
we finish with your statement."

"I'll do that."

With graceful discretion Ellen turned to her husband. "I believe we
have an appointment, dear."

"No we don't." Harry had his head bent over the chessboard, but he
didn't fool anyone.

"Harry?"

Yes, Brad concluded, all women came with the raised eyebrow and the
tone as part of the package. It worked on Harry just as it seemed to work
on most of his gender. Harry sighed, but he stood up.

"In that case, we have an appointment. See you next week," he promised, "if I don't see you before. I expect I'll be working pretty closely with
Evan on our angle of the case."

"Just don't let the board find out you are using ancient Chinese divi-
nation tricks to solve its largest theft in a decade."

"Just an avocation." Harry gave him the barest nod of a bow. "Just
an avocation."

As the couple passed him on their way to the door, Ellen paused, her
hand on Brad's arm. "Dougherty could be a problem if you are trying to
hide anything."

"I have nothing to hide." He was an expert at lying, and he looked
into her eyes with all the sincerity that had convinced Gwen Davis' jealous
lover to free him. But Ellen Li was a woman, like Evan's mother. He figured
she was inclined to take Gwen Davis' story seriously. She was also a cop
who had seen through more than one good liar in her time, which made it
a more interesting contest.

"About this case, no, I don't think you are holding out on us," she
agreed. "But Dougherty isn't concerned with art theft. His attention is
focused on you, and he'll be just as happy to bust you for jaywalking or
stock fraud as for stealing the Empress' treasures."

"Thanks for the warning."

He knew in that instant that he'd given himself away. Ellen Li patted
the arm she'd been holding. "Whatever it is, make sure Evan hears it from
you first. Oh, and—I don't want any surprises from Joe Dougherty either.
You owe me that much."

Brad figured that was true, though she wouldn't thank him for any of
his secrets.

The couple left him deep in his own thoughts until a slight cough
reminded him that Mai Sien Chong had stayed behind. And she'd heard
every word.

"Blue suits you," he said, admiring the drape of her sable hair against the shimmer of her cheongsam.

"More lies, Mr. Bradley?" she asked him with a sardonic smile.

He returned it with mock innocence. "I never lie," he said, then added: "When silence is an option."

"In that case, would you like to play?"

Brad cataloged the meanings that simple sentence suggested in her eyes. The tingle was back, uneasy restlessness prickling at his skin. Startled, he discovered that more than the hair on arms and the back of his neck was reacting to that itch. On impulse he reached out and touched her face with his fingertips. Interesting. For a moment his mind went completely blank, and he wondered if his face had shown the same brain-gone-south slippage of expression that Evan tended to get when Lily licked her lips.

She gave him the hint of a knowing smile. "I believe I would like to play. But not here."

Yes. Apparently, it had. He'd seen Evan get himself into enough trouble that he realized he needed to think *now,* not later. Before he could decide what to do about her offer, however, his stomach growled. He'd read that romantic reactions like that were usually psychological in origin and culturally based. Which meant that the lizard brain at the base of his human spine had started making decisions for him. Not a comfortable thought.

"Shall we eat?" he asked. Food would get them out of the club and buy him some time to think.

"That was part of the plan." She flashed him a knowing smile; his resolve nearly evaporated when she added, "Do you like Chinese?"

"Of course." She stood up, taking her time about it, and stretched languorously to pick up her purse. Brad shook his head in grinning bemusement. She moved with the self-conscious grace of a Siamese cat pretending to be aloof while it demanded attention with every flick of its ears. So that was the game. He reached for her hand, let his fingers slide across hers and drift up her arm before coming to rest just above her elbow, and enjoyed the way her eyes widened. "Check," he said.

Her irises had almost disappeared, but still she raised her chin in a defiant tilt. "It's not mate yet. How about Susanna Foo's?"

"Won't we need a reservation?"

"I don't have any reservations at all." She cocked her head to give him the slantwise come-on that had been Poor Tony's downfall. "But she has private rooms."

Not a single chess piece had moved in the room since Ellen and Harry had walked out the door, and Brad found himself suddenly commiserating with Poor Tony. Time to end the suspense, for the chess club if for no one else. "Shall we go?"

"Anything you say."

She let him lead her from the room and down the hall, and he knew it was part of the seduction. In the stairwell she turned into his arm to give him a feather-drift of a kiss. "This is going to be very interesting," she promised; her smile made a joke of the inscrutibility of the East. And half a block down Walnut Street, Susanna Foo had no tables but could always find a quiet room for Madam Chong's party.

The duck-filled potstickers were divine, the Mongolian lamb fiery, and Mai Sien Chong played an elusive game of lowered eyelashes and cool smiles over conversation about the food. And when dinner was over and compliments given to the chef, each went home alone—Brad to do some thinking. He hoped Mai Sien's sleep was as troubled as she'd made his.

# Chapter 17

STILL HALF ASLEEP, EVAN WANDERED INTO THE STUDY. HIS BRUISES STILL HURT, though they'd started to change colors, and the stitches itched—by Monday, he'd be rubbing the knots out of his hair. But the trustees of the Philadelphia Museum of Art wouldn't wait forever for him to get their precious crystal back. He found Brad in his tapestried wing chair, left ankle propped on right knee, the printout that hadn't given them any clues yesterday spread across the makeshift workspace of his leg. Seagrave's revisionist study of the Dragon Lady, the last empress of China, lay open, facedown, on the small table next to his father's chair.

"You've been working," Evan noted. He dropped into his own chair behind the desk, where more books lay scattered. The computer was running, the screen open to a chat room in Hong Kong.

"Anything new?"

His father colored briefly, and Evan caught a look of confusion on his face before he dropped his gaze to the printout on his lap. Not an expression Evan had ever seen on his father's face before—he wasn't sure he liked the idea that a daemon lord of the host of Ariton might be plagued with the uncertainty of a mere mortal.

He would have pursued the insight, but Lily materialized in the doorway and closed the space between them in a few steps. Or not. However she got there, she perched on the arm of his chair and clamped her lips onto his like a moray eel in heat. He considered shifting her off his lap to make the thinking part easier, but she felt good right where she was, so he filed the questions away for a less distracting moment and concentrated on the problem in his hands.

But all good things, even Lily's kisses, came to an end. Eventually, Evan surfaced for air. "Good morning."

"A contradiction in terms." Lily slid off Evan's lap and perched on the desk. "What were you up to before I got here?"

"I was just wondering what has Brad looking confused, and I'd swear he looked embarrassed, when I asked him what he had on the case. *Do* we have a problem with the case?"

"You didn't ask about the case."

Evan needed a second glance but, yes, Brad was fidgeting under the combined stares of his host-cousin and his son.

"You asked if anything was new. I was thinking about someone at the time . . ."

"Someone?" Lily was pushing, and she was enjoying her host-cousin's discomfort.

"She's my problem. I'll deal with it." Brad dismissed the topic of conversation.

She. The number of shes involved in this case was limited. Ellen Li, perhaps? Evan knew his mother had interfered, brought Dougherty down on their heads, but she *wasn't* Brad's problem to deal with. Certainly not the way his daemon kin usually dealt with their human problems.

"Leave my mother out of this."

"I didn't bring your mother into the discussion. But since you mention it, what are you going to do about her?"

Somehow the conversation had gotten away from Evan, taking a direction he couldn't follow let alone control. He took another shot at it anyway. "If not my mother, what woman are you talking about?"

Brad took a deep breath, as if he might actually answer the question; then Evan saw the moment of indecision, and the next, when Brad decided against the confidence. He hadn't closed down, just moved to something else vying for attention in his head; Evan could almost feel the mental tick against an imaginary checklist.

"*You* were talking about women, Evan. I was just thinking. But since we are on the subject of your mother, what are you going to do about her?"

"Talk to her. I told you that." Just, not now, when his head was throbbing in the back, where the monitor had collided with the outside of his skull, in the front, where his brain had collided with the inside of his skull, and on the side, where Brad had left streaks of bruises that blended into the gash where Lily'd hit him with a lamp. He wasn't having a good week, and explaining his father to his mother didn't seem likely to make it any better. Brad was shaking his head, which boded no good either.

"That still leaves us with Joe Dougherty," Brad added. "Now that he's got his teeth into us, Flint thinks he'll stick with it. Dougherty's a cop. He probably figures you can talk your mother around, but he won't stop until he's got evidence one way or the other."

Lily had her usual suggestion: "We could kill him."

Evan had his usual answer: "Dougherty alive hasn't convinced Ellen Li yet that Brad is guilty. Dougherty dead will put him on the FBI's most wanted list. You can leave town. Hell, Brad could show up at Ellen Li's office four inches shorter, twenty pounds lighter, with crooked teeth and a comb-over and confess to the crime, and Ellen would send him home with a complimentary supply of thorazine. But my life won't be worth shit if we start killing cops." Never mind that he'd grown up with Joe Dougherty, who'd always been a pain in the ass but was still somebody from Rosemont Street, a link to the time when Evan was a human adolescent with problems and not a half-daemon monster with more power than control.

"The boy has a point," Brad admitted, privy only to the spoken part of Evan's objection. "More to the purpose, our attorney, for whose advice we pay a very high annual retainer, has suggested a simple solution. We give Dougherty his evidence."

"Of what?" Evan asked him. "A deposition about the color of my mother's bedroom curtains won't convince anyone you slept with her. If you're lucky, Dougherty will assume I told you. If he's feeling suspicious, he may decide you've been stalking the family for years."

"Khadijah Flint thinks we should have DNA tests done. She seems to think that we might need the results to prove paternity in case the relationship were challenged in court. Or in case Dougherty wanted to use the lack of relationship to support a motive for whatever crimes he's trying to dig up."

"That's not likely to happen, is it?" Evan asked. "The police in New York know you were looking for Paul Carter, but they have nothing to place you at the bar when it blew up. No one can place you in Venice when Ca' Dacosta collapsed; I'm the only suspect there. And other than abandoning a BMW in front of expired meters, I can't think of a thing you've done they can put on the record."

The record was an important distinction. Brad had fifty dead in the East Village to pay for if the New York Fire Department had a supernatural category for arson. Evan had trained his mind to stay clear of that bit of family history, but every once in a while it sneaked up and bit him in the ass.

Brad was answering the question, not the queasy memory of a case he'd rather forget.

"Joe Dougherty has already contested paternity on your mother's evidence. I am not sure what my motive for the pretense is supposed to be. Couldn't be your money, because you had none. Couldn't have been for sex. You've made it clear that close human relatives don't have sex together, and you were old enough to walk away from a proposition before I ever met you. Given the condition in which I found you, I wasn't likely to have picked you as the choicest candidate for a proposition anyway."

Evan remembered. He didn't like to, and he still couldn't figure out why his father had bothered to keep him alive in the weeks that followed, but he certainly hadn't been anybody's idea of a dream date.

"Then why? What motive does he think you had?"

Brad frowned slightly—not displeasure—his father was gnawing on a problem that didn't quite make sense.

"Khadijah suggests that while looking for a long-lost son, I found you, who were yourself looking for a long-lost father. Faced with years of disappointment and searching ahead as well as behind, we ended the search with each other."

"Is that possible?" For humans it was more than possible—mothers had been passing off "premature" babies to new "fathers" for centuries. The thought gave Evan a cold chill. Omage—but no, Evan was of Ariton, not Azmod. He'd been accepted by the Host of Ariton, and the Princes of the second sphere didn't make mistakes when it came to recognizing their own kind. But there were 833 daemon lords of the host of Ariton—

"No. It's not."

Evan could tell that Brad wished it *were* possible, wished that he could leave this mess of human flesh and emotional tangles to some other of his host. "The Princes sent me to deal with you because the essence of your daemon nature called out to me and to no other of our kind."

Evan nodded, unable to speak through his relief, but he knew it showed and regretted the answering grief in his father's eyes. It took him a minute or two, but he managed to sort medical reality from emotional need.

"That has nothing to do with DNA. Or does it? Will your daemon nature show up in my DNA?" It didn't seem likely. Daemon lords didn't, in their own sphere, their universe, have corporeal form. No body, no DNA. Seemed pretty clear. "All a test will prove is that we don't share genetic material."

"We will." Brad stood up and walked toward the desk, and it felt to Evan as though his father towered over him. Brad took Evan's hand and exposed the wrist crossed by the fine ridges of scar tissue left by Omage's silver knife. He held out his own free hand, palm up. As Evan watched, a cut opened on the palm and welled blood.

"I can't," he said, knowing what Brad asked without words.

"You can," Brad answered, and meant the ability to set aside his fear as well as to reshape his flesh. Memory lay in his father's eyes, of cuts poorly sealed with infected scabs and an alabaster bowl stained brown with Evan's blood.

It only seemed the same, Evan realized: not his sacrifice this time but his father's. Brad was offering him the life they had made here; all he had to do was move beyond his past. He closed his eyes, ignoring the tears that gathered at their corners, and concentrated on the shape and feel of the scars on his wrist. He chose one, remembered the night he'd received it, the closest Omage had ever come to letting him die of blood loss. He remembered the quick slice, scarcely felt until Omage separated the lips of the wound with his teeth and then held it open with his fingertips, tilted over the bowl. He remembered the pain that followed and the terror as he catapulted into the second sphere and raged his fear and anger until, too weak to live divided in place, he tried for the first time to drag his body after him. He'd been too far gone and had ended up trapped in Omage's chains, body and soul, while he felt his life drain away and prayed, with what bit of mind he had left to him, that this time Omage wouldn't stop in time.

"That's enough."

Not Omage, the voice, but Brad, his father. Louder, sharper, than he usually spoke. "Evan!"

He opened his eyes, met Brad's and saw alarm there. Why? Oh. He looked down at their hands, Brad's clasped firmly over Evan's wrist. The blood leaked between the fingers clenched over the wound.

"That's enough. You can stop the bleeding now."

"Can I?" He felt dazed, as if he'd been dragged from a dream.

"Yes. You can."

Evan nodded his head. "Okay." He concentrated on the wrist, remembered how it looked today, not four years ago. The pain faded. The blood stopped.

They stared at each other, not yet able to break the contact, until Lily brought them back to the problem at hand.

"You are going to have to clean up the blood you dripped all over the desk, or we will never get another cleaning crew in here again. And I don't intend to do it."

"I'll get a cloth," Evan offered, still in a daze.

"No, you won't."

The revulsion in his father's voice hit him like a blow, and in Evan's confusion it was almost enough, right then, to break him. Then Brad did something that woke them all up with the crack of thunder, and the desk lay in splinters on the floor.

"We'll get a new desk."

Oh. His father was angry at something else, at least for the moment. That was okay.

"Better get another computer monitor while you're at it," Lily added. "Now, can we get back to the case at hand, or have we decided to make our living at the casinos instead?"

Back to work seemed like more than he was capable of, but some part of his detecting experience seemed to be working. Evan figured the books must have taken most of the blood he'd lost. As he looked at the debris on the floor that used to be a desk, he didn't see nearly enough paper.

"What happened to the books?"

"Incinerated."

Evan hadn't realized until now that his father must be carrying some memories of the bad old days too. His mind was still muzzy and working at half-speed, but he found the notion reassuring.

"Does he need a doctor?"

Brad's voice, and he didn't want to explain to the doctors the scar on his arm still raw from the morning's work.

"Not for this, I shouldn't think." Lily gave him a reassuring peck on the lips. "He's made a mess, but blood is like that. I expect he hasn't lost more than a cupful."

He didn't know how long he'd bled before his father got through to him, but he was still on his feet, so he figured Lily was probably right. "Just some juice," he said. "They make you drink juice at the Red Cross after you give blood." He started for the kitchen, but Lily pressed him back with a hand over his heart.

"I'll do that. You lie down."

Suddenly, flat seemed like a really good idea. By the time he'd stretched himself out on the couch, Lily returned with a glass of orange juice. The glass felt blessedly cold in his hand, the juice even colder running down his throat. "Brad—"

"I'm here." And he was, grim as the shadow of death standing over the couch.

"Thanks."

Evan didn't quite understand why that simple word made his father flinch, or why his father wouldn't look at him, but stared at the splintered desk. He thought he understood that look, the fascination mixed with loathing. He'd felt it often enough in his Omage years. When Brad said, "We have a long way to go before thanks are in order," Evan figured they were both seeing more than a few artifacts they were contracted to find.

"Make that go away, cousin." Lily was looking at the kindling that used to be a desk as well, with simple distaste that Evan found easier to deal with. "When the police are likely to be picking through your garbage, you don't want to make the cleaning staff any more nervous than you have to."

"Later," Brad answered her. "Right now I have an appointment at Major Crimes."

"Tell Liz I'll be there in a few minutes," she answered. When Brad disappeared, Lily turned her attention to Evan. "Get some rest; you look terrible." She took the empty glass and handed him a second full one, though where she got it from he didn't want to ask. "I'll look in on you when I get back."

She gave him a kiss that was a promise more of comfort than her usual leer and followed her host-cousin through the second sphere. Evan fell back onto the sofa, splashing the juice on his thumb. Hell and damnation. He drank it down, decided Lily was right that he needed rest. Sleep hit him like a brick wall.

# Chapter 18

MAJOR CRIMES HEADQUARTERS TOOK UP THE SECOND STORY OF THE POLICE station at 39th and Lancaster in the middle of Mantua, one of the more seriously drug and crime infested parts of the city. For a few minutes at home Brad had considered dressing down to blend with the surroundings, but he gave up the idea. At the best, he'd look like a tourist lost on his way to a golf course.

A suit, however out of place there on one of the hottest days of early summer, gave him armor against the police, a reminder that he was no common criminal but a wealthy and respected businessman in the elite community of the city. The local bad element would likely take him for a crime boss and leave him alone as well, a good idea given that the police generally frowned on dead bodies, or the ashy remains of same, on their doorstep. He chose navy, over one of Carlo Pimi's swiss cotton shirts with simple gold cufflinks, added a blue and gray regimental-striped tie, and combed his hair, thick and black with just a hint of silver traced through it. The subtle intimidation of wealth and maturity: yes, that would do it. Ellen would think it was funny, but she'd said Jaworski would be there as well. Best to start the junior on the right foot.

Ready, he brought to mind the landing behind the fire doors that opened into the reception area at Major Crimes—the floor of vinyl tiles with grime at the broken corners, the green ceramic blocks that lined the walls, the suspended ceiling with brown stains marking the places where pipes had leaked, and the swinging doors with the metal showing where the green paint had chipped away—and walked through.

Liz sat at a desk behind a counter fronted with bulletproof glass. She held the phone receiver to her ear but gave him an editorial roll of the eyes and motioned him inside.

"Just a minute, Sid. Got a customer." She put Sid on hold, and Brad gave her a sympathetic smile. Sid Valentine was FBI. Brad had run into him a couple of times on cases and didn't like him much.

"The feds giving you a hard time?"

"Just Sid," Liz said, "and he only counts toward Karma-points." Sid didn't have the imagination to be as overbearing as the ones on television, but he still seemed to think he could ride to a cushy pension on the work of other people. His assistant had twice the smarts and got half the credit. If Sid was on the line, he must figure there was a collar he could snatch somewhere. Brad just hoped his own collar didn't enter into Sid's figuring.

"They're waiting for you in the captain's office," she told him. "He's at a meeting downtown, but Ellen is here, with Mike. Deej arrived a few minutes before you did, and that guy from the Northeast, Joe Dougherty, asked to observe. Deej just about bit his head off, but Ellen said he could stay if he kept his mouth shut and his hands in his pockets."

Ellen probably had said those very words. She didn't have a lot of time for fools showing up on her turf and complicating a case that was difficult enough already.

"Thanks, Liz. Oh, Lily's right behind me—" He stopped, brought up short by the apparition on her side of the desk. "*What* are you wearing?"

She stood up, laughing—"That's why they call it undercover—" to model the outfit: Pearls. A knubby pink cotton sweater with flowers embroidered around the throat. A golf skirt even pinker than the sweater. The door opened while he was absorbing the transformation. Lily walked in wearing an identical outfit in blue, right down to the canvas tennies and the golf club stuck on the skirt by some magic of women's clothing. She carried an oversized canvas bag, and Liz pulled a similar one in straw from the filing drawer in her desk.

"Hey, Vinnie, I'm out of here!" she called, and a uniformed policeman wandered out of the coffee area with a disreputable looking mug of pale mud in his hand.

"Happy hunting." He sat at the desk, put the mug down where Brad watched in horrified fascination as the cream circled in oily uncertainty on its surface, but it was that or stare at the thinning spot in the middle of the policeman's flat-top.

"Who's on hold?" Vinnie asked.

"Sid," Liz answered before she closed the door behind her.

"Oh. Okay." Vinnie left the phone on the desk and picked up the mug.

"Lily said she and Liz were going shopping." Brad figured he could pull an answer out of Vinnie if he masked the question as conversation, Vinnie was smarter than he looked.

"They're checking out the weekend flea markets. Not likely to find anything, but you can't overlook the possibility." Vinnie had a reminiscing gleam in his eye. "I suppose if Ms Ryan were my partner, I wouldn't be too picky about reports either."

"Wouldn't do you any good," Brad admitted. "Evan is the only one who cares about the paperwork."

He wandered in the direction Liz had pointed, leaving Vinnie with no more excuses. As Brad reached the door to the captain's office, he heard the uniform on the phone: "Hey Sid, howyadoing? Liz had to go—you know women." The window blinds were drawn, so he couldn't see what waited on the other side. Had to figure he was the last one in, though, and whoever else was in the room, Ellen Li was the key. He had to keep her on his side. Wishing he had some of that apocryphal knowledge about women himself, Brad walked through the doorway.

"Ellen!" He put on his best debonair act, both hands outstretched across Captain Marsh's oversized desk, knowing that Joe Dougherty, sitting deep in the corner on his left, would see the gold cufflinks, maybe know they were real and hate him more for it, which suited him just fine. Dougherty was a hothead, worse than Evan, and humans riding an emotional wave made mistakes. Khadijah Flint, on his right, never let emotion get in her way on matters of business. She'd let him play out his game while she watched for leverage, and she'd take it when it was given. They'd worked enough together that she'd expect Brad to win those leverage angles for them any way he could.

He hadn't done business with Ellen Li until this case, but he'd sat across the chess board from her enough to know how she ticked. She'd be taking it all in as well, just as she was doing when she let him take her hands and clasp them over the portable tape recorder on the desk.

"How is Evan?" she asked.

"Back to work, though he's still on short hours. The boy has an uncanny knack of landing on his feet."

"Looked more like he landed on his head this time, to me. Tell him we haven't given up on finding your bomber."

She took her hands back and, after he closed the door, motioned for him to sit in the one empty chair in the room, next to Khadijah Flint on his right. Mike Jaworski sat in a short-sleeved shirt with no tie to the right of Khadijah Flint, at the desk—backup for Ellen and as watchful as if he expected someone among them to spring up and attack the lieutenant with an AK 47. Not a comfortable-looking man, but at least you knew where his loyalties were. It put Joe Dougherty on Brad's left, at his back, where Brad couldn't see him. He didn't much like the arrangement, but he smiled anyway.

"Ms. Flint. I'm glad you could join us today." He greeted her with a long clasp of her hand before he sat down. Trouper that she was, she didn't show by a flicker of a lash that his behavior surprised her, but she squeezed his hand with a knowing sympathy he should have expected, perhaps, but hadn't.

"Evan's been spending some time on that investigation as well." Settled in the chair with his hands resting lightly on its arms, he addressed himself to Ellen's last statement. "We'll let you know if we turn up something useful."

Evan already knew who'd hit him, but Brad figured the lie people expect always beat the truth that would complicate his own life. He studiously avoided any overt recognition of Dougherty's presence but gave Mike Jaworski a brief nod when Ellen introduced him with, "You remember Detective Jaworski? He's assigned to the case, so he'll be helping to take your statement. Mike will do most of the liaising with outside contacts, so you will probably see a lot of him in the next few weeks."

"Does that mean we will see you at the club on Wednesday?" he asked Ellen, "or would it still constitute a conflict?"

From Joe Dougherty behind him, Brad heard a disgusted sigh, but only the twitch of the muscles around Jaworski's mouth showed that the detective had reacted at all. Brad smiled.

"I need you there—Mai Sien will eat me alive without you there to protect me."

"I suspect that wouldn't hurt at all." Ellen gave him a wry smile. "But until we check the details of your statement, I am sure some sort of police protection can be worked out. Perhaps Detective Jaworski would act as bodyguard in the meantime."

"I wouldn't ask something so dangerous of the detective."

"You're just worried that he'll throw himself on the suspect to protect you."

Brad laughed appreciatively. He figured Ellen had the same picture in mind, and he didn't think Jaworski or Mai Sien Chong would object. "That goes without saying. I'm just afraid she won't bother to throw him off again."

"Somehow, Mr. Bradley, I can't see you being afraid of anything," which hit too close to the mark even though Ellen Li was still smiling.

"Is this a police investigation or a social club?" Joe Dougherty, of course, sounding more querulous and short-tempered than anything else.

"Mr. Bradley has been charged with no crime here, Sergeant, and is cooperating voluntarily with the police." Ellen Li asserted rank with an ironic chill in her voice. "There is no reason to bring out the rubber hoses and the brass knuckles just yet." Which told Jaworski as much as Dougherty where she stood. Brad could feel Dougherty's animosity seething at his back, but Jaworski's smile was almost as bland as Brad's own.

"Shall we begin, then?" Brad asked, taking the initiative for starting the official business out of the hands of the police. Or, rather, Ellen had engineered it that way. Interesting. "You folks are on salary, but I'm paying Ms. Flint by the hour."

"Just you remember that when the bill comes due." She reached over and patted his hand where it lay on the arm of his chair, the touch creating the illusion that they were a unified front. But her hand felt warm on his; perhaps there was more truth to the fiction than he had realized. The fact shut Dougherty out and left Jaworski with a decision. Mike Jaworski was the new kid, a bit older than Evan, but not by much, tall and barrel chested with short blond hair and a cigarette stain between the two first fingers of his right hand. On the third finger, he wore a school ring. Brad would have bet money on a couple of tattoos, at least, and he figured them for the kind that sailors found in any liberty port when they were drunk enough, not the fashionably daring ones the kids were wearing these days.

Police hierarchy and class reticence denied him entry into the closed circle of his superior officer and her personal friends at the table. Socially, Jaworski would seem to be aligned with Joe Dougherty, but Dougherty had clearly made a nuisance of himself. So Brad took a chance.

"Anchor?" he asked, casting a glance at the shirtsleeve covering Jaworski's upper arm.

The detective seemed confused for a moment, then gave Brad a searching glance. "Semper Fi," he turned his wrist to reveal the tattoo on the inside of his arm.

Brad didn't think the indignation was a ruse, but he knew Jaworski was following. He nodded once, slowly. "Good man to have in a tough situation." He made it sound like a judgment.

Jaworski took the offer: "So, where do you play chess?"

Oh, yes, this young man had scoped the territory and knew where the high ground was.

"Franklin Mercantile."

Dougherty was not happy. "Why don't you just turn around and bend over, Bradley. Make the ass-kissing easier all around."

"You are not part of these proceedings, Sergeant. Another outburst like that and I will have you removed." Ellen Li took control away from him again, and Brad relinquished it freely. He had, after all, seen her play.

Dougherty was standing up now, keeping his voice below a shout with an effort that corded the tendons on his neck.

"The guy is a fake!" he said. "We don't know who he really is, or what he's hiding, or what he's doing here claiming to be Evan Davis' father. And we don't know why he was in the Chinese gallery with an unconscious guard and half the stuff in one case gone."

"Mr. Dougherty!"

"No." Brad held up his hand, placating Ellen Li. "We can't fault him for caring about Evan. It's hard not to, after all." He smiled at Dougherty, who returned him an incredulous look. Yes, he'd known Evan all right.

"Ms. Flint and I talked about this over lunch yesterday. I have resisted doing anything to prove my relationship to Evan on a clinical level because I wanted to leave the past behind us."

He paused for effect but found he did need the moment to gather his thoughts. The memories ached strangely somewhere that he wouldn't give a name. "I don't speak of the time when I found Evan, but you have to understand, he was in pretty fragile condition." Completely, suicidally, insane, actually, but he'd win no points for accuracy here. "How would I have explained a request for blood tests? That I didn't trust him to be who he was? And what would Evan have thought? That he wasn't good enough to be my son? That I was trying to give myself a scientific reason to abandon him?" He realized his arguments echoed the ones that Khadijah Flint had made to him the day before and didn't want to admit they'd made an impression. Paternity was not in doubt, but that didn't answer the questions that he still found haunting Evan's eyes at times like these, when the question to go or stay trembled on the brink of his father's desire for home.

"I didn't need a doctor in a lab to tell me Evan was my son: A father knows his son, soul to soul." Quite literally, in this case. In the second sphere, Evan sparked with the same blue flame as his immortal kin, the daemon lords of Ariton.

"But a father's recognition of himself in his son hardly seems proof enough in a suspicious world. Fortunately, Evan is no longer the emotionally distressed boy I found. He's grown into a man with a good head on his shoulders. So we talked this morning and he agreed. As soon as he's recovered from the injuries he suffered in the recent attack, we will make an appointment for DNA testing. I know the results won't be available soon enough for Sergeant Dougherty, but it will stop future efforts to destroy what Evan has built with his paternal family over the few years we've had together." Brad carefully modulated his tone to convey a degree of resignation and just a bit of his anger. He even managed to control the gag reflex. It struck him, once again, that he'd really be better off if he just fried the bastard and went home.

On the other hand, he did like chess, and it seemed that all his games were coming off the board and into his life these days. He'd like to see if he could win against the police and the thief. As to the game he was playing with Mai Sien Chong, well, he thought maybe losing that one wouldn't be so bad. But right now he had Joe Dougherty temporarily out of the game; his next move had to block Jaworski while keeping Ellen on his side.

"Now that we've taken the question of my personal early indiscretions off the table—and I do hope you noticed that I've gone quite beyond what the law might require to answer a question that had no business on the table in the first place—can we move forward, to the case in question? I don't know about you, but I have an investigation to conduct. The faster we can exchange information, the faster we can all get back to work."

So, he placed himself firmly on the side of the angels and co-opted their questioning to one of mutual exchange of information. Given where Lily was right now, he figured the point was a technicality anyway. But he wanted it on the table to haunt Joe Dougherty throughout the meeting. He couldn't very well kill the man, but he could make his life miserable for as long as he had contact with Bradley, Ryan, and Davis.

Jaworski turned on the tape recorder and spoke in the date and the names and relation to the case of those present; he identified Brad as a witness, and for Dougherty he said, "observer." Then he asked for a voice identification from each of them for the tape. When the formalities were completed, Brad began by reminding them:

"We have already covered the night of the burglary, so I assume you want to know what we have learned since."

Clearly that was not Joe Dougherty's agenda, but Ellen Li nodded agreement.

"Harry confirmed that the trustees at the museum had hired the agency for a security evaluation. He was surprised that you went in after hours without giving the board or the police fair warning. I would like to hear again your explanation why you didn't follow procedure that night."

"Not to implicate Harry, about whom my only suspicions revolve around the chessboard, but I believe there is a possibility that the theft at the University Museum was an inside job. Harry was afraid, correctly as it turns out, that the PMA might be next. Logically, if our burglar, or burglary ring, should have inside access to both institutions, I didn't want that access to include information about our security evaluation."

"And you don't mean to implicate Professor Li?" Jaworski sounded skeptical, but Brad gave a very confident little laugh.

"Not at all," he explained. "Given the reputation of Bradley, Ryan, and Davis, he'd have been a fool to bring us on if he were guilty of the crime himself. Harry may be many things, but a fool isn't one of them."

"No it isn't," Ellen Li agreed. "But you didn't mention your visit to Evan or Lily either. Did you suspect either or both of them?"

"Of course not. Lily was out of town, and Evan was handling his usual end of things. I thought I'd be in and out of the museum in a matter of minutes, that I'd have some information about how scrupulous the guards were at setting the security systems, but nothing of consequence. I don't think any of us, Harry included, expected the burglars to hit the museum so soon after the university job. I certainly didn't expect to find the burglary in progress when I arrived, which supports my contention that we are looking for someone with immediate access to policy decision making at the institution."

Joe Dougherty bounced out of his chair with a disgusted grunt. "I can't believe you are buying this shit." He glared at the room in general. "He knew damned well there was a burglary going on—he just didn't know his accomplice had triggered the alarm. And he didn't tell Evan because they need a dupe in the agency, somebody who really *is* innocent to put the police off the track. If you take a good look at the agency's record—a really good look—you'll see that the tactic of feeding Evan to the police has worked in half a dozen countries. Evan fronts for them. Evan is genuinely innocent, so the police walk away with nothing. Evan isn't going to complain even if he does find out the truth, because Evan has been an emotional cripple since he was a kid."

Dougherty whipped around then, and pointed an accusing finger at Brad's nose.

"I don't buy any of this long-lost son crap. You stumbled on some poor half-crazed kid and realized you could put him under your control by offering him the one thing he'd been looking for all his life. Was it some kinky sex fantasy of yours that the three of you were playing out, or did you just want an unwitting accomplice you could throw to the wolves when the police got too close?"

Brad was trying with little success to imagine Evan as an innocent dupe. He wondered what Lily would think of that and why this fellow, who claimed he was a friend of Evan's mother, seemed so obsessed with the idea that Brad was having sex with Evan. He didn't have time to frame a question, or to do more than note with a corner of his mind that Khadijah Flint had stood up with daggers glinting in her eyes, because a voice behind him stopped them all in their tracks.

"You're out of the loop, Joe."

Evan. Brad hadn't heard the door open, but now he understood what that sick expression on Ellen Li's face was about, and why Khadijah Flint looked like she was watching a bomb tick down its timer.

"There was a time when I fit the description my mother gave you—dupe and then prisoner at the Black Masque, and more than half crazed even before then. You probably remember how it was from the old days. But I haven't been insane for about four years now, not since I got to know my father."

Brad stood up and faced his son. By all the Lords of Ariton—he hadn't seen that expression on Evan Davis since he'd faced down Franklin Simpson in a battle for two universes, and his immediate reaction was to kill the man who had put it there now. He took a step toward Dougherty, and Khadijah Flint gripped his arm at the elbow and squeezed. The sharp pain focused him again. Dougherty posed no real danger. Brad had already matched DNA types with Evan. When they disproved his most damaging claim, the others would fold after it. And, more important, Evan wasn't the half-crazed boy Dougherty described. The expression marked Evan going into battle, and when he thought about it, he figured maybe Khadijah Flint should be holding onto the son instead of the father.

Evan gave his father a quick glance that made it clear he would tolerate no interference and faced the enemy again.

"I'm not under anyone's control, no one has thrown me anywhere, but my father has gotten me out of a jam or two when a case blew up in our faces. We don't have arrest records because we try not to break the law."

"You've come close on more than one occasion," Ellen Li pointed out. She was looking at Evan, not at anyone else, gauging something that she saw there, and giving him something in the look that Brad didn't quite understand.

Evan did understand it, apparently, because something inside him came off danger mode. "Close," he agreed, and whether that was an admission or an apology or an agreement to stand down, Brad couldn't figure. Khadijah Flint seemed to, though.

"My client has nothing more to say." Flint's voice lived up to her name, cold and cutting and final as a knife. She stood up with Evan behind her, and intimidated Joe Dougherty with her cold anger, but spoke to Ellen Li. "Unless you are going to charge my clients with a crime, we suggest that you keep Sergeant Dougherty clear of this case."

"Deal." Ellen Li gave Dougherty a look as cold as the one he got from Flint. "You have worn out your welcome here, Sergeant. I'd suggest you leave right now, before Ms. Flint files a harassment suit against you."

"You just made a big mistake." Joe Dougherty turned to leave, but Khadijah Flint stopped him with a question: "Was that a threat, Sergeant Dougherty?"

Dougherty threaded his fingers through his hair and surfaced with a look of disgust. "I'm one of the good guys, remember? I'm here because I told his mother I'd make sure the wheels of justice didn't grind him up over a fraud and his promises. So, no, Ms. Flint. It was not a threat. It was a genuine warning, to a friend who is in over his head with no one looking out for him but me."

"I'll talk to her tomorrow. You'll be off the hook." Evan nodded, a brief admission that maybe Dougherty meant better than he knew how to do. Dougherty returned the nod, but he was shaking his head as he picked his way between the desks. He didn't look back when he went out the door.

"Now." Ellen Li didn't sit down again, so everyone else remained standing as well, except for Mike Jaworski who hadn't gotten up for any of it.

"I think we've all had enough for one day. Brad, do you have anything useful to add, or can we sign off on this and be done with it?"

"You had all I knew on Wednesday night. All I could do today is answer your questions with the same old information."

"Your investigation hasn't turned up anything?" The "either" hung unspoken in the air.

Brad shrugged. "You'll have to ask Evan," he admitted. "Or maybe Lily, but Evan's likely to have the best information. I've been a bit preoccupied lately."

Ellen gave a glance after Dougherty and followed with a little bow of her head in agreement. Then she gave Brad a more searching look, but she didn't say what had crossed her mind.

"In that case, here is the deal I will offer you. No more Dougherty. Promise. In exchange, Mike will accompany you back to your offices, where you will show him the files on this list." She pulled a sheet of paper from the corner of the desk blotter and handed it over. Notepaper, Brad noticed; not a warrant, but not worth fighting over if it got Dougherty off his back, he figured. Ellen hadn't finished yet.

"Evan, I want you to go over the computer data you've compiled on the case with Detective Jaworksi."

She didn't wait for Evan's agreement, but turned to Jaworski and added, "You are authorized to share information at your discretion, Mike. Just don't let his father sucker you into a chess game for money."

"Anything you say, boss lady." Jaworski pulled himself out of his chair and straightened his shirt.

"Then, I think we are finished for today. Thank you all for coming."

That was flat out sarcasm, and Kevin Bradley wasn't going to dignify it with an answer, but her final words, "Bring money on Wednesday; we'll play for dinner," sent him on to his next appointment feeling that perhaps this case wouldn't end in disaster after all. With no clues, no motive, an MO emerging but nothing in the records to flesh it out, perhaps the facts did not warrant his optimism. But he had his freedom, and Ellen Li had gotten the flea Joe Dougherty off his back, so his decision to stay on the material plane for a while didn't sound quite as masochistic to his own ears. And Wednesday they'd be playing chess for dinner. He'd make a reservation, Susanna Foo, or perhaps George Perrier's new Brasserie, just in case.

# Chapter 19

EVAN OPENED THE FRONT DOOR AND USHERED DETECTIVE JAWORSKI IN AHEAD of him. As a matter of policy strangers did not have access to the private study in the living quarters. He suspected that Jaworski had taken a look around after Lily had blown out of town, while Evan was still in the hospital. He wasn't getting a second shot at it, particularly now, with the desk doing a good imitation of kindling on the floor.

The blue Aubusson carpet hushed his footsteps across the reception room; Evan noted in passing that the moldings on top of the white painted wainscotting needed dusting, but the Hepplewhite sideboard and scattered armchairs gleamed with polish and energetic rubbing. They went straight through to the formal office where the agency received clients. Late sun cast lace-curtain shadows on the desk and mottled the cup on the corner with light.

"Have a seat, Detective."

All the spindle-backed chairs scattered in the office were wood, authentic antiques in the corners and almost-authentic reproductions in areas of heaviest use. None of them were particularly comfortable. Jaworski sat in one, hitched his back a twitch, then seemed to realize it wasn't going to get any better, which Evan figured showed good sense.

Bradley, Ryan, and Davis specialized in retrieving stolen artwork. They had a sideline in cases involving the occult which brought in the occasional crackpot and the even more rare authentic haunting, demonic possession, and once a telekinetic Peeping Tom with a habit of leaving his targets feeling as though they'd been clawed by a raptor. Clients had to feel confident, but, as Lily often reminded him, they ran a detective agency, not a counseling service. Comfortable chairs just encouraged the customers to linger. That rule of thumb didn't have an exception clause for the police.

Evan went around the desk and snapped on the computer and monitor before he sat down at his considerably more user-friendly high-backed executive arm chair. "Mac takes a while to boot up." He tilted back in the chair, splitting his attention between the computer screen and the police detective. They'd put the computer on the desk because clients seemed to expect one, but they used it so seldom that Evan was almost surprised to see the computer happy face appear on the screen. "While we wait, maybe we can compare notes."

"You know what I'm here to look at." Jaworski pulled the sheet of paper from his breast pocket. "Here's the list, in case you've forgotten something."

"I haven't forgotten." Evan took the list and glanced at it briefly, then dropped it on the desk. "But we aren't going to find anything there. I've already cross-checked our client database, and we don't have anything in our background checks or case histories that points to a similar MO." He clicked the mouse, moving the cursor to a file that listed the client records by contract type, and quietly deleted the Simpson/Carter case. He scanned the list Jaworski had handed him, checked it against the database, deleting all the cases but those on Ellen Li's list, and hit a prompt to print it out.

"Here is the information Ellen wanted. I haven't found any connection with the museum case in them, but maybe you'll have more luck."

Jaworski took the sheaf of papers and glanced at the names and contract types, all retrievals of art objects. "Do you have hard files?" he asked. "Anyplace someone could have slipped a stray notation or telephone message that didn't get into the computer?"

Evan shook his head. "We don't keep paper files here. We put it all on computer when we do the summary final report. Then we ship everything out to a service that records all the telephone calls, correspondence, travel, or any other expenses we need to document. They send the completed file to our billing service, and they pass it to a temporary storage facility where we pay to have it kept for about three years. After three years, all paper records are destroyed."

"Aren't you worried that you may lose your records if your computer crashes?" Jaworski looked nervous, and Evan realized that the man didn't doubt the truth of his statement but had some real misgivings about the safety of computerized records.

"Sometimes we do lose the database," he admitted, "but we make a taped backup every night. We could lose a day's work, but anything we are working on is likely to be in the office anyway. It's the old records you have to worry about, and we keep several backups, one in the safe and one with the storage company, just in case."

"And this is everything there is?" Jaworski held up the sheaf of papers, which looked pretty thin.

"Those are the summary final reports. If you see something that interests you, I can pull the billing records or even get the hard copy out of storage. But there isn't any point in going to the trouble if you don't see anything worth your time."

"It's not my time," Jaworksi pointed out. "It's Ellen Li's time, and she wants these records checked." So much for the uncomfortable furniture. He spread the papers on the desk and pulled out his own notebook.

Evan sighed. This wasn't how he'd planned to spend his afternoon. In fact, he'd awakened from his unplanned nap with the dream of undressing Lily in the garden still making itself felt on his body, and he'd been kind of hoping she'd come home early ever since. Spending the rest of the day with Jaworski in the most uncomfortable part of the house didn't appeal to him one bit.

Resigned, he stood up and went to the door. "If you're staying, we might as well get comfortable."

Jaworski followed him down the hall to the kitchen, where Evan pulled a Guinness out of the refrigerator. He stared at the dark bottle long and hard, then passed it to Joe with a sigh and went fishing again, for a bottle of Coke.

Jaworski gave him a hard look. "Got a problem with this?" He tilted the bottle to show his meaning, and Evan felt the embarrassment fuel his anger. Jaworski stared him down, not judging but waiting, as though he'd just given Evan some kind of dare and wanted to know if Evan was man enough to take it.

"Yeah." No point in blaming Jaworski, who had nothing to do with the craving that could still turn him inside out on days when Lily didn't come home or his father seemed more likely to disappear and be rid of a half-human bastard son. "Sometimes." And he wanted that bottle so bad it took all of his self-respect not to rip it right out of the man's hands and crack the seal on the countertop.

Jaworski knew, could see it in Evan's face, and fed him back the knowledge. "Yeah, well. I've known a good man or two with more nightmares than a bottle could handle. Do you have another Coke?" He leaned over the refrigerator and exchanged one bottle for another. Couldn't help but notice there wasn't a hell of a lot else in the fridge. "Don't eat much, I guess."

Evan shrugged. "It's just the three of us. None of us likes to cook, and we've got enough money that we don't have to."

"Don't let my wife hear that."

He wondered what Detective Michael Jaworski knew about nightmares, and what Mrs. Jaworski thought about her husband's job that gave his mouth that bitter twist. But the exchange shut down the line of easy talk with the realization, sharp as a knife, of the difference between them. Mike Jaworksi and Evan Davis might have the basic skills of their jobs in common, but Evan paid more in taxes than a police detective earned in a year. Jaworski probably figured that Evan did it without risking his neck as well, which was incorrect and raked up too many memories to be even ironically funny.

Jaworski took a swig of Coke, and Evan squirmed under the cold examination of the bruises on his face, the scabbed wound on his arm. He knew, Evan could feel it, that the life that came with the money sometimes asked more than a man could reasonably pay. Then Jaworski let his gaze slide away, giving Evan the option to call him on it or pretend it hadn't happened.

"Living room," Evan said, and the choice was made. "There's a couch calling your name."

Jaworski followed, accepting the line Evan had drawn between work and confidences. "Looks like Jackson Pollack's dropcloth," he said, and Evan laughed.

"I thought I was the only one who saw the resemblance."

Jaworski responded with a question: "Who picked it out?"

"Lily," Evan said, and Jaworski answered, "Oh."

It was all the explanation he needed. The cop was only a man, after all, and Lily was . . . Lily. It would take more than a flattop with a tattoo to stand up to Lily's supercilious frown, and Jaworski clearly empathized with any other male trying to enforce a matter of taste against that hauteur.

"Comfortable, though," Evan admitted. He opened the sliding glass door to let in a breeze from the garden, then excused himself. "I've got something I think you will be interested in. Be right back."

He left Jaworski reviewing the printouts of old case files and went to the family's private study. The computer now sat on the floor next to the splintered remains of the desk, but Evan found the materials he wanted on the beaten brass coffee table and swept them up in his free hand. He took a long drink of his Coke—it wouldn't settle his nerves any, but it would at least keep him awake—and headed back to the living room where Jaworski was staring at one of the Georgia O'Keeffe's on the wall, the papers in his hand forgotten for the moment on his lap.

"Are they real?"

"Uhuh. Lily likes them." He took the chair set at right angles to the sofa and didn't tell Jaworski what Lily said about O'Keeffe—that she liked a woman painter with the balls to paint genitals in pretty colors and sell them as flowers. Evan had pointed out to her on more than one occasion that O'Keeffe didn't paint genitals with balls, which would have been difficult to sell as flowers, but details never got in Lily's way.

"I think I may have a lead."

Jaworski gave up his contemplation of the paintings immediately. "What did you find?"

"I'm not sure how much it means to the case," Evan admitted. He handed Jaworski the sheaf of papers he'd carried in from the study. "Look, the objects stolen from the Philadelphia Museum of Art and the objects stolen from the University Museum. Do you see anything?"

Jaworski gave him a pained look. "I've looked at those lists until my eyes crossed. All of the items stolen were carved or sculpted out of jade, ivory, wood, or crystal. No snuff bottles. They're kept locked in a separate cabinet at the PMA, and scattered in a number of exhibit cases at the University Museum. The case the burglar broke into at the PMA had no snuff bottles in it. There was a snuff box in the burgled case at the university, but it was not taken. No textiles, no calligraphy or paintings were taken either. That's why we dismissed Harry Li as a suspect early on. He's primarily interested in ancient Chinese calligraphy. Nothing stolen matched the profile of his collecting interests by type or age."

He should have figured that Harry would be a suspect, though he'd dismissed the idea himself on the evidence that he was the only trustee taking action to prevent a burglary. While that might look like deliberate misdirection to the police, the agency's reputation didn't lend itself to that kind of manipulation. They'd caught and turned in their clients on more than one occasion. And on one, the client had ended up dead. No, Harry as burglar or mastermind didn't make sense.

"Of course he didn't do it. And actually," Evan admitted, "I'm not sure how much closer to finding the thief my discovery takes us. Look—here, here. The objects all originate in the same collection."

"Nope, check again, or I can bring over the printouts from the FBI databases. The objects were donated by at least three different individuals, at widely varied times." Sometime during the conversation Jaworski had stopped thinking of him as an annoying duty and started talking to him as a colleague. Evan hadn't noticed right away, and he was careful now not to call attention to it. He didn't want to call attention to his own change of opinion about the police detective either, but he acted on it, holding out the challenge:

"Not the donors; they're all white and English or American, not Chinese. The collection goes further back than that."

"You mean one person in China owned all that stuff?"

"Three guesses who."

Brad had started to put it together. Evan had noticed Seagrave's biography of the Empress on the desk this morning. Then the problem of Joe Dougherty and the damned DNA tests had pulled his attention away from the short-term task. Evan had remembered the book when he woke up in the study, but it was gone, burned as part of Brad's angry attempt to obliterate old memories. Once the idea had started gnawing away at the problem in Evan's head, it didn't take long to set the ferrets running in the system, and he'd come home to find they'd done their job again. He couldn't tell Jaworski how he'd pulled the information together, but the detective already had the data he needed.

Jaworski didn't take long. The light dawned with a smack to his own head. "The crystal ball stolen from the university is called the Dowager Empress Stone. It's from the Dowager Empress' collection? She died in, what?, 1910 or something?"

"1907," Evan confirmed the close date. "Peking was looted on a pretty regular basis from the Boxer Rebellion right up through Chairman Mao. There are pieces in the museum collections from a variety of great houses of the nobility, but the thieves only stole those items that came out of the Dowager Empress' personal quarters at the Imperial Palace."

"I don't know that much about Chinese art." Jaworski handed back the sheets of data. "If I remember my military history"—and Evan suspected that Mike Jaworski hadn't forgotten a thing about cold-war history—"the Chinese Communist government has spent most of the twentieth century trying to wipe out every vestige of the old empire, right down to destroying their own libraries.

"Besides, we're supposed to be buddies these days. All they'd have to do is ask nicely, and the State Department would be stripping museums as fast as the trucks could haul stuff out."

"Maybe—"

The sound of a door chime stopped the discussion. From the sound, it came from the side gate into the garden. Evan hit the lock release and stood in the doorway watching Joe Dougherty push the gate open and step cautiously onto the brick patio.

# Chapter 20

BRAD HADN'T EXPECTED TO FIND HER IN CHINATOWN, WHICH HE USUALLY associated with cheap restaurants: sticky linoleum tables and a deep cynicism hiding behind the submissive expressions of the staff. But there it was, the simple glass door of a million small businesses all over town sandwiched between a bustling warehouse on one side and a noodle factory on the other. On the top half of the door, the name of the company appeared in Chinese characters above and western transliteration below: Chang Er Imports, painted in red and gold for luck. The figure of a woman holding the moon flanked the written forms of the company name. If he'd had any doubts about the address, the rendering in a few sharp lines of Mai Sien Chong's features on the goddess put them to rest.

He tried the door, found it locked, and rang the bell. When the lock release clicked, he opened the door and stepped up into a tiny vinyl-tiled entryway and waited again until the street door closed and the door to another world opened on the inside.

"May I help you sir?" The woman at the polished mahogany desk watched him with a bland smile across a vast expanse of Chinese knotted-silk carpet.

"You can let Ms. Chong know that Kevin Bradley is here on business."

"Of course, sir. Would that be Ms. Lisa Chong, in sales, or one of our other Ms. Chongs?"

"Mai Sien Chong."

She pulled the mouthpiece of her telephone headset into place and pointed to a fragile looking arm chair tucked between an equally fragile small table on one side and a thick stand of bamboo rooted in a concrete tub set on the other.

"Have a seat, Mr. Bradley."

Brad wandered in the direction she indicated but remained standing, letting his gaze drift over the sweet green bamboo while he listened to the receptionist speaking rapid Chinese on the telephone. He should have thought to learn the language before coming, but he'd only have been guessing on the dialect.

"Mr. Hsi will be right here to escort you to Ms. Chong's office." The receptionist gave him a more welcoming smile this time, and returned to answering her telephone console. After a moment the door to the inner offices opened and a tall Chinese man in a suit with a bulge under the arm stepped through.

"Mr. Hsi, I presume?"

"This way." The man neither smiled nor indicated in any other way that he had heard the question. He waited at the door until Brad passed through, then followed him and pushed a button on a small panel. An elevator. It opened again on a hallway with marble-chip floors and Chinese watercolors on the walls that extended the length of several buildings the size of the facade out front. Brad figured Chang Er Imports had the upper floors over both the noodle factory and the warehouse, but none of the noise from the street seemed to penetrate the hushed elegance of the offices. The man—Brad presumed it was Mr. Hsi or the receptionist would have stopped him—headed down the hall to the southwestern corner of the block and knocked on a door which opened to reveal another impassive mountain with an automatic weapon strapped to the inside of his jacket.

"Brad! How did you find me?" Mai Sien Chong looked up. Her hair smoothed back and pinned out of the way gave her features a sharp quickness he hadn't noticed about her before. In some indefinable way, it reminded him of Lily. She rose from behind an oversized rosewood desk and came toward him across another carpet of tightly knotted silk laid over a teak floor. "I'll take care of Mr. Bradley."

She dismissed the guards, who made no pretense at any other function. When they had stepped out and closed the door, Mai Sien took his arm to draw him into the room. Hsi and his buddy would be waiting for him on the other side whether he spent five minutes or five hours in the office, he guessed. And they'd be inside with their guns drawn in less than a second if Mai Sien made the smallest sound of protest, which added a certain zest to the meeting. Kevin Bradley smiled.

"You know the board of directors of the Philadelphia Museum of Art has hired my agency to locate and assist in the return to them of a number of Chinese artifacts stolen from the museum earlier this week."

"Mmm." She guided him to the low platform sofa against one parchment-colored wall and pulled him down to sit beside her. "The discussion you had with the Lis at the club yesterday had something to do with your case, then?"

"Exactly." Brad paused to take an appreciative look around her office, a hybrid blend of West and East common among the intellectual ranks of the nobility in late-nineteenth-century China. Large stone pots holding a bamboo plant or two were scattered in several corners. Carved rosewood screens with greased parchment inset in the upper portion of each panel flanked one wall. Golden light glowed through the parchment; Brad figured the screens must hide the windows on the street side of the building.

A couple of delicate armchairs like the one downstairs were placed about the room, as were some fragile carved tables and small desks with the tools of a Chinese scribe on them—a carved wrist rest, an inkstone, and an alabaster cylinder with a few calligraphy brushes standing in it. She had just a few hangings on the walls, examples of fine calligraphy except for one watercolor scroll over the couch.

The room didn't surprise him much, but she did. At the chess club most of the players dressed casually, including Harry and Ellen. Brad usually wore a suit. He didn't think it likely that any human currently alive— except Evan, of course—would guess his real name and bind him to his or her will. If he were inclined to believe in a talisman, however, it would be the three-button single-breasted business suit. When he wore it, he felt invulnerable; a golf shirt or tennis shorts just didn't compare. Mai Sien Chong usually wore a traditional cheongsam in brilliant silk, so he hadn't expected to see her wearing tailored linen slacks and a wide-sleeved open-necked shirt of pearl gray silk, and he felt a sudden dislocation, as if time had shifted. For a moment he had a flickering awareness of another figure imposed upon Mai Sien's: a shorter woman, with a massive headdress and heavy robes embroidered in pearls and precious gems.

Then it was gone; he realized, for a distracted minute, that he'd never seen her throat before, had never seen the delicate hollow at its base that drew his eyes down past the open collar to the promise of breasts, just out of sight unless he took the point of her shirt collar and spread it, like so . . . She looked down at his fingers, watched him as he folded back the collar with a gesture like the caress of a flower petal, and smiled.

Mai Sien took his head between her hands, tapered nails polished a deep blood red carding through his hair. "Your timing could have been better." She pulled him toward her mouth, rubbing the side of her face against his before taking him in a kiss. "I have an afternoon appointment."

Brad sat, fingers poised at the opening of her blouse, beset with more sensations than he'd ever felt at one time. Well, perhaps second most sensations, but this time none of them included pain, and his mind stopped, overpowered by the confused and confusing responses of the flesh he wore. He wanted to merge with her as his kind did in the second sphere, to become her, to open his soul to the universe and fill it, fill it with his sensations as she would fill it with hers, and he would know her as he knew his own kind, and revel in their sharing.

But she was mortal, and flesh had ideas of its own. His hand fell, curled around the curve of her breasts and found them infinitely softer than he had imagined when he'd watched them press against the tight fabric of her cheongsam. He didn't know what to do when her lips found his ear, but he felt the insistent pressure of her hand on the back of his head and bent to her neck, his lips playing across the soft skin behind her ear, where the hair swept away in its disciplined coil of pins. She smelled of incense and midnight, and when he couldn't pull together a coherent thought if Azmod himself came down to accost him, Mai Sien lifted his head away and asked him again, "How did you find me?" She nuzzled his jaw to take the sting out of the words. "Not that I'm complaining."

"The case." He wanted to touch her, but when she held him at arm's length, out of the immediate influence of her perfume and her skin, the words came back to him. "Evan compiled a list of collectors. Your name was on it."

"I'm a dealer, not a collector," she corrected. "And a small dealer at that, as a courtesy to our customers."

"Your primary business is industrial—textiles, small machine parts," Brad completed. For some reason he didn't mention the Hong Kong chat room where a computer name he traced to her offices had come up in a discussion of high-level gold trading. Nothing illegal in it, but he'd come to see her because it was a fact that didn't fit. Unfortunately, her fingers were working their way around the back of his head again, kneading at his skull and sending an overload of conflicting messages, soothing relaxation and tingling awareness, to a part of his brain that he hadn't known he possessed until this moment. The body he wore moved closer to her of its own volition, as if the gravitational pull of her skin had taken control of his movements.

"Stop!" she said, and his muddled brain wondered who she was talking to, until she clarified with "Brad!"

But she was smiling when he looked at her with a question in his eyes, and she rubbed her forehead affectionately against his.

"If this continues in the direction it seems to be heading, the Hsi brothers will come crashing through that door in about five minutes to rescue me," she explained, "and I don't want to be rescued. At least not until morning."

Taking Brad by the hand she pulled him to his feet. "Let's get out of here."

"Your appointment—"

"Another reason to make our escape while we can."

She went to the door and opened it a crack to talk to the guards, giving Brad a chance to clear his mind. He remembered sex from the last time, with Evan's mother, but it hadn't been like this. They'd both been awkward. She'd been frightened and eager, and he'd tucked his rage away in the coldest part of his soul and had played out his part without feeling much of anything. As he recalled, she hadn't gotten much pleasure out of it either, but it had done the job. She'd lost her virginity and her fiancé, and nine months later Evan made an appearance. By then the jealous boyfriend was dead, and Badad the daemon had gone home to his eternal darkness and the business of Princes. He'd experienced nothing like this before, but he finally began to understand what Evan saw in it.

"We'll take the back elevator to my car." The Hsi brothers had disappeared, and Mai Sien reached for his arm again, guided him out of the office and down the short bit of hall to the elevator on the end opposite where he'd come in. "No one will see us," she promised.

The elevator stopped at an underground parking level and Brad followed her to her car, a black Seville with corporate tags, and slid into the passenger seat.

"We'll be home in no time."

She promised more than a short ride with her smile, and Brad sat back, wondering where they were going, and what they would do when they arrived, and what connection a firm that imported textiles and machine parts from China had with the gold trade. And did that connection lead any further than a conservative investment philosophy?

# Chapter 21

"WHAT DO YOU WANT?" EVAN COULD FEEL THE SUBTLE SHIFT IN THE AIR AS Mike Jaworski came to attention behind him.

"I came to apologize." Dougherty held onto the gate, clearly unsure of his welcome, and afraid to let go of his lifeline to the street. "I didn't mean for you to hear that, in the meeting this afternoon."

"No," Evan agreed. "You just wanted to convince my father, my lawyer, and the police I have to work with on this case that I am an emotional incompetent. You want them to believe that I had such a sick need for a father that I'd latched onto the first rich older man who offered for the part."

"He's dangerous. That security guard he nearly killed at the museum is still unconscious, and they can't figure out why." Dougherty let go of the gate and took a step forward, but Evan didn't move aside or invite him in.

"That's your theory. Doesn't jibe with Brad's story or the evidence gathered by the police actually working the case either." Which didn't mean Dougherty was wrong, except that while Brad might lie to just about everyone else on the mortal plane, he hadn't ever bothered to lie to Evan.

"I don't have proof I can take to a judge," Dougherty continued, "but I know he had something to do with the explosion in New York a few years ago, the one that killed fifty people in that bar. We have the connection—you met him there—and we know he was supposed to be working on a case for the owner, who turned up dead. All we need is a witness who puts him in the area and we've got him."

"You have no evidence." Certainly no witnesses. They'd all died when Badad of the host of Ariton lost his temper.

Dougherty read some part of the truth in his eyes and took a step back. "Can't you see what he's done to you?"

"You're the one who can't see, Joe." And now there could be no mistake about the threat in the set of Evan's face. "I was always as dangerous as my father."

"That's why you spent two days unconscious in the hospital, right?"

"Happens sometimes, when you ride the whirlwind." Evan smiled. He didn't think about it, that smile—ironic, with secrets peeking from the corners of his eyes—but it seemed to unnerve Joe Dougherty more than anything Evan had said, and when Evan finished with, "Go away, Joe. You are out of your league," the sergeant took a step back as if he expected Evan to strike him dead on the spot.

"There isn't anything I can say?"

"Try good-bye." Evan turned to the living room, leaving Joe Dougherty holding the gate open in indecision. Evan had more important things on his mind. Like smoothing things over with Mike Jaworski, who was studying Evan's face now with the same alert attention he'd given the conversation he'd eavesdropped on in the garden.

That, too, would have to wait. Evan heard a mumble of pardon me's and then Harry Li's voice. "Evan, do you have a minute? I need to talk to you."

And damn it, Mike Jaworski was laughing.

"Betsy Ross House is five blocks north and two east." Evan pointed to the front of the house in an exaggerated show of giving directions to tourists, but Harry just patted him on the shoulder and gave him a nudge into the house and out of the doorway.

"Detective Jaworski, Ellen said I'd find you here. I'm to fill you both in, since it was my discovery. She'd have come herself, but she thought you'd take it better from me."

Evan didn't like the sound of that, especially when Mike Jaworski added, "Isn't that a bit irregular, Professor?"

"How long have you been working this case, Detective?"

Jaworski nodded. "Point taken. It's been irregular from the start. I hope the lieutenant knows what she is doing."

"Be assured."

Evan filed Harry Li's answer away for later. Right now, his attention focused on the laptop computer tucked under Harry's arm.

"I believe that belongs to me," he said.

Harry Li cast his eyes down in apology. "May I have a seat, Evan?"

That didn't bode well. "Do you really mean a minute or two, Harry, or should I call for supper?"

Harry perked up and smiled. "French would be very nice."

Evan hit the direct dialer. "Anybody specifically hate anything French?"

"Sweetbreads," Jaworski answered. He already had his cell phone out, and he fell into muttered conversation while Evan gave his order on the ground line.

"Be here in an hour or so." He pulled a second chair over to join Jaworski on the sofa and Harry in the chair closest. "Okay, Harry, what is it that Ellen is afraid to tell me."

"You left this in the board meeting room at the museum." Harry gave the laptop to Jaworski, who handed it on to Evan. "Ellen had her computer experts at headquarters crack your password."

Evan stared at the machine as if it had grown horns and curved fangs. *"Et tu, Brute?"* he muttered under his breath. He wondered who had cracked the password, and if they had used a random number generator, or someone had actually psyched him out. And he wondered what insights they may have gained into his mind just picking through his files. But they weren't his shrink, he wasn't a kid anymore, and he had an expensive lawyer who made sure he didn't have to put up with people trashpicking through his life anymore.

"That's an invasion of privacy I didn't expect from you, Harry." He found it hard to admit to himself that he'd just scratched Harry Li off the short list of people he trusted, and he wondered at the cyclical wave of his life, that had taken him for a brief span of years into peace and a bit of confidence that the universe didn't have a personal grudge against him and now seemed to be grabbing him in a nasty undertow. Shit. "If I'd known, I'd have ordered pizza. With anchovies."

Harry gave an elaborate shudder, but Jaworski interrupted before Evan could tell whether he meant to apologize or justify his actions.

"Ellen's list called for the police to have access to specific files, including your case files on the present investigation. Were those files on the laptop?"

"Some notes on the current case. The rest had nothing to do with the museum's case."

In fact, he didn't keep much of anything on the laptop. The access software to their internet service provider and to AOL just because they were big and sometimes worth keeping an ear on. Some old software he'd never gotten around to deleting, and one or two specialized programs of his own that would take some work to get past standard browser functions. Evan didn't think the police had had their hands on the computer itself long enough to figure those items out, but he'd bet that some keyboard jockey at the roundhouse had pulled them off to diddle them on his own time. His mind drifted for a moment over a menu of possible fixes.

"Evan? Evan!" Harry was standing over him with a stern frown. "Don't do that, it frightens the policeman."

"Is he okay?" Jaworski did look worried. "Did he have a fit or something?" The question carried a subtext he'd heard a lot as a kid, less since his father'd gotten his head straight. The real question was always, "Is he freaking out? Does he need a padded cell and a straightjacket?" Evan had never quite understood it, but fortunately Harry knew him all too well.

"He's fine, detective. He gets that glazed look when he is doing in his head the sort of thing most of us do with paper and pencils or computers. What was it this time, Evan? Figuring a way to make your password tamper-proof?"

"Trying to remember if any of my software has cracks in it." He thought he'd been pretty cryptic with that answer, but Jaworski looked indignant.

"Lieutenant Li asked to see only document files, not software. And if you are as smart as the professor here thinks you are, you won't give me any reason to ask a judge to add software to the list and make it official with a warrant."

"Ellen said to tell you, specifically, that they only looked at the files on her list, that she stood next to the cryptographer while he worked on the machine, and he never went near any other files, but she suggests that you retire any software you think may have suddenly become obsolete." Harry gave a moment to reflection. "Oh, yes, and perhaps you should take your time replacing it."

"That's the message?"

"Part of it. I didn't want to deliver her message at all. I have valued your confidences and feel that the invasion of your personal computer has compromised my honor with you. For myself, I have come to beg your forgiveness and to humbly ask for your continued assistance." Harry bowed low before him, a sight which Evan found more shocking than the idea that Ellen Li would hack his laptop.

"What can I do that Ellen can't?" Evan challenged him, but Mike Jaworski stole the floor with a snort.

"You are not a stupid man, Evan Davis, and I suspect that our Sergeant Dougherty has about as much sense of what you are about as the man in the moon. But clearly Ellen, and our professor here, have you figured well enough to guess what the software that 'isn't on your laptop' does. It's homebrew if I make my guess, and I *don't* want to know what it does. But you've already given me a lead we didn't have, so I'm with the professor. And one thing I will vouch for—if Ellen Li said nobody looked, it's the truth."

Evan covered his eyes with one hand and let his head fall back against the putty-colored cushion, the down stuffing cradling the back of his neck. "Okay. Okay." Evan couldn't believe he was saying it, but he decided that it was easier to give in, to accept that maybe trust with humans could be as complicated as the kind he had with his daemon kin. "Will somebody get the door—it's the side gate, with the food."

"You got a wallet, rich boy?" Jaworski was standing in a patch of late afternoon sunlight, stretching out the kinks in a long reach for the ceiling that twisted into a craning effort to see beyond the garden gate.

"Julien knows to put it on the tab. Have him bring the boxes into the kitchen." Evan wandered out of the living room with Harry trailing behind him and Jaworski's plaintive cry—"Don't say anything until I get back"— floating on the air behind them.

Mike Jaworski scooped up a forkful of venison in a wild berry reduction sauce. "So, what is the big news that Ellen sent you over with?" he asked before popping the forkful into his mouth. Harry gave him a moment to recover from the pleasure of the flavors and then tossed his news onto the table.

"Although a number of collectors over several decades donated the artworks stolen from the university and the art museum in our two related cases, when you track the artwork back to its original owner in China, you find it all belonged to Lady Yehenara."

"Who?" Jaworski asked. "Evan had it figured as the Dowager Empress."

"Yehenara *was* the Dowager Empress of China." Evan delivered the *coup de grâce* with a smug grin, partly out of humor, and partly out of the sort of challenge that in tribes of chimpanzees would be carried out with much beating of chests.

"Yes," Harry said. "But Ellen put in a call to the State Department, and the Chinese government hasn't said a thing to them about repatriating the art. State figures they've got their hands full with Hong Kong, so it's unlikely that the government is behind it."

"Are there any royalists left in China?" Jaworski asked between mouthfuls of the venison and the honeyed carrot mousse.

Harry shook his head sadly. "Westerners just don't get it," he said. "There weren't any royalists when the Ch'ings were in power. In the first place, they weren't Chinese, they were Manchu, and they took power the same way the Japanese did—by invasion. In the second place, they were weak rulers at a time when China needed a strong government to meet the Western encroachments. The Chinese never forgave the Ch'ing for losing the Opium Wars to the British—that was the beginning of the end for them, though they hung on, what with one thing and another, for sixty years or more. Then, when the Communists came to power, they finished the job the British had started on the nobles and the intellectuals. By the time the Red Guard were finished, you had a country in anarchy running solely on its hatred of education. Anybody who would have cared about the emperor or the treasures of empire was dead."

"Taiwan?" Jaworski suggested, but Evan and Harry shook their heads in tandem.

"Has its hands full keeping Mainland China off their doorstep," Evan filled in the reason, and added, "Could be a job a professional syndicate took on for one of half a dozen collectors in America or Europe with an Empire fetish. If it is one of them, we should be able to solve the case in a week or two."

He didn't mention that the agency's methods included travel through the second sphere into the vaults of those collectors and traveling back out again with the artifacts in tow, and no one the wiser for their having come and gone. Ellen wouldn't be pleased if they came home without a suspect to put on trial, but Bradley, Ryan and Davis only contracted for the art, not the burglars—they felt a kinship with that side of the trade too keenly to give up their brother thieves.

"If one of the offshore Chinese syndicates contracted the job, we may never find it," he finally admitted a bit glumly.

"Ah," Harry said, "but we have the coins and the book. They have a tradition of centuries, we have a tradition of millennia. I will put my money on our methods."

"The coins?" Mike Jaworski was looking a bit disgruntled. "You know, if we were talking about a Vermeer, I wouldn't sound half so stupid."

"Just think of it as therapy for the emotional cripple," Evan suggested. "I haven't had anyone to feel superior to since we got rid of Joe."

"He's really not such a bad guy when he bothers to pull his head out of his butt." With that last half-hearted endorsement, Jaworksi wiped his mouth and got up from the table.

"My wife will be mad enough when I come home late with French food on my breath, gentlemen. If I don't want to sleep on the back porch tonight, I'd better be going. Evan, I'll take those papers home with me and look them over. For all our sakes, I hope it turns out to be one of your Western collectors."

Evan followed him to the living room to make sure he picked up the sheaf of laser printed documents and saw him to the garden gate. "I'll let you know if we find anything," he promised.

Jaworski nodded. "You've got my number."

When Evan turned around, Harry was watching him with that gleam in his eyes that Evan had learned to mistrust. And he had his battered, leather-bound copy of the *I Ching* in his hand. "Shall we get to work?"

"Tomorrow, Harry. Around nine, my office, with the *I Ching*?" Evan figured if his mother had waited this long for an explanation, a few more hours wouldn't hurt. He'd make the trek out to the Northeast in the afternoon. Maybe Harvey would be there to calm his mother down after they'd had their little talk.

"You've gone away again, Evan. Got to watch that."

Evan waited in the doorway until Harry took the hint. "Very well. Tomorrow morning. But you won't find the crystal ball in some European bank vault." With that last parting shot Harry gave him a slight bow and let himself out through the gate. Evan meant to return to the house, but he found himself moving deeper into the garden, thinking of Lily and the long ago Empress who had treasured the three mysterious crystals. Lily won out, and his dream came crashing back with such power that he could almost feel her skin beneath his fingers tracing the vee of her shirt, growing deeper and wider as he undid one button, then another, then another. Her fingers, cool and sure teasing his body for the pleasure the power over him gave her. But Lily hadn't come home yet. Neither had Brad. And he had files to review. So he left the breezes and the growing dark and went back into the house.

# Chapter 22

After the promised few minutes the Seville turned down the ramp to a parking garage under a fashionable high rise in the Rittenhouse Square area. Brad climbed out of the car and followed Mai Sien Chong to the elevator, thinking. She'd gone from the underground parking at Chang Er Imports to the underground parking at the Rittenhouse. The members' entrance to the Franklin Mercantile Chess Club likewise let them into the building through the parking garage; after dinner at Susannah Foo's, he had walked her back to the club for her car, not the four blocks or so to her building.

"Do you have a problem with sunlight?" he asked when she keyed in her floor on the elevator panel. It was a gauche question, and he regretted it almost as much as the one he really had on his mind but refrained from speaking aloud: Are you hiding from someone?

She slanted him a mocking smile. "Don't tell me you believe in vampires!"

"Just beautiful women with delicate skin," he corrected her apprehension, not mentioning that someone in the Hong Kong chat room had referred to her computer identity as a vampire of the economic kind.

"An excellent save," she granted him. "And you don't have to admit your ignorance about the ghouls in the dark that frighten Chinese children at bedtime. Our vampires are the souls of the dead ancestors who have not been properly honored by their relatives. As vampires they are a hardier breed than your Western ones and would never dream of evaporating in sunlight."

"Have you always honored your ancestors?" She seemed so completely Westernized today that he wondered about the cheongsam and the ghost story, but Mai Sien tilted him a wry nod.

"Always. Who wants old grandmother nagging after she is dead?"

"If grandmother is a nag, then placate her by all means," he agreed.

The elevator doors opened to a hallway carpeted in a plush beige that would have shown any dirt that had the temerity to land on its hallowed halls. Mai Sien passed an electronic key over a swipe pad and pressed five buttons. Brad thought the door would click open then, but nothing happened at all except for the sounding of chimes. After a moment a middle-aged Chinese woman in a domestic's uniform opened the door. She bowed her head as she welcomed them in.

"Mr. Hsi called ahead and said you would be bringing company." The domestic closed the door after them. "There are several items in the refrigerator for dinner—a lovely salmon, and a beefsteak with spicy seasonings the gentleman might enjoy."

When she turned to pick up her purse from the table next to the door, Brad noticed the snub-nosed thirty-eight snugged against the small of the housekeeper's back. He waited until she had taken her leave with a final, "If you need me for anything before morning, madam, I'll be downstairs." Then he turned to Mai Sien, who seemed to anticipate the question:

"Are we expecting an invasion?"

"Not 'we.' Uncle Chong." She took his arm and led him into the living area, a room with sweeping scale heightened by the sparse but elegant furnishing. "He pulled a great deal of the firm's money out of Hong Kong before the takeover, and he believes with all his heart that Beijing will send spies and strongmen to take it back." A western-style couch the color of champagne marked a sinuous curve through the width of the penthouse; most of the seating faced out into the room, except for one arc that curved in around the serpentine fireplace. Brad thought that she would stop there at the fireplace, but she walked past it, her arm tucked in his, across a broad expanse of pale carpet to a small altar set in an alcove close to a wall of windows. She stopped a moment to light three sticks of incense at the altar, then drew him through a sliding glass door onto a narrow balcony with a breathtaking view of the city.

"Uncle Chong says the Mainland Chinese are waiting until after they repatriate Maçao." She leaned on the railing, the light from the apartment gilding the curve of her back and her arms and casting her face in shadow. "Beijing wants to prove it can co-exist with the capitalists because it wants Taiwan. Once Beijing achieves its goal of unifying China's territory, Uncle Chong believes that the strongmen will target the overseas corporations like Uncle's. So he ensures that the family take precautions."

Which explained the gold trading and even the armed guards, he supposed. Brad wondered what other precautions good old Uncle Chong was making for the future. At the moment, however, he was more interested in the curve of Mai Sien's neck. Strange, that he had known her for a year or more and had never noticed the elegance of it, or the way her throat, her jaw, her temple, demanded his touch. He reached for her, to reassure himself that the cool sculpt of her face had not truly faded in the night, and she turned into the curve of his hand, brushing his palm with her lips.

"Old soul," she whispered into his palm, and the feel of her breath on his flesh tightened the skin on his arms and on the back of his neck. Old soul. Tonight he felt time as flesh did, in the beat of his heart and the pulse of his blood, and he would have contradicted her: not old, but new, just born in this moment.

She was right, of course. He had known the court of the Sun King and in his own true form had experienced the creation of her universe as it washed over the spheres. Alfredo Da'Costa had called it an accident, interpenetration of two spheres never meant to meet. The material sphere came into being as a patch on the weakened barrier between the spheres, and in its creation it knew both time and space. But he could not believe that the response of his human body to the feel of her tongue on the palm of his hand was the product of an accident. Some things, he decided when she looked up at him, her eyes crinkled at the edges in a smile, had more purpose than anything the Princes had ordained in all their eternity.

"Old soul," she repeated looking up at him with eyes that suddenly seemed older than her body. "I see it in the way you look out at the world, as if you've seen it all before and wait only for the wheel to turn again, the next lesson to begin."

Brad wondered what she saw, how much she understood, and for a moment he knew an old fear. Did he have a name in China? Did she know it? Or was it all a game, a psych-out calculated to amaze like a store-front fortune-teller? She took his hand in hers and led him through a different door, to a room with a bed covered in emerald satin, and she kissed him. His mouth skimmed lightly over her lipstick until that gravitational pull exerted itself on his body again and he moved toward her, body against body, mouth against mouth, and he wanted to taste more of her: her throat, her jaw, her breasts, her belly, the curve of her ankle and the curve between her legs. He knew he wanted more, but his memories of when he had done this before did not bring pleasure, and he didn't, exactly, know how to make it better.

She must have felt his sudden reticence, because she took a step back and looked up at him, puzzled.

"We don't have to do this if you don't want to," she said, and smiled to show she meant it. "I am attracted to you"—she touched his face, and the icy flames of her fingertips tightened his body all over.—"The only *game* I want to play with you is chess."

He didn't believe her, of course, but he wanted this thing that his body craved, and her body seemed to know what that was. Her hand traced a path down his throat to his breast, and he held it there, pressed over his heart, which was turning over in his chest in a manner he hadn't known internal organs could do. "I'm not sure what I should do."

"Anything you want." Then her expression changed as a new idea struck. "You have a son?" She took her hand back and linked it with the other behind her back, out of his reach.

"That was procreation."

She seemed about to offer a tart witticism but backed off it. Instead, she looked him up and down and began to circle him. "You didn't love her?" Mai Sien was behind him now; his back itched as if she held a knife to it.

"That wasn't part of the bargain."

She seemed to take that in and mull it for a moment, circling round again, but with her eyes down, studying his body. "And since?"

She swept a quick glance at his face. Brad gave her a rueful grin and shook his head. "That wasn't part of the bargain either."

"I see." She was circling again, passing out of sight beyond his left elbow. The tension made him dizzy. "You're not attracted to women, then?"

"I didn't give it much thought until today." Which was a lie. He'd been thinking about Mai Sien's body yesterday, watching Evan with Lily in his study. He'd been thinking about touching her later, over dinner at Susanna Foo's. When he'd walked her back to her car and seen her on her way home, he'd suppressed the urge to follow her and wrap her sleep with his being as daemon lord of the host of Ariton. Even then he'd known that only flesh would satisfy the craving for the touch of flesh she'd ignited in his brain. But she was behind him and had only the tension in his back, the sharply erect way he held his head, to read.

"Men, then?"

"Not lately, no." Not the right answer, he suspected. Gender wasn't relevant to his kind, and he hadn't quite figured out the protocols of sex and gender among humans. But Mai Sien, circling to the front, just raised an eyebrow, appraising him like a sculpture. Or a lamb chop.

"And how do you feel about women today?" Out of sight behind him again, she whispered the question in his ear, and he shivered in anticipation—

"I feel," he told the empty wall in front of him with perhaps more force than he would have liked to show. Those two words told more than she would ever know of how she affected him. Because she would not understand, he completed what he had started: "that, if you continue to stand just out of reach like that, I will burn away at your feet. Which would undoubtedly ruin this fine carpet."

"Ahhh." Circling around, she faced him again. "We wouldn't want to ruin the carpet." All promises and mischief, she smiled. "Much better to ruin the sheets."

"But how?" She must have read the frustration in the lines of his body, because Brad was certain he'd kept expression off his face. After a leisurely moment of consideration—of the question and of his body—she smiled. "Slowly, I think. And with great attention to detail."

He should have asked Lily, maybe practiced while they were at it. Then he wouldn't be standing here in the middle of Mai Sien's bedroom with no idea what to do next that would lead them anywhere but toward disaster and Mai Sien looking him over as if he were her own personal birthday present and she was trying to decide how to unwrap him. And there was a realization that broke him out in a cold sweat. Whatever else he might be ignorant of, he did know he couldn't do this in a suit.

"Sit down." Mai Sien pushed him into an upholstered boudoir chair. She seemed to glide over to the bed, one arm curved around her head, pulling the pins out of her hair. When she reached the bed she kicked off her shoes and tossed the hairpins onto a cabinet, next to a chilling bottle of champagne and two graceful flutes.

"Do the honors?" she asked, bringing the bottle back to Brad in the chair. In her other hand she carried the flutes. He took the bottle and she stood too close, shaking out her hair while he twisted the cork out of the bottle.

"Mr. Hsi's idea?" Brad asked as he poured the wine into the glasses.

"Mrs. Zheng's, actually. She is quite the treasure." Mai Sien waited until he set the bottle down and then handed him a sparkling flute. She stood so close that he could feel the heat from her inner thighs against his knees. "A crack markswoman as well," she finished, "trained in the PAL until the lure of the West and family loyalty brought her to us."

"To Mrs. Zheng, then."

PAL: the Red Army. He wondered how deeply Uncle Chong's mainland connections ran, and to what purpose. But when he thought about connections running deep, his mind wandered to his body again, which wanted to run itself as deep into Mai Sien Chong as it could and didn't give a damn about Uncle Chong or the PAL.

He began to raise his glass to drink the toast, but she stopped him with a touch.

"No," she said, reaching for the buttons of her blouse. "To our night. Let there be joy here." And he would have dropped the champagne flute, except that her hand left the buttons to close over his and squeeze until he had a firm grip on the glass again.

Watching her, he lifted his glass when she raised hers, touched his glass to his lips as her glass touched her lips. When the muscles of her throat moved, he could feel the golden wine pour down his own throat, and when she licked her lips he could taste her kiss on his mouth. When his eyes fell to the front of her blouse she smiled and returned to work on the buttons, freeing them slowly. One by one. Until he would have reached for her and torn them open, except that part of the wanting was in the tension, and he wanted to savor that feeling as well. So he held his hands still as her blouse opened and fell away to reveal a tiny bra, just a scrap of satin holding her up, and she released the hook. The bra fell to the floor and her breasts relaxed against her rib cage. They were softer than he expected, and they swayed gently when she moved.

Still he held back, so she handed him her champagne glass, grinning at the way she had hobbled him with a glass in each hand now. She undid her belt and released it, unhooked her slacks and slid the zipper down—he would have offered to do that with his teeth, the idea had a certain piquant charm, but he kept his silence, waiting, while the slacks fell to her feet and left her in nothing but a satiny scrap of underpants.

"Tell me what you want," she said, slipping out of the last bit of satin. "Tonight you are a king."

Naked, she knelt at his feet, rubbed the side of her face against his knees, and she did not smile when she looked up at him, but let him see the mystery deep in her eyes. "Tell me what you want."

"I want to touch you." He dropped the glasses to the carpet where they rolled, spilling a few golden drops of wine until they came to rest at either side of the chair, and then he reached for her, let his fingertips trace the delicate line of her collar bones, smoothed his hands nearly the length of her, following the curves of breast and waist and hips. The mounds of her buttocks filled his palms with smooth flesh glowing gold in the room's shaded light. He wanted to crush her to his body, to take all of her inside of himself and know her from the inside out, as if she were a host-cousin at home in the second sphere. But she was human, and flesh was giving him enough to think about. Right now, it was telling him it wanted out of the business suit.

She reached past his questing hands and he felt her fingertips, deftly separating buttons from their buttonholes on Carlo Pimi's fine swiss cotton shirt. The buttons were open, and she slid closer, between his legs, holding the layers of jacket and shirt open with a hand on either side.

"What do you want?" she breathed against his skin, and then her mouth found his belly, his chest, her tongue licked at the base of his throat while her hands worked at his belt. "What do you want?"

But he was awash in sensations he hadn't known existed, and he could not speak, could breathe only with an effort of will because all of his awareness wanted to focus down tight on the feel of her fingers and her mouth and the slow glide of her breasts against his belly, and he wanted her to touch the penis that rose out of the trousers and briefs she had pulled out of the way, wanted to feel all of her against his skin, and when she moved and her breasts brushed against his swollen flesh, he grunted softly, not sure what was polite, when flesh had a mind of its own.

She kissed him there, and he thought he would die, that the heart in his chest would simply explode, and he wondered, if he shaped a new body to replace the one she killed with her touch, would she do that to him again, if he asked very nicely?

She smiled. "Here or on the bed?" she asked, and that question, phrased as a simple option, clicked his brain into gear.

"Bed," he said, thinking of satin against his skin, against hers, and she rose between his legs and pushed the jacket and shirt off his shoulders, let them drop onto the chair before she took his hand and pulled him after her, to his feet.

There was no graceful way out of the trousers and briefs at his ankles, so he made them disappear. Fortunately, Mai Sien had turned toward the bed just then, drawing him after her with small, sinuous steps.

He followed her to the bed, followed her down when she lay upon it, and she curled her arm around his back, holding him close, and asked again, "What do you want?"

This time, he knew the answer, though it surprised him when he said it. "I want to make you smile."

"Then touch me." She traced the line of his temple, the curve of his ear, and when her fingertips moved to his mouth, he reached up and took her hand, pressed each finger to a kiss, and caressed her palm with a whisper touch of his lips. He kissed her wrist and licked it, feeling the warmth of life pulsing through it, and nuzzled at her elbow, her shoulder, until his mouth found her breast and she sighed, her body drifting like a petal on the sea of green sheets. Like a lotus petal. At the thought, petals fell like a gentle rain in the room, on the bed, in her hair. He rolled over, covering her with his body, and their weight crushed the flower petals beneath them, releasing their mysterious perfume to mix with the scent of their heated bodies and the moist earth smell of sex.

He smiled when her arms wrapped his head and dragged his mouth to hers, when her body curled up to meet his, and when he put his hand between her legs she rode him, hot and ready. And he entered her, confident that the one thing he had learned about this body over the past four years was how to prevent fertility.

She cried out beneath him, her nails scratching at his back, and the sensations were too much; he felt his shape waver and firmed it again, but as release approached, he felt himself grow larger, change. She shivered inside, holding him, and he lost control.

While his body pumped of its own volition, he heard a scream, not pain but terror, and tried to pull his senses together around the elation and the lethargy. Mai Sien was beating at his breast and shoulders, screaming and weeping, and he pulled away, wondering what he could have done so wrong until he saw his own hand on the sheet. Blue. With scales. His carefully buffed fingernails looked more like claws of dirty horn. Shit. When had that happened? He bolted upright in the bed and tried to cover himself with the satin sheets, but the claws on his hands poked holes in the fabric, so he tried to maneuver it with just the pads of his scaled fingers, with little more success.

"I can explain," he tried to say, but the words rumbled out of a strange throat an octave deeper than his own voice, and Mai Sien was cowering in a corner with the coverlet wrapped around her. She was naked underneath it, he knew, and that thought stirred his anatomy—his entirely too blue, too impressive anatomy—currently holding the sheet at attention. He *did not* want to know what face he wore at that moment. And, oh lords of Ariton, they were banging at the door. Mrs. Zheng, no doubt, and a Mr. Hsi or two, with weapons that couldn't hurt him, but would take some explaining to the management when the repair slip came in. He pulled his scattered mind together enough to regain his human form and hold up his hands, palms out, in a gesture of surrender.

"Please. I won't hurt you." A human voice, thank the lords of Ariton; not quite his own yet, but getting closer. "Don't make me hurt anyone else."

She stared from him to the door, licked her lips as she thought over what he'd said. He wanted to kiss her when she did that, but he didn't think now was the time to mention it. Finally, as the bedroom door began to open from the other side, Mai Sien climbed to her feet, still wrapped in the coverlet, and met Mrs. Zheng, snub-nosed .38 drawn and ready in the doorway, with a Mr. Hsi right behind her. Mai Sien said a few words in Chinese, Mrs. Zheng answered more sharply, and Mai Sien said a few more words with a deprecating shrug and a shaky smile. Mrs. Zheng didn't seem to buy the story, but she let the door close in her face. Mai Sien seemed calmer, but she skirted the bed and went over to the chair where his coat and shirt lay. She did not look at him until she had settled herself into the chair with her coverlet wrapped around her.

"I told them I saw a spider. Mrs. Zheng didn't believe me, but I told her I thought it was a poisonous one and that you killed it for me."

"Did she believe you the second time?" Brad asked, relieved to hear his own voice again.

Mai Sien shook her head. "Probably not. I expect she thinks that you are beating me, but she doesn't want to interfere if that is what I want from you."

The thought made him queasy. He'd pulled his son out of enough bad situations to know that Evan hadn't liked being hurt, and his own few experiences with pain hadn't demonstrated its appeal either. "Do you often want abuse from your lovers?"

"No." Mai Sien pulled the coverlet more tightly around herself, though it hadn't slipped, Brad noticed. Her answer left him wondering if she liked abuse occasionally or not at all, and what she expected him to do about it. He rather hoped that her lover turning blue and scaly during sex would suffice as adventuresome romance.

Mai Sien appeared to regain her composure; at least, she didn't seem to anticipate an imminent death. She'd even gotten enough of her usual nerve back to ask a question. "What are you?"

"Right now, I'm a man." He checked under the satin sheet. Yes, all of him, still a man. "I can be something else, if you have a preference." That answer didn't go over well, but he figured he'd make the offer.

"Are you an evil spirit?"

Trick question.

"Not particularly evil, I should think." At least among his own kind he didn't seem out of the norm. He considered disappearing—he could be out of there faster than her mind could register the experience—but that would pretty much put an end to Wednesday night chess. So he reached for his clothes in the space between the spheres, envisioned them on his body. Unfortunately, Mai Sien was sitting on his shirt, but he only had to zip and hook to make himself respectable from the waist down.

"No. Don't," she said as he stood up and began to zip. His hand poised over his crotch, he waited for her to finish what she wanted to say.

"Are you a god?" She was still looking at him, but much of the fear had gone from her face, replaced by something else—her tongue flicked out, licked at her upper lip.

"Maybe." He thought about his answer for a moment. "In China, yes, probably. But a very minor one."

"Do you have a proper name I should call you?"

"As deities go, I am far too minor to have a name," he lied, and wondered if he could risk getting rid of the clothes again.

She stood up and the coverlet slipped from her fingers. "Then may I call you by your father's name, Chu-Jung, blue god of the south wind?"

Badad shuddered; the words, sounding through the body he wore, found the lines of connection that tied to his host-cousins in the second celestial sphere. The mind of his Prince stirred in the dark, called into being by his name.

"Call me Brad." He tried to sound calm, but he was shaking.

"Brad, then." She walked toward him again, smiling the challenge he sometimes saw over the chessboard. "Let me do that." Moving his fingers away from his zipper with a caress of fingertips, she pulled the zip down and with a hand on each of his hips, she dropped to her knees, bringing the trousers with her. When he was naked, she rose, letting her hair drift over his body in a caress that tingled all the way up, and when she stood facing him again she put a hand to his heart.

"Lie still." She pushed him down, gently but inexorably, until satin cradled his back and then she straddled him, so that her breasts hung over him like ripe fruit. Braced with one arm on the bed by his side, the other still holding him down, warm above his heart, she teased his mouth with her breasts until he could have screamed with the frustration, and she smiled with all the knowledge of the world in her eyes and leaned closer, let him taste her salt and skin and the slick oil of her heated body.

"Can you be anything?" she asked, and he answered, "Anything," while she crouched over him and slid down, finding him waiting for her under the sheets.

"But you want to feel this first?" She moved her hips, and his body clenched under her. He bit his lip, afraid that she would call him by the name of his Prince and transform him into some creature with different senses reading her damp skin, her heat, and he wouldn't get it right, this human sex thing, ever. But she slid into his arms like a swan riding home and whispered nothing words that guided him until he realized that this time they'd gone all the way to exhaustion and he hadn't turned blue.

He thought perhaps she would move away then, and he didn't want to let go of her. She felt warm in a wholly different way now that he wanted to experience as well. Apparently she felt the same, because she stirred only to drag the coverlet over their bodies, cooling where they did not touch each other. "In the morning, show me what you can do?" she asked. Then she snuggled down, her breasts flattened against his stomach and her right leg wrapped over his left. "The flower petals were nice." She gave him a kiss over his heart for emphasis. "Can we do that again?" She sighed, gave a final wriggle to draw them as close as they could be, and drifted a good-night kiss on his left nipple.

Brad lay quietly, thinking about the spicy beefsteak waiting for the microwave. But her hair slipped through his fingertips like a river of silk when he stroked it, and soon the rhythm of her breathing lulled him into sleep.

# Chapter 23

THE DOOR CHIMES WOKE EVAN; HE ROLLED OVER IN—OOF! HE FELL OFF, ONTO the floor, from—not bed, then. That damned couch. His face ached with a gnawing throb where he'd been lying on the bruises, and there went the damned door chimes again, starting the dull ache behind the eyes. In the old days he'd have known it for a hangover, but this morning he figured the headache came of not enough sleep mixing uneasily with a mild concussion. Once he got moving, he'd get it under control, but at the moment he felt nauseated and stiff, his head hurt inside and out, and the intruder rang the bell, again. The office bell; he could tell by the chime, and at the ungodly hour of . . . nine.

Harry. Damn. Lily hadn't come home last night—she wouldn't have left him on the couch if she'd seen him there—why didn't Brad let him in? By the time Evan got to his feet, the bell was chiming in a deeper tone. Someone wanted to get in at the garden gate.

"Evan? Are you in there?"

Harry, with a note of panic in his voice. He'd given up on the front door, then, and stood on the brick patio, beating on the sliding glass door to the living room.

"Just a minute!"

But Harry didn't wait; he slid the glass door open and popped his head inside, giving a cautious look around. "Evan!" The rest of the professor followed his head. "Why didn't you answer the door? I'm not sure what upset me more—that you didn't answer the bell, or that your back gate and the sliding door were unlocked."

Evan winced. Stupid to leave it unlocked, though he'd gotten out of the habit of worrying about human dangers.

"When you didn't answer, I thought you'd had a return visit from our burglar. I half expected to find you dead on the floor."

"Feel like it," Evan admitted. "Sorry I scared you. I didn't sleep much last night." He'd pretty much given up on it, actually. "I went out to the garden for some air and must have forgotten to lock up afterward. Finally fell asleep on the couch around three, and I didn't wake up until you rang the bell."

"I'm sorry I woke you." Harry looked him over more keenly than Evan appreciated, and the disapproving frown said he didn't like what he saw. "Are you sure you don't want to make a quick visit to the emergency ward, have them take another look at you?"

"It's nothing." Evan couldn't think of a single reason they should be having this conversation on their feet, so he sat down on the couch. If he could think of a way to get rid of Harry, maybe he could rest a bit.

Nope. Mother at twelve o'clock. The words had the sound of a heads-up to his ear, and he imagined training a turret gun on the little house on Rosemont Street, lobbing words instead of shells with the same capacity to destroy whatever peace his mother had found there. And he couldn't do that without a full load of caffeine. He hauled himself back to his feet with the kitchen in his sights. Coffee.

"Evan, sit down!"

Evan sat.

"You have tea?"

"In the cabinet." He started to get up again, but Harry pushed him back down.

"Don't move." He retreated, leaving Evan to drift in and out of a half sleep with the whistle of a teakettle somewhere in the distance.

Harry returned too soon, with two cups of tea and a roll left over from dinner on one saucer. "Eat this." He set the tea on the table next to the couch and handed Evan the dinner roll. When Evan had torn off a chunk with his teeth, Harry handed him one of the teacups.

"Drink. Believe me, your stomach and that coffee were about to engage in open warfare. I didn't know white people could turn that shade of green."

"It's an art," Evan acknowledged. But the tea did make him feel better. So did the roll, which he bit into again.

While he chewed and sipped, Harry was scanning the second-floor balcony with narrowed intensity. "Where is your father?"

"I don't know. Could be in bed, I suppose, but I've never known him to sleep late, and I didn't hear him come in last night." Evan would not admit to waiting up for his father. Stupid idea. Brad was an adult. Hell, he was older than the known universe, and Evan wasn't exactly a latchkey kid. No, he wouldn't admit that Brad's absence had kept him awake, worried in some indefinable way last night, because it wasn't . . . true. Exactly.

"It's not your fault, Evan."

Which hit close enough to the mark that Evan wondered if the professor had more than powers of observation going for him. Harry settled himself in the overstuffed chair next to the couch and picked up his teacup, set it down again in a sequence of nervous gestures that brought rumblings of tension to Evan's already queasy stomach.

"I'd hoped to find him here, but I may be too late."

"Too late for what?"

"To warn him."

The nausea was back with a vengeance. Evan had thought that if Brad were in trouble, he would know it, but some link between them had changed when he'd set his father free. He couldn't feel it anymore. Another Simpson could have bound his father already, and he might not even know.

Harry dug up the battered leather *I Ching* out of his pocket and opened it to the place he'd marked with several sheets of lined yellow paper folded into quarters.

"Every time I try to ask the *I Ching* about the crystals, it answers with a changing hexagram. Never the same changing hexagram, mind you; but each time I run the coins, they seem to point to your father and a woman. It appears that for some reason not yet clear to me, this relationship may put the treasures we are seeking out of our reach forever."

"What woman, Harry? Khadijah Flint? Ellen?"

"Certainly not!" Harry straightened his backbone to rigid indignation, difficult to do in that chair, as Evan had reason to know. "Actually, Ellen thinks Mai Sien Chong may be the woman. Brad seems smitten with her, but the police have nothing to connect her to the burglaries except us."

"Brad? With a woman?" Hadn't intended to let that slip, but Badad the daemon had made it very clear that he'd had enough of humans and sex when he'd been forced by a binding spell to impregnate Evan's mother.

Harry laughed softly. "Parents don't lose their sexual feelings just because their children have grown old enough to have sexual feelings themselves," he pointed out.

"It still seems unlikely." His father's avowed disgust at the means of Evan's conception just didn't mesh well with the idea of his father picking up women at a chess club. Ellen Li notwithstanding, he found it hard to believe that the sort of women who might intrigue the daemon Badad out of his determination to avoid human entanglements frequented the chess club. The whole notion seemed a bit surreal.

Harry shrugged. "Actually, I would have agreed with you in this case. Ellen and I had crossed paths with Mai Chong at a number of charity events, both for the museum and for causes involving the Chinese American community. About a year ago, she began to join us at the chess club. She was fairly matched against me; Brad and Ellen usually play a little better than either of us, but not enough better to make play terribly uneven when we change opponents."

Evan ate the last bit of his dinner roll, hoping it would settle his stomach. Harry had relaxed a bit and seemed to be thinking out loud to himself as much as talking to Evan; he figured with Harry that was a good sign, and the warning was not quite as dire as it had sounded.

"Ellen seems sure that Brad didn't know her at the time—certainly not in the biblical sense. In fact, he seemed to find her rather sexual approach to the game amusing, at least until this week."

"And?"

"He still seemed amused," Harry admitted. "But when we saw them together this week, Ellen felt certain that they were going to take their amusement to the bedroom—if not that very night, then soon. I wouldn't say your father fell in love, but he certainly began showing more interest in the sexual game she was playing than he had in the past."

"This is none of my business, Harry." Evan knew it was true. He remembered his father sitting at the desk in the study, looking beyond the computer screen and the stack of printouts to something that Brad had admitted concerned a woman. But romance? Brad? The daemon who had vowed he would never become physically involved with a human being again and who had never, in the four years Evan had known him, maintained a relationship of any kind with a fully human being.

Except that, of course, he had done just that, had a whole different life on Wednesday nights with friends he knew well enough for long enough to ask an enormous favor for his son. And now, it seemed, he also had a girl friend he'd told Evan nothing about. His *father*? He wondered if Lily knew.

"I really don't want to know this, Harry. It would be different if she really were involved in the case, but if her only connection is that you and Ellen happen to be acquainted with her . . ."

"I know, I know, Evan. But remember, the last time we talked I said that there was a woman involved and that if Brad became involved with her, we could lose the artifacts. Now, I've run the coins again. And again, they point to patience. Here, see—the hexagram of the present is *Hsu*, for patient biding of time. The upper trigram is misery, *K'an*, the lower, *Ch'ien*, the flowering of ideas, but they are held back by *Li* and *Tui*, nuclear trigrams of pleasure that is marked by bondage."

The word sent a jolt of adrenaline through Evan. He reached out, unconscious of the motion, and gripped Harry by the arm. "What did you say?" He needed to hear it again, though he'd already broken out in a clammy sweat from the first time.

·   Harry stared at Evan's hand on his arm until Evan moved it with a low rumble of embarrassment.

"It is as if he is in thrall to the joy of this woman, so that he rushes forward, oblivious to the obstacles in his way, when he should be patient and consider the consequences of his actions. *Hsu* stands for love. Patience, holding back, will bring love, but rushing forward will result in failure, disaster.

"That is the present. The future shows intimate relations with a younger woman, which sets aside all good sense. Obligations to home and family and ethical living are broken in the name of lust. Evan, the hexagram promises only a bad end for this relationship, for any goal he tries to reach while under the influence of this woman. And its name is *Kuei Mei*."

Evan rubbed at the stitches at his temples and wished the gnawing pain in his gut would go away. Shit.

"If your interpretation is correct, and Brad is considering an affair with this woman, I don't see that it is any of your business, or mine. I was over the age of consent when he found me, so he doesn't owe me a thing. If he wants to throw away everything he's built here for this woman, he has every right to do so. And neither you nor I have the authority, moral or otherwise, to tell him he can't do what he damn well pleases with his life."

"Even if he is bound to get hurt in the process?"

There was the word again; he flinched at the sound of it.

"Is there any risk of that?" he asked, and knew he couldn't tell Harry the real fear—what binding meant to his father's kind, not a metaphor for attraction, but enslavement to the will of one's captor. "Any risk that this woman is forcing my father to do anything against his will? Does she have the power to hold him prisoner if he wants to leave her?"

Harry gave him a reassuring smile and shook his head. "If you mean a real, physical imprisonment, no, of course she poses no such threat to your father. He can well take care of himself against aggressive violence were she to offer it. But Mai Sien Chong has the power some women have to distract a man with her body if she chooses. She has chosen your father. Not for his money—for the challenge, I think."

Not a real risk to his father, then. Perhaps to Evan, but that wasn't Harry's problem.

"People get hurt, Harry. It's part of life."

"You're right, of course," Harry agreed. "And if I had been so lost to proper action toward a friend as to ask the *Book* about your father's personal life, I would agree with you and humbly beg your pardon for the gross rudeness of this conversation. But I did not ask about your father. I did not ask about Mai Sien Chong. I asked about the Moon Stone. Whenever I ask about the crystal, the *Book* gives me your father and this woman."

"Perhaps it's your interpretation that's off," Evan suggested. "The treasures were owned by the Dowager Empress. That could be the allusion to a woman. Brad's relation to her may mean his relation to the search for her lost objects."

"I wish you were right, Evan, and I would agree with you except that in each circumstance when I have asked the book, it has given me a changing hexagram. Always, duality: man and woman, past and future, and always the outcome is the same. Objects lost go further away, further beyond our ability to find and retrieve them. The man in this duality does not act out of malice or evil but out of impetuosity and passion.

"Each time the answer is the same, and each time the redress is clear. We must stop this romance of your father's. Mai Sien Chong will hurt him, and, in the process, we will lose our only chance to retrieve the lost treasures."

Evan looked at the professor as if he'd lost his mind, and he realized that he'd come to an uneasy acceptance of this new version of his father. "Sorry, Harry. If my father has found a woman who makes him happy, even for a little while, the only thing I am going to say to him, if he should ask for my opinion, is 'congratulations.' And if that means we don't get the museum's lost artifacts back, I will happily forfeit the fee."

"I was afraid you would say that." Harry stood to go and Evan followed him to the door, where the professor made one last effort. "There is, perhaps, more urgency to regaining the lost objects than we may have understood."

Evan leaned back against the frame of the sliding glass door, watching the day lilies sway on their long stems in the breezes whispering through the garden. Part of his mind followed Harry Li's argument, but another part searched his awareness of the universe for his Lily: Lirion, the lily of heaven. He needed her advice this morning as badly as he'd wanted her body last night.

"Do you remember when I described the crystal ball to you as suspending the present, frozen in a drop of water turned to stone?"

"Yes." Evan didn't tell him that he'd felt that power of the stone himself.

"For the security guard at the museum, that has more than a poetic meaning. He has still not regained consciousness. I believe the cause is the crystal. It has, in a sense, drawn out his soul, captured it and frozen it in the moment when he reached out, perhaps, to take it from the hands of the thief."

"Isn't that a bit farfetched, professor?" While he was saying it, Evan knew it was true, but he still couldn't accept it. "If it were true, why didn't we find the thief unconscious next to the guard?"

"An interesting question, yes?" Harry patted him on the shoulder. "But I must go—summer school starts tomorrow, and I haven't prepared a thing. Take care of yourself. And when you are deciding between the case and the fleeting physical gratification of your father's sexual appetite, remember that a man's life may depend on your answer."

Harry went out the gate, turning only to remind Evan, "Lock up behind me."

Frozen in time. Evan knew the one person who could give him an answer about that. But the last person he wanted to see right now was Alfredo Da'Costa, who had tried to kill him in one memorable discussion over the consequences of humans and daemons meddling in the spheres that separated time and space. Alfredo Da'Costa, who'd been doing more than sleeping with Lily Ryan last night when all Evan had to hold the night terrors at bay was the memory of his daemon kin in her shape as a woman in his arms.

And he had promised his mother he'd see her for lunch. This was shaping up to be a very bad day.

# Chapter 24

SPICY BEEFSTEAK WITH VEGETABLES. THE THOUGHT THAT HAD FOLLOWED HIM into sleep became a scent that woke Kevin Bradley in the morning. Mai Sien's side of the bed was empty, and the bedroom door that Mrs. Zheng had tried to beat down the night before stood open, letting in the smell of the hot food. Brad considered putting his clothes back on, but the idea didn't appeal. Neither did making an exit for home, through the second sphere, for clean ones.

For the first time since he'd returned to Earth to guard the spheres from his son, he'd taken real pleasure from the flesh he wore, and he wasn't ready to let go of the imprint of her skin on his, the feel of silk sheets sliding against the skin, cool and hot and slightly sticky all at the same time. He figured he'd made the right decision when Mai Sien returned wearing nothing but the honey of her skin and carrying a tray with steaming plates of food.

"Mrs. Zheng will have a fit if we don't eat this up," she said with a laugh.

He took the tray from her and held it until she had unfolded a bed table between them, then he set the food down and began to eat the spicy beef. He didn't care if Mrs. Zheng did pack a .38 and report to the Red Army, he was going to kidnap her and make her cook for him forever. But he forgot all about Mrs. Zheng when Mai Sien leaned over the tray and kissed him deep, so deep—that she'd stolen the spicy beef from his mouth, and sat crosslegged on the bed laughing at him. "You are permitted to beat me, but not to starve me!"

Brad gave that some thought as he scooped another forkful of beef into his mouth and chewed. When he'd bought himself all the time he could reasonably do, he swallowed the food. "Do you want me to?" he asked. "Beat you, I mean?"

"I hate brutal men."

An expression of such loathing transformed her features that for a moment she looked like someone else entirely—someone far, far older, features creased with age and disappointment.

"But Mrs. Zheng believes differently. That you do like it?"

A bit of sauce dripped from his fork, and he wondered if Mai Sien would like a taste of Kevin Bradley in a spicy sauce. The thought crawled across his lower abdomen, muscles clenching pleasurably in its wake, and Brad heard her answer through a haze clouding his brain.

"Some men, with no talents of their own and no conscience, use women to gain power or to feel powerful in a world that treats them with the contempt they deserve. If Mrs. Zheng thought you were one of them, she would have shot you last night."

She gave him a smile full of sharp white teeth, and he had second thoughts about making suggestions that involved that mouth and his vulnerable flesh. "I assume a bullet or two would not have hurt you, but it would have ruined a lovely evening."

"Would have made things awkward." A bullet in the gut wouldn't have done any permanent damage, but it would have hurt like hell until he'd transformed the body. It certainly would have spoiled the mood. He'd been hoping she'd forgotten what he was. But then, he supposed it had been a landmark evening for her as well. She might have more experience at human sex, but he doubted her other lovers had shown their appreciation by turning blue and scaly. And he didn't want to know what his face had looked like.

"Sometimes, though," she added, "between a man and a woman"—she gave him a long, measuring glance that made him nervous—"or a man and a man—the pleasure is more complex, bitter with the sweet and salty, rough with the gentle."

She gave a little wave as if to turn aside the conversation. "You promised you would be anything for me today."

He'd forgotten that. "Yes I did."

"But I have to go to work soon." She sighed and set the bed table on the floor. "And tonight I have to be in Vancouver. Business." She made a face. "Come to me there?"

"Where?"

"I usually stay at Uncle Chong's island, but I have an apartment, on the bay, for when I need privacy. We will want lots of privacy. Say yes." And she'd found the bit of sauce decorating his body, licked it off and kept up the search while he flopped back on the bed, flattening everything but the part of his anatomy she was presently examining, which expanded to make it easier for her tongue to find what it was looking for. And when that growling, hopelessly hopeful sound escaped his clenched teeth, she pulled herself up to give his nose a merit badge of a kiss. "Does that mean yes?"

Of course, it did. But he felt that, as a daemon lord of Prince Ariton, it wouldn't do to let her know that his capitulation had been so utter, so complete, and so quick. So he waited until after she had wrapped her legs around his hips and fulfilled all the promises she had made to his body. Then he took her face in his hands and kissed it, eyes and nose and mouth, mouth deep enough to savor the flavors mingling on her tongue.

"Yes."

"I knew you wouldn't disappoint me."

And there were so many layers to that simple statement—last night, and the games she had played with him, teasing over chess, and acknowledgment that his answer, "yes," had meant all of those things and tonight as well—that he could think of nothing else to say.

"A gentleman would make promises," she teased him again, "that he would never disappoint me."

She left him on the bed, pulling clothes out of a chest and heading for the bath, and he watched her with Ariton smoldering in his eyes as his answer. Not a gentleman. And not given to promises. Now was all he had, all he ever had. But tonight in Vancouver, they would have another now. When she closed the bathroom door between them, Brad thought of his bedroom in the house on Spruce Street. Dark furnishings gracefully curved, old Persian carpets in layers underfoot, and he was home, standing naked in front of his closet. He took a deep breath, wanting to hold in his lungs the smell of sex rising like a memory from his body and headed for his shower. He would have to talk to Evan about the Harry Li burglary case, but first he needed to talk to Lily.

He found her essence and followed it, materializing in the shadow of an all too familiar church. Lily sat across a small table from Alfredo Da'Costa at a sidewalk cafe in a piazza with the church on one side and a sweeping view of the Grand Canal on the other.

"Cousin!" She greeted him Venetian style, with a kiss on the cheek, and looked him over, casually at first, then more sharply. "What have you been up to? You look like the cat who caught the canary but doesn't know what to do with it."

"I figured most of it out." Brad pulled a chair from a nearby table and joined them. "Returning to the scene of the crime?" He glanced at the Grand Canal through an area of gardens and paving stones that used to be Ca'Dacosta.

"I like to keep an eye on it," Da'Costa admitted."We plan to rebuild as soon as the architects and the city planners come to an agreement. At the current bribery levels, I'll run out of money about the same time that we receive our license to build." A rueful smile played in the depths of liquid brown eyes, but little of whatever emotion he felt about the question, or the place, showed anywhere else on his face. His ageless features still had the chiseled look of a finely sculpted bronze.

Brad understood, of course. As a guardian from the third celestial sphere, where time existed without space, Da'Costa could wait out as many generations of city planners as necessary. But time meant change in the material sphere. Da'Costa had tried to execute Evan for the crimes he might someday have the understanding to commit. The guardian, Count Da'Costa, had failed, and the Titian frescoes on the high, domed ceiling of Ca'Dacosta were gone forever. Brad liked to remind him occasionally of the cost to renew the conflict in case he experienced a sudden onset of conscientiousness in his guardianship of the spheres.

A waiter in a short white jacket approached the table and Brad pointed at Alfredo Da'Costa's glass. "I'll have one of those."

He didn't know what the glass had held, but he didn't care much either. He had more important matters on his mind, like Mai Sien, and why this human body he wore had suddenly started making his decisions for him, and what had Mrs. Zheng thought they were doing that involved Mai Sien's screams but no retaliation from her guards. He needed to talk to Lily, but Alfredo Da'Costa had other things on his mind as well.

"We've got a problem."

"Who's we?" Brad sincerely hoped that DaCosta didn't plan to fight Evan again. Fortunately, DaCosta had other problems to worry him today.

"There's been a disturbance in the time stream," he said.

"Evan didn't do it."

"Probably not, directly," DaCosta agreed, "but the anomaly is located, spatially, in the area where you maintain your business."

"It's the Empress' crystal balls," Lily explained.

"The crystals have created an anomaly in time? What kind of anomaly?" Brad accepted his drink—a gin and tonic—from the waiter and sipped from the glass while he waited for Da'Costa to take a drink of his own refill and answer.

"It's created some sort of knot, stopping time and holding one particular moment frozen inside the stone."

"And you never noticed the stones could do this?"

"I knew the possibility existed. The shape, the particular type of crystal used in the process, and the process itself, all serve to create a harmonic representation of the spheres themselves, much as an orrery does the solar system. But the effect of the crystal depends on its size and the purity both of the base matter and of its finishing."

Da'Costa stopped, looked from Lily to Brad, with tension deepening the pools of his dark, liquid eyes. "You must understand, Lord Badad, that to make such a crystal sphere, the artisan begins with a single, naturally grown crystal of at least one hundred fifty pounds in weight. And then he must carve out the ball and polish it for months in a sandbath of ruby dust. During those months, the crystal must never stop turning, or the polishing will produce an imperfectly spherical ball. And, when the ball is finished, the artisan is more than likely to discover that the crystal did have some flaw in it that was not obvious when he began."

Count Da'Costa took a drink from his gin and tonic and seemed to be trying to gather his persuasive arguments. Brad remembered when he'd last seen the guardian look this serious. Evan might have died then; he couldn't help wondering who would die this time.

Da'Costa set down the glass with exaggerated care. "There are many lesser crystal balls, but as far as I know, only three exist large enough, and perfect enough, to create the effect I've experienced this week. To use the crystals in this way, one must either know how it is done, or be extraordinarily unlucky.

"All these conditions came together to freeze time only once before in my memory; that was during the reign of Yehenara, the Dowager Empress of China. The Empress did understand the power of the crystals. She collected three whose size allows the adept to create a significant temporal effect in a very small space. She knew how to wield their power and did so on occasion. But the process to create the crystals was lost before she died, and since her death no one has broken the mystery of the Dowager Empress' crystals. Now they are gone, and time has been disturbed. While Yehenara used the crystals sparingly, we don't know who has them now, or to what use they will be put. But if the crystals should fall into the hands of someone like your son, he could destroy our three universes with a word. He wouldn't have to physically travel through the spheres, so his discomfort doing so, and his dread of exploring the reaches of the second sphere in search of the boundary beyond it, would no longer deter him."

"I don't believe he is starting this again." Brad ignored Da'Costa; he hadn't liked or trusted him since he'd tried to kill his son, and nothing he'd said today had changed any of his ill feeling. But Lily—"If you'd wanted Evan dead, all you had to do was hit him in the head a little harder with the computer monitor. You could have burned him to ashes, or stopped his heart while you rode him in bed. Why wait this long and come to him"—he gave a sharp nod in Da'Costa's direction but could not bring himself to speak the guardian's name—"and why ask me to listen? If I want Evan dead, I will kill him myself. If I don't, this story won't convince me any more than the last one did."

Da'Costa raised a hand to interrupt. "But Evan doesn't *have* the crystals," he said. "And as long as they don't fall into his hands, he presents no more than his usual danger. The question is, who does have them? And how can we get them back and destroy them before the thief learns how to use them to greater effect?"

"And," Lily added, "how do we keep them away from Evan when he is the only one in the agency currently looking for the Moon Stone?"

"It appears you have more incentive than a fee and a challenging recovery for Professor Li." Trouble still brooded in Da'Costa's eyes, and if Brad looked deeper, he saw beneath emotion, to where judgment had lain through all history. Da'Costa was the guardian of this space, protector of universes, and no more human than Brad himself. It wouldn't do to forget that. He was tempted to leave the whole mess in Da'Costa's hands; Mai Sien and the reaction of the body he had fashioned for convenience were enough to keep him busy right now. But while his mind had wandered on thoughts of golden skin and silk hair dark as home, Lily had made the decision for them. She stood up, smoothing her short linen dress in place.

"It will be fun." Then she leaned over to kiss Da'Costa with a lingering promise that Brad was only now beginning to appreciate.

"Come, cousin. We have work to do."

He followed her into the shadows of the church and transformed into his true form, heading home, where flesh did not exist and he could revel in the darkness and in his kinship with the host of Ariton. And where he could meet Lirion mind to mind and understand, through her, these new feelings of the flesh.

# Chapter 25

ROSEMONT STREET HAD CHANGED: NOTHING MAJOR, BUT A HUNDRED LITTLE things that made him even more a stranger than Evan had felt growing up. He pulled the Mercedes to the curb, noticing that fewer children played on the narrow street these days and that the parents who used to sit in their lawn chairs on their small front porches had turned into grandparents. They'd watched their own children grow up from those same porches, cigarette in one hand, glass of iced tea in the other. Watched those children build their own lives, move across the country or around the block, and now took up sentry duty for another generation. Fewer of the watchers as well. Those cigarettes had taken their toll, as had the jobs that swept away their children and grandchildren to new lives in suburbs that smelled of paint and wet cement, where they rolled out the lawns like carpet. His mother didn't belong here anymore, had nothing in common with the people on either side growing old on stories about the corporate successes of their children and the dance recitals of their grandchildren.

Her face, looking out at him from the parlor window, had that tight but hopeful expression he remembered from when he was a kid—ready for the worst, she was willing to believe that he'd had a normal day until he'd proven otherwise. He'd hated that look as a kid because he knew he'd see the hope disappear as soon as she read the note from school. Today wouldn't change his record. He opened the gate in the chain-link fence that surrounded the postage stamp of a front garden and reached for the doorknob.

"Evan, come in!" His mother opened the door and greeted him on the doorstep with an awkward hug before taking his elbow and pulling him into the parlor. The room was too small for a modern sofa, but she had an Early American loveseat in a tartan plaid, a recliner for Harvey, a rocking chair with her cross stitching dropped in one corner, three small tables with lamps shaped like ginger jars on them, and a twenty-five-inch television on a swivel stand with a copy of *USA Today*'s sports page sitting on top. Memories filled the walls: photos and knickknacks scattered in cases and on shelves or rising on the far side of the stairway. More recent souvenirs, of summer vacations his mother hadn't been able to afford when Evan was growing up, sat on the windowsill between the chintz curtains tied back at either side. As a small child he'd felt clumsy in this room, wary of breaking her treasures. He discovered that nothing much had changed since those years except that, because he was bigger, he was more than ever likely to damage something.

"Should you be out and driving? With a concussion, I mean?" She reached to touch his temple—"You've still got stitches in your head"—and he let her do it, relieved when he felt just a whisper of fingertips.

"I'll be fine," he assured her. "I'm almost as good as new already." He didn't mention the headache pounding behind his eyes; there wasn't anything she could do about it, and the last thing he wanted to do was admit to a weakness going into an argument. She didn't sit down, so neither did he.

"Harvey will be down in a minute; then we can have lunch."

She smiled, and Evan smiled back. "Fine." He wondered if his effort looked as false as hers did. But Harvey was coming down the stairs, his tread heavy on the sagging risers, and then he was crossing the blue-green rug like Poseidon crossing the sea, his hand out, his smile genuine, with a strong trace of irony.

"Come on in, Evan. Your mother's been in a tizzy since yesterday about lunch—shall we eat before she dumps the shrimp salad over our heads?"

His mother gave her husband a little punch in the arm, and Evan decided that Harvey Barnes was proof enough that a God did exist, and that he hadn't abandoned them on Rosemont Street. He smiled, the first genuine article since he'd decided to come here and have this talk with his mother, and followed her into the dining room with Harvey behind him. They could talk later, after lunch. Evan determined to give her that much—an hour for shrimp salad and crusty french bread, for lemon pound cake and iced tea—before he took on the task he'd come for.

But the awkward pauses in the conversation and his mother's worried glances combined with the headache he hadn't quite shaken to form one fervent wish: to get out of there, away from the memories that hung over the street and the house and came to rest in the haunted expression in his mother's eyes. If Harvey Barnes hadn't been there, he would have cut and run, but Harvey had taken the measure of the situation and did his best to ease them all through the meal. He told funny stories about the current crop of freshmen "moving up" to senior high amid a flurry of pranks and confusion, and recounted the outrageous gossip he'd heard about the vice principal for discipline and the French teacher who always wore high heels and black leather pants to school. He even repeated a few rumors he'd overheard about himself that made Evan's mother blush and Evan choke on a shrimp.

Then, when lunch was over, he'd kissed Evan's mother on the top of her head and sent her off to the parlor for her "visit" while he cleaned up. When Evan stood up to follow her, Harvey Barnes gave him a wink, then disappeared into the kitchen, his hands full of cake plates.

Evan's mother settled herself on the rocker and put aside the needle-point she'd been working on before he arrived. "It's been a while, Evan." That seemed a bit obvious even to her; she knotted her hands in her lap and gave him another weak smile. "I'm glad you could visit."

Not likely, this time at least. She had to know he was here about Joe Dougherty, about his father. He'd have done this part of the job with his hand wrapped around the front door handle if he could have gotten away with it, but he had to give the afternoon at least the pretense of a social visit, so he swept a glance around the room, choosing—not the recliner, Harvey Barnes had that territory staked out with the *TV Guide* stuffed between the cushion and the arm. Evan threw himself down on the loveseat and winced: too late. His mother had told him not to fling himself at the furniture every day of his life.

Shit. He was a grown man, and the woman in the rocker wasn't much above five feet tall. Which didn't much matter and never had. She used extensions, like Joe Dougherty to do the dirty work and Harvey Barnes to smooth things over. But now it was just the two of them, and nothing would get said if he didn't start.

"We have to talk."

"I didn't think you'd come by for the shrimp." Now that he'd begun, something inside her seemed to let go. The tight knot of her entangled fists relaxed, and she leaned back in the rocker, her hands resting on the arms of her chair.

"Brad had a talk with our lawyer, and we've decided to have DNA tests done. She thinks that's the best way to rule out any false claims against either of us."

"What will you do if the test disproves paternity?"

"It won't." We made certain of that when we made the decision to go ahead. But he didn't add that part out loud, for all the good it did him.

"How can you be sure? Preliminary blood tests? They don't really prove anything, you know, Evan. At most they rule out half the men in the city. You've still got half the population that fit the blood type."

At least she was talking. That was something. Evan figured he'd measure the success of the visit by how long they managed to keep talking before her face stiffened and her mouth pursed tight around the words she would not utter.

"We haven't had any matching tests done." He took a deep breath, but it didn't calm him as he'd hoped. "You can't tell anyone what I am going to tell you, Mom. If the wrong people knew, they could, well, it could destroy my father, and I don't want to think of how many innocent people could be killed in the process."

"You're not trying to tell me he's some sort of secret agent?" She didn't quite sound as if she disbelieved it and Evan wished not for the first time that it were so simple.

"No. But you've got to promise to keep this afternoon secret, even if you hate my father more after I've explained. And you have to get Joe Dougherty off our backs. It's my life he's going to ruin, because Brad won't give a shit. He'll—"

"Watch your language around your mother, Evan." The last thing Evan wanted was Harvey Barnes coming in from the kitchen and sinking into the plush recliner, but that was what he got.

"This is private." Evan held onto his patience, but only just.

"Not if it has anything to do with your mother and the scoundrel who left her pregnant and alone all those years ago."

Outside, a storm had rolled in, darkening the sky. Harvey Barnes took his time, turning on a lamp next to his chair—"That's better"—with a deliberate nod of his head.

"Then you do believe Kevin Bradley is my father."

"I believe your father was a scoundrel and that if this Kevin Bradley thinks he's your father, then he must've been a scoundrel, with somebody's mother, if not with your own. But I'll tell you the truth: I believe him when he says he is your father. I don't know what his story is, but if it needs to be so secret, your mother's going to need help to carry that knowledge around. Better you should know right off the bat that I'm carrying it with her."

Harvey gave him the same glare that he'd dished out all four years of high school, and Evan knew he wasn't going to budge the man. But telling the story was infinitely more difficult with one more reminder of a disastrous youth sitting in the recliner. And it had started to rain. Not just a summer shower, but a downpour, with hail the size of marbles bouncing off the parlor window, as though hell itself were beating to get in. Harvey

Barnes looked out at the storm with a slightly worried air before turning to Evan.

"If it helps any, I'm probably more prepared to hear what you have to say than your mother is." The glare was gone, but something much grimmer took its place. "I think it's time we got the elephant out of the living room, don't you?"

That probably made sense somewhere in the mind of a high school principal, but the intent of the message stood out in bold letters. Harvey Barnes knew something, and Evan had an ally in him. As long as he didn't swear in front of his mother.

"He's not human."

"Who isn't human?" Evan's mother looked from her son to her husband for an answer. She shrank back into her chair as another bluster of storm threw more hail stones at the house. Harvey Barnes seemed neither confused nor surprised. He looked out at the street with a weary expression, as though he'd been proved right the one time out of a million he wanted to be wrong.

"My father. He's not human."

"I'm sorry to disappoint you, *son,* but the angel of God only did that once. The basics of procreation are simple. If he weren't human, you wouldn't exist, let alone be a normal human being."

She always escaped into science when the emotions got too strong, too negative, but Evan knew she'd come back to the point if he waited a minute while her last statement sank in. Normal. All the experts she'd trotted him past had agreed on one thing: Evan Davis was not a normal little boy. He shrugged his shoulders.

"I came to talk about my father, not about me. But if anyone finds out what he is, guesses his real name, the consequences could be devastating. Because he's not human, he doesn't think like us or care about the same things, and he is more powerful than you can possibly imagine."

"You sound like he's a terrorist with an atom bomb in his suitcase." His mother made it sound like an exaggeration. She wasn't going to take it well that her example was a vast understatement of Badad's power as a daemon lord of Ariton. But she didn't need to know the full extent of Badad's power or her son's. No need to tell her he'd almost blown up the sun himself once.

The wind was whistling an eerie siren through the windows that he'd helped her weatherproof last year; his mother had picked up her needlepoint, as a shield or just something to hold, he guessed, and he didn't feel any closer to telling her the truth he'd come for.

"If he's so terrible, why are you trying to prove he's your father when you could walk away and use the doubt as an excuse? And why are you so anxious to have Joe Dougherty taken off the case when you may need him to protect your life?"

"Joe Dougherty isn't on the case. He's just getting in the way of solving it, because he's targeted the wrong suspect. My father didn't do it. He's incapable of bungling anything that badly." Which told her more than he'd intended about Brad's uncertain ethics, though she didn't seem anxious to pursue the notion. Harvey, however, edged another sideways glance at the window, where the rain was lashing the Mercedes and the sky had turned a sickly shade of green.

"Um, Evan. As a demonstration of your point, it's pretty impressive. Is your father looking for you, or are you doing that—"

Evan stared at the window for a moment, and it slipped out—"Holy shit"—before he reminded himself that he'd better get a grip on his emotional state before Rosemont Street made the front page of the *Daily News*. Control.

"That's what I thought. Could you stop before the storm drops us on Oz, or wherever else unnatural twisters drop people?"

Harvey was taking it all a good bit more calmly than Evan was. He couldn't just stop it—the imbalance that would create in the localized air pressure would rupture eardrums and windows in a three-block radius. Instead, he clenched a fist and focused on it as an image of the storm. Gradually, gradually, he loosened the fist until his hand lay open and relaxed on his knee.

"Sorry," he said, not sure if he was more embarrassed, terrified, or contrite. The storm had passed, the sun shone again, and Harvey Barnes looked vaguely uncomfortable.

"My God. Evan? My God. My God." His mother twisted the needlepoint between her fingers, pricked her hand with the needle stuck in it and didn't seem to notice until Evan reached over and took the cloth from her. "I don't understand."

He'd heard that tone of voice before. For the past four years, he'd offered what comfort he could with the answers his clients didn't want to hear as a detective working with Bradley, Ryan, and Davis. His name appeared on the door with his father's and Lily's. He knew how to do this. And suddenly, he did know, and he distanced himself from the problem, calmly, as if he were reporting that Brad had stolen the silver. "There was a man, Carl Adams." He kept his voice low, and held out his hand for her to hold onto. "Do you remember him?"

"Yes, I remember Carl. Harvey, what did you mean, asking Evan to stop the storm? How could he—"

"Mother." Evan called her attention back from his stepfather. "The storm did stop, didn't it?"

"That was coincidence! Bad storms like that come in fast and pass by just as quickly. Human beings do not tell storm cells where to go."

"Humans don't." Evan took her hand, closed his more tightly around it when she tried to pull away. "What do you recall about Carl Adams?"

"He was a friend, and certainly human! He was a graduate student in the history department while I was finishing my master's degree in chemistry. We didn't know each other very well; we saw each other at a few social events on campus, but Tom and I were planning to get married. I wasn't paying attention to other men."

Which came too close to the point, really. When Kevin Bradley had shown up, shorter than he was now, with red hair and a few freckles but those same blue, blue eyes, Gwen Davis *had* noticed, and all her plans had gone up in smoke when the pregnancy test came back positive. She sounded angry; she always did when he'd frightened her, and he was scaring the bejesus out of her now. She didn't need the reminder that Evan wasn't normal, and she didn't want to know that her one indiscretion hadn't been normal either.

For some reason, hearing the familiar anger in her voice, he regretted all those other times when he'd raged against her fear, frightening her more in a cycle of terror and grief that neither of them had ever understood. Evan understood it better now. But he'd had a lifetime of fighting the labels people put on him, of looking for the answer that would make him whole. And he'd had four years of living with the answer to get used to it. Still, it sometimes freaked him when the realization hit that other people couldn't light matches with a glance, couldn't raise a storm or knock a building down just by thinking it. She wasn't going to like this at all.

"Carl Adams was human."

"But he wasn't a friend." Harvey Barnes kept his voice low, but he couldn't disguise the hard edge to it. "And for him, it wasn't casual."

"What do you know about this, Harvey?"

Harvey Barnes had grown up in the neighborhood and headed to Temple a year or two ahead of Gwen Davis for an advanced degree in education and social work. Evan could see as well as his mother could that Harvey knew more than he'd ever let on. For a minute Harvey just looked at his wife, a question in his eyes. Finally, with a sigh, he told her what she didn't want to hear.

"Just that he had a thing for you, Gwen. Didn't you notice that he hung around the lab building an awful lot for a history student? He knew he didn't have a chance with you, and it made him crazy. Tom warned him off a few times, but he kept coming back. Finally Tom dragged him out behind Conwell Hall and beat the crap out of him. Wasn't three days later Kevin showed up, out of the blue, and the next thing anybody knows you are calling off the wedding, and Tom was leaving school."

Tears filled the hollows at the corners of her eyes, and Harvey pulled himself out of his recliner and went to her, giving a nod of thanks when Evan stood up to give him the place on the loveseat closest to his mother. Evan couldn't quite bring himself to sit in Harvey's recliner, so he leaned an elbow on the television set and fervently wished he were anywhere but listening to his old high school principal discuss with his mother the man who should have been his father.

"It wasn't your fault he died, Gwen."

Evan hadn't known that part of the story. Hadn't known the way his mother felt about the old boyfriend until she shook her head, tears escaping their corners, and contradicted Harvey.

"Whose fault was it, if not mine? He left school because I wouldn't, and he died in a stupid training accident, blown up against the side of a mountain. They couldn't even find a body."

"There was a war on," Harvey reminded her. "Lots of men died, or worse. Blame fate. Blame the government. Blame Carl Adams. All of them had more to do with Tom dying than you did."

"I betrayed him, Harve. I slept with a man I didn't even know a week before we were supposed to be married. What could Carl Adams do that comes close to what I did to Tom?"

Evan had an answer to that question. Until that moment, however, he'd actually thought he could get through this without discussing his mother's sex life with her. Hope springs eternal, until it trips on reality—

"He sent Kevin Bradley to seduce you. Adams was human, but he conjured a daemon to punish the girl who wouldn't love him. Carl Adams bound that daemon to his will and forced that daemon to attract the girl to him, to have sex with the girl, and to report back to his master the details of the seduction."

"If that's a joke, Evan, it's in very poor taste."

Harvey shook his head. "I don't think it's a joke, Gwen. I knew Carl Adams and he was into some pretty strange stuff. Nobody took his obsession with the history of black magic seriously—all of us tended to get a bit obsessed with our research specialties, and we didn't believe it could work anyway. But Tom took Carl's obsession with you seriously, and he never trusted what happened between you two at the end."

"It wasn't your fault," Evan told her. "I don't know how they do it, but the daemon can control certain aspects of the material world when they are in it. Sometimes, if the human who binds them commands them to do it, they can direct the actions of others, the way my father directed yours."

He stared out the window, his voice growing colder as he tried to protect himself against the truth that had cut worse than Omage's knife all his life. He was the living evidence of his mother's most devastating mistake. Later, he'd added his father's hellish bondage to his account, and now he knew that two men—his mother's fiancé and his father's captor—had died because Evan Davis had lived.

"It wasn't Kevin Bradley's fault either," he said to the window and the street beyond it, because he couldn't say it to his mother. "A daemon *can't* enter the material sphere unless he has been summoned and bound at some time. Our universe changes them, and the memories, always begun with bondage, are never pleasant. No daemon would enter the material sphere unless forced by a human, or unless something here is threatening the continued existence of the spheres."

"Carl Adams died." Harvey Barnes had a slight quiver in his voice, but that was nothing compared to the shaking Evan was doing inside. Neither his mother's love nor his father's uneasy tie to the spark of Ariton within him could change the fact that all of their lives would have been better if he'd never existed. But he did exist, and he had to finish the job he'd started here.

"You can't imagine what Carl Adams did to my father. I've seen his kind driven insane by it." He didn't mention that he'd been held prisoner by just such an insane daemon, or that he had himself bound his father, for his protection, but that hadn't made it any easier, and ultimately he could have died for it.

"I don't believe this."

Evan turned from the window. He owed her that much—penance—to face her with the dreadful knowledge of his birth and to live with her fear and disgust. She did believe, of course; it hurt more even than he thought it would to see the thought, "Monster," written on her face when she looked at him.

"It's insane." Gwen Davis looked to her husband for confirmation, but he kept his eyes on Evan, forcing her to do the same, and Evan met her flinching glance with as much equanimity as he could summon.

"It's true," he said, and lifted a photo from the table. All he'd ever been good at was destruction, and this time didn't seem any different than the rest. He looked at the photograph in its glass-fronted frame—his mother, in front of the gangway to a cruise ship—and shaped a tiny ball of energy deep inside, pressing it down, until he could contain it no longer and it exploded out of him in a hail of shattered glass.

"I'll replace the glass." Then he put the picture back on the table.

"I wasn't there"—wasn't born yet—"so I don't know if Brad killed Carl Adams accidentally when he broke free of the binding spell, or if he did it with conscious anger out of revenge for the agony Carl Adams had put him through."

"Did he do that to you?" She looked at his face, and he didn't know if she felt concern for him, or disgust. After all, what kind of lost soul would stay with a man who could kill him with a thought, and nearly had? He gave her a self-mocking smile.

"Not exactly. I thought, once, that he would kill me just to rid the universe of my presence."

His mother flinched as if he'd slapped her, and Evan wondered if she'd heard the suggestion before. "But we've come to an understanding." Which was vastly overstating the facts. He didn't know what motivated his father, he just knew that for now, Kevin Bradley had accepted him for the glimpses he caught of Ariton in his son.

"Have you killed anyone?"

God, they were determined to flay each other alive today. Evan couldn't face her with that answer, even if he deserved the punishment of seeing the horror and fear in her eyes. "Yes. Two. I could say it was self-defense, or that it was an accident. Both are true, more or less."

"How can you sound so casual?" The note of hysteria was creeping into her voice later than he'd expected, but he knew she was close to the end of her endurance.

"You are talking about murder!"

Self-pity whispered in Evan's ear: No one had ever asked if he had surpassed his ability to endure and survive. He smiled, neither a pleasant expression nor a happy one, and his mother caught her breath.

"That was years ago. I hadn't learned more control of my daemon nature than to keep myself out of trouble on a good day. When I was a prisoner of Marnie Simpson and her husband, I didn't have any of those. Marnie was into torture." He shuddered, remembering too much—Omage, with his silver knife and alabaster bowl, Marnie Simpson's cigarette, burning tracks across his chest. Jack Laurence dead, his body a pile of charred bits and ashes on his kitchen floor.

"When I realized that my father's nature made it possible for me to escape, I found the Simpsons weren't the only ones who had an eye on the bastard monster from hell"—Alfredo Da'Costa, but he wasn't handing out any names she might give to Joe Dougherty. He had enough on his hands without worrying that Da'Costa would start regretting his decision to let Evan live.—"That one didn't want it to hurt, but he wanted me just as dead. During our discussion, I convinced him that killing me was a bad idea.

"Unfortunately, by then I had already knocked down his house. More unfortunately for the Simpsons, they were in the house at the time. I didn't set out to kill them but, at the time, I didn't really care that I had."

"I did this to you—made you a murderer."

It felt like a fist to the solar plexus—he couldn't breathe for a minute, absorbing the words. Murderer. It didn't compute, but his mother was weeping openly now, repeating over and over into Harvey's shoulder, "I just wanted you to be happy, I just wanted you to be happy."

He considered telling her that, mostly, these days he was happy, but he decided that might not make her feel better. He wondered if there was a lack in him somewhere that he didn't feel more guilt for what he had done, but when he thought of Marnie Simpson, he saw her playing sex games with the daemon who had killed Jack Laurence and felt her cigarette burning a map of her pleasure on his body. He couldn't help it. He was glad she was dead.

"That's in the past," he said, but he knew it wouldn't be that easy. "Joe Dougherty is in the present, and the lords of the second sphere don't feel the same way humans do. If Dougherty crosses my father at the wrong time, he could die, and all for nothing. Brad didn't commit any burglaries, but he surely did father me."

Evan thought about the Black Masque, and fifty dead for what Omage had done to one of his own Prince's half-human monsters, and for what he had done to Evan. "I've got enough dead on my conscience already. I don't want to add Joe Dougherty to the list."

His mother sat rigidly upright in her chair with both hands in fists, tears leaving a glistening track down each side of her nose. Evan looked to her for a response, but Harvey shook his head. No more today. A good call: Evan didn't think he could cope with any more either. He gave Harvey a sharp nod in acknowledgment, all he could manage at the moment, and left the house. The Mercedes gleamed in the bright summer light that had followed the rain. Evan slid in behind the wheel and listened to the low purr as the motor turned over, afraid to let his mind wander farther than the task at hand. In spite of his determination, he drove through the city streets on automatic and didn't notice that he'd turned in at the garage until he found himself in his own kitchen again.

# Chapter 26

FREE OF THE CONSTRAINTS OF FLESH AND THE DISTRACTIONS OF SIGHT AND SOUND and touch, Badad of the host of Ariton spread himself through the now of the second celestial sphere. He felt the presence of others of his kind drift like threads across his mind—Agibol and Rigolen, messengers between the Princes of Ariton and Amaimon, and Diopus of the host of Azmod, enemy to Ariton, and Hepogon, servitor lord of Magoth, messenger to Kore—and felt their passing as they moved on. Caramos laughed a greeting, merged entities as they raced through the darkness, filling it with the presence of their Prince. Then Lirion joined them, sparking pleasure through the void.

"What did you want to know, cousin?"

Not words. He knew her thoughts as she knew his, and he showed her Mai Sien Chong, naked and strong, flushed beneath the honey of her skin, and Lirion saw in his mind the body he wore in the material sphere, saw it engorge with the fine trace of Mai Sien's long fingernails, the touch of her lips, and Lirion laughed in his mind. "What do you need of me?" The asking told him the answer to his question before it formed, but she read it in the flicker of his own field of being.

"Human flesh has few uses," she told him mind to mind, and they both saw broken flesh littering their knowledge of humans. "Too fragile, and they die quickly."

Existence gone in the pulse of an energy node that burned as a sun in the material sphere. Evan would die one day like that. Mai Sien would. Badad remembered death. He hadn't liked it, but he *had* learned to measure time in the heartbeat of human flesh, to recognize the passing of life in the stuttering halt of that beat, in the distancing of flesh-bound pain. Lirion offered him the other side of flesh, Mai Sien, whole and firm and eager, leaning over him, her smile one of conquest rather than submission. Mai Sien, reaching from under him to touch his hair, his mouth, while her sighs brushed heat on his lips like a kiss, and in the image his eyes looked inward on nothing, mind gone away, absorbed in the spell of Mai Sien's hands, her body, and in the sensations tensing the flesh he wore in its rhythmic explosion.

"Yes, flesh does have its uses."

And she saw the source of his confusion, the memory of scales and horns and dismay as he became in material shape the form their Prince had taken in Evan's world. Lirion laughed. A star in Cassiopeia would wobble on its axis in the material space that paralleled the energy flowing in knots and vortices of the second sphere, but in their home, her mocking humor filled the dark expanse of infinity.

"I don't think you need another teacher." Not words, but he knew Lirion's thoughts when she left him—"You seem to have found a native guide, and she seems to know the territory."—And he felt her laughter ripple through the second sphere when he opened in his mind to her the words Mai Sien had said and his confusion about pain and its relation to pleasure.

"No, not Evan." He felt her agreement in his head. "Humans seem to like that sort of thing out of anger or curiosity, or because those feelings have been so tangled up for them that they don't understand pleasure without pain at all." She thought about it for a moment. "The Carter boy was probably like that—he couldn't stay away from the pain, because it was all he knew. If Evan ever had curiosity about the mix of fear and pain for sport, Omage cured him of it, though sometimes the rage still bubbles up, and I think he'd like to tie me down, just to show he has the power."

That confused Brad. Evan had the power, had held them bound to his will for three years, until he willingly gave it up, an offering to Lily that could have gotten the boy killed. He didn't understand what Lily showed him, that Evan feared his own rage. It made no sense, but that was common for Evan, and right now, he wasn't interested in his son.

"Sometimes," Lirion added, "it's just a game, playing at power and fear out of curiosity, for people who have never had their limits tested the way Evan has, or Paul Carter." And at the question in his thoughts, she showed him her own human shape in tall spiked heels, a naked human male tied with scarves to the spindles of a balustrade. They laughed together as her image walked away, leaving him for his wife to find.

"The question you have to answer for yourself is simple," she reminded him. "If Mai Sien Chong knew your real name, would she bind you to her will, or would she have no interest in a daemon slave?" He felt her smile tingle through him. "If your answer is yes, ask yourself again, does it make your human flesh tingle when you look at her and know that you are playing close to the fire, that at any moment the game could become real?"

He knew what the answer would mean, knew that the line between the game and the reality resided in a word or two; and he wished in that moment for flesh, to feel it tighten in response to the image he saw in his mind. He would never trust Mai Sien the way he trusted his own kind, but the idea of testing his wits against hers in the bedroom as well as the chess table set sparks of energy pinwheeling through the empty dark. Lirion plucked from him the question that hovered almost unthought.

"Sometimes, with Evan, I have the fantasy," she admitted as her presence faded to nothing. While she shaped energy into the stuff of human flesh, she added, "But he's afraid of the impulse. And I'd be afraid of him if he weren't." Her presence left him then, shifting into the material sphere.

Alone once more with his unsettled thoughts, Badad knew he should go to Evan. If Da'Costa was right about the Dowager Empress' crystals, this case had just gotten more dangerous by orders of magnitude. But the tug of the material sphere he felt had nothing to do with work or a son who brought with him a host of feelings more complex and considerably less pleasurable than the ones he was contemplating.

Mai Sien waited, in Vancouver. And she wanted him to be . . . something else. Shaping himself a form to please her, a large orange cat with black stripes and a huge head, he focused on the material, on Earth, and found her in an office building high above the city skyline. Not a good moment to surprise her, he decided, and he searched out the sense of her presence that would take him to her home in this place. He materialized in a bedroom. She'd been here recently; her half-empty suitcase lay open on the bed, a tumble of silk underwear spilling out. A rumpled suit hung in the closet, and he snuffled it for her scent. Yes, she'd worn it recently and then changed for her meeting. A long split tunic, very sheer, with slim silk pants hung next to the suit, but in the body of the cat he could not quite tell what color it was, nor could he identify the fabric until he rubbed his head against it. Silk. It felt cool against his fur, and contentment rumbled deep in his throat for a moment before he pulled his head out of the closet and began to roam the bedroom, looking for something that marked the place as hers, and not just as a stopping point.

On the dresser he saw her hairbrush and an ivory comb, too yellow with age to come under current protective laws. A bottle of perfume and a small figurine stood on the nightstand. He passed on, considered leaping onto the bed for a nap, but thought better of the idea when he remembered the damage he'd done with his claws the last time. He felt the thought of a sigh form in his mind, but the sound came out of his cat's mouth as a low roar.

Then a memory out of his human time intruded on thoughts grown increasingly catlike. He'd seen that figure on the nightstand, of a sleeping child, before. A word leaped out at him past the sense-rich now-brain of the cat. Jadeite. A stone. But it had no smell, and so he let the image go and followed his exploration, looking for signs that Mai Sien Chong lived here. The bathroom, showroom-clean, was empty of personal items except for her travel kit on a shelf over the sink. He saw a screen with a country scene painted on it and circled around it, into a sunken living room with marble chess tiles in the floor, alternating pink and white. Sunlight sneaked past the foliage of a roof garden that obscured the view from windows slung low under a sloping roof and filled the room with dappled shadows and streaks of dusty gold. Curious, Badad stretched and made a circuit of the room.

Mai Sien had told him that she used this place when she wanted more privacy than her Uncle Chong's island compound afforded her. He didn't entirely comprehend privacy or its value, but he could tell that she spent very little time here—with the heightened senses of the animal body he wore, he would have caught the scent she left behind, or that of any regular visitors, but the room felt sterile, as if she never used it. The furniture, boxy modern pieces that didn't seem to suit her at all, gave no sign that she had used that either. Even the small altar cabinet seemed strangely neglected, with no offerings of incense or pictures of loved ones on it.

It wasn't a sign of Mai Sien, but the thick Chinese rug by the hearth of the huge fireplace drew him closer. Giving a long, luxurious stretch that nearly doubled his length, he reclined in boneless ease on the carpet, licking his orange paw with long strokes of his tongue. Contentment rumbled deep in his throat. He could think of no reason to resist the pull of his great eyelids, so he settled his massive striped head over his paws, flicked his tail lazily a time or two, and let sleep fill him with animal dreams.

The gasp of a woman's voice half-roused him, but she called his name, and he lolled a huge pink tongue at her, lifting one sardonic eyelid when she laughed. She wore a red silk robe, and he guessed that she wore nothing underneath it. Badad felt a rich satisfaction when he saw her breath catch.

"Chu Jung?" Tentative at first, she put her hand out to touch him, and she smiled when he gave her fingers a cautious lick. "My lord, you came to me." She fell to her knees, plunging her hands into the fur behind his ears.

"Chu Jung," she repeated, and "My Lord," combing her fingers through the thick fur.

It might not be as good as sex, but it had to be the second best thing he'd ever felt in a physical body. The rumble in his throat grew louder, and she laughed again. This time he let her keep the illusion of power, and she leaned over him and wrapped her arms around his neck, laid her head on his side, and closed her eyes. But the smile lingered, and her fingers continued to stroked his fur into sleep.

He woke to the feel of Mai Sien naked and heavy on his side and the scent of her in his head, and the sound of rubber-soled shoes squeaking closer on the marble floor. Lifting heavy eyelids, he looked into the terrified eyes of Mrs. Zheng, and into the third eye of her thirty-eight. His roar of protest didn't help the situation—he heard the bark of the gun, twice, three times, four, and the screams of Mrs. Zheng and the angry commands in Mai Sien's voice, but in a language he didn't know, and then the rubber-soled shoes were running, and more footsteps followed them back, more shots punched into his hide.

As he lay bleeding from the many gunshot wounds, Badad the daemon felt death wash in to fill the emptiness left by the lake of blood he lay in. From a distance he heard Mai Sien calling for him, but the .38 slug that had tumbled through his brain had taken the meaning of her words with it.

"Chu Jung, Chu Jung," she called to him, but he could not raise his huge cat's head to answer her. He was dying again, but differently this time, the cat-life ending like a shutter closing. Darkness . . .

# Chapter 27

THE AGENCY KEPT A BOTTLE OF TWENTY-FIVE-YEAR-OLD SINGLE MALT SCOTCH IN the credenza in the front office. Evan headed for it like a drowning man diving deeper for the surface. Damn, and damn. He usually didn't let himself think the sort of accusations that rattled around in his head: If his mother had kept her pants on around Kevin Bradley for just one more week, Evan would be normal, human, with a father who hadn't died because Gwen Davis had dumped him for a passing stranger. Carl Adams would still be dead, but it wouldn't have anything to do with Evan Davis.

Resentment he hadn't recognized until now bubbled on the surface of his rage. It wasn't so much that she'd married Harvey Barnes—she was entitled to a life—but that she'd taken Harvey's name. Mrs. Harvey Barnes. Gwen Barnes. He'd never had his father's name, but the last name he had used to mean something—the son of Gwen Davis: well-loved penance for his mother's sins if nothing else. Now he had nothing, was no one, because that son of a bitch Harvey Barnes had taken not just his mother, but her name. The one thing she'd given him with his miserable, monstrous life, that one slim thread of belonging, her name, was gone.

Why it hit him now instead of at her wedding, or at his belated college graduation, or in the hospital, or at any one of a thousand small moments, he didn't know. But it had, with the suddenness and fury of the afternoon's storm and hard on the heels of his retreat in the face of her tears. Damn. Damn. He reached for the bottle and stopped at the sound of Lily's voice behind him.

"Evan? I was about to call you—"

She sat behind Brad's antique Hepplewhite desk; Evan turned around and saw in the flicker of her eyes the quick catalog she did of his disheveled appearance and the shell shock on his face. The green and yellow streaks of bruises tracking his face didn't help, but she settled on his eyes, where he figured he was showing way too much of the battle going on inside him. Ellen Li sat across from Lily at the desk, neat in a trim charcoal linen suit, taking inventory as efficiently as Lily did. And next to Ellen, a stranger, a man slightly past his prime, slightly over his fighting weight, and slightly underprepared for the company he was keeping if the expression on his face—smug in a way that told Evan right off he didn't know the score—was anything to go by. Just great.

"Were you looking for something?" Lily asked. She knew what they kept behind that door in the credenza and waited for him to tell the truth or come up with a convincing evasion. So he took it as said.

"Yes," he said, "but it was a bad idea."

She lidded her laughter behind a drop of lashes, but not before Evan had seen the rueful mockery. Home sweet home. He threw himself into one of the uncomfortable spindle-backed chairs and faced his inquisitors. "Who's your friend?" He nodded in the stranger's direction. "And what did you want?"

"Want?" Lily's eyes widened in a travesty of innocence. "Nothing at all, except to invite you to a party."

Ellen Li shook her head, but whether she disapproved of his rather desperate appearance or Lily's glib response he couldn't tell.

"We've got a lead," Li explained. "Liz got the call from Customs this afternoon. They turned up a couple of our missing artifacts in a shipment of collectibles heading for Hong Kong via Vancouver, and we are on our way to the airport to take a look. This is Special Agent Sidney Valentine, Federal Bureau of Investigation, assigned to crimes involving the movement of stolen art across state lines. Sid, Evan Davis. Evan, Sid. He'll be coordinating our investigation with the Canadian authorities."

Evan gave the FBI agent a nod. Lily was grinning at the agent in a way that made Evan think of gristle and bits of bone between her teeth. Ellen Li showed none of her feelings on the matter, if she had any.

"I thought Brad might like to be in on the fun of tearing up boxes and looking for loot," Li explained.

Ah. That meant there were too many boxes, not enough people, and they would be spending the rest of the day up to their armpits in styrofoam peanuts and bad reproductions of the liberty bell while Customs tried to figure out who would bother to smuggle Chinese artifacts into China under cover of a shipment of tourist junk that no Hong Kong shopper would ever see. Wise of Brad to make himself scarce. But Lily was looking at him strangely, and he didn't like her next words. "Have you seen your father, Evan? I thought he would be with you this afternoon."

"Not since we all left Captain Marsh's office yesterday." He'd been annoyed about it. They had a case to solve, and so far Brad had put the firm under suspicion of stealing the objects themselves, but he'd done nothing to help them solve the case or get out from under the suspicion. He figured Ellen Li must be wondering if she'd made the right decision when she talked Marsh into not pressing charges, but she just gave a little laugh.

"I think perhaps he found a more interesting pillow to sleep on. Harry will be pleased for him." She gave a wry little smile, as if she'd just got the punchline of a private joke. Sidney Valentine didn't appreciate the humor, private or otherwise.

"Maybe you can discuss the sex lives of your suspects some other time, Lieutenant. Right now, we have United States Customs waiting for us with several of the items on your want sheet, and you have stopped to chat with the associates of our primary suspect in lieu of the suspect himself with the intention of inviting them to participate in the search for said objects."

As he grew more indignant, Valentine's neck and cheeks grew redder. He bounded to his feet and paced the length of the room. Turning, he raised his right arm and pointed a rigid finger at Ellen Li. "If you worked for me, you wouldn't be on this case at all, and this behavior is just more proof that Marsh should have taken you off the case as soon as he realized that you had a conflict of interest."

"If I worked for you, Sid, my name would be on the class action suit currently pending against your office for discriminatory promotion policy, so don't try to second guess the way I conduct my investigation."

She turned to Evan with the vestiges of her wrath still clinging to her words. "Mike Jaworski is on his way to the airport now to start looking through the boxes, but I don't expect him to find much more than we already have. The shipment totaled about fifteen boxes of materials purchased from The Franklin Mint by the Xiamen Private Trading Company, Limited, out of Singapore and shipped to Vancouver for final destination Hong Kong."

The case information snapped Evan's brain into work mode, as he figured it was supposed to do. He rounded the desk and took up a position over Lily's shoulder. She had the computer on, so he didn't have to boot up, just find the right browser.

"Spell that?" he asked. Ellen handed him the notebook where she'd written the information in crisp printed letters. "Odd," he said, as information filled the screen. "The name Xiamen means 'Mansion Gate.' I suppose the mansion could refer to the company's headquarters in Singapore, but it's also the name of an island, part of Fukkien Province."

Valentine's ears pricked up at the hint of a clue. "Let me see that."

Damn. Ellen Li had a way of treating him as if she'd known him forever that slipped past Evan's defenses like they didn't even exist. Being married to Harry, she probably did hear more about him than Evan wanted to know, but he trusted Harry and, by extension, his wife. He'd forgotten about the FBI man, though, an inexcusable loss of concentration that left him with his hacker programs hanging out and a federal officer in a position to arrest him for it heading for the screen.

Lily slithered out of the chair with an unnecessary wriggle. "Why don't you stay here with Lieutenant Li and work your magic on the machine from hell, while Sid and I take a look at those boxes Customs is holding at the airport?"

"Thanks." He sat down, noting with relief that Lily slipped her arm through the crook of Valentine's elbow and led him out of the office with a look of utterly false adoration on her face. Valentine, his detecting skills honed and ready, was lapping it up like a puppy left alone in the basement too long. Evan wondered how long it would take the man to do something actionable in court, and if Lily would let him live if he tried anything, or if she would take him to bed for the amusement value. The thought curdled his stomach.

"She's very good at that," Ellen Li observed. "But you are going to owe Miss Ryan quite a bit for that little maneuver."

"I know." He needed something worth the sacrifice of Lily's evening, but he didn't think he had it yet.

"According to their tax statement, Xiamen Private Trading Company specializes in importing for the Asian market American popular culture collectibles. The company does a steady business with The Franklin Mint— high-end souvenirs—but they don't crack the surface of the art world. Why would Hong Kong need to import collectibles through a Singapore trading company with a Fukkien name?"

"We are assuming the final destination is Hong Kong because that is where the bill of lading ends," Ellen cautioned. "But most Asian markets are mad for American popular culture these days. Once the shipment enters China, the receiving address can send it anywhere with little suspicion. If Xiamen Trading is stealing artifacts and sending them to China on a regular basis, those boxes of fragile collectibles make an effective cover, and they can sell the legitimate product in those markets for a reportable income."

Evan knew how that worked—the detective agency of Bradley, Ryan, and Davis existed to do the same for his daemon kin. But Ellen Li didn't have to know that. "The government probably doesn't know about the stolen art objects, though." Evan followed the train of thought. "If Beijing filed a formal request, we'd have to send the objects back anyway, particularly the ones with a clear provenance showing ownership by the Imperial Household. So they must be going to a private collector, or collectors."

"Smart boy." Ellen patted him on the shoulder. "Can you check the names and addresses of the Xiamen officers and primary owners on there? The company may be registered in Singapore, but that doesn't mean the owners necessarily live there."

Evan returned to studying the computer screen. "Give me a minute." He hit a few more keys, narrowing the search. "Did you have something specific in mind?"

"Maybe." Ellen Li shrugged. "The city of Amoy is located on Xiamen. Many Singapore Chinese consider Amoy their true home and still have family there as well."

"Still doesn't explain why they'd be smuggling carved jade elephants to Hong Kong in a box full of Scarlett O'Hara dolls and zircon-studded models of the Enterprise."

She was looking over Evan's shoulder; he knew he shouldn't let her see this, but the puzzle had them both. So he wasn't particularly surprised, when the list of owners scrolled by, to hear her whisper something in Chinese, the delivery of which suggested an epithet of dismay.

"What is it?"

"Chongs," she answered. "Way too many Chongs."

"Mind telling me the significance of the name?"

"Could be nothing," Ellen Li suggested. Evan didn't buy it. Neither did she. "Could be that the Chongs stole the artifacts and set your father up to take the fall."

Evan didn't like the cold lump that settled in his stomach. "He didn't come home last night."

"I don't think she would hurt him, Evan."

That brought a twist of a smile to his lips. Not likely, no. Except that something *was* wrong. He could feel it. Badad still had his freedom, but a disturbance had rippled through Evan on a wave of nausea when he thought of his father. "Who is she?"

Ellen looked at him for a long moment. "Mai Sien Chong. Do you see her name on the list of owners?"

Evan scanned the screen quickly, found it on the second pass. "Here it is. She's a small holder, not one of the major players in this company, but it looks like there are ties through other entities." He highlighted the name, Mai Sien Chong, and searched again. "Here, 'Chang Er Imports. Mai Sien Chong, principal shareholder.' All other shares held by major and lesser stockholders in Xiamen."

"Nothing subtle about their company names."

"What?" Evan looked up at her, waiting for Ellen Li to explain.

"Chang Er, the Moon Goddess. She is said to have stolen the draft of immortality from her husband. Damn!" Ellen pounded him on the shoulder she'd just patted. "I've known her for over a year, played chess with her once a week, and never suspected a thing!"

"Neither, apparently, did Brad," Evan pointed out. "But Harry did. His book told him." And Evan hadn't listened. Damn.

The computer beeped, and he turned back to the screen. Financial records scrolled into a cache file for later study, but he caught enough to make some guesses as the data passed by.

"It looks like both Chang Er Imports and Xiamen Trading pass through the Empress Holding Company, along with at least half a dozen financial entities listed here." He interpreted out loud for Ellen Li. "Empress had extensive holdings in Hong Kong until last year, when the company divested suddenly. Some of the money seems to have moved to Singapore, some scattered throughout the United States, but a good portion of it seems to have landed in Vancouver."

"The Flight of the Millionaires." Ellen Li nodded as if that part of the equation made sense. "Many wealthy Chinese did not trust the national government to keep its economic promises when Hong Kong changed hands. So they withdrew their wealth and invested it more heavily in the West."

"Empress seems to be at the center of their corporate structure." Evan looked up for a moment, a frown pulling at the stitches in his head. "Isn't that unusual for Chinese? Naming their companies after women, I mean? I didn't think women rated very highly on the Chinese scale of things."

"Not one of my culture's more endearing qualities," Li agreed. "But, if the Chongs are organizing their business interests symbolically, then we can assume they've been planning the theft of the Dowager Empress' treasures for over a decade."

"Why choose her for special attention?" Evan asked. "The Dowager Empress wasn't exactly a benign figure in Chinese history, and she's not the only Chinese imperial figure whose possessions are on display in world museums."

"Tzu Hsi was Manchu, not Chinese," Li objected. "She wasn't the evil schemer most Westerners make her out to be, but you're right, it doesn't make sense."

She straightened up. "We'll have to ask Chong Li-huang when we catch him."

Chong Li-huang. The principal stockholder in Xiamen and a major holder in all six of the other companies that Evan had traced so far. Clearly a ringleader in the scheme to steal the Dowager Empress' collection. Evan wondered what other irons old Li-huang had in the fire. He pulled up an address and printed it, then set the search programs to keep digging and turned off the monitor.

"The next search level will take longer," he explained. "No point in sitting here watching the minutes tick down."

Ellen Li nodded and reached for the paper in his hand. "Chang Er Imports, I presume, Dr. Watson?" She pushed away from his chair. "My car is at the curb."

"After you, Sherlock." Evan stood up and followed her to the office door. He didn't mention the search program again, and neither did she.

# Chapter 28

In his incorporeal being, Badad watched the scene that unfolded in Mai Sien's living room. Without his will and essence to hold it together, the body of the tiger faded and vanished, too slowly for Mai Sien's bodyguards to deny its existence or the supernatural mode of its disappearance. Their dread of the dying beast came as no surprise, but he hadn't expected the mortal terror that Mai Sien inspired in her henchpeople.

Trembling, Mrs. Zheng had led the Messers Hsi in dropping to the floor, where they lay facedown in abject obeisance to their naked and screaming mistress.

"Old Mother," he heard Mrs. Zheng whine, "forgive your servants who thought to protect the sacred Empress from the beast of her enemies."

"I have no enemies but my servants!" Mai Sien screamed, landing a well-placed kick in Mrs. Zheng's side. "And now, I have no lover!"

"We saw a *beast,* Blessed One, not a lover," Mrs. Zheng wailed, her righteous indignation mixing strangely with her miserable penitence. "We would not dare to harm one under the protection of the sublime presence!" The object of Mrs. Zheng's worship clearly had fallen in her estimation by consorting with a wild beast, even one as sleek and powerful as the tiger. Badad gave himself over to a bit of preening as Mai Sien kicked her servant again.

"And did it never dawn on you that I was under *his* protection, you fool?"

"But *whose* protection, My Lady?" Mrs. Zheng persisted. "Surely not your uncle's, who has charged me with the care of the sublime presence as he has charged Hsi with protecting your heavenly presence! The honorable uncle would surely not entrust that care to the jaws of a terrible beast!"

"He was not a terrible beast, you fool!" Mai Sien planted another solid kick against the housekeeper's head. "He was a god in the form of a beast, beautiful and strong, and you have destroyed him with your stupid gun!"

Badad decided it was time to put in an appearance in human form, before Mai Sien's did some serious damage to her foot or Mrs. Zheng started asking questions about gods consorting with her mistress. He settled into his more accustomed shape, with the black pants and sweater he'd left in the space between the spheres, and politely rang the bell.

Alone in the pink marble hallway, he waited for a long minute until Mrs. Zheng limped to the door. She did not look pleased to see him. He didn't really care; he didn't plan to take Mrs. Zheng to bed.

"Tell your mistress that Mr. Bradley is here to see her." He didn't bother with a please or thank you; he didn't feel much like being polite to the woman who had just ventilated him with a .38-caliber service pistol. He did hold her glance for long enough for recognition to set in. Not just of the night before—he let her see the tiger in his eyes. She looked away quickly, but not before he caught the fear and loathing in her eyes—and the jealousy. Mrs. Zheng did not like sharing the honors of protecting her mistress. Her royal mistress, if the conversation he'd overheard meant anything. Tough. He didn't like the old bitch anyway.

"Your mistress?" he reminded her.

Mrs. Zheng didn't exactly invite him in, but she did loosen her hold on the door so that he could slip by. Mai Sien, he noticed, did look quite lovely when she was angry. Temper brought a flush to her skin like a ripe peach. A rosy glow suffused the warm honey of her skin even in those places she usually kept hidden but which were now on quite vivid display, to the disapproval of Mrs. Zheng and the extreme discomfort of the Messers Hsi. Brad liked it just fine.

Fortunately, Mai Sien was suitably relieved to see him in one unperforated piece. She smiled as if he'd done a particularly clever trick and ran to him barefooted across the marble chessboard of the floor. When she stood so close that the tips of her nipples brushed lightly against the nap of his sweater, she stopped. "I knew you would come back." She raised a slim hand that trembled slightly as it stroked his cheek. "Chu Jung."

"Of course." He leaned into the stroke as she drew her hand back, until they stood mouth to mouth. He didn't quite remember if he'd answered yes to the fact of his return or to her use of the name that sent a cold chill fizzing up his spine. He knew he should care—there was danger in admitting too much to a human—but her excitement, sharp in the brittle glitter of her eyes and in the quick pant of her breath as it caressed his lips, ignited his own tension. Teasing the tiger. The danger turned her on, and she didn't seem to mind the audience, either. He took the final step toward her, touched her lips with his, and reached for a thigh.

Mai Sien broke their kiss long enough to sigh into his mouth. The audience seemed less sanguine about his actions than Mai Sien; Mrs. Zheng hissed her disapproval and made a quick gesture to dismiss the Messers Hsi, who looked ready to strangle him and take his place. This time they didn't try to shoot him, however, which he considered an improvement in their relationship.

"I'll take care of Ms. Chong, now," he said without looking away from Ms. Chong's mouth. "You can have the night off."

The shorter Mr. Hsi, who was frowning the most ferociously, seemed about to respond, but Mrs. Zheng gave a curt command and he bowed rigidly and left the room. She gave Brad a considerably more chilly bow, and, with a last look around the living room and a darker look for her mistress, she followed the taller Mr. Hsi from the apartment.

"I thought you said you came here for privacy," he said when the door shut after the departing bodyguards.

She smiled up at him. "This *is* privacy. At Uncle Chong's, we would have grandmother and grandfather and uncle and aunt and their children and their children's children, and here we just have Mrs. Zheng, who will swear her brothers to secrecy and send them back to Uncle for the night."

Her answer seemed more comprehensible than most he'd received from humans. The Chinese, he decided, were very much like his own kind, tied in alliance to their families as daemon lords were to their Prince, and it mattered just as little how the individual daemon, or Chinese business-woman, felt about it.

"Thank you for the gift of the great tiger." She laughed deep in her throat, her fingers drifting a delicate trace along the curve of his ear and the line of his hair along the temple. "But next time, perhaps you should wait until you are sure we will be alone before you give me the gift of your many faces."

"I'll remember that," he promised, and she took his human body to her bed in the room that showed little of her presence but the carved jadeite child on the dresser. As he finally drifted off to sleep, he noted with a bit of pride and a great deal of pleasure that he hadn't torn her sheets at all this time.

# Chapter 29

ELLEN LI GAVE THE UNPREPOSSESSING FRONT DOOR AT CHANG ER IMPORTS A sweeping glance. "This is the place?" she asked Evan, with a sniff and a twitch of her nose. The smells of cooking food, and the bustling cacophony of the traffic on the street behind them, and the shifting of sacks and boxes in the warehouse to the side hardly suggested the corporate offices of a wealthy business.

"That's what it says on the door." He added the comment he knew Ellen Li was thinking: "You'd think they could afford better office space, given their tax statement."

"And the business that never reaches the tax returns," Ellen Li added. "Could be an address of record, I suppose."

Evan shook his head. "Doesn't seem likely. The only other address listing we found for Chang Er Imports is in Singapore. Xiamen has offices in Singapore, San Francisco, Vancouver, and Hong Kong, but none in Philadelphia."

"But their boxes landed in our airport, with objects stolen from our museums," Li reminded him. She hit the buzzer at the side of the glass door. "So Xiamen is probably using Chang Er Imports to ship from. The question is, where is The Franklin Mint shipping to?"

"San Francisco." Evan shrugged when she gave him a sharp look. "Call it intuition." She might look the other way if he saw more than he was supposed to about the records of a criminal organization, but clearly his ferret programs would earn him closer scrutiny if applied to upstanding companies like The Franklin Mint, whose only crime was their prices. A staticky voice interrupted this thought.

"Who is it?"

"Lieutenant Ellen Li, Philadelphia Police. I'd like to speak with Ms. Chong."

"Just a minute."

The lock release clicked. Evan opened the door and followed Ellen into a vinyl-tiled entryway too small to hold them both comfortably. When the street door closed, the lock on the inner door clicked open to a nearly empty office.

"May I help you, sir?" the woman at the polished mahogany desk asked.

"You can tell us where we can find Ms. Chong," Ellen said.

"Of course, just a moment, please." She spoke into the mouthpiece of her telephone headset for a moment, then broke the connection.

"Ms. Chong will be with you in a moment. Make yourself comfortable, please." With that, the receptionist returned her attention to her telephone console.

Evan looked around the reception area, wondering how they were supposed to make themselves comfortable. With the exception of the receptionist's desk and chair and a cement pot of bamboo, all more expensive looking and tasteful than he would have expected in that location, the room had no furnishings at all. The floor, a rich hardwood set in a complicated pattern, showed a slight difference in color where a rug must have lain until recently. It looked as if somebody was packing for a quick exit.

A bell chimed softly behind him, and he turned around as an elevator door he hadn't noticed before slid open.

"You wanted to see me?"

This was the woman for whom Brad had given up on his determination to avoid complications with humans? She was short and plump, with streaks of gray shot through her shoulder length hair. The lime green linen suit she wore didn't exactly clash with her skin tones, but the overall effect was one of earnest frumpiness.

"We are here to see Ms. Chong on a police matter," Ellen Li said, and Evan found her confusion reassuring. So, this wasn't the girl friend.

"I am Ms. Chong," the woman answered.

"I'm afraid there has been a mistake." Ellen smiled her patient police officer's smile. "We were looking for Ms. Mai Sien Chong."

"Ah! That explains it! I am Mai Lu Chong, Mai Sien's cousin." The woman opened her arms in a gesture of apology. "Unfortunately, you will not be able to see Mai Sien Chong today, as she is out of the country on business. But I will be happy to leave a message for her to contact you when she returns."

"Which will be?" Ellen left the end of her question dangling, and Mai Lu Chong clasped her hands with a little bow, more apologetic than before.

"I am sorry, but we do not expect Ms. Chong to return for several weeks."

"I see. And you are authorized to speak for her?"

Mai Lu Chong gave a tiny laugh. "No one is authorized to speak for the company in Ms. Chong's absence. All decisions will wait until she reaches Singapore next week. If you want to leave her a message, I will see that her secretary receives it and that it goes into the message pouch for Singapore. After that, we must wait until she checks in. But I will help you as much as I can."

"I see. Can we speak to her secretary directly?" Ellen asked.

"I am terribly sorry, but Ms. Chong's secretary took advantage of Ms. Chong's absence to take her own vacation. We do not expect her back for two weeks." Mai Lu Chong wrung her hands in obvious dismay, but Evan figured by now that distress had more to do with the continued presence of Ellen Li and himself than with the absence of Mai Sien Chong.

Ellen merely nodded. "Can you give us the address where she is currently staying?"

"Of course!" Mai Lu Chong scurried to the reception desk where she tore a pink message sheet from the pad by the receptionist's elbow. "She will be at this number when she reaches Singapore sometime next week. If you would like to leave your number, I can ask her to call you if she calls in before then."

"Thank you for your help." Ellen took the message slip but didn't bother to look at it before putting it in her pocket. "If we need anything more, we'll be in touch."

"Of course. And good-bye."

Mai Lu Chong gave them a curious little bow, but did not shake hands, and returned to the elevator hidden behind the carved panel on the wall. Dismissed, Evan followed Ellen Li out the first door, waited until it had closed and locked behind them, and opened the street door. Once outside, he took a deep breath.

"She knows more than she is telling," he said, breathing easily for the first time since they'd entered the offices of Chang Er Imports.

"Of course she does," Ellen Li agreed. She started walking down the street to where she'd left the car and Evan followed, listening as she admitted, "I expect the receptionist does too, and that's why we got the legal department Ms. Chong, instead of the one in sales or the one in shipping. She was careful not to lie, but Chong was clearly avoiding telling a number of relevant truths."

Like the present whereabouts of Mai Sien Chong. "So, what's next? The apartment at the Rittenhouse, or the airport Customs office?"

Ellen rounded the car and gave him a wry look over the roof. "Now we call Mike and see how his end went. We hope they found enough for a search warrant at the Rittenhouse, and tomorrow, with paper in hand, we check it out." She opened the car door and slid in behind the wheel. After she'd unlocked his door and Evan had settled himself beside her, she rummaged in her purse and pulled out her cell phone. "Hit the third button; it will connect you to Mike's cell phone."

Evan followed her instructions, and Jaworski's voice answered with the first ring.

"Ellen?"

"No, Evan Davis. Ellen is right here."

"Ask him if they found anything."

But Mike Jaworski didn't wait for the question to begin his report. "We didn't find much, but we did seize the bills of lading. Sid is contacting Interpol Hong Kong, in case any of the items on our want list already made it through."

Evan passed along Jaworski's information, and then repeated Ellen's next question: "Anything to connect the boxes with Chang Er Imports?"

After a short wait, Jaworski gave a hesitant answer.

"Sid doesn't think so. He's pursuing the Hong Kong end, and San Francisco."

Evan didn't wait for Ellen to ask: "But you think you've got something?"

"Maybe. There's a Philadelphia phone number scrawled on the side of one of the invoices. I tried calling it, but I got a recorded message that the number has been disconnected. I'm heading home now, but I called it in, and we should have billing records on it tomorrow."

Evan relayed the message, and Ellen took the phone from him. "Mike," she said, "get some rest and meet me in the office by eight. If Chang Er Imports ever paid that phone bill, I want a search warrant for their offices, their warehouse, and Mai Sien Chong's Rittenhouse apartment. Got it?"

Evan didn't hear the reply, but it made Ellen laugh. Then she handed the phone back to him. "Hang it up for me, please?" and by the time he had done so and stuffed it back in her purse, they were parked on Seventh Street, by the garden gate.

"Sorry I can't invite you to the search party tomorrow, Evan," she told him as he climbed out of the car. "But there are privacy issues, and the fourth amendment—"

"No problem." He smiled so she would understand that he had no hard feelings. "But I do expect to hear all about it later."

"As much as I can," she promised, and pulled away.

Evan waited until her car had disappeared around a corner, and then he went into the garden and pulled a piece of paper out of his pocket. He looked at the address, an apartment on the twentieth floor of the Ritten-house, and tried to visualize the building and the distance from the ground. And then he willed his body to pass from the material sphere to the second sphere of his father, and shifted again, back into material form, in the living room of the apartment that his father's lover called home. Except that the living room, at least, was empty. The kitchen still had a few items in it; the vegetables in the refrigerator still looked fresh, but the bath was empty.

The bedroom looked empty as well, but Evan could feel the presence of his father in the room. Brad had been here. As if he'd needed the evidence, two objects sat together in the middle of the wall-to-wall carpet. An alabaster figure of Kwan Yin, about ten inches tall, stood with one arm raised in blessing and the other outstretched. Looped over her outstretched arm, there was a gold cufflink engraved with Brad's initials. Evan picked them up and turned them over in his hands. He recognized them both, and a chill ran up his spine as he read the threat in them. Where had Mai Sien Chong gone? And how much, he wondered, did she really know about his father?

Neither object gave him an answer. He gripped them so tightly that the folds of Kwan Yin's robes bit into the flesh of his palm, but he set the pain aside and remembered the lesson he'd learned from Lily on the river-bank. He could find his father if he concentrated hard enough. So he stood very still, with his eyes closed, the cufflink clasped tightly in one fist and the Kwan Yin in the other, and he reached outward, feeling for the con-sciousness of the daemon lord. Flinging the essence of his daemon nature into the second celestial sphere, he let his mind thunder the name of his father. He drew some unwelcome attention he recognized as Azmod flick-ering with the green flame by which the lords of that Prince appeared in his mind, but he felt no answering presence of his father.

Returning to his body, which had remained frozen in the position of intense concentration he left it, he sent a thought out into the material sphere, searching for the resonating pattern that would echo the presence of his father. For a moment he thought he heard the echo, but jumbled and unclear, and then it was swept away, as if the mind he'd touched had ceased to function. But that couldn't be. Whatever happened to the body he wore, Badad of the host of Ariton could not die. Evan shivered, as though a clammy presence had touched him, but he felt nothing, not even a breeze to account for it.

The Kwan Yin in his hand mocked him. Goddess of Mercy indeed. He could use a little mercy right now, but as usual, none was forthcoming. He remembered the impression of chaos, and then nothing. Had Mai Sien Chong bound his father? Was that the reason he'd lost a sense of his father so suddenly? The thought of his father bound to the will of someone who cared only for the power Badad could give them and nothing for the creature who was bound made him ill. But he hadn't felt the struggle or the torment he remembered from his own experience binding the daemon. Maybe they still had time, if he could just capture again the sense of his father he'd held for that brief moment.

"Damn you," he muttered, and visualized home, listened for the sound of the fountain splashing in the corner of the garden, and felt for the scent of late spring blossoms floating on the breeze. Suddenly he stumbled against the rough brick paving.

"Find anything interesting?" Lily walked out of the shadows.

"Where's my father?" Evan demanded.

Displeasure tightened her lips. "You don't own me anymore," she reminded him. "I can kill you if I don't like your manners."

She meant it. Lily never made idle threats. But she almost never moved without warning, at least on him, so he figured he still had time to explain. "I can't find him. I found these at Mai Sien Chong's apartment." He held out his hands, the cufflink in the palm of his right, the statuette of Kwan Yin wrapped in his left. "It's a message—she's got him—and I can't reach him."

Lily reached for the Kwan Yin but stopped short of touching the ivory figure. "Oh." She smiled a twist of irony at him. "She's got him all right. Had him might be a better phrase. He's sleeping—you can probably reach him now if it is necessary, but I don't think he'd appreciate the intrusion."

"Then he's not in danger?" Oddly, the thought that his father did not need rescue made him angrier than he had been when he thought someone was holding his father captive. Jealous? He didn't think so. But maybe disappointed that he wouldn't get to play the hero tonight. Lily seemed to follow the play of thought across his face.

"I didn't say he was safe." She reached a finger to Evan's temple and caught a lock of hair, curled it lazily around her finger tip. "But I don't think he'd appreciate rescue tonight."

"You mean—"

She pulled him toward her by the lock of hair. "Even parents," she confirmed, then caught his lower lip in sharp white teeth and nipped. He decided now was not the time to make demands about Alfredo Da'Costa or the meaning of fidelity in a relationship. According to Lily-logic, she was always faithful when they were in bed together; it was just the rest of the time that he had to worry. So he let her lead him to her bed. Tomorrow would be soon enough to worry.

# Chapter 30

BRAD AWOKE WITH THE SCENT OF MAI SIEN'S HAIR IN HIS HEAD. THE THIN GRAY light that promised dawn cast her planes and curves in a million shades of shadows as she slept, insubstantial except for the warmth of her body heavy against his side. He smiled to himself and stretched, finding pleasure in the play of languorous muscles and the way his skin slid against hers when he moved. But human bodies also had bladders, so he drew his arm out from under her and headed for the bathroom.

On his way back to bed, the jadeite figure caught his eye again. The last time he'd seen it, the figure had been reclining next to an alabaster Kwan Yin on a shelf at the Philadelphia Museum of Art. But Mai Sien Chong wasn't looking at his eyes. Beneath sleep-heavy lids her gleaming eyes had fastened on his morning erection.

"Is that for me?"

"It could be," he agreed. Interesting to find it had a purpose after all. She gave him a lazy smile; Brad almost lost his train of thought when she licked her lips. "If you can explain this."

He set the figure of the reclining child on his side of the bed and waited.

"Beautiful, isn't it?" Mai Sien wistfully traced a finger over the smooth jadeite surface.

"The curator at the Philadelphia Museum of Art thinks so."

"I suppose he does," she sighed, then reached for his head, pulled him down to her kiss with both hands. "Wait for me."

She slid out of bed and wrapped her red silk robe around herself, a bit late for modesty, Brad thought, but it did make it easier to think. Not a lot easier, though. She stopped at her closet before the bathroom. Probably a good idea: Brad dug up his clothes and put them on because he wouldn't give much for his chances of keeping the next conversation at the level of work if his flesh had easy access to hers. He figured he was finding out about the down side of being human now, and he didn't much like it.

When Mai Sien returned she wore the silk pants and long split tunic he'd noticed on the other side of his cat-death. With human eyes he realized the clothes were a brilliant sapphire blue with a delicate swirling pattern in green worked into the tunic. She held her head erect, and age peeked out of her eyes.

"Good morning, Empress." Brad stood next to the bed, one eyebrow cocked in question. "But Empress of what, I wonder?"

"As a dutiful niece, I must ask you to wait for your answer just a little while longer." She reached out to touch him, hesitant in the way her fingers sought his but dared not take them. He did not oblige, but stuffed his hands in his pockets, waiting for her to explain.

"My uncle will expect us to call on him this morning, a duty to family I cannot escape. When we have paid our respects, I will show you all you wish to see, tell you what you want to hear."

"I have a feeling I won't want to hear any of it," Brad muttered, but he followed her out of the bedroom and waited while she called for her car and a driver.

She accepted his help with her coat, slid her arms into the sleeves and shifted the shoulders carefully into place without allowing her body to come into contact with his hands. He could find no guilt or shame in the way she had withdrawn into herself, no insecurity in the demure downcast of her eyes. It was as if another personality had overwhelmed the one he knew, or as if the manners of a different time and duty shaped the way that personality lived in the world. It seemed ominous enough that he wondered if this was the effect on time that Alfredo Da'Costa had warned them about.

But the car was at the curb, and the driver was silent as he held the door for them. Brad would have preferred to take the direct route, but he didn't know where they were going, so he leaned back in the plush seat and watched Vancouver fall behind them.

When the car approached the wharf, he figured they would get out and take a boat, but then he saw the small ferry painted like a Chinese junk, docked between two massive freighters. The car did not stop, but continued down the dock and into the ferry's open loading bay. Then the driver stepped out and held the door for them again, and Mai Sien invited him to attend her on the deck.

He'd much rather have found himself a nice soft chair in the cabin below and indulged in a few of the Sunday rituals that he'd learned to appreciate—a fat newspaper, a cup of coffee, and most important, the way that Evan had insisted the firm set aside Sunday as downtime—nowhere they needed to go and nothing they needed to do. Gusting clouds leached the warmth out of the spring day, and Brad wondered if the water ever gave up its threat of winter. But for more than his usual reasons he didn't want to let Mai Sien out of his sight, so he followed her to the bow of the boat and watched the dark line on the horizon draw closer, hoping he was seeing the island home of the Chong family and not the line of murky fog it looked like.

After about fifteen minutes of biting cold wind and bitter spray, the rocky shore and the jetty reaching into the sound resolved out of the murk.

"Home?" He nodded in the direction of the island, but Mai Sien Chong shook her head.

"Safe harbor, perhaps," she corrected him, "but China is home."

"Have you ever seen China?" he wondered, and she laughed.

"In this life, many times in my dreams. But China is old, and some take longer than others to reach enlightenment. So yes, I have seen China. I have lived many times in China; husbands have taken me to their mothers' houses to raise families, and I have watched them die of famine or war or disease."

"And you've died?"

"As many times as I lived, save one. Sometimes I died as young as the children I lost in other lives, other times I lived as long as my old grandmother." She made a dismissive gesture with her hand. "Once when I died, I went to heaven with a large black pearl in my mouth to pay my way. Other times, more numerous than I can count, I went to the world beyond with no rice in my belly and not even paper money burned in my honor."

The thought of so many deaths seemed to make her more somber than sad. For a moment, as she talked, Brad felt as though she were the older of them, and the wiser. He wondered how Mrs. Zheng had had the nerve to chastise this mistress. But of course she hadn't. Mai Sien Chong, the woman he knew in this life, was aggressive and headstrong with a temper like flashpaper. She had nothing in common with the woman on the ferry except for the body she inhabited. But the eyes were the same, older, stronger, and the desire still burned in them, wanting him and knowing that all of it was temporary.

"Were you a woman in all those lives?" he asked while his body fed him fantasies of Mai Sien stretched beneath him on the bow of the ferry, her clothes pushed out of the way, her legs cradling him.

"I *am* a woman," she answered him. "The body is just a reflection of who I am." And she slid her arms beneath his coat to wrap them around his waist and buried her face in his breast.

"Don't let them make you forget that." And the way she looked up at him when she said it demanded a promise in return.

"If I am ever in danger of forgetting, just do what you are doing now," he assured her. "I won't be able to forget. But—"

"No more questions!" She took her arm from his coat to place a tapered index finger across his lips. "Don't ask! I should not have spoken of it at all, but you are a god, and must know these things already."

"I'm not that sort of god," he pointed out, but her driver came to tell them they would soon be docking, so he didn't get a chance to show her what kind of god she had made him.

The driver didn't lead them back to the car as he'd expected, but took them through the cabin—as warm as he'd known it would be, with the smell of hot coffee lingering in the air—and out a side door on the lower level to a gangway leading to the dock. A car waited with a driver and a guard who opened the door for them and gave Brad a baleful glare when he entered. They drove away from the shore along a road of crushed shell that lead upward into a small forest. When he had begun to wonder if there was a house on the island at all, or if the drivers had conspired to bring him here to kill him where no one would find the body, they rounded a last curve and he saw the Chong compound.

He could understand why he hadn't seen the house on any of their turns until they faced it across a small clearing. The roof and sides were made of wood the exact color of the trees that surrounded it. The windows reflected those trees so that, even this close, one had to look straight at the house or it would seem to disappear. On first seeing it, he'd thought the house too small to comfortably hold all the Chongs, but when the car pulled up at the front door, he saw how wrong a sense of perspective can be. The double door stood twice his height, and the house itself, stretching away on both sides, dwarfed him. One of the doors opened before he reached it. Mrs. Zheng. Wonderful. The housekeeper bowed to Mai Sien and ignored Brad.

"You must be chilled, Lady," she scolded like an old amah. "You will catch your death one of these days."

As Mrs. Zheng herded her away, Mai Sien grabbed his hand. "Don't leave me." It sounded more like a plea than an order. Brad found himself drawn after her by her eyes more than the hand that held him, but he resolved to step carefully. He didn't know what Mai Sien had told her uncle, or how the bodyguards had explained the fact that she'd sent them packing.

Mrs. Zheng seemed less than pleased with the arrangement, but she led them through halls and up stairs, past rooms decorated in a mix of styles both Chinese and Western. He tried to identify the artwork on display through the doorways they passed. All of it seemed worth a second look, but he recognized none of it from the list of objects stolen from the PMA or the University Museum. He supposed Mai Sien might have bought the solitary piece from a fence, but he doubted it. The rest of it was here somewhere, but they'd reached the end of the hall, where Mrs. Zheng stopped to hold a door open on a room with a bed and a walk-in closet.

"You will wait outside now, demon," Mrs. Zheng commanded. She reached behind her back, as if to warn him that she could shoot him again, but he beat her to the gun and stuffed it in his pocket.

"I don't think so," he corrected her, and she blushed deeply, huffing her embarrassment.

"This is no time for man-woman thing! My Lady's uncle waits! She cannot dishonor her grandfather in this house!"

"Then she won't. But she will change into dry clothes, and I will fetch some clean things from home myself. And then we will join Mr. Chong."

"Your home is Philadelphia. Go home for clothing, then, and stay there! You should not be here!"

Mrs. Zheng's head bobbed as she scolded him. If she hadn't already shot him once it would have made him smile. Since she had shot him, he closed the door on her protests. But she was right about one thing—he was far too damp and miserable in his present condition to consider the "man-woman thing."

"I'll be back before you are out of the shower," he told Mai Sien, who was stripping off her own damp clothes. He waited a moment to appreciate the naked curve of her hip, then disappeared, heading home for a quick change of his own.

He looked the same in his bedroom in Philadelphia as he had in Mai Sien's room in Vancouver, but he'd abandoned the matter of that body when he entered the second sphere. The body he now wore would pass all the local medical tests designed to determine physical identity, but he'd shaped it in his mind out of the energy of the second sphere, leaving the cold and the damp and the sweat with the floating detritus of the planet's energy nexus. He could have shaped the clothes as well, he supposed, but it took more energy than it was worth, and the results never had quite the feel of Carlo Pimi's tailoring.

Feeling far more sanguine about his human form again, he pulled from his closet a charcoal suit and one of Carlo Pimi's shirts. The crisp cotton fell into place impeccably across his shoulders, the feel of it cool and precise on his skin. As he dressed, he heard voices downstairs—Evan and Harry—but figured the amenities would keep. Mai Sien Chong, however, might not. So he closed his eyes and searched out the presence that he recognized as Mai Sien and let her draw him back.

# Chapter 31

EVAN IGNORED FOR THE MOMENT THE LIST OF ADDRESSES BELONGING TO THE Chong family of Xiamen trading and related companies, including Chang Er Imports, on the screen and took a tentative sip at his coffee. Too hot, but the sting of it took his mind off the profound stupidity of sitting in his father's tapestried wing chair, brooding. He knew he was brooding because Lily had told him so in no uncertain terms before rolling over and going back to sleep. He supposed it was true, though he preferred to think of it as rational concern. The focus of that concern, an ivory Kwan Yin with one of Brad's cufflinks in its arms, stared back at him from the rubble where he'd propped her. What did she mean? Had someone known he would find her, or had she been intended for the police? Had his father's lover left it as a challenge, or had someone else placed it there as a warning? Ellen Li's search this morning might give her the key, but she'd barred him from the chase because he was a civilian, and because Sidney Valentine still considered his father a suspect. And now that he had the missing Kwan Yin, the police might even suspect that he'd stolen it himself, as his father's accomplice.

He checked his watch again. Ten-thirty. By now, he figured, Ellen Li must have nagged the evidence she needed out of old Sid and she'd had time to wake up a judge for a search warrant for Chang Er Imports. She'd have the satisfaction of closing in on the quarry and proving that her mind was sharper, her skills better than those of the thief she tracked, while Evan waited with the Goddess of Mercy mocking him from the ruins of his desk and a decision to make in his hand. At which address would he find his father? He figured it had to be Vancouver; if Mai Sien Chong had gone directly to Singapore, or Shanghai, or the island from which Xiamen Trading took its name, she would still be on a plane and Brad would have been sleeping in his own bed. If Mai Sien Chong took a flight to Vancouver, she could have arrived as early as yesterday afternoon, and Brad could have been waiting for her. But at the condo in Vancouver belonging to Chang Er, or on the nearby island where the Chong family seemed to have its North American base of operations? And more to the point, perhaps, would his father appreciate Evan rushing to the rescue? Which took him back to Kwan Yin.

Evan didn't like waiting. He'd just about decided he'd done enough of it when the doorbell to the back garden rang. Figured. Could be anybody, because nobody on this case bothered with the front door anymore. He doubted there'd ever been a suspect on more personal terms with the authorities determined to lock him up. Ouch. Worse than brooding, he was working on a full-blown sulk, and if he didn't want to hand the advantage to whoever waited at his garden gate, he had about thirty seconds to shake the self-pity. He hauled himself to his feet, grateful that at least his head didn't hurt this morning. He'd given it until today, figuring that if it got worse, he probably had some sort of slow-leaking hematoma the doctors had warned him about, and if it didn't, he'd probably survive. Looked as though he was going to live.

Harry waited at the gate, hands in his pockets—no book this time. Evan released the lock and opened the door. "Any news?" he asked.

"Quite a bit." Harry stepped inside. "Ellen is off to Vancouver with Special Agent Valentine. They left Mike Jaworski to cover the search of the warehouse kept by Chang Er Imports. Neither Valentine nor the police officers who just lost their Sunday afternoon in Vancouver seemed much pleased with the speed with which Ellen is moving, but she didn't want to wait, figures the goods might slip out of our hands again if they don't move quickly."

"And you are telling me this because?" Evan didn't have to say anything more. They both knew why he'd been left home, and he couldn't imagine that Valentine would be happy if he knew Harry was warning Kevin Bradley's son that the police were on their way.

"Ellen isn't usually as forthcoming to me as she's been on this case." Harry gave him a little shrug. "I rather got the feeling that she expected me to tell you everything and that she was making sure I had all the pertinent facts handy for you."

"In that case, let's see what we can make of her information." He led Harry toward the public offices at the front of the house. As he passed under Brad's room, he thought he heard the soft pressure of footsteps crossing the carpet, but it was gone before he could be sure he heard it. Probably Lily, or a trick of acoustics in the old house, but Harry had heard it too and stopped to look up.

"Has your father come home yet?"

"I haven't seen him."

"I thought perhaps he had contacted you." Harry sighed. "Ellen is worried. Neither of us believes that Brad would be an accomplice to a felony, but we hadn't expected Mai Sien Chong to be involved either. If they have developed a romantic entanglement, as Ellen believes, it will be difficult to convince a judge that they didn't commit the burglaries together."

"It sounds like Ellen was beginning to have her doubts as well."

Evan ushered Harry into Brad's office, with its side windows looking out on the garden, and gestured to a side chair before taking his place behind the desk.

"I don't think so." Harry sat absentmindedly, frowning in the way he had when giving the full weight of attention to a problem. "But Sid Valentine is going to be a problem unless we can prove that Brad's interest in Mai Sien is only professional. You haven't met her, but Chong . . . let's just say that, the evidence being equal, a judge is not likely to believe there was nothing personal between them. Chong is beautiful in a way that can be very dangerous for a man. She uses her attributes shamelessly to win at chess; if she truly is involved in illegal activities, I would think she would do the same."

"Then we'll have to make sure that the evidence isn't equal. When did Ellen and her FBI-geek leave for Vancouver?"

Harry gave him a disapproving glare, but he answered the question. "Their flight took off about an hour ago. Ellen stopped at the Rittenhouse with a search warrant for Chong's apartment this morning, but it turned out she didn't need one. Chong had already sold the place and moved out, lock, stock and barrel. The cleaning staff were scheduled for tomorrow morning, but Ellen had the apartment sealed for forensics.

"She said the place had been emptied by an expert. Most people leave something behind—open cleanser under the counter, jar of pickles in the refrigerator, but they didn't even leave the toilet paper on the roll when they cleaned out the condo."

They'd come back, then, and cleaned up after he'd gone last night. "They did leave something."

"Your name didn't appear in the guestbook, or Ellen would have mentioned it."

Harry didn't waste time on the obvious. Evan wondered if Ellen Li knew he'd been there. "Don't you want to know what I found?"

Harry looked at him then. If Evan hadn't known better, he'd have said his teacher was afraid. "Ellen said that she'd put a watch on the door last night. No one came or went except a couple of people on hotel security's list of Chong's domestic employees who live in the building. Neither of them fits your description."

Of course, Evan realized, he didn't know better. Harry *was* afraid, but curious as well.

"I suppose I should want to know what you found," he said, "but I'd rather know how you did it."

"No," Evan laughed a little, to himself . . . "You really don't want to know that, Harry." He was scaring Harry more now, but he shook his head.

"Evan Davis! I want to talk to you right now!" Joe Dougherty, thundering through the back of the house, pulled them both out of an uncomfortable silence. How the hell had he gotten in?

Harry gave him a rueful laugh. "You are going to have to remember to lock that gate, Evan." The fear wasn't gone, just set aside, but the fact that Harry could put it aside gave Evan some hope.

"Yeah, I know."

"He doesn't sound happy," Harry noted. "Better get out there and face the music before he starts chewing on the furniture."

"Wait here." Evan took a breath, remembered who he was talking to, and what he owed the man. "Please. While I take care of this."

"I presume that, since your father has not come down the stairs to deal with the interloper, he has already made a successful getaway?"

Evan nodded. "Probably, if it was Brad at all. It's more likely that it was Lily." And he didn't want to think about the explanations he'd need if Joe Dougherty clashed with Lily in one of her moods.

"Then I think I'd better accompany you, Evan. Perhaps a third party present will keep the discussion below the level of fisticuffs." Harry couldn't have known what Evan was thinking—not even with his *I Ching,* which he didn't have with him.

Evan figured he could deal with a fistfight. Harry, Joe Dougherty, and Lily Ryan together in the same room, though, might be more than he wanted to tackle in one lifetime.

"Doesn't anybody take Sunday off anymore?" He'd meant it as an aside to Harry as he opened the office door, but Joe Dougherty had already reached the other side and heard him.

"This *is* my day off, you bastard, and *this* is completely personal." Dougherty grabbed Evan by the shirt and swung him against the wall so hard that Evan's head bounced against the plaster before finally crashing into the wall to stay. The hallway was too narrow; a fragile decorative table crashed to the floor, and Dougherty had an arm pressed across Evan's windpipe, not hard enough to stop his air but tight enough to make the threat of strangling to death real.

Evan panicked. The office door crashed back against the wall as the air pressure in the house rose, and the leaded-glass panes in the street door bulged outward for a moment before Evan pulled the tempest back under control. Dougherty didn't seem to notice, but Harry stared at Evan with a mixture of fascination and dread on his face that reminded him too much of all the years of his childhood. But he wasn't a child anymore. Control. His father had taught him control.

"What did you do to your mother, you son of a bitch!"

Evan froze, cold dread settling in his stomach at Joe Dougherty's words.

"I didn't do anything! Where is she? What has happened to her?" Evan dragged at the arm across his throat. If some enemy from his hideous past had attacked his mother for revenge or leverage, he would find it and kill it, or bind it and consign it to the deepest ring of hell for the rest of his natural life.

"I don't believe you, Evan!" Dougherty applied more pressure to Evan's throat to emphasize his point. "I never have, and I will beat your head into the damned wall until I get some truth out of you now! What did you do to your mother?"

"Sergeant Dougherty, this behavior is completely inappropriate." Harry Li stood behind Joe Dougherty with a hand on the sergeant's shoulder. "Take your arm off that man right now, or I will report this to your supervisor. And unless you have a warrant, I'd suggest you leave this house immediately. You'll be very lucky if Evan doesn't file charges for felony assault and battery."

Harry's words were having about as much effect as the hand on Joe's shoulder, but at the moment Evan didn't care. Joe could beat him to a bloody pulp if he wanted, as long as he answered the question.

"Damn it, Joe," he gasped out, "I didn't do anything! Is she hurt?"

"She called me, told me she didn't want me checking into Kevin Bradley's background anymore." Dougherty increased the pressure on Evan's throat, but he kept talking. He didn't seem to care anymore whether Evan answered the charge or not. Which was just as well, since he couldn't have answered if he wanted to. Couldn't talk, couldn't breathe. Sparking light pinwheeled on the periphery of his vision, but Dougherty didn't seem to notice, or didn't care, what he was doing to Evan. He just kept talking, with his arm pressed against Evan's throat.

"She sounded scared, so I went to see her, and she's terrified all right— she couldn't even hold a cup of coffee without spilling it! She'd been threatened by an expert; when I asked her what had happened, she cried. She looked like she'd been doing a lot of that, but all she would say, over and over again, was that it was all her fault, and that there was nothing anyone could do. But she is wrong. There is something I can do."

Dougherty tightened the pressure on Evan's throat. His head was singing with high-pitched pain again, but he didn't break away. It was all true. He had done exactly what Joe Dougherty accused him of; he'd battered his mother with the truth of his existence, of what she had done that made him what he was. He'd told himself that he'd done it to stop her from bringing the life he'd made down around his ears, but he had to admit that he'd wanted to punish her for all the years of misery his divided nature had caused him. Maybe, if he just let go, they'd all be better off . . .

"If you don't release my cousin immediately, I will have to kill you." Lily. Should have known. He couldn't see very well; the light had dimmed around the edges and the center was fading fast, but the tone of voice left no doubt she meant what she said.

"I would already have killed you, just for disturbing my bubble bath, but Evan doesn't like the mess. He's big on fair play and warning shots, so consider this yours."

Dougherty eased up on his windpipe, and Evan's vision cleared enough to see Lily standing at the end of the hallway in a lace robe that hid nothing but its practical value as clothing. She should have looked vulnerable and alluring in it, but the expression on her face, and the sure and deadly way she moved, made a lie of the lace's fragility. In that mood she terrified Evan, and she was doing a good job of scaring Harry. Dougherty looked as though he'd been hit with a two by four, but he was making an orderly retreat.

"This is not the end of it, Evan." Dougherty released him but did not move away. "I'm going to keep on looking until I find something to nail on you people, and I'm going to slap your asses in jail until they rot. I just want you to know that your mother did what you ordered her to do. She told me to stop looking. This is my grudge now; it's got nothing to do with her, so whatever you were using to threaten her—blackmail, violence, whatever—it's pointless now, because she's got nothing to do with it."

"You've got it wrong, Joe." Evan cradled a hand around his throat, trying to think past the ringing in his head to something that would convince Joe Dougherty. He took a deep breath, then lost it again as a scream cut through him on a searing wave of fear and rage. In its wake it left a silence that dropped him to his knees.

# Chapter 32

BRAD FOCUSED ON THE BEDROOM IN THE CHONG COMPOUND WHERE HE'D LEFT Mai Sien Chong and willed it to grow solid around him. As the walls sharpened in detail, he scanned quickly, looking for Mai Sien. He located her in time to see her head reappear through the neck of another long tunic, this time in yellow over silk pants the color of spring grass.

"You are beautiful," he said.

She screeched, her eyes wide with shock, then quickly threw a hand over her mouth. "Don't do that!" she snapped.

"Don't do what? Tell you that you are beautiful? I thought women liked that." He smiled at her, but she waved her arm at him, mimicking the fright she'd just experienced.

"Don't leap in and out of existence like a monkey god, frightening poor maidens out of their maidenhood!"

"I think the monkey god is too late," he pointed out, and wrapped her in his arms, holding her tight against his body. It felt good. He rested his chin on the top of her head and mused at the strangeness of the universe, that something so simple could feel at once so peaceful and so stirring. But Mrs. Zheng banged on the door again, and insisted that they come, right now, as Grandfather had no more patience, and Uncle had run out of excuses for her.

Back down the hall, down the staircase, into a wing of the house he hadn't passed the first time, Mrs. Zheng led them to the parlor where the Chongs waited in straight-backed chairs ranked on either side of a stiff old man with iron gray hair and eyes like stone.

"Grandfather." Mai Sien gave the old man a little bow, which he returned with a tilt of his head.

"Blessed One. How kind of you to pay respects to an aged grandfather such as myself."

"My duty is my pleasure, Grandfather."

"Then sit beside me, my child." Irony sharpened the basilisk glint in his eye. Grandfather Chong gestured to the empty chair to his immediate right, and Mai Sien bowed again, took the hand he offered, and let him seat her next to him.

No one had offered Brad a seat and, looking around him, he saw no empty chair in the room. So he lounged against the doorjamb, arms crossed over his chest in a pose calculated to annoy Mai Sien's relatives arrayed in front of him, and studied them as they studied him. The middle-aged man with the sour expression to Grandfather Chong's left glared at Brad, while the rest of the family watched with varying degrees of greed, jealousy, boredom, and fear layered like paint on their features. Whoever had said the Chinese were an inscrutable people had never met the Chongs.

But Grandfather Chong was speaking again, and the mood in the room altered subtlely, in the expectant way the Romans in the Coliseum had perked up when the lions joined the Christians at center ring. "Tell an old man why you have brought this foreigner from your bed into the presence of your family and the man who would be your husband, my daughter."

"And why you dismissed your bodyguards," the sour man next to Grandfather Chong said, "when to do so is to risk not only your own life, more precious than pearls, but the fortunes of your family."

"Uncle Chong is kind." Mai Sien gave a fleeting smile to the uncle in question, whose frown belied the compliment. "But my affection for his wife's nephew is that of a cousin, and I do not wish to dishonor those feelings in the marriage bed."

"Your feelings do you honor, daughter."

Uncle Chong clearly thought nothing of the kind. Brad wondered which of the weak-chinned, nervous-eyed younger members of the clan had the dubious honor of being the unwanted intended of the woman next to Grandfather Chong. One or two had promise, if the occasional glint of humor was anything to go on, but he felt pretty sure that Mai Sien Chong would make potstickers out of the best of the lot.

"But you must consider the fortunes of your family. My wife is dead, and we can not succeed without the good will of the Hsis."

The Hsis? As in the brothers Hsi, Brad wondered? Had Uncle Chong actually sent the family's choice of a husband for Mai Sien to serve as her bodyguard, knowing she was taking other men to bed? No wonder the man had wanted to kill him. Had killed him, actually, but that didn't quite count, Brad supposed. He remembered the guns, though, and wondered what the Hsis were bringing to this plan that Grandfather and Uncle Chong were hatching.

"But we can."

Brad recognized Mai Sien's smile. He usually saw it over a chessboard, right before he heard the words, "check and mate."

"I bring you no foreigner, Grandfather," she explained, "but a god whose favor can bring us success in our endeavors, who chooses to appear before us in the form of a Western man."

Shit. Brad stood straighter then, a warning glint in his eyes. Temper had likely blurred the outline of his features as well; the assembled Chongs squirmed uncomfortably in their straight-backed chairs and looked away.

"A Western god, perhaps." Uncle Chong must have heard the reports from the Hsis about yesterday's altercation, for he looked decidedly nervous as he glanced from Brad to Grandfather Chong. "But what god of our people would choose to appear as a foreigner? What god of our people would choose to make love as a beast."

That was a tactical error; Brad could see the gears working in the heads of the gathered Chongs. Grandfather seemed able to come up with several gods with peculiar reputations. He nodded. "If your lover is a god, then let him show himself as a god. If he is a man, a Western man, then we must ask ourselves what is a fitting punishment for a woman who would be Empress of All China but yet would dishonor her family and her intended husband by bedding a foreigner and bringing him into the very heart of our plans."

Until this point the gathering had reminded him vaguely of an aggregation of daemon lords for the purpose of making alliances among Princes, but this talk of plots and power and punishment were more than he'd signed on for. He would have vanished, giving them their proof but not the assistance they seemed to expect, when Mai Sien stood up and reached a hand to him. She was beautiful, and his body remembered what she felt like with a shivering ache, but he did not move, waiting to see what she would do next.

"I said this morning that if you waited, you would find your answers." She stepped away from her grandfather and uncle, to a small carved screen set on a chest by the wall. When she moved the screen, he saw the crystal balls, all three of them, set on their silver waves like moons rising out of the sea. "To the museums, I have stolen the crystals." She gave him the answers with her promises grave in her eyes. "To me, to my family, I have simply reclaimed what is mine."

Brad felt a buzzing in his ears and shook his head to clear it, but the sound remained, just at the limits of awareness. In spite of the annoyance, he focused on her words. Not stolen but returned to the rightful, if long dead, owner.

That explained much. "Tzu Hsi, I presume?"

"Once I was called by that name," she confirmed, "and I was Empress of All China, until the Westerners came with their opium and their gunboats. Then I was Empress of a dying court. Then . . . Empress of nothing. But that flesh died. Now as in the past, however, I bow to the wishes of the men of my family who would rule through me.

"Ironic, I suppose you would call it. A Manchu in my former life, I ruled as Empress of All China. And then, as Hokkien Chinese, I was reborn in the home of a Chinese merchant in Singapore, not in China at all, to find my treasures looted, my country held in the hands of avaricious peasants, and my own family living in exile. But I will return home."

She took the largest of the crystals from its stand of silver waves. He remembered reading on the police report that the ball weighed fifty pounds, but she held it up in her two hands and stared into it as if it weighed nothing. "With the god of the South Wind at my side I will return the rightful center of Chinese rule to the south."

The crystal drew him as surely as the grave sorrow in her eyes, and he knew, in that moment, that she had betrayed him. Too late, he saw his danger. The crystal held him, paralyzed him.

"Chu Jung," she said, "come to me."

As she spoke the buzzing in his head rose to a roar like an oncoming tornado, and he felt the power of that wind sucking him in.

"Chu Jung," she said again, and "My god, my beautiful tiger, my Chu Jung, demon of the South Wind, come to me!"

She held the crystal ball over her head, calling to him above the roar of the wind, and he felt his daemon essence break free of the flesh that had held it, and he screamed in pain and terror as the crystal swallowed him whole.

# Chapter 33

"EVAN! EVAN!" HARRY, DOWN ON ONE KNEE BESIDE HIM, WAS SHOUTING IN HIS face, but the sound came to him thinly, as if filtered through a dense mist that still echoed with the sound of his father's scream. He saw Harry's mouth move, saw him face Joe Dougherty with his anger.

"Not his fault." Still hoarse from the pressure Dougherty had put on his throat, Evan grabbed Harry's sleeve to make him listen. "It's Brad." Evan hadn't realized he was feeling the connection until it winked out of existence. "Something's happened to my father."

"It's concussion," Harry objected. "I'll file charges against him if you don't, Evan."

Evan shook his head. Didn't help under the circumstances, and the core of dead silence grew in his mind until it blotted out all thought except the one impossible fear: Brad had died, somewhere, alone. Impossible, he knew, daemons were immortal. Badad couldn't be gone. Must be the concussion.

He looked for Lily, but she'd felt it too. She waited only long enough to tell him, "It's Badad. He's gone."

It was true then. "Dead?" he asked. Not possible.

"I don't know. But Ariton will need me."

Not Brad, the temporary manifestation of his father, but the daemon lord Badad, and the house of Ariton, needed them. Then she disappeared so fast the air imploded with a soft crack, leaving Joe Dougherty staring at the place where she had stood, his face white, his eyes glazed with shock. He would find a rational explanation for himself, or not, but Evan discovered he didn't much care which.

Closing his eyes, he gathered his strength. Not too bad. His breathing had eased, and with a return of oxygen it seemed he'd escaped a second concussion. The gash in the back of his head had opened up again, but he felt nothing more than a smear of blood, nothing that would get in his way.

He gave an apologetic little shrug that he knew Harry wouldn't understand, then he focused his mind. He didn't think he had the nerve to follow where that scream had gone, but he *could* follow Lily.

So he imagined the shape of the second sphere, the empty reach where the essence of daemonkind fought and made alliances in an eternity of darkness, and set his soul free to find it. When the familiar disorientation took him, he summoned his body and it answered, leaving a local atmospheric disruption behind him that sent Joe Dougherty slamming into the wall where he'd been bouncing Evan's head.

The last thing he heard was Dougherty's "Jesus, Mary and Joseph!" and he realized he'd made a tactical error. Two vanishing suspects made it considerably less likely that Joe would find a comfortable explanation for the day.

But that was on the other side of the universe. Evan figured he'd come up with something to tell Dougherty later, after he beat the shit out of the man. But first, he had something more important to do. He grabbed the darkness around him and shaped it to meet the needs of his body for gravity and breathable air, then sent his thoughts in search of Lily.

He found more than he bargained for. Daemon lords with names he did not know, but who carried the essence of Badad and Lirion and Evan himself within them, boiled down on him. They gathered with the speed of thought, shaping of their combined being their celestial Prince, Ariton, out of the blue flame by which he saw them in this sphere.

They did not have the power to kill him in this sphere. He knew that now, though he also knew that his life depended on the integrity of his mind and soul. He could die here if he forgot for just one moment who he was, and what he was, and that he lived in the material sphere. So he held close the sense of flesh, the reality of a heart beating in his chest, and stood against the hatred of his father's kin battering his mind from the inside with the knowledge that he was a monster, an abomination, and that the daemon lord Badad had suffered too much already for something that had never been his fault. And now Badad was gone, and there was nothing to stand between Evan and the dark hatred of the second sphere.

He sensed the approach of Lirion, Lily Ryan in his own reality, and for a moment he almost crumbled under the fear darkening his mind. He needed her, couldn't find his father without her, but his determination to hold onto life faltered in the onslaught of the wailing terror that filled him with the maddened lust of his father's kin, for his death. If Lirion merged with the host of Ariton against him, he would have no hope.

Then she was in his mind like a cold light, and she shared colder thoughts with him. Ariton did not know what had happened to his father, only that he'd gone where Ariton could not follow. But maybe, Evan figured, *he* could go there, to bring his father back if possible, or to know the truth of what had happened to him if that was all that he could do.

"I have to find him." The words formed in his mind; her answer came so fast after it that it might almost have been his own thought—"There won't be anything to find."

Of course. Without the daemon essence of Badad of the host of Ariton to animate it, the body that he wore as Kevin Bradley would cease to exist. But still Evan persisted—"I have to try"—and his despair shivered through the presence of his Prince.

"Yes, I guess you do." He felt Lily's thought, like a kiss, though she wore no body. Then stillness. "This way," and she set off after the thread of Badad's last passage through the spheres, to the place from which that terrible scream had come.

Evan followed and found himself standing next to her in a room paneled in dark carved wood, with carved chairs and a table of antique artifacts that he recognized immediately from the fact sheet the police had distributed. A cluster of people, all Chinese and all bearing a family resemblance, sat in the chairs watching a woman who held a large crystal ball over her head. The one exception, Alfred Da'Costa, stood with his hands in the pockets of his raw linen slacks, facing the woman who held the crystal ball.

No one moved, which surprised Evan for a number of reasons. Most people would find two strangers appearing out of nowhere in their parlor a bit of a surprise. And according to the police fact sheet, the crystal ball weighed fifty pounds, yet the woman held it over her head as if it weighed nothing at all.

"Where is my father?" Evan demanded. At his words, the whole room seemed to wake up. Da'Costa's hawk-shaped face twisted in a wince. The woman screamed and let go of the crystal ball. Da'Costa leaped forward to grab it with an oath muttered in a language Evan didn't know but felt fairly certain had been dead for several millennia.

As if released from a spell—ah yes, of course—a middle-aged man in a business suit leaped from his chair. "Who are you, and what are you doing in my house? Do you have a warrant for this intrusion?"

"Bad timing, kid," Da'Costa muttered. "Really bad timing."

Evan ignored him. "Chong Li-huang, I presume?" he asked of the middle-aged man in the business suit, then answered the question. "We don't have a warrant. We are not the police." Lily was prowling around the table which held the Moon Stone crystal belonging to the PMA and another

Evan felt reasonably certain belonged to the Smithsonian. He waited until she reached out to touch the crystal to make his point with Chong: "Which means we can pretty much do as we damn well please if you don't tell us where my father is."

The click of a bullet chambering sounded behind Evan, but Lily just cocked an eyebrow. "Not a good idea," she said, and the man who had entered the room behind him let out a sharp yelp. The gun clattered to the floor and went off, but Evan didn't let it distract him.

"Who is in charge of this pop stand?" he asked.

"I was, until you blew in."

Evan ignored Da'Costa's sarcasm. "Mai Sien Chong, I presume?" He tilted his head in acknowledgment.

"You must be Evan." Chong considered him with a look much older than her years. "Are you as dangerous as your father?"

"Right now?" he asked, and considered the question before answering "More. Brad wasn't looking for treachery, but I am. And he liked you. I don't."

She nodded her head, accepting his answer. "Then send the rest of the family away," she asked him. "They do not understand this quarrel and should not have to die for mistakes they had no part in."

"Uncle stays," Lily objected, "and Grandpa there."

Mai Sien nodded agreement, and Lily added as an afterthought, "We'd better keep Mr. Gun Happy as well."

Lily picked up the gun and motioned to the man behind him, who slunk around the edge of the room. He avoided Lily with suspicious awe and settled behind and to the left of Chong Li-huang. Evan watched him cautiously but did not try to stop him. Lily, however, shifted her position to stand between the bodyguard and Evan while a line of nervous-looking Chongs filed out of the room. They hadn't checked the room for more guns, which wouldn't matter to Lily or Da'Costa. But Evan didn't enjoy the thought that a stray bullet might take him down before he found out what had happened to his father. Fortunately, Lily seemed willing to stand in the way of danger at least until he figured out how Brad had run afoul of the Chongs. When the last of the departing clan had filed out the door, Lily gestured the three men who remained to reclaim their chairs.

"What if they try to break in with reinforcements?" Evan asked.

Lily shrugged. "I sealed the doors and windows. They won't get in until we leave."

With the numbers in the room more in their favor, Evan allowed himself to relax a bit while Alfredo Da'Costa explained:

"May I introduce Lady Yehenara, Dowager Empress of China."

"Tzu Hsi," she corrected him. "How did you know?"

"We've met before," Da'Costa answered. "You have an unusually tenacious spirit. But your time is over."

"I don't know what you mean." She lied, but Evan held his temper in check. Da'Costa seemed to know what was going on here, which he couldn't say for himself. If it helped him find out what had happened to his father, he'd put up with the sparring. But he needed some answers.

"Lady Yehenara was the concubine of Emperor Hsien Feng," he pointed out. "She had his only son, as I recall, and reached a position of power in the Chinese court primarily by outliving several emperors and a number of military coups. But that was a century ago—she's been dead since 1908. A revolution overthrew the Ch'ing Dynasty a few years later, and China hasn't had an emperor, or an empress, since."

"And yet," Da'Costa explained, "this is she, the Empress Tzu Hsi, returned from the dead to lead the Chinese back to impoverished oppression by a half insane and completely debauched monarchy."

"Is that worse than a central government that is entirely insane and only half debauched?" Mai Sien objected, "Either way your argument is irrelevant. I am no longer Manchu, but Hokkien."

Chong Li-huang interrupted her with his own explanation. "The Ch'ing Dynasty of the north is dead, and the Imperial peasants of the north will follow it into the past. The Chong Dynasty will return the country to the true Chinese of the south. Tzu Hsi will work for China as its servant, not its conqueror."

Evan wasn't buying the altruistic motive for a moment. "Chongs never did anything that wouldn't make them richer."

"Good servants are paid well, that is true." Uncle Chong bowed his head to acknowledge the hit.

"And what do you get out of this?" Evan asked Mai Sien.

She shrugged. "The opportunity to help my people, of course. To free my country from its tyrants and to give them the justice I have wished for my countrymen for many lifetimes."

Lily snorted. "I don't think that is what Uncle Chong has in mind."

"Our people are still children in the ways of freedom," Chong agreed. "They must be led to self-rule slowly, with the guidance of a clan that has known the freedom of the West."

"And where does Ms. Chong—excuse me, the Dowager Empress Tzu Hsi—fit into that equation?" Lily asked. "The last I saw, the Chinese don't exactly value women."

Uncle Chong smiled. "Chong Mai Sien will be the new model of Chinese womanhood," he answered. "When she marries Hsi Fong and joins our families in rule together, she will retire to raise his children and bestow upon our poor country the blessing of their Mother."

"And Chang Er Imports?" Evan asked.

"Being dismantled even as we speak," Uncle Chong answered. "The mother of our country will lavish her love and her attention on her children, the people. With her uncle as the economic and civil ruler and her husband in command of the army, she will have at her right hand and her left the power of a country in prosperity and peace."

Chong Mai Sien did not seem happy with this version of her future, and Alfredo Da'Costa was quick to follow up on her displeasure.

"Sounds like old times, Lady Empress. Let the men bungle the governing and prepare to take the blame again."

"Not this time," she asserted. "I have explained to my uncle that I will not marry Mr. Hsi, who only wishes to marry me to strengthen his attachment to my uncle and thereby his claim to command of the armies when we take power. My uncle believes we need the clan of the Hsis for their connections with the military, as they need the Chongs for their claim through my soul for the right to govern. But I have a weapon more powerful than my uncle yet understands."

"Which is?"

Chong Mai Sien smiled. "I control the daemon in the crystal."

Evan turned to the crystal ball Alfredo Da'Costa cradled like an oversized basketball in his arm. Da'Costa looked a little sick but not surprised; that fact set cat's claws tearing at Evan's gut from the inside.

"How do I get him out?"

"Carefully." He shifted the crystal—"Would you mind?"—and Evan took it.

"What is it?" Evan wrapped his arms around the crystal and held it close. He hadn't forgotten his experience with it as a child; his fascination for it still scared the hell out of him. But if it had something to do with his father . . .

"A crystal ball." Da'Costa answered Evan's glare with a wry twitch of a shoulder. "There aren't more than three of the crystals on this planet large enough and perfect enough to create a distortion in the space-time fabric. Individually, each crystal has the potential to produce a very minor distortion field in its near vicinity. In concert, however, their effect can be magnified beyond imagination. Only Tzu Hsi, Empress of China in the nineteenth century, knew about their special properties, as far as I could ever tell. And for the first time since she died, the three are together in one room again."

"What kind of distortion," Evan persisted. "And what does it have to do with my father?"

Da'Costa seemed unwilling to discuss it, then changed his mind. "He might be gone, Evan, frozen forever in the moment the crystal took him, or torn to shreds in the vortices at the center of the crystal. Or it could drive him mad. But if we don't get him out soon, we run the risk that he will find his own way out, through the portal the crystal creates to the third celestial sphere. If that happens—"

"I think we've had this conversation before." Evan stopped him, trying to absorb the implications. Everything that humans knew and called the universe had come into being in the cataclysm when the third sphere of Alfredo Da'Costa's universe, which existed along the dimension of time without space, forced an entry into the sphere of his father's kind, who inhabited the timeless empty space of the second celestial sphere. Alfredo Da'Costa existed as a guardian on this planet to make sure that the two spheres never came into contact again. If they did, the destruction could be minor on the cosmic scale—the obliteration of the material sphere, Evan's universe, along with those of his father and Alfredo Da'Costa.

Or, the effect might be sufficient to wipe out all the seven spheres, leaving chaos in the place of an ordered heavens. No human could understand the enormity of the danger, because no human could experience the reality of the celestial spheres beyond the material one they inhabited. Except for Evan Davis, half-human monster of a daemon father. He'd feared the universe of his daemon kin all his life, dreaded the creatures that inhabited it. But he knew that place; he belonged to Ariton as surely as his father did. And he knew to his soul the devastation one misstep now would wreak on all creation.

"My father is inside the stone?" He knew in his gut, but he had to hear it to make it real.

Mai Sien Chong answered "Yes," her head held at a defiant angle. "It can be frightening, perhaps painful at the moment of transition, I am told, but imprisonment of a man's spirit in the stone creates no damage to the body."

"But Brad isn't human," Evan told her, careful not to give away his father's real name. "You imagine that his body anchors him here, in our world, as a human's would."—As the museum guard's body did, lying comatose in the hospital in Philadelphia—"But it doesn't."

Not an explanation, he knew, but he was having a difficult time containing his revulsion at the thought of Badad trapped in the stone. Evan knew the tug of home, knew that without it he would never have survived his travels in the second sphere. How would it be to find himself trapped in a reality not his own, with no sense of where home was, and no hope that he would ever feel the ground beneath his feet again? He would do anything to find his way home again. His father would do the same, but there *was* no way home for Brad: just the prison of the stone or the destruction of all their universes in his struggle to be free. That realization set his skin to prickling.

They could all die. Without a moment to prepare, his universe, and those of the other spheres of creation, would cease to exist. He wondered if the destruction would kill them before they knew what was going on, or if they would suffer through the horror of their whole reality breaking up around them.

Lily flickered in and out of material form like a ghost, bathed in leaping blue flame. Evan felt her panic and distress amplifying his own. The only thing keeping Chong alive, he knew, was her connection to the stone. If Lily believed for one moment they could rescue Brad without the woman who put him there, she would have torn Mai Sien Chong to pieces by now.

The sound of incantations spoken softly in Chinese broke through the paralyzed tension in the room; the gunman had covered his face with his hands and muttered softly to himself in Chinese, while Uncle Chong stared in disbelief at the flaming apparition of Lirion as close to daemon form as the material sphere allowed. Only Grandfather seemed unaffected: He looked to Mai Sien, who seemed only to catalog the fact that Lily existed.

"Get him out of there." Lily. If Evan hadn't realized the gravity of the situation before, the panic in her voice would have convinced him they were in deep, deep shit.

Mai Sien Chong gave Lily's flickering image a long, thoughtful study. Then she turned to Da'Costa. "Yes," she said, "perhaps it is time my lord Chu Jung joined us." She reached for the crystal and Evan looked to Da'Costa, who gave a single nod of assent. Reluctantly, Evan handed over the crystal ball, and Mai Sien took it back to the table and placed it on its stand. Taking up an incense stick, she lit it and waved it in a circle around the crystal while she chanted a short command in Chinese. Nothing happened. She repeated the move, placing one hand on the crystal, and called for him again. Nothing. "I don't feel his presence," she admitted. "He does not come when I call."

"I was afraid of that." Da'Costa, looking grim. "You've got to get him out of there, Evan. No one else can."

"What makes you think I can do it?"

Da'Costa shrugged. "Maybe you can't. But at the moment you are the only reasonably sane creature in the universe that shares the substance of daemonkind and the heritage of the material universe. Lily could reach him, perhaps, but she couldn't bring him back, and she'd be more likely to find herself trapped just as he is."

"What if the stone traps me?" He wanted reassurance, but Da'Costa didn't have it. In the exchange of glances Evan knew that Da'Costa was thinking of the museum guard in the hospital.

"If that happens, we are all lost." Da'Costa managed to compress all of their history in his rueful smile. Ironic, that smile seemed to say. If I had killed you as I knew I must, Badad of the host of Ariton would be free now, home and safe. All our universes would be safe. Now it was time to pay for his life. Evan gave a little nod to show he understood, and faced the stone.

# Chapter 34

PAIN. FOR THE FIRST TIME IN FIFTEEN BILLION YEARS OF EXISTENCE HE COULD have wished for pain, for anything that would replace the emptiness pressing in all around him, obliterating the "I" of his existence. Badad felt nothing, experienced nothing but his own shattered thoughts. He was a daemon lord, but he was nothing. He was of Ariton, but Ariton did not exist; something had torn away the awareness of shared being with the host of his Prince that was the greater part of him. He had a son, but in this place of nothingness his son did not exist. He would have been alone, except that in this place *Badad* did not exist, and that which did not exist could not be alone.

In an agony of nothing-feeling he tried to build within his fractured mind the image of the second sphere, tried to send his being out, out, to fill the universe with his presence, but could not. He thought himself small, dense as a point, but could find no point of space to occupy. Only the crystal existed, a drop of time frozen outside of space, and he was trapped, with not even a facet in the stone to anchor his awareness. He imagined claws to dig his way free; the horny stems sank into the stone and broke off when he tried to move them. He grew teeth in his mind and tried to gnaw his way free, but this mouth closed on stone that sealed up after him.

He screamed and screamed, but he heard no sound, no answer, not even his own scream, and cursed Mai Sien who had trapped him, and Lirion who had warned him of the flame but could not stop his fascination with the danger. He cursed Evan for existing and because the sense of his son had gone, like the presence of Ariton in his being; and he knew that his son would not save him and he was doomed to this eternal oblivion. He tried to imagine time as he lived it in the material sphere and sensed something, distorted and flawed and infinitely incomprehensible, and he tried to move toward it, but he could not move, for there was no space. It was there, time, not like Earth, but running forward and backward and sideways and a million-million other ways that he could not begin to comprehend but that twisted back on themselves so that all time led back to moment when the crystal had called to him and drawn him to its frozen heart. And it would have driven him mad, except that he found a thread of minutes and followed them, rolled them up in a ball in his mind like string and followed their track, minute by minute leading out from the center of a maze. And if they should lead nowhere, he was no more lost than he was when he started, but perhaps a little less mad than he had become.

# Chapter 35

"You'd better sit down." Da'Costa shoved a chair at Evan, and Evan sat without thinking about it. His mind was thousands of miles away and ten years in the past, reliving the moment when the crystal had caught and held him. He would not grant the object a will of its own—it was not, after all, a living thing—but it had called to him once. The thought that he could end up like the museum guard, comatose with his mind trapped in stone, frankly terrified him, but he could not say that to Alfredo Da'Costa, who already regretted that he hadn't killed Evan four years ago. He could not admit to a weakness to Lily, who tolerated him only because his father demanded it of her.

But Lily was behind him, her form steadying, her hands cool on his temples. She caressed the fading shadow of the bruise. "I won't let go," she said, and he realized she already knew.

"Thank you." Inadequate, but words didn't matter. Later, if their universes survived, they would share their minds as they shared each other's body. And in the meantime, he accepted that no human knew him so well or accepted as much of him, flaws and all, as she did.

"Clear the room," he added. Da'Costa nodded, and Chong Li-huang seemed eager to comply. He took the gibbering gunman by the elbow and shoved him toward the door, showering the man with insults and curses.

Old Grandfather Chong looked at Evan long and hard, breaking away only to give his granddaughter an approving nod. Mai Sien Chong had not moved. Neither did Grandfather Chong, except to gesture with his hand. "Begin," he said, and added in a gently chiding voice, "It is unseemly to bargain with spirits for the power to rule our own country. If we cannot win and hold it with our virtue, then perhaps we are not yet ready to rule."

"Yes, Grandfather." Mai Sien bowed her head, but the old man chuckled.

"You listen now, when your uncle has revealed his intention to usurp your position and rule with your power. Perhaps you would not be so docile if your own plans to rule had come to pass."

"I have time, old man."

The eyes that looked out of Mai Sien's face were old eyes, filled with patience and humor, and Grandfather Chong bowed his head to acknowledge the truth of her words. "But now, we must free your lover from the rather uncomfortable position you have placed him in."

The old eyes laughed, but Mai Sien Chong's face remained otherwise tense. Evan noted the complex of emotions on her face and the calm humor on the face of the old man. Something here did not add up, but he did not have time to think about it now. The fate of all the universes wouldn't wait forever. So he set his hands on either side of the crystal ball and focused down, down, into the place where the world turned inside out. And when he felt himself sinking, he called out to his father.

Nothing.

Don't panic. Brad was there somewhere. But no, not Kevin Bradley. He remembered what Lily had told him, back on the other side of disaster: to find his father he had to think of his father, not of himself, not of his need for a father but of the creature that father was, independent of Evan's hold on him. Evan realized he'd been looking for a mirage, a fantasy. His father, his real father, was Badad of the host of Ariton, and Kevin Bradley did not exist except in the mind of Badad; and so Evan took a last deep breath and let go his hold on flesh. He let go of the image of flesh that he knew as Kevin Bradley and searched instead for the blue flame of his father's mind, the connection that spoke of Ariton in his soul. Nothing.

Think. Da'Costa had said the crystal froze time, could even act as a portal into the third celestial sphere where time existed without space or material form. He still existed, the crystal still held him, so Badad could not have passed through into Da'Costa's universe. But if the daemon somehow sensed the portal, he could be deeper in the stone. Because he was himself a creature of time and space, Evan could feel the pull of the stone, could feel it wrenching time out of true, but Brad would not know the danger any more than a blind man knows the danger of staring into the sun.

Evan followed the twisted whorls of time, aging, then growing younger again as time moved forward along his life or turned him back on his beginnings. As a way to distract himself from the immediate incomprehensibility of the crystal, he tried to count his own fears. He could become lost forever, alone in the tortured passages of time that sometimes swept him along with them and sometimes washed over him and left him stranded in nothingness. He would find his father, but they would remain lost to-

gether in the stone, growing increasingly mad, and perhaps, as Da'Costa
had warned, find themselves torn to pieces in the currents of time raging
at the center of the crystal.

His father might find the portal to the third sphere while Evan was
trapped inside the crystal; he didn't know what would happen to the crystal,
but Da'Costa had made it clear that there would be no home to return to
for any of them if the daemon breached the portal. Perhaps the most
wrenching fear of all, he would find his father and lead him in the wrong
direction. It would be Evan who breached the portal into the third celestial
sphere, Evan who caused the death of all the spheres and every being that
lived in them. He would die torn to pieces in the wave of chaos he would
unleash, knowing that the same would happen to his mother, to Harry Li
and Joe Dougherty and the kids who played in the schoolyard a block down
Seventh Street. Ariton would die, and Azmod, and Da'Costa's people, whoever the hell they were. Structure would dissolve. Perhaps a new order
would take its place, and perhaps after another ten or fifteen billion years
humans would rise up again in a new form somewhere in the creation that
would follow the devastation. But that would all be too late for Evan.

When he realized that he was using his fears to keep him company,
Evan put them firmly in the back of his mind. Instead, he drew from his
memory images of his father as he had appeared to Evan in the second
celestial sphere, and he remembered what it felt like when his father's mind
had touched his own. Curiosity, and surprise, and sometimes understanding,
all layered over with an alien sense that Evan recognized as the wild core
of his own soul. It was that wild core he sought in the heart of the crystal,
and when he found the echo of it, he wondered if he had sensed himself
along a time vortex, or if it was Badad, and the feeling mirrored truly the
nature of the daemon.

He reached, reached, through the layers of hours and weeks, skirted a
shortcut through a time before he was born—he wasn't sure he'd exist at
the other end of the passage—and flung his call out on a wave of panic
moving toward the future. The echo was real. It came back to him changed,
something more completely of the second sphere, and Evan followed, moving into the future, while the stone's hold on him seemed to thin, and time
seemed to move backward and forward at once.

The portal. Evan called again, with all the terror and anger he could
muster, sending one command ahead of him:

"Come back!"

Time stopped. Rocked him where he waited. Then he felt it. His father,
resisting the call to go back into the maelstrom, anger and confusion and
absolute determination in the feeling shivering through the stone.

"No!" Evan opened the doors he had closed on his fears, drove them with the beat of one word—"death"—flying through the stone to his father. And the presence he recognized as Badad stopped. Evan sent out tendrils of summoning, calling with the words he had used when he bound his daemon kin "I conjure you . . . come to me . . ." past the moment that had ended the binding so disastrously. And Badad came.

Slowly Evan moved back through the stone, afraid that they would be lost there forever and afraid that if he saw the fear, Badad would break free of Evan and make for the portal again. So Evan tried to summon the images Da'Costa had fed him, of universes in ruin, of the souls trapped in the crystal, shattered, destroyed.

They had reached the center again when Evan realized that he could not find his way. All time seemed to meet here, so that no time meant anything. He tried to choose a time line to follow but found himself knotting back into the center.

And he had begun to realize something else about the crystal. Somewhere on the third or fourth try, when he discovered he had led them back to the center again, he began to realize that the crystal ball was a physical representation of the third celestial sphere, like a protected bubble in which all time met. Evan could exist here, could even sense the time thread. As a human, part of the material sphere, Evan could find himself trapped here indefinitely. His essence shared in time and in space, the result of their creation. His father, however, was entirely of the second celestial sphere.

Badad did not share in the elements of matter as the crystal did, nor did he share in the dimension of time. So far they were still alive in there, but the crystal had to become increasingly unstable as Badad's presence remained. Badad would become increasingly unstable as well. But the crystal, while acting like a portal to the third celestial sphere, also acted as a barrier against it. In a sense, while the stone of the crystal remained whole in the material world, the thing that the crystal *created* outside of the spheres must likewise continue. Portal, yes. Also, containment vessel protecting the universes from the power and energy passing through it. But, if he could create a reaction greater than the crystal's capacity to hold it, and he was close enough to direct that reaction into the material sphere, they might be able to destroy both portal and containment vessel. He didn't expect the stone to hold the reaction, didn't know what would happen when he'd started it. He did know that he was mortal and that his body was sitting in front of the crystal ball with its hands wrapped around it. He could die. Just once he'd like to have an idea that didn't end with those three little words. But a vivid imagination had never been his problem. Ideas weren't his strong point, and if by some fluke he lived through this, he was going to pass the honor of coming up with solutions to save the universe to somebody else.

In the meantime, how was he going to create that reaction? Bringing together the spheres could do it, but how . . . Ah, of course.

Evan turned around and moved back along the path he had most recently taken, searching the threads of time for the essence of his father. He was there, following blind and half mad, but following the summons; Evan reached for him, touched minds.

He expected an explosion, expected to die instantly. He didn't expect to feel the slow build of outward pressure, or to hear the crack of the stone, or see the fissures in the stone grow along fault lines that hadn't existed a moment before. Most of all, he hadn't expected to see old Grandfather Chong, laughing at the center of the stone. Then the crystal was flying apart, and his mind was flung into the air, raw, and confused, and he felt the thread of his own living body drawing him back.

"Are you all right, young man?"

Evan's body hurt; he moaned slightly coming to, wondering why he felt as though a great weight were pressing him down. And why was Grandfather Chong's voice in his ear? Ah. Grandfather lay draped across Evan's back, and while his next words didn't explain what he was doing there, Evan was glad to hear them:

"Would someone please help me up?"

"Of course." Alfredo Da'Costa's voice. Da'Costa's handmade Italian leather shoes moved purposefully into Evan's range of vision, and then the old man was grunting his way to his feet and Lily was looking down at Evan with a bemused expression on her face.

"You're back," she stated the obvious.

Evan crawled to a sitting position on the floor and rubbed his head where a new bruise was freshening the green and yellow of the one that preceded it. "What happened?"

Lily kicked at a shard of broken crystal before she spoke. "I rather thought you would be able to answer that."

"I don't exactly know," he admitted. "I mean, I know what happened in there, but not what you saw."

It must have been spectacular, he figured. Fragments of crystal were embedded in the wall behind the table where the ball had stood. More fragments lay scattered in a wide semicircle around the table. Given the number of fragments on the floor behind him, Evan figured he wouldn't have a head on his shoulders if Grandfather Chong hadn't knocked him down. But how the old man knew the crystal was going to shatter, and how Evan had seen him inside the crystal right before it did, remained a mystery. As did the source of the wide crack that started on the wall behind the crystal and divided the floor into two pieces, the half with the table two inches to the right and four inches higher than the other bit. Earthquake?

"Did I do that?"

Alfredo Da'Costa followed Evan's gaze to the slip line in the floor. "Indirectly."

Evan shuddered. They'd come closer to disaster than he'd known. He couldn't think about it, or he'd lose control completely, and he couldn't afford to do that yet.

"The police," he said, stumbling to his feet. "We've got to get out." He looked for Grandfather Chong to thank him for saving his life, and to ask him some pointed questions about how he'd done it but the old man had disappeared in the commotion, along with Evan's father and Mai Sien Chong. That, at least, was no surprise. Evan just hoped they could get out of Vancouver without leaving a trail of bodies. Thanks to Grandfather Chong, his body wouldn't be part of the trail. Now to return the favor and stop Brad before they had the body of the Chong woman to explain along with the demolished crystal ball.

Lily was a step ahead of him. She picked up the Moon Stone crystal. "I'll drop this off with Liz." She grinned. "Should please her no end."

"Not if you don't supply a suspect," Evan pointed out.

That gave Lily a moment's pause, then she brightened. "I'll leave it with Uncle Chong and tell Ellen where we've left him."

"Good idea," Evan agreed. "And I'd appreciate it if you would stop my father from killing Mai Sien Chong. I'd like to wring her neck myself, but I don't think Sid the Fed has a sense of humor."

"I'll leave that to you." Lily disappeared in the Cheshire-cat way of hers, leaving nothing but the memory of her wicked grin, and Evan grumbled. How could he stop his father from killing someone when he didn't know where they had gone? And how was he going to get past Alfredo Da'Costa when the guardian had that "You cost more than you are worth" look in his eye?

"I had nothing to do with the damned crystals," he said, and Da'Costa sighed.

"Guilt or innocence has never been part of your equation, Evan. You are not to blame for your birth. You agree, your father agrees, I agree on that point. Your continued existence is still a danger to all the seven spheres. Life struggles to make sense of the universe, on every level, and you could end it all, out of maliciousness or clumsiness or even as the victim of someone else's ignorance. How am I doing my duty if I let you hold all of creation hostage?"

"I'm not doing a damned thing," Evan pointed out.

"The young man is correct." Old Grandfather Chong. Where did he come from? And why did Alfredo Da'Costa look so uneasy? "Of all the fault in this room today, young Evan shared least in it. You yourself must take more blame than Evan—you knew what the crystals were, and you could have stopped this before it ever began, but you valued their beauty more than you feared their power. My granddaughter should not have encouraged Mr. Hsi to help her steal the crystals, she should not have panicked and stolen the soul of the man whose job it was to guard the stone. And she most assuredly should not have tried to hold a daemon captive. Her uncle should not have tried to use her for his own ends. Why, then, should Evan be the only one to suffer for the heedless acts of others?"

"I have no intention of letting Mr. Da'Costa kill me, sir." Evan smiled. "And when Ellen Li arrives, I believe justice will fall heavily on Uncle Chong and your granddaughter. But I thank you for your concern."

Da'Costa shrugged. "He's right. Evan and I came to an agreement some years ago, and it stands, not least because he dreads the consequences more than I do. But it doesn't hurt to remind him once in a while that his continued existence is a great inconvenience to the rest of the sentient universe."

"That's what keeps it interesting." The old man patted Da'Costa on the shoulder and picked his way through the rubble. "But I don't think the police are going to find my granddaughter."

He was laughing softly to himself as he passed through the door and disappeared. Evan should have seen him move away down the corridor, but Grandfather Chong was just gone. When Evan turned back to the room, Alfredo Da'Costa stood in front of the Moon Stone crystal with a hand on either side of it. He stared deeply into the stone, and Evan felt a wave of nausea pass over him. Alfredo Da'Costa swayed, and for a moment he wondered if it were an aftershock, but Da'Costa shook his head, as if clearing his vision, and said, "The guard is home."

"That was you, then?" Evan waved a hand to take in the broken floor that had seemed not quite real beneath his feet and the carved paneled walls that had rippled like silk just a moment before.

"Yes." Exhaustion. Evan had never heard that tone in Da'Costa's voice before, hadn't thought the guardian of the spheres capable of such mortal limits.

"Thank you." Evan owed him that much.

With his hands still curled possessively around the crystal, Da'Costa considered him with that grave expression he remembered from a ceiling fresco of an ancient god sitting in judgment of mere mortals. But the guardian surprised him. "It's I who owe you thanks, Evan."

Da'Costa stopped, as if considering what to say next, then he admitted, "We came close to losing it all today. My fault, as Old Grandfather said, for leaving the crystals intact. I should have destroyed them when I first realized their danger, more than a hundred years ago. But they were beautiful, and there is little enough of beauty in this universe or any other. They are safe now."

He moved away from the crystal and Evan thought he saw a change, a flaw like a mist swirling in its depths. "What's safe?"

But Da'Costa had disappeared. Evan was really not in the mood for introspective games with his deadly enemies, particularly those who disappeared before he could complain that their vague assurances didn't tell him a thing. He figured if anybody deserved the brunt of his smoldering temper, it was Brad. So he focused—it took almost no effort this time—and went.

He found himself in a bedroom. Brad wasn't alone.

# Chapter 36

"COME BACK!"

Time stopped, held Badad where he strove toward the end of the trail of minutes he had followed. Then he felt it. His son, calling him from the maelstrom. Badad heard the call through anger and confusion and his absolute determination to escape the stone. Evan could follow him or stay behind, trapped in the madness that lay behind him, but Badad of the host of Ariton was going home.

"No!" Like a dam cracking, Evan's fear washed over him, pulsing with the beat of one word beating through the stone like a heartbeat. Badad stopped, knew it for a mistake when the tendrils of summoning caught him, wrapping his brain in memories of his son, binding Badad to his will.

"I conjure you . . . come to me . . ."

The spell of conjuration did not hold him any longer, but a stronger binding did. Ariton called to him through his son, host loyalty drew him. He turned, moved back toward the center he had escaped, and met the word that he'd been running from: death. Evan was before him, and Badad followed, slowly, as they moved more deeply into the stone. They would be lost forever; the fear drove him back, but Evan drew him forward with images of universes in ruin, of souls trapped in the crystal, destroyed.

They were lost, and Evan's despair tangled with the waves of Badad's own madness. Then something began to change. The crystal pulsed with forces building in the mind of his son, and the old man, Mai Sien's grandfather, appeared before him in the stone, laughing, with a wink and a compliment—he'd raised a clever human. Then the crystal shattered, and Badad was free, home and the currents of the universe running through him. And Evan was—he looked, could not find his son, or Lily.

At some point the house had rocked on its foundation, and out in the sound he noticed another small island where none had been before. He wondered briefly if Alfredo Da'Costa would have an explanation for that, and if that explanation involved Evan. It couldn't have been his fault, though, because Brad could still feel the life of his son thrumming somewhere in the back of his consciousness. So Evan wasn't happy, but he wasn't dead. Brad figured he'd deal with that problem later—they had a lifetime to argue who did what to whom and who deserved what as a consequence. Mai Sien Chong, however, he would have to deal with now. He found her in the bedroom they had briefly shared in the Chong island compound, shaped a body, and entered through the door.

Mai Sien looked up, startled, from packing a suitcase. "I didn't expect to see you again."

"No, I don't suppose you did."

She smiled at him, but he didn't miss the wariness in her eyes. "I've offended you."

His expression told her what he thought of that understatement.

"I wouldn't have kept you locked in the crystal. I love you."

"Try again." Brad smiled. "You usually play a better endgame than this."

"Perhaps not love." She shrugged. "All right. My uncle was pressuring me to marry Hsi Fong, I didn't want to marry him, and I certainly didn't want to hand all of the power to my uncle and his toady. But Hsi Fong had the army. I had to find a way to hold off my uncle until I could establish myself in power. When I realized that you were a god, well, it seemed the perfect play. My bishop against Uncle Chong's knight. I was bound to win."

"I told you," Brad reminded her, "I'm not that kind of god."

"But Uncle Chong didn't know that." She wrapped her arms around his neck, carding fingers through his hair. "And you really are quite lovely in bed."

"I had a good teacher."

She couldn't hide the triumph in her smile. "We can still win—"

"Alfredo was right." He set her away from him, and her smile faltered. "Times change. You wouldn't like being Empress today. Think of the long hours. The ungrateful losers. And then, there's the war to gain control. Chess is clean, war is messy. How many do you think would die to put you on a throne? How many would die to keep you out? And what would you have at the end of it?"

She looked at him for a long time, but he had a feeling she wasn't actually seeing him. There were centuries passing in her eyes, and he understood about time a little better now, having passed through centuries himself in the center of the crystal. Good times and bad times passed across her face, and he couldn't help noticing that there were more of the bad than the good.

"I think Xiamen Trading Company will be looking for a new CEO next week," he commented. "In a way, it's not a bad empire."

"Uncle Chong . . ."

Evan chose that moment to appear in the middle of the room, looking ruffled and irritable and as though he had something important to say. "In less than half an hour, I estimate, Uncle Chong will be explaining to the FBI and the Canadian authorities what he is doing with priceless artifacts belonging to various institutions in the United States."

Brad smiled with paternal pride, which Evan didn't seem to appreciate.

"I have no idea why you would want to help her, given that she almost destroyed you and that you almost took your home, mine, and Alfredo's with you while you were floundering around mad as a hatter in there. But if you don't want her arrested, I suggest you get her out of here, now."

"The ferry's gone," she said, "but my uncle keeps a boat at the landing."

"You can leave the museum's property here," Evan added, and Brad followed his gaze to the suitcase on the bed. The figure of the reclining child lay snuggled between the underthings and the negligee she never seemed to get around to wearing. He picked it up and Mai Sien wrapped her hand around his, traced the shape of the figure through his fingers.

"They took my son away when he was very small," she said, and Brad could sense that she was not speaking of this life but of her life at court. "I was a concubine, not a fit mother for the future Emperor, so they gave my son to Tzu An." Tears glittered in her eyes. "Much later, when my son was Emperor and I was Dowager Empress, I had an artisan make up this child to remind me of what I had lost."

She looked at him sharply out of her old eyes. "He made a very bad Emperor. I know that. But once, he was a good child. And if they had given him to me to raise, China would be mighty still."

"China is pretty damned mighty without you." Evan was showing all the earmarks of running out of patience, but he did have a point. And the next one made more sense: "The police will be searching your apartments here and in Philadelphia. I expect Interpol will get onto Singapore as well. As far as I know, the Singapore police do not accept reincarnation as sufficient cause for committing burglary. If they find that thing, they'll arrest you."

"If they find it," she agreed, but she did not let go of Brad's hand, and he did not let go of the figure.

"It is hers, Evan." Give or take a hundred years. But years meant nothing to a daemon.

Evan sighed. "I don't want to know," he said. "When will you be home?"

"Shortly." Brad grinned at him. "I'd rather not meet Ellen in Uncle Chong's parlor."

"Good point." Evan vanished. As far as Brad knew, Evan had never done that in front of a full human before. The boy was sincerely rattled, or he just didn't give a damn. But Mai Sien Chong had a boat to catch.

# Chapter 37

"DAMN! WHAT ARE YOU DOING HERE?" EVAN STARTED SWEARING BEFORE HE finished materializing in the sheltered study in the house on Spruce Street.

"Waiting for you." Harry Li sat in Brad's wing chair, holding the ivory statue of Kwan Yin. Evan figured Harry must recognize the figurine—he'd hired Bradley, Ryan, and Davis Detective Agency to find the damned thing, along with a number of other items. Evan couldn't decide which would be harder to explain—why Harry had found the stolen Kwan Yin in the private office of said Bradley, Ryan, and Davis, or how Evan had just materialized out of thin air to do the explaining.

But after a momentary start, Harry didn't seem surprised or disconcerted to see Evan appear out of nothing in front of him.

"Sit down, Evan, you look as though you've been through a war. Which reminds me: Your mother called. New stepfather, actually. I think your mother was afraid that Brad might answer the phone. They'd like you to come to dinner on Tuesday. Stepfather will be barbecuing. Unless you can do something about your technicolor face, before then, I'd suggest you postpone dinner in favor of a hospital."

"Thanks, but I'll be fine." Evan looked around, located his desk chair but decided that would draw attention to the wreckage of mahogany kindling in the middle of the floor, and dropped into a corner of the leather couch instead. "I didn't steal the Kwan Yin," he began, "and neither did Brad."

"Of course you didn't." Harry ran a thoughtful finger around the outline of the ivory statue. "Given what I've seen today, it's unlikely you would have alerted the guard if you had. I doubt you would have had to break the glass, either."

This wasn't going quite the way Evan thought it would. "Harry, we have to talk."

"I know, Evan." Harry set the figure down on the small table next to his chair and gave Evan his attentive, understanding look. "You're not human."

"I am human." Evan couldn't lie in the face of Harry's calm acceptance of the truth. "Or, mostly I'm human. With just a few . . . differences." And what Harry would make of that Evan didn't know, but he figured he wouldn't have to wait long to find out. Harry didn't disappoint him.

"I noticed some of those differences when you disappeared. I have to admit it surprised me, though I did not react as badly as your friend Sergeant Dougherty. I told him you'd knocked him out, the vanishing part was just a hallucination, and that you'd gone upstairs to clean yourself up after the contretemps. It seemed to calm him down a bit, though he did want to arrest you for assaulting a police officer. I reminded him that he'd invaded your home without invitation or warrant and that he'd done the attacking, that you had only defended yourself in a life-threatening situation that he had created, to which I volunteered to attest as a witness. He showed no remorse for his behavior, but he did warn me that I, too, would be in danger from you if I didn't help him put you away.

"I managed to persuade him to leave before you returned, and I'm afraid that I did make a promise in your name, not to press charges against him if he left quietly with no more disturbance. He did so, but he threatened to come back with a warrant. It's been a couple of hours, and I assume he either thought better of it, or could find no judge on a Sunday afternoon willing to issue a warrant for an arrest with no charges."

"Thanks, Harry." Evan waited for the other shoe to fall. When it did, it wasn't quite the one he expected.

Harry picked up the Kwan Yin. "I was able to restrict Sergeant Dougherty's movements to the living area of the house. If he had come in here, of course, he would have found this, and he would have had his warrant. Where did you get it, Evan?"

"I didn't hear you come in, Evan, but I'm glad I brought the whole pot." Khadijah Flint entered the room as if on cue. She was carrying a fresh pot of coffee and set it next to the telephone on the brass table. "You look like death, child. Just give me the word and we'll slap the police with an abuse charge. Harry, get some cups while I consult with my client, please."

"I forgot to mention, that's when I called Ms. Flint." Harry set the Kwan Yin on the table next to the wing back chair and scuttled out with a wary look back at Evan. "Don't tell any of the good parts until I get back."

"I didn't steal it." Evan stood up and wandered over to pick up the Kwan Yin. "Neither did Brad. We haven't been lying to you."

"I'm glad." Khadijah Flint settled into the opposite corner of the couch. "Innocence doesn't, as a rule, make defending a client easier, but it does help me sleep better when I enter a not guilty plea. But if you didn't steal it—and I'm not doubting your word—where did you get it?"

"Where did Evan get what?"

Brad, looking about as casual as Brad ever did in a pair of black slacks and a black sweater, entered the room through the door to the private part of the house.

"I thought I heard someone else wandering around in the house." Harry came into the room behind Brad, carrying a stack of cups in one hand and a stack of saucers in the other. "I brought extras, just in case." He set them down on the brass table next to the coffeepot and poured a cup for Khadijah.

"Black?" When Brad nodded, Harry poured him a cup and passed it over, then poured for Evan, who took it and retreated to a corner of the room, where he set the Kwan Yin on a bookshelf and stood with his elbow resting in front of it.

By the time Harry had poured for himself and everyone had a cup, Brad had taken his chair, so Harry took the one next to it. "Now what were you asking?"

Brad set down his cup and glared at Harry. "Have we had enough of social trivia, yet? I want to know what Evan found that Khadijah thinks will get him arrested."

"This—" Evan nodded at the Kwan Yin. "I went to Mai Sien Chong's condominium," he explained. "The apartment was empty, except for the statue and this." He went to the low beaten brass table and picked up the cufflink, held it out for his father to examine. "I found them together in the middle of the carpet in what looked like the master bedroom."

"Mrs. Zheng." Brad took the cufflink and tossed it in the air. "A mediocre housekeeper but a good soldier. She took an instant dislike to me; I suspect she disapproved of Mai Sien bringing home strangers. Uncle Chong thought he was paying for more than her services as a bodyguard for Mai Sien, but I suspect that Mrs. Zheng's loyalties remained with the People's Liberation Army. And I would guess the Red Army has no need of an Empress, or of Uncle Chong, at present. Mrs. Zheng probably figured she could be rid of me at the same time that she rid her country of the threat of civil war. Ironic, isn't it?" Brad asked.

Evan could see no irony in the situation at all and told him so. Brad just smiled.

"But think about it, Evan. Mrs. Zheng wanted to stop Uncle's plot. But she also hated me. Killed me once, in fact, but that's another story. Ultimately, however, I stopped the Chongs' conspiracy."

"You don't think too much of yourself, do you, Brad? Ellen was on her way; she'd have stopped them if you hadn't." Harry's ironic response took Evan by surprise, as did Brad's laughing response, "But I stopped it first."

"And how did you do that?" Khadijah Flint asked him sharply.

The phone rang just then, saving Brad from an immediate answer to Flint's question, and Evan picked up the receiver. "Bradley, Ryan, and Davis," he answered. Ellen Li's voice came to him across the wire.

"Evan!" she said, "Is Harry there? I couldn't reach him at home."

"He's here. So are Brad and Khadijah Flint. Can I put you on the speaker?"

"You might as well. It will save time."

There was a brief pause while Evan reached for the button that would turn on the speaker. "Okay," he said, "we're here."

"We are at the Chong family estate off Vancouver. They had a minor earthquake out here; the house is in shambles. Unfortunately, the university's crystal was destroyed somehow in the quake, but we've recovered many of the objects stolen from the university and most of the objects stolen from the PMA, including their crystal ball."

"Did you make any arrests?" Evan asked.

"A number of them. Mai Sien Chong has disappeared, but we managed to round up Chong Li-huang and a number of other relatives who seem to be involved, and the Canadian authorities seem willing to release the suspects to the FBI for extradition to the United States, which pleases Sid. We also turned up several members of the Chinese army who seem to have been working one side or the other of national security in the case. The Chinese government has already put in a request for their return. Given their involvement in the Chong burglaries, I expect they will be reclassified as undesirables and sent home. What the Chinese government does then is out of our hands."

"But you can't find Mai Sien Chong?"

Ellen sighed through the phone. "No sign of her. Singapore police will be watching incoming flights, but we don't have any evidence that she was more than an unwilling dupe of her uncle. We just received word that the museum guard is awake and recognizes his surroundings, so it looks like there won't be any capital charges. He is talking, but he doesn't remember the burglary, which is pretty common for a traumatic head injury. He may never remember who hit him. We've recovered or identified all but two of the stolen items, all of them in the family home of the primary suspect, so I don't expect more than a perfunctory search for her as a witness."

"Thank God the guard is recovering," Khadijah Flint broke in. "But make that all but one item recovered. We seem to have the Kwan Yin here. Mr. Bradley thinks that one of the Chinese operatives left it to implicate him in the burglaries, both to confuse the issue and out of personal animosity."

For a moment only static crackled through the telephone. Then Ellen returned. "Where did Brad find it?"

"Mr. Bradley didn't find it, Mr. Davis did, in the empty apartment of Mai Sien Chong. He would seem to be guilty of tampering with evidence, but I don't believe he had anything to do with the original theft, and he has returned the object to the trustees, as contracted." Flint raised a questioning eyebrow at Harry, who didn't look happy but nodded his agreement.

"I'm still here, Ellen, and I've got the Kwan Yin." He turned a quick frown on Evan. "You're not holding out on me, are you, Evan? If Ellen, or Mr. Dougherty, return with a search warrant, will they find the last missing object tucked away somewhere in your offices?"

"This is all of it," Evan reassured him. "They can search all they want."

"No, they can't," Khadijah put in, but Harry shook his head.

"I think our young friend has been very foolish," he said, "but unless you have better evidence than we have, I don't see any reason to start doubting his word now."

After another pause, Ellen agreed. "We will leave it at that for now. But it would help if we knew where the last item had got to. According to the list, it's a small figure, made of jadeite, in the shape of a reclining child."

Brad never twitched. Evan wasn't sure he'd maintained his veneer of innocence when he heard the description, but Ellen, at least, couldn't see him. After a moment, Ellen finished with, "We will keep looking. Harry, I have to go, I'm patched through the Vancouver police line, and I have already imposed enough on their hospitality. I'll be home late tomorrow. Don't get into any trouble while I'm gone."

Evan had the feeling that last was not meant for her husband, but an open line patched through a foreign police department didn't offer the best opportunity for confidential discussion. When she cut the connection, he hung up.

Brad smiled. "It looks like we have scraped through again," he said. "Khadijah, thanks for coming over. I am sure that we would not have fared so well if you hadn't been here." He was on his feet, his hand out, and Khadijah Flint took it.

"When you get that look in your eye," she said, "I know it is my cue to leave. If you plot anything nefarious in my absence, please do not tell me about it later!"

"On my honor."

"And make sure Harry Li gives you a receipt for that trinket!"

Brad laughed and led her through the offices to the door. Evan waited in an uneasy silence for his return. Harry seemed to be doing the same, but with a great deal less unease, and he was the first to speak when Brad returned.

"How was Vancouver?" he asked.

Brad gave Evan a sharp, questioning glance.

"I didn't tell him anything, but I made the mistake of materializing in front of him." Evan gave him an apologetic shrug. "I didn't expect anyone to be here."

"And you couldn't convince him that he'd been mistaken?"

That was harder to explain. "I sort of left the same way."

"I see."

"It wasn't Evan's fault," Harry began, then retrenched when Brad glared at him. "Not entirely at least. As you know, I've been consulting the *I Ching* on the matter ever since the burglary. It has been clear from the beginning that supernatural forces were at work and that, as I discussed with Evan on a number of occasions, they concerned yourself and a young lady who was more than she seemed. I have not entirely concluded what sort of god or demon or ancestor you may be, but I did know that if Evan were truly your son, he would share in some of those supernatural traits.

"You seemed far more certain of paternity than a mere ruse could account for, so I assumed that you were correct, that Evan was your son, and that he could perform some feats that would attest to his supernatural birth. And he did. I assume your associate Lily Ryan is also of your supernatural number?"

"You don't seem very upset." Brad pointed it out, but Evan had been wondering the same thing since he'd materialized in front of the man. Harry smiled.

"I must admit I was taken aback when the *I Ching* first led me to this conclusion," he admitted. "But I have known you for a number of years and have pitted my mind against yours in chess. I had seen your concern for your son, and your pride in him, and the pleasure you take in your work and in the game. Gradually, as I watched you with the new eyes the *Book* gave me, I became convinced that while you are capable of evil, you are not, intrinsically, evil of yourself. You are even capable of good, and the love you have for your son is perhaps the most admirable of your virtues."

"I don't," Brad started to say, but Harry laughed at him.

"It is called the *Book of Changes* for a reason. Whatever you are or have been, your life here, your son, have changed you, and the *Book* records those changes.

"Ellen does not know. I would rather not know myself," Harry admitted, "but if you can learn to live as a human being, I can learn to live with this knowledge."

Harry took Brad's hand and shook it solemnly. "I am honored to number among your human acquaintances," he said. "But since we are sharing the truth with each other today, I will admit I would rather not experience any more proof of your supernatural origins for a very long while."

"I think that can be arranged," Brad admitted.

"I'll find my own way out." Harry stopped in the doorway. "And Evan, it's not too late to come back to finish your degree."

"I have my degree, Professor. I have two of them."

Harry grinned at him. "But wouldn't a Ph.D. sound nice after your name?"

"Not today, Professor," Evan said aloud, while he privately swore off art for the rest of his life. He figured that life would be a lot longer that way. When Harry had gone, Evan looked at the empty sofa.

"Where's Lily?"

"With Alfredo." Brad let him brood on that for a moment before adding, "Saying good-bye. Alfredo explained about the crystal ball. It seems the earthquake in Vancouver was just the beginning of what we would have unleashed if we'd come out of the crystal in the wrong direction. It was enough to convince Lily that the game she was playing with Alfredo might have consequences even she would regret. She should be home soon. And gloating doesn't become you."

"I know." Evan flung himself lengthwise on the leather sofa and grinned. "I just can't help myself."